NANCY HALE (1908–    ) was born in Boston, where her parents, Philip and Lillian Westcott Hale, were successful painters. She published her first short story in the Boston *Herald* when she was 11, and in 1935, having already been an assistant editor at both *Vogue* and *Vanity Fair*, she became the first woman reporter on *The New York Times*. In 1942, she married her second husband, Fredson Bowers, a professor at the University of Virginia, and has ever since made her home in the lively academic community of Charlottesville. Author of numerous short stories, many of which were first published in *The New Yorker* and frequently anthologized, she has written such novels as *Never Any More* (1934) and *Dear Beast* (1959). She has also written a life of Mary Cassatt, as well as a partially fictionalized autobiographical work, *A New England Girlhood* (1958), and *The Realities of Fiction: A Book About Writing* (1962).

MARY LEE SETTLE is the National Book Award-winning author of *The Beulah Quintet*.

# THE PRODIGAL WOMEN

*by*

Nancy Hale

Introduction by Mary Lee Settle

PLUME AMERICAN WOMEN WRITERS
SERIES EDITOR: MICHELE SLUNG

A PLUME BOOK

**NEW AMERICAN LIBRARY**

NEW YORK AND SCARBOROUGH, ONTARIO

## PUBLISHER'S NOTE

This book is a work of fiction. Names, characters, places, and incidents either are the product of the author's imagination or are used fictiously, and any resemblance to actual persons, living or dead, events, or locales is entirely coincidental.

NAL BOOKS ARE AVAILABLE AT QUANTITY DISCOUNTS WHEN USED TO PROMOTE PRODUCTS OR SERVICES. FOR INFORMATION PLEASE WRITE TO PREMIUM MARKETING DIVISION, NEW AMERICAN LIBRARY, 1633 BROADWAY, NEW YORK, NEW YORK 10019.

Grateful acknowledgment is given for the following:

"The Sheik of Araby," by H. Smith, F. Wheeler (T. Snyder). Copyright © 1921, renewed 1949 Mills Music Inc., c/o Filmtrax Copyright Holdings Inc. Copyright renewed. All rights reserved. Used by permission.

"Mickey," by H. Williams (N. Moret). Copyright © 1918 Mills Music Inc. c/o Filmtrax Copyright Holdings Inc. Copyright renewed. All rights reserved. Used by permission.

"April Showers" by B. G. de Sylva and Lewis Silvers. Copyright © 1921 Warner Bros. Inc. (Renewed) All rights reserved. Used by permission.

"Sweet Child" by Al Lewis, Richard H. Whiting and Howard Simon. Copyright © 1925 Warner Bros. Inc. (Renewed) All rights reserved. Used by permission.

Charles K. Harris for the use of the two lines "Often a Bridesmaid, etc." appearing on page 237.

 PLUME TRADEMARK REG. U.S. PAT. OFF. AND FOREIGN COUNTRIES
REGISTERED TRADEMARK—MARCA REGISTRADA
HECHO EN CHICAGO, U.S.A.

SIGNET, SIGNET CLASSIC, MENTOR, ONYX, PLUME, MERIDIAN and NAL BOOKS are published *in the United States* by NAL PENGUIN INC., 1633 Broadway, New York, New York 10019, *in Canada* by The New American Library of Canada Limited, 81 Mack Avenue, Scarborough, Ontario M1L 1M8

**Library of Congress Cataloging-in-Publication Data**
Hale, Nancy, 1908–
  The prodigal women.
  (Plume American women writers)
  I. Title.  II. Series.
PS3515.A273P7  1988    813'.54    88-17940
ISBN 0-452-26140-6

First Plume Printing, October, 1988

1  2  3  4  5  6  7  8  9

PRINTED IN THE UNITED STATES OF AMERICA

*To*

ELIZABETH NOWELL PERKINS

# Introduction

A classic, Roger Shattuck has written, is "at the same time, a period piece and forever young." Nancy Hale's fascinating novel of its time, *The Prodigal Women*, first published in 1942, is such a work.

I interpret a "forever young" novel as one in which we find our timeless selves, our hopes, our fears, our neighbors, never-ending, never-changing sorrow and joy and pride. Anna Karenina is echoed whenever a woman has to choose between son and lover, Emma Bovary whenever a middle-class romantic makes a fool of herself; and all of us have known, identified with, and still recognize vestiges of the three principal women in *The Prodigal Women*.

To relegate a novel to history, or to condemn it as "dated," which is the pejorative way of saying the same thing, is to miss this very quality. But it is just as essential not to ignore a book's own view of its time. It is a view that can be found nowhere outside of good fiction, neither in the certainties of history nor in the lesser novels by contemporary writers who did not use their senses to record their surroundings.

The fact that the *The Prodigal Women* takes place between 1922 and 1940 is irrelevant to its essential meaning. Yet it is, at the same time, a perceptively observed documentary of the *mores* of the period and the daily ways people lived.

It is too easy to categorize it as an early feminist novel. It most certainly is "feminist"—though the use of that word is far more "contemporary" than the book itself—but it follows the tradition that existed long before women began using a self-conscious language in their appraisal of where they were and what they wanted. Nancy Hale is, and it is not quite the same, the most essentially feminine writer I know. Her female revenges are as ancient as Medea or Electra. But neither does she condone the excesses of "feminine wiles." These, too, are punished—terribly.

The "feminist" novel, if that is what is meant by novels where men are interpreted in a less than heroic manner, goes back to the great classics by women. The list is formidable: George Eliot's *Middlemarch*, where Dorothea's choice between Casaubon and Will Ladislaw is hardly a choice, and which is enough to frighten any sensitive woman out of marrying; Ellen Glasgow's Jason Greylock in *Barren Ground*, the author's terrible revenge on Southern men for losing the Civil War and drinking too much; Edith Wharton's Newland Archer in *The Age of Innocence*; Willa Cather's Jim in *My Ántonia*. Here they are—strong women, frail men—a genre, a tradition, and a revenge for all the natural insults that female flesh considers itself heir to. Like these great women novelists, Nancy Hale's women are more alive, stronger, both more sympathetic and more destructive than her men.

A contemporary critic compared *The Prodigal Women* to the work of Thomas Wolfe; I suppose because it was long. Nothing could be farther from the truth. Nancy Hale's prose is controlled, her sense of place precise and vivid. She had the gift of making places resonate behind her characters, and become a part of them. Her introduction to Leda March, one of the "prodigal women," is at the beginning of the book. Scott Fitzgerald wrote that a professional writer has "a sense of the future in every line," and within this lyric passage of an eleven-year-old girl walking in the woods, there is an ominous forecast of her destructive isolation.

Now that she could be alone, she was happy . . . The woods were old. Parts of them were virgin forest; none of them had been cut for a century. Stoney Road was a lost segment of an old post-road. The paths that led among the woods were the same trails that Indians had followed before the settlement of New England. She loved them. Through winters and summers she had learned to walk quietly like an Indian along

the paths, setting her feet down without breaking a twig . . .
It was as though in the woods her awkwardness left her and
she became full of useful grace. She supposed that other
people, in the real world, felt all the time as she felt here:
knowing the land, sure of themselves and belonging there.

Leda March is the coldest and most self-concerned main
character I can think of since Julien Sorel in Stendhal's *La
Rouge et Le Noir*. The second of the novel's three leading
female characters, Maizie Jekyll, is a marvelous picture of
what can happen to transplanted, and not very smart, twenties flappers, cheerleaders, or small-town girls (north or south),
who try old female survival techniques in new environments.
She has the self-destructive urge of the conservative, clinging to the old ways at any cost. In Maizie's case, inculcated
"feminine wiles" are a way of life. She knows nothing else.
They destroy her.

The third of the women is Betsy, Maizie's younger sister
and Leda's first friend, used by her and then thrown away.

Betsy is two women: The first is a bright, charming, lively
young girl who works, plays, reflects the fashion world of
New York in the late twenties and early thirties, falls in
love lightly and out again, and accepts the world she finds
herself in with more joy than anyone else in the book. In one
magic moment she embodies all the longing of all those
thirties girls to "go to New York City."

On an afternoon in June Betsy Jekyll Jayne stood on a curb
on Park Avenue waiting for the lights to change . . . She was
charming . . . she stood quite still, in a red print dress and
jacket and a white straw hat with a red ribbon. She looked
like a picture in a fashion magazine, all except for one heel
which showed a hole above the shoe . . . She had never been
afraid. She had never visualized defeat or despair or shame.
She was like a shining, brown, uncracked nut.

The second avatar of Betsy comes after a sea change caused
by what Hale must consider a disaster: falling deeply in love.
In reaction to one of the nastiest men in modern fiction, Betsy
develops into a closed-off, calm, strong earth mother who

finally, in the most ancient woman's way of all, uses the man to make a mother of her, then tolerates him the rest of the time, instead of shooting him and dumping him down a well, as he richly deserves.

> Betsy's world was round and compact and workaday; it seemed to her now that Hector roamed in some vast ringing stratosphere. He had left her world at a tangent . . . She cooked the summer meals, she bathed the baby, she swam and lay in the sun, she went to bed with Hector when it was night. His new preoccupation did not trouble her. She did not see how it affected her and her small full life . . . He had gone off and up in such a curve while she marched straight on from sunup to sun down.

Hector, first the lover, then the husband of Betsy, then the puritan sadist, reminds me of the definition by Dostoevsky of a minor artist: "He lived the life of a man of genius but he had no talent." Petty tyrant, demanding man, failed "artist," Hector is Hale's picture of the writer *manqué*. In one of the best scenes of the book, a Hollywood director who has gotten drunk tells him, and us (and we read it with true relief), the truth about Hector and his ilk.

The second of the men in the novel, James, cousin and then husband of Leda, begins as a very attractive young doctor, and seems to fade into a kind of dim civility. Maybe it is because he is Leda's victim. He ends up marrying her worst schoolgirl enemy, and it is hard not to wish them well.

The third, Lambert Rudd, is the most interesting and self-redeemed man in *The Prodigal Women*. He is, or starts out to be, a very good painter. But caught in the trap of the women, he diminishes throughout the book. First there is Maizie, who drives herself into recurring mental collapse and him into debilitating guilt by trying to change his home truths into promises. Then, at only one time in their lives do he and Leda have a chance to become what they seem meant to be—he a good painter, she a good writer.

But it is hard to see such a future for them. Buried in the character of Leda from the first scene is her classic fatal flaw: She has no heart. And buried in Lambert is his fatal flaw.

He rides roughshod over anyone who stands in his way, and, alas, Maizie, square in the middle of his road, trying wiles she learned as a teenager in a Southern drug store drinking Cokes with her chums, is run over.

Her pathos is the only "dated" attitude in the book: such women were accepted in the thirties as tragic; now their self-destruction is recognized. She reminds me of a dreadful line in Noel Coward's thirties film, *The Scoundrel*, "I don't want your love handed to me on a platter like the head of John the Baptist or lying in the road where I can run over it. . . ." The only two truly decent men are the two fathers, and they are both failures. One commits suicide, the other is seen mostly through the destructively critical eyes of Leda March.

What makes *The Prodigal Women* a joy and a discovery to reread is a quality that Nancy Hale's contemporaries in the forties could not have seen. They saw the women then as products of their environment; reading the book now we can see them in the added dimension of their times.

But it is all too tempting to see their attitudes toward men, their overdependence on their mates for fulfillment, and their acquiescence, as dated, until we read the morning paper. And there they are still, the battered, the victims of moral and physical sadism *who have stood for it* until the event—the shot, the beating—happens that makes the headlines.

At the time it was first published, the honest sexuality of the book obscured both the structure and the characters, according to Nancy Hale. People tended to read it for its shock value. To a reader today that aspect of it seems very mild. Now, over forty years later, the sexuality can be taken for granted and admired for its honest picture of what life was, and is, like for women.

A good book is a good book, but a good book that sells a million copies within a few months of publication is a mirror as well to the people who read it. What is astonishing about the overwhelming popularity of *The Prodigal Women* is the special and frightening period that it came out: 1943, a year after the United States went to war. At a time when the accepted picture was of brave men going off to fight and leaving their heartbroken wives, *The Prodigal Women* was made into a best-seller by people who recognized a far different picture of life between the sexes. There is, at most, only a vague mention of the coming war, and that is thrust aside by Betsy: "Don't pay any attention to them, Maizie. They get like this when they've had a couple of drinks. Hector is always talking about war. Don't pay any attention to him."

A wonderful visual presence in the book is a history of women's fashion in the twenties and thirties. Hale makes the years go by in the length of a skirt and in the change in passions and admirations: "What [Betsy] had now was glamour instead of 'it'. She admired Marlene Dietrich instead of Clara Bow." She makes a shirt speak for the woman who wears it. She uses the color of lace to show what was acceptable, what was not. She makes us see why the way one girl dressed in 1925 was right, and why another was so very wrong that you could see her disastrous future in what she wore.

Nancy Hale worked as a fashion writer for *Vogue* and as an editor for *Vanity Fair*, either of which in the early thirties could be called the *Women's Wear Daily* of its era. She was the first woman reporter for *The New York Times*, and many of her stories had already been published in *The New Yorker*. All of her training and her knowledge is evident in *The Prodigal Women*.

Her recognition of the power of simple objects can release a magic memory when *The Prodigal Women* is read today. Details glisten with recognition, and for those of us who have any memories of the time, they evoke a piercing recall. A woman spits into a mascara box to dampen the little brush that came with it, and a whole world flashes into a new reality: the mixture of coal smoke and clean linen which was the smell of thirties trains, the scent of *Evening in Paris*, the feel of silk stockings, the swish of a short beaded skirt that those grand and gallant girls of the twenties slipped into—as the book says, "WITHOUT UNDERCLOTHES"—while we peek at them dressing and the talcum powder flies.

She revives the space and dirt of the old railroad stations when coal dust colored the mist of winter days. She goes with two young girls playing "hookey" from school, and explores Boston of the early twenties. The Copley, the Ritz, the Harvard Yard, all of it is here and alive again in its time, for places change as people do. What remains the same is their familiarity, what changes is a revelation of time.

Color, and the use of space itself, are both claustrophobic and free. A girl walks through snow into the woods, a woman is trapped by her own madness in a hospital room: All of these images are enhanced by her acute visual sense. Nancy Hale was trained first as a painter and it shows in every scene she writes.

Much has been made, too, of her knowledge of the mores of the North and the South. Indeed, she misses little of the way people live, of their habits, of their choices, whether the habits and choice rise to the level of tradition or sink to the level of fashion. She was forced in her own life to be aware of this—to take nothing for granted.

She came from a large and highly respected New England famiy of artists, thinkers, and writers. There was no question about their place in both the intellectual and the social life of Boston. She was blessed when she was young by having her decision to become a writer freely accepted and honored by her family.

Edward Everett Hale, writer and Unitarian minister, was famous for his essays and stories, one of which is an American classic, *The Man Without a Country*. He was Nancy Hale's grandfather. One of her great aunts was Harriet Beecher Stowe, the author of *Uncle Tom's Cabin*, who was welcomed to the White House by Abraham Lincoln in 1862 with the remark that she was "the little lady" who wrote the book that started the Civil War.

Both of her parents were painters. Her mother, Lillian Westcott Hale, was the most successful and honored portrait painter of her time in Boston. Her father, Philip L. Hale, had lived and worked near Monet in France, and was known as the American Impressionist. He was a distinguished critic

and art teacher at the Boston Museum of Fine Arts, where
Nancy Hale had her first training as a painter.

Then she married a Virginian. It must have been a profound shock to realize that the social South treated writers as
*deracinée*. It colored her early writing about the region. Some
of her people can't get the mush out of their mouths. She
became the prime recorder of Southern tacky. Maybe it was
an act of revenge.

Then, in 1942, her life changed completely. She was
married again—this time to Fredson Bowers, a distinguished
professor at the University of Virginia. She has lived ever
since in Charlottesville, one of the intellectual and social
oases of the South, a city where university life and county
life have balanced each other, and where writers and artists
have always been welcome. She says that over the years,
living there has altered her ascerbic view of the South. Later
her mother came to live nearby, and house after house in
Charlottesville has Lillian Hale's superb portraits on the
walls.

I hope that one of the positive side effects of reviving *The
Prodigal Women* will be to lead a new generation of readers to
Nancy Hale's other work. Her family memoir, *The Life in the
Studio*, read in conjuction with *The Prodigal Women*, illumi-
nates both books. *A New England Girlhood* is a later and more
tender study of the same material out of which the early
sections of *The Prodigal Women* came. She has replaced the
fury of the novel with compassion, and while there is little
nostalgia (I suspect that Nancy Hale would decry it), there is
greater understanding of the past.

The depths of the past, the urgency of the perpetual
present, and a sense of life seen and recognized and sensu-
ously recorded in full light are the marks of her work. Here,
in *Life in the Studio* she recalls her father's voice: "Where the
light falls is the light. Where the light does NOT fall is the
shadow. *Chiaroscuro*, the clear and the obscure. Don't go
mucking up your drawing with half-lights."

And she never has.

—Mary Lee Settle

# THE
# PRODIGAL
# WOMEN

# CHAPTER 1

ON A SATURDAY MORNING late in April a fifteen-year-old girl named Leda March stood at the bend in Stony Road and looked back across the orchard and the swamp to her house.

She had two full days before her to be free from the self-consciousness, the shame that came with being with the other girls at the Hampton Country Day School. Except for a birthday party of one of them this afternoon, and church tomorrow morning, she could be free; she could go back into the woods alone and think her own thoughts. She could find her special pleasures there and forget for a little while that they were silly pleasures that would not be pleasures at all to anyone else, anyone who was busy and popular. The morning was young and fine. She could forget for a short time her life, which in this year, this spring, was becoming more lonely, more frightening, more unhappy. She could pretend that she was still a child, playing alone, engrossed in the small symbols of her privately lived existence —not a young girl odd and different from her contemporaries, hopeless of ever being loved or possessing anything or controlling the great attraction and power which she believed that all other girls had.

When she had been a child she had been, in her own way, happy. But that was before school and the girls in it had taught her that that kind of lonely, secret happiness was wrong; contemptible. Pleasure in loneliness seemed to be something only for children. Now, for the rest of her life, she would have to face people and live in relation to them. And they would never like her, she was sure; they would avoid her and make fun of her, and she would live in a world where she could not learn the common language. She had come to face herself as an unattractive girl, uncoordinated, shy, without social talent, full of awkwardness and embarrassments and silly fancies. That was the way the girls at school saw her, and now she saw herself that way too. The illusions, the secret feeling of importance, had vanished with childhood.

Leda looked back across the land to the small white house, set on a rise in the fields, where her mother was, where her father was. It was a mile from the village of Hampton. There were three similar New England houses near by. In them lived the Marches' neighbors; but none of them were friends. An egg or a cup of sugar might be borrowed once a year with smiles and inquiries, but the Marches had no friends; none anywhere in Hampton. They were timid people who did not care to involve themselves in friendships. There was no one who disliked them, no one who thought of them at all.

But from this distance Leda could pretend that the house belonged to busy active people with a full life, engagements, and a popular daughter. It did not depress her now, in her Saturday freedom, as it did when she walked up the path from school and saw it as one more token of her life—all wrong, just as her parents were all wrong, and her clothes, and herself.

Now that she could be alone, she was happy.

She turned and walked on up the white, stony dirt road that led back to the woods. When Leda was a child she had pretended that the stones were dragon's teeth, spit by a gold and scarlet monster who had come down the road slashing its tail and been wounded by a knight.

The woods were old. Parts of them were virgin forest; none of them had been cut for a century. Stony Road was a lost segment of an old post-road. The paths that led among the woods were the same trails that Indians had followed before the settlement of New England. Few people but boys with guns and slingshots ever went to the woods, and for all these years of her childhood Leda might as well have owned them. She knew them well.

She loved them. Through winters and summers she had learned to walk quietly like an Indian along the paths, setting her feet down without breaking a twig. If people came she would slip away and they would never hear her. Once she was in a part of the woods far from home, back from the road; a part she did not know. She came upon a shack built of boards and tar paper; even looking at it gave her an uneasy feeling. A man came suddenly to the door. He was a horrible creature, unshaven, his dirty shirt open down his chest, his trousers sagging. He was drunk. He said something in a loud, blurred voice. Leda turned and ran away, with her heart pounding. She could hear him running after her, stumbling; she glanced over her shoulder and saw his red-rimmed eyes, his fuzzy, filthy hair. He ran, but she slipped down the trails and away from him.

It was as though in the woods her awkwardness left her and she became full of useful grace. She supposed that other people, in the real world, felt all the time as she felt here: knowing the land, sure of themselves and belonging there.

She walked up the road past the old, abandoned well, the high knoll of pines, to the decayed red gate. Beyond the gate lay a long marshy hollow that narrowed to a path and then gave onto an open circular clearing that, as a child, she had thought of as her secret garden. In late spring the clearing was filled with bluets; edged with silver dogwood trees; there were lady slippers. Now the place was brown and empty; there was only a haze of spring over the slender trees. She passed through it and climbed the trail that slanted up the side of the rocky hill.

At the top of the hill was pine forest. The path was smooth and slippery. Leda descended the other side of the hill into thick second growth; she held her hands before her to push back the branches that hung across the path.

The trail led down into a hollow, dark under the boughs; pushing through Leda came upon a small pond covered with dark gray scum. No one else would have known the pond was there at all.

There was a rich, sickish smell of skunk cabbage. She squatted on her heels beside the sluggish water and dipped her fingers into the cold.

Under the slimy leaves and the scum her fingers found a slippery mass; she lifted it and looked at the tiny frog's eggs like black seeds. She dropped the jelly back into the water.

A little farther, beside the pond, was a sloping broad rock. Leda climbed up it and sat holding her knees in her arms and looking up at the sky.

It was clear blue and without clouds.

She stared up, broadening her focus so that she seemed to see the whole sky, curving down to the tops of the trees, and at its base the circle of the thick, bare woods. It was like a cup inverted over her alone. Slowly peace began to fill her; a sense of vastness and still beauty.

Her mind drifted in a long, deep swell. She thought of New England, stretched over the miles and miles of hills, fields, river-beds and swamps, to north and south and west of her. The lands of early spring, empty sighing woods, long marshes: her spirit seemed to walk through them. She heard the tall trees whisper, felt under her fingers the stir of the buds at the twig-ends. This country was without people, New England before the Indians, before human life.

A feeling of possessing and being all the world filled her. She was a part of all this land. And the feeling was like an answer. Everything was beautiful, simple, and true. It was a moment of the fullest peace.

Slowly, gravely, the feeling dissolved and Leda was left feeling weak and empty. She went on staring at the sky, trying to regain that sensation which was so strange, so wild, so lovely. It would not come back.

After a while she stood up and began to walk back along the trail. But her mind swam still in the shallows of its exaltation, and she was hardly aware of walking.

She found herself back on the white, stony, dry road.

Down the road a group of boys came straggling. She saw them, and the last rags of her ecstasy whisked away; she was at once tense and full of the fear of people. She knew these boys. They were high school boys from the town, in leather wind-breakers and checked mackinaws, laughing loudly and pushing each other about. Their faces were grinning, red, mottled. The tallest had black curly hair and a red mouth; his name was Theophile Tracy; he carried a big knapsack. The younger boys hung about him, shouting and laughing shrilly. They saw Leda coming toward them and one of them began to mimic her, holding himself stiff and pulling his face down long and glowering.

They came nearer.

"Hello, Leda," one of them called in a falsetto voice.

She did not speak. Her fingers were clenched inside their woolen gloves. She made herself go on walking, looking straight ahead.

"Hello, Leda!"

"Hi, Leda!"

"Leda, Leda, such a reader!"

"Leda, Leda, is a bleeder!"

She stared ahead of her down the road toward her own house, without seeing; all of her was rigid, blind. She heard their voices moving away from her, going farther up the road. She heard Theophile Tracy's voice, deeper and huskier than the others:

"Leda, Leda, y'r father's full of hooey."

There was yellow sunshine all over the table at luncheon. The maid, Bridie, moved in and out from the kitchen with the cold lamb, the creamed potatoes, the cauliflower; her face was broken out in red blotches, with greasy black hair combed slantwise across the bumpy forehead. Bernard March sat at the head of the table, chewing his meat with his rabbit teeth, and Laura March sat at the foot. Leda sat between them on the side. Outside the April wind had risen; the twigs of the snowball bushes scratched against the panes of the dining-room window.

They had apple dumplings for dessert.

"Do you suppose Bridie would give me some more apple dumpling, Mother-Cat?" Bernard said, smiling across the table.

"Oh, *Father!* Don't!"

"Don't what, Kitten?"

"Talk that way, say things like that. Why can't you be like other people?"

"Do you want me to order you and Mother-Cat around? All right."

"Oh, Father. Don't be disgusting."

Bernard's poor face fell. Laura smiled at him across the table; her big pale face comforted him.

Leda said nothing more. Her face was heavy and dark with misery as she ate her dessert.

"Baby's going to Adèle Macomb's birthday party this afternoon," Laura said.

"That's fine. I hope you have fun with all the nice little girls," Bernard said. He knew he was not saying the right thing, but he could not think of anything else to say.

"Sweetest, you don't have to go if you don't want to," Laura said. "You don't look as if you wanted to."

"I've got to." Leda's voice was strangled.

"But, sweetest, don't do things when you don't want to. You can stay home and help me dig in the garden instead. I know those girls tease you."

"I've got to."

"Leda's too clever for those other girls, that's what it is," Bernard said.

Leda looked wildly from one gentle, loving face to the other. Under the table her hands screwed the napkin into a hard string; she began to sob.

"Precious Baby, don't cry, sweetest." Laura got up and put her arms around Leda. "There. Sweet Baby. Don't go to the party if it makes you feel bad to think about it. Stay with Mother."

Leda wrenched away from Laura as the maid came in and stared at them.

They got up and went out into the garden. Inside the maid was clashing the dishes together. Laura put her arm through Bernard's and they stood together looking at their barren garden; a few crocuses were sending up spikes. Leda had walked away from them. They saw her kneel down by the crocuses and begin to push the dry leaves away from the spikes.

"She's so awfully excitable," Bernard said.

Laura nodded. She smiled into his face and for a moment they felt the warmth of their intimacy. Then they both looked away to where their daughter knelt.

Bernard March did not look like a son of one of the great Boston families, and he did not feel like one nor had he ever lived like one. He was, however, the youngest son of Josiah Arlington March, the grandson of James Treat March. He had gone with his brothers to St. Mark's and to Harvard, but unlike his brothers he was neither athletic nor possessed of business acumen. For him to be part of the family firm of March and March on State Street was as unthinkable to him as it was to his father, uncles, and brothers. His only ability was a musical one, not great but definite. He had been sent to the Conservatory after Harvard. When he met a young lady from Worcester and married her his family were as glad as he to have him settle in a little house in Hampton, ten miles from Boston. Since then, eighteen years ago, the family had seen little of Bernard. His family had always frightened him; he felt and was a fool in their large, commanding presences—a little, giggling, buck-toothed fool. He was very happy with Laura, and they liked living in their own snug little house together. Bernard had an adequate income as his share of the family fortune.

Laura's family-in-law terrified her, and she bored them. At the occasional teas to which she went at her family-in-law's, she stood about like a timid, pleasant cow. No one could have suited Bernard half so well.

She met him when she was an unhappy, timid student at the Boston Conservatory. She had a bloodless talent for music. Her family, shrewd, pushing Worcester Yankees, had forced her to develop that talent for all it was worth. Boston frightened her; the other students frightened her; the idea of making a living for herself teaching music frightened her. When the rabbit-faced young man named March, who was taking a class in counterpoint with her and was quite as shy as she, began to call on her at her boarding-house, she found that they were very happy together, once they had got past any fear of each other. One night on the boarding-house sofa he put his head in her lap and asked her to marry him. She stroked his thin sandy hair away from his forehead and said yes.

For the first years of their marriage they were completely happy, together and with the baby. Bernard loved to play with the baby; it seemed so tiny and pink. There was a picture of Bernard holding Leda, at two, on his knees; his rabbity face radiant with pride and pleasure.

But as Leda grew older she spoiled their cosy happiness. She was a child of the March strength and the Haskell ambition, sprung from Bernard's weak loins and Laura's timid body. She had all their timidity, all their fear;

but she could not, like them, be happy within the walls of her own shyness. She was frantic with self-consciousness and envy and desire.

## CHAPTER II

HAMPTON was both a town in its own right and a suburb of Boston. The people who lived in Hampton were of two kinds, the native Hamptonites whose ancestors had settled in Hampton in the seventeenth century, and the suburbanites. The former were narrow, bigoted, thrifty, proud people, who looked down upon the rich commuting Bostonians. The suburbanites lived in architected houses of concrete and stucco and brick, set within grounds, out from the town in the direction of the Country Club and the Country Day School. They did not look down upon the natives of Hampton because they were oblivious of their existence. Their life centered on Boston. There was, in addition, a third group, the Irish, who ran the local politics. The children of the Irish and the native Hamptonites went to the public school, the children of the suburbanites to the Country Day School.

The parents of Adèle Macomb were among the richest of the commuting class. They were people who had made a place for themselves in their life-times; their power lay in the offices in State Street where they had been able to make so much money. Financially they had supplanted the older merchant families of Boston. Their daughters were making debuts in Boston, joining the Junior League and even the Vincent Club; their sons were being sent to Groton. They and their kind were becoming the ruling class of Boston, more potent to the outsider's eye than the old families that lived in shabby houses on Beacon Street and the Hill.

Mr. and Mrs. Macomb lived in the manner of Boston's new rich. They played golf, drove motors, served cocktails at their dinner parties, travelled de luxe to Europe in the summers, seldom read a book, and it was their ambition to be taken for New Yorkers when they were away from Boston.

The Macomb's house was square, large, ugly, made of concrete. It lay back up a driveway from the road a mile or two from Hampton. Halfway up the neat gravel driveway was a concrete garage that held two Packards, and an adjoining stable for the girls' saddle horses. The front door to the house was of plate glass, and over it was a cloudy glass roof, supported by iron braces, so that people could pass from their cars into the house without getting wet.

Adèle was the prettiest of all the Macomb girls; her nose had been broken when she fell out of a swing as a child, turning the tip upwards, a strangely becoming effect. Her voice was low and rapid and set a fashion for voices among girls of her age. She had brown hair and brown eyes and a scornful mouth. Her legs were too big. But almost, she had made other girls wish their legs were piano also. Adèle was a leader, like her father, like her sisters; she dominated her class in the Country Day School.

This was her fifteenth birthday. She had asked to her party all of her class in school. They all came, the fawning, imitative ones, and the little wretches like Leda March, upon whom all the force of Adèle's inherited bullyism was wreaked.

Adèle was very happy; she ran to meet her guests in a blue dress, laughing and flashing her brown eyes and talking in her low, rapid voice. She led the new arrivals through the big, oak hall to the staircase, up the red velvet-covered shallow steps to the upper hall, where doors opened into sunny, luxurious bedrooms and a faint smell of expensive perfume hung in the air. Her own bedroom was the perfect bedroom for a young girl: the dotted swiss curtains, the white painted furniture, the snug little bed, the small desk, the little bureau—and all painted in blue forget-me-nots. Blue was Adèle's favorite color, and the favorite color of every girl in her class.

Leda March arrived in a hired cab. All the way over she had been as tense as though she were facing death, holding her tissue-wrapped package stiffly before her. There had been tears at home over the wrapping of the package. Mrs. March had wrapped it in plain heavy white paper. Leda turned red. "But, Mother, all the girls take presents wrapped in tissue-paper! I can't take it like this! I won't go!"

Adèle met her at the door, a group of attendant girls close behind her.

"Hello, Leda."

"Hello, Leda."

"Hello, Leda!" There was a burst of muffled, hysterical laughter. They all ran toward the stairs together, in pink, and white, and yellow, and blue dresses.

Leda took her coat and hat off slowly in Adèle's bedroom; Adèle sat on the bed to open the present.

"Thank you so much, Leda. Look, Betty, Vera, isn't this just beautiful? A cake of soap!—and a washcloth. I'll have to give you the same thing when it's your birthday, Leda, thanks for giving me the idea."

Laughter—idolatrous, hysterical laughter.

"Wouldn't you like to use it now, Leda—there's a bathroom right in there. You must be dirty after that horrible old taxicab. Leda came in a taxicab," Adèle informed the girls. They all laughed.

Leda felt the blood in her face, but she felt icy cold, too. The present had been something Mrs. March had bought for Christmas, left over. Leda had known it wouldn't be right. Nothing would ever be right. She lowered her face, groping in the pocket of her coat as though she were looking for something.

"Go on, Leda, I mean it. Go right into my bathroom and wash," the low, rapid voice went on. Adèle got up from the bed and pushed Leda. For a minute it seemed as if it were in fun. But all the others joined. They were really pushing her, pushing her hard; they pushed her into the bathroom and shut the door, laughing outside.

In the bathroom Leda sat down on the white stool. She was shaking all over. She felt as if she wanted to be sick. That wretched little present—for a bathroom like this, with its thick blue turkish towels, and a soft rug on the floor, and shining porcelain and nickel. Slowly she began to see the sunshine. It was warm and pretty in here, and she was alone. She wished she need never go out. They didn't want her, and she would be so much less miserable. She got up and washed her hands and face in the bowl, knowing that they would know if she hadn't. Then she put her hand on the doorknob and opened the door.

"—Poor church-mouse," Adèle's voice was saying.

"Leda, how much money does your father have?" It was one of the other girls, laughing, giggling, watching Adèle's face all the time to see if she was amused, or whether, suddenly, someone would have said the wrong thing and Adèle would have to be propitiated.

"About five thousand dollars," Leda muttered.

"Five thousand dollars! Isn't that lovely, Adèle? Why, I should think Mr. March could afford to buy Leda plenty of soap on that, shouldn't you, Adèle?"

But Adèle was tired of it now. She jumped up and ran out of the room, with all of them after her.

The huge living-room was full of deep velvet sofas and chairs; Oriental rugs, and lamps with Chinese shades. They all sat around, Adèle in the middle of a sofa like a little queen, and the others on the arms of the sofa, hanging over the back. Leda sat alone in a green velvet armchair. Inside her mind was beating like a hammer: "It's ugly, it's ugly and I hate it. I hate you. I wish I could kill you, I wish I could kill you."

"What are we going to play, Adèle?" one of them asked.

"We're not going to play anything. You can all go and play outside, if you want to. But we're not going to have games, like children. I want to sit and just talk."

"Oh, that's much more fun."

"Who wants to play games like a kid?"

"Let's just talk."

I can sit here, Leda thought. I can just keep perfectly still. I won't have to play tag football and have them laugh.

Talking was something Adèle ran her own way. She would turn her pretty, brown, scornful eyes on one of them and say something, pick at some raw spot. Then they would all turn like a pack of wolves and tear that one apart. The victim would giggle feebly, and sweat in her chair, looking adoringly, wretchedly at Adèle until the torture was over and another one was getting it. A few did not get it at all. They were the ones that were Adèle's best friends, who lied for her, licked her boots, did her work of torturing for her.

"Are you going to Country Day next winter, Vera?" Adèle asked, in her abrupt, point-blank way, her mouth uncompromising.

Vera Blaine blinked.

"Why, yes, I guess so. Aren't you, Adèle?"

"Of course not. I wouldn't stay out here in this little hick town and go to that old place now I'm fifteen. Naturally, I'm going to Miss Sheraton's in town. *Aren't you?*" demanded the low, rapid voice.

"*I* am, Adèle."

"So am I."

"*I* wouldn't go to that old Country Day any more."

"Mother says I can go to Miss Sheraton's if Betty's father will drive me in with her when he goes to the office."

"You mean you haven't got a car, Anne?" The low, rapid voice.

"Well, my father could perfectly well afford one, but he's just so funny, he doesn't want to have a car, he likes the train better."

"How crazy."

"But I'm going to make him get one," Anne's voice went on, racing, breathless. "I'm going to tell him he's just *got* to get one."

"I'll bet Leda's going to Country Day next year, aren't you, Leda?" Another voice, high, shaking with excitement.

"Are you going to Country Day next year, Leda?" Adèle asked.

"I don't know."

She knew her parents expected to send her to the same school next year. She wondered once more, as she always wondered, why she always did the wrong thing, why her parents always picked the wrong thing for her to do. She and all that was hers was odious, miserable, forever and ever to be apologized for.

"We'll miss you, Leda," Adèle said. "Won't we all?" Another burst of laughter.

A butler came to the doorway and announced the refreshments to Adèle gravely, as if she had been grown-up. Adèle nodded carelessly. They all began to squirm in their chairs, but Adèle did not move and they all sat on, smiling anxiously at her. Finally she got up and strolled toward the door. Leda was just behind her. She looked with dull fascination at the back of Adèle's head, that bright brown hair with a blue bow. She wondered how it felt to have the hair everyone else would like to have, and always say the right thing in that perfect voice, and live in this house, and know you were the best of everything.

Suddenly Adèle turned and put one arm around Leda's waist. In agony Leda tried to put her own arm around Adèle with nonchalance, as though she walked thus daily. It was Heaven to walk like this—Heaven and agonizing embarrassment—to be within the circle of Adèle's arm, where all of them would love to be, walking as her intimate. Leda smelled the fresh, clean smell of Adèle's skin. It was so terrible the way the hate and shame dropped away and all there was left was pride, joy and delight to be walking with Adèle.

"Leda's an old cutie," Adèle said. She put her hand over Leda's.

They came to the red plush portieres of the dining-room doors. Leda was walking on air. The strangest sudden visions packed into her head: herself as Adèle's friend, her confidante; a new life under the supreme patronage of Adèle. She tried to walk lightly, in step. She cleared her throat thickly.

"I'm going to see *if* I can't go to Miss Sheraton's next fall," she said. Her heart was fluttering.

"You didn't get your nails clean when you washed your hands, Leda," Adèle said, in her low, light, rapid voice. "Go on upstairs and clean them, will you. It'll make me sick to look at them at the table." She dropped her arm indifferently from Leda's waist, and led the others to the big table.

Leda turned and went up the broad stairs. She could hardly see before her; everything was black and shaking. She stumbled through the hall to the bathroom where she had been before.

I'd like to kill you, she kept thinking. I'd like to kill you. I'll get even with you if it takes the rest of my life. I'll kill you.

The warm water running over her hands quieted her. It was not just the old hurt, the old fear and pain; it was the humiliation: the pleasure that she had got from Adèle's momentary intimacy, the ease with which all past hurts had been wiped out, and herself become slavish and adoring.

She braced herself, leaning against the bathroom door, to go down and enter the dining-room again.

Leda drove home in the darkness, later, in the taxi, that smelled of stable, just as the old horse-drawn hacks had smelled that had been driven in Leda's childhood.

The evening was very black, very quiet; the yellow street lights shone like blobs of gold along the country road as they drove by; blobs made iridescent by Leda's tears. She felt strange; melting. She could not stop thinking of when she had been a child; and the thought of home ahead of her, with a warm supper and her mother and her father waiting for her, seemed sweet. Suddenly she could hardly wait to get home.

They drew up and Leda jumped out and dashed into the house. Her mother was sitting by the side of the fire in the living-room, sewing; her father was just coming downstairs. The fire and the two lamps threw a yellow light over the room. A sob rose in Leda's throat. Her father came to the bottom of the stairs and she threw her arms passionately about him.

"Oh, Father, I love you so!"

"There, Kitten, I love you. Why, you old darling. Laura, she's crying."

Laura got up and came across the floor. She put her arms around Leda and Leda turned her face into her mother's neck.

"What's the matter, Kitten?" Laura asked. "Did you have a horrid time, sweetest? I wish you'd just stayed with me."

"I wish I had," Leda said. She cried quietly.

They had supper with candles on the table. Leda ate and looked around the little room as if she had never seen it before; its white walls, checked curtains, the plain Colonial furniture.

After supper Laura went back to her sewing. Bernard went into his own room, across the hall. Leda sat on a stool before the fire, watching it snap and flicker and burn into glowing purplish depths of heat. She looked at her mother's big, pale, shiny face and wondered how she could ever be so angry with her. She felt no anger at all now, only fatigue and the desire to stay here, where it was warm and safe. After a while she went up to bed.

She undressed in the dark, feeling the familiar objects around her in the darkness, the bureau, the chest that held the secret notebooks in which she wrote long, passionate outbursts, the small bookcase. She went to the window and opened it, knelt down on the floor and leaned out, breathing in swallows of the cold early spring night air, hearing the occasional pipe in the swamp that was the beginning of the full chorus of the spring frogs. She looked up at the white stars in the black sky.

Now, once more, she could feel that there was no life outside of this house that held her. She could forget the menaces, the fears and humiliations that assailed her outside of its walls. Now, because everything was black outside, it was as if the blackness wiped the people from the earth; only the bare curve of the world stretched away on all sides from that one house, that stood alone in the night, alone in the universe, holding her in her room; like someone high in an enchanted tower in a deserted world.

Again, like warmth, the consciousness of the still forested mountains and the waters and the dark fields of the world crept through her nerves. It all lay there in the night, in peace and loneliness, in the night wind. Inside the house she lay, as quiet as the world. Downstairs her father began to play a Chopin mazurka—fast, delicate, melancholy music that made her sad and happy.

It was only the future, the world outside, the world of people, that was heavy and ominous and full of fear.

In the morning the sky was gray. It was an agitated morning, with an irritable wind that smacked at the windows.

Leda and Laura dressed to go to church; Bernard was waiting downstairs, in an old brown tweed suit, smoking a pipe. Leda had seen him standing at the window as she went upstairs; his rabbit's face was vacuous.

Now was a new day, a bad day, with church to be faced. Leda put on her best blue serge dress. It had broad shoulder-straps, and a white cotton crepe guimpe. She put on her best brown low shoes. She put on her heavy brown coat, and her brown felt hat. She felt miserable in them.

She went into her mother's room.

Laura was putting her black sailor hat over her hair. She looked grave, and tearful, and foolish. Leda stood at the foot of the big bed, itching with irritation. Everything in her rebelled at the pomposity of going to church.

"Sweetest, don't look so glum," Laura said, taking a *papier poudré* from the little blue book and rubbing it on her nose.

"Mother . . . do I have to go to church?"

"Why, yes, dearest, I think you'd better. I think we're all better for church."

"I don't see why. I don't get anything out of it. I hate it. All those awful Hampton people."

"They're nice people. Besides, it isn't the people you go to church for."

"Well, I hate it! I hate it! It's horrible, and I don't believe there is any God anyway, so what's the use of going?"

"Leda! Of course there is a God, darling. Are you all ready?"

"Prove there's a God."

"Oh, Leda, I can't argue with you when you get this way. Of course there's a God. All the greatest people in history have believed in God."

"I can't believe anything unless it's proved to me. I'm not going to believe something just because somebody tells me it's so. I think it's perfectly horrible, disgusting, just accepting something because somebody else has accepted it. I hate religion and church and being all serious and sad and sorrowful."

Laura March looked frightened. She picked up her purse and her white gloves, and gave a few little pats to herself.

"We've got to be starting, sweetness. Come on."

"Oh, Mother. You're so stupid. You can't argue with me because you don't think."

They went out of their front door and down the street to the village. Bernard hummed through his rabbit-teeth, walking along stoop-shouldered and knock-kneed. Laura took little quick steps. Leda took longer steps than either of them; her face was sullen and she hung her head. Now and then she would walk ahead of them.

"Sweetness, don't go so fast. We can't keep up," Laura said.

"You great big girl," Bernard said, with his giggle.

Leda said nothing.

The Congregational Church, where the Marches went, was not the fashionable church of Hampton. The rich commuting citizens went to the Episcopal Church that the Marches passed on their way; an affluent, modern stone structure. The Congregational Church was old New England, a white wooden building with a spire; the native Hamptonites went to it. The Marches went because Bernard, who was indifferent about his religion, had readily resigned his family's Episcopalianism to the religion of Laura's family; she would not have cared either, but they had begun that way, and they rarely changed any habit they got into.

The people of old Hampton streamed in to church: garrulous old gentlemen, members of the Historical Society; brisk housewives, severe mothers and excellent cooks; old maids, young people, outstanding in High School, deep in church affairs; all the Yankee types, alive today in the same old guises. They were keepers of failing stores; members of the G.A.R. Post; librarians, Sunday School teachers; High School valedictorians; bee keepers; deed lawyers; under-educated doctors; proprietors of little book shops and flower shops quartered in musty front parlors; dressmakers—people rooted three centuries deep in Hampton soil.

The Marches went to their pew on the side, halfway up the aisle. Mr. Butler, who also stuffed birds, produced reedy music from the organ up in the chaste white gallery. The congregation rose and sang "Oh, worship the King." The pews were painted white, and had pads of old green damask. In the high square pulpit the Rev. John Fuller stood, simple, sincere, and ineffectual, in a dark suit. The subject of the sermon was "Our Path As Christian Citizens."

As Laura March sang the hymns, her face grew sadder; she seemed about to weep. On the other side of Leda, Bernard March sang an accurate baritone; as his mouth opened wide his chin receded into his throat in a gather of skin-folds. When the congregation was seated for the sermon Laura sat with her hands folded, like a child's, in her lap, gazing with serious moist eyes at Mr. Fuller; Bernard fingered the edges of the hymn-book in the rack in front, and sniffed from time to time; he could not breathe well through his nose.

Leda was watching a pewful of strangers in the center of the church, well forward. There was a father, tall and lanky with a bullet head covered with short, curly hair. There was a mother, a diminutive creature with an ugly, mobile, alert face. There was a young lady who must be in her twenties, strikingly pretty, with curly light-gold hair and a babyish, bee-stung upper lip. There was a girl of Leda's age; and two little girls, yellow-haired, that wriggled and whispered.

They fascinated Leda. They were different from any people she had ever seen. They were not like Bostonians nor like Hamptonites. They were dressed somewhat fantastically: the mother wore a hat very much on one side of her head, showing her hair skinned back rakishly behind her ear; the oldest daughter wore a bright red hat and a pair of green earrings that showed beneath the masses of soft curly hair; and the daughter that was Leda's age wore earrings too, and an old, raddled, squirrel fur. The littler children were dressed in motley, unmatched clothes. The father was the only one of them that bore an air of normality, of conventionality. And yet around all of them was an aura curiously distinguished, an air not of cheapness but of character, energy, life.

Leda watched them. She forgot about herself. It was like watching a play. The lazy-looking father crossed and re-crossed his legs, cupped his hand behind his ear. The mother moved restlessly, like a bird, and once she whispered something to the oldest girl and they both laughed behind their hands, their eyes sparkling. The girl Leda's age gazed with enormous solemn eyes at the minister, and yet somehow as if she were about to burst out laughing. When the younger children began to whisper a little too loud the mother hushed them, but in a friendly, casual way, as if she did not really care whether they hushed or not.

After the last hymn and the blessing the congregation waited a moment while Mr. Fuller hurried down the aisle to the front door. Then they all began to move out, talking; down to Mr. Fuller, with whom they all shook hands and spoke for a moment.

The Marches reached the door just as the strange family, in a group, were talking to Mr. Fuller. Mr. Fuller was laughing, and all the family was laughing, and the oldest girl was showing deep dimples in her cheeks, rather prominent white front teeth, and a dent under her lower lip that swelled out again into a round white chin. Mr. Fuller caught hold of Bernard March's hand.

"Mrs. March—Mr. March—I want you to meet our new parishioners. Mr. and Mrs. Jekyll, Miss Jekyll, Miss—Betsy Jekyll, is that right?—and little Jane and Glory Jekyll. There, that's quite a family, isn't it?—The Jekylls have bought the Cameron house, up on Crompton Street, and we hope they're going to settle with us for good."

The Jekyll family turned in a body on the timid Marches, exclaiming, laughing, creating a strange, exciting atmosphere. They all seemed to talk at once, except Mr. Jekyll, who shifted from one long leg to the other silently and seldom took his eyes off his wife. They all moved, while the Jekylls talked, out into the gravel churchyard, to allow people behind them to speak to the minister.

These new voices were marked by a strong accent of the South. They had a way of breaking from words into a low, breathy laugh, and back into words, high, rapid, nearly shrill. Bernard and Laura March looked ashamed and self-conscious under the barrage. Leda only stared. She and the girl her age looked at each other; the other girl smiled, brilliantly, and Leda found her mouth widening into a smile too.

"A real interesting sermon, Mr. March," Mrs. Jekyll was saying, her bird-like head cocked on one side. She had drawn a package of cigarettes from her purse and was lighting one; she continued to talk, with the cigarette thrust in one corner of her mouth and the smoke rising in a screen close to her plain, animated face; she blinked her eyes impatiently in the smoke. "I do think this is the nicest town, just real pure New England, isn't it?—I've always thought New England must be the finest place to live, all the cultural advantages, and a bracing climate. Talk about the sunny South, down home where we come from, in Annestown, Virginia—I believe it's every bit as cold as you have it here, but not near so bracing. I don't believe there's a particle of difference in the temperature. . . ."

". . . . Mrs. March, it certainly is the funniest old house," the pretty older girl was saying. "You've never seen it?—just the funniest old place, we love it. Up top of the house there's a tower, like a tower, and Betsy's all decided she's going to have it for her own private personal place. You all must come down and see us in it. We're in the wildest confusion you ever saw, boxes and things all over everything, but we certainly would be glad to see you any time."

". . . . Yes, did you hear that?" the fifteen-year-old girl said to Leda, smiling all over her pug-dog face. "I've got my own room to myself for the very first time in my life. I've always had to sleep with the Brats. Why don't you come down this afternoon and I'll show you my tower and we can fool around. Maizie—she's my sister, isn't she just the most beautiful thing?—she's making herself a new dress, and we can help and . . ."

"Ma-ma . . . Ma'am . . . come on, let's run all the way home," shouted the oldest of the two younger children. The very youngest was a queer, shrewd-looking little girl, with her mother's quick, snapping eyes. She was playing some complicated form of hopscotch on the gravel.

"I reckon I've got to get home and feed these starving children," said Mrs. Jekyll. She took the youngest child's hand, and started to move off toward the gate of the churchyard, still talking. "I hope we'll have the pleasure of seeing you all soon. Just come any time. The house is a terrible mess of confusion, but I'd be delighted to see you."

"I'll see you this afternoon, won't I?" said Betsy to Leda.

"Yes," Leda said. She had never in her life seen people like these or had an invitation given to her so casually and gaily, or one which it seemed so easy and natural to accept.

The Jekyll family turned and trooped out of the west gate of the church-yard. Leda walked up the street toward home between her parents, behind and before members of the Hampton congregation. Sober, musty, stiff, they seemed to dispel that sudden vision of gaiety and easy laughter. All people in the world were austere and dismal and forbidding, like these. All people were to be feared. Gradually self-consciousness and diffidence crept over Leda again. There was nothing in the world she dreaded so much as arriving at a strange house: there were the frightful moments of hesitation outside, the doubt that she was wanted, the impulse to run away; and then cold, questioning faces behind the door. Now she doubted her impression of the Jekylls; it was an illusion, and they would be like everybody else. If she went there, this afternoon, she would regret it. Walking between her father and her mother she was aware of their timidity, and clung to it. She was forever safe with them, however much she resented them. She doubted, more and more, that she would go to the Jekyll's this afternoon.

## CHAPTER III

MINNIE MAY JEKYLL inherited her love of pleasure from her mother and her grandmother. She was heir to two traits from the line of Virginia women behind her: that love of pleasant living, and a hotter love. The sexuality of those women now dead was a stronger thing than that of the men they married; they were women who lived consciously in their physical lives and fed upon their husbands' virility with a hunger that consumed all of it. That appetite was retroactively destructive to the women who owned it: it made them as tractable as drug-addicts; these women lived under their husbands' domination, worked for them, sacrificed for them, obliterated their own personalities willingly. The total effect of each woman's life was that of the docile, dominated, will-less wife; and yet this fate had been brought by the woman upon herself; she had through years willingly as-sumed an aspect that brought her what she must have: the whole force of her husband brought to bear upon her.

In all this Minnie May was like her forebears. In two other things she was different from any of them. The demands of her appetites, although they burned inside her with as hot a fire, were never capable of consuming her energy entirely; she retained a restlessness, an ambition, an active curiosity toward life, which were as characteristic of her as they were unheard of in her line. And unlike the rest of them she was plain. They had been beautiful and lush; all her life Minnie May had been little and thin, knobby-boned, with dun-colored hair and an intense, plain face—muddy skin, no color, long upper lip, thin, mobile mouth.

She was born Minnie May Green. She was brought up in Annestown in the weather-colored frame house to which her grandfather had moved the family when Fern Hill, the Green house up toward the mountains, had burned just after the Civil War. The Greens were poor. They lived on

Minnie May's father's salary as a professor of philosophy at Annestown College. But they were no poorer than any of their friends, and Minnie May and her beautiful sister Glory grew up with the understanding that they were the equals if not the superiors of any family in the South.

They lived easily, lazily, pleasantly, a life full of sunshine and big meals and long summers and the sound of women's high-pitched voices. There were always plenty of people about, and never any social feeling but of friendliness, intimacy, casualness among their equals and pleasant patronage of the negroes. There were plenty of desirable things—clothes, carriages, horses—that their money would not buy, but there was never anything to worry about, never any stay to the comfortable knowledge of equality with any aristocracy the world had to offer.

When Minnie May was seventeen Glory was nineteen. One night—a Sunday night—Glory was having a party in the old house. It was raining. A number of students from the college were coming, most of them Glory's suitors. The kitchen was full of ham and turkey and hot bread. Somebody pointed out that the wall of the front living-room was leaking; dark rivers were running down the red wallpaper, making a shallow, spreading pool on the Brussels carpet.

"Now why do you have to call attention to a thing like that right at this time?" Mrs. Green cried, laughing. Her soft, ravaged face was as full of anticipation of the party as Glory's. "You know those students aren't going to see anything but Glory. It doesn't make a particle of difference how much water comes in, long as nobody drowns!"

It made no difference to Minnie May, either. She had her family's, her class's indifference to matters that could not be helped. That class never outgrew the feeling that if anything had to be fixed, the negroes could fix it, and if there was no one to fix it, it could go. They lived according to their desires, having as much of everything as they could get by the use of all cash in hand and all available credit; they did not comprehend the principle of saving; they lived happily in the hour, and although their connections were no wealthier than themselves, they were so extensive that in the end none of them came to very sorry grief.

So, while the roof rotted slowly over their heads, Minnie May grew up as the homely younger sister of a college belle. For someone like Minnie May, that was not easy. She was full of energy and flirtatiousness. She was obliged to witness the spectacle of her sister strolling slowly, interminably, on the campus of the college through spring after spring with a succession of courtly, hopeful suitors. Minnie May never forgot the beauty and enviability of that scene: the shadows of the great trees falling over the smooth grass on the campus, the shadows of the columned cloisters, and walking through them the figures of her sister and some young man, Glory tall and ripening into the family figure, her face luscious but still unconscious and unawakened to the sensualism that was her future, turned dreamily as if half asleep toward the assiduous, attentive suitor that walked by her side. Herself, Minnie May, was only a shadow in that scene, Glory's plain little sister— although she, far more than Glory, was awake to desire; she already understood and longed for the passionate and full-time occupation of being a woman.

In the end Glory married none of the eager young men on the campus. By chance a young Italian, Count Ruggero Venti, came through Annestown on his tour of America, to inspect the Italianate architecture of the college. It was one of those somewhat preposterous, romantic things which Annestown people took quite for granted. Count Venti was entertained in their mouldering old houses as an equal—a titled foreigner, but after all someone who was approximately the equivalent of themselves, of their own deathless nobility. And he fell in love with Glory, and that was no more of a surprise than his being there in the first place. She was a Green, one of the Green beauties and hence one of the beauties of the world. Minnie May watched her marry Count Venti in Christ Church, and stand beside him in the red-papered front living-room receiving the good wishes of her friends; the old stains still showed as dark as ever on the wallpaper. Minnie May watched her, and would have given her right arm to stand there in her stead; her instinct was right; the life that Glory went to would have just fitted Minnie May, this marriage would have suited her to perfection.

Next year in Annestown there was a young law student named Tom Jekyll. He had never seen Glory. He was tall and had long thin legs and a close-cropped bullet head and a funny, pug-dog face. He came from West Virginia and hence was not considered socially first-rate by the Annestownites. He was lazy, good-natured, tolerably intelligent, and he used to call on Minnie May, perhaps impressed by her social eminence and stimulated by her energy. He would sit on the horsehair sofa in the old red living-room, his long legs out in front of him, and Minnie May would tell him how to make something of himself.

"Now, don't you go back there to West Virginia. How in the world could you amount to anything buried out yonder in some little town? You just get yourself an office down by the Court House, and set up, and be somebody."

"You reckon anybody'd come to me to handle their cases, a country boy like me?"

"Certainly they would, Tom. They would if I were to tell them to. There's not much money in this town, but there's a practice for a young man who works hard. Later, maybe, you might go North to practice law—New York, maybe. Who knows?"

"You know I wouldn't go up North. But it's right kind of you to take an interest in me, Minnie May."

One night he asked her to marry him. Perhaps she willed him to. She accepted with alacrity, and they were married soon after. Everybody in Annestown was delighted that Minnie May Green had got herself a man. Glory, who had borne twins, sent a cable. The Greens purchased as fine, as expensive a trousseau for their plain second daughter as they had for their beautiful first daughter, and went further into debt to pay for it.

If she had been completely her mother's daughter Minnie May would now have been happy for the rest of her life. She adored her lanky, lazy

husband and drew his healthy virility from him like honey. In body as well
as mentally and spiritually she really possessed him. Now that she was able
to expend her great store of desire, he had grown to be almost unconscious
that she was not a beautiful woman; her desire awoke his, and he wanted
her. At night, when the long pent-up heat of all her youth was released, it
would have diminished her pleasure to remember who she was, how she
looked. In the dark she could pretend to herself that she looked quite differently; in the dark she was, to herself, a beautiful woman. It was nothing
vague, it was a very clear embodiment: she had thick, long, corn-colored
hair that filled the hollow of her neck, she had full red lips, she had a fragile
waist above hips that went down into lovely thighs. It was this woman that
filled Tom Jekyll's arms at night, and although she never mentioned a word
of this illusion, Minnie May managed to make it as real for Tom as for herself. After marriage he was convinced that his wife was as voluptuous as she
was voluptuary.

Within a year of their marriage Minnie May had borne a child, a girl as
beautiful as she could have wished, with her aunt's fair curling hair and a
pink, dimpled little face. Minnie May thoroughly enjoyed everything to do
with her pregnancy. In reality she was one of the women pregnancy sits
least gracefully upon—she became pinched and gray-looking. But her illusion
persisted mercifully. She gloried in her swelling girth. The pain of childbirth was exciting to her; like her mother and her grandmother and all the
women before her she enjoyed the anguish, the screaming and tossing.

Little Minnie May, who was called Maizie, was an affectionate and prepossessing child. She had her mother's adoration, and grew up not spoiled
but expecting and receiving love wherever she went. Two years after she
was born, her Aunt Glory died in Rome in childbirth. Minnie May was
wretched at the loss, but she was conscious of a dignity in the cause of
Glory's death. She herself would have liked to bear a child every year, as
Glory had done, but she did not become pregnant again for six years. Then
Betsy was born.

Betsy had her father's pug-dog face, made whimsical and appealing by
her enormous eyes. In the years before her birth the closest kind of relation
had grown up between Minnie May and Maizie, and it was a relationship
into which Betsy was never able to penetrate. Her mother loved her, but
more reasonably than Maizie; Betsy's childhood was spent trying to make
her mother notice her and love her more. Five years after Betsy, Minnie
May gave birth to Jane and, a year later, to Glory. After Glory she knew
that she would never have any more children.

In the years of their marriage Tom Jekyll had become a fairly successful
lawyer in Annestown. He had a ground floor office in an old brick building
on the Court House Square. Nearly all of his clients had been sent to him
by Minnie May; their business was small, for the most part the re-deeding
of property, wills, the prosecution of petty thefts; Tom made enough to
live on. He always felt unsustained in his office, and frequently telephoned
home to ask Minnie May's advice. He felt inadequate when he was on his
own; Minnie May had possessed him completely. He began to come alive

when he rounded the corner just before their house. He would walk into the house and all the children would come tumbling, shouting down the stairs to kiss him; the smells of cooking floated out from the kitchen, cheerfully; a meal would be served presently somewhere, possibly in the dining-room but quite as probably somewhere else, by some new servant whose name he did not know. And his wife, a fascinating woman, would talk and laugh and joke with the children, flirt with him, smoke her innumerable cigarettes and make him feel that his life was the happiest in the world.

He was more content than Minnie May, now. Those deep resources of her energy had hardly been tapped by her years of child-bearing and now she was as fresh, as restless, as curious about life as ever. The outlets for her were few enough: her physical life with Tom, whose lust was wearing out long before hers, her life with the children, whom she led a merry dance, and the social life of Annestown, where she managed most things and had a say in everything. It was not enough.

She was growing impatient of Annestown. She realized that with all her pushing Tom could not get much further than he had. She was curious to see new faces, live in a new place, encounter new ways of living. It was not until Glory was ten that an opportunity came to move elsewhere. Tom had an offer from a firm in Boston; the firm had dealings with companies in the South, and they felt it would be well to have a Southern member of the firm. That, too, was really Minnie May's doing. She had met the representative of the Boston firm when he was in Annestown, looking over the lawyers in town; Minnie May had had no way of knowing that, but just because he was a stranger, just because he was something new, she asked him at once to dinner. It was a strange meal: the cook had left in the middle of the preparation of dinner; Maizie had finished it, and they sat in the littered, crazy dining-room and ate turkey while Minnie May was so diverting and so gay that the Boston lawyer left town with the confused impression that Tom Jekyll was a clever lawyer with a wonderful wife, both of them just as full of Southern charm as they could be.

In reality Tom Jekyll was not full of charm. He was a pleasant man who had fallen into the way of letting his wife think for him, a West Virginian who had never had sufficient confidence to forget that he was not a Virginian. He had plenty of men friends in Annestown. He liked to play pool and tennis with them, to get drunk with them. He was happy in Annestown, and he was surprised and disturbed when he found that he had accepted an offer to go to live in Boston.

"What in the world will I do up North?" he inquired of Minnie May, pulling off his shoes on the edge of the bed before going to sleep. "Whole pack of lawyers up there practicing fancy law I don't know anything about. Honey, you know I belong down here in Annestown."

"Annestown's poky," Minnie May said firmly. "You and I know this old town inside out and there's nothing more for us to know about it. Tom, I've always wanted to get out and live somewhere else. I've just got this one life, and I certainly would like to see a little something in it. Up North will probably seem strange to us, but we've got a lot to learn. Seems like we ought to be able to adjust ourselves to a new kind of living. We're ourselves wherever we may live. I reckon we ought to have a pretty good time any-where." She brushed her thin, dun-colored hair with determined strokes. Her eyes gleamed with anticipation.

"Minnie May, darling, it just doesn't seem quite fair to Maizie, somehow. It's tearing her away from all her beaux down here, now she's grown-up and about ready to marry. She'll have to get started all over again up North. Boston sounds like a right unfriendly place."

"Maizie's a Green, isn't she? I'm not afraid. I reckon I'll like Boston and the people up there will like me."

"Everybody always likes you, Minnie May," Tom admitted. Personally he was frightened; but he had confidence in his wife.

They moved. Minnie May carried all of them with her on the wave of her enthusiasm. Nobody wanted them to go; there was a round of parties before their departure; someone high up in the city had the name of the street the Jekylls lived on changed to Minniemay Avenue, hoping to induce her to remain. But they moved. Only Tom and Maizie were unhappy.

All her young men sent flowers and promised to write to Maizie, but she felt a deep disturbance inside her at this breaking off short of her life. She had spent all her youth in Annestown. She was a Green woman; the con-tentment and resignation that had skipped Minnie May had come out again, true to type, in Maizie. She felt the deepest nostalgia at leaving the place, the cool, quiet reaches of the campus at the college, the familiar lazy pattern of life, the cohorts of her admirers just as she was ready to begin choosing from among them. But deeper still than this love was the love between her and her mother. They had always been singularly close. Anywhere Minnie May wanted to go Maizie would go too.

It was different for Betsy. Although she looked like a pretty version of her father, it was her mother she resembled temperamentally; the impatience and adventurousness had cropped out again, with a strong romantic streak, an inability to accept reality, that was Betsy's own. Like her mother she was excited to be going somewhere else to live; her enormous eyes were wide open with anticipation. It was like her to believe that the strange was the beautiful; she saw irresistible enticements in the unexplored.

The little ones—the Brats—were unmoved at the prospect of departure. To them it was just another of their mother's schemes, as ever full of amuse-ment and delight. The family moved North, and took a house in Hampton within commuting distance of Boston.

## CHAPTER IV

THAT HOUSE was a strange one. On a skeleton of roomy, simple Colonial architecture had been added the queer limbs of late nineteenth century building—an enormous circular bay-window that thrust out from the living-room, a wide porch that dripped with wooden icicles, a high square tower at one corner that rose two stories above the rest of the house, and a long wing that sprawled out from the rear, holding pantry, kitchen, servants' bedrooms above, and beyond a succession of useless, cold rooms that might have been used as laundries or storerooms. Into the capacious, eccentric house the Jekyll family poured, shouting, laughing, exploring, and dumping their belongings all over the place.

None of them, certainly not Minnie May, had any conception of how to make a house orderly, to make it function smoothly; none of them had the ambition to know how. What they laid down they rarely picked up until they needed it again. Maizie had some feeling for neatness, but this was displayed only upon her person; she was always delightfully appetizing. All of the family took baths at all hours of the day, whenever the water was hot, and threw the wet towels about the bedrooms.

Minnie May had the big front East bedroom; Maizie had the opposite room, on the West; the Brats slept in the room behind hers. Betsy had immediately found and claimed the tower for her own; its height and seclusion seemed to her redolent of glamour. Tom had a dressing-room off Minnie May's room, and slept in the big bed with her.

Downstairs one half of the front of the house was all living-room, a long room with a great rounded bulge at one side. On the other side of the front hall was a dark panelled room which had been named Tom's study; it had windows framed by square panes of vari-colored stained glass; all the children threw their coats and hats in there when they came in; Minnie May and Tom sat there in the evenings when the children had gone to bed. Behind it was the dining-room, filled with all of Minnie May's assorted dining-room furniture; it was always full of sunshine, and the remnants of the last meal.

On that Sunday afternoon late in April the house was noisy with laughter and loud music. The ruddy rays of the sun came in through the western windows of the dining-room where Glory sat eating a fried-egg sandwich that she had made for herself; she had been playing outside when the others ate their lunch. Jane was sliding down the varnished banisters; a stout child, she would run thunderously up the stairs and slide down, to land with a bump against the carved post at the bottom. Tom was in the study, surrounded by three Sunday papers that had been pulled apart into chaos by the whole family; the late sun shone down on his curly, close-clipped bullet head and he wore a pair of horn-rimmed glasses; his long legs stuck comfortably out in front.

In the living-room Minnie May sat at the out-of-tune upright piano, playing loudly, carelessly, with tremendous gusto, the dance tunes that came into her head. She wore an old black skirt and a satin blouse. She smoked as she played, and the smoke drifted up over the skin of her face, yellowing the long upper lip. Her dun hair was screwed into a French twist up the back of her head. She played the bangy dance tunes with heavily-marked rhythm, singing sometimes with the cigarette wagging in her mouth, for Maizie and the young men to dance.

The young men were Hampton young men. Maizie had immediately attracted them. She was "a Southern girl," and her voice and pretty face and laughter, and the unheard-of life that went on in the old Cameron house, had already set up around her an aura of excitement and danger. No respectable God-fearing family could live as the Jekylls lived. Respectable families lived parsimoniously and neatly, with meals on time. There was a feverishness, a devilish look of excitement, about the young men in the Jekyll house that day. They felt they were up to something unorthodox. One was a young teller at the Hampton Savings Bank; one was a student at M.I.T.; the third was at Harvard; all of them went to the Congregational Church and were members of old, rusty Hampton families. They were not very personable young men; they looked callow, and over-excited, and their manners were both over-confident and ill at ease.

Maizie was as pretty as a flower. Her curly hair, soft and clinging like milkweed, puffed out from either side of her round, dimpled face. Her cheeks were bright with rouge. The jade-green earrings swung against her small round neck, and she wore a jade-green dress of cheap silk. As she talked and laughed her blue eyes shone with pleasure, and her under lip caught under the two prominent white front teeth.

The young men danced with her in turn to Minnie May's loud dashing music. Betsy hung about, admiring Maizie; now and then one of the young men would ask her and she would dance, rapturously and painstakingly. Her wide-eyed pug face was solemn with the effort to follow properly. She wore one of Maizie's dresses, scarlet silk with a flaring skirt, and the same green earrings she had worn to church. She looked up into the young men's faces in imitation of Maizie's gay, flirtatious look. She had attempted to cover the freckles on her snub nose with an application of pink powder, but she still looked childish, round, and enthralled.

The long floor was bare and partly littered with papers and cigarette ashes. There was little furniture. The marble mantelpiece was thick with letters and ashtrays. The younger children drifted in; Jane stood watching the dancing, and Glory came over and rubbed her head against her mother's back.

Minnie May played on, stressing the beat heavily and experimenting with high trills that as often as not were false; but the effect was gay.

> Mickey—pretty Mickey—
> With your hair of raven hue,
> With your smiling so beguiling
> There's a bit of the Blarney, bit of Killarney, too!

Minnie May sang the words, cocking her head, in a high voice that was cheerful and a little bit flat.

> Childhood in the wildwood—
> Like a mountain flower you grew!
> Pretty Mickey, pretty Mickey,
> Can you blame anyone for falling in love with you,
>                         Boom, boom!*

*"MICKEY" by permission of the copyright proprietor, Mills Music, Inc.

Minnie May paused a moment to light another cigarette.

"Betsy," she called. "Come here. There's that little March girl we saw this morning, walking past the house in the wrong direction like she's scared to come in. Run out and tell her to come right in, hear?" She returned to her playing with gusto.

That was the scene that Leda came upon, led by Betsy. Mrs. Jekyll stopped playing and beamed.

"Hello, Leda dear," she said as if she had known her well. "Certainly am glad you came. Now wouldn't you like something to eat? Betsy'll get you something. An apple, or a nice fried-egg sandwich?"

"No, thank you," Leda said. She could not help smiling back.

"Hello, Leda," Maizie said. Her face was pretty and affectionate.

Leda looked toward the young men. They were sheepish and confused at seeing someone they knew. They lit cigarettes and strolled about with studied maturity.

"Come talk to me," Mrs. Jekyll continued. "I declare I'm tired to death playing for these children. Now, Leda, tell me something. Where do you go to school around here? I feel like I've got to do something about getting these children some education."

"Well, I go to the Country Day School now," Leda said shyly. "But next winter I guess I'm going to Miss Sheraton's in Boston. That's where all the girls are going my age. At least, I haven't asked Mother yet, but that's where everybody else is going."

"I see," Minnie May said reflectively. "That's *the* place for older girls to go around here, I reckon. Well, Betsy, you can go to Miss Whatyoumay-callem's next winter, too. Don't see why you have to go to school any more this year."

"Gosh, I'm glad," Betsy said. She grinned at Leda and Leda laughed.

"I reckon we'd all like something to drink," Minnie May said, getting up briskly. "Maizie, you want to go make some lemonade for everybody?"

"No, Ma'am, you go on do it."

"Well, Betsy, you and your guest can play together. I'll go make it myself."

As she went down the hall she popped her head into the study and waved to Tom.

"Hello, honey, you getting along all right by yourself in there?"

"Unh-hunh. Who was that just came in?"

"A little friend of Betsy's. I declare, Tom," Minnie May said, going further into the room and lowering her voice, "she is the most peculiar child. Just as shy, and kind of miserable looking. You know, we all saw her this morning after church. I'd like to be nice to her. She's a pretty child, with those dark eyes and that heavy black hair, too. She's pale, but it's sort of becoming. Besides, Tom, Mr. Fuller was saying after church this morning, these Marches come of a real fine family around here. Boston. She'd be a nice friend for Betsy. I don't think much of these whipper-snappers Maizie's got here this afternoon."

"Common-looking," Tom agreed.

"Besides, this March child—I've got a funny feeling about her—I can just see her looking at me feeling the way I often feel—kind of wanting to run things and not knowing how."

Tom looked over the top of his horn-rimmed glasses at his wife.

"Do you want some lemonade?" she said. "I'll fix you a nice glass with whisky and a little sugar."

High in Betsy's tower Betsy was demanding,

"When are you going to be sixteen?"

"Next August. When are you?"

"June. Seems like I'd never get to be sixteen. Ma'am says I can wear rouge like Maizie when I'm sixteen."

Leda stared.

"Let's fix our hair," Betsy went on. "Come on. I can make mine look real snaky this way, putting a little water and making curls down over the forehead."

"How—would you fix mine?"

"Haven't you ever fooled with it? Look. You've got marvellous hair, so shiny and dark. I just *hate* my hair!"

"It's curly. My hair is perfectly straight."

"I know, but you can get a perm. Lots of girls down home are getting perms. They're right expensive, though."

"Permanent waves?"

"Unh-hunh! Did you ever see such beautiful hair as Maizie's got?"

"No, never."

"And she's the sweetest sister. I'm just so crazy about her I don't know what to do! Everybody is. Why, down home you should have seen all the beaux. Every student in the college was in love with her. She's got *five* fraternity pins and she uses two of them to pin her brazeer straps to her teddy straps."

Leda looked uncomprehending and fascinated.

"Brazeer's our family word for brassiere," Betsy explained. "The girls in the shops call them that, and we think it's funny. Teddies are under-clothes, kind of all in one, top and pants. Maizie has just heaps of them. Blue ones, and pink, and orchid, and some with ecru lace. . . . I just can't wait to grow up and have a time, can you?"

"I don't believe I would have a time."

"Don't be coo-coo! Why, I think you're just fascinating looking. Ma'am does too. She said so, at lunch. You're kind of mysterious, with deep-set eyes and that dark hair. You'll be a knock-out. . . . Leda, let's be great friends and go after beaux together and fix each other's hair and everything. Want to?"

"Yes," Leda stammered. Her dark eyes were shining.

"Maizie'll help us learn to fix our hair and fix our faces and things. She's so sweet. And she always gets such a rush, she'll be able to help us. You wait and see. She'll have millions of beaux here like everywhere. Honestly, I have got the most marvellous family. Don't you think so?"

"Yes, I do," Leda said.

"Ma'am said she thought you were shy. Are you shy?"

"I guess so."

"Well, you don't feel shy about me, do you? Because I like you loads. I want to be friends and have fun. You don't have to feel shy with any of us, because we all are crazy about you. And we're all kind of crazy anyway and there's nothing to be scared of. . . . Oh, I'm so glad we've started being friends, because now we can do things together and get to be popular. I want to be popular more than anything in the world, don't you?"

"Yes, I do," Leda said. Slowly her mouth curved into a smile. Betsy had pushed a pile of tumbled, soiled underclothes to one side of the bureau and was leaning anxiously toward the mirror, solemnly plastering curls down over her forehead with water.

Leda picked up the box of pink powder and dabbed a little of it on her nose. She looked over Betsy's shoulder into the mirror and saw herself as if for the first time. In the greenish, streaky glass her face was slender and pale, with deep dark sockets of eyes, a delicate nose, and masses of dark hair above her forehead.

From downstairs the bangy music blared out, and the shouting of the younger children as they scuffled in the hall.

> Though April showers
> Fall all the day
> They bring the flowers
> That bloom in May!
>
> So though it's raining
> Have no regrets,
> Because it isn't raining rain you see
> It's raining vi-o-lets!

Betsy sang the words to the distant music in her cheerful, high-pitched little voice. She turned from the mirror and grinned, wriggling all over with puppylike pleasure.

"Do you really like me?" Leda said in a low voice, looking away.

"My goodness, yes. Do you like me?"

"Yes."

The music changed and grew still louder, bangier.

## CHAPTER V

BETSY JEKYLL had her first friend in the North. She admired Leda March extravagantly. She considered her mysterious and beautiful. Leda appealed to all those deep sources of romanticism in Betsy that made her idealize

Maizie's prettiness and imagine Maizie's successes as extravagant conquests. She was never content to see things as they were. She made all events into dramas, and all the girls she admired, like Maizie and Leda, into heroines. Her tower was an enchanted turret, Leda was a strange, thrilling friend, an only child; Maizie was the toast of the town, a heart-breaker, an enchantress. Her mother was a fascinating personality, a wit, the source of all plans. Every day Betsy jumped out of bed filled with the elixir of her health and with the overwhelming conviction that she lived in a family of seven-day wonders, of whom all glamorous things might be expected.

With her romanticism she had a friendliness, a gift of interest and intimacy, that made her like an affectionate, trusting puppy. All people were interesting to her, and it had never occurred to her that someone might not like her, might be cold or disdainful or unfriendly. She saw the people of Hampton as new and extraordinary; she imagined for them exciting private lives and made friends with them with unembarrassed energy.

The first time she went to the Marches' house was a case in point. She had seen Leda nearly every day for two weeks, but always at the Jekylls'. Leda never asked her to her house, and into this difference Betsy read mystery and enchantment. Finally she asked herself—arrived at the house back up the road toward the woods just after lunch, and came in beaming and bright-eyed. Leda's shyness and inhospitality she translated into reserve. She went up to Mrs. March and shook hands.

"Mrs. March, I've just been dying to see Leda's house. It's so pretty. I never saw such pretty things. I *am* so glad to see you again! Leda's such a friend of mine now, I just felt I had to get to know her mother."

She sat down on the sofa next to Laura and wriggled up close to her, grinning at Mr. March.

"I hear you're a great musician. Won't you please play something? It's terribly exciting to know a real honest-to-goodness musician. Please, Mr. March."

Bernard got up and played Chopin for her. Betsy didn't really listen. She had turned again on Mrs. March, looking into her large gentle face, trying to extract the wonderful secret of her personality. Laura's timidity vanished in the face of this warm, chattering child. She had always prided herself inwardly on the arrangements of her house. But it had always been an inner pride. She felt that Leda didn't care about such things; certainly she never said a word of praise. Bernard was frankly indifferent to his surroundings; it was their peace, their snugness, that was important to him, and he was oblivious of decorations.

This child seemed to take the deepest interest. Somehow, Laura didn't know how, she found herself talking of the trouble she had had with the green chintz curtains in the room, how there hadn't been enough of the material, and she had had to send for more that didn't quite match; how she loved the look of oranges heaped in the pewter bowl set in the south window; how she disliked carpets on stairs, and had left hers bare, and admired the simplicity of New England furniture. This child seemed rapt and entranced.

Bernard played on. He liked the child's enormous eyes fixed on him with wonder and respect, as if she considered him mysterious and important. No one had ever thought that of Bernard. He felt that he was playing very well, and although the child's admiring exclamations showed that she knew nothing of music, he felt a warmth and liked her being there.

Leda sat across the room. She had never asked children to play at her house since she was quite little; she was always ashamed and self-conscious. The house seemed all wrong, queer, and her parents ridiculous and unlike other children's parents. She still felt embarrassment at having Betsy see her house and her family; but it was vanishing. Increasingly she felt the new hope that had begun to exist in her since she had known the Jekylls—that now she had friends, that she could forget about queerness and have some pleasure besides those lonely pleasures in the woods that she seemed to be outgrowing.

Later that afternoon, after Betsy had gone, Leda asked her mother to call on Mrs. Jekyll. She had conceived a vision of intimacy between the two families—a familiar interchange of friendship; it was almost too exciting a thought to be borne.

"Oh, Leda!" Laura said. "Do you really think I ought to? I do dread calling on strange people so. I never know what to say."

"You've got to. They're so wonderful, they're the most wonderful family you ever saw. You won't be scared, they make you feel good right away. You've got to go. I'll *die* if you don't."

"Sweetness, don't scream at me. Of course I'll go, if you really want me to so much."

But Laura did not enjoy her visit. She felt awkward in the dirty house and was made uncomfortable and uneasy by the disregard for order. Mrs. Jekyll was like a foreigner; a rakish-looking, chattering woman with lipstick on her mouth and dozens of cigarettes following each other between her lips. Mrs. Jekyll did all the talking, for sure enough, Laura could think of nothing to say. She could not talk of domestic matters to this restless woman who had apparently never given a thought to her house in her life. Laura felt stupid and frightened and uninteresting.

"I'm afraid I'm not like that kind of people," she said to Leda when she got home. "That oldest girl—she was painted so. I felt uncomfortable in that house. There was dirt in all the cracks of the chair I sat in."

"Oh, *Mother!* They're the only nice people I've ever known."

"I don't know whether your aunts would approve of your seeing so much of them. They're not our kind of people," Laura repeated. Her standard for correct behavior was based on what Bernard's sisters approved of.

"Mother, if you don't let me see them you'll ruin my life. I've got to see them. I've got to! I've never had any fun before or been happy in my life. I suppose you want me to be miserable always."

"Darling, don't talk that way. Of course I want you to be happy, more than anything in the world. I just don't want you to do anything your aunts wouldn't like. They can help you a great deal when you're older."

"They've never done anything for me. I'm having some fun now. I've never had any. I've never had any friends or been able to have people here or anything."

"I wish you weren't so ashamed of us," Laura said miserably.

When Mrs. Jekyll returned Laura's call it was equally uncomfortable. Mrs. Jekyll came in in an old black suit with a pink blouse, her hat tipped far to one side of her head. The sight of her frightened Laura. She hurried out to the kitchen to hurry the preparation of tea. She fussed with the tea-table linen, and brought out her wedding china. She was ill at ease pouring the tea and offering Mrs. Jekyll the sandwiches, the cookies. Mrs. Jekyll seemed oblivious of such things. Laura felt a fat, stupid fool. Their acquaintanceship rested there.

But Betsy remained the friend of the family. She saw Leda every day. Most often they played at the Jekylls'. Life was gayer there, more exciting. The Jekylls were in the thick of church affairs. The house was always full of people, goggling at the casual arrangements and acting a little stiff; but Minnie May's personality had made itself felt, and the Hampton housewives accepted her as an organizer and leading spirit, whose odd way of living could be excused and laid to her coming from the South. The Brats had made friends; they were always busy, and hordes of screaming children ran through the house all afternoon. Maizie had a multitude of local swains who called on her in the evenings and took her walking and driving in their cars. Betsy, in her queer, stubborn little way remained faithful to Leda; she had seen Leda's embarrassment and closed face when they were with other girls. She admired Leda more than any of them, and for her sake saw them less and less. Leda was her special, her close friend.

"Seems like you never play with anybody but Leda March," Maizie said one evening at supper. She was planning to go out on a date afterwards, and was dressed in a new jade-green suit; her cheeks were bright and her blue eyes sparkled.

"Leda doesn't get along with other girls. I like her best," Betsy said, with her mouth full of chicken.

"I don't know but what it's just as well," Minnie May said reflectively. "That March child's got more style than the rest of the children. Seems like she's more somebody than these Hampton people."

The dance at the Parish House was Leda's first party. Mrs. Jekyll had helped organize it, hung the bare little hall with crepe paper and balloons. "Don't seem to be many dances around here," she had said. "Maizie, you'll be forgetting how to dance, and I declare I miss hearing an orchestra." Maizie had a new dress for the party, a bouffant green taffeta trimmed with gold tinsel from Filene's basement in Boston. "I declare the styles are right pretty up here," Minnie May said, viewing it. "It's much easier to get something pretty here than in Annestown. Cheap, too. Now, what's the use of paying big prices when you can buy clothes like this—and Maizie's not going to want to go on wearing it for the rest of her life, either."

It was at the end of May. Betsy was bursting with excitement at being allowed to go to the dance. Maizie had bought her a taffeta evening dress too—pink, with a bunch of silver grapes at the hip. Betsy spun around in it before the mirror, the day before the dance, to make the skirt stand out.

"You've just got to go too, Leda," she said again.

Leda sat on the bed. She was torn apart inside by her fear and her new, wild desire to go to the dance. Some unfamiliar nerve inside her said that she would like it; itched to go and to dance. But her life's habit made her afraid.

"I can't," she said.

"Now, Leda. You're so coo-coo! You'd have a rush, I know you would. I'll just die if you don't go too. I tell you what. You come and get dressed here and go with us, and spend the night afterwards. Now will you?"

Finally Leda consented. Her heart was beating. There was a dress of Maizie's, enviably bright and tinselly, light blue, which Maizie promised to lend her: an exciting dress, of the kind the Jekylls wore. Leda could not resist it. Somehow she felt that in a Jekyll dress she would be like one of the Jekylls.

"Oh, Leda," her mother said. "It seems so funny to spend the night with someone in the same town."

"You've got to let me. I've got to go. I'll die. . . ."

"All right, darling, of course there's nothing wrong about it. But I can't understand your wanting to go to the dance. You know how you hated dancing-school. You were the most wretched, pathetic little thing. . . ."

"I can't help it. I want to go."

Betsy's heart was like a bubble that Saturday night. She and Leda and Maizie dressed together in Maizie's bedroom. The floor was littered with underclothes, the tops of the bureaus with spilled powder and hairpins and little boxes of rouge. The window stood open and the soft May breeze wandered in and cooled Betsy's hot face.

She squirmed into her pink dress and hooked the side up; she patted the bunch of shiny grapes and spun around once more to see the skirt stand out in a big circle around her knees. Then she attacked her face. It looked annoyingly young and round in the mirror, but she drew sophisticated butterfly eyebrows on with a pencil, squinting grimly at herself to get the line even. She covered her freckled face with pink powder, and painted her mouth a luscious, curving red. Standing back, she got the effect. She did look much older.

She sat down on the bed to watch Maizie and Leda. Maizie looked brilliant in the jade-green that was so becoming to her yellow hair. She had put coral-colored rouge on her soft cheeks and was now applying mascara carefully to her eyelashes, spitting into the little box to moisten the cake. She looked like a girl on a cover, Betsy thought.

Leda's face was flushed. She looked slim and distinguished in Maizie's blue dress. She was painting her mouth hesitantly. They were all laughing.

Jane came dashing into the room in her pajamas.

"How many baths did you all take, anyway," she demanded. "There isn't a drop of hot water. How'm I going to get clean?"

"You'll have to go to bed dirty," Betsy sang. "We each had a long, long bath with lots and lots of the hottest water *and* the best soap. How do we look?"

Jane squinted at them critically.

"You look like Maizie's face pasted on top of yours. Leda looks prettiest, she looks like a princess."

"Oh, *Janey!*" Betsy cried, dabbing anxiously at her cheeks.

"How do I look, Janey?" Maizie asked.

Jane gazed at her and then ran and buried her head in the green taffeta skirt.

"You look beautiful," her voice came in muffled tones.

They were ready to go down. Betsy stuck her arm into Leda's and smiled at her. She felt rather scared, beautifully scared, herself. She attempted to glide down the stairs, her chin held high, her eyes dreamy, like a heroine in a book. But her heel, her new, high, gold kid heel, caught in the hem of her dress and only Leda's hand saved her from falling head-long.

Tom Jekyll was waiting at the bottom of the stairs in his evening clothes, and he bowed solemnly over Betsy's and Leda's hands as if they had been young ladies. Minnie May was all keyed up and talking ceaselessly, in an old red evening dress with ostrich feathers round the hem. They all swept off to the dance in a hired taxi. Even the smell of stable in the cab was thrilling.

The Parish House seemed a palace of light as they came in; the blare of the orchestra struck at them as they opened the door. Inside a crowd of young men were waiting for Maizie. Betsy watched her sister's face, dimpling with laughter, as she was propelled on to the dance floor. A panic took hold of Betsy. She wanted so desperately to be a belle. She lifted her chin. She assumed a look of rakish gaiety, and took hold of Leda's hand. It was cold. Betsy threw her a brilliant smile, and they followed Mrs. Jekyll in to the chairs along the wall.

A group of women took Mrs. Jekyll into their midst. Mr. Jekyll was standing out in the hall with the older men, smoking. Betsy and Leda sat side by side, looking with fixed smiles at the dancers. Suddenly one of Maizie's young men detached himself from the group of stags. Was he actually coming their way? He was. He was coming nearer, bowing—but to Leda. Betsy watched them dance off. She felt a momentary throb of pleasure that Leda had been asked to dance. Then she intensified her expression of delirious joy.

The dance ended, and she was still alone. Leda was standing out on the floor, talking; she looked lovely, Betsy thought. A chill seemed to clutch at her heart as the music began again and she was still there against the wall, smiling. The music came to an end again. This was the second dance she had sat through. Maizie was surrounded with a swarm of men, and Leda had been cut in on and was talking to the new man.

Now someone was really coming toward her, Betsy. It was rather a horrid little man, older than Maizie's beaux, a short, stocky, bald man who sometimes called on Maizie and made conceited jokes. But this was no time for criticism. Betsy rose and drifted into his arms. The floor was as smooth as glass, the orchestra enthralling. She felt as if she were flying in the clouds: this was what she had always dreamt about, dancing in a man's arms, to swooning music, a creature in a rose-colored dress. This was the life she wanted—dancing, music, new dresses; all the poetry and illusion that went with them.

The man, whose hand was warm and damp, was holding her very closely. "Cute little thing, aren't you?" he observed, squeezing her waist.

She threw him a flashing smile. His cheek, that he pressed so close to hers, was moist. But she remembered something Maizie had said at one of those times when Betsy had been begging for tips on how to be popular— "You have to be nice to the pills, no matter how gummy you think they are. That's what popularity at a dance is made out of—lots and lots of pills and just a few snaky ones. But the snaky ones won't dance with you unless you seem to be having a rush, and the only way to get a rush is to encourage the pills."

Betsy responded slightly to the clutch in which the man held her. He was certainly one of the pills. At her touch on his shoulder he increased his pressure.

"I think you're wonderful," he breathed in her ear.

She laughed ringingly, and like magic another man cut in. The bald man poked the other man in the ribs as he walked off.

She was enchanted by the number of partners she had. Between the dances she made "peppy" conversation, tipping her head pertly to one side in an imitation of her mother and laughing. She was too busy even to think of Maizie or Leda.

Above her shining brown head the colored balloons bobbed and occasionally popped, yellow and orange and red and silver. The orchestra was a confusion that she saw drunkenly, the dizzy streak of a violin-bow and the long yellow highlight along the tube of a horn. She was drunk with illusion; she was not herself, she was her super-self, someone dancing and dancing and laughing and being all the time a picture she had seen, a dream she had dreamed.

It was twelve, and in Hampton Sunday began at twelve. The orchestra intoned mournfully, brassily "Good . . . night . . . ladies. . . . Good . . . night . . ." and Betsy stood still, breathless, in the center of the floor, not even seeing who she now stood with, clapping her hands without sensation and talking on, cocking her head, saying "Cinderella. . . . Oh, why does it have to be midnight . . . and where are the coach and horses?" —in that pert voice that she had mastered that night, laughing that high, excited laugh she had just learned.

In the hall there was a small group, that without sound or confusion exuded the atmosphere of tension. Minnie May was in the group, in the center of it, and Betsy stared at her—the red dress, the flounce of bedraggled ostrich—a haze before her eyes, still rapt in the tower-high illusion. Her father was there, too, swaying gently from side to side.

Suddenly Minnie May had swept them all together, Betsy, Leda, Maizie,

Tom, and out into the waiting taxi. Betsy woke up out of her trance with the confusion, the sudden hurried concentration of the disturbed sleep-walker.

"Tom." This was Minnie May's voice, very level and definite in the dark taxi. "Where in the world did you get anything to drink . . . because they didn't have anything there, not even punch."

"I'm fifty-one years of age," Tom remarked carefully. "I took it with me in a bottle. You are not going to begin when I am fifty-one years old to tell me I couldn't take it in a bottle, Minnie May, darling."

"Your father's had too much to drink," Minnie May explained to them casually. "No. I wouldn't mind for an instant, you know that. It's just here. They feel different. Remember about the girls, because the whole point is—you know. They've got to have a good time. I shouldn't think you'd want. . . ."

"They are a lot different," Tom explained laboriously. "I don't begin to understand what in the world they do. Not one man I can talk to. Not one. You see, don't you?"

"You'll get used to it."

"Certainly hope so. Certainly do hope so. . . . Do you want to know who I want? Jack Randolph. The exact man I want. A mason jar of corn whisky and . . ."

"Now hush, Tom. I know. . . . Were you all belles?"

"Oh . . ." Betsy sighed. She was aware of her feet throbbing inside the gold kid slippers.

"I had a lovely time," Leda said suddenly, very clearly.

"I'm so glad, child," Minnie May continued. "Certainly was sweet to see you dancing round with all those beaux. Betsy, Maizie, you look sharp now or Leda will cut you out. She's got the makings of a belle."

There had not been a sound from Maizie.

"Maizie," said Minnie May sharply. "What's the matter, darling? Didn't you have a good time? Now don't tell me you weren't the belle of the ball, because you know you were. What's the matter, honey?"

"Nothing," Maizie said. "I was just thinking about down home."

Betsy and Leda staggered up to bed. They could not even wait for the hot chocolate the others were making. They kicked off their clothes, left them in heaps on the floor; fell into the two beds.

"And you did have a good time, didn't you?" Betsy muttered foggily.

"Yes," Leda said. "I danced, and danced, and . . ."

In the morning Betsy woke up with a rush of buoyancy. She yawned and wriggled luxuriously in the sheets, and looked over at Leda.

"Wake up!"

It was late by the time they had breakfast. The whole family and Leda sat about the table eating fried eggs and reaching for things. Leda got up from the table and went and stood by the window looking out at the gray day.

"I hate to go home," she said.

"If you'll stay, we'll make the beds," Betsy said.

"Don't go home just yet, Leda dear," Minnie May said. She sat at the head of the table in an old turkish-towelling dressing-gown, smoking cigarettes and reading the papers that she threw down into a heap around her chair.

Leda looked unhappy, Betsy thought, as they attacked the beds upstairs.

"I hate to go home," she said again. "I feel as if life would begin again the old way as soon as I get out of this house. All last night was just like a dream—the way I think things ought to be."

Betsy stared at her admiring her pale slender unhappy face.

"I wish I was one of you," Leda continued. "You always have things so that they're exciting. My house is just awful." She wrenched viciously at the sheet. They were making Glory's bed.

"Get that sheet smoother, Leda. Glory's not going to be comfortable with it this way."

"I don't care," Leda said.

"Don't you care whether Glory's comfortable?"

"Nobody ever worries about me," Leda said. Her voice burst out in a kind of fury. "It's never been like last night any other time. I've been hurt, and hurt, and hurt. I just . . . don't . . . care whether I hurt anybody else or not. Nobody ever cared whether they were hurting me."

"Leda . . ."

"I'm sorry," Leda said. "I know you'll hate me for talking like this. But you don't know."

"Oh, Leda." Betsy ran around the bed and threw her arms around Leda. "You know I just love you. You're my best friend."

"Really?"

"Of course."

Betsy was crying with pity and love. She pressed her wet cheek against Leda's. Leda's cheek was quite dry.

## CHAPTER VI

THE JEKYLLS stayed in Hampton that summer; the Marches never went away. The Country Day School closed early in June. Leda was free to be with Betsy, to be at the Jekylls', all she liked. The end of school was always a day of exaltation; a day that seemed to be opening into another life. But in the years before, the day had never really opened into anything: the exaltation died. There was never anything but the long, hot summer months, the fields shimmering with heat, the woods full of a million caterpillars that crept interminably up the trunks of the trees and dropped off noiseless onto the hot ground; the woods were full of the murmur of their eating. There was never anything but loneliness and a sultry melancholy that broke with the afternoon thunderstorms that came up in a few moments and pelted rain that ceased suddenly, leaving the night as hot as the day. After such summers it was almost a pleasure to have school to go back to in September; after the languor and the long idle heat, there was the sharpening air of early autumn; and there was always the hope that things would be different by a miracle. But they never had been.

This year was different. Betsy and Leda had a hundred plans, a hundred secret jokes and favorite spots and little passwords that sent them into gales of laughter. They used to sit in the loft of the barn behind the Marches' house, in the open doorway where long ago hay had been pitched up from the barnyard—and talk about boys. They made up private names for the town boys—"Greetings," and "Bubblenose," and "The Hokey-Pokey Man"—and spent hours analyzing looks they fancied had been thrown at them. "I saw him looking at you," Betsy would say. "You were wonderful, you just gave him one of your long, mysterious looks." "He's got a passion for you," Leda would say. "He's crazy to ask you to go out driving with him but he doesn't dare."

They used to saunter very slowly down the streets of the village of Hampton, looking into the windows of the shops. They spent every cent of money they could beg, on college ices; jewelry in the 5-10-25 cent store; tin bangles that clattered on their arms, and necklaces in bright colors; and quantities of women's magazines. They read the stories luxuriously; from the articles on entertaining they planned the parties they would give next fall—the oranges cut to resemble baskets, the invitations written in verse, the complicated games, the costumes made of crepe paper. They sent money in stamps for the samples of cosmetics that were offered in the advertisements, and waited for the arrival of packages that contained minute quantities of face-powder, nail-polish, rouge, cuticle remover, hair-tonic. "A man always notices a woman's hands. It's terribly important to have exquisite nails," they said to each other. "You have to keep your hair spotlessly clean to have it glossy and thick." "A man always notices pores in a woman's nose. Leda, look at the horrible pores in my nose!"

Minnie May and Maizie watched them with amusement. "Mother," Maizie said, "I declare I believe Betsy thinks she's Barbara la Mar. She paints the most ridiculous mouth on her face these days and looks down her nose at me with her head tilted back like she's got something in her mouth she wants to spit out. I never saw such children. I heard Betsy tell Leda she looked like a vamp, and now every time she thinks you're looking at her she narrows her eyes up like she can't see and sticks her under-lip out."

Minnie May said, "I know. Aren't they just cute? I reckon they're going to be right attractive girls."

They strolled interminably along the streets of the village. In the heavy heat, along the village pavement, they walked, parading their new hair arrangements, their new way of walking with the chest held in hollow and the stomach thrust out.

The rich commuters had moved away to the summer resorts and their houses were closed. The town belonged to the natives for the summer. The square was full of sunshine and a cheerful, provincial atmosphere with no expensive motors hurrying through. The drugstore hung itself with banners advertising a One-Cent Sale. Miss Violet, who sold hats, could relax and talk of the new styles to her Hampton customers without feeling the insecurity that came from seeing the millinery of the rich women passing her windows. The Federal Market announced Week-end Specials on stickers in its plate-glass. The candystore had a sign "Take home one of our Neapolitan Bricks and surprise her." Housewives stood about in groups, in the heat, and talked comfortably in the ownership of their own town.

Leda and Betsy would saunter into the drugstore and sink gracefully into chairs at one of the marble-topped tables. Black Walnut Sundae, they would order, or Lemon and Lime, or Orange Phosphate, or Hot Fudge Sundae with Vanilla Ice Cream and Chopped Nuts. They would consume these staring slantingly at the boys at the soda-fountain and breaking into fits of giggling; they did not know what they were laughing at. But everything had a veiled importance: the boy behind the soda-fountain was sleek and dark and mysterious; they found out his name; it was Rex; "Rex" they used to say to each other, sitting in the loft in the summer mornings, and break out again into laughter.

Betsy sent for a ukelele and a book that promised instruction in eight simple lessons. They picked out the tunes, slowly, in the book from the charts—"There's Egypt in your dreamy eyes," and "Kalua." They sang, and their eyes grew vague:

> Your love . . . belongs . . . to me.
> At night . . . when you're . . . asleep
> Into . . . your tent . . . I'll creep.*

Sometimes in the hot afternoons they went swimming in Bestley's Brook, in the hollow by the Power House where there was a dammed-up pool. They wore tight red bathing-suits. They slid off the big rock at the edge, launched themselves like ducks into the water. There was always a crowd of town boys there, swimming in trunks and diving off the roof of the Power House. Leda and Betsy watched them, imagining what they thought about. The boys splashed and ducked each other and shouted from the roof; their voices were husky. Theophile Tracy was the leader; he dove best, and swam twenty times back and forth; he never spoke to the girls, neither did any of the boys; but Betsy said, "Leda. Did you see Theophile Tracy staring at you? He's crazy about you. You can tell, because he doesn't *dare* speak to you." "Do you think so?" Leda said. Their eyes met, large and speculative.

One day Betsy climbed up the ladder to the Power House roof and dived off. She landed flat on her stomach and came up puffing but very proud.

The boys cheered, raucously. Betsy came back to Leda and they sat talking rapidly about nothing on the bank. Three or four of the boys came up out of the water just by their feet.

"Hello, Annette Kellerman," one of them said.

*"The Sheik of Araby" by permission of the copyright proprietor, Mills Music, Inc.

"Hi, Neptune," Betsy replied pertly, lifting her chin.

"You going up to try it, Leda?" Theophile Tracy asked.

"Oh, I guess not today," Leda yawned. "Athletics bore me."

"They bore her," Theophile told the other boys. "Cute swimming suit you've got there."

"It's an old one," Leda said.

"It's still cute. You girls ever get out in a canoe?"

"No, but we haven't signed a pledge not to," Betsy said.

"How about it?"

"All right," Betsy said.

"Meet you here tomorrow, about four. Hunh?"

They nodded. They could hardly wait to get away to burst into laughter. The next afternoon the boys were in the canoe, angling about in the stream.

"Want to come aboard?"

"Oh, we'd just as soon. We don't care."

There were Theophile Tracy and another boy. They brought the canoe in to the bank and Betsy and Leda stepped in. They started up the stream through the banks where the pine trees came down close to the water.

"I suppose you haven't got any name," Betsy said to the other boy.

"If you'll give me a penny I'll tell you."

"I haven't got a penny to waste."

"Okay. Bill Herbert. Mr. Herbert to you."

"All right, Mr. Herbert, I could use a little more room, thank you."

Leda watched Betsy with admiration. She turned to Theophile with an arch and truculent look.

"Did you ever win a prize paddling?" she asked.

"No remarks from you. Want to be the motor yourself?"

"I'll let you do the work, thanks." She wondered what to say next.

Theophile pulled the canoe in close to the bank.

"How about a little relaxation, boys and girls?"

"How about *mosquitoes*, mister?" Betsy said, flashing her eyes at Bill Herbert.

"Oh, we wouldn't let any mosquitoes bite a couple of nice girls."

"Aren't you the most chivalrous things?"

"You owe me something," Bill said to Betsy. He was sitting up close to her in the bow.

"I can't imagine what."

"A kiss, bright girl."

Betsy ducked away a minute later.

"My goodness, are you always such a fast worker?"

Leda watched him kiss her again.

"I'm getting cold," Theophile said.

"Bad circulation?"

"No, I just get cold when I get lonely. How about coming a little closer?"

"Oh, I'm comfortable here."

"How about this?" He put his arm behind her.

"Haven't you got any use for your arms? I haven't any."

His mouth was down over hers, wet and hot and soft—horrible. She twisted her head away. A wild distaste took hold of her and she threw her weight away from him. The canoe tipped over.

"Clever, Leda, clever. Fine place to go swimming."

"Leda, what on earth happened?"

"Leda had a rush of blood to the head," Theophile said.

They righted the canoe and climbed back in. Leda said she wanted to get home and change her clothes.

"I must be a *wreck*," Betsy said.

In August the Marches took Leda away on a weekend visit to Bernard's brother Treat's on the North Shore. They were asked, once every summer, and they always went: Bernard fidgety and working his rabbit-jaw, Laura dressed in the wrong clothes for her comfort: a blue serge suit in that August weather, with a white linen blouse that had a jabot with embroidery at the edge; Leda mute and sullen.

The Treat Marches were milder people than the other Marches. The other Marches also lived in summer on the North Shore, but it was unimaginable that they should want the Bernard Marches to visit them.

The Treat Marches' house in Manchester was like the other houses on the North Shore that belonged to their friends. A gray-shingled house of the ugly architecture of the end of the last century, it had porches providing a magnificent view of the ocean, and, within, large cool rooms. If Treat March had been asked from a point of view of aesthetics what he thought of it he would have said it was ugly; but he would still have chosen to go on living in it, because it was their house and it was where they wanted to go in summer, and they liked living in it. Grace liked it, Treat Jr. was unaware of its appearance; only James, the doctor son, asked them sometimes why, with plenty of money, they didn't build themselves something decent. But such a move would have required pride, dissatisfaction, and ambition; the elder Marches felt none of these things.

They were tolerant and adjusted: happy. They did not suppose themselves to be any better than anyone else; merely different; in a new sense they claimed the ancient, inalienable right to worship what gods they chose in their own way. They were not snobbish, because it was not in their heritage to have conceived snobbishness. Only such outsiders as were utterly baffled by that elusive philosophy—See whom you choose, Live as you choose—fell down in exhaustion and laid their defeat by the simple forces of individuality to snobbery. It was true that outsiders did not come to be friends of the old Bostonians; but that was because the thoughts they thought, the lives they lived, were unnatural and unappealing to the Bostonians. There was no lure, no bait, to be offered to these quiet people in exchange for their friendship; because they were too content for any lure on this earth to have a glitter for their eyes, for any bait to deflect their tastes.

The Treat Marches saw little of the Bernard Marches since Bernard

March bored his older brother. The one August invitation was always issued not because of any feeling of family obligation, but because Grace March was quite simply sorry for her brother-in-law, and did not want him to imagine that the Treat Marches avoided his company. Of Leda, the daughter, they knew little. It would have surprised and distressed them to know that they, their establishment, their way of living, aroused the most violent feelings of envy, despair, humiliation in her.

She knew it was ugly, and yet she admired it, as she was driven from the station up the long gravel drive to the house. She was impressed with the polished hall floor that swept back to the French windows opening out on the sea; the vista of the cold blue ocean; the boats that she could see rocking gently at the end of the long pier. Her uncle and aunt were in the living-room, having tea. The floor seemed interminable as she walked across it with her father and mother.

Her uncle was a tall, soft-cheeked, soft-lipped man, immaculately dressed; he was stooped, he spoke in a low voice. Her aunt was small, with a face like a toasted marshmallow; her hair was archaic, her clothes might have been taken from a trunk locked in 1900. Leda said to herself that they were unimpressive, without sparkle. And yet—they were impressive. Leda saw without understanding why, that they were three times as impressive as the commuters of Hampton. They had grandeur. But why? They owned nothing grand, there was nothing grand in their appearance or talk.

"Hello, old boy. Glad to see you," Treat March said, extending his soft, effeminate hand. He smiled at Bernard, at Laura, at Leda.

"Hello, Treat. Nice to see you again." Leda felt suddenly proud of her father. He was his brother's brother. He said the right thing.

"I do love your view, Grace," Laura was saying in that panting voice of hers; it was quite cool, but she sounded hot. "It gets lovelier every year. I do love . . ." Leda felt ashamed of her mother. She was not talking in the idiom.

"It's as much as our life is worth to keep it open," Grace March said. "The locusts grow up like weeds. It keeps a man and a boy up on ladders all summer long to keep it clipped." She was impersonal, and yet completely interested in what she was saying. She led Laura out on to the porch to point out trees to her.

Treat balanced on his heels, teetered to his toes and back again, swaying his long body before the fireplace filled with boughs and regarding his brother with amusement and a certain affection. Bernard did the talking, mouthing his words as if there was a hot potato in his mouth, laughing so that his receding, rabbit-jaw trembled, looking up at his brother and glancing down foolishly. Leda sat in an armchair.

It was bitterly humiliating that they didn't think her, her family, sufficiently important to invite them to their house but once a year. They had an invulnerability that was maddening. Why should two dowdy, eccentric people have this atmosphere of power? But it was nice to be related to them. It was deeply, stayingly satisfying to know that you belonged to them and they belonged to you, that they could not disown you, that your name was also theirs. In her hours of most hideous humiliation with Adèle Macomb, and people like her, Leda did have that tiny, useless comfort that she dug her nails into, bit on: her family was real, not spurious, not parvenu; her family was unquestionable, rooted forever. She would have liked to hurl it at them. But something—part of being one of the Marches was apparently that you did not consider being one of the Marches anything. It exasperated Leda; she would have liked to ride roughshod on her patronym over the bodies of the Macombs, the others; it was ridiculous not to; not to let them know, insult them with the fact, that they were nothing and less than nothing, upstarts. What was position for, if not to raise yourself up as on a pedestal? But she didn't do it. She didn't know why. It gave her a feeling of inverted pride, too, not to do it; to hold inside her breast the consciousness of her superiority and not to show it to them; if they did not know it for themselves then that was just one more lift in the rise she stood on above their heads.

A young man came into the room, in a white shirt and trousers. It was James, her cousin. He was dark; she realized he looked something the way she did herself; but he had a rapidity, an unconsciousness about him.

"Oh, hello," he said. "Uncle Bernard. How are you? Is this Leda? Good God, what a big girl. Does that make you mad? It would me, if I were you. Insulting to be told what a big girl you are."

Leda felt self-conscious but not unhappy. She liked the way he looked at her. This summer, with all the fussing over her face with Betsy, must have done some good. She smiled mysteriously at him. Laura and her Aunt Grace were coming back through the long windows.

"Hello, Aunt Laura." The easy grace, the charm. Unlike his parents, James looked gay and handsome. "I'm going up to change, Mamma. I'm all dirty. I'll be down directly." He ran across the hall to the stairs, his rubber soles squeaking.

Leda sat still. 'I'll be down directly.' Directly. It was a magic word, used by magic people. In it was implicit a whole atmosphere.

When they were dressing, later, in the big, cool, chintz bedrooms Laura said to Leda,

"I wish you wouldn't put all that stuff on your face, darling. I know Betsy does it, I know it doesn't do any harm and I haven't spoken to you about it—much—before. But don't do it now. I don't believe your uncle and aunt would approve of it."

Leda opened her mouth to snap back at her mother. But she closed it again. For once, Laura was right. She did look wrong, suddenly, with paint on her mouth, with so much powder. She took a cloth and washed it off. Why did it look different here? It looked cheap. She put a minute quantity of lipstick on her mouth and rubbed it in carefully. It made her eyes brighter and did not show.

In the evening after dinner they all sat about in the wicker chairs out on the veranda, listening to the long shush and swing of the ocean. Leda sat between James and her father on a canvas hammock that moved slightly under them.

"Leda's going to that school in Hampton again next winter, Laura?" It was Grace's voice, quiet and old-fashioned and clipped.

"Well . . . She wants to go to Miss Sheraton's. We haven't known quite . . . I suppose I should have done something about it if she's going to."

"I suppose all your friends are going to Miss Sheraton's, Leda. Well, Laura, I think she ought to go if she wants to. She'll make the friends she will know when she comes out, of course."

Leda sat quite still, listening to them, liking to hear her aunt concern herself with her life. She was very conscious of James beside her, smoking cigarettes. His tweed coat sleeve was against her arm.

"I don't know . . ."

"Well," Grace's voice was brisk and thoughtful at once. "We must do something about that. I don't suppose it's too late. I shall see Lowell Rice tomorrow, and he's on the board. . . . If you're willing to let me attend to it, Laura."

"I wish you would."

"That's sweet of you, Aunt Grace," Leda said. Her voice, coming out after a long silence, cracked and she cleared her throat.

"I think it's about time you did go to school in town, Leda," her aunt said. "You'll need to know the girls. . . . You're getting such a big girl now, I hardly realize it. Your uncle and I will give you a party the year you come out."

"Thank you, Aunt Grace," Leda said.

She felt James's hand on hers in the dark.

"What an old man I'll feel with my little cousin a debutante. I'll be an older man, do you know that, Leda? You'll say, 'Oh, I do love to dance with older men, they're so *interesting*'—but really you'll wish to God somebody your own generation would cut in. Why, I'm twenty-eight now! Isn't that hideous, Leda?" James laughed, and in the darkness he squeezed her hand.

It did not matter that she knew some of her cousins, her other important, self-assured cousins would be coming out that year too, other near years. She—would she still be a frightened, sullen little thing that people were contemptuous of? With a catch in her throat she thought, very slowly, Well . . . perhaps . . . not! Perhaps in that year ahead James really would dance with her. James, who was important and busy and used to his cousins that were like himself.

In the meantime, he did not take away his hand.

When Leda got back to Hampton she had a feeling of having lost her balance. It was hard to reassume the rhythm of her life. She had the sensation of returning from a foreign land to which she had given an enthusiastic allegiance, to a home which was tiresome, petty, and familiar. She came home on the Monday morning; all that day she stayed by herself, sitting in the chairs out in the dusty August garden, or in her room leaning on the window-sill, staring with eyes that did not see, imagining a future. She had no impulse that day to rejoin the Jekylls.

It was Tuesday afternoon before the old attitudes, the familiar desires, had reasserted themselves and she wanted to see Betsy. She walked down the road to the Jekylls in the hot afternoon, between the wilting elms whose leaves were sprinkled with a white powdering of dust. She liked the lush green, the exhausted limpness of the landscape; it gave her a feeling of relaxation and of comfort.

An inch, perhaps, had been added to the shape of her life; or a stone wedged into its foundation. After the weekend she felt, now, a rise of confidence, little enough, but sufficient to make her, for once, in no hurry to reach the Jekylls; sufficient to make her interesting enough to herself to walk slowly and not hurry to join that atmosphere of gaiety.

She opened the Jekylls' front door and walked in, as had become her custom. There were voices, talking loud, in the small panelled room to the right, and she paused.

It was Maizie's voice that was crying out, sounding so wretched and wild. "I can't stand it. Honestly, I don't believe I can. Ma'am, can't we go home where we belong? There isn't one—not one—of these men that I like. I declare I don't see I'll ever find anybody I want to marry up here. They're all so trifling."

"Maizie. Darling." The lower voice was Minnie May's. "We've only been here such a little while. Naturally you're bound to be homesick, sometimes. But don't feel so bad. The winter hasn't even begun. Then you'll meet a whole lot of men that amount to more than any of these town boys you know. I admit they aren't much. But the ones you will meet. You know they're going to be more interesting, amount to more, than anybody you'd be likely to marry down home. I'd hate to see you marry a small-town Southern boy, to tell you the truth, Maizie. I may as well admit that's one reason I had for moving up here. I want you to have more of a life. I want you to marry someone who is somebody."

"But I'm getting old! I don't care anything about all this marrying somebody important. Honestly, I don't. I just want to be happy. I just want to marry somebody I love."

" 'Course you do, darling. I want you to get somebody who's worthy of you. I don't want to see you all tied down to some little old poky marriage. You know you're too pretty and attractive to waste yourself like so many of the girls you know down home who've got married. Just think of what a good time you'll have next winter, and all the men you'll meet in Boston."

"Ma'am, I don't believe I want much more of just running around. I guess I've had about enough fun. I'd like to get married and have a home."

" 'Course, that's what I want for you too. You can be happy and be somebody in the world, too. Look at your Aunt Glory. She was just crazy about her husband and all those sweet children, and she had an interesting life. My goodness. That palazzo in Rome, and all those princes and counts for friends, and all those dinner parties—I wish you'd seen her, Maizie; I never did see anyone who got more out of life. That's the kind of thing I want for you, don't you see, darling?"

"I know, Ma'am. I don't know as anybody like that'd ever want to marry me."

"Maizie, you're every bit as pretty and just as sweet as your Aunt Glory. No reason on earth why you shouldn't marry someone just as attractive as Ruggero. Now you take Boston. Why, Boston's just full of nice people; there are dozens of young men with good family and plenty of money that will be courting you next winter. You know you'd like that."

"I don't believe they will."

"Now, Maizie, why do you say that?"

"Oh, Ma'am, you expect everything wonderful's going to happen to us children just because you're so wonderful yourself, because you've always made things happen the way you want them to. I know I'm all right looking, but I'm not such a raving beauty as to break down any barriers in this place."

"I swear I don't know what you're talking about."

"We aren't going to be able to get anywhere in this place. We aren't going to be taken in and be part of things the way we were down home. Every single thing I've heard makes me just know that coming to Boston like this we're going to stay strangers forever. I'm not going to get asked to any of the parties in Boston next winter, because I don't know anybody and because if they knew me they wouldn't ask me. They wouldn't know who I was."

"What a way to talk. You're a Green, aren't you? I reckon a Green is as good as anybody anywhere. You're just depressed, honey. And even if these people are exclusive around here, I never heard of that making any difference to a young man who's in love. As for parties, I guess we'll manage to get you to any parties you want to go to. Mr. Rathbone's been helpful, I reckon he'll continue to be. He's devoted to your father. Just let all these Boston young men start courting you; you'll marry one of them, and then you'll be in things all you want; you'll be one of them yourself."

"Ma'am, I know you mean to be sweet, but I think you're awfully mean. I'm so miserable. I'm so homesick. I just don't belong around here. I know you feel all right, because you can fit anywhere, but I can't and I'm just miserable. And so is Daddy."

"Your father takes a long time to get into the run of things."

"I'm sorry for him, Ma'am. He hasn't any friends. He says he can't understand the men he sees in Boston; they just don't act like any people he's accustomed to. And he can't understand the men out here in Hampton, either; the ones that go to our church. He says it seems like they're all dried up into hard little nuts. Seems to me the only friends he's got are those awful Irish men he sees on the train. He says he gets along fine with them."

"I declare it would do your father good to get shaken up out of his rut for once in his life. That's another reason I thought it would be a good thing to come here. He wouldn't do anything, ever, if he wasn't pushed or pulled into it."

"Ma'am, if you were to see that we weren't going to get anywhere here, that we weren't going to get to know anybody, then would you be willing to go on home where we belong?"

"Maizie, you sound like you hadn't got good sense. You know there's no reason on earth why we shouldn't get to know anybody at all we want to know. I certainly am not going to go on back home with my tail between my legs."

"Oh, Ma'am, I just wish you'd remember I'm getting older and older all the time."

Betsy came running down the stairs, her round face grinning with pleasure, and threw her arms around Leda.

"I'm so glad you're back! My, I've missed you. Did you have a wonderful time? Or were your old relatives just poky? Come on upstairs. I've got a new box of the most marvellous powder. Called 'Illusion.' It makes kind of a film over your face, kind of glowing looking. You'd look wonderful. My, I'm so glad to see you!"

They went up into Betsy's tower. What Leda had heard drifted in the back of her head. She felt strangely excited at having looked secretly into the private lives of other people. She felt confident and faintly superior.

"I had a wonderful time," she said. "My cousin, the one called James, held my hand out on the porch one evening. He's a doctor. He's terribly good looking, and he has black hair and he says he's going to give me a rush when I come out."

"Leda! How marvellous! Weren't you excited—having your hand held, I mean? He's probably perfectly mad about you. He's probably thinking about you right now. You probably seem mysterious to him, and he's furious because you're his cousin so he can't marry you."

Betsy had a way of building things into a credible dream of glamour. Leda let herself be led along. Having someone else say it for her, not having to manufacture it for herself, made it seem true. They sat on Betsy's bed, half lying, on their elbows.

"My aunt says she's going to give a party for me when I come out."

"Won't we have fun? Gosh, I can hardly wait for them. We'll be the twin knockouts of Boston. Maybe Ma'am will give me a ball—or anyway a dance in this house."

Leda felt patronizing.

"My aunt's going to get me into Miss Sheraton's this winter. Mother hadn't done anything about it, but my aunt's going to get me in."

"Oh, Leda! I'd forgotten all about school. I've just got to go to the same school you do. We'll do everything together. I'd just die if we didn't go to the same school."

"What if you can't get in?"

"Ma'am will fix it. Ma'am could fix anything. You wait and see. Now, come on, try this powder. Oh, Leda, you look heavenly! You are the most mysterious looking thing."

"We would have fun going to Miss Sheraton's together, wouldn't we?" Leda said. She felt the old warmth returning for Betsy. Certainly Betsy made life seem exciting and kind, and herself, Leda, a kind of heroine.

## CHAPTER VII

TWENTY YEARS before, Miss Sheraton's school had been a brownstone house on Beacon Street, with fifty girls chosen from Boston's old families and a headmistress who sprang from one of them herself and had a combination of liberalism, idealism, and energy characteristic of her age and class in that city. Along with such pioneers of female education as Samuel Brearly and Caroline Ruutz-Rees, she was brave enough to believe in women's ability to absorb a college preparatory education, in their capacity to be more than elegant females. Her energy raised the school out of a city always tolerant to higher education into an institution whose scholastic standards were recognized by the women's colleges. Her idealism led her to preach to her girls a text whose burden was "Women are individuals. Women can have careers," and to prophesy to those under her a day when women would move as well-informed human beings with an equipment, mental and even physical, on a par with men. She introduced gymnastics into her school; not much, but a great deal for her day; before she died she had instituted compulsory field sports on a tract of land on the outskirts of Boston. She was essentially large-minded and democratic. In her last years she received as pupils girls who did not come from the old families of Boston, who belonged to the new, the richer, families. She would have scorned to recognize a difference in births, to concede a priority to those old Boston families of which she was naturally a member; she asked a large tuition fee because it was essential to her plan of acquiring the best equipment and the best instructors available. It was material she was after, not names or prominence; material capable of being moulded into the New Woman, a released being with brains and courage and health and independence.

Like most faiths, after the death of its founder this faith suffered a sea-change into something richer and stranger but by no means as rugged and idealistic as what Miss Sheraton had dreamed of. After her death, the school was controlled by a board of trustees; rich, important men who took their responsibility seriously as connected with that increasingly sacred subject, Education.

They kept it financially successful, they expanded it in size and equipment. They increased its enrollment to two hundred, moved it into the outskirts of Boston where, on the old athletic fields, a new and sumptuous building was erected and larger, better-equipped fields for sports added to the property. They maintained a large, able faculty of teachers and athletic instructors.

From being an institution which derived its character from the spirit and philosophy of its founder, it became a place whose character was moulded by its pupils. Since Miss Sheraton's day, hundreds of rich, socially secure girls had gone there; among them were daughters of old, simple Boston families of the unostentatious tradition; among them were daughters of the new rich, socially self-conscious, Boston families. It was the latter group that gave essential color to the school; perhaps something in the potency of new blood. It had become a school subdivided within itself into layers of social desirability.

And yet, such is the stubbornness with which a city's institutions become rooted, the Sheraton School remained an educational absolute even in the minds of those parents of an older, simpler tradition, who were deeply contemptuous of all that was socially pretentious. It had become *the* school of Boston, as well for the pure in heart as for the consciously ambitious.

Leda March and Betsy Jekyll entered Sheraton in the Seventh Class—the next to last of the school's divisions. On the first day, a late September day full of sunshine and clear blue air, they stood about with the hesitation and crazy hopefulness that is the essence of the spirit of New Girls. At any moment some kind older girl might appear and offer to take them under her wing; one of these alarming, strange girls who knew their way about, who laughed and called and ran up and down stairs, who groaned loudly at coming back to the old place.

But there was no chance for the realization of any of Betsy's or Leda's hopes in that school from the start. Girls asked other girls what they knew about such and such a newcomer—was she anything, or was she wet?

"That one?" Adèle Macomb said on one of the earliest days, sitting at recess in the lunchroom drinking cocoa—"That's Leda March. Yeah, Hampton too, but awful. She was the drippiest girl in school out there. Family never goes anywhere.—Yeah, they are cousins of those Marches. But a lot different.—That one? Her name's Jekyll. They live in Hampton too. They come from the South or something. Mother doesn't know them. They aren't anybody. I don't know how she got in here."

Thus were new girls relegated to their places in the Sheraton School, as neatly as a dealt pack of cards. These are the wet girls, these are the grinds, these are the nobodies, these few we will take in with ourselves. To Leda this fate was no surprise. She had seen a sample of its workings in the school in Hampton. With the old resigned sense of inferiority she accepted it as what she should have expected. It was true that on that first day there were those idiotic hopes—but she should have known better. She should have known.

Betsy did not grasp it for a little while. She went around grinning at girls, sitting next to girls in class she should not have dared to sit next. But it did not take too long, or too many of those deliberate, withering cuts from Adèle and the others like Adèle to make her see where she might sit, whom she might talk to, whose arm she might link with.

Hockey was the autumn sport. In the afternoons, after lunch, the school streamed out on the playing fields in middies and bloomers. Four teams could play at a time, the others sat and rested on a bench in the fall sunshine. Neither Leda nor Betsy had ever played hockey; Leda was sullen and did not try to learn; Betsy paid a puppy-dog attention to the coach's instructions, ran up and down the field. At the end of her team's play she came back to the bench and sat down. A minute later one of the big girls—

one of Adèle's friends—strolled up to the bench and sat down almost on top of Betsy. She was a big, frizzy-haired girl, with ruddy cheeks and the muscular look that characterized the girls of Sheraton's inner circle.

"Hey!" Betsy said, laughing, "you're sitting right on top of me."

The girl turned her head coldly without moving her body.

"Well, what are you doing under me? Get up. You don't belong here on the bench. Go over there where you do belong."

Betsy got up, confused, and went where the girl pointed. That was a little group of girls sitting on the ground on their sweaters. They were girls with spectacles, thin unathletic girls or pretty girls with a crestfallen look; Leda was sitting there.

"That girl kicked me off the bench," Betsy said to Leda, sitting down beside her. "She told me to get over here."

"I hate them," Leda muttered. "They're always like that. You don't know them. I'd like to grind my foot in their eye. I'd like to bang their heads against a stone floor."

Betsy stared at her.

"Gee, Leda. They can't be that bad."

"Oh, yes they are. You wait and see."

"Well, I guess we better stay away from them, then," Betsy said. She began to smile again.

"That's what they want. They want us to stick with these . . . these." Leda rolled her eyes around at the girls they sat with. "I won't. If I can't be the best I won't be anybody."

"I bet they're really a lot nicer girls anyway. The best thing we could probably do is make friends of these ones, and let the awful old ones do anything they choose. *I* don't care."

"I won't. I won't be stuck off with the wet girls. I won't be part of something nobody wants to be part of. If I can't be with the top ones I'll be by myself."

"You've got me."

"I don't know what I'd do without you." Leda looked miserable. "Do you realize you're the only friend I've got?"

"Oh, Leda. I don't see what you want the other ones for friends for, anyway, if you hate them so."

"They're horrible and athletic and they have piano legs and they're stupid. You just wait. I promise you that I'll get even with them somehow if it takes the rest of my life."

Betsy looked reflective.

"They're not so awful-looking, though. I don't know—I think they're kind of glamorous."

"I know," Leda said miserably in a low voice. "But I wouldn't admit it!"

Their true life was lived at home, and on the way to and from school.

The Jekylls' house that autumn was more gay and noisy than ever. The Brats came roaring home from school; they were banging and carousing by the time Betsy would get home, in the late afternoon. The house would be blazing with lights, in empty rooms as well as occupied ones; and the living-room would be full of lounging young men. On Saturdays Leda and Betsy hung around while Maizie dressed to go to Harvard games; she went to all of them, in bright hats and her new coonskin coat, with earrings swinging out under her soft gold hair. Those were the best days of all: the smell of spilled perfume in Maizie's bedroom, the powder and cheap jewelry and high-heeled shoes for tea-dancing; Mrs. Jekyll playing football songs loudly downstairs on the piano; and the rush away after a quick lunch, Maizie beside some young man in the front seat of a roadster that would skid the corner going out of the drive.

But in November Maizie found what Betsy told Leda was a "heavy beau." That was exciting to them. It meant romance and what Maizie said to the young man when they were alone and whether he kissed her and whether they two would be in the wedding; for they were sure there would be a wedding.

He was a very young man; he did not go to any college; he was an artist, and had a studio in Boston. They did not know very much about him except that his name, Lambert Rudd, meant that he belonged to the Rudd family, who were rich. He had a Chrysler roadster, and he had a dark face and he smoked a great deal. Maizie began to smoke more too; soon she was smoking nearly as much as her mother. She was obviously in love. The other men gradually stopped coming to the house. Betsy and Leda watched Maizie like hawks: she ate little and seemed always excited and ran to answer the telephone when it rang; she took a long time doing her face and hair upstairs when Lambert Rudd came to the house; she looked as if she were listening for something when he was not there, and she looked almost agonized with intensity when he was there.

Betsy and Leda had little enough time to be at home to watch. They used to take the train from Hampton village in town to school at 8:20 every morning. Betsy walked down with her father every day; he took the same train. Leda would meet her there and they would immediately leave Mr. Jekyll and launch into one of those long, hushed conversations that ended in a burst of stifled laughter. On the train they would sit together in the red plush seats, dusty with sharp grit, and talk on in those low, private tones, or study a lesson that should have been learned last night. The train got to the Back Bay Station at 8:42. There was just time to hurry down Dartmouth Street to where the street-car stopped, on which they went the rest of the way to school. In the street-car they did not have the same sense of privacy and intimacy that they had on the train, that they had at home in Hampton. There were apt to be other Sheraton girls, Boston girls, going to school on the street-car. There never were on the train. All the Hampton girls that went to Sheraton were sent there in their families' motors.

Coming home, later, it was the same. In the late, sunset afternoons they would take the street-car from school and have to talk with some of their classmates—about the work, the games, the teachers. Then they would stand, alone together, in the black cavern under the Back Bay Station where the trains came in, waiting for the Hampton train with their lungs full of coal gas and their eyes stinging. The train used old New Haven cars; the light in them came from gas jets that the trainman lit with a long pole, flipping the glazed domes back over them. There was an agreeable melancholy and comfort after the day in sitting in the dirty red seats, not talking much, hearing the stations called in the conductor's hoarse voice—"Stone Pit . . . Forest Vale . . . West Hampton . . . Hampton!" Then they would go out into the sharp cold, the darkness, and walk through the lighted streets of the town before they separated to go home.

They had been best friends, but their friendship grew more essential to them that winter. They did not like the school, and they went through its routine close together always. Going to Boston to school made them alone again in Hampton, where any other girls they might have known went to the local school. All their talk was secrets, all their jokes and stories and thoughts confidential. Now Betsy needed Leda quite as much as Leda needed Betsy. They were each other's mainstay in the days they were living. They had achieved an instant sympathy, and thought the same, joked the same, were unhappy the same about everything.

When Thanksgiving came Betsy wanted Leda to have dinner with the Jekylls.

"Come on, Leda," Mrs. Jekyll said cordially. "Betsy feels just like you're her sister. We're all so used to having you with us we'd miss you. Of course I guess your family wants you then. But if they wouldn't mind, Leda, I certainly would be delighted to have you here."

"Leda, please," Betsy said.

But Leda suddenly didn't want to. She had very little use for her family these days. The life she lived with her friend was far more real than the hours she had to spend at home. She had grown to pay almost no attention to what her father or mother said to her, to hear their words as if in a dream. Her family contributed nothing to her that she wanted; neither gaiety, interest, nor support. She never confided in them. They hardly knew whether she was happy or not at school.

But she wanted to be at home for Thanksgiving. It was a sudden stab of sentiment that she did not understand.

She was furious, the day before Thanksgiving, when she heard her mother arranging to have soup for the dinner.

"Mother! That's all wrong. We never used to have soup. We had turkey, stuffing, cranberry, creamed onions, mashed potatoes, giblet gravy, mashed squash and we had mince pie and squash pie. That's the way it has to be."

"All right, darling. I had no idea you cared so much about the tradition. We'll have just what you want."

Her parents were pleased, not understanding but loving her, touched by her efforts to recreate the old Thanksgivings they had always had. She lived the day over carefully, like a rite. Snow fell the night before, and that she accepted as a dispensation; it gave the last touch.

In the morning she read in the living-room, close by the window whose panes were edged with the light, wet snow. She was aware of smells—the dinner cooking, the clear fresh smell of the snow when she opened the door. When they ate dinner in the middle of the day she tasted each dish solemnly.

After dinner she went for a walk alone. The woods were scattered with the shallow snow; the snow slid from the upper branches in heavy falls, that broke the cold, infinite stillness. She walked through the woods, along the paths, seeing each tree, each rock. In the snow at intervals were the tiny tracks of a rabbit; the fallen leaves of the autumn were black with wet. The woods smelled cold and sweet and damp.

She came out into an open meadow that was white; only the sharp tops of tall grass broke through the snow in spikes all over the field. It was getting late and the sky was lead-colored; far off a dog was barking, melancholy and unreal. Leda stood in the wet snow and looked up at the sky. She felt utterly alone. The wide, silent field sloped away to the woods that rose in a black hill beyond an old, crumbling stone wall.

There was only this sense of perfect joy, perfect solitude; a sense of being one with the cold silence and the calm.

When she got home it was pleasant to come in to the snapping little fire in the living-room and warm her hands and feet. She felt subdued and satisfied. She wondered dreamily what the explanation of this happiness could be; for in the past few months she had thought herself happier than ever in her life before because she had found friends. And yet today, that she had spent alone, without friends, in the old solitude, was the happiest for a long time.

When Christmas came it was different. She accepted her parents' presents hurriedly, investigated and appraised them, and went as quickly as she could down to the Jekylls'. They had an enormous tree. Dozens of presents lay all over the floor among the piles of disordered wrappings, the mess of tinsel ribbon. Everyone was shouting and laughing.

She was shown all their presents, given some for herself, told all the jokes of the day and the thrills and the disasters. It was a big, noisy, family Christmas. Betsy was tearing about with a crown made out of a holly wreath on her head. Loud, bangy music came from Mrs. Jekyll at the piano, with a necklace of dozens of Christmas ribbons thrown around her neck, and smoke ascending up her face from her cigarette.

Only Maizie was quiet. She had a new bracelet on, made of lapis lazuli, that her beau had given her. She sat in the bay-window, looking out; Betsy whispered to Leda that she was waiting for her beau to come to see her. Maizie's face was painted brightly and her hair was lovely, but she looked nervous and strained.

When Leda left no young man had yet appeared. She went home through the deeper snow to her supper. Later she lay in bed listening to her father play Chopin downstairs.

She was torn apart with bitterest regret. She suddenly knew Christmas had been all wrong and it was her fault. She should have done the old things, the things of her childhood. She should have hung up her stocking; waked up in the dark dawn to pinch its crackling fullness. Last night she should have tried to lie awake to await the hour when the fairies are allowed to come back to earth at midnight for a yearly revel; she had forgotten to listen for the village church-bells ringing for the midnight services, to think of the camels striding across the desert two thousand years ago. She had ruined her Christmas.

She got out of bed and went to the window. The cold air struck her hot face and she breathed it in in deep gulps. Under the snow the land was infinitely still. The stars were white and luminous in the sky. It comforted her. She stayed there at the window. "O little town of Bethlehem, how still we see thee lie. . . ." She tried to pretend that this was Christmas Eve.

Why was it that she felt this way about people? Did they save her life or did they ruin it? She had been lost without friends, and yet now that she had some they spoiled certain things that she must have alone, that were more lovely and precious to her even than the friends. There were certain high moments that only came in solitude; their pursuit was almost worth the loneliness that came like an accompanying disease. But not quite: she realized that now that she had found friends, she was a different, a happier person. But the friends and the ecstasy worked at cross-purposes; they meant different, opposing forces in her life.

She wondered, when she was lying in bed, if she would ever fall in love with a man who would be close to her; like herself; someone with whom she could experience these moments that she knew she would always desire. Some deep source of skepticism within her said no; she could not believe that any man would ever be anything but a stranger to her. She wondered if she would, then, always be alone, in the highest moments of her life.

Near the end of January, Maizie was suddenly married, and went away on a honeymoon to South America. Leda and Betsy were bitterly disappointed. There had been no wedding, no special clothes, no show. There was only that day when Maizie came home, late in the afternoon, with Lambert Rudd, and said that they had been married; she was glowing and dimpling, transfigured with happiness. They watched her sitting on the window-seat with her hand in the hand of this dark stranger; this difficult man whom even Betsy called Mr. Rudd. He talked almost not at all, just sat there smiling slightly, looking as if he were thinking about something else, holding Maizie's hand.

In a way, however, afterwards, they thought it was very romantic. Maizie and the man had gone away so quickly after that, to New York and thence to South America. They wondered constantly where she was, what she was doing; they conjured up pictures of strange, tropic ports, full of moonlight, where Maizie and the man embraced and said . . . what? . . . to each other; a fictional couple, not real to them any longer. They knew she was happy; happier than they were able to imagine; they had seen her transported face that day when she sat in the window-seat. She was now a heroine, full of mystery.

Somehow her going made them feel older; now they were the older ones, the ones that would have beaux, soon. School seemed more unbearable than ever. That spring they formed the habit of playing hookey, that took them into a secret life of their own.

Nobody could know about it but themselves. They perfected a technique. They would wait until they felt that they could bear the girls, the teachers, the intolerable routine of school no longer. Then one morning, when they reached the Back Bay Station, they would not hurry out into the cold street, but walk quietly back into the women's room of the station.

In the women's room it already seemed queer, dreamlike. The attendant sat in her soiled uniform reading a pink tabloid and the sunlight streamed in from the snowy city over the dirty white tiles of the floor. There was a smell of old cosmetics, and there were fat, greasy women applying rouge to their faces in the big mirror, while their little boys waited in knitted helmets. Leda and Betsy would fix their own faces, arrange their hair, taking plenty of time, letting all the Hampton people get well out of that part of town.

Then they would go out into the waiting-room, where the voice of the train-announcer echoed drearily, and go to the telephone booths. One of them would telephone the school, speak to the secretary, represent herself as her mother, and ask that she be excused from school that day, on account of—a cold, or indigestion. The other one would wait, not to bring the calls too suspiciously close together. She would telephone in about an hour, from wherever they were by that time.

They would pass through the waiting-room, past the booth of magazines, cigars, and toy animals, out into the city. On those mornings it always looked unreal and a little sinister. The streets were full of piles of shovelled snow, and sunlight, and sharp cold. They would walk down Boylston Street to Washington Street.

The movie houses there had morning rates of twenty cents. They showed two pictures continuously, and inside they were almost empty when Leda and Betsy slipped into their seats. A few men sat about in the auditorium. Why were they there? Why weren't they at work? Betsy and Leda used to sit far away from other people; they had heard stories of men injecting drugs into girls that sat beside them in movie theatres. There was something melancholy about the loud organ music playing in the theatre.

When they came out again, the sunny street increased the sense of unreality. They would go into a warm little candy shop and have lunch—a sandwich and soda, feeling luxurious, powdering their noses in the mirrors of their compacts and looking about at the other women. Afterwards they would go into the shops in the downtown part of Boston. They went to the basements of Filene's and Jordan Marsh's and Hovey's. They would scuttle along the sidewalks like rats and dive into Kresge's, that smelled of cheap candy and cheap perfume; they pawed over the things on the jewelry counter, talking and laughing excitedly. In the bargain basements they looked at the racks of evening clothes, pulling the dresses apart from one another and looking at the beaded ones, the jade-green ones, the ones with feathers round the hem. Sometimes they would sit down at the lunch counter in the basement of Kresge's and eat a mid-afternoon roast beef sandwich with gravy.

They felt apprehensive and daring. They never knew when they might see someone on the street—a friend of their families', or in the afternoon one of the teachers from school. As far as they knew, they never did, but fear made them run from shop to shop, skulking along the walls of the buildings and dodging into doorways.

They loved those queer, lost days. They loved the realization that nobody knew where they were; their parents thought they were at school, and the school thought they were at home. To Leda this gave a feeling of power, of control over home and school; she was outwitting both. To Betsy it seemed glamorous, mysterious.

Sometimes in the late afternoons they would go and sit in the lobby of a hotel. Of all the things they did it was most luxurious, most unreal. The lobby was warm, and full of palms and marble and soft carpets and tapestry chairs. In a few minutes they would forget their rough coats, galoshes and round felt hats—and lean back dreamily listening to the string music that played for teatime. The important and unknown people hastened to the desk from the golden revolving doors and thence to the elevators.

They played hookey all through the spring. It cancelled out the consciousness of inferiority that was forced upon them at school. Each strange day they spent that spring made them look forward to the next one; it made them closer friends than ever. They were bound together in the secrecy of those days.

In late April the weather grew softer; they took off their galoshes the first of May. They were conscious of dressing differently from the other girls in school, and they did not care; they wanted to. The other girls wore wool dresses or plaid skirts with cashmere or Fair Isle sweaters; the arrogant ones with an air, the others imitatively. Betsy and Leda wore brighter dresses, sometimes of silk. They were what Mrs. Jekyll thought Betsy looked pretty in, and because Betsy wore them Leda demanded them, with the rage which her mother could not resist. They were not allowed by the school to wear any make-up; but they wore their galoshes open and flapping; they thought this dashing; the other girls buckled theirs.

By quarter of four in the afternoon the big cloakroom in the basement was filling with girls, who had changed from bloomers back into their dresses or sweaters; they would slap their piles of books down on the shoe boxes at the foot of the racks. In the drive outside, which was on a level with the basement windows, the motors waited to take the rich girls home; girls went to the windows and peered out for a glimpse of their chauffeurs, and went back to talking. It was a scene cluttered with dropped coats and scattered books and pads and bundles of middies to be taken home to wash, girls combing their hair before the mirror, and standing in queues before the doors to the toilets. In May the scene was further complicated by baseball bats and bathing caps, used in the swimming pool, strewn about the floor.

Leda came down to her hook to get her hat and coat. The racks were divided alphabetically into twelve sections each, with hook and hat stand and shoe box. Leda's hook was next to Adèle Macomb's. When she looked at her hook it was bare. Her coat and red felt hat lay on the floor, covered with dust. A group of girls lounged at the end of the rack, Adèle and some of her friends, watching Leda. Leda straightened up and looked at them.

"Did you kick my clothes around?"

"It's none of your business what we do," Adèle said rapidly, indifferently.

"You've got them all dirty," Leda said.

"They were dirty anyway. You can't hurt clothes like that," one of the other girls said.

Adèle came toward Leda. She stooped quickly and picked up the red hat.

"I don't believe I'll let you have it," she murmured. She tossed it to one of the other girls. Betsy had come up and was listening.

"Give me my hat," Leda cried. She started for the girl, named Molly Parker. The girl laughed and ran off toward the stairs.

Blind, shaking, animal fury possessed Leda. She ran after Molly, without calling to her, consumed by this passion to get her, reclaim her property, batter Molly's head again and again on the stone floor. Molly ran upstairs to the open hall; Leda ran after. They ran up the next flight of stairs, past the doors of the lunchroom, through the corridor to the next flight of stairs, Molly running easily and glancing back at Leda. Molly dropped the hat down the well of the stairs so that it fell two stories. Then she threw her leg over the banisters and slid down, laughing up at Leda.

Leda went slowly downstairs. At the bottom she picked up her crushed hat and dusted it, straightened out the crown. She went on down to the basement to get her coat. She was shaking with rage; she felt sweat breaking out all over her.

Betsy was standing facing Adèle, looking more than ever like a pug-dog, scowling, her hands on her hips.

"It serves her right," Adèle was saying lightly, disdainfully. "She's nothing but a poor church mouse. She's *wet*."

Betsy lifted her right arm from her side and slapped Adèle in the face, hard. Girls stopped and looked.

"Why, you fresh little thing," Adèle said slowly. She looked Betsy up and down. Then she walked away with her friends.

In the train Leda said to Betsy, "That was wonderful of you to stand up for me. It wasn't even your fight."

"You're my friend. She's a horrible bully and she ought to be slapped oftener."

"I think you were wonderful to do it," Leda repeated. "Not many girls would have. She has too many ways of getting even."

"She can't do anything to me," Betsy said truculently. "I'll show her."

When they got off the train the town was full of the sweet-smelling breeze of spring. A few lights glowed delicately in the dusk. They wandered along the street, carrying their books, up to the Jekylls' house.

The Brats were eating pieces of bread with molasses on them; they had molasses all over their chins. Mrs. Jekyll sat with a pair of horn-rimmed spectacles on her nose, reading a magazine; she looked peculiar and out-of-character in the glasses. She looked over them at Leda and Betsy.

"Hello. Why don't you get yourselves some oranges or something? I'd get them for you, but my back aches like fury. I must be getting old. Seems like my back aches most of the time." She laughed as if she did not believe what she was saying, as if she were trying out a joke.

When they came back from the kitchen they joined Mrs. Jekyll in the study.. They sat sucking the oranges through a lump of sugar in the hole.

They heard a car drive up, and a door slam. Betsy peered out.

"It's a taxi," she said vaguely.

The door opened and someone came into the hall.

In the doorway stood a woman, with a white face, sunken cheeks, wispy hair. It was Maizie.

"Mother!" She had come in a second across the room and was on the floor with her head in Minnie May's lap, weeping. Terrible sobs came from her throat. "Mother!"

"Darling. Darling Maizie. Darling. . . . Why. . . . Has that man been treating you badly?"

"No!" she cried. "No! No! No, he hasn't!"


## CHAPTER VIII

WHEN MAIZIE JEKYLL first met Lambert Rudd at a party he seemed to her much more distinguished, much more the real thing than any of the men who had paid her attention since she had come North.

He took her to several parties given by his friends, to which she had not been invited; she felt nothing demeaning about being brought to a party by a man, as an outsider. She liked the feeling that she was his girl. His appeal, his distinction began to grow in her mind like a fever. He was younger than she, but that never worried her or seemed to matter very much. She felt very young; she looked very young; she knew that there was nothing that was aging, nothing that had grown dim about her.

He had a studio in the Fenway Studios on Ipswich Street in Boston where he took her several times, in the afternoon, to look at his work. It was a bare, messy barn of a place, canvases stacked against the wall, a long high table covered with tubes of paint and scraped palettes and boxes of pastels. It excited her to think that she was in love with an artist; it must be wonderful to be an artist's wife. He showed her his pictures with an abrupt impatience, putting them away again after she had said that they were pretty. She would sit on the old couch and look at him, feeling impressed and almost afraid of him, as he talked in his hurried, passionate way about his work.

Watching him, with his sharp jaw thrust out, his dark eyes flickering, his thin lips forming words with hardly any movement, Maizie suddenly knew on one of those afternoons that she was terribly in love with him. She wanted him with a great wave of the possessiveness that was bred into her. Her blood awoke and burned and demanded this man, and that she should live for him in the old way, giving him everything that she might get everything.

It was some time in November when he first took her to his studio at night. They had had dinner at one of the small Italian restaurants where Lambert went. They came back to Ipswich Street in the sharp cold; into the stuffy heat of the building; up in the slow, groaning elevator run by a reeking colored boy. The old floor-boards creaked as they walked along the corridor to Lambert's door. He lit a light or two, blue glass bulbs that shed a white glare; all one side of the big room was glass—the north light—grimy with soot from the Boston & Albany trains that rumbled by at intervals.

When they came in they were laughing. They sat down on the old couch and lit cigarettes. Lighting hers, Lambert leaned nearer and then knocked away her cigarette and took hold of her and kissed her.

She pushed him away, laughing, and patting the soft, thick hair over her ears.

"Don't push me off," he murmured as if in his sleep; his eyes were closed. "Maizie. Pretty lovely thing with gold hair and soft skin—dimples. Come here."

He put his arms around her again and kissed her with that hard, urgent impersonality. She could feel his hands move in her hair, nervously but with assurance; hurriedly. He was leaning on her, pushing her back, absolutely hard in his desire. He had hold of her, he was kissing her neck, his lips and his chin thrusting into her.

"—Don't!"

He straightened up, looked at her and shrugged his shoulders.

"All right. Just as you say."

Then, as if it had never happened, as if his mind had switched entirely away, he got up and walked across the room, and began to look at a drawing.

He might never have kissed her. He was a hundred worlds away from her, talking about his work. He did not care that she did not understand. He needed to talk.

"They're so easy . . . those smart effects. An unfinished drawing's got twice the style, the smart effect, you see, don't you. . . . It's how to finish em up and still keep the freshness, the sharpness—and yet have the stuff, God damn it, the solid knowledge of what you're doing, and get it all in, the structure . . ."

Maizie did not hear a single word he said, talking and talking. All of her nature was gathered, drawn up in a knot, wanting him and seeking about for a means of getting him, shattered and abruptly shocked by the removal of his arms from about her. All of her was pointed at him there across the room, needing him, insisting on him.

He was still talking. He was looking around her, past her, even at her, but never seeing her. Something lifted her to her feet; something inside her was goaded to desperation by his remoteness, by her impotence to engage him. She walked over to where he sat, with his legs apart, his chin thrust out, leaning forward upon one knee. She slipped her hand around the back of his neck, feeling the stiff separate bristles under her palm.

He was impatient at first, interrupted from a train of thought. Then he looked up at her, smiled, perfectly friendly, perfectly willing for change from his mood. She leaned her cheek down to his and he put his arms up around her, as willing for the moment to hold her as to talk.

There was no conflicting caution at all for a while. Then they were quiet on the sofa, lying with his arm relaxed under her. Then the other nerves began in her again.

"Darling," she said. "I love you so."

"Love you. . . . Sweet thing."

"Darling . . . you're the only man I ever loved in my whole life. You're so wonderful. I'm so happy with you."

"Mmmmh," he murmured in her hair. A little while after he pulled his face back from hers and looked at her. He lit a cigarette and gave her one, got his elbow under him and lay on it.

"Look," he said. "It wouldn't be fair if I let you get the wrong idea. I haven't any intention of marrying anybody. I don't mean to be rude. But just in case you didn't understand. . . . You're a lovely thing, and a sweet thing, and I love having you here. But I'm a painter and I think about that, you know, not any other kind of a life."

She said nothing. All the cautious, wise blood in her told her that what he said did not matter. Men never wanted to marry; men must be led into marriage, and then made happy, given the deep and lasting satisfactions they had not known they wanted. Tonight had been unwise, but not too unwise. A man like this would never notice a woman unless she was brought closely to his attention. Perhaps this was best. Somehow Maizie knew that this particular man would not have the code of a Southern man. He would not think of disrespecting her; he would only be more likely to be aware of her.

And so after that she went often to the studio at night. At home, going to sleep in Hampton, she would remember the huge, dim room; the great wall of glass; the roar of the trains passing; the smoke of their cigarettes rising into the void between their faces and the ceiling. She would remember the deep satisfaction of Lambert's arms. For a while it was so much better to her than just looking at Lambert and loving him, across a room, or hearing him talk with his eyes unseeing, that she had no worry about any future.

One night he said, casually, going on smoking, that he was going away, in January or February.

". . . South America, I think," he said. "I've always wanted to see it. I have a feeling I'd like to paint it. I like the idea of all that . . . big bare mountains and decayed pink buildings and wild green jungle. It ought to be swell."

"I'd miss you . . ." she said faintly.

"Miss you, too. I don't suppose I'd stay longer than May, or June."

She was not listening. All her nerves were running about, preparing ways and means, proposing desperate expedients.

"I've always been crazy to go to South America," she gasped. "My, I'd love to go. I can't imagine anything more wonderful than going there."

"I thought I'd go first to Panama, and then . . ."

"I'd love to be there with you, darling. I could look at all the sights, and things, while you painted."

He looked at her, smiling, puckering his heavy brows.

"Uh-uh!"

It was after that that all her anxiety, her nervousness and wretchedness began.

It was the logical result of her new unhappiness, that instead of feeling frightened or forlorn at the beginning of January, she was quietly elated, comforted by what she knew about herself. Her instincts told her that she had found a solution.

"Lamb. I'm going to have a baby, I think," she said slowly. They were sitting in the studio at night; the corners were full of shadows. She interrupted Lambert in his talking; he stared at her vaguely without understanding what she said. Then he started forward in his chair.

"Good God! Why, you poor kid! Well, don't worry. We'll do something about it. Really, don't worry. I know a man that knows . . ."

"Lambert! Oh, I couldn't! Oh, Lambert, don't say such a thing. I'd rather die than do that, go to one of those people. I don't care what happens, I won't do that."

For one moment she was filled with the wildest longing for home, for the South; where the code was fixed, where she would not have done what she had done with Lambert, where people knew her and her family, where she would in time have fallen in love with a man she understood, who would have married her. She was alone. It was suddenly the sheerest nightmare, and she longed to be able to awake and find herself back in Virginia, among people who loved her, with a happy safe life before her. This man was a stranger, with dark eyes and a hard mouth; it was an insanity, a disease, that made her desire him so and feel that it would be death not to have him marry her.

"It isn't such an awful thing, you know," he said. "Other women have done it."

"I don't care. I'm not like the women you mean. I wasn't raised to be like that. I couldn't, I couldn't. You can't make me do it, I won't."

"Don't get excited. Well. What do you want me to do?"

"There's only one thing you can do," she said stiffly, from an old pattern; words put in her mouth from somewhere long ago.

"You mean marry you. You mean you want to play this trick on me."

"Don't speak to me like that, darling. It isn't a trick. It kills me to have you say that. I couldn't help this happening to me."

"You could help . . . Now listen. You just think about what I said. Just think about it quietly. I promise you it isn't so awful. So many women wouldn't do it if it were. I'd take you there, and it would be all over in a few minutes. Then you'd have nothing to worry about any more."

"I think you're being low." She stopped. She knew, somehow, that the old standards would not work with this man. He was a stranger to all the things she knew. She loved him so; it was pain to her to look at him.

And yet nowhere in her did she feel hard, or tricky, or grasping. She only loved Lambert with all her heart; her whole being needed him. She knew how good, and sweet, and gentle, and patient she could be with him if only he would let her; how happy she could make him, for after all he was a man, and men were to be made happy in certain eternal, unvarying ways. She would be all that he could ask, she would give to him as no other woman he would ever find. She would not hurt him for the world. She only wanted happiness, and peace, and love.

He said: "You know I don't want to marry you."

In that next week she lived a fantastic life, waiting, wondering what was going to happen. She made long, dreamlike, involved plans; pictures of life with him; themselves at breakfast, walking, at a party, talking in bed, buying a house, reading the newspaper: aged thirty, aged forty, aged sixty. She thought of him and his person and·his life out of all proportion to reality, in phrases that were heavy with beauty and mystery and significance; thoughts put into words as: He is a painter; his hair is thick and black; he wears blue shirts; his mother's name is Eugenia; his ears are small and flat; he has black hair on the backs of his wrists. All the mesh of a hundred tiny known facts about him made a nebulous aura around that central, beating name in her consciousness: *Lambert Rudd*. She waited in the window, watched the streets, at all hours when he would not come; her blood trembled incessantly for his coming and throbbed like a wound at the sudden shut of a door, the ring of a telephone. She wrote his name on a piece of paper, over and over; combined her name with his; stared at his name in the telephone book; whispered it, thought it, all day long, and in dreams too, so that she awoke heavy and flushed from sleep that was crowded with him.

She saw him in a week. He came unexpectedly in the afternoon, driving his car through the sunny, white, creaking snow. She ran to get her coat and they went out and got into the car. They drove along the hard white roads; a loose link of the wheel-chains slapped quickly, merrily, against the ice, rap-rap-rap-rap. Lambert had a blue muffler up around his chin, folded neatly inside his gray coat; his face looked straight ahead. Maizie simply sat beside him, engrossed with the satisfactions of feeling his arm, knowing that it was his car, seeing a picture of herself sitting there beside him.

"Well," he said, suddenly, "have you changed your mind about getting this business attended to? I hope you have."

"I can't do that," she said.

"You refuse to?"

"I can't do it."

"Well . . ."

The deep red sun was heavy along the pure line of the horizon. The shadows on the snow were blue. The air was still.

Again suddenly he spoke: "All right. I can't just let you go ahead and have it. I don't know why I can't, in a way, but I can't."

There was such peace in the cold afternoon.

"Darling," she said. "You mustn't be miserable. I'll . . . work all my life to make you happy."

"I know you're a swell girl. But I can't help feeling that you aren't a very good sport."

It didn't make any sense. His words were something that hurt and that had to be thrust away, in these last moments of waiting until everything would be all right. Then nothing would ever hurt any more.

"I love you more than anything in the whole world. I don't care about anything but you. All I want is to do everything you want."

"I don't really *want* anything, though," he said, wryly: "All right, you win. There must be something that can be done about it later."

That slid off her mind like water. All that mattered was the present; once the present was accomplished, the future could be made happy.

". . . I'll get a license in the morning," he said, talking without moving his lips. "And we'll go down town and get married on Friday."

She murmured something vaguely. She felt the deepest peace.

"Do you want to tell your family?"

"I don't know."

"Well, then don't. We might as well get it done quick and quiet."

"All right."

"God in Heaven knows why you want this," he said, his voice much louder. "You aren't going to like being married to me. I'm not going to change anything for you. I'm sorry, but this wasn't my idea and I don't see why I should. I've got my work to do. I don't know how you're going to fit in. You might as well realize you're going to have a hell of a time."

She didn't believe him at all.

"I just want to be near you," she murmured, out of the roar and chaos of her love.

They were married and went home to Hampton and sat on the window-seat in the living-room and told Maizie's family about it. Even from her mother Maizie felt worlds removed; there was no reality except Lambert, and she could not hear any voice or see any face but his. She went upstairs and packed her clothes while he talked to her family, and came downstairs again. She kissed them all, and Leda March, who was there, without feeling their skin against her lips.

They had dinner with his mother in her house on Commonwealth Avenue and later took the night train to New York. They were sailing on Tuesday for South America.

## CHAPTER IX

THE NIGHT TRAIN was hot and stuffy. Lambert went into the smoking-room at the end of the train, and Maizie lay awake for him for a long time, but he did not come.

They stayed at a large hotel in New York. In the daytime the streets were full of sun and dirty snow, and Maizie bought summer clothes for the tropics. Every night they went to a theatre; it was difficult to talk between the acts when they went out to smoke, for Lambert did not answer her; he seemed almost unconscious of her presence. Afterwards he would not go to bed for hours. She sat up with him in the plush sitting-room of their suite; her attempts at talk ceased from exhaustion; he sat and smoked one, two packages of cigarettes, his face dark and closed, far away from her, while her heart pounded, her eyes ached. She kept thinking ahead to when they would get on the boat. She believed superstitiously that everything would be all right then. That was when their life would really begin. This was only a sort of nightmare.

On Tuesday they got up after four hours' sleep. Lambert looked just the same, dark and unscathed; Maizie was heavy and nervous with exhaustion. They took a taxi across Manhattan to Brooklyn through the snowy streets, to the docks. In an hour they had sailed.

The ship was very cold, not arranged for Northern weather. They sat in the small smoking-room on the promenade deck, drinking whiskies, muffled up in coats; Lambert was remote and preoccupied. Maizie was in a fever of anxiousness, for this was when she must make their life begin.

She talked scrappily, in little bits, keeping her eyes on his dark, unlistening face. She chattered about the other passengers that went by, about the draughts, about the arrangements of their staterooms—anything. She said something about how pleasant it would be when they got further south and it began to be hot.

"What?" he said suddenly, loudly, looking at her. "Yes! It will be nice, won't it? After all, it's a good trip in itself, isn't it?"

"Yes," she said eagerly.

"We might as well have a big time, mightn't we? There's no reason why we shouldn't have a big time and get drunk and dance and enjoy ourselves, is there? Why not?"

She looked at him timidly. She could not understand his sudden, noisy mood.

"You look pretty with your little red, cold nose," he said, leaning toward her. "You're a lovely thing, aren't you? I can't imagine a prettier woman to have around me. Do you want another drink?"

"No, I don't believe so," she said. Already she was responding; she understood this; she smiled and dimpled. Her wretched heart quieted.

"Well then, come along below, my pretty," he said. He tucked her hand under his arm and went down the stairs with her, smiling down into her face with a ferocious intensity.

All the way to Panama he was like a new person. He danced every evening with her, and swam and lay with her on the hot sun-deck covered with canvas, and made urgent, insatiable love to her; he was different from any way she had ever before seen him. Gradually she became happy; confident. He never left her alone. He seemed to be spending a deep reserve of energy upon her. He could dance till the orchestra stopped playing, holding her very close and pretending to flirt with her in his queer, violent way. Lying on the sun-deck he would look her over, slowly, voluptuously, with a possessiveness that made her happy. When he came into her stateroom with her, in the afternoons and at night, he appeared possessed by his desire; he hurried her through her undressing and took hold of her, shook her, held her off and jerked her close to him; he seemed to be given, with the most excessive abandonment, to physical living. She felt sure, now, that he loved her, but she was frightened of him. She liked feeling a little frightened of him. It was part of what she wanted. This was the way she was created to live.

Sometimes he would take her up on the boat deck, at night, when the sky that moved slowly by above the ship was full of stars. She would stand at the rail, looking at the wide, phosphorescent water, conscious of his presence beside her; she was where she belonged, beside him; and now everything was all right, and he was never cold to her any more.

And then he would take hold of her shoulders with his fingers, and jerk her around to him, not saying anything. He would look at her in the moonlight in her evening dress.

She enjoyed it all as her right. She only wished he would speak to her.

For she could not get him to say he loved her, except sometimes impatiently, hurriedly, in the heat of his desire. She thought it was pride. He felt she had made him marry her. He would forget that. She would make him happy. She would be indispensable to him. She was laying the foundations. She went into his stateroom and mended his socks, repaired his shirts, did many little things that gave her pleasure and were the coin in which a woman paid a man; the little ribbons that held him to her so that he could never escape.

He came in and found her sewing in his stateroom one day.

"The little wife," he said. "My little domestic blessing." He smiled. "You come here, you pretty thing."

She continued to sew, with a virtuous, feminine air.

"I said come here."

He came over to her and pushed her sewing on to the floor, jerked her to her feet with his lips set hard. She told herself that men spoke violently to the women they loved.

By the time they reached Panama she felt confident and possessive.

She liked the hotel in Panama City: a big place built around a dim patio, with rooms that had balconies looking out over the square. She hurried about, unpacking their clothes, stepping out on the balcony for a minute to breathe the sweet tropic air, with a domestic, proprietary sense of being Lambert's wife and owning him and taking care of him.

"Isn't this nice?" she said. "It's so comfortable and cool, and such good bathrooms. I think we'll like it here."

"For Christ's sake, let's have a good time in Panama," he said.

"Of course, darling. Let's. Didn't you have a good time on the boat?" she asked conversationally, hanging up a dress.

"What did you think? Didn't you know I was in hell? Listen, my girl, this trip was something I planned to take alone, my own way, without bothering with someone else. Don't forget that."

Tears came quickly into her eyes.

"Oh, darling. . . . I didn't know I was in the way. I'll try not to be." She didn't know what to say.

"Just shut up. Just try for God's sake to leave me alone."

She went downstairs with him to the bar, quietly, in terror; she gave her order for a drink almost in a whisper.

"Oh, don't be wet," he said.

The bar was a marble-floored place; the wide, old, red doors were thrown open making the place one with the sidewalk. Maizie liked the foreign murmur of Spanish at the tables; gradually she became calmer; men were subject to crazy bursts of temper that meant nothing.

Lambert saw, across the room, one of the men they had met on the boat, and beckoned to him to join them. He began to talk gaily, almost wildly, with the man, a middle-aged American. He ignored Maizie; they drank round after round, and after the first neither of them asked her to join them. She began to feel indignant. By the time the other man left she was pink with anger.

"Lambert. How could you be so rude to me? After all, I'm your wife."

"Will you kindly shut your head? Just as a favor to me."

"Lambert! I should think you wouldn't speak like that to any woman."

"I will say exactly what I please. Just because you tricked me into marrying you by the most completely stinking piece of bad sportsmanship I ever saw, is no reason, as I see it, why I should treat you as if the whole thing was my idea. *If* you get my meaning."

"Darling. . . . You wouldn't be so horrid if you knew how I love you."

"If you love me you'll shut up. You'll kindly go to hell."

She was trembling all over with the effort not to cry. They went up to their room after dinner, Lambert in a stony silence, Maizie wild with alarm. She did not know what to do, what to say; everything she tried seemed wrong. She began to take off her clothes and go quietly to bed.

"What the hell do you think you're doing? Come here."

"I only thought you wanted to be left alone. . . ."

"Oh, quit that. You'll sit up here so I can talk to you."

"Yes, darling."

He talked for hours, then, of his painting and what he planned to work on in South America. She stared at his dark face; he seemed further away from her than he ever had. It was after four when he stretched himself and got up. He smiled at her, suddenly, and her heart came to life.

"You're pretty sweet, I hand you that," he said. "You're a pretty baby, if I ever saw one. Who do you love?"

"You," she said, with all her heart.

She woke up the next morning to the ringing of the bells in the Cathedral across the plaza; a full-bodied, orange sunshine flooded all the room, and a rugged heat ringing like brass. She got up and looked down at Lambert sleeping. For a moment as she looked at him she was entirely conscious of loving him and hating him, two clear, separate, tremendous emotions.

She went out alone and had breakfast of coffee and sweet rolls in the hotel cafe, tasting each mouthful of the bread and the strong, burnt coffee with an agonizing perception. She walked across the plaza; it was full of little dark children in white, running with balloons, and people reposed for the day on benches; along the curb were open black automobiles with white linen covers on the seats. The streets were lined with shining plate-glass windows displaying embroidery and perfume and straw hats and Chinese robes.

She went into a chemist's and asked for the name of an American doctor. She was given an address just across the street. She went up a flight of stairs and sat down in a dusty waiting-room with several dark, ill-looking women and their children.

The doctor, when she went into his office, was a paunchy American; white haired, white moustached, pleasant, lazy. He leaned back in his swivel chair and smoked a cigar and was not surprised nor interested nor anything but comfortable and kindly when she told him that she was pregnant, that she thought her husband did not want her to have the child, that she would like to know if there was any medicine she could take. Without leaning forward he scribbled out the words "quinine . . . castor oil!" on a prescription pad and dropped the paper in her outstretched hand.

"Don't believe it will do a thing for you," he said. "But you probably want to feel you're doing something. After you've tried it out just forget about it and go on and have the baby. Husbands often feel the way yours does. There isn't anything they can do about it, once the child comes. They get to like them."

"How about having it stopped?" She realized that she was on the point of tears. It was something about this old man. He seemed so happy and safe and untroubled.

"Oh, I don't like that sort of talk, not at all. I don't like things against nature, no I don't. My dear child, stop thinking about anything like that, I beg you. Things like that are very dangerous, yes they are."

The tears had come, in torrents.

"Oh my God. . . . I don't want to, but . . . you don't understand . . . it's so horrible . . . so horrible."

He contemplated her.

"You couldn't tell me?"

"No, I couldn't, I couldn't. . . ."

"Husband mistreat you?"

"Oh, no! . . . You wouldn't understand . . . it's all so mixed up and horrible."

"Well . . . you go home. You're upset. Don't do anything silly."

She got up. She wiped her eyes and stared at him mutely.

"Goodbye. I'm sorry I can't help you further. You passing through the Zone?"

"Yes. We're going on to the West Coast for two or three months."

"Tch. Well, behave yourself. Too bad you can't go home, instead. . . .
If you *should* need anybody—there is a doctor in Guayaquil. Jackson. You
needn't tell him I recommended you to him. But forget about the whole
thing if you can."

She left him and went out into the street. There was no one on earth who
could help her. There was no way, ever, for her to come close enough to
anyone for them to understand or help. All people were strangers. For her
now there would never be anyone but Lambert, and whatever life he dealt
out to her.


## CHAPTER X

THEY STAYED in Panama a few days, lunching at the Chagres Club in the
shade of the balcony, drinking at the bars, listening to the raucous singing
in the cabarets on the Avenida Central at night, dancing at the Union Club.
The days were full of strong sun and the nights of stars and the crazy calling of women from upper balconies.

They boarded a ship that moved out into the enormous, oily waters of
the Pacific. The weather was burning hot at Buenaventura; everyone went
ashore and wandered through the tin-roofed town, up and down the mud
streets among negroes and loose horses. The day they crossed the Line all
tyros were to be initiated into Neptune's Court, held at the side of the ship's
pool by seasoned passengers disguised with paint and whitewash.

Maizie lay on her berth in her promenade-deck stateroom, sapped by the
heat, listening to the procession that was rounding up victims, parading
round the ship, to the loud music of a fife and drum. "*Hinky-Dinky Parlez-
vous*" squealed out over and over and over above the march of feet, and the
music turned sour and ominous; on and on. There was a loud triple rap at her
door. She got up in her bathing-suit and went out to join them. Why did
she feel so numb with terror? The shrill monotonous tune sounded like a
death march. Lambert was already with them; he was laughing.

"I can't do it," she stammered. "Can't I pretend I'm sick or something?"

He spoke to her abruptly, sharply.

"For God's sake, behave yourself. This is all in fun."

There was nothing to it. She was judged and convicted, thrown by polite
figures in disguise into the pool, slathered over with whitewash and squash-
pulp. It was nothing alarming, and she did not mind it. But she felt something horrible hanging over her, that was still unseen.

That night after dancing she went up on the top deck with Lambert. She
came close to him and slipped her arm around him.

He pushed her arm away.

"What are you always touching me for?"

"I'm sorry, darling," she said.

"Oh, stop apologizing for everything. Can't you tell by now when I want
to be quiet and think?"

"I wish you didn't hate me so."

"Oh, I don't hate you so. Stop exaggerating everything. I just think you're a fairly unscrupulous person, who's got her own way pretty much at my expense."

Her nerves ached with pain.

"I don't see why it's unscrupulous for me to have loved you and wanted you so that I had to have you."

"Don't you?" he asked.

"Why can't you just let me love you? I promise you that I'd make you happy if you'd let me."

He looked at her with obsessed, tormented eyes.

"I can't believe anything you say. I can't trust you. You're scheming . . . unscrupulous. . . . I don't believe you were going to have a baby at all. I think you just used it to trick me."

"Lambert!"

"You don't seem pregnant. You look just as well as you ever did."

She thought of all the time she spent working on herself, trying to make herself pretty.

"You think that," she said slowly.

"I'm not such a damn fool as I look. I know I've been a sucker, an easy little boy for you to hook. But I'm not entirely crazy."

"Lambert. I swear to you that it is true."

"Balls."

She walked away from him, down the deck, and to her cabin. She sat there for an hour, waiting for him to come and knock. The longer she waited the more absurd appeared her idea that he would ask to be forgiven. At last she went down the deck to his stateroom and knocked on the door.

"Who's that?" his voice said.

"I'm so sorry. It's all my fault." She was prepared to apologize for anything.

"Oh, go away," he said.

"But, darling, *please* let me come in and talk to you. I can't stand knowing you're there thinking untrue things about me."

"Will you go away?" he said, wearily.

She lay awake for hours, thinking and thinking and thinking.

In Guayaquil they went ashore to buy Panama hats. Maizie knew now what she had to do.

She was cold, in the equatorial weather.

They hired a car and drove through the streets, lined with wattled fences, tin roofs, the crumbling pinkish stone of buildings.

At the hat store Lambert got out and turned. She smiled at him, stiffly.

"I think I'd rather drive around," she said.

"All right."

She leaned forward to the black driver.

"I want to go to Dr. Jackson's office. Do you know where that is?"

She was shown directly into a small office whose open windows gave onto the lush green of a garden. After the glare of the streets she could not see.

The first thing she saw was that Dr. Jackson had negro blood. It was in his thick, bluish lips, and his crinkly hair, turned white. He was bland and unctuous. He played with a china ashtray in the shape of a hat, with his long, delicate fingers. His eyes were very large behind round glasses. He moistened his lips carefully from time to time. His white linen suit was immaculate, and he wore a stickpin in his tie. His skin was the color of strong tea.

"It will be impossible to give a general anaesthetic," he said. "In these climates. . . . If you are to take the boat when it sails tonight a spinal is also out of the question; you would not be able to walk."

"Oh. . . . How much will it cost?"

"Let us say a hundred dollars."

There did not seem to be anything else to say. She stood up. Suddenly her stiffness broke, just a little.

"Will it hurt terribly?"

"Well . . . we must expect to pay for what we do," he said. "Pain is the price we pay for something we hope to gain." He added, "Plenty of young girls from the families here about can stand it. Plenty of young girls who have made a little mistake—you know what I mean? Their families are wealthy, and it is not too hard to remedy. . . ."

"I'll be back in three-quarters of an hour," she broke in.

"Everything will be prepared."

She got back into the open car and drove by the hat store for Lambert. She felt little numb chills in her veins.

"Let's go somewhere and have a drink," he said.

"Yes. I want to tell you something."

They sat in the patio of a hotel and drank whisky. Maizie drank hers down fast.

"Well . . ." he said when she had told him. "What in God's name do you want to do that for?"

"Oh, Lambert, you're so wretched and I thought and thought last night, and this is all I can do. I want to do it. I can stand it. I want to do the only thing I can."

"Don't be so melodramatic," he said absently. "What do you want to do it for, is what I want to know. It seems kind of late to be so brave now, doesn't it?"

"It's all I can do," she mumbled. She drank her second drink. She could not realize, actually, what was going to happen to her. Her mind thought around it, and above it and below it.

"Don't be a damn fool, that's my advice," he said. "Everything's about as lousy as it can be, and there's nothing that can be done about it now. I think you'd better stop acting like an abused heroine."

"If I do this, then you'll be free, don't you see? You'll have no obligation to stay with me any longer."

She finished her drink.

"What kind of a man is this? How do you know he's not a quack?"

"The doctor in Panama sent me to him," she said.

He stared at her.

The wholly fantastic thing about the operating room was the way she found herself and Dr. Jackson talking as he moved about, completing long ablutions, being put into a long white coat by one of the tiny brown South American nurses that had led her down the corridors to this room, that now trotted about lifting instruments from sterilizers.

She lay on the table covered by a sheet. Far back in the point of the cone of her mind was that frightful little terror . . . but in the meantime she and Dr. Jackson talked.

"And where do you come from in the States?" she heard herself asking.

"I am a native of Philadelphia," he said.

"Oh, yes. I love Philadelphia; that is, I love all I've ever heard about it. It must be very peaceful."

"It is peaceful," he said. "I don't know about how it is now, however. I am a member of the older generation. I have been doing a great work, over many years, in these parts."

"Have you really? It must be very interesting."

"You have no idea of the ignorance of the natives," he said, holding out his hand for a nurse to dry. "They must be shown the most elementary matters of hygiene. It has been thirty years since I instituted my work in the country; I can assure you that it fills a crying need."

"I'm sure it does. Why do they all have tin roofs on their houses?"

"I have no idea. They have no conception of what is good for them. . . . Now if you are ready, I think we can commence."

The preposterous part was that now she felt no fear, only an idiotic curiosity. Odd thoughts presented themselves to her mind. Mickey, Bolshevicky, with your hair of raven hue. . . . And with the irrelevant words came an exact, colored picture of the living-room in Hampton, her mother playing the piano and herself and Betsy dancing with a number of young men who had no faces. How curly Dr. Jackson's hair is, she thought. The nurses were like little smiling monkeys. They kept nodding at her, showing their pretty white teeth. Outside the window the sky was glaring blue, and the tops of trees waved in vivid, shattering green.

"Modern science is very remarkable," she said out loud in short gasps.

Dr. Jackson nodded seriously without looking up.

His hands moved toward the table beside him, picking up and laying down steel instruments.

This was sheer, exquisite agony, like sugar melting down her spine. It was sweet and sickish. It was the normal state of life, and it would never end.

"There," he said suddenly, standing up. "That was a beautiful job. I want you to be quiet in bed now until you have to go. The nurses will come if you ring, and you will have your supper here. I will send your husband up to see you after a time. Everything is perfectly all right."

And now she was crying, without being interested in crying or thinking about it. She found herself in another bed, in a small dark wooden-walled room; only the window was a patch of light, with the thick lush green leaves swaying outside. She rang a bell. A nurse came.

"Can I see my husband now?"

After a while she began feeling rather well, like a heroine. She had done something very brave, but she was not sure just what. She was sure that Lambert was going to think that she was very brave about something. Her body felt whole and neat and unhurting, but she liked lying still, watching the bubbles of reflected sunshine skip up and down the walls. She felt that she had been here for several days; it seemed quite time to get up, if she was going to catch the boat. But it was too delicious lying still and she thought she would miss it. There were people talking on the other side of the wall.

Suddenly Lambert was standing by her bed, his face flickering with green light; she had not even heard him come in.

"Poor darling," he said. "Brave girl."

She pressed his hand. "Now do you love me?"

"What?"

"I couldn't have done it for anyone but you."

"I—I didn't ask you to do it. Now, darling, get this straight."

"You did," she said, and the tears began to fall from her eyes. "You asked me and asked me, and you hated me because I wouldn't. You thought I was lying to you about having a baby. Now you see. I couldn't have done this if I hadn't."

"Funny kind of act," he said. "I don't understand. You didn't want to before, and I married you, the way you wanted. Why did you do it now? Just to prove something?"

It was not according to the book. He should not be thinking like this, he should not be thinking at all. Sympathy and admiration and amazement and remorse ought to fill his mind, he ought to have his head in her outstretched hand. She found herself pushed into replies foreign to her nature.

"Now you can leave me," she said. "Now I've made you free of me."

She saw the gratitude in his face under the livid green light from the window.

"Did you really do that?" he said. "You poor little kid."

"Now you can go off by yourself," she said. "I can go back on the next boat." Deep within herself she knew that she did not mean to let him go, she could not, but nevertheless the tears came into her eyes again at her own sacrifice, spoken in those words.

"You can't stay here. I don't like that coon downstairs worth a damn. I'll get you back on the boat in a little while and we'll go on to Callao, and then we'll see."

She never remembered how she left the clinic nor how they got to the water front. She remembered the trip out to the ship in a small rowboat. The ship stood out in the harbor in the darkness like a great shimmering meteor. She sat in the stern of the skiff, frightened of the water and frightened of the Ecuadorians who rowed the boat, and yet happy feeling frightened, with Lambert's arm solid behind her back. He helped her up the gangway and along the decks to her stateroom. He helped her to undress, and tucked her into·bed.

"There, now. You keep still for a day or two, in bed, and you'll be all right."

"Yes, darling," she said. She wished he were more frightened for her, more alarmed about the condition she was in, but she was beginning to know that he was not that kind of man—not a man as she understood the word 'man,' but a special, strange, free being whom by mischance she loved to distraction. It was wrong that she should feel all the anxiety, the mad desire to please; that she should do all the pleading, make all the sacrifices. That was the man's part. She saw that he did not even realize the odd maladjustment of their positions.

She knew what she wanted—for him to love her as a man should love a woman. It remained for her to find the ways to make him into that kind of man. She did not know them but they must exist, and, she thought, she would find them if it killed her.

## CHAPTER XI

THEY CAME TO CALLAO in the middle of the morning. It was hot and yellow and sultry. Maizie dressed for the first time, and packed her clothes, feeling weak, but knowing that because it was three days since Guayaquil, she must be well. She stood on the dock with Lambert, waiting for the customs man. Lambert was dark and strong and stimulated-looking, in a white linen suit. Three girls waved to him as they got into a car and drove away.

They drove from Callao up to Lima in an open hired car with their bags piled around their feet. The country was flat and exhausted; there were stone walls on either side of the road; and from miles away, through the mists, Lima could be seen, like a mirage, ominous and ancient.

Their hotel was around the corner from an open plaza. The city looked brooding, very different from the lightness and gaiety of Panama. The windows of their rooms were hung with oppressive brocade curtains. Maizie felt the need to lie down; she was weak and trembling. But Lambert walked in through the door that connected the rooms.

"Well, how do you feel?" he said. "Let's go out and catch a bite of lunch somewhere. It looks swell. Did you notice that church just before we got here? The whole place is the most decadent, weird sort of spot I've ever seen. Ready?"

Maizie took his arm and they walked out into the hot street.

In the restaurant she talked and laughed. But inside her fright was growing. This place was filled with an ominous corruption.

"I don't guess we'd better eat any lettuce or such," Lambert said, smiling at her. "This is part of the dysentery belt."

They ate shrimps in mayonnaise and some sort of hash made out of chicken. It was all she could do to laugh and flirt with Lambert, to take out her mirror and put on fresh lipstick, to look casually at the sleek, well-dressed·Limans lunching all around them.

After luncheon they walked through the streets, across the plazas, into the old Spanish churches, the Palace of the Inquisition, past modern blaring department stores and drugstores with their windows filled with soap. For blocks now Maizie had been aware of an overwhelming weakness; the sun seemed to melt and rot her.

"I'm terribly tired," she said at last; she stared up at the great, rapacious statue of Pizarro in front of the Cathedral. "I'd like to go home."

Lambert looked at her. She could see the annoyance at interruption of his enjoyment, in his face.

"All right," he said. "You go on home and rest. I'll be back later."

She could not endure it.

"Oh, no," she said. "I'm not really so tired. I'll get a good sleep tonight. What'll we see next?"

"If you're tired go on home and rest. Don't wear yourself out and then blame it on me."

But she could not endure to let him wander about this city alone, apart from her, glad to be rid of her perhaps. She must stay with him, no matter how she felt.

"I'm fine," she said, looking up at him gaily.

When the sudden twilight had fallen over the city, they stopped at a cafe on the sidewalk of the plaza near their hotel for a drink. Lambert ordered "Dos vermouths con soda," and Maizie suddenly knew she was very ill. The day lay like a nightmare behind her. She was afraid of everything, and most of all afraid of Lambert.

"Had fun?" Lambert took her hand and squeezed it. "You look a whole lot better."

She wondered what would happen if she should faint, or die, at this moment, before him. She tried to push away her illness with pretense that it was not there. No. . . . Oh, yes; yes, she was ill.

"I'm sorry," she said. "Please don't hate me, darling. But I'm sick. I've got to go back to the hotel."

He looked at her quickly and led her across the plaza.

She listened to him telephoning in the other room, asking the desk about doctors, as she lay on the bed. She turned on her side and looked out of the window into the dark blue night. There, on top of a silhouetted mountain behind Lima, burned a gigantic cross. She closed her eyes and opened them, and it was still there: a monstrous cross of white light.

Lambert came back into her room.

"Do you think you can get up and drive out to Callao again? The best doctor seems to be a man at the British-American hospital there. I've called him and he can see you if we come out now."

She climbed off the bed obediently. She went downstairs, got into the car, sat there while it bounced and swayed out the road to Callao. It stopped at a low building. They went in, to a room opening on a patio. A little dark nurse came and took their name and went away. Then another nurse came, a big fat white one with a Cockney accent. "Come this way," she said to Maizie.

She led her into a small office and sat down with a pad of paper before her and began to ask questions.

"But can't I see the doctor?" Maizie asked.

"Dr. Mackenzie will have to see your history first. Now then. On what date was this operation performed?"

At last the nurse went away with the sheet of paper and there was a long wait. The nurse came back.

"Come this way," she said.

They went through a passage into another patio, and into an examining room.

"When can I see the doctor?" Maizie asked.

"Now be a good girl, and he'll see you presently."

Maizie felt angry; they had no right to speak impertinently to her. She had never heard of a doctor treating his patients like this. She thought, I'll get up and walk out of here.—But he's all there is, she thought in a panic; this is Peru, and he's all there is.

A young man walked in. He did not even look at Maizie.

"Patient prepared?" he asked.

"Yes, doctor."

"How do you do," Maizie said, distinctly.

The doctor glanced toward her.

"Oh," he said, and nodded. He went on with his examination.

"Well, young woman," he said, as the nurse pulled off his rubber gloves. "You've got yourself into a pretty pickle. Can you be here at eight o'clock tomorrow morning?"

"Can't you make it a little later?"

"No, I can't. That's the only free time I have tomorrow to operate. This must be done at once."

"Suppose it isn't?"

"If it isn't, you'll be on your way to heaven, young woman. Eight o'clock tomorrow."

He was on his way out of the room. "Will you give me an anaesthetic?" she cried after him.

"Yep. You should have had one the other time. Probably wouldn't have had this trouble. Can't tell." The doctor had gone.

As soon as they had got back into the car Maizie began to cry. Lambert put his arm around her.

"I wonder how much that boy really knows," he said. "There must be other doctors. When we get back to the hotel you go to bed and I'll scout around and see if I can't find someone to come and see you."

He patted her shoulder.

"So he said you'd be on your way to heaven, did he? That's a hell of a way to talk. For Christ's sake. There, darling. Don't be frightened."

She lay on her bed alone for hours, staring out at the cross that burned on the mountain. Lambert did not come back until after midnight.

"Oh, where have you been?" she cried as he switched on the light.

"Aren't you asleep?"

"How could I sleep not knowing where you were, and thinking perhaps I'll die? How could you go off and leave me?"

"Listen. It may sound like a cinch to you to go out in a strange city to find a doctor to save your wife's life, but it isn't. Anyway, I've got hold of the name of a man. If we call him early in the morning we may be able to get him. A Peruvian boy, but apparently he knows his stuff."

"What do you mean, we *may* be able to get him? What if we can't? Suppose we don't get hold of him? Will I go out there to Callao?"

"Maizie, for Christ's sake, what's the use of worrying about what *may* happen? We'll do our best to get hold of him. I've put in a call to be waked at seven."

"You don't care whether I live or die."

"Kindly stop heckling me. What the hell do you suppose it's like to be responsible for whether you do go out there to What's-his-name's or not?"

She turned her face into the pillow; her cheeks were burning and she ached all over.

"Good night," she heard him say.

She raised her face.

"Darling! Tell me where you were all that time—what have you been doing?"

"I told you. Trying to get the name of a reliable doctor."

"But where have you been?"

"With some people I met on the boat. At the other hotel down the street."

"But why did you have to take so long? You don't know what it was like waiting, all this time."

"Darling, please quit crabbing. You can't walk right up to someone and say, 'What's a good doctor to see whether my wife has to have an operation?' I had to sit around with them for a while. I had a few drinks, that's all."

"Oh, darling—were there girls there?"

"Ye-e-e-s," he said. "There were girls there. Is that all you want to know? Because I want to get some sleep. Good night."

She slept in fits and starts through the rest of the night. Her eyes would open and see again that enormous cross burning on the mountain; still burning there after the dawn came and the mountain turned to dark yellow. She stared at it in horror and feverish apprehension, and wondered what Lambert had been saying all those hours, what girls he had been laughing with.

## CHAPTER XII

THE LITTLE MAN with the silky black moustaches came right over. He walked into Maizie's room, bowing decorously, and asked her a question in Spanish. She looked at him helplessly. She had dressed and was standing by the window. The doctor tried a question in French, and Maizie stammered out an answer. He seemed no more at ease in French than she. She was not even quite sure of the meaning of his questions; she had to guess at them. Finally he nodded his head firmly.

"*Il faut, Madame, que vous veniez chez moi, à la clinique. Il faut faire une examination.*"

They walked, all three of them, the little man in the middle, down the long, straight streets, around corners. The doctor's office was in a large stone house. Maizie got on the examining table in response to the doctor's sweeping gesture. He drew on a glove and approached her.

She remembered the precautions that had been taken yesterday, that were not being taken now. Suddenly she realized that the doctor had not understood.

"*Vous ne comprenez pas! Il y a quatre jours seulement depuis l'opération à Guayaquil. Ne faut-il pas faire l'examination stérile?*"

"*Madame. Je n'ai pas compris.*" He lighted a little alcohol flame in a burner and began to hold his instruments in the flame one by one. Maizie's heart turned cold. This was such inefficiency as compared to what she had seen yesterday.

He made his examination.

"*L'opération, ce n'etait pas bien fait,*" he said finally. "*C'est ça.*"

"*Mais, ce que je veux vous demander, c'est si c'est nécessaire à faire encore une autre opération? Le docteur Mackenzie a dit hier. . . .*"

"*Mackenzie? Vous avez vu le docteur Mackenzie?*"

"*Oui. Hier.*"

"*Voyez-vous,*" said the little doctor, snatching a photograph from the wall. It was of himself and Mackenzie, both in surgical coats, together. "*Le docteur Mackenzie, c'est mon cher collègue. C'est un homme de génie. Allez chez Mackenzie, Madame. Je ne séduis pas des gens.*"

She felt wildly gay driving out to Callao with Lambert.

"He said he didn't seduce people," she said. "Wasn't he cute?"

Suddenly Lambert kissed her.

"Such a brave girl," he said. "I'm sorry if I seemed cross last night. You do feel lots more cheerful today, don't you?"

"Oh, darling, when you're sweet to me like this I could do anything. I don't care if I die on that operating table, if you love me, darling."

"Don't talk that way," he said. But he kissed her again.

In the room they showed her to she undressed and put on a hospital nightgown; they wheeled her into the operating room. Doctor Mackenzie and another doctor were washing in two basins.

"Good morning, doctor," she called. "I believe I'm on the dot."

Mackenzie only glanced at her, but the other doctor grinned, and at once she found it easy to joke with him.

"What kind of knockout drops are you giving me?"

"Spinal. Ever had it?"

"No, is it fun?"

"Maybe you'll think so. Anyway, you won't feel a thing from the waist down."

"Good."

All her thoughts were oddly light, gay, they swooped like little bright-colored birds into her mind and out again. She wanted to laugh at every-thing. In one of those moments it occurred to her how preposterous was her situation now: she had never been sick before in her life, and now she was very sick, had undergone one agonizing operation and was about to undergo another in an attempt to save her life; she had learned the names of anaesthetics, of parts of her own pelvic anatomy, she was living, had been living, in an atmosphere of illness and emergency, a fantastic, exaggerated world; how queer.

The operation went through with speed; she talked all through it; the assistant murmured replies; Mackenzie worked silently, not glancing up, his square, pale face set and the round jaw-muscles in his cheeks contracting.

Maizie was wheeled back to her room. In a moment Lambert was shown in. She lay in bed, paralyzed from the waist down.

"God, I'm so relieved everything's all right!" He dropped down on the edge of a chair by her bed and took her hand. She smiled at him gaily.

"I've been through hell waiting," he said. "Suppose anything had hap-pened to you! Get well now quick, won't you, darling?"

"I will," she said lightly.

It was all quite clear to her. It was her desperation and need of him that drove him away; be casual, be light, and he would love her. She hung on to that knowledge in her mind, gripped at it; she would never for a minute forget it. He was her husband now; that initial victory was won. Now she could make him love her and keep on loving her, by dissimulating her passion for him, by always laughing and seeming to be apart from him, by being gay and by not eternally reaching for him.

On the last day of the seven she spent in the hospital she expected Lambert back. The day after her operation he had spoken of taking a painting trip back into the mountains, and out of her new wisdom she had insisted upon his going.

Once a day Dr. Mackenzie and his assistant had made a call; he was silent, abrupt, made his examination and departed. She was unutterably lonely. For hours she was alone in the hot dim room; she could hear people walking along the arcade, people chattering in nearby rooms. She spent her time thinking of her resolution to be casual and gay with Lambert. She kept her face covered with cold cream. She manicured her nails.

Lambert returned late in the afternoon. He was burned dark and his hair was ruffled and shining. He kissed her and sat down near the bed. It was only by strictest self-control that Maizie could preserve her planned gaiety; if she had given way she would have thrown herself out of bed into his arms and cried wildly, meaninglessly, against him.

"—The damnedest sort of a trip I heard about. Just what I've been look-ing for. First the railroad over the mountains, then you take a car and drive. Did you know these mountains are hell? Terrific altitudes, and you get the *sirroche*, mountain sickness; bleed at the nose and ears and faint and what not. Then you meet the mules you've arranged to have meet you, and go through the jungle for five days, or more; good God, can you imagine? Orchids and snakes, lush and green and stinking. When you get to this river you're met by a launch if all goes well, otherwise you wait for it, that takes you down a week or so to the Amazon, where you get on a river steamer and go on down the river to Para in Brazil. Can you imagine anything better?"

"I'm not strong enough yet," she said faintly.

"I know," he said. "I thought this: We'll wait around Lima a couple of days, three, arranging about the mules, the launch, the car, all the rest of it. Then we have to get riding breeches and so on. You can take it easy and lie around resting up."

"Can.a woman do it?"

"Sure. A woman told me about it, woman who keeps the inn where I've been.staying back in the hills. Berta Baker. She's done it several times. Said once her mule refused to step over a log on the trail in the jungle and she gave it a whack whereupon the log wriggled off the path. Snake."

Maizie's heart was beating heavily, rapidly. Under the covers she had clenched her fists. Above the covers she smiled at Lambert, nodded.

"In the jungle you stop at night in shacks along the trail. They call them *tambos*. Pretty luxurious, not having to camp. It would be something, wouldn't it, if you had to camp in that jungle?"

Her imagination raced crazily through the putrid, lush green jungle; only her lips curved gaily.—And the charm did work. He leaned over and kissed her on her cheek, on her eyes, on her mouth.

"I'll be so glad to have you well, baby," he said. "Need you."

She kissed him back, her lips ardent enough, cool enough.

The next day she was dressed, and the nurse had packed, and Lambert was waiting outside. She was told that Dr. Mackenzie wanted to see her. She went along the hot arcades, weak in her limbs. Mackenzie sat behind a desk, fidgeting.

"You ought to be all right now," he fired at her. "You've been a very lucky girl."

"Can I do things?"

"You ought to sleep alone for a month. You ought to get out of this climate. You planning to stay in Lima?"

"My husband wants to go on a trip over the Pichis Trail. Could I do that?"

"Certainly not. Tell him I say it's out of the question. You're not out of the woods yet. Take good care of yourself, get some fresher air than you'll get here, and you'll be all right. See?"

"We were going to go down to Chile, before my husband had this idea."

"That's O.K. Sea air first, then a fresher climate. Do that."

In the car driving into Lima she told Lambert that Mackenzie had forbidden her to go across to Brazil. After she had finished speaking he said nothing for a long while.

"Then what do you suggest we do next?" he asked stiffly.

"We could just go on to Chile, as we planned."

"All right," he said.

"That could be marvellous fun."

"All right."

"You know you wanted to see Chile."

"Yes. I did. I suppose you won't want to do anything tonight."

"Do you want to do anything?"

"Well, to tell you the truth, I don't specially like sitting around in a strange city doing nothing. I mean, I'm not an invalid."

"I know you're not, darling. Of course I want to do something tonight. Anything you say."

"We could go out and have dinner at this place outside Lima. There's dancing."

"Marvellous!" She wondered from whom he had heard about the place.

They came in around midnight and Maizie got undressed. She got into bed and smiled with one last effort up at Lambert, walking around smoking, his face eager and restless.

"Are you coming to bed?"

"I don't feel awfully like it, no. Too bad about what the doctor told you."

"Yes," she said.

"Look, would you mind if I went back there and had a couple of drinks? I won't stay awfully long. I don't feel like going to bed."

"All right," she said, stiffening herself with her last strength and smiling, smiling at him. "Go on, darling."

She had been so exhausted that she was sure she would drop to instant sleep, but now that he was gone her eyes were wide and sleepless. That cross burned on the mountaintop beyond the city. She stared at it and thought over the evening. It had been a success and proved her new wisdom. She had joked and been silly about little things, danced and walked back to the table ahead of Lambert without looking back to be sure that he was there. He had laughed too, and kissed her while they were dancing. It was only when she said that she was tired and would like to go home, that his face turned stiff and bored. Then she offered to stay on; but he insisted on taking her back to the hotel. In the taxi she leaned against his shoulder, and put her face up to be kissed. He kissed her lightly, and then she had to turn and throw her arms around him and kiss him as she needed to, deeply and wildly. She had missed him so, all these long days in the hospital. . . .

"There!" he said, putting her away from him gently.

"Oh, darling. . . ."

"It's very nice, darling, but Dr. Mackenzie's little prohibition makes it difficult for a gentleman to kiss his wife with much enthusiasm. *If* you see what I mean."

Now she lay in the bed in the hotel and looked out at the electric cross. She felt as if all the blood had run out of her veins. . . . Why didn't he come back? She fell asleep after a long time.

She woke when Lambert came in and switched on the light.

"Oh, darling, where have you been?" she cried.

He grinned at her.

"Your husband is just the tiniest bit drunk," he said. "All ready to go to bed, thank you."

"I've been dreaming horribly, something about you with a girl. . . ."

"You're turning into an awfully *gloomy* girl," he remarked. "Better watch that. Might stick."

She forced a laugh.

"Darling, I'm still sleepy. Tell me there isn't anything to it but a dream, won't you? I can't get it out of my head."

"Don't use your head too much. Never does anybody any good."

"Oh, please, darling, just say you haven't been out with a girl. Just so I can go back to sleep."

"Well, baby, if you insist on knowing, I have been out with a girl, in a small way. Just a little bit out with a girl."

"Did you kiss her?"

"You go back to sleep and stop talking."

"I *can't* go back to sleep. You've got to tell me."

"Well, Mrs. Rudd, your husband did kiss a very little girl just a very little bit."

"Oh. . . . Christ! . . ."

"Please do not be melodramatic in public. About five—small—kisses underneath a moon on a night club terrace do *not* constitute a major catastrophe."

She turned on her side, away from him, and stared out at the cross.

"I *was* going to ask for the honor of sharing your couch this evening, madam," he said. "But seeing as you don't seem to like me very much I'll just trudge back to my own lonely room."

She sat up and reached out to him.

"Darling, please, please do stay here. Oh, Lambert, darling . . ."

"Thankyouverymuch."

He switched out the light and jumped into bed. In two minutes she could tell from his breathing that he was asleep.

His legs and arms were spread heavily across the bed, and Maizie could not move them. She lay on the extreme edge of the bed. Dawn was beginning to turn the mountains dirty yellow.

There was no love for her, no sentiment, no lovely happy things that came to other women, no love, no strength, nothing, no love.

She saw them, Lambert and a girl, a girl Maizie never saw, taking his kisses that Maizie was not allowed to have; and they laughed. They were both very young and free and full of strength and health, and they kissed. While she was here, staring forever at the burning cross, with sickness in her flesh, corrupt, unlovely, not a lovely woman but sick. Her husband did not love her, her husband kissed a pretty young girl, on his honeymoon with a sick woman older than he.

When the dawn had broken, Lambert sighed and rolled over in the bed. Maizie put out her foot and caught herself from falling. She put her lips to his shoulder and kissed it.

She was unable to lie on that side of the bed. She got up and went around

to the other side, where there was more room. She took Lambert's hand in
hers. In a minute Lambert sighed again, and heaved his body around so that
he lay flat in the middle of the bed with arms and legs spread. There was no
room for her on the bed. She took the quilt that was rolled at the end of the
bed and doubled it twice to make it thick, and spread it on the floor beside
the bed. She lay down on it and in a little while she went to sleep.

## CHAPTER XIII

LAMBERT awoke in the middle of the morning, stretched himself, yawned,
and without opening his eyes felt the heat of the sun on his body. His
waking mind turned at once to the things he had been seeing and to a slow
going over of them, cataloguing them; thinking about painting. At the same
time he was aware of the pain in his temples that meant that he had been
drunk last night. He understood it and was amused at it; he would get up,
bathe, drink coffee, and feel more conscious of well-being than if he had
waked without such pain.

His ears heard the morning clang of the streets of Lima. He ran his
tongue over his teeth and stretched his arms out to either side.

The things that came into his mind were a golden, rotting palace bathed
in sunshine, its cornices and statues crumbling in pink and eyes and a mouth
held up for him to kiss. He saw an Indian woman yellow and white; the acute
silhouette of the mountains where he had lately been. He saw a small face,
shaped like a heart, with tipped-up nose, walking with her husband along a
mountain path; they wore blankets woven in stripes of green and white and
red thrown over their shoulders; their faces were dark and triangular, the
eyes pushed up by the cheekbones into pockets of stolidity; the man wore a
hat of red straw on the side of his head. He saw a string of llamas led along
a village street, waving their long virginal necks, their eyes sad; at the end
of the street was a gold-colored church. . . . His mind switched back to
the heart-shaped face and his body stirred uneasily. He opened his eyes.

He looked about, wondering why he was in this room, and where Maizie
was. Suddenly his eyes found her face, lying on the floor. Her eyes were
open and looking into his; they looked as if they had been looking at him
for a long time. They were sorrowful and meek; it made him want to shout
at her. He thought for a moment that she had lain down there on purpose
to make herself infuriating. Why did she have to lie on the floor and stare
at him with sad eyes?

"Good morning, darling," she said.

He turned his face away from her and looked out into the sunshine of the
street.

"I'll order breakfast for you," she said. He felt her coming. She bent over
and kissed him. "Oh, darling. I've had such a horrible night. You wouldn't
let me sleep in the bed with you. You pushed me out. I had to sleep on the
floor. Oh, darling!" She sounded as if she were going to cry.

"What the hell are you doing sleeping there? You've been sick and you ought to take care of yourself. If you get worse don't blame me. I suppose I must have been drunk if I pushed you out. But why didn't you go into my room and sleep?"

"I wanted to be near you."

"All right. Let's have breakfast. We're supposed to start at noon. We're to meet them downstairs at twelve."

"Meet who? I didn't know you'd planned something. I feel so awful, I thought you'd let me stay in bed."

He turned his head and looked at her. He noticed how old she looked. She was older than he. He wished he could get away from that face.

"You don't have to go. Certainly you can stay in bed. What do you mean, let you? I told these people we'd drive out and have lunch in Chosica. It's the place where I stayed last week. But you don't have to go."

"Who are they?"

"Man and a girl I met last night. Brother and sister. Americans."

"Is it the girl you kissed?"

"Yes!"

"Oh, darling . . . darling. . . . You left me for her. She's laughing at me now."

"Don't be such a damned fool. Is that what you've been thinking all night? Listen, it was just kissing someone, and that doesn't mean the world's coming to an end."

"It's so awful, having your husband unfaithful to you on your honeymoon. . . ."

"Maizie, for Christ's sake, snap out of it. Haven't you got any sense of humor? You don't seem to be able to take it at all."

She was crying now, tears that ran down her old-looking face.

"Can't you try to understand what it's like for me to have had such awful things happen to me, and love you so, and then as soon as I get away from that hospital and back to you, to have you leave me and kiss girls?"

"I kissed . . . precisely . . . one . . . girl," he said.

"I've gone through hell for you."

"I didn't ask you to have that operation in Guayaquil. That was an idea of your own. I married you so that you wouldn't have to have an operation. God knows you didn't have it for the reason you said you had it; you didn't mean a damned thing by that."

"What?"

"Oh, forget it. Listen, go to bed now, and keep still and take care of yourself, and maybe you'll be a little more normal by tonight."

"I can't let you go without me . . . with that girl . . . You'll kiss her. . . ."

"Look, if it will make you pull yourself together I'll tell you that I won't kiss her."

"You'll be with her and she'll think she's got you away from your wife, and laugh at me. It's going to be so horrible, going downstairs and having her see me."

"She hasn't got me away from you. Because I kiss a girl doesn't mean one . . . God . . . damned . . . thing."

"She thinks it does. She's trying to make you leave your wife."

"Look. She's a nice little young girl and she doesn't think any such thing. I don't think you'd better go."

"I've got to go."

"All right, go then. But let me get dressed in peace, will you?"

In his bath, relaxed, Lambert felt sorry for having been so angry. If she would only fight back, instead of always crying. . . . He supposed he should guard himself, try to be kind and not to speak sharply, since she had been so sick. . . . Suddenly he smiled a little, thinking how odd it was to find himself a sort of a nurse to a woman, a woman whom he could not enjoy nor find any pleasure with, whom he must guard and save from exertion; a fine kind of a wife, a fine kind of a man to become. . . .

## CHAPTER XIV

THE BOAT between Peru and Chile was a slow one. It cut a smooth swathe into the green Pacific water. Multitudes of sea birds flew over the ship all day; at night the water was black as satin, and the stars were cooler and whiter as they moved South. Along the shore line there was the eternal outline of the mountains. They were queer, bulging, clumsy, swollen. They were like great distended stomachs thrust up at the sky; like malformed monsters crawling over one another from the womb of the earth.

It was a relief to Lambert that Maizie had ceased to hang on him, and had ceased to weep. She was very gay, and did whatever he did; she danced every night with him and went down to gamble afterwards. They never got to bed before three, and when Lambert went into her stateroom at eight in the morning she was always awake and smiling at him from her pillow. Lambert believed she must be getting well fast. He thought that those days when she had cried and never let him alone must have come from her being so ill. He felt a queer urge to keep telling her that she was well now; he hoped she realized that. In Lima she had acted like a hypochondriac. Certainly she had been ill, but she had never been anywhere near death. Yet she had acted as if she were dying.

He would go into her stateroom in the mornings and she would be lying in bed with a pink jacket thrown around her shoulders and her yellow hair pinned up on the top of her head. She would make some joke and he would go over and give her a kiss.

"The beautiful Grainger was just the tiniest bit stinking drunk last night, wasn't she?" she said one morning. Lambert noticed that Maizie was picking up many of his own expressions; it was rather sweet of her.

"Are you being catty?" he asked, and laughed.

"Certainly not. But you know she acts sick and tired of Compson and the whole idea of going on a trip with him. You ought to console her."

"Are you doing a little light procuring for me?"

"Would you like me to?"

"I hope to have my own wife in good running order shortly, thank you."

"Seriously, would you like to have an affair with Lila? It would probably let off some of your steam. I'm not an awful lot of good to you."

"Get it in your head that you are practically well, will you? You mustn't get the idea that you're sick."

"Yes, darling, I know. But wouldn't Lila do you good?"

"You've changed a lot. It's funny to hear you recommending infidelity."

"I'm sorry, Lamb." She put her head down and spoke in a low voice. "I was horrid about it. But I'll never be any more. You can go out and have all the affairs you want with women, as long as you'll come back to me afterwards. You would do that, wouldn't you?"

"Why, you sweet thing. I recognize that as being pretty remarkable. I suppose that's what a man needs most, a woman who can see when he needs something and lets him have it without raising a stink—who understands what's going on and what it means, no more. Would you really be that way about me?"

"Yes. . . . I would. . . . We could laugh about it, couldn't we, when you came back from wherever you'd been, and you could tell me all about her. Oh, darling! I do want you to be happy so much."

Her voice was turning the slightest shade too intense.

"We'll be frightfully famous in Boston," he said. "Do you know Mrs. Rudd, she picks out her husband's floosies for him."

"I mean it."

"I appreciate it. But I don't believe you'll have to bother much with that for some time. Seeing as you're practically well now."

"Yes, darling."

"All you need is to exert yourself once more. Get up now and don't lie around. There's nothing the matter with you now."

He went on deck. People were strolling slowly round the deck in the sunshine. Lambert threw himself into a deck chair and watched the brilliant blue ocean heave slowly up and down.

"Hello."

Lila Grainger was sitting beside him. She had a handsome face, dark and powdered a rich orange; her hair was blue-black and vital. For the past few days her look had varied between vivacity and a sullen boredom.

"Hi," he said.

"How much did you lose to the old skinflint?"

"I won. I've won the last three nights. I think my wife brings me luck or something."

"Listen, do you play a system or what?"

"I've got my own private system."

Maizie passed just at that moment. She smiled and waved and did not even pause.

When they were dressing for dinner that night she called through the open door to him.

"Did you make any time with La Grainger?"

"I didn't even try. I told you I was all right for a few days, my love."

"I want you to have what you want."

"I don't believe you'll ever have to worry much about that," he called cheerfully, tying his tie. "I think you can take care of me very nicely."

"I want to, darling. I wish I could:"

"Oh, don't you worry. I can't think of a time when you wouldn't be able to keep me in condition, except maybe when you're having a baby, something like that."

"Lamb . . . would you *then?*"

"Would I what?" he called.

"Would you be unfaithful to me when I was having a baby?"

"You'd be pretty busy yourself and probably wouldn't give a damn," he said.

"I wouldn't care if you were sweet to me," she said in a low voice, coming into the room. Her green crepe dress made her hair look like a mass of polished brass shavings. She was very thin.

"I've got a very good-looking wife," he said.

She laughed loudly and excitedly, and they went up to the smoking-room for a cocktail.

Near three, they came down again from the roulette game to go to bed. Lambert had won again and he had had a wonderful time and talked to everyone on the boat.

"Darling," he murmured, with his arm around her as they stood at her stateroom door. "You're an extraordinary woman. Wonderful looking girl." He kissed her.

"Do you love me?"

"Crazy about you."

"Do you love me more than all those Chilean girls you danced with? Or Lila?"

"Don't be dumb." He looked at her and there were bright pink spots in her cheeks. Getting her color back, he thought approvingly.

"How about a little attention to your husband?"

"Oh, darling . . . the doctor said. . . ."

"All right. I bow to Dr. Mackenzie." He bowed elaborately and turned to his own door.

"Darling . . . Lamb . . . don't be mad at me. Darling, come back here." He walked slowly toward her.

"Sure?"

"Oh, darling, I'm crazy for you. Don't you know that? Don't you know that I can't live without you?"

"That's more like it."

They went into her stateroom with his arm tight around her. He felt dazed and foggy and intent on what he was doing.

That night awoke the appetite which he had had to deny, and for the rest of the trip he was happy and intent upon its satisfaction. He knew he could not live normally without it; it was hard for him to think of painting, of what he saw, when that appetite, by its denial, was continually forcing his mind away. He was rather proud of how long he had gone without insisting on his rights; he had taken damned good care of his wife, at expense to himself.

He felt that perhaps there had really been no need for his waiting so long. Maizie was perfectly well now. It had been days since that second operation which had fixed everything up. In the mornings now he woke in her bed with a sense of things having come back to normality. The only thing that bothered him any more was that she might have some idea that she was not yet well.

Waking, he turned his face on the pillow and smiled at her.

"Happy?"

"Yes, darling." It did annoy him that she made her voice so weak; trying to be pitiful, perhaps.

"You're a big, strong girl, you are, able to take care of a man. And very nice care, too."

"Do I, sweet?"

"You certainly do. I hope I do the same for you?"

"Yes, darling."

"You and your Dr. Mackenzie. Old Dr. Rudd knows the sure cure. I guess I've cured the hell out of you."

She laughed and kissed his fingers that lay beside her mouth.

"Now come on, jump up and get yourself into some clothes and we'll go up on deck and get some fresh air. Not that fresh air's as good for you as I am."

They were active days and long evenings of dancing and gambling; afterwards he could hold Maizie in his arms and complete his days fully and go deeply to sleep.

They came to Valparaiso in the evening of the tenth day. They went to a hotel and dressed quickly in evening clothes and drove out to the Recreo on the road to Viña Del Mar. There was dancing in one room to a marimba orchestra, and two rooms of roulette. The place was full of brilliantly dressed and jewelled Chileans and Argentines. He danced for an hour or two with Maizie to the deep, thrilling tango music and went in to the roulette tables with her and won twenty thousand pesos.

"You bring me such luck, my beauty," he said, smiling at her over his shoulder. He liked the way she stood, very straight and still; her white face inside that blaze of hair. He thought being married, living with him, had made her much better looking than the pretty little girl he had met in Boston.

They went home at five, but Lambert was so stimulated he could not go to sleep. He sat and talked about the Lakes, about going across to the Argentine, about going back to Peru, now that Maizie was well, and taking the Pichis Trail through the jungle. The daylight was filling the room when he got up and came across the room to her.

"You're a lovely thing to be going around with," he said, and kissed her on the lips.

"Am I?" Her voice was like a sigh. It excited him, and he put his arm under her back and lifted her body up to him.

He slept until afternoon the next day. When he woke she was lying beside him, quite still, with her eyes closed.

"Wake up. We've got to catch the four o'clock up to Santiago."

She opened her eyes.

"I'm not asleep."

They packed their things and got the train. The lounge car was furnished with wicker chairs. Everything seemed very pleasant and he felt well. The train wound through broad fields under cultivation, and up through the mountains; only a few cactuses grew there. The colors of the rocks were superb; orange and scarlet and crimson.

"Look out, darling," he said. "You shouldn't be missing this."

She sat back in her chair with her eyes closed.

He did not care if she did not want to look. He ordered a drink from the car steward and went on looking out until it was too dark to see any more.

They had not wired for rooms, and when they got to the Crillon there was no accommodation for them. Lambert turned to tell Maizie. She was sitting in a lobby chair with her eyes closed.

"Listen, there is no room at the inn. We'd better go out and find a stable. The man says there's a good pension if we can get into it. He's telephoning now."

"All right," she said, without opening her eyes.

The Pension Valdez would have a room vacant on the following day, but for tonight they must go to the Hotel Nono. They climbed two flights of stairs to a lobby, hung with travel posters. They were given a room papered with crimson cabbage roses.

"It's magnificent," he said, walking around the room. "I've never seen anything like it."

Maizie did not answer. She lay on one of the beds, with her eyes closed. Lambert wished she would try to be more cheerful. This was not a pleasant room, it was grotesque; but the only thing to do was to have a little fun about it.

He felt full of energy, and suggested going out for a drink and dinner at the Savoy Cafe down the street, that they had passed. Maizie got up and went to wash her face. When she came back she walked slowly around the room.

"It's like a nightmare," she said.

"For Christ's sake, quit being so gloomy," he said, and they went down the long stairs to the dark street.

Walking home after dinner they were not sure where the Hotel Nono was. There was a large sign proclaiming "Fajas," that Maizie remembered as being above the hotel.

"What's that mean?" she said.

"Corsets, I think."

"We will now go back to the Corsets Hotel," she said in a faint voice; he smiled at her affectionately; this was more like herself.

But when they were in their room she stripped off her clothes and got into bed and closed her eyes. He was annoyed; he was far from sleepy, and he resented her leaving him to himself like this. He sat up until two drinking from a bottle he had brought back from the cafe.

When he woke in the morning Maizie lay in the other brass bed with her eyes closed.

"How about some breakfast, baby?" he called.

"I can't get up. I think I'm going to die."

"What the hell. . . ."

She opened her eyes and looked at him steadily for a moment and did not answer.

"You've been so well and cheerful. Baby, I think it's your imagination. You just get yourself up and you're bound to feel better."

She did not move.

"Well, what do you want me to do? Get another doctor?"

"I don't care whether you get a doctor."

"Of course I'll get you a doctor. We'll be on intimate terms with all the doctors in South America before we get through, won't we?"

She did not answer. He dressed in silence and went out to the desk to ask about a doctor. When he came back she had not moved.

"They say the best man for us is a Dr. Campbell. Speaks English. Lots of Chileans have Scotch and English names, I hear. I've made an appointment for you to see him in an hour."

She sighed but did not open her eyes.

"Well, do you want me to get him to come here, or something?"

"No," she said. "I'll get up."

He took her in a taxi to the address on a long, white street. The doctor was a pink bald man, who looked like a fat child. He asked Maizie to come in, in a very British accent.

Lambert sat for a long time in the dusty sunshine that filtered through the long lace curtains, smoking and waiting. At length the doctor came to the door and beckoned.

When he went into the office Maizie was sitting in a black leather chair. She had her hat off, and she had been crying. The office was small; there was a black leather examining couch in the corner. Campbell sat down behind the desk and folded his fat little hands and smiled.

"Your wife is a bit ill," he said. "Matter of fact, she has an acute inflammation. It may be quite possible to clear that up by the use of diathermy. I have a machine here, just behind you. Treatments every day for a bit may do the trick. It is of course impossible to promise anything. I have been telling your wife that she must not be too disturbed about the possibility of an operation.

"No, there's no necessity for her to go to hospital, nor to stay in bed. She should take good care of herself. At least nine hours' sleep at night.

I understand that you have been planning to continue your trip across to B.A. I really can't advise it. She oughtn't to be moved. I wouldn't even recommend your taking her back to the States for a bit, not for a month, p'raps. If you want to avoid an operation, of course. . . .

"A quiet, restful life for a bit, that's the ticket. I think you'll find Santiago pleasant. There's polo, you know, at the Jockey Club, and cinemas, and all that. . . .

"You see, in addition to the main condition there are other complications. The anaemia appears to be quite advanced. Nothing alarming, you know, just run down. Injections every day for a bit would bring the blood up to where liver in capsules would be quite sufficient. And then of course the low blood pressure is in order. The improved blood count will take care of that. I shouldn't be at all surprised if a month of rest wouldn't put everything to rights. Your wife says you've reservations at the Pension Valdez. Very nice place."

Lambert listened, his eyes moving between the doctor's face and Maizie's. The doctor talked on and on in the dusty sunshine. Lambert thought he sounded like a judge delivering a sentence.

## CHAPTER XV

IT WAS THE MONTH OF MARCH; late summer in that hemisphere. The Rudds lived in a large room in the pension in the Portal Fernandez Concha on the Plaza de Armas.

They used to wake up in the morning in the two beds when the pension maid brought in their breakfast on a tray and planked it down on the table. She was a pretty girl about fifteen with a loud voice.

"Señora! Señorito! Desayuna!"

They would lie for a few moments, listening to the cheerful sound of hammering all over Santiago. Then they would get up and drink the thick, black coffee and eat the hard rolls.

After breakfast they would dress; then they would go out into the warm, fresh sunshine. The Portal Fernandez Concha was lined with pastry-booths displaying horns filled with whipped cream, napoleons, meat-filled empanadas. Lambert and Maizie would buy a cream horn apiece and sit on a green bench in the park in the middle of the plaza, watching the children go by with their nurses, as they ate the pastry.

They would walk down the broad clean streets to the hill of Santa Lucia. The hill was like a rich man's garden. Blankets of morning-glories hung over the rocks and there were beds of red and yellow flowers along the path that led up the hill. They climbed by slow stages, resting on the benches by the way, to the top of the hill. They could sit up there in the sunshine and look all over Santiago, and beyond it to the mountains.

Soon it would be time to go down the hill for a vermouth and soda before lunch. Luncheon consumed an hour—hors d'œuvres and soup and eggs and two meat courses and salad and dessert. The families in the pension sat at separate tables, and the Rudds used to watch them, and imagine who they were and make up stories about them. But the Rudds never got to know anybody.

About twice a week, they would lunch at Henri's, downstairs in the Portal. They would eat tiny Chilean alligator pears stuffed with cold chicken; *pastel de choclo*—chicken and ripe olives and fat raisins covered with chopped fresh corn and brown sugar. For dessert they would have a concoction of ice cream and layers of cake and whipped cream and almonds and sugar, made in a big block and cut into slices. Then they would go upstairs to their room and lie down on their beds and go to sleep for two hours.

When they awoke, Maizie would dress to go to the doctor's. Lambert lay on the bed and watched her dress; he would go back to sleep when she had gone.

She would go in to the doctor's and have her treatment and talk pleasantly with him while she lay with the diathermic appliance crackling beside her; while he injected the hypodermic full of concentrated liver. Walking down the street afterwards in the late afternoon she could feel the blood running warmer in her veins; a new vitality creeping through her after the chilly lassitude that her body felt increasingly until it was time for another treatment. She would stop on the way home and buy a lump of ice for cocktails, a bottle of vermouth, a box of crackers, a tube of anchovy or some cheese, a jar of strawberry or raspberry jam for breakfast, a small bag of oranges; a jar of ripe olives, or a quarter of a pound of sardines.

She would go up to their room and switch on the light. Lambert would be lying on the bed, with his hands clasped behind his head. She would put the things down on the table and he would get up and open them, guessing what each was. Then they would drink cocktails. They kept the left-overs from the food on the outside of the window-sill. Sometimes something fell off and smashed in the courtyard below, and they thought that was very funny, hanging out of the window together to see the mess. Everything was very childish and lazy and unimportant.

Dinner at the pension was at nine, another enormous meal that took up an hour. They would sit there and watch the waiter, the old lady with four bottles of medicine beside her plate, the British couple at the next table. They would finish just in time to go to the *noche* showing of one of the movies down the street.

When they walked home afterwards the streets were quiet and all the shops were closed; the lights were going out in the houses. Maizie used to be tired out by that time; they went down the long quiet corridor to their room, walking slowly. Lambert would make himself a drink while Maizie undressed and went to bed. Then he would talk with her for a little while until she went to sleep. After that he sat up alone for an hour or two and drank.

By the end of the month she was growing stronger. She had grown easy and calm with Lambert in this life they were living. The doctor said that now they could plan to go home. He also said that she must continue to be quiet, to rest, if she was to avoid an operation.

There was a boat sailing in early April that would take them to New York without changes. They took passage, and planned to go by train to Valparaiso a day or two before, so as to give Maizie a chance to rest. Their trip was done and now they were going home.

They were leaving for Valparaiso on a Thursday; the boat would sail on Saturday. Monday they lived their life as usual, the wakening, the walk, the lunch, the siesta, the treatment, the dinner, the movie. When they came into the pension the German proprietress was on her knees in the hallway scowling over a lock.

"Ah, Herr Rudd," she said. She was a black-haired woman with a serious face. "Perhaps you would be so kind as to help me with this lock; the key has been broken, so, off in the lock, and with this wire I am trying to get the broken piece out. Perhaps you can. . . . Thank you."

She made pleasant conversation while Lambert worked over the lock and Maizie stood by.

"I am so sorry that your visit will end this week," she said. "It has been pleasant to have you here. I hope that when you come back you will again stay here.

"Frau Rudd, you are looking better than when you came. Our food, I hope. And Santiago is restful. You have a kind husband, Frau Rudd, who looks well after you. Many people have spoken to me, yes, of how gentle Herr Rudd is, such a quiet, considerate man. I do not flatter you, no, Herr Rudd. It is such a man one meets too seldom."

When the lock was fixed they went on down the corridor to their room. Maizie got undressed and went to bed. Lambert sat sipping his long rattling drink. Maizie was nearly ready to fall asleep. But there was something not just right about Lambert's quietness.

"Darling, is anything the matter?"

"No. What makes you think anything is the matter?"

"I can always tell about you. Oh, darling, have I done anything you don't like?"

"Not a thing. You go on and go to sleep and get a nice, long rest."

She sat up in bed.

"I can't possibly go to sleep knowing there's something the matter. For God's sake tell me what it is. It's so much better if I just know what's the matter."

"Lie down and go to sleep. If you get all excited you'll get sick and blame it on me."

"I won't blame it on you. Just tell me."

He sipped again from his drink and did not speak. His face was suddenly dark and closed. She felt the choking in her throat, the fast painful flutter of her heart-beat.

"Darling, darling, tell me what's the matter. I can't possibly sleep. . . ."

"Wouldn't that be awful? Imagine if you didn't get your sleep."

"Lambert, is that the matter? Do you want me to sit up and talk with you?"

"I wouldn't think of asking for such a sacrifice from you. Go to sleep."

"Oh, please, be nice to me."

"Haven't I been nice to you? Didn't you hear what Frau Thingummy said? She said I was a model husband, so good and quiet and considerate. A kind of a stuffed trained nurse."

"She was admiring you."

"I'm admiring myself. I'm a wonderful man. A man with a real future, the perfect nurse."

"I didn't know you had been feeling that way. I thought you were happy here too. . . ."

"I have been happy. Just like a nice quiet cow. There's nothing better as a training to be a painter than a course in nursing. You know that. This is a swell life. Wake up, breakfast, lunch, dinner, go to bed, wake up, breakfast. . . ."

"I wish you'd told me you felt like this. I thought you were enjoying a quiet life. I thought perhaps you were tired, too. . . ."

"Not being an invalid, I'm not tired. Yes, I'm an invalid, too. I've been sick ever since I've been here, sitting around all day without an idea in my head, never doing anything, sleeping all the time, eating. I've never felt so sick in my life."

"If you'd only told me. You could have gone out and painted. . . . We'll change everything right away."

"I've gotten used to it now. I'm resigned to being an invalid. To hell with being a painter. We'll just be two dear old sick people and take beautiful care of each other. It's a fine life. It's O.K. I'll take wonderful care of you and never let you lose your sleep. You do the same for me, will you? Watch my sleep and my diet and my bowels and don't let me overdo. We've got a long, long, marvellous life ahead of us, looking after our health."

"Oh, darling, I just can't bear to have you talk like that. I'll be well so soon, now. It was only for a short time, all this. . . . You don't think I've enjoyed being sick, do you?"

"I know damned well you've enjoyed it."

"No, I haven't! I hate feeling old, and tired, all the time. I'm young, and I hate not feeling young. The only way I can stand it is to realize that if I'm careful I'll be well soon and then everything will be lovely."

"Hell, you're too optimistic. You aren't going to get well. You're a born invalid. You'll be sick all the rest of your life, and I'll take care of you. That's the schedule."

"I won't. . . . I won't be sick if I'm just careful. One can't get well unless one's careful."

"Can't one? All right, one had better get the hell to sleep and shut up. I'll just sit here. Don't worry about me. This is the one time I come alive and act just the teentsy-weentsiest bit like a man. The rest of the time I'm a good, quiet, considerate guy."

"You know I'll do anything you want me to."

"No, I don't know that. Why should I?"

"All the time in Lima . . . all the time on the boat. . . ."

"Oh, you're crabbing about the way I treated you, are you? I wondered how long it would take. All right, go ahead and give me hell."

"I'm not crabbing. I just want you to realize that I want to do anything you want me to. I didn't realize you weren't happy the way we've been living."

"I don't suppose you did. You aren't very discerning, are you? Any God-damned fool would know that the life I've been living isn't exactly ideal for a young, able-bodied man who had a vague idea he wanted to prove something in the world."

She was crying now; tears ran helplessly down her face.

"Just tell me what you want me to do, darling," she said. "Forgive me for not having understood. I've been so sick. . . ."

"Will you quit throwing that at me? I made you sick, and so I spend the rest of my life taking your temperature to make up for it. Christ, what a responsible man I am! Responsible for making you sick, responsible for your getting plenty of sleep. . . . You're going to get your pound of flesh out of me, aren't you?"

"I don't feel any of those ways."

"The hell you don't. I've seen those nasty little eyes, that little cat's face looking at me." He had had three drinks now.

"I haven't meant to look at you any way. . . . What have I done?"

"I'll tell you what you've done, by God. You tricked me into marrying you by the slimiest trick known to woman."

He took another drink and went on talking with a deadly gusto.

"You said you'd let me go. You swore to me in Guayaquil that that was why you went to Jackson's, so that I would be free. You didn't have an idea of giving me anything like that. Hell, no. All you're thinking about is what you can get out of me.

"You just want a nurse to croon over you and talk baby-talk to you all day long. You want to take every drop of strength out of me so that I'll be weaker than you. You've been trying to reduce me to your own level. You get sick and make me responsible for the whole thing. You . . . little . . . swine. My painting didn't mean a damned thing to you, did it? You used to listen to me talk, sweet like a little cat, before we were married, but as soon as you'd hooked me all you thought about was yourself, yourself, yourself, and how you could turn me into a weakling."

"If you'd just tell me, darling, what I can do for you now. . . ."

"The hell with that. The hell with you doing things for me. I know how much that means. You were going to go over the Pichis Trail with me, weren't you? You knew how much that meant to me, didn't you? It was just what I needed, something to get the smell of medicine out of me. The hell you knew. Doctor says I caaan't, I have to get plenty of sleep. Sure, you were going to be a super-woman and understand about my seeing other women. You're a slimy little liar. You didn't mean one word you ever said to me, you were just trying to get your hooks into me, turn me into a wet-nurse for the rest of my days. Christ, I'm proud of myself. I'm a swell man."

His face was tortured.

"Darling . . . if you'd just say what you want now . . . I'd do anything. . . ."

"Don't give me any of that stuff. I've been too God-damned soft, feeling sorry for you and guilty as hell and doing what you want. I've got my work to think of. That's worth ten of any women of your kind. I'm through."

"You mean you're going to leave me?"

"You're damned right I'm going to leave you. You can get all the sleep you need. You can sleep all day long and all night long. I don't think I'll want to sleep again for six months."

"What do you want me to do?"

"You can go to hell."

"I can't stand it. . . . I love you so."

"I'm going to get out before I go completely nuts. If you really meant all that about loving me you'd want me to be a man instead of a cow. I'm going to take that plane out of here at six."

"It's four now. . . ."

"Well, there's just time. You'd better go to sleep, you might miss some of those nine hours and the world would come to an end."

He got up unsteadily and pulled his suitcase out from behind the big wardrobe opposite the beds. Maizie watched him bending over the bureau drawers. Then she got out of bed and began to pack his bag for him.

The plane flew north to Antofagasta where it stopped over-night. Lambert swam in the pool there and walked in the dark streets and went back to the hotel to bed. He was haunted by that month of sloth in Santiago, the weeks of sickness, and the memory of himself as he had been, a young man whose thoughts were clear, a young man whom he was no longer. He wanted to weep for his lost integrity, the long dreams of art that he had had, that seemed now the dreams of a dead man. All that he could regain of them was the longing for them. All he could do was loathe his life of the past two months and through his melancholy thoughts feel the stabs of conscience.

He lay awake all night until the plane flew north at seven. He could not put Maizie out of his mind. She had possessed him with her sickness, her pain, the things that she had suffered; guilt destroyed his mind's peace.

He thought all the next day flying to Lima, and all the next when he drove up to Chosica through the yellow mountains.

Berta Baker met him with cries and a kiss on the cheek. He felt old following her up the stone steps to the terrace. He let himself be put into a wicker chair and fed brandies and soda. Berta sat with him.

"What's the matter with you?" she demanded. "You act like a sick cow. You get dysentery down there?"

"No," he said. "Maizie got sick when we got to Chile. We've just lived there in Santiago. . . ."

"What's happened?" Berta asked. "You left her? She joining you later? Or what?"

He wanted to come out and say that he had left her. But he could not.

"She's sailing for New York from Chile," he said. "I expect to join her when the boat touches at Callao."

Now that he had said it, it was true. It was ridiculous, because he did not want ever to join Maizie again. He wanted to be alone for a long time.

"Well, you look sick yourself," Berta said.

"I'm all right."

"You'll get the hell out of here and do some painting while you're here. I won't have you slopping around. You got your painting stuff with you?"

"Some."

"Well, tomorrow you clear out of here and do some work."

He smiled gently.

The mountains were full of light. Lambert went out every morning to paint. He painted out of his technique, taking pains, but seeing nothing with his inner eye. After the second day he hardly attempted to paint at all, but sat on the camp stool with his head in his hands. He could not forget Maizie for a moment. He felt sick and confused and devoured by sorrow and hatred. Then guilt would stab him and pictures would form before his eyes of Maizie ill, perhaps dying; he had again and again the impulse to wire her that he would join the boat at Callao.

Something stopped him. If he did, it would be the ultimate surrender. He knew that his one chance lay in keeping away from her, conquering his confusion and clearing it.

The days went by and he accomplished nothing. One evening in his room he took the canvas he had worked on at first and slit it into ribbons with his penknife. Then he came closer to crying than he ever had since he was a little boy. He lay on his bed and despised himself for this melodrama; for the base hurly-burly that his mind had become. The fat, honey-colored Peruvian stars shone in the sky outside his window. It did not matter any more whether anybody did anything. To lie in some comfortable land and stare successively at the sun, the stars; to weep at intervals for dead dreams that could not clearly be recalled; and then sleep, and then again the sun.

"You're a mess," Berta said to him at breakfast. "I'd never think you were the same young man. I guess you're this damned type that goes to hell in the tropics. It's just as well you're going back to Boston in a couple of days. I like you, Lamb. But you look like a betrayed cow."

He smiled at her. A wild hope awoke in him. He wanted to go home. Perhaps that was the matter, not Maizie. This continent had destroyed his purpose. This continent had brought disaster, misery, and sloth.

It was new to him to feel this longing for his home. He thought of Boston. It was like a salt breeze. He thought of its streets deep in snow, its high houses, the unbending beauty of its architecture; the formality of the Public Gardens, the Common, the faces of its people. Everything had always been well with him there. Everything was quite simple. In this haunted continent people became symbols; at home he would be himself, his work would be his work, his friends his friends, and—Maizie would be simply his wife.

The thing was solved for him. He was suddenly recovered. He did not try to paint any more. He had fun with Berta, laughed with the other guests at the *quinta*, went riding, and at last said goodbye and drove down to Callao.

He had not wired to Maizie. He wondered as he boarded the ship where he would find her. The porter put his things into his stateroom, and he left his hat and went up on the top deck. He wanted to find her out on deck.

And she was. She was standing, leaning against the rail. She turned just before he reached her. She wore a green dress, and she was thin, and her face was white.

"I knew you'd come," she said. "I just knew you would. I couldn't have gone on living if you hadn't."

He put his arms around her and kissed her. Everything was all right now. Maizie was alive, and in the back of his mind there had been the fear that she might have died. She loved him, and she was happy, he could see from her face. It was so good not to be worried any more.

"I couldn't leave you, baby," he said.

"I've been through hell," she whispered in his ear.

"There, poor baby." He kissed her to stop her mouth. It felt good to kiss her again.

"How did the doctor say you were?" he asked. "You're just about well, aren't you?"

"I have to keep hot water bags on my side, he said, on the boat. And get a lot of sleep. Then go to see a doctor when I get home."

He felt a strong wave of impatience. How long was this going to go on? He moved his arm.

"Oh, darling, don't be mad," she said. "I didn't mean to say that. I won't say it any more."

"Naturally, I want you to get well," he said stiffly. "I'm not a monster."

But he felt happy and reassured. He was going home, and Maizie was all right. It was queer what a relief it was to him that she was not dead, considering that it would have been ridiculous to suppose she might have been dead. . . .

His energy increased as the boat moved northward. His conscience felt light. He tried to forget that Maizie was a woman and that he wanted a woman; he did not want to hurt her any more. He did not kiss her any more than he could help. He came into her stateroom in the mornings and grinned at her and gave her a pat and went swimming. She had her breakfast in bed and sat all day on a deck chair, and went to bed again for dinner at night. Those had been Campbell's orders, and Lambert was not going to interfere with any more doctors' orders.

He shared a table at dinner with a Venezuelan engineer who had had malaria and dysentery and looked like a corpse; he was woman-mad and made propositions to every woman on board; he went ashore at each port and made for the red light houses. He amused Lambert. He would say, at table, "My friend, you are such as the ladies cannot keep their hands from. My God, that scimitar of a nose! Now listen to me and come ashore tomorrow at noon. Too early? My God, you furtive Anglo-Saxons! I tell you noon is a fine time. It's healthy! Now me, my liver is all gone and the mercury has wrecked my heart; I am one to appreciate health. But be a fool; I shall go ashore tomorrow at noon and I shall be very hot and comfortable and happy."

At Guayquil a Colombian girl came aboard, going as far as Buenaventura. Mendez, the Venezuelan, introduced Lambert; they leaned together over the rail and watched the loading going on; the bales being lifted from the barges in the Guayas River into the hold of the ship. The air shimmered with heat, the blue-black skins of the stevedores glittered with sweat; Guayquil lay pink and gold and dusty. The hot waters of the Guayas lay quite still between their flat banks; an officer stood at the rail above the loading deck and shouted orders in an exhausted voice.

The woman, Lya Rivas, laughed a great deal. Her skin was pocked slightly. She had a kind of style about her. She and Mendez joked in Spanish and switched back into English for Lambert to join. Mendez left them and went ashore in a launch. Lambert walked with her back to the outdoor cafe on the stern deck, and they drank rum and lime juice and laughed a great deal.

"I have to get off again at Buenaventura," she said. "But why do you not come too? We will go up on the train to Bogotá. Sit still, I take a picture of you."

She had a new camera, and snapped him leaning back in the canvas chair with his drink at his lips.

"I'm going home to Boston. My wife's with me; she's been ill. Come on, we'll go up and see her."

Lya Rivas lifted her black eyebrows and pulled down the corners of her mouth. They went up the companionway, where the brass rail was too hot to touch. Maizie was lying on her deck chair in the shade. She wore a white linen dress; her hair spread out around her face against the white pad on the chair.

"This is Señorita Lya Rivas," said Lambert gaily. "—My wife. Are you burning up in this heat, baby? They'll be sailing when the tide turns. Look, you take Señorita Rivas' camera and take a picture of us together. She's been taking them of me."

Maizie held the camera and snapped them as they stood at the rail together, arm-in-arm. Then Lambert took one of Lya and one of Maizie.

"I want a drink," Lambert said. "Maizie, you come down to the bar and have one with us."

"I don't believe I will," Maizie said. "I think I'll just sit here."

"Your wife, she's pretty sick," Lya said in the cafe. "What shall we do tonight? There is dancing?"

"Sure, there's dancing and I think horse-racing."

"I'm so hot," Lya said. "I want to change from these terrible, terrible clothes I've been in forever."

Lambert wandered up again to the upper deck, but Maizie was not in her chair. He thought he would bathe, and went back to his stateroom. When he went into the bathroom he heard Maizie crying on the other side of the door. He went in.

She was lying on her berth and her shoulders were trembling. She heard him and turned over. She lay on her side and looked at him with swollen eyes.

"What's the matter with you?"

"Nothing."

"Come on, get it out."

"Nothing."

"I don't see what I can do about it if you're not going to tell me."

"I know."

"Well. . . ." He went back into the bathroom and closed the door and started a bath. He knew what was the matter with her. But he had had nothing to do with Lya Rivas. He felt a little stab at his conscience, and that was not fair, for he had done nothing. If he could not even talk to a woman and be photographed with her, then nothing was possible at all.

Lya Rivas got off at Buenaventura and the ship sailed on. He had drunk with her and laughed, and she had sat at table at dinner with him and Mendez, but he did not touch her ever. He saw that she was puzzled by him, because he was plainly attracted by her. He did not touch her because he wanted his conscience clear. He wanted to be happy. That way he could always feel resentful when Maizie looked at him with the question in her eyes.

He had met Wendie Gray at the beginning of the trip; after Buenaventura he saw more of her, because after Lya she was the most amusing woman on the boat. She was a funny, ugly young girl with a mass of curly hair. When the ship stopped briefly at Cristobal on the Atlantic end of the Canal he went ashore with her and they walked all over Colón while she bought perfume to take home. She had been living in Peru, and she was going home to Delaware. She was not more than twenty, an impertinent little girl with a boy's figure.

Colón was vibrating with color and noise and sunshine and profanity. The sky was electric blue; the streets were gold; the women were in scarlet and green and purple, their skins were black and purply-brown and russet and their eyes shone in their faces.

For the first time in weeks Lambert felt the old excitement; what he saw took form in his mind and he suddenly had something he wanted to paint. The relief was heart-breaking. He felt a wave of gratitude to Wendie.

She made him his old self. She walked beside him in her starched dress, bareheaded; she was interested in everything. She laughed, she talked, she listened to him, not patiently nor politely, but with a clear, young attention that was precisely right. She said "Nuts."

He had almost forgotten that there were girls like this. But America was full of them.

The ocean was blue beyond the poison green of the palms. A ship whistled from the harbor. Before they went back to the boat he stopped and bought a big bottle of perfume for Maizie.

They walked down the long dock to the gangplank, and he saw the spot of jade green on the deck that was Maizie, sitting there, waiting for him. Suddenly he realized how much he loathed that color: jade green. And in the same instant he thought—Christ; a painter oughtn't to have any personal feelings about color.

Two nights before they reached New York, Maizie stayed up to see a movie that was being shown on the after deck; he sat beside her in the darkness. She laughed at the jokes and kept touching his arm and whispering comments.

She held him in the corridor outside her stateroom.

"Darling, it was fun, wasn't it? It was awfully exciting to stay up and go to a movie with my husband."

He kissed her and gave her a pat and a slight push toward her door.

"Who do you love?" she demanded.

"You."

She threw her arms around his neck.

"I love you so. Don't ever forget that as long as you live no one will ever love you the way I do."

"I know."

"Won't we have fun when I get well?"

He realized that she was flirting with him. He was sorry for her and embarrassed and uncomfortable and a little disgusted; he only wanted to get away. They would be home, in Boston, soon; then they could sort this thing out, this marriage, and make a go of it somehow. But he did not want to face it until they were at home and he could sit down and put his mind to it.

"Now you get a good sleep," he said.

"Couldn't you go to bed now?"

"Well, I'll just stay up a little longer."

"You'll stop in and kiss me when you go to bed, won't you?"

"Yes."

He joined Wendie in the smoking room. She was drinking a glass of Perrier water. Her bright hair stood up all over her head, and she wore a white chiffon evening dress.

"Wheeeee," he said, as he sipped his drink.

"You're a louse," she said.

"Don't be fresh."

"You are."

"Why?"

"Oh, nothing. It's none of my business."

"That's the girl. Don't make remarks about your elders and betters, you just concentrate on coming in out of the rain and other elementary things you can understand."

They sat for two hours or so, talking in snatches; comfortable and relaxed. Some time after midnight they went up on the promenade deck and leaned over the rail watching the phosphorescence in the water. A breeze blew against their faces and fluttered the white chiffon dress.

He felt her looking at him and turned. He put his arm around her waist and kissed her. He felt very happy and unconcerned. There was nothing desperate or wretched about this. He kissed her cool lips and she smelled fresh and her body was very firm under his hand.

After a while he took her to her stateroom door and they said good night. He smoked a cigarette at the rail and went to his stateroom to go to bed.

He opened the door to Maizie's room and peeked in. She was sitting up in bed with the light on, smoking, with tears running down her face. She called him in a low voice.

"It's all right," she said. "It's all right, darling. I just want to kiss you."

"What's the matter?"

"I just saw it, that's all. I said it would be all right and it is. If I just hadn't had to *see* it! You both looked so beautiful and young! It's all right," she said again. Then she sobbed terribly. She lit another cigarette and smiled.

"How did you see?" He sat down beside her and patted her shoulder.

"I just was looking out of my window. You were standing up there at the rail. I suppose I shouldn't have kept on watching. I couldn't help it. It's funny! It was the most beautiful thing I ever saw."

There was nothing to say.

"You go to bed," she said. "It's all right. Really it is."

"Will you sleep all right?"

"Oh, yes. I'll sleep all right. You go to bed."

Next morning it was much cooler and the swimming pool had been emptied. There was a strong wind blowing. Lambert walked round and round the deck with Wendie. She had lunch with him and Mendez. Maizie had not come on deck, and Lambert thought she must be asleep.

In the middle of the afternoon he came around the corner and she was sitting in her chair in a big coat. He sat down beside her. Her face looked very queer.

"You're not seasick, are you?"

"The morphine has been making me sick, that's all."

"What morphine?"

He looked at her uneasily. He felt very guilty.

"I told you I didn't blame you and I don't. Only I lay there all those hours after you went to bed and I couldn't sleep. I couldn't stand it. I went down about six o'clock and woke up the doctor and he came up to my room. First he gave me some pills and I took them and they didn't do anything. I sent a bellboy for him again at eight and he came up to my room and gave me some morphine. I was so awful. I couldn't stand it at all by then and I cried all the time and he couldn't do anything for me and he thought I was insane, I guess, and finally I did go to sleep. When I woke up the morphine made me sick."

"I'm sorry," he said.

"You'd be glad if I died, wouldn't you?" she said.

"Will you quit saying things like that? Of course I don't want you to die. I want you to get well."

She looked frightened and he hated her for being frightened of him and for thinking that he wanted her to die. He hated her more because it was true.

"We'll be home day after tomorrow and then you can take it easy and get well and then we'll straighten all this out."

"Are you going to leave me?"

"No, I'm not going to leave you."

She lay back in her chair. Her skin was green around her nostrils and her upper lip. After a while he got up and strolled away.

He had dinner that night with Mendez and one of Mendez's women, a big red-faced Irishwoman. Mendez was elaborately courteous to her. Lambert was bored. He joined Wendie after dinner.

Later, after most people had left the smoking room, he asked her to go up on the boat deck with him.

"No," she said, "I won't."

"Why not?"

"Because it's too cold, I haven't got my wrap with me, and I don't want to."

"I'll get your wrap."

"But I don't want to."

"Don't you like me?"

"Oh, you want to get pompous, do you? No, I don't like you very much. I think you're a lot of fun, but I think you're pretty nasty. God help your wife. I'm going to bed."

"Oh, sit down."

"You're a bully and a conceited ass and one of the temperament boys and underneath rather a nice guy. And I don't want any part of it."

"I said, sit down."

"All right, if you want some more. You think you're the most important thing God ever made. I don't think you are. I think I am."

"And?"

"And you're just what I could fall in love with, but since you are a dose of poison, I will now say to you, good night."

He sat and drank and smoked. He wished there were somebody for him to talk to.

He went out on deck and met Mendez.

"Come on back to my room and have a drink and talk," he said.

"Not I. Extreme fatigue has come upon me, my friend, and I go to do my sleeping."

"I don't feel like going to sleep."

"Unless I am greatly mistaken, La Belle Feeney is still awake in her stateroom which is number 398, C Deck. But you didn't see the ineffable charm of La Belle Feeney. Now I have the perception, the finesse, to perceive what depths of majesty lie there, in that Hibernian bosom, what essence of femininity, what. . . ."

"Oh, dry up," Lambert said crossly and passed on.

He went up on the boat deck and looked at the water. What about the woman? He didn't like her. But she was just what he needed.

It would be doing one more thing to Maizie. But one more thing would make it no worse. This was the last night, and in Boston he could start fresh.

He went down to C Deck.

The boat was to dock at noon, and when he got back to his stateroom Lambert started to pack. He did not feel the need of sleep. The wind swept across the deck, strong and salty, as the ship moved up the Narrows. He had breakfast and at length went in to see if Maizie needed help with her packing.

She lay on her bed, dressed.

"Why didn't you come in last night when you went to bed?" she asked.

"I didn't get back to my room until a short while ago."

"You stayed up all night?"

"I don't like to be cross-examined."

"You were with a woman." Her voice was absolutely dull and blank.

"Yes."

"That girl you kissed?"

"No."

"I just wanted to know."

"I'm sorry."

"It's all right."

"It was just a woman, I hardly know her."

"I know, darling. Listen, when we get back I think I'd better go home. I think I'll get well quicker."

"You're sore as hell, aren't you?"

"I swear to you I'm not. But I must get well for you or I'll go crazy. If I can be alone I'll get well quicker and then I can come back to you. I'll never get well this way."

"All right," he said stiffly. "Do just as you think best."

"You said you wouldn't leave me."

"I'm not leaving you."

"Just try to understand. . . . I love you more than anything in the whole world."

She looked as if she really might be going to die, he thought uneasily.

"Can I help you pack?"

"No, the stewardess did it."

"I'll just walk around for a while. You'd better come out on deck and get some air. It will do you good."

"Yes, darling. In a few minutes."

He walked around the decks saying goodbye to people. When he came back to his stateroom there was a slip of paper lying on the floor under the door. He picked it up.

"I love you," it said. "This has been such a wonderful trip and you have been so good to me and I'm sorry I've spoiled so many things for you. But I love you so. Maizie."

## CHAPTER XVI

THE BIG, sprawling, affectionate Jekyll family gathered Maizie back into its arms and cherished her. None of them knew what was the matter with her. Because they saw she suffered, their hearts were torn, and to comfort her they did all that a family could to assuage those wounds whose nature puzzled them. All of them believed that her husband, that dark, reticent stranger named Rudd, was somehow responsible for the straits to which Maizie had come; and their instinct was to blame and hate him. But Maizie's last energy was spent in defending him, picking up the slightest hints of criticism and throwing them back in the giver's face. She was not their own Maizie any more; she did not belong to them any more; she was not a Jekyll girl, she was Mrs. Lambert Rudd.

With her out of the room, they said what they chose. They were in the dark as to why Maizie looked like the corpse of her old self, why she was shaken with nervousness and unable to sleep, why she made a daily trip to a Boston doctor, why she wept bitterly behind her closed door, why she was living apart from her husband although she would not hear a word against him; she made it understood that their separation was temporary. She said she wanted to get well before she began to establish an apartment in Boston with Lambert. But of what was she ill?

None of them knew. Maizie was closed to them. They knew only what she did and said, and that was terrible enough. When she was not in the room Tom Jekyll cursed his son-in-law and threatened to have the thing out with him, punch him in the nose for mistreating his little girl. Betsy and the two little girls understood nothing, stared and wondered and were afraid of the pale, haunted-looking woman who had come back instead of their sister, lovely, laughing Maizie. There were not any more new jade-green dresses, or spilt bottles of perfume, or cars driving up to the door; no dancing in the living-room. This frightened woman had furrowed cheeks, wore old dresses, always seemed to be listening for something, or looking for it, with apprehension and terror. The two little girls were merely confused; one of their certainties had been upset. But Betsy's mind attempted to explain the thing; unlike the children, she felt frightened herself.

Minnie May was tortured with love and pity and fury and sometimes with a kind of remorse, an uncertain remorse. She and Tom used to talk about it, that summer, after the children had gone to bed. They would sit up together in Tom's study with the windows open on the hot night; Tom drank and Minnie May smoked.

"I can't understand it," she said. "I truly can't, Tom. Even if he'd *beaten* her—I don't see how it could have done this—made her so scary and weepy and sick. Oh, Tom, it's so awful to see Maizie like this. I declare I've heard her every single night, crying in bed—and sometimes she screams out in her sleep. You've heard her. If she'd just tell me. If she'd just admit that it's that man's fault. I feel so helpless. I want to tell her to divorce him, yes I do, and come on back here and live and forget about him and be happy again. But you know how she acts. She won't hear a word against him. She says he's just wonderful and that she is perfectly happy with him. Happy. . . ! She adores him; I never saw a woman so mad about a man. You know she writes to him every day. There's something awful the matter. It's just driving me crazy. And I can't *do* anything for her."

"I'd like to knock that fellow down," Tom said, and drank his whisky moodily. He had no other solution and no other anodyne for the pain he felt all the time in his gentle, stupid heart.

"I want to know what's the matter with her insides. She won't tell me and apparently she's made the doctor promise not to tell me, because he won't. And I'm her mother. . . . Seems funny to think a daughter of mine could let a man destroy her like this. Because he has. You can't tell me it's not him. He's a monster, but I don't know just what he did. I want to know what she's so scared of. I declare it makes me shocked and ashamed to see how scared she is of her own shadow. Apologizes for things all the time. That's not Maizie. Nobody in this family ever apologized for anything. That man's just beaten her into a pulp. Is it my fault, Tom? But what could I do?"

"I don't know. I don't know anything about these people up here. Seems like I never will understand them," Tom said. "Never. There isn't a man I can talk to. They're like foreigners. Maybe this Rudd is all right. But he isn't my kind of man. I just don't understand."

"But they're human beings, just like anybody else. They can't be all that different. I reckon there are bad men everywhere, in Virginia too. If Maizie had any sense she'd tell him to get out, get a divorce, start over again. I just don't understand. . . . She was so lovely looking, you know she was. She could still make a place for herself, be somebody, like I wanted her to. Like I thought she would if she could marry somebody up here and amount to something."

"I wish we hadn't come," Tom said. "I wish we'd stayed down home where everybody knows us. We don't belong here. Maizie would be all right; this wouldn't have happened, if we were just down home where we belong."

"Now, Tom Jekyll, don't start that again. Seems like you want to be no-body all your life. Places don't make all that difference. I know they don't to me. Like I said, Maizie could have found a bad man any place we happened to live. It's just luck. I still believe this is the place for us. The children can amount to something here, and they'd never be anything but little country stick-in-the-muds if they were down home. You're just an old stick-in-the-mud yourself. If you'd just shake yourself up a little, look around, not be so opinionated. . . . I've made plenty of friends here in Hampton already. Seems like Northerners make friends slower, but they do if you give them time. I guess I'm still a Green. I guess it would take more than Boston to lick me."

"You're different," Tom said heavily.

"I'm thinking of the children. . . ."

They heard it then, that sharp, terrible cry in the darkness of the house; muffled, full of terror. They looked at each other and then went upstairs and stood outside Maizie's door. The cry came again. It was a cry out of sleep, not conscious, a bitter, bewildered, unendurable sound: "Oh. . . . Oh. . . . Oh. . . ."

They stood side by side outside their daughter's door, in the dim upper hall, and looked at each other's faces. Minnie May held both her hands out a little, unconsciously, helplessly.

It was another long, lazy summer for Betsy and Leda. But it was not the same as the summer before. They were a year older and that made all the difference. Both of them had the sense that things were about to happen, life was about to begin. One more year of school, and then what? Whatever it was, it would be life, as this was not. This was marking time until life began.

But they were, as ever, by what seemed now lifelong habit, inseparable. Still they walked the hushed, drowsy streets of Hampton, drank sodas, window-shopped. Still they went swimming in Bestley's Brook, made up stories about the boys they saw in the village, sent for samples of cosmetics, talked for long hours in the loft of Leda's barn, with their legs swinging over the edge of the pitching door. But it was all a little different. Neither of them knew what it was that made them feel different, but it was there.

They were bound together by the same bonds: Leda by her confidence in Betsy, by her uncertainty and lingering fear of other people and the outside world; Betsy by loyalty and love. They always talked assuming that they would be best friends forever: they made up stories of their futures. Sometimes, in a moment's burst of sentiment, they made vows of eternal friendship; then they would imagine for themselves contingencies in which the one would rescue the other. Their imaginations ran to alarm, to vague and terrible happenings, that summer; there was fear and mystery in the atmosphere ever since Maizie had come home. They used to speculate with large eyes as to what was the matter with her; they were sure it had something to do with the strange dark man that was her husband.

"Maybe he got her down there in South America and tortured her," Betsy suggested; her face held mingled pity and excitement. "Maybe he whipped her or something."

They were strolling, slowly, aimlessly, down the main street of Hampton, arm-in-arm.

"Maybe she made him jealous and he tried to kill her," Leda said.

They stared at each other.

"She's so beautiful—she was—probably somebody, a South American, fell in love with her."

"I can't stand having her look all homely and awful," Leda said.

"My goodness, suppose it happened to *us!*"

"It couldn't."

"Leda, I don't think I want to get married for a long time. It's so *terrific*. It's so different from having fun. Either it's stupid or maybe it's like this. My goodness, do you remember how in love with him she was?"

"She still is. You know the way she acts about the postman. Well, I don't want to get married either if it's going to be like that. But it won't. I don't think I ever want to be too much in love with anyone."

"I'd hate to miss being terrifically in love."

"I want to marry somebody who's terrifically in love with me. I want to be fascinating and have people in love with me!"

"You will, too. You're fascinating-looking now. Didn't you see the fat one goggling at you in swimming yesterday? . . . You'll marry somebody who's mad about you and everybody else will fall in love with you too, and he'll be wild with jealousy and he'll probably kill them and maybe he'll kill you too."

"No. I won't marry that kind of man. I won't be hurt. I've been hurt enough. All the rest of my life I'm not going to be hurt."

In August Leda went away with her family for their yearly visit to the Treat Marches. Betsy was left alone without a friend. The Jekylls' house was different now than it ever had been before, and the change made her unhappy. By temperament she was accustomed to feeling happy, and this queer unhappiness was all the more acute, unnatural. It was queer not to want to stay at home with her family; it was unnatural to prefer to walk alone through the tired, dusty town. But at home the unhappiness was unavoidable. Maizie was like a burning wraith in the familiar rooms. And her mother was not the same either: Maizie seemed to preoccupy her so that she was almost indifferent to her other children. She was always taking her breakfast on a tray, sitting for long silent hours with her, making something to tempt her appetite, accompanying her to Boston on the train. The whole family life was different, with Maizie and Minnie May different; the others got along by themselves. Betsy, who all her life had idolized her mother and courted her approval, felt left out now, and lonely and at loose ends when Leda went away.

That afternoon in August it was scorching hot; the leaves were very limp on the trees, and the bright green color had been washed out of the landscape. Betsy sauntered alone down the road past the brook, trying to make up her mind to go swimming. But she did not want to go alone.

It was curious how empty and without energy she was when she was alone. She knew that Leda, alone, had a secret life, her own thoughts. But Betsy's life seemed to stop short when people left her, when she left people. Without someone to say it to, no thought came into her head. Without a companion she had no plans, no desires to do anything whatsoever. She realized now, dully, walking alone along the road, that she had never had to .live alone in all her life for more than a few moments at a time. There had always been plenty of people, and always her large, affectionate, noisy family. Her life in retrospect meant companionship, experiences shared. Leda had been with her constantly since they had met. Now that Leda was away, and Maizie a million miles away, and her mother with Maizie, Betsy was without impetus, in a vacuum. She had no resources in herself.

A Ford roadster with the top down drove past her fast, going in the opposite direction. In it sat two young men, both light-haired, and, she thought, handsome and excitingly older than the boys she knew. She wandered on down the road after the car had passed, her mind again a disconsolate blank.

She heard a car come slowly up behind her. When she turned to see it was the Ford roadster; it pulled up to a halt beside her. The young men were smiling down at her, but diffidently, without impertinence.

"Can we take you anywhere?" The one at the wheel spoke. He had light brown hair and large gentle brown eyes. They both wore white flannel trousers and blue coats.

She could not possibly resist.

"I'm not really going anywhere," she said hesitantly.

"Well . . . would you go for a ride? My name is Sam Welldon; this is my cousin, an oaf named Harry Welsh. Pay no attention to him," the young man said rather shyly, smiling at her with his brown eyes. The other young man opened the roadster's door and stepped out. Betsy looked at them and got in; Harry got in after her and closed the door and they drove on.

She knew she ought to feel guilty and frightened, for she knew that this was the way girls got into trouble, accepting rides from strange young men. But these were so disarming. They seemed shyer than she, and for a while they drove almost in silence, with sudden bursts of artificial conversation which attempted jocularity.

"I'm supposed to be taking Harry to town," Sam said after a while. "Would you go that far, and then I'll drive you home?"

This was of course a worse situation, but somehow she could not feel frightened. They dropped Harry on Huntington Avenue. He stood for a moment next to the car, looking at his cousin.

"Watch yourself, Sam," he said.

"Hey," Sam said, and looked annoyed. He turned the car around in the street and they drove away, out of town. Betsy felt happy, being with Sam. He was so gentle and shy. He must be at least twenty-one. Something was really happening. Perhaps he would fall in love with her.

"I tell you," he said. "Would you drive out to my house and go swimming? I've got a pool, and an extra bathing-suit, and everything. It's so hot today. Of course if you want to go home I'll take you."

"I'd love to go swimming," she said. It was an enchanting surprise.

They drove out into the real country; the trees were fresher green out there than in Hampton. Sam's house was a big brick one up a long driveway; he took her in, where it was pleasant and cool, and introduced her to his mother, a gentle oldish woman lying on a straw lounge. Betsy was taken upstairs to a bedroom and given a bathing-suit to put on.

They swam together in the pool and lay drying off on the edge, talking.
Sam told her all about himself, with his brown eyes looking at her smiling.
He was in Harvard, he was twenty, he had gone to Middlesex to school.
He asked her how old she was.

"Eighteen," she said. She could not bear to have him think her too young.
She said several things about herself, small things, that were not true.
She was so anxious to have him think her a fascinating person. And being
just Betsy Jekyll was not fascinating. It was essential to embroider the truth,
to invent stories of high dives taken the previous summer, of visits made to
New York, to make herself the sort of person she wished she were. And
once said, the lies assumed a wonderful verity; there was not one thing she
said that she did not at least half-believe the moment after.

They went afterwards and dressed and had lemonade on the terrace at
the side of the house with Mrs. Welldon. It was cooler by then, and a light
breeze swept from west to east, the length of the terrace. The garden was
lovely, and the ice tinkled in their glasses.

Sam drove her home to Hampton, and came into the house for a moment. The children were sliding down the banisters, shrieking. Tom Jekyll
was at home from the office, reading his paper in the middle of a pile of
debris; Minnie May was calling cheerfully some long story to Tom from
where she sat at the far end of the living-room, darning a stocking in a
desultory sort of fashion, spools and stockings and bits of cloth all around
her. She got up and came to meet Sam when Betsy brought him in and introduced him.

"Certainly am glad to meet you, Mr. Welldon," she said, smiling her own
inimitable gay smile. "Won't you stay and have supper with us? Glory!
Run out and tell Norah there'll be another place at table, you hear?"

"I'm sorry—my mother expects me at home," Sam said. Betsy went out
with him, and stood on the steps as he got into the Ford.

"You've got a wonderful family," he said shyly. "It must be an awful lot
of fun. I've always wished I was part of a big family."

Betsy felt full of pride.

"They are wonderful. Mother's so clever. And my sister Maizie—she's
sick now. But I wish you could have seen how beautiful she was. . . ."
Until that moment she had forgotten about Maizie. It came back to her
now, the unhappiness in that house that had always been so carefree and
noisy. The remembrance was a dimming veil over her happiness of all
afternoon.

"When am I going to see you again?" Sam asked. He leaned over the side
of the car. "May I see you again?"

"You call me up," Betsy said. Her eyes sparkled again. This was exciting
and new and just what she had always wanted to begin happening to her.

She had so much to tell Leda when Leda came back a day or two later.
She telephoned her to find out if she had come home, and hurried up the
road to the Marches' house. Leda came out and they went up into the musty-

smelling loft; it was hot, almost stifling up there, but it was a habit with them. They had so many little habits.

"Leda!" Betsy said intensely. "You can't imagine what has happened. I've got a beau."

"How?" Leda asked. She seemed very far away, reserved; Betsy remembered that it had been just the same last year when Leda came back from her aunt's. It had taken her a little while to return to the old intense intimacy; she would again; but Betsy wished she were more excited now about the news.

She told Leda how it had happened. She had thought over the circumstances again and again; telling it was even more fun than remembering it. Now it seemed true to her when she said that Sam had told her she was the most wonderful girl he had ever met, and when she said that he had asked if he could come to see her every day, and take her to dances next winter at Harvard. She believed those things, now.

"But I said, 'You can call me up,'" she concluded. "I wanted to kind of lead him on and not promise to see him."

"I don't think you ought to have let them pick you up," Leda said. "It's not very nice to be picked up." She was being just the way she had been last summer after her visit, constrained and queerly superior.

"Why, Leda! Don't be silly. I guess they could tell that I'm not that kind of a girl, I mean usually."

"I don't see how. I don't want anyone ever to think I'm easy."

Betsy wondered suddenly if Leda was jealous.

"Well, I'm not easy. They weren't that kind and I'm not that kind. Sam just saw me and I guess he felt he had to get to know me. If he'd had to be introduced he never would have met me."

"You're awfully romantic. You make up things. You're always thinking people feel all sorts of ways they don't really feel."

Betsy kept silent. She felt hurt. It was hard to talk to Leda when she was like this. After a while she remembered her other piece of news.

"Leda, I forgot, there's something else too. Something awful. You know what?"

"What?"

"Mother had a letter from Miss Chapin at school. I can't go back next year. They said my grades weren't satisfactory and that I didn't mingle with the others and that from my uncooperative attitude they had decided that I was an undesirable influence in the school. They said that. Leda, isn't that horrible?"

"Oh, Betsy! What am I going to do there without you? You were the only friend I had. Where are you going instead?"

"Mother says I'll have to just go to Country Day here. Now, Leda, listen. Couldn't you go to Country Day too? I'll just die without you. You're my best friend. You don't want to keep on going to Sheraton's, do you? I've been thinking it all out since I found out. I know you hated it at Country Day, but we'll be together."

"Well . . ." Leda said. Betsy stared at her.

"We *couldn't* go to different schools," she said. "We have to be together. Don't forget about the oath. . . . Leda, if you went in town to school and I stayed here, we'd *never* see each other!"

"We could see each other in the afternoons late and weekends," Leda said slowly. "I just couldn't go back to Country Day again."

"But you hate Sheraton's! You know you do!"

"Yes, but at least it's better than this old place. We'd be able to see each other after school."

Betsy began to cry. She had never for a moment expected this.

"Don't cry," Leda said. "I'll miss you, all right. You know I haven't any friends there."

"But I want to be where you are," Betsy sobbed. "I always want to be, you know that. We were going to stick together. . . . I won't have you, and everything will be horrid. Oh dear . . . what *is* the matter with everything lately?"

"Don't forget about your beau. Now you've got one, you'll begin having lots."

"You don't think I ought to have spoken to him. Leda, you're so *mean.* . . ."

"You know you're my best friend. You always will be."

"Honestly?"

"Honestly. All my life. I promise."

"I promise."

They shook hands.

"Let's go down to my house and make up," Betsy said, feeling better. She put the thoughts out of her mind. Things could not be as bad as she had felt; things couldn't be that bad. The thing to do was not to think about them, and then they would get fixed up somehow.

"I'm not going to wear make-up any more," Leda said. "Just a little lipstick and nothing else."

"Well, you can," Betsy said cheerfully. "You've got such marvellous eyes, and that skin and everything."

They went down the hot road together to the Jekylls'.

"Maybe there'll be a call for me from Sam," Betsy said. She was happy again and skipped a little.

Leda said nothing. She was growing more and more beautiful, Betsy thought without jealousy. Now especially, since her return from visiting those relatives, she walked with the beginnings of elegance: slim, looking still taller than she was, holding her head up on the long, slender neck. She did look so different from other people. She's going to have lots of people mad about her, Betsy thought.

"Why do you suppose they had to kick me out of school?" she asked as they walked along.

"You know it's a snob school."

"Yes, but . . . what's that got to do with it?"

"Well, your family don't—belong in Boston, you know," Leda said delicately. "It's practically impossible for outsiders to ever get in in Boston."

"Yes, but my family . . ."

"I know, but that's Southern. That's different. Of course *I* know about it. But lots of marvellous people are probably failures here in Boston."

Betsy considered the possibility, the fantastic thought, that her family, her mother, the Jekylls, could be failures. She walked slower. She could not conceive of the thing. But it was curious, unpleasant, to hear it from Leda. She had always accepted without surprise Leda's admiration and interest in the Jekyll family; everyone, always, fell under its charm. . . . Leda had clung to them, worshipped Minnie May, adored Maizie, just as Betsy did; laughed at the Brats, loved the crazy gay atmosphere, just as everyone did. But now Leda was different; it was as if she were subtly, just a little, pulling away from them all. But Leda was such a lonely person; they had all felt her loneliness and spoken of it, and freely, warmly, offered their effulgent capacity for friendship to her, and she had been comforted.

Everything was different this summer. Everything was changing. The old verities were no longer in force. Something unpleasant and vague was working, spoiling everything, taking away confidence and solidity. Betsy felt it without understanding it, like a shadow creeping up from the furthest corners of her consciousness. The old order had been based on the absolute unity and assurance of the Jekylls as a cemented family, sure of itself and its charm and its power; complete loyalty and mutual admiration and love. But now Maizie was another person, and Minnie May had turned all her love and attention to that one of her children. The Brats, even, were different, Betsy suddenly realized; perhaps it was that they were turning into little Yankee girls, while all the rest of them carried as essential covering their Southernness. Even Tom was different; he was unhappy. Betsy did not know why; but in this moment of sudden, brief realization she saw how unhappy he was compared to the Tom Jekyll of Virginia; he looked different, he acted different; he was becoming a different man.

Then the instantaneous, sharp flash of insight left her, and deposited no trace on her mind; Betsy walked on down the road with Leda, glad to have the depressed sense of facts leave her, happy to be left free and thoughtless; she did not want to realize unpleasant things. As far as she could be said to have a philosophy, it was that unpleasantness existed only in its appreciation; if unhappy facts were not faced, they ceased to have existence. She wanted to believe that her family were the most wonderful and successful people in the world; by continuing to believe them so, they continued to be so, for her.

As they came nearer to the Jekylls' big, ungainly house, like an elephant grazing in the New England country, they passed the Brats playing with some other children in the back yard. They waved and passed on.

Tom Jekyll took the 5:38 home every night from the South Station. He sat down in the hot, gritty red plush seat and opened the evening paper. He bought the *Traveller* every night on the way to the train. He stretched his long legs into the aisle and tipped his hat back from his forehead; the short hair stuck to his scalp in wet curls. At Back Bay another man from

Hampton came into the smoking-car and sat down in the other half of
Tom's seat; he was a business man whom Tom knew slightly. They nodded
at each other and muttered the other's last name. The other man opened his
paper and the train racketed out into the suburbs in the late summer afternoon. Tom read the news and the three pages of sports, and dropped the
paper down on to the floor under his feet. He looked without interest out at
the dusty green landscape they passed, the rows of neat wooden houses
backed up against the railroad track, each with a tiny, meticulously tended
vegetable garden; in some of the gardens a man, home from work, was
already on his knees weeding; the look of the country, the frame houses, the
gardens, was unfamiliar and unnatural to Tom; he hardly saw them. All his
ideas had formed and petrified when he was a young man—his conceptions
of beauty, of comfort, of honor, of honesty. They had crystallized embalm-
ing the sights and tenets of the land of his youth. His conception of good
fellowship was limited to good fellowship as practiced in the South, his
conception of a beautiful house was a red brick mansion with white pillars;
he had no conception of a beautiful small house.

It was a habit with him to forget the day's work when he had left the
office. All he looked forward to, all that any day really held for him, was
the time that he spent at home with his family, where the life, the voices,
the words, the manners, were part of the tradition he knew and did not
want to see beyond, where at last he felt himself because his surroundings
were familiar. By training and intelligence he was an able enough lawyer;
the law seemed the same matter to him in Boston as it had in Annestown.
But he was without curiosity as to how others not of his tradition thought
and lived; he knew his own way of living and wanted no other. In his new
life of the past year and a half he was a lonely and homesick man.

He lit a cigarette and the other man took out one; Tom held the match
for him.

"Seems Virginia may get herself some kind of a team this fall," he said
tentatively. He would have felt no more tentative if he had been speaking
to a Chinaman.

"Where?"

"University of Virginia."

"Oh . . . yeah."

"My old school."

"That so?"

"Uh, believe Virginia's coming up here to play Harvard this fall."

"That so?" the man said. "You see the Harvard-Yale game last year?"

"Unh-unh. My daughter Maizie got to all those games, though, I believe."

"My wife was saying she'd been sick. Hope she's better?"

"I guess so. She's been mighty poorly."

"That's too bad. Mrs. Jekyll well?"

"She's fine, thanks."

Tom felt foolish, as if he had been talking to a ventriloquist's doll. All
his conversations with these Northern men were like this, pointless, mechanical, without ease.

The train jerked along over the rough road-bed of the local route, stopping at short intervals. The brakeman would open the door and shout the stations into the smoky car. Tom got up and climbed past the man and went out and stood on the platform.

"How you, Mike?" He nodded to the brakeman.

"Okay. How's it with you?"

"I'm fine. You win that bet on the fight?"

"Sure, and got paid, too. Took the wife and kids to Revere Saturday. My luck's running fine. I'll be winning the Sweepstakes next."

"Well, I hope you do, Mike."

"And how's your daughter, the one that's sick?"

"Not so good, I'm afraid. Looks like that little girl's real sick, to me."

"She ain't any better? Tchk, tchk," the brakeman clicked his teeth and shook his head gravely.

"I reckon she's some better. The doctor says she's right much better. But I don't like to see her looking so peaked and jumpy."

"My, no."

"Will you catch a quick one?" Tom asked in a lowered voice. He put his hand back to his hip pocket.

"Ah, no, not on the train, somebody'd be looking. But thank you all the same."

"Some other time," Tom said.

"Sure, I'd welcome it any other time. That stuff's hard to get."

"I've got a man, brings it to my office."

"Uh-huh? It's not so easy to get."

The brakeman grinned at Tom and went to open the car door as the train slowed. His voice bawled out the station as the wheels ground noisily to a stop. Tom stood on the platform looking out across the dusty grayish fields. There was a quality of sadness, in that late afternoon sunshine. Far down the track he could see the spires of the Hampton churches shining remote and golden in the sinking sun.

He got off at Hampton and walked through the village and out Crompton Street, taking long strides, his gray worsted trousers flapping about his thin ankles. There were fifteen or twenty other men walking home from the train. Tom nodded to a few of them as he passed. But he walked alone, and did not stop to speak to any of them. Not one of them was his friend.

## CHAPTER XVII

THERE WAS NO PEACE and no hope in all that summer for Maizie. All through May, through June, through July, until now in August, she had been torn without hope between those two impossible decisions. When she thought of going back to Lambert it was the same as thinking of going to death; when she thought of not going back to him, of staying with her mother who loved her, it was as bad; neither worse nor better. Both were terrible, full of horror, full of more pain, more anguish; of death.

She dragged through the days. Her sickness was treated in Boston by an excellent doctor until now she was physically cured, all was normal. But sickness had become her nature. She was absorbed in sickness. Her sisters, her father, even her mother, passed before her eyes beyond a veil. Nothing had reality for her but the present fact of her unwellness, the living vision of Lambert, and the unfading pictures of her old anguish during those past months. She lived in them, and in imagined scenes more real than her daily life, in which she reproached him for all his unkindness and her pain, in which he said he loved her and repented the past, in which he promised to be good to her. Those scenes were the nearest to comfort that approached her. But there was one of them to a hundred of the wrenching memories of the past, in which she heard his voice again cursing her, and relived his neglect and brutality and indifference.

She could not pull herself out of the morbid world where she lived and suffered. She did not try. It was an ordeal to her to go anywhere, to the doctor's in Boston. She had hallucinations that the walls of rooms and trains were falling in upon her; she had waves of sick dizziness, and even after the doctor reported her blood and blood pressure to be normal she felt again the old sensation of bloodlessness, utter exhaustion. There was no peace for her. Away from home, she wanted to return where she could relax from the sensations that assailed her; in the daytime she wanted to return to bed; at night she was in hell. The very love and solicitude of her family made her wretched, because it could not touch her, because she felt barred out from human comfort, alone with her sickness and the anguish of her love.

She wrote to Lambert every day. It was the one positive exertion of her life. Into her letters she put all her energy, trying to make them good letters, trying to make him love her, always trying to do that. Sometimes she would feel a weary panic for fear she was writing him too often, boring him. He wrote her about once a week, short letters about his work and hoping for her recovery. She would mean to wait, sometimes, for a letter of his before writing to him; but a counter panic would wake in her, for fear without tangible reminder of her he would forget her altogether. She would write an incoherent, overflowing letter full of her love and unhappiness—and then lie awake and agonize for fear it had disgusted him. When the doctor pronounced her condition cured, she was queerly reluctant to write him about it; when she knew that, it would be time for her to go back to him; and she feared and dreaded that as much as she longed for it. She was torn apart in everything, between her love and her terror. In the end she wrote him the doctor's pronouncement. She was unable to keep anything from him; she knew she was all his, whether he wanted her or not, no matter what he did with her.

That day she had been lying on the sofa in the living-room, reading a novel. For a little while she got pleasure from reading; it soothed her to read about other people, to lose herself in lives which were happy and normal. But then something would distract her; she would look up from the book and come back into her own life. She would cry weakly, lying there, with envy and longing for anyone else's life than her own; everyone else in the world was healthy and confident and happy.

Beyond the iron veil moved Betsy and Betsy's friend Leda, coming into the house, going upstairs. Beyond the veil was her own mother, going about the house on various errands. Beyond the veil was her father, coming from the train in the late, hot afternoon, and the younger children when they came home from play. She watched from the cell of her isolation as Betsy's new beau came to the door, as her mother let him in, as Betsy and Leda came downstairs to him. She spoke to them all from her lost distance and was not with them. She sat in the room with them, watching them, listening to them; but she was alone with herself, her sick, ruined self that she loathed, and the living presence of Lambert whom she loved with all that there was of her. From her distance she heard the telephone ring in the hall.

Her mother walked across the room to her, unnaturally slow.

"Maizie, darling. That man is on the telephone. He wants to speak to you."

"That man . . . ? *Lambert?*"

"Don't talk to him, honey. . . . He'll want you to go back to him. . . . He'll take you away."

But she was running, for the first time in months and not knowing she was running, to the telephone.

His own voice was there, actual, clear and real somewhere beyond the mouthpiece that she held to her lips.

"Hello, baby! I got your letter."

"Oh . . . did you . . ."

"So you're a well woman, able to do your own work! I bet you're proud of yourself."

She simply could not think of anything to say. The reality of his voice was overwhelming. It woke her up out of a long sleep.

"How about coming back to your husband? He needs you. You ought to see the way the studio looks. It needs the feminine touch."

"Oh, Lamb!" Suddenly she felt . . . happy; she was laughing. He was *real*. He was a human being; only a human being, not a nightmare monster; he was a human being, and she was another.

"Suppose you come in town tomorrow and I'll meet you and we'll go to lunch somewhere. We can stay at Mother's till you've found an apartment for us. Sound all right?—I could come and get you, but I thought it might be fun to meet you at the station, as if you'd just arrived from Europe."

"I'd love to. . . . I'll take the twelve o'clock train."

"Think you can get packed, all that?"

"Oh, yes. . . ."

"How do you really feel now? All well?"

"Oh, yes, I'm all well, darling, all well."

"I'm glad as hell. You know, I'm sorry about . . . you know what I mean, but I am a lousy carer for the sick, I guess."

"Oh, of course, darling. . . ."

"Well, that's all right. We'll start all fresh. See you tomorrow. I've been doing a lot of thinking about us, and everything's going to be all right."

Maizie went back into the room.

"I'm going to Lambert tomorrow," she said towards her mother, without seeing her or any of them.

Minnie May sprang up and threw her arms around Maizie.

"Darling child! You shan't. I won't have you going back to that man. He'll make you sick again, just as you're beginning to get better. You're not anywhere near yourself yet. I won't have you kill yourself over that good-for-nothing brute of a . . ."

Maizie saw that they were all staring, the strange young man and Leda too; her mother seemed beside herself, shaking with intensity; tears were in her eyes, that never cried.

But all she could think of was packing; the little plan formed itself in her head that she would wash her hair tonight.

"Maizie," her father said. "Maizie. Don't you do it. Don't you go 'way. Maizie. . . ." His voice petered off into inarticulateness; his square, bull-dog face was heavy and anxious and the low forehead puckered.

All of them surging around Maizie; there were tears and agitation beyond the veil that shielded her. She appreciated that it was an important time, a time of distress, for them. She wondered what she would wear on the train. The young man calling on Betsy excused himself with an abashed face and went away.

"Maizie . . . Maizie . . . Child, get some sense into your head. Maizie. . . . Darling. . . . Don't you go back to that man. . . . Maizie, you haven't the strength. . . . You haven't the health. . . . Maizie. . . . Maizie. . . ."

Maizie had never seen them so upset. She was sorry. But after a little while she went away from them and upstairs to go over her clothes. When she had been alone for a time she began to feel exhausted and ill. But it did not matter. She heard Lambert's voice talking to her over the telephone. It was a kind and affectionate voice that held no fear for her. She went on packing, the core of her being fixed on the moment of meeting tomorrow; the thoughts of all this summer had vanished.

In the beginning of dusk Leda walked home alone. She walked slowly, half thinking, half allowing her emotions to direct her mind. She had been oddly repelled by the scene at the Jekylls'. There had been something naked about it, a baring of too much pain, an excess of suffering. She was glad to get away from it. She felt purified by walking alone through the delicate and unextravagant countryside.

An excess of feeling. . . . Leda was repelled by excess. She herself had suffered much, given herself excessively to rage and resentment, to frustration, and despair. But her desolation had been a lonely thing, living out its emptiness within herself and dying and being reborn in the secrecy of her private being. All her life she had lived in desire and envy of beauty, order, the control of lives that she had jealously observed in the people she admired and wished she were. Her own excuses of longing and hate were an essential part of her self-contempt; because these fires did burn within her she believed herself an inferior being. The people she envied were empowered persons, calm and potent in their absolute control over circumstances and people, living in order and untouchable peace.

Now she had seen leaping out into air uncontrolled fires comparable to her own shameful emotions—from people who had been people she admired. She had believed the Jekylls to be powerful in that personal sense she so envied, in their lightheartedness, their carelessness. They had seemed to live their lives with more pleasure than other people. Their living had seemed to have more air, more style, than that of the timid and tentative New Englanders. This afternoon they had fallen out of their niches; the people Leda had watched were frightened, unhappy people. She did not know just what they were afraid of. But they were not running their own lives. Something outside was being too much for them.

People she saw to be as weak as herself shared the contempt she gave to herself. She had believed Mrs. Jekyll to be wise and confident, above the touch of fear; she had believed Maizie to be a symbol of loveliness and attraction; now she had seen that neither were those things. They were susceptible to all the diseases of the heart that Leda had suffered. They were not persons whom she envied any more. She was fond of them, but affection and love were not among the prizes she longed to wrest from life.

She wanted power, and control, and order, and proud untouchable beauty. Her parents loved her, and it had never done her any good. With a sort of resignation she loved them too, but it had never helped her or made her happy. The only acute happiness she had ever felt had come from those moments when by mischance she had experienced the sensation of power. When for a moment she had believed herself to be exerting her own will against some obstacle with success, she had been happy to a point which forever defied comparison with smaller, more timid pleasures. For the years of her youth she had believed that the things she wanted were by bitterest irony those things she was of all people least equipped to achieve. She had felt inferior; not even normally endowed with the muscles for seizing power. Lately chinks had appeared in the iron that bound her; she did not any longer believe it inconceivable that she should make herself happy. She was beginning to perceive her assets; she knew that she was going to be beautiful; she realized that she was intelligent and that intelligence was not the liability it had been for an ill-adapted child; she saw that Boston offered a social safe-conduct to people named March, something that she had appreciated through observation of her uncle and aunt; her parents' avoidance of all social life had kept her ignorant of the fact that to the outer world she could be anything but the unimportant daughter of unimportant parents.

She was prepared to remodel herself; rip out her worse qualities and substitute whatever acquired beliefs, habits, manners, might help her. Having no confidence in her own nature and character, which had failed her, she was open to all attributes of other natures and characters which had proved themselves to be more useful. She had no pride in herself. Anything she could remove from it, anything more valuable she could graft on it, she would do gladly. There was little of herself that she would defend or cherish. She was ready to imitate, to renounce, to swear new allegiances, to remould herself in all ways. She had the intention to use for all its worth every one of her assets; to acquire more, to use them fully.

Walking along the road, in the twilight, away from the Jekylls' house and towards the house of her parents, she perceived that the Jekylls could help her no more. They had given her friendship, companionship, more confidence in herself, many things; but they could help her no more. Now they were as small or lesser than herself; they owned no mysteries; she knew all that they could teach her of conquering an obdurate and stubborn world.

The twilight fell in tiny ways over the New England land. The weeds by the side of the road were powdered with the finest dust; the long shadows lengthened by minute degrees across the wilted fields. In a swamp one frog, exhausted from the summer, piped tremulously, and from everywhere in the limp grasses crickets sang. As the twilight increased a firefly sparked above the fields, and a moment later three, and then a dozen.

Leda forgot the machinery of her thinking, that hardness that was of the very nature of the world of people. She loved this country with her heart. The smell of it was perfume made more perfect by its familiarity. She knew it well, each turn of a season, each way in which nature conducted a New England year. Each year was exquisite like the last, a formal dance of the seasons, an intricate progression through heat to bland airs to chill to acute cold which again, always, sloped to liquid heat.

Sometimes Leda thought that if she could live alone in this country she would be happy. If the world held no people there would be nothing to distort the rhythm of her peace. When she was alone, this country gave her all she needed of pleasure, calm, and ecstasy. There were two worlds: this perfect and ordered country, and the hard, inaccessible, cruel world of people; in the two she was two different people. If there were no people, if she could live alone in this country, she would never encounter despair or hate or envy or pain, but live in freedom and beauty.

But that was impossible.

That autumn Leda went back to Miss Sheraton's school without Betsy. When the weather turned cool, and clear, and bright blue and copper, she felt panic at going back there without her only friend. They had been together nearly every day. Suddenly Leda appreciated what a mainstay Betsy had been to her life: an admiring chorus, a supporter always. Nobody else had ever admired her, stood up for her, fought her battles. What would she do, alone?

They spent the last day of vacation together; when the September sun sank and Leda had to go home, they both cried, standing in the middle of the road. From tomorrow on it would all be different. That evening they swore to spend every weekend together; Betsy promised to meet the train every afternoon when Leda came home from town. But it was the end of something.

Leda walked the rest of the way home alone in the clear and singing twilight of early autumn; this was the weather of expectation, of change from old to new ways, and she felt the tremor of new days beginning, the unquenchable hope that is born every autumn.

Everyone who has been a child has known it, the eagerness, both timid and brave, for the year of school ahead. There is a highness in the air, in the sounds of the birds so soon to go, a brilliance and recklessness in the late September, early October, weather. This brilliance dulls the aspects of reality, so that even the most unfortunate and least successful child feels, on the day before he starts back to school, that now, *now*, everything will be different; surely this luminosity, this spirit in the air, will continue and make clear the days before him; it is impossible to believe in the old hardships, the old shames, however deep their causes may be sunk in the character of the child who stares at the sunset, smells the burning leaves.

Betsy met the train on most of the afternoons of October; toward the end of the month she missed several days, and after November she stopped meeting the train altogether. By that time there was little to talk about; they were thinking so differently, living such different lives. Sometimes in that first winter one of them would make an abrupt effort to revive the friendship; but that was worse than nothing, and killed it faster. The embarrassment, the over-eager effort to pretend that nothing was different, that they were still best friends—it was strained and they were glad to get away from each other. There was no reinstating it now. Both of them felt, in private, warmly about the other; after all, nothing had happened to kill their friendship; it ended like most final endings, for no reason at all; simply there was no reason for it to live.

The time, the circumstances, the need for each other was over. They did not know that, and each carried a sense of guilt. Leda's guilt was deepest, for she saw that she was the one whose life was now become more fortunate, to whom new things were happening, and she knew that really she did not want Betsy any more. She was occupied with learning how to deal with the new things, the new friends—how to become a different person.

She sometimes thought, at night, of Betsy left behind and lonely; she thought that Betsy was timid of encroaching on her own more important life. This was because if she, herself, had been left behind she would never have dared to recall herself into the other's life; she was never able to imagine that other people did not have this sensitiveness, this envy and awe and fear of lives that were full and important; to her all positions were relative on an envious scale; each rank below hated and envied and worshipped the rank above. She thought of herself now as a rank above Betsy, and assumed that Betsy felt it too.

Betsy's feeling of guilt was simpler and more sentimental. It came from her emotional sense that something lovely had ended and been allowed to die. But it was not very deep, because Betsy's nature could not blame itself deeply for anything. Life, change, the swing of living, swept things away, moved people about, altered everything. She allowed herself to be carried along by the currents of her admirations and her desires, to be enchanted

by the colors of things as she saw them with her imagination; she was like
Leda in that she had no standards of living, of right, of wrong; but Leda
had thrown hers away because she did not believe in anything of her own,
and Betsy had never had any.

Glamour, romance, were actualities to her, and she believed in thousands
of little things that to other people were only fictions—the glamour of wick-
edness, in men worshipping women, in such things as low, husky voices,
colors and music as intoxicants. It never even occurred to her that other
people did not have the same admiration for the same things, that these
things were not accredited coin of the realm.

Both Leda and Betsy retained the faint sadness. It seemed to both of them
sad that their friendship which had taken root in their youth and grown
and thrown out shoots should thus shrivel. But that was their only sadness.
Although they might not have believed it, this year that they lost each other
was the happiest and fullest so far for either of them.

Those were the long autumn days full of red-gold falling leaves, of broad
bare skies wildly blue; the days of autumn when Leda suddenly began to
like school, to find friends, to open her vitality and use it and move forward; those were the autumn days when for the first time Leda dreamed
the dream of her youth. The two counter influences of her life began to
turn real and powerful, to tug at her from opposed angles, although then
when she was seventeen they did not seem to tug, but only to sway her
dreamily from one vision to the other and back again, neither self-exclusive.
The dream of order, the life of the mind, of delicate values, that seemed so
brilliant and beautiful when it sprang from her head out of the confusion
of childhood, from useless loves and timid tastes; when her nature's predi-
lections suddenly came together, cohered, had a name, emerged as a way
of life. And the conception of power and influence now for the first time
appeared tangible and attainable, full of rewards. They both seemed beautiful and true; both contained the flavor, the orderly and delicious atmosphere that enchanted Leda's imagination. She was unaware of the conflict
that lay implicit in their juxtaposition. She saw only that there was a life
to be had that was beyond worlds important, desirable; and that it was for
her, promised to her, if she had the wit and the drive to take it. And she
had; there were no old convictions in her, no standards that she would not
willingly abandon, to become the kind of person to whom rewards were
given.

## CHAPTER XVIII

NORAH HUNT'S OFFICE was only a desk on the landing of the third floor of
the school building. That floor was under the eaves, split up into two huge
studios and another big, peaked room used for declamation classes. Girls
coming and going from art and speaking classes used the front stairs, and
Norah Hunt's landing was nearly private. Above in the high white ceiling

was a sky-light, and so the landing, the upper stairs, the desk littered with
papers and periodicals, was always blazing with sunshine on clear days, and
lighter than the rest of school when it rained.

Each time Leda climbed the stairs into the sunshine she came more
eagerly. Her schedule had been arranged so that she had these two periods
of an hour each week for what was called 'Sp. Eng.' on the schedule card.
Actually her hours with Miss Hunt were no more English classes than
they were Latin classes, French classes, or any one of a dozen different things.
Norah Hunt gave the hours a liberal interpretation; she was a vague woman,
with all her violent enthusiasm and memory for the million things in literature
that she loved. She might read to Leda from Blake for an hour, translate
Theocritus before her eyes, talk about Dreiser and Lewis and Millay, read
Tennyson's *Ulysses* with the tears starting from her eyes and spend the rest
of the hour explaining why Tennyson had no value for this century. Her
tastes were catholic and intense; she was a natural linguist, she had an Irish
flair for recitation, and she loathed what she loathed as hotly as she loved
what she loved.

It never occurred to Leda to be afraid of her. Here was someone who
poured out enchantment and knowledge, who knew everything, lines and
cadences like gobs of honey, great chanting stanzas like trumpets sounding
from another world.

She was not prepossessing physically, and perhaps it was her dowdiness
that disarmed Leda's natural attitude of suspicion at once. She was a short,
fat, soft-skinned, flaming-cheeked, straggle-haired woman of perhaps thirty-
five, innocent of all worldly knowledge or even the ability to cross a
crowded street with dispatch.

Leda's reading had been disordered but acute. She had the taste and the
appetite for reading, the same itch that inflamed Norah Hunt. Miss Hunt,
at first, laid out a sort of rough chronological outline for their reading; but
they never stuck to it, they wandered up and down like notes upon a five-
barred scale.

Now Leda's tastes burst into form like flowers turning out their heavy
petals. Something new, discrimination, a sense of the pure and a sense of the
ill-achieved, came into her mind, giving her a queer pleasure. Now they
read Milton, and the lines came sweeping into the questioning, empty beach
of her mind like breakers. Virgil, and she could not understand the words,
only the things that formed by themselves within her from the sound of
the large syllables. She became aware of her capacity for awe, for pain,
and these for things outside herself; she learned what it was to feel in the
mind for things half-forgotten, for things far away and recaptured for a
second by sound and sense. For weeks words would sing in her head without context and she would hear them only as a strange music in her inner
ears, somehow affecting her, shaping her. . . . "No, no, go not to
Lethe. . . ."

They read in French: Villon and Victor Hugo, De Musset, Baudelaire
and Verlaine. The different sounds, the syllables, made other shapes in her
mind, and this poetry rang in her head too, quickly, like little bells: "*A*

*Saint-Blaise, à la Zucca. . . ."* and *"Dans le vieux parc solitaire et glacé,*
*Deux spectres ont tout à l'heure passés. . . ."* But it was English, not French
nor Latin nor the syllables of Greek, that made the music that possessed her
ears. They read Wordsworth, Shelley, Coleridge, Keats, Byron. And it was
when they were reading Byron that Leda's sympathies started and ranged
themselves forever with the poets. Norah Hunt was telling her of the attack
on Byron in the *Edinburgh Review;* she read her Byron's empoisoned re-
tort. . . . "O Amos Cottle! Phoebus, what a name!"

Leda laughed suddenly, with queer delight. She could not see how any
Amos Cottle could have survived that. She felt the strangest pleasure at
Byron's revenge, a sense that she was avenged too by him. She felt that she
belonged with him, them, the poets; it was the Amos Cottles that perse-
cuted and tormented them. And that one time they had gotten their deserts;
instead of cringing, weeping, or dying like Keats, this one, Byron, had
turned and given it back to them, but so much more venomously than they
knew how! It seemed to strengthen something in Leda to see that Byron
had done it; it showed that there was a fight to be made, that the others
need not always win. She was so glad. She was so glad, that day, that she
belonged with the poets and not with the others. For the first time she had
a reason for being glad to be different.

She wandered away at the end of the hour, her ears ringing. Words
seemed to beat upon her, and syllables fell into place beside others without
sense, only the loud brazen sound like trumpets. Her next period was a free
one, to be spent in the library studying. She went in there. There were large
oval tables surrounded with arm-chairs, and the walls were lined with bookcases. She sat down and stared at a bust of Homer blindly, until her eyes
slid away and out of the window. They were burning leaves in a pile below
the windows; the smell of the smoke drifted in. Outside the playing-fields
had the bare, clean look of November; Leda stared at them and at the road
where the motors streamed by against the strong blue sky.

It was mid-morning. The sun lay in oblongs on the floor, and the room
was hushed. She looked down the room to the statue of Minerva placed in
the window-niche. She could not write any of the things that had been
shouting in her head; they still shouted, chanted, rang, words and sentences
without sense, great sounds that lifted her heart. But they were not sense,
she could not write them. She had to write something. She looked about for
any small thing that she could write about, and back at the white statue in
the niche, and began to write, very slowly; she formed her letters meticulously as if she were just learning to write.

> Perhaps her very soul is marble, too.
> But then, perhaps . . . perhaps she is not dead
> But palpitates and breathes. . . .
>
> Perhaps within the cloister where she stands
> She sees the gods of Athens walk again.
> Perhaps at night, her head bowed in her hands
> She weeps for her lost city, its lost men. . . .

She finished it and folded the paper up very slowly and carefully and went to her next class. She felt strangely. Something had happened to her. She did not look at what she had written again until her next hour with Miss Hunt. Then she laid the paper on the desk and said, abruptly, "You might just look at that. It's . . ."

Norah Hunt read the lines. She turned around to Leda, her face flaming with excitement and pleasure.

"But Leda! You can do it! Now this is grand, I might have known. My dear girl, what a grand thing to have happen to me! Ah, this is what I've been hoping. . . . Now I'll tell you what's the matter with it."

That began a month or more of verse-writing for Leda. It seemed as if all her thoughts fell into metre and rhyme. She was intoxicated with the sharp ecstatic pleasure of dropping sense into the mold of verse. She wrote a new set of verses every day, sometimes more than one, and brought them when she could to Miss Hunt, who ripped them up and shouted her deep-voiced cry of enthusiasm over them, and introduced to Leda old and intricate verse-forms—ballade and rondeau redoublé.

Leda had never done anything with energy before. Now she tore into this thing that she found she could do. In those weeks she was unconscious of and indifferent to the other girls in the school—she did not care, now, whether they liked her or not. She had something she could do and loved to do, and she had an inner sense of comfort and pride because she knew that they could not do it. She belonged to something.

She wrote free verse about the rain that fell in long white lines outside the library window. She imitated Shelley and Millay and Sara Teasdale and Sandburg and Keats and Shakespeare. But the finest times were when something came into her mind that really fell into natural expression. Generally the thing was not that spontaneous. But sometimes she felt something very deeply, when she was reading, and then the work was harder, but the pleasure was deeper and there was an actual necessity to put the emotion into words and rhythms.

She was reading a collection of the Pythian odes of Pindar. It was afternoon in the school library, and she was supposed to be out at sports. But the cool November sunlight streamed through the leaded windows, and she read the book instead. "Pindar . . . took the world as he found it and thought it would last forever. . . . Sophocles is nearest to him, but Sophocles knew the human heart too well to accept the world as Pindar accepted it. . . . Pindar was not Ionian but Boeotian. . . . Science and philosophy meant nothing to him, and though he lived in the fifth century before Christ, a contemporary of Simonides, Aeschylus, and Pheidias, for his inspiration he looked to the legendary past. The qualities denied by Athenian intellect survived in him, and he is their inspired interpreter. In him the beliefs which sustained the Greek oligarchies found a voice, belief in breed, belief in religion, belief in song. More than Theognis, more than Homer, he saw the glamor of the Greek nobility and the Olympian gods, and he wrote what he saw. . . . Pindar was the last lyric poet."

She felt a warm thrill of understanding. She more than comprehended the

words. She had never felt this warmth about anything real in the world
about her. She wanted to write what she felt, and drew the pencil to her.

> The book was Pindar.
> Over that sod
> The sun was kinder
> Because it was God.
> The lightning flared
> But it could not startle
> Because it fared
> From the hand immortal. . . .

Miss Hunt read the verses when Leda brought them to her. "You felt
that, didn't you?" she said. "I think you ought to send that to the *Spyglass*."

Ever since she had been in school Leda had read the issues of the school
magazine with mingled scorn and envy, loathing the naïve little pieces of
writing in it, and longing too to see her own name in its pages. She had
never dared to send anything. The whole process frightened her to contem-
plate—whether rejection or acceptance would prove more paralyzing she
hardly knew. Now she felt an unaccustomed security. She knew her verses
were better than the little sonnets to the moon with which the *Spyglass* was
peppered.

The verses were accepted for publication in the next issue. Leda received
a note in her desk to call at the *Spyglass* office. She walked around the
gymnasium several times, summoning her courage to knock on the small
brown door.

The three girls who ran the paper sat in chairs with their feet up on the
table. They wore middies and gym bloomers, and looked very rough and
ready.

"Hello, Leda."

So many terrible times had begun with that pair of words. . . . "Hello,
Leda." She hated the sound of them . . . but she could see something different in the regard of these girls.

"This is terribly good," one of them said, waving the paper Leda had
written. "We think it's marvellous. Really, it's terribly good. I didn't know
you wrote poetry."

"Yes," Leda said.

They all looked at her. Even she could see that they looked at her differently than girls had ever looked at her before. Self-assurance flooded her.

"Of course we're crazy to use it. We hope you'll write some more for us."

"I'd like to."

"Why haven't you ever sent us anything before?"

"I was never asked for anything . . ."

"But, honestly . . . we never *ask* anybody, you know. All you have to
do is just drop it in the box . . ."

She went out into the gym trembling with contempt; at what, she was not
sure. She felt crawling with distaste. "Anybody . . . who wants anything

from me . . . must ask me for it," she whispered. "I couldn't . . . come
around to their box . . . with my poems."

She was filled with a new kind of hatred. She was not afraid, now. She
was only disgusted by the girls' fat, healthy faces, their frizzy hair, their
loud, cheerful voices and stupidity. . . . "All you have to do is just drop it
in the box. . . ." She felt she would like to step in their fat, ruddy faces . . .
and she was not afraid.

How she hated Boston girls! Their ankles were so thick, their clothes so
good and warm and ugly; if they would only be a little vicious or underfed
—if they couldn't be lovely, brilliant or extraordinary. They stumped up to
school on their low brown heels, or drove up sitting beside the Irish chauffeurs of their parents' serviceable closed cars—never a town-car, or any car
that was not conservative. They spoke in loud, pleasant voices; there was a
stubborn innocence, an unworldliness about their tones; they knew nothing
and wished to know nothing; they were insufferable. They had all the means
towards the life Leda imagined, and they were powerful, but stupidly,
charitably powerful. They drove in station-wagons for the fresh air, opened
their eyes wide when they did not understand something; they had not even
the decency to pretend that they knew what they were ignorant of. They
were rotten with honesty, stinking with frankness. They had no imagination, and their houses and way of living were as serviceable as their ribbed
woolen stockings.

Leda hated people, or envied them, or scorned them; sometimes she was
fond of them: she was fond of her father and mother, of Norah Hunt, she had
been fond of Betsy. But it was inconceivable to her that people, human beings,
could ever awaken the kind of hesitant tenderness, the warmth, that came to
her when she read great words, or when words formed themselves in her imagination. There was something both majestic and pitiful about great poetry;
it made Leda want to stand straight and reach up to the sky, and cry forever
too. In the school library she read of Darius abandoned by his generals, left
to die from the stabs inflicted by his own men, in a cart in Asia while the cohorts of Alexander rode swifter and swifter to kill him finally. Tears came
into her eyes; she heard the man groaning, saw him sweating, in that miserable cart, while above the broad glaring blue of the Asiatic sky burned, and
across those interminable plains the horses of the Greeks galloped untiringly,
their riders bent slightly forward, their cold eyes gleaming. . . .

> Then all the frightened generals ran away.
> But first they slashed and jabbed at him with knives.
> To the invader, and to save their lives
> They left him, bleeding, in the early day. . . .
> When the impatient Macedonian
> Rode up, victorious and strong of heart,
> He found this pitiful subject for his slaughter:
> Omnipotent Asia, dying in a cart;
> The King of Kings, a lone abandoned man,
> Who choked, and rolled his eyes, and called for water.

That poem was accepted for the *Spyglass* too. Leda read the verses when they appeared, with cold, proud eyes. She was beginning to feel stronger, and wiser, and above the other girls, not afraid of them any more. But they could not know that; it was still necessary to learn the ways to show them that she was better than they.

Norah Hunt began to talk about Boston to Leda. She talked about the Massachusetts Bay Colony, about the three hills on which Boston was built, about the Boston forms of speech, the Boston pronunciations. She had read her from Henry Adams, and the *Letters and Journals* of George Ticknor, and tried her on Mather's *Magnalia*. Out of her profound and informal erudition she told her snatches, stories, of the old Cambridge crowd, of Bowditch, of Webster the grammarian, the founders of State Street, among them the first March.

In the afternoons, now, when she was not at school, Leda wandered through the old streets down town in Boston, this Boston which now was so different to her from the strange misty place that she and Betsy had hurried through, truants, the year before. Now she looked with imagining eyes at the frozen flower-beds, the stiff and orange walks of the Gardens; the little hill, the monument, the Frog-Pond in the Common. She saw the amethyst window-panes on Beacon Street and explored the tiny eighteenth-century alleys through the Hill. West Cedar Street, Pinckney Street, Louisburg Square, Mt. Vernon Street; they were steep and rocky with cobble-stones, lined with old pink brick Bullfinch houses from another era. Her love, that was so little drawn to people, awoke at these sights which she had seen from time to time for so many years that now began to live for her: the steely, ice-rimmed water of the Basin, the Mall lined with skeleton trees, the austere shape of Faneuil Hall lost among market carts; the names of the wharves off Atlantic Avenue—India Wharf, Rowe's Wharf; she could see the sailors on the ships of a century ago, brown from the tropics, Chinamen and negroes and Lascars, their heads bound, their hands tarry, gold hoops in their ears. Her own roots went far down into this soil, under the old houses, under the famous fence of the Common; she saw the memorial at the top of Beacon Hill and burned at remembrance of the words "Robert Gould Shaw —'buried with his niggers'." It did not occur to her to wonder at the contradictory hate that consumed her for the people of Boston today; she loved the place and knew that it was hers as it had been her ancestors'. She liked to be lonely in it; in those afternoons she had no wish to be a part of Boston's present life, to have friends in it, live a practical life in it; she wanted to walk as though invisible through its streets, learning its names, finding its oldest alleys.

She took a subway to Cambridge, sometimes, and walked down Brattle Street between the wineglass elms, between the commodious red or yellow houses, thinking of their old inmates, the books that had lain upon their library tables. She walked about the Yard, among the naïve brick buildings faced with white, where it had been so wonderful and so difficult to find learning. She was, then, disagreeably shocked out of her daze when one of the sauntering students caught her eye or spoke to her; it turned things into a reality she did not like, in that mood. She would hurry out, and go back to Boston in the subway.

It was in those days when, at night, going to sleep, she dreamed the dream of her youth. It seemed to her that she would live, in some inchoate time which was the future, and when she was *herself*, in a pink brick house somewhere on the quiet, dreaming Hill. There would be a door beneath a broken arch, painted white, with a brass knocker. There would be a small drawing-room: the chairs would be French, painted white, with flat cushions of gray satin; there would be a faded wreath of flowers, ashy pink and mauve and palest brown, on the flat, thin rug.

And above, at the top of the house, she imagined her room, the room where she would study all the days. In plain walnut cases stood the thousands of books, the millions of books. And there was nothing else but the large square table in the middle of the room, and the chair with arms, with cushions of dark red damask.

She thought of what she would study, what she wanted to study, to learn, to find out about. She would read Aeschylus, Sophocles, and Euripides, Homer and Herodotus, Sappho, Theocritus, and Moschus. She would read Horace and Virgil . . . everything. She would study French, and Italian, and Spanish, and Russian, and German. She would learn Hebrew for herself and translate the Bible. She would read all the philosophers from Plato to Bergson. She would learn Anglo-Saxon, and ancient Celtic, and read the Book of Kels and the Cuchulain saga. She would learn of the Middle Ages, of Byzantium and the Irish monasteries, of the low dark peasantry in old France and High Germany. She would read Gibbon. She would read all of French literature. She would read all the memoirs on Shelley, on Keats; read all the Victorian novels; read the works of the Countess of Pembroke's circle. She would learn the whole of the Chanson de Roland, and Paradise Lost, and the Kalevala of Finland.

She listed them over, said them in a whisper to herself, in those long evenings when she lay in bed and dreamed of the life she desired.

This was the dream of her youth. Her life would be pure, and severe; spent in learning, absorbing. Her life would be as white as alabaster, never smeared with the soil that came from living minds. When she talked, it would be with precision, beyond all touch, all power to shatter.

This was the dream of her youth.


## CHAPTER XIX

A CLASSROOM in the Sheraton School, on the second floor, where French history was being taught. It was November, and the windows were closed; beyond their broad oblong panes was the brick-walled hockey-field; beyond the wall rose the white, stripped trunks of the sycamore trees; the sky was pale, clear blue and the thin clouds raced across it propelled by an impatient wind.

The teacher stood behind her desk at the head of the room. She was French, and wore a red coat-sweater, and her hair was done in a hundred tiny locks of black that scalloped her forehead. Her face was big and white; her nose was large, and her emaciating lips pointed out stiffly like the mouth of a fish.

There were fifteen girls in the class; they wore plaid or blue serge skirts and heather-mixture, Brooks, or Fair-Isle sweaters. Those with long hair wore it done up; most of them had short hair, parted on the side. A few had powder on their noses, carefully put on to avoid the notice of the teachers; these few had curled their hair, or had it permanently waved; they wore a dozen ringing bangles on their wrists, imitation pearls around their throats, and they looked bored and discontented; the sturdy girls were bland as cows. There were only two in the class unlike those two groups, and those two were different from each other. One was Leda March. She sat on the side of the room. She was tall with dark, thick hair and a white face in which were deep-set eyes; her neck was very long and straight, her hands were thin and played with things the eyes did not see, pencils and the edges of paper. She was wearing a blue woollen dress with a red belt, and she looked a great deal at the other 'different' girl. The other girl was Nicola Kruger.

"Mademoiselle March, what is the date of the death of Charles Quint?" Mlle. de Mostouac asked Leda in French.

Leda had been thinking of the way Nicola Kruger looked. She was very fair, her skin cream and her hair short twisting strands of honey. She had a short, straight, cream-colored nose and a wide red mouth, a short white neck and wide shoulders. She wore a tan gabardine suit and a blouse made of white crepe with rows of tucks down the front. She had a heavy gold-link bracelet on her wrist. She looked very quiet and polite and self-contained. Leda wondered what she was like. . . . Now she started.

". . . I don't know. . . ."

"Mademoiselle March, you have studied the lesson?"

"I forgot to take home the book. I left it here," said Leda, who had taken home the French history and spent the evening writing.

"Mademoiselle Wheeler?"

"I don't know."

"Mademoiselle Kruger, then, tell us the date."

"*En quinze cent, cinquante-huit, Mademoiselle.*"

"*Très bien, Mademoiselle Kruger.* You can tell us also the date of his resignation of the imperial crown to his son?"

"*Oui, Mademoiselle, ce fut en quinze cent, cinquante-six.*"

"You have lived for a long time in France, haven't you, Mademoiselle Kruger? Your accent is very good."

"Yes, Mademoiselle. For eight years."

"One sees that. You have lived in Paris?"

"Yes, Mademoiselle, and also in the country, at Éze and at Socoa, near to the border of Spain."

"Ah, you know Socoa? *Vous connaissez St. Jean-de-Luz? Il y a beaucoup du monde là.*"

"*Oui, Mademoiselle. De quelle partie de la France êtes-vous venue, Mademoiselle?*"

"I am from Touraine, from the environs of Tours."

"*C'est charmante, Touraine.*"

"*Oui, oui, la Touraine! C'est la plus belle partie de la France.* You understand what I say, Mesdemoiselles? *Eh bien.* At what battle did Charles Quint take prisoner the King of France? *Dites-donc, Mademoiselle Feeshaire.*"

"*Je ne sais pas,*" said the girl with a strong Boston accent.

"*Et pourquoi pas?*"

"*Je n'ai pas lu la leçon.*"

"*Vooo n'avvy pas loooo la leçon, hein?*" cried Mademoiselle de Mostouac. She thrust out her pointed lips and made them quiver like those of a goldfish. "*Lu. Lu. Llllll—u. U. Comme en prune. Dites-moi 'prune,' Mademoiselle.*"

"*Prune,*" said the girl. She shuffled her feet.

"*Prooooon. C'est quelque chose d'epouvantable. Prune. Prrrrune. Pru-ne. Et lu. Lu. Dites-moi 'lu,' Mademoiselle Kruger, s'il vous plâit.*"

"*J'ai lu,*" Nicola Kruger said carefully. She spoke quietly, looking directly at the Frenchwoman without raising her head.

"Good. You have heard that, Mademoiselle Feeshaire? You see that it is not impossible. Mademoiselle Kruger can say it, quite simply. It is a question of the lips. Hold them like this, draw them together. '*Lu.*' '*Lu.*' '*Lululul—lu*'.''

"*Lu.*"

"No, my God! Listen. With the lips, now, form the sound so, *u, u, u.* Now say: *Lu.*"

"*Lu.*"

"Are you an imbecile? What is there that is hard, that you say Loooo, Loooo, Loooo? Now then. Pay attention. *Avec les lèvres. . . .*"

The wrangling went on and on. The electric clock above the door went click . . . click . . . towards the hour. The November wind battered the window-panes against their frames, and the girls bent over the desks and drew pictures heavily with soft lead-pencils, and designed fancy initials for boys they knew, in the fly-leaves of their books. Nicola Kruger continued to look steadily in front of her, not bored, not interested, her lovely creamcolored face composed. Leda watched her. The electric clock ticked its final step, and a sharp buzzing bell rang throughout the school, and in less than a second everyone was on her feet, books scrambled together, carried on the hip, all pushing to the door, pushing out of the room. . . .

"*Un instant, s'il vous plâit, mesdemoiselles, un instant. . . . Pour la prochaine fois. . . .*"

But nobody listened, nobody stopped; it was recess-time and through the corridors streamed the hurrying figures in sweaters and pleated skirts, out of every classroom poured more, calling, laughing, pushing, carrying each her stack of books on one hip.

In the lunchroom they dropped into chairs at the long tables, piled their books on the tables, went and served themselves to hot chocolate, soda-crackers, milk.

Leda sat down slowly, hesitantly, beside Nicola Kruger.

"Can I sit here?"

"Do. I'm not with anyone."

"It must be awfully nice to speak French so well."

"It doesn't mean very much if you've just learned it by living there." Nicola smiled at her. It was a strange sort of smile, because it was so absolutely matter-of-fact and practical. The girl was so lovely that she appeared unusual; but she spoke and smiled in the most completely conventional way. Nevertheless she fascinated Leda. There was something attractive about the faintly English accent, the very stolidity of Nicola's smile. There was nothing in the least alarming about her. Clearly, she was anybody's friend. Leda wondered whether she had any likes or dislikes.

"How do you like this school—compared to being abroad, I mean, and other schools?"

"It's very nice. It's very different. I don't think the girls are very attractive, do you? But I don't think they want to be."

"No, they love not being. The worse you look the grander girl you are, you see."

Nicola looked at Leda with that lift of the eyebrows of a child who has suddenly seen the joke, and is delighted. Then she laughed out loud, peals of laughter.

"Leda . . . you are terribly funny. . . ."

Nicola's face had that ineffable look of having been executed by the finest artists, as smooth as porcelain; the tucks in her crepe blouse were sharply ironed, finely sewed; her shoes were made of bright russet leather; her stockings had clocks running up the sides. She was exquisite and enviable and cut after the most expensive pattern.

"Are you . . . going to the Friday Evening next week?" Leda asked suddenly, taking herself by surprise.

"Yes, Mummy says I have to go, although I expect I shall get stuck with everybody. I'm not a bit good at a dance, I lumber frightfully and I never can think of anything to say. But Mummy says they're about the only really chic thing in Boston for my age, so I suppose. . . ."

"My aunt's giving a dinner for me before it. Mrs. March. Will you come? I'd like to have you; there aren't many girls I like enough to ask. That is, I guess they don't like me. Nobody likes me, you know," she said with a sudden burst of confidence. "You probably wouldn't like me either if you knew how unpopular I am."

"But that's absurd, Leda. I think you're so much more attractive than the other girls in our class. Mummy would think you chic. Your hair. . . . I'd love to come to your aunt's dinner."

"I'll have her write you."

Leda was warm with an inexplicable sense of victory. She had been able to see that Nicola—*Nicola*—liked her and admired her, and Nicola was the most enviable, foreign girl in the school. She felt, too, with queer sureness, that she was the stronger character of the two, and that she could make Nicola do what she liked; this with her feeling of respect for Nicola's life, her cosmopolitanism, her clothes and accent and manner. In an odd way Nicola reminded her of Betsy, not in any way but in her attitude of admiration; this was another Betsy for Leda, but one grown up to her ambitions and needs; a Betsy on a grander scale.

"I've told Mummy about you, how brilliant and unusual and lovely-looking you are. Mummy says the Marches, your family, are terribly distinguished Boston. Mummy says . . ."

"Really?"

Nicola's face was at once as sensible as a grandmother's and as gullible as a child's; her short upper lip trembled slightly in a way that showed interest and affability; it was both touching and sophisticated. Her face was a blend of style, worldliness, kindheartedness, and ignorance. She leaned her chin on her palms, propped her elbows on the table, with an instinct of grace; she had manner.

Leda took a sharp breath.

"Will you come home and spend the night with me after the Friday Evening?" she asked. "I mean, there isn't any school. We could go for a walk in the woods. They're lovely in the winter. Perhaps there'll be snow." She had never before felt this courage to praise the things her lonely self loved. She was not ashamed, before Nicola.

"I should love to. I haven't been in the country for so long. I should love to take a good walk and get health. We used to take marvellous walks at Heathfield."

"Heathfield?"

"Heathfield School, in England."

Something inside Leda trembled with pleasure.

Mrs. Treat March gave a dinner for her niece Leda before the first Friday Evening dance of the season.

There was very little fuss about it all. Grace March had not exactly taken Leda under her wing; she was not especially drawn to the child. Her seeing that Leda got into Miss Sheraton's, her planning this dinner, her vague but certain expectation of seeing Leda through her coming-out year, came from a general benevolence. It was obvious to the Treat Marches that poor, rabbit-jawed Bernard, and timid Laura, could never cope with giving Leda any of the things which she might reasonably be supposed to expect in her youth. They would flutter, and forget, and push the matters fearfully out of their minds, until it was too late and Leda had never got to a party, to a proper school, never met any of her contemporaries. Ergo, it seemed to the Treat Marches, they must. They knew the other Marches, the stern and busy and impatient brothers and their high-headed wives, would never lift a finger. By a process of elimination all her own, Grace March accepted responsibility for Leda; that way was duty constructed.

Along with her own press of obligations she had attended to these things for her niece; seen that she was invited for the series of Friday Evening dances at the Somerset that were given every winter for girls of the sub-debutante age. Now quietly, among the orderly and useful procession of her days she had planned this dinner: ordered the champagne, enough for one glass apiece, up from the cellar; ordered the dinner early, because the dance would be over at eleven; invited such sons of her friends as were Freshmen at Harvard; and enlisted her son James to jolly everyone along and keep the party from degenerating into the dullness and silences of extreme youth.

James said, "Good God, Mamma. I'm a busy doctor, had you heard about that? Not an amiable tutor for the young. Darling, you manage your own children's picnic and leave me to my sick. Seriously, I haven't the time."

They were in the upstairs sitting-room the afternoon before the party. James lived in an apartment of his own out near Peter Bent Brigham, but he generally dropped in every day at some time to see his mother and father. He sat straddling the old red-corduroy bench that fenced off the fireplace, wagging a cigarette on his lower lip and grinning at his mother. She sat, as usual, before the writing-desk, half turned around towards him; her face of a crumpled flower regarded him gravely. The room was full of the spice-smell of dark red carnations.

"I thought you particularly liked your Cousin Leda, James. I thought you said she was your best cousin."

"Oh, *Leda*. Oh, *that* one! Well, why didn't you say so, Mamma? I should be enchanted to assist at your baby-party. Yes, indeed. I shall be here on the dot of whenever they eat—five? Let the patients blow their own noses. My medical knowledge, such as it is, will come in handy for changing diapers."

"James!"

"Forgive, darling. But Leda. She is lovely. I don't suppose you see it, you old angel. She's a remarkable girl, those eyes and that hair and—I don't know. She's a cut beyond the rest of us Marches."

"James, you're very extravagant," his mother said mildly.

But Leda looked beautiful at her party. Her thick dark hair shone like satin and her eyes were very dark and she wore a dress made of blackberry-pink crepe with little bunches of flowers made out of beads scattered over it. Her mother had disapproved of the dress. She said it was too low in the back. Leda said, "If you don't let me get this dress I'll die. I can't stand it. I'll die. . . ."

Her mother and father were not at the dinner the Treat Marches gave. Grace had asked them, but they did not accept. Leda had told them that she did not want them to come. "It's the first party anyone ever gave me," she said. "You'll ruin everything." They looked frightened and hurt and adoring.

The house at the foot of Beacon Hill was full of lights. There were roses and carnations and Freshmen everywhere. Grace liked her house when it was full of people, and young people were especially decorative. The young girls were a little stiff and awkward, but that was refreshing and right.

There were too many to seat at table, and the boys brought the girls plates of food where they sat in the drawing-room or on the wide red-carpeted stairs. Leda had been responsible for asking the girls; Grace March had wanted her to invite her own friends; now she saw that she knew most of them, knew their parents; they were nice little Boston girls and a little heavy in the ankle, Grace observed with wry amusement; Boston girls had always been like that.

The prettiest girl, besides Leda, was some friend of Leda's from school, Nicola Kruger. Her parents were not Boston people; New York people, Grace March thought. But the girl was lovely, peaches and cream and gold, very quiet and self-possessed, and of all the girls, by far the most polite. She was the best dressed of all of them, and the most appropriately, too; she wore a blue dress made all of pleats, and beautifully made blue crepe slippers. Grace liked her, for her simplicity and her manners. It made her like Leda, too, that she had made this girl a friend. Perhaps she was not a Bostonian, and perhaps people here would be a little chilly to her on that account, but Grace March made up her mind that she liked the girl. Nicola was so charming, and so gentle. Leda was so strange. But Leda was her niece, and that was the end of it. Grace March sat at a small table eating lobster with a handful of her contemporaries; from time to time she observed Worthington, the butler, coping with the situation.

Champagne, lobster, chicken salad, and raspberry ice; the clatter of March plates; the sound of young male voices with a break in them; the sound of young female voices talking steadily, rising slowly to a high pitch and breaking off in indignation, amusement, or contempt. The two drawing-rooms, one dark red, the other dark green, opened one into the other, and the long mirrors at each end reflected two crystal chandeliers. Forty young people of Boston sat on Georgian and Victorian chairs, leaned against black walnut banisters, and set their champagne glasses on the mantelpiece. Some-one said, "Isn't it about time to get started for this thing?" A Freshman said, "Eleven o'clock to end a party! Why won't you women grow up? God, in New York. . . . God. . . ." and a girl's voice cried, "Honestly! If you haven't got any school spirit, honestly! . . ."

On the stairs Leda sat next to her cousin James. They held glasses in their hands; they had set their empty plates on the step behind them. Leda's cheeks were hot, and she felt as if she were stronger than ten thousand armies.

"You've got the most beautiful back I think I ever saw," James said.

This was the beginning of her life, Leda thought.

"Nobody's ever said that to you before, have they? They're going to. I kind of like it that I got there first."

She only looked at him, with tranced, blind eyes. She did not see her cousin, only the man who had paid her a grown-up compliment.

"You hurry up and grow up, will you?" he said. "I've got a lot more I'd like to say to you. When you come out next year, look around for me. Those flowers will be from me. I've got you all picked out for my debu-tante. I suppose you think of me as a hundred. I'm thirty."

She continued to stare at him blindly, her vision suffused with rose color, all of her lifted from the step where she sat and floating in an ether of triumph.

"This is the first time I ever in my life wished I was a Freshman," he said. "I can't go to this party of yours. I'm too old. Mrs. Wolcott and Mrs. Saltonstall wouldn't let me in."

"You wouldn't want to go to a children's party," she breathed automatically.

"Oh, but I mean it," he said.

Mrs. Treat March's chauffeur drove Leda and Nicola out to Hampton after the Friday Evening. They leaned back against the cushions side by side. Through the night outside flickered a few snowflakes; others whirled in eddies before the headlights of the car; it was quiet and calm and beautiful driving out into the country. Leda looked straight before her into the whirling maze of the illuminated snowfall; inside she was calm and warm.

"You had the best time of any girl at that party," Nicola said in her low, safe voice.

"Do you think so?" Leda murmured.

"You couldn't dance two steps without being cut in on. You looked too lovely. But not just that, you look so shining from inside. Mummy says some women simply draw men to them by that radiant thing."

Something stirred in Leda at Nicola's generosity. She didn't know at all what kind of a time Nicola had had.

"You have the best-looking clothes of anyone I ever saw," she said. "You were the best-dressed girl in that whole room."

"Oh. . . . Mummy buys my clothes. But I'm not like you. I get stuck. I haven't got that quality."

The next day, the Saturday, the country lay under a light snow. They arose in the guest room, where Leda had slept in the next bed to Nicola's, and went in their nightgowns to the open window and leaned out. The air was as fresh as flowers above the fallen snow. There was a watery sun that made pale blue shadows. They closed the window and dressed. Nicola put on a brown tweed dress, clocked lisle stockings, and calfskin shoes; she called these 'country clothes.' Leda listened to all she said, learning from her: names of things, turns of expression, even ways of enunciating. This was the kind of person she wanted to be. She drank in Nicola's precise beauty, her finish in little things; she envied her her calm, her somehow desirable stolidity. There was something in particularly good taste about Nicola's unemotionalism and her blank manner of conformation to some foreign, but nevertheless conventional, standards. Leda could see that everything Nicola did and said and wore was according to the tenets of some group of people who had a law for everything; she did not know the people, but she felt that they were important. She smelt opportunity in Nicola's presence; she perceived that Nicola belonged to something she would like to belong to; and Nicola was her friend and for some reason saw something she admired in Leda.

Leda's course was imitation; by assuming the manner, the code, of that unknown group she could become one of them and in time by the sifting of like to like be with them. This she felt in the back of her mind. On the surface, from minute to minute, she liked Nicola. She liked her simplicity, which held nothing that was frightening. She liked her calm, natural way of breaking into laughter. It made her feel happy and attractive to be liked and confided in and admired.

And all the time in her nerves was the warmth of memory of the night before. The success she had had, the ease she had felt on the dance-floor, trembled in her imagination like something dreamed but not quite true. She had had a victory. She had found something she was good at. She did not want to think clearly about it; it was so pleasant to let the filaments of memory quiver in the back of her mind.

She was very happy. Things were being moulded to her desires.

When she had asked Nicola to spend the night she had chanced the possibility that she would feel ashamed of her parents before her. Last night, when they came in, her mother had called to her from her bedroom, to ask if she had had a good time. Leda had hurried through an impatient good night, answering her mother's queries, and gone back to Nicola. She had felt unsure; that there was something stupid and provincial about a mother's calling her daughter in late at night to ask about a party. She felt that the mothers of Nicola's kind of people would have been asleep, or busy with their own thoughts and affairs, not living in their daughters' pleasures. . . . But Nicola said, "Did you tell her that you were a belle? She must have been pleased. Poor Mummy, she'd be so pleased if I should tell her I'd been having a time when I came home from a party. She always wants to know."

They ate a late breakfast, feeling like women of the world. Nicola was charming to Mrs. March, and when Bernard wandered in, goggling his eyes and working his weak chin, she smiled at him and let flow a stream of light, calm conversation. . . . Leda watched her parents react to Nicola in so much the same way that they had reacted to Betsy; with delight and affection and surprise that they were not snubbed by Leda's friends as they were snubbed by Leda. . . . Leda felt a vague doubt, a wonder, stir inside her. She observed her parents as if she had never seen them before. Perhaps she was mistaken about them, perhaps they were all right. First Betsy, then Nicola, both people that Leda had looked up to and envied, treated her parents with politeness and more, as agreeable people. Why did she feel that everything they said was always sentimental, embarrassing, wrong?— why did she blush inwardly and writhe at their way of living, their ingenuousness? She wished so that they were hard, worldly, invulnerable people.

But they seemed all right to Nicola, who knew. Leda framed in her mind, tentatively, a new attitude towards her parents, one in which she would be proud of them, take pleasure in talking to them. But the vision refused to jell. It remained a conjecture. There were too many years of being a misfit and blaming it on her bringing up; there were too many memories of hours full of frustrated tears, of opportunities denied her that other children of more worldly parents achieved, of feeling forever that she was an odd, unattractive girl and that it was all her parents' fault.

Now she was happy. Now she saw that life was going to be open to her, that she was going to be able to seize as much or more of the rewards as other girls. But sharply the thought came to her: I did it all myself. Anything that I get I will have got for myself. They never did anything for me.

And she felt warmer than ever. She had found a new sort of self-approbation. She felt that she was going to become someone lucky and remarkable and happy, and all through her own efforts, her own will. She would cure her shyness, her oddness, she thought boldly. She would conquer all the defects that had hindered her from satisfaction, and become whatever she pleased.

In the early afternoon they took a walk through the woods. The early snow was damp and clinging; it hung in festoons from the twigs of the trees.

"This is frightfully pretty country you live in, Leda," Nicola remarked. She walked through the snow with small, ordered steps, watching where she was going, seeing only what was there. "There must be any quantity of woods. Do your parents own all of this?"

"No, not all," Leda said. She wished they did, so that she might say so. "It is rather nice. You should see it in the autumn. It really is beautiful then."

"Yes, I do think autumn in America is the best time. I don't actually ever want to live in the country in the winter, that is, live all the time. It is a bit bitter and wearing. I like the city best in winter."

"Yes, of course," Leda said. She had been walking with Nicola's small neat steps, instead of her own long, wandering stride. She had consciously limited her vision to the realistic things that Nicola spoke of. She was trying to talk like Nicola, feel like Nicola, act like Nicola; *be* her. She wanted to be different from her old self. She would prefer to be Nicola. It was curiously easy to be with someone else; you adapted yourself completely to their way of thinking, agreed with them, let them make the absolute statements; that way you could get along with anybody.

"You must come in and spend the night with me very soon," Nicola said. "Perhaps after the next Friday Evening. I'll ask Mummy when."

"I'd love to," Leda said carefully.

"I know Mummy's going to adore you. She'll think you're *bien elevée*. She was so relieved when she found that your aunt was going to have us driven home last night. She thinks it's frightful—rather cheap—for young girls our age to go about at night with boys. I must say I think it would be rather fun."

"I know what you mean. . . ."

"But I suppose that's silly. If you let yourself get talked about, get a bad reputation, you simply lose out by it, that's all. You're not invited, and all that. It's a bore, but I suppose Mummy's right."

"Yes," Leda said thoughtfully.

"I'm so glad you asked me, Leda. I do hope we're going to be good friends. I think we should have a good time next year when we come out.

I do think you are so much more amusing than the other girls in our class."

There was a pedantic quality about Nicola's speech which was fascinating.

"I'm so glad." That was all right, but not an especially interesting thing to say. It would be fun to be witty. . . . Leda had never thought of that before.

"Of course you have so many more friends than I in Boston. Mummy says your family is related to everybody. I really know nobody at all, after living abroad so long, and just moving to Boston last spring."

"I'd love to meet your mother."

"Mummy's marvellous. I mean she's really divine, it's hard to explain how. Just exciting, somehow, and yet so orderly and perfect. . . ."

Nicola talked on as they set their feet into the snow. Leda understood her, the things she talked of, instinctively; it was not learning from what Nicola said, it was almost like remembering a lesson taught long ago; she seemed to know how these things were, how people lived that kind of life. She remembered that mathematical geniuses are said to acquire knowledge, as children, almost as if recollecting something; not as if learning a task. She thought, Perhaps I am a genius at this kind of living Nicola has lived, and her mother; perhaps I know how it is done instinctively, and I shall be naturally adept at it.

She looked quickly at Nicola in the growing darkness and laughed, suddenly, a way children laugh out of happiness and well-being. Nicola caught her eye and laughed too; it was just for a second, but afterwards they were friends, they had shared something.

Across the spiky fields in the dusk, up through the long and familiar pasture in the twilight, they walked. They came around the curve in the field and as they saw the yellow lights of the small house shining beyond the darkened snow, something changed sharply in Leda and she felt a quick, terrible pang. Something like regret, nostalgia, a stab of consciousness of perfidy, tore at her heart, quite without warning.

This was the place she knew, that she had hated and been lonely in, that she had felt imprisoned in, and yet that she knew as she would never know anything else. Those yellow lights from the house; the quiet snow; the woods behind her, all known, all her own for the tortured years of childhood: these suddenly seemed acute to her, made her want to cry from longing and shame at her betrayal of them, and from unutterable confusion. They were her actual self, the thing that was good and simple and young about her, and she had betrayed them to the bright and unnatural, the lusts of her old unhappiness. For she had walked all afternoon in her own woods and not seen them, not felt anything about them; walked as a new person, one of the world of people that she had hated and feared always; talking of people and affairs and laughing and giving herself to change. Not for a moment had she surrendered herself to the lonely enchantment; she had not become a part of that country in the old way, felt its pulse beating in her own. She had not seen nor felt where she walked, and it all lay behind her untouched, untrod.

The lonely, bare, beautiful woods, full of the damp of winter, the black boughs, the whispering of the stark twigs; the sound of it, the small wet drip of snow from the boughs on to the snow beneath. It lay behind her unseen. The pools lay in their dark and hidden hollows; the ancient paths made first by moccasined feet led on between the rotting trees, up the naked hills and down in to the still valleys. She had a feeling that now she would never see them again, that now she had closed her eyes to them, and the old magic of the tranced imagination would never respond to her wish again. She had denied that part of herself and willed to be something else, and now she must be it. She would never be wretched and lonely, wandering frustrated in the woods, again; but she would never have that delicate comfort either, nor the queer occasional ecstasy of union. Now she was a person, like other people: capable of victory, equipped for conflict.

But now, suddenly, she was not sure that she wanted to be a normal person after all; suddenly she loved her old, despised self, she felt the nostalgia of loss, grief for what was dead, and for a moment she almost hated Nicola and everything that Nicola stood for. An unexpected questioning started in her head: what had she longed for and now possessed but something that everyone had, that she had only wanted because it had been difficult for her? What she had had alone was precious and rare. That life, and added to it that other life of the mind that she had found with Norah Hunt, made a whole. It was her whole, surely: and Nicola, and what was Nicola's, was none of hers. Why. . . .

And then they had come up the short slope to the kitchen door, old, wooden, and familiar; it was with a kind of inner insistence that she came this way, opened the kitchen door, smelled the dinner cooking on the stove, saw the yellow warmth of the kitchen spreading into the outer darkness. Then the door was shut, they walked across the worn brown boards of the kitchen floor; there was the black stove, the step down to the little store-room, the soapstone of the sink, the cups hanging in rows from hooks at the under edge of a shelf. Leda did not look at Nicola, she wished she were not there. They went into the half-light of the living-room where a small fire glowed into the shadows behind the piano; it was all quiet and safe. She sat down on the low chair beside the fire and stared into the blurred quivering red of the embers. She did not care whether Nicola had sat down or not.

And then the telephone rang.

It was one of the boys she had met last night. Now suddenly, she changed inside again and was the other person. She was a person in the world of people, and her armor was apparent to her, and her blood rushed up and she felt strong. In a second she had forgotten all the other. . . . This was life and she liked it. The boy asked whether she and Nicola would go to the movies with him and another Freshman that evening.

She hesitated. She looked through the doorway into the living-room, the pretty, half-lit scene with Nicola's fair head gold in the firelight. Leda was part of it, that kind of scene, this kind of situation. She turned back to the telephone and said that she was sorry, but they weren't allowed to go out alone in the evening, and would the boys like to come over after dinner? She hung up and went back into the room where pleasant things could happen with other people, that were attractive and busy. It was fun dressing later, with Nicola, for the call the boys paid them. Leda put on a dress made of orange shantung, and Nicola wore a dress made of water-blue crepe, pleated in a hundred tiny pleats.

After the first of the year, after Christmas, it was all that way with Leda. She had her two classes a week with Norah Hunt, but the fire had died out and it was only once in a while that she saw the visions she had had in the fall; she still wrote verse, but carefully and with a consciousness of her own facility. She was becoming more and more confident; she had a good time at all the parties she went to; she was seldom afraid of anybody any more; and her self-confidence fed upon itself, filling her sometimes with a wild elation. She went to all the Friday Evenings, and to the private dances given for girls of her age; generally she stayed in town for the night afterwards, either at her aunt's or at Mrs. Kruger's.

Mrs. Kruger was a woman, originally from Kansas City, naturally endowed with taste and a feeling for decorative, orderly, gay living. Her husband was a New Yorker of good family, lazy and good-natured, who was content to let his wife amuse him with her parties and friends when he was at home; the rest of the time he was in an office in New York, Paris, London, or, now, Boston. He was not a personality and had never felt the itch to be one. It was a tradition in his family for the husbands to husband the fortune, and the wives to be beauties and hostesses.

Mona Kruger loved to be a hostess, she loved the thousand details of a large menage with plenty of income behind it, and she loved to establish herself in new places. She was one of those women without any inner, private intelligence; her mind flowered as she spoke, as she listened, and although she was not accounted a wit she was considered a damned amusing woman. Likewise she was not beautiful, but she dressed exquisitely and made of her person something at once delectable and surprising. She was very tall and slim; she had soft, thick brown hair arranged in a beautiful shape; and her features were mobile and generous: of them nothing but the large gray eyes and the mouth, wide and painted red, could be remembered. She was a woman practically without ambitions; she had no memory for the past and little interest in the future; she desired to be entertained in the present, and to be entertaining. It made her happy to be the center of a group; ardor, unhappiness oppressed her and she was a singularly faithful wife, but not from virtue. She was loved and admired everywhere she had ever lived; it suited her to observe the conventions, to teach her daughter exquisite manners, to go to church, to dress with imagination—to conduct her days with restraint, seeking in people and things and places the attractive, the entertaining, the social qualities.

She was living in Boston because the idea had come to her that she would rather have her daughter make her debut in that city than in any other. Abroad it was impossible. New York was too big, it was expensive and rather vulgar. Philadelphia was noisy and too horsy to be endured; Boston was just right. Old school, studded with conventions, tradition, it did not offer too much competition for a young girl to cope with, and a successful entry into society in Boston meant something even today. Mona Kruger was very much interested in her daughter just now. She was lovely looking, beautifully brought up, sweet and good-natured; there was something missing, a fire, that kept her from enjoying the sort of extravagant admiration from boys that Mona had had as a girl, that she rather wished for Nicola, but her qualities equipped her admirably for making a superlative wife; there was no reason why she should not make a good marriage. It suited Mona's tastes perfectly to face a year of parties for Nicola, to plan a series of dances in the house for her and plot out a wardrobe. She was interested in the preliminaries now taking place, the friends Nicola made, her contacts in Boston. During the winter Mona met most of her daughter's classmates; Nicola brought them home for lunch, to spend the night, asked them to dinners before the sub-debutante parties. Of them Nicola seemed to like Leda March best, and on the whole Mona did too; her instinct for such things recognized in the girl more potentialities for activity, excitement, than in the somewhat stolid others; Leda had that fire Nicola lacked; and her family were distinguished. Mona thought she was a good friend for Nicola.

The Krugers had taken a large house on Commonwealth Avenue. Mona had the dark, huge furniture removed and arranged her own beautiful things in their places. There was a large hall paved with black and white marble; she had Venetian mirrors set all about it. Her drawing-rooms were white and green and crystal; her dining-room was pale blue, with carnelian-and-white striped seats on the chairs. In the vast closets off her bedroom hung the rows of beige, green, red wool dresses from Chanel, the white, the black, the coral, the emerald green evening dresses from Vionnet; on long racks stood the shoes—sports shoes, calf walking shoes, black shoes with high heels in suede, kid, patent leather, gabardine; the evening slippers made of crepe, of satin, of brocade and gold mesh.

Mona was not as gay in Boston as she had been in all the other cities, but she had not expected to be. She had no intention of seeking gaiety where it could be found if the sources were second-rate; she knew that Boston dinners that were first-rate were not intended to be amusing. She was here for Nicola's sake; she intended that Nicola should have all there was to have out of a debutante year, and she saw the necessity for a preliminary year in which Nicola could make friends. For herself, she saw many people for the sake of Nicola; people with sons, with daughters, people who gave the right parties. Occasionally she had parties of friends over from New York, which gave her brief snatches of real gaiety; but she did not intend too much of that. Just enough; it would add to Nicola's prestige to have New York friends visit her for the parties when she came out; but she did not mean to be caught sneering at Boston. She realized that as an outsider and as a well-dressed woman she was the object of some suspicion in Boston society; but she relied on her husband's unquestionable position in New York and her own tact and friendliness to dispel those suspicions in time enough for Nicola's year. She thought it might be very nice if Nicola married a Boston young man. If not, never mind; it was the Boston debut she wanted for Nicola. There would be years enough afterward, wherever they went next, London again, or New York or Rome or perhaps Washington, for Nicola to find the right husband; for Mona to find him for her. It would be very nice to move on, away from Boston; on the other hand, it would be very nice to be here for a bit; Mona Kruger had unlimited equanimity and a happy nature.

## CHAPTER XX

IT WAS into this life that Leda came in her last year of school. In the back of her mind, Leda realized how useful Mrs. Kruger could be to her. Her example was precisely what Leda needed to show her how one acted, one spoke, one reacted, when one was an easy, charming member of the social world, always at home with people however difficult. And now that Leda began to realize how well guarded she was in Boston by her own family connections she was the more aware that she needed people to introduce her into the world outside Boston. Already, among the younger people whom she knew at school and dances, she had learned to sneer at Boston, to bewail its provinciality, to long for New York and to speak of her own city as a prison. To be content with Boston was to brand one's self as a stodgy, dowdy Bostonian; one must gibe, one must imitate the girls that came over from Philadelphia and New York, one must have the air of accepting Boston under sufferance. Leda was no longer in terror of the world as represented in Boston; she had made up her mind to be important in the world of people; she intended to prove her domination over a larger area than home. In Mrs. Kruger she saw the person who could introduce her into further, larger worlds.

But it was not all as scheming as that. In the front of her mind she gave herself to enjoying that last year at school. She was learning the ropes fast. Buoyed up by her outstanding success at parties, her new manner, her new way of talking, her new clothes, she began to believe in her new self. It was fun, in particular at the Krugers', staying there, going and coming.

She would spend a weekend there. Nicola's big room was pale green with white Venetian blinds, and on the Friday night they would lie awake talking in the two green beds, with the light coming in from Commonwealth Avenue and lying in stripes upon the floor. The quiet sounds of the city, the passing cars, the muffled hoot of horns, came comfortably into their conversation. They talked of boys, and parties, and of New York and Paris, and of the girls they liked and did not like at school, and of clothes, and of all the things they meant to do next year together, when they came out. How they would dress, how they would behave, what they would say to the young men, whether they would kiss anyone or not, whether they would get engaged and whether they would do it seriously or not, how they would get to New York for the parties in the holidays, how they would always do everything together and back each other up.

On the Saturday they would go skating at the Boston Arena, in black velveteen skirts, very short and full, and bright colored sweaters. They saw the other girls from school, all seriously practicing outer edges, doing exercises to strengthen their muscles for fancy skating. Later they would walk down Huntington Avenue together in the early dusk, walking slowly with shoe-skates in their hands, talking. They would stop to look in the lighted windows full of dresses, shoes, underclothes, filled with a lazy contentment at the hour and the prospect of a party before them.. They would stop at Schrafft's and eat ice cream and cake that had hot chocolate sauce poured over it. Then they would come out into the twilight. Boston was pretty and gay under the winter's snow, and the lights in the streets were bright; people hurried by in overshoes along the icy pavements. They would walk along Arlington Street opposite the snow-bound Gardens, and turn down the Mall on Commonwealth Avenue. It was only a short way under the bare branches to the Krugers' house. The house was full of lights, and it was pleasant to go up the steps and have the butler open the door to preparation for festivities. They would run up the stairs and go to Nicola's room to dress.

Their clothes were laid out on the two beds, and there was something exciting about seeing them there, the small pile of crepe de chine drawers, brassiere, and thin silk stockings; the evening dress, spread out carefully, ironed; the pair of gold or silver or colored shoes placed side by side on the floor. They would undress slowly, and go into the two bathrooms that had a door between so that they could talk. By a special concession from Mrs. Kruger, who did not believe in serving cocktails to Freshmen and schoolgirls, they were brought a small Martini apiece while they were bathing, and these they drank with luxurious sloth, lying in the warm tubs and washing with perfumed soap. There were so many details of dressing that they indulged in with joy: the lotions, the perfume (floral), the nail polish (pink), the brilliantine for the hair, the red salve for the lips, the peach-colored powder; the jewelry that they wore with their dresses. They ran into the bedroom from their baths and proceeded to dress. They stood in their knee-length evening dresses before the pier-glass and revolved slowly. That year they wore metal 'slave necklaces'—hoops of gilt in one curved piece. Their necks rose from the stiff hoops like stems to support their brilliant, excited faces, their shining hair.

They went very slowly down the stairs to the dinner party below; the green and white drawing-rooms were full of girls in pink taffeta, in lavender georgette with a frill of feathers at the knee, in lace dresses finished with colored chiffon flounces at the hem. The Freshmen wore dinner coats and starched white shirts below their ruddy faces, their damp hair. Among them moved Mrs. Kruger, illuminating all the scene, setting it at a pitch well above itself. So beautifully dressed, with the shape of the hair, the friendly gestures of the hands, the mouth always talking—she colored all the atmosphere, she gave them all a promise that parties were gay and that everything was fun. Her voice was curious: it was almost harsh, quite metallic. It was a cosmopolitan voice, without an accent; it was a composite of all the voices of busy, gay women all over the civilized world.

In the spring of that year, when they came home from the parties late at night, the faint fuzz of leaves on the trees of the Mall would be pale green in the street light. It was cold and fresh, and their feet hurt from dancing; Leda's mind was always in that fog of after-pleasure, the trance of triumph that always came and always surprised her because it was too wonderful to be true. If there were boys who had accompanied them home in the Krugers' car, they would all go in and sit and talk in the small sitting-room near the front door. There were no sounds from the street outside; Leda, Nicola, the boys, sat and lay about the room in relaxed attitudes, eating the sandwiches, drinking the hot drinks. They talked: Nicola quietly, sensibly; even at that hour after a dance rational, amiable, conventional; her face calm, her fair hair shining in the light. Leda herself felt divorced from reality, talking in a dream; the boys, who might be a little in love with her, talked to her with their eyes dazed, about things none of them knew anything about: voyages, and poetry, and Europe. The little sofas, the chairs, were soft and deep; the flowers in the vases, hyacinths and narcissus, sent out an odor that was strange and bemusing.

Then she and Nicola would rise, gravely, and tell the boys it was time to go home. There was a lot of talk about modes of conveyance out to Cambridge; the last subway had gone; the Krugers' car was put away; generally they ended by hailing an ancient cab and cabby that waited all night along Commonwealth Avenue—Freddy and Freddy-the-horse. The boys stood in a group by the open front door; their faces were still ruddy and shining; they laughed, and repeated once more old jokes of the evening; the fresh cold scents of Northern spring came in through the door, and then it was closed, and Leda and Nicola went upstairs to bed.

On the Sunday more boys would come to tea; in the spring Leda and Nicola sometimes went driving with them in the afternoon. They would drive back to Boston and have tea in the drawing-room with other boys who had come. There was an agreeable lassitude; a slight fatigue, a soreness of the feet that had danced; it was easy to talk and laugh, and to drink tea and eat small bacon sandwiches and hot rolls with cheese in them.

As the end of school drew nearer for the girls who were graduating, their boredom and familiarity with the place dissolved and they found themselves anticipating nostalgia; feeling affectionately towards the teachers, filled with school spirit; now, suddenly, they could not bear that it was over. The May weather filled the playing fields with green, swaying leaves, bright shadows, and the graduating class was allowed to do its studying out on the benches around the brick wall, instead of in the library. They sat in cotton dresses on the last days, half studying, half looking with love and regret at the brick pile that would forget them so much sooner than they could forget it. It was 'School.' Each luncheon became a ceremonial meal, something fine and united, instead of a time to gabble and complain about the food.

Even Leda felt it. She became aware abruptly of the significance, the beauty, of that once-hated, lately-tolerated place. There seemed to be a dignity about the class-rooms; something pitiful and fine about this organization for the perpetuation of learning. She saw the quietness and integrity of the library, with its busts of Homer, Beethoven, Socrates—men in whose name this solid, routined building was dedicated. Now she walked with a feeling of solemnity through the long corridors, and saw the sense to the place's being—now that she was going to leave it.

Girls gave luncheons, teas in the country, for their classmates; girls whom they had never seen much of; in a last stab at realizing themselves as a class. Old cliques were dissolved for the time. Leda went to the houses of girls she had never seen at home before; felt friendly towards them and saw the same look in their eyes; girls whom she had ignored, or who had ignored her; girls who had been too timid, or too athletic, or too studious, for her. Now for a little while she liked them.

A day or two before the last day of school Adèle Macomb gave a tea at her house in Hampton and did not ask Leda. She asked Nicola. The tea was a large one, composed of more than Adèle's own crowd at school; she had asked nearly everyone in the class. Quite naturally, Nicola asked Leda if she were going.

Leda had almost forgotten what this feeling was, this frustration and despair. She was left out. Suddenly all that had happened during the winter, all the slow growing of her confidence and security, were thrown over and she was despising herself for being the wrong kind of person. She might have known. All of her pleasure, all of her success, had meant nothing to Adèle Macomb, who had always despised her and seen her for what she was, a miserable outsider in the world of people, trying to pretend to be what she was not. She was sure—and all of this in the instant of shock and disillusion—that Adèle had been laughing at her all winter, sneering at her little successes; and now she was showing that she still thought of her as she always had, as a mean, insignificant, loathsome little creature. It was the old defeat. It had always been Adèle who destroyed her. It had always been Adèle who represented the terrible ease, the domination, the unlimited power, that Leda feared and longed for.

How she had deceived herself! The winter crumbled into dust. She was no better than she had ever been, for all she had tried so hard. Adèle despised her. She had asked everyone of the slightest importance in the class to this tea. The thing was real, it was deeply significant. Leda felt complete defeat.

She was in the deserted class-room, after lunch, with Nicola. Nicola stared at her, her calm, polite face disturbed.

"I don't see why you care," she said. "Adèle's not especially attractive, I shouldn't think. She's never been a particular friend of yours."

"That's not it. . . . You wouldn't understand. . . . Oh, Nicola, why does everyone despise me, why can't I ever be like other people? I want to be, so. . . . People hate me. She hates me. . . ."

"That's not so. People don't hate you," Nicola said reasonably. "You

aren't like people because you're more attractive than they are. She probably is jealous of you. You have a much better time at parties. I can't see
why you're so upset."

"She despises me. . . . She always has. . . . You wouldn't understand, it
goes way back into my childhood. She's so strong. I'm afraid of her. She
hates me, and she'll ruin my life yet. I feel it. She wants to ruin my life.
She's always wanted to. . . . Every time I'm a little bit happy, she wrecks it
all somehow, she just waits until she can hurt me. . . ."

Leda was so frantic that at last even Nicola began to believe that there
was something queer in Adèle's not inviting Leda to her tea. Her simple
loyalty made her ask Adèle why, in a way. She found Adèle in the cloakroom and told her that she herself would not be able to come to tea.

"I'm so sorry," Adèle said. "Can't you really?"

"Well. . . . I promised Leda to do something with her, and as she's not
going to your house I don't believe I can either."

"Oh. . . . Did Leda get you not to come?"

"Not at all, Adèle. Had you any especial reason for not asking her?"

"I suppose she got you to ask me that."

"Oh, she didn't at all. I wanted to know myself. It seems so odd your not
asking her, you must have known her for a long time. . . ."

"Yes, I've known her for years. I simply don't like her, if you want to
know. There's nothing so queer about it, I just don't like her."

But this one defeat had the power to shake Leda's new confidence. It
awoke in her all the old, insistent drive for power; for a potency which
could destroy Adèle. She had a dream, the night that she heard of her
exclusion from the tea-party, in which she murdered Adèle with a stick,
beating her on the head until she was dead. She awoke with a sense of relief,
and satisfaction. Then she realized what she had dreamt, and lay thinking
about it. It seemed to her to mean that while Adèle was alive she, Leda,
would never have any peace or security of spirit. She wondered what it
would do to her if she were really to murder Adèle. She knew she would
never have the courage to do it. She wished she could, and rid herself
forever from the fear, the menace that laughed at all her little triumphs and
reduced her again to tears and despair. What was it Adèle had?—what was
that power, that rightness? She knew again as in the long years of her
childhood, that there was something essentially right about Adèle, some
innate capacity for triumph, and that in her, Leda, there was only wrong
forever, and shame and the groping for a little happiness, a little balance.

She cried into her pillow as miserably as she ever had. The winter behind
her was only pretense; she did not do those things by instinct, by nature;
she was only an outsider, aping the manners of the strong and secure. It was
a secret that could never be learned. It was born in a person and managed
as easily as a hand, a leg.

The next morning at school she felt drained and weak, but fierce with
resolve: she was back to three years before, she was again a body of determination to get power, to control her life, to make people do as she wished.

She was walking along a corridor, her head lowered. The warmth of sentiment for school which had filled her was drowned in the flood of despair and then of necessity for making more of herself. She was thinking, looking at the floor, of the summer before her. The Krugers had invited her to spend a month with them at Bar Harbor; she had a number of invitations for shorter times. She thought of the arrivals, the stations or boat-docks filled with people meeting their guests; she would be part of that. She had opportunity before her; she was planning how she could make the most of it. She saw, now, that it was not simply a question of finding pleasure; power was something more, it meant even sacrificing pleasure to gain hold on more that would aid one's eventual strength. She did not mean to jeopardize her future in one tiny thing. She would be more than conversant and easy in the world of people; she would control at least a part of it, hold it in some sort of subjection. She could not tell what particulars of living might lie before her, in what manner she might help herself forward. But she was formulating a sort of credo for her guidance. She would never allow herself to do anything that might be criticized by the old and mighty; she would make the most powerful friends possible; she would avail herself of every tiniest scrap of information, of example, of precept, which might teach her how potency is achieved, how the will is made dominant.

She walked slowly down the corridor. Someone called her name.

"Leda!"

It was Norah Hunt. Short, squat, she waddled down the corridor towards Leda. Perspiration stood out on her smooth, shiny face; her hair trembled in loops. She transcended the indignity of the fat woman. Carrying her weight impatiently, she was alive with purpose; her broad forehead was calm, her mouth mobile with intention.

"Leda, I've been trying to get hold of you to talk to you."

Leda stared at her through a mist thrown up like a screen before her eyes by the intensity of her separate conflict. Norah Hunt was like an apparition from another life; she meant something that had been fine, exalted; but all that was over, unreal. . . .

"Look here, Leda, I know you haven't taken the college course, but I want you to take the College Boards. I'll recommend you for English. And I've talked to your other teachers, and although they won't recommend you they'll mark your application consent. It's too late, really, but the thing can be arranged. I want you to so much, to show you what you can do. I'm not trying to persuade you to go to college. I know you are after something else right now. But just take that English exam. I want you to see how well you come out on it. I know you will. You'll get a high mark. And you can coach for the others. Leda! I want you to try."

"It's awfully kind of you to bother, but . . ."

"Don't say 'but.' Look here, you're leaving school and I want to tell you how much I've enjoyed reading with you this year. I want you to know that. You've got a good mind, Leda, a good mind. Don't throw it away. Go on and make something of it. It's a fine life, the life of the mind." It was strange, the incongruity of Norah Hunt's body and voice. Her body was grotesque; her voice was strong and moving.

Leda regarded her. Almost she wanted to do what she knew Miss Hunt wanted her to—take these examinations, pass them, go to college next year, begin the preparation for that life that they had talked of together. But Leda could not. She was committed to a salvation of herself, an establishment of herself upon the hills of power. The other life, Norah Hunt's life, seemed to her now easy; gentle. The other defied her, and frightened her, and she must conquer it.

"I wish I could take the exams, Miss Hunt, but I've got to go on a visit to Buzzard's Bay. To Marion Bentinck's," she said.

Norah Hunt gazed at her quietly, her eyes moving slightly in her face; moving over Leda's face. She lifted one fat hand as if to make a gesture; her hand fell. She stared a minute longer.

"*Buzzard's Bay!*" She spat the words out.

Then she lifted her hand again, shook hands with Leda, made a pleasant remark or two, and waddled off down the corridor. Leda never saw her again to speak to. Only on the platform at graduation she saw Norah Hunt's bulk on a chair, listening with that odd, grave air, compounded of comprehension and skepticism, to the address to the graduating class.

Two weeks later, when she was driving through the Fenway with Nicola, they passed the hall of Simmons' College where the girls were going in to take College Board examinations. The morning was sweltering hot; the dust lay on the leaves. The windows of the halls within stood open. Suddenly Leda wanted to be in there, as if she were wanting an apple to set her teeth in hard; she felt craving for the work. She knew that she could do well; even the examinations she was not recommended for she could pass. But it was too late. School was over forever. Nicola's roadster slid on along the curve of the Fenway and left the big brick hall behind, and in a minute Leda forgot it. They were going to pick up Nicola's bag on Commonwealth Avenue and drive down to the Cape for a visit together to Marion Bentinck. It was going to be a house-party. There would be sailing, and tennis, and parties in the evenings. Leda had a lot of new clothes. She was full of purpose; this visit, all visits, were training; proving-grounds for her will to power.

## CHAPTER XXI

LEDA sat waiting in James March's Buick coupe, outside the Peter Bent Brigham hospital. It was late February, in the midst of a winter thaw. Water dripped from the trees along the street and from the gutters of the building, on to the blackened, pitted snow; as cars drove by they ploughed through lakes of slush that splashed up on either side. The late afternoon sun shone through the clouds over Brookline; a dreary, smug atmosphere; the weariness, resignation, muddy sunshine of late winter afternoons. Leda felt as if she had known a thousand of these peculiar winter afternoons when the air, the quality of light, seems to commit one to a life of boredom; a comfortable life where one is content. There was something significant about this sort of afternoon; she felt that if she were to give in to it she would be lost forever and succumb to a lifetime of quiet, sunshiny afternoons in Boston, with cars splashing by forever in the slush.

She lit another cigarette from the old one, and threw the butt out of the window; she watched it float down the rushing flood in the gutter, turning slowly round and round. She was impatient at being left so long while James paid his calls at the hospital; at the same time she had a feeling she ought to be taking this time to see what she wanted to do about James. But it was always impossible to think at the times best suited for thinking; clear thought came inconveniently, startlingly, at times devoted to other things— at a concert when there was music to be listened to; at a party among the babel of voices and the whirl of color; in the middle of a conversation. Now she had been sitting here for half an hour waiting for James; she realized how ideal was the moment for deciding whether she wanted to marry him— or whether the other impulse, the impatience with him and with all he stood for, Boston, medicine, was worthy of action, was the truer instinct to follow. He had not asked her to marry him, but she knew that he was going to; sometimes she felt the wildest irritation from her very knowledge of his intentions, at the things she knew he would say when he proposed to her, and the way he would kiss her. She anticipated that serious look in his eyes, and it made her flesh crawl with impatience. Already she had lived through the moment of his proposal a dozen times, and turned hot with exasperation, and thrown back at him a variety of stinging dismissals. She had said "I loathe the very sound of your idiotic voice," and "What made you ever think that I would marry a Bostonian fool like yourself?" She had said seriously, "I think that would be impossible. Too many Bostonians have married their cousins, and look at them."

Actually she knew that no such consideration as that would deter her from marrying James if she came to the conclusion that that was what she wanted to do. She was, leaving out her instinctive emotions—and she intended to leave them out—quite open to the possibility that such a move might be the wisest she could make. He bored her; it was inconceivable that only a year before, when she was still in school, she had thought him important and desirable. But at the same time she saw the advantages that would attach to being his wife, and besides she felt a sort of weary affection for him. He was like this kind of afternoon; eternal, and sunny, and depressing.

Leda leaned her head back on the seat cushion in an attempt to relax; she was tingling with irritation; with an impulse to get out of the car and walk away through the slush very fast and never see James or his gentle eyes or hear his voice and laugh again. When she felt this way, when she was especially annoyed or impatient at waiting for him, she wished she could hurt him. She wished she knew someone evil, whom she could prefer to James, to show him that his loving kindness was really the most cloying stupidity. She would like to shock him, to outrage him; not from any desire to sin but only to explain to him how boring he was.

And yet it was necessary not to be stupid about this.

If she married James she would have a good deal of money and an excellent position in Boston society. She would have formed the nucleus of power. Supposing that she was to spend the rest of her life in Boston, she could do no better than to marry James; she could make no better start toward bringing the society of the city to heel—and that was what she had always wanted to do; she told herself that she must not forget that; it was possibly unintelligent to let slip this chance to accomplish all the frantic hopes of her youth. . . . Her mind slipped away from the argument, already tired of it, to fragmentary scraps of thought.

Three hundred parties in a hundred nights. . . . Billy Lossez's orchestra. . . . Bert Loew's orchestra. . . . Paul Whiteman at the Copley-Plaza for a ball given by people who made patent-medicine and owned horses. . . . A Senior from New York telling her she was the most beautiful girl he had ever seen. . . . Five Sophomores serenading her under Nicola's windows in the early morning of the city street; the sparrows chirping on the Mall as the sky grew bright. . . . The dances in the holidays in New York, staying with friends of Nicola's on Park Avenue; Sherry's, Pierre's, the Ritz, the Plaza. . . . And Nicola's friend, Janet Bellingham, of New York, asking Leda to stay with her, Leda alone; that had showed so wonderfully that she could make these friends for herself, friends outside of and transcending Boston. . . . All the football games in the fall, the great roaring push of people over Anderson Bridge, the flasks of whisky in the Stadium, the man who was in love with her playing on the winning Harvard team. . . . The dancing at teatime at Shepard's Colonial with Lewis Grainger, the best dancer in Harvard; strange quick little steps beautifully executed, and his olive face smiling down at her as they danced. . . . Nicola saying as they undressed in the light of dawn after a party, "Everyone's jealous because you are the most successful debutante this year." . . . Mark Hamill carrying her picture in the back of his watch. . . .

That was the difficulty of being a debutante in Boston: all the men you met were still in Harvard, unable to marry and unsure of their prospects; she knew that she was lucky to have James, a grown-up man with a fortune, in love with her; none of the other debutantes had found anyone as eligible. There was the alternative of waiting until your Harvard beaux graduated, made money, and then marrying one of them; but she knew now that she did not want to wait. She saw the advantages of marriage. She saw nothing valuable in remaining single; she did not want to go to the parties year after year, a post-debutante and a post-post-debutante and a post-post-post-debutante. James was ideal, equipped with all she wanted; but he was such a fool. . . .

The banjo player in Lossez's orchestra who played "That Certain Feeling," whenever she entered a party for the first time. . . . Buying clothes in New York with Nicola in the fall—eight evening dresses besides the brocade *robe de style*, twelve pairs of shoes, two tailored suits, the black tea-dancing dress with pleats, and the deep purple crepe, three woollen dresses with leather belts. . . . The amethyst dress when she wore it first, at the dance Aunt Grace had given, not the early one on the North Shore in October, but the big one in late November; and the two hundred presents of flowers. . . . Betsy Jekyll, whom Leda's mother had made her ask to Aunt Grace's dance; how strange she had seemed, dancing cheek to cheek with those slick-haired inferior Sophomores, in that skin-tight green beaded dress, her hair in little points pulled out on each cheek; that imitation jewelry. They had a moment's conversation in the dressing-room; Betsy was so blatant, so "peppy" in her own phrase; it was queer to think that she had once been Leda's best friend. "And how is Maizie? . . . Oh I'm so sorry she's not well *yet*." . . . "And how's your mother?" "And how's your father?" . . . It was all over, and nothing left of it; just a little jazz-girl with a high laugh. . . . Nicola and Leda receiving with Mrs. Kruger at the party for both of them. Nicola was always the same, always calm and polite and conventional, and yet with that ineffable style; always in exquisite taste; not popular with the men at parties, but liked, admired, a grand girl, and such a perfect friend for Leda; there was still something about her that Leda envied, that she had not mastered; something that was absolute security, self-assurance; Nicola could not be upset, she could not be hurt; there was something about her that was the grand manner. . . . James sending her gardenias every morning; that had seemed such a glamorous, un-Bostonian thing to have happen, and everyone had talked about it, envied it; but now. . . .

James had been in love with her since the party his mother gave for her on the North Shore in the fall; he had gone to debutante parties where he was the oldest man, and had taken her out to dinner and told her bit by bit all about himself. She had known all about him; he was her own cousin and she knew his history; but he told her about all the girls he had ever been in love with; narratives that he went on with a little at a time. She realized he was laying his life open to her. It was with each additional thing that she learned about him that she grew more and more contemptuous of him. There was something repulsive about his honesty; sometimes she thought that she might be able to feel attracted to him if he could once tell her of something really wrong that he had done. But it was all virtuous, honorable, boring. He was so Bostonian, and she was impatient of Boston and of him. She did like the idea of putting Boston in its place, ruling it; her old dream; and he was the means by which it might be done. But those gentle eyes; that considerateness; there was nothing in him that caught her breath, and more and more, now that the rush of parties had subsided for the winter, she felt the itch to be surprised, provoked, excited. In a way it had all been so much easier than she had expected, her success; there had been no fight to any of it, nobody had opposed her, all the old fears and panics had been reasonless; she had been backed by the Marches and upheld by Nicola, and nobody had denied her anything. And yet this could not be all; she distrusted her victory because it had been easy, and doubted that it was a victory after all. Perhaps, she felt, she had missed the way to triumph, mistaken her success for what she really wanted; she had an uneasy sense that she was missing something.

Perhaps she was being stupid about James; perhaps it was a perversity in her that created the impulse to deny him. She did not trust her instincts, she never had. Perhaps James was her wisest course. She wished she knew.

Lying back against the seat, she opened her eyes and saw him coming out of the hospital. He was a tall man, slender, dark, in a gray tweed overcoat cut straight and loose and a gray felt hat. He carried a black bag. He looked toward the car and waved at Leda; his dark moustache widened with his smile. She stared at him, watched his way of walking, and did not wave back.

He came across the street and opened the car door. He stowed his bag behind the seat and got in beside Leda, tucking his overcoat under his legs and slamming the door. He started the car and smiled at Leda at the same time.

"You've been a very . . . long . . . time," she said without smiling.

"Isn't it hell? People get sick just to spite me." He looked at her beside him and suddenly switched off the motor and took his hat off. He hung it on the gear stick and leaned back, looking in front of him at the wheel he held in his hands.

"Now what are we going to do?" she asked. She pulled her Persian lamb coat around her.

"Did I ever tell you you were perfectly beautiful? Did I ever tell you you've got night-black hair and skin like a camellia?"

"You're very poetic, aren't you?"

"Please don't laugh at me."

"I'm just restless from the long wait. I think I deserve to be taken somewhere and given a good time now."

"I'll take you anywhere in just a minute. Look."

"What?"

"I'm in love with you. What do you know about that?" He smiled at her with such sweetness that she shivered with repulsion.

"And I want to marry you. There you are. Would you be horribly disappointed not to change your name at all? It would be very economical, you know, to use your old things and all that."

She leaned her head back and examined the ends of her gloves. She did not know what to say. She wished that some answer would come to her with a certain amount of finality.

"I've been thinking you did like me rather a lot. . . . You get mad at me and I don't think we do that unless we love someone."

"Don't say 'we'," she interrupted. "I can't stand it when you get medical and say 'we' and talk about a 'group'."

"Maybe you do think I'm ponderous, darling. But you know I'm not actually so old, just you're so miraculously young to be so strange and beautiful and old for your age. I'm a damned fool. I ought not to be sitting here talking to you. I know perfectly well I ought to tell you that God damn it, you'll marry me and shut up. But I don't feel that way. Perhaps I'm afraid of you. Please marry me."

She continued to stare at her finger-ends.

"Suppose you think about it. I don't mean for you to crash through with your mind made up this instant. I think we could have a good life. You know the money part is all right. I'm very lucky, of course. I don't think that in the long run you'd have to worry much about practice, you know it's research I want to go after and that's easier on the wife. I want to go to Vienna in a year or two and we could live over there for a while."

She looked at him, her imagination caught. He felt the difference in her regard and took her hand quickly.

"Darling, I love you so much. I want you to have everything that goes with the way you are. I know you are bored with Boston. I am too in a way, but I love it and I think you will when you grow up; it's in us to love it. It's a pretty good place in the long run. It doesn't consume you, bleed you like New York and it isn't ugly like most cities. It nourishes you, I think, and lets you be an individual. But we wouldn't have to live in Boston always. Vienna, and we could build a house up near Mamma's —I know you like it there."

She felt now tangibly the advantages in a life with James. She was not looking at him, but through him, towards a life she had not quite realized before: herself adored and indulged by him, given all that she needed for the conquest of power, gaining all that she desired; forcing a world to her will.

"I'll . . . think about it," she said.

He put his arms quickly around her and covered her face with his. She felt an inescapable revulsion from the touch of his lips on her own. His moustache disgusted her; but at the same time she was somehow attracted by her own feeling of repulsion, and did not push him away. She felt slim and immaculate in his arms, as if he were incapable of truly touching her; she felt removed and impersonal, and watched with fascination his own loss of self. It gave her a queer feeling to hear him breathe, to see the top of his head as he dropped it to her breast, and feel his arms tighten around her. It was almost as if she were not there at all. She imagined that she was somewhere else; this was a shell, of crystal and porcelain, that he embraced, and herself, her reality, stood outside and saw the man lost in love, in passion, believing that he held a woman in his arms.

"I hope your colleagues in the hospital are interested," she said.

He took away his arms and smiled good-naturedly. She watched him straighten his coat.

"Now will you take me down to the Copley-Plaza?" she said. "I told Nicola we would meet her there. She's there with Dicky."

"I like that Dicky," he said as he drove through the slapping slush. "Is Nicola going to marry him, do you think?"

Leda felt herself stiffen.

Dicky Fenton was Nicola's only faithful beau, and he took her everywhere, but it was inconceivable that she should marry him. Leda almost hated James for thinking that Nicola might. It was just like him. He did not realize what Nicola was, what Dicky was beside her. Almost she felt enraged. She spoke slowly.

"How could she possibly marry a creature like that? . . . Nicola is

fond of him, of course, as one is fond of a wretched little mongrel dog,
but to imagine that she could marry him is as if you thought that the
Queen of England could marry a Cockney." Leda had to control herself
to keep from trembling.

"All right, darling. Don't bite me. I didn't mean to insult your friend.
But I think Dicky's a nice kid, nicer than most. I think Nicola'd do very
well to marry him, I honestly do."

"He comes from Newton," Leda said slowly and viciously.

James laughed.

"That's pretty bad. Does he wear a clean shirt every day?"

"You simply don't understand," she said with all her contempt. "You
don't know anything about Nicola."

"I hope I do," he said gravely.

When they came up to the table in the ballroom where Nicola and
Dicky were sitting, Leda felt suddenly, shockingly, the desire to run away.
Adèle Macomb was sitting there with them. Leda had not seen her to
speak to, beyond a moment in a dressing-room or two, all winter. She had
driven Adèle out of her mind and believed that she had passed the need
for fear of her. But now the fear was alive.

There she sat, confident and invulnerable, in a small black hat, her heavy
legs prominent in flesh-colored silk; but somehow even those ugly legs
gave Leda no feeling of superiority; because they were Adèle's, it was
almost enviable to have such legs. Adèle's pretty, proud face smiled charmingly. Her voice, when she spoke, had a rapid, musical tone.

They sat down. The music was playing the dance tunes of the year, and
at the table they were drinking tea and eating cinnamon toast. Nicola
smiled at Leda with the calm solidity of their friendship; then she went
back to talking to Dicky Fenton. Dicky was a bond salesman, not more
than twenty-two years old. He had not gone to college, and his family
were undistinguished, and Leda could not imagine where Nicola had
met him. But now he was her constant companion; she had invited him
to all the dances that winter; he was enjoying new friends, new experiences,
through Nicola. He was short and stocky, ruddy in the face, with a disarming, childish look.

Leda was stiff with tension. Simply having Adèle at the table cast over
her the veil of her childhood diffidence. Now suddenly she was glad to
have James beside her; she looked at him with real gratitude; his presence
meant something, established her, restored in her a confidence that had
evaporated at sight of Adèle Macomb. She found herself smiling encouragingly at him. He was not bad: he was sure of himself, and good
looking; she realized for an instant that he was a natural inhabitant in the
world of people, and always had been; all that had been so difficult for
her had been birthright to him. Any place that he might ever find himself
in during his life would seem easy to him; he could like it or dislike it.

"How did you like the Barneys'?" Adèle asked. Her arms rested carelessly on the table, their bracelets turned sidewise against the cloth; her

voice was rapid and careless. Her face and shoulders expressed the whole attitude and manner of their year; the hair was cut short, shingled; the eyes were indifferent, the nose turned up in a sheer pure curve, the mouth was painted orange. Her neck was thin and long, and she wore a choker-necklace of immense artificial pearls which fell over the straight neckline of her white crepe blouse, cut after a model of Vionnet's which was imitated everywhere; there were hollows below the collar-bones, inside the shoulder muscles, as a result of her posture; her chest was flat and hardly marked by the faintest peaks of breasts.

"I thought it was amusing," Leda said.

"My!" James remarked.

"That wasn't champagne," Adèle said. "Jack says it was alcohol mixed with white grapejuice. *Honestly*."

"It was wonderful in Washington after all that sort of thing, wasn't it, Leda?" Nicola asked in her low, calm voice. She and Leda had visited a girl in Washington during Christmas and gone to two Embassy parties. Leda smiled at Nicola. Nicola was her friend, not Adèle's. Nicola was someone to be envied by anyone, even Adèle. And Nicola liked Leda best. That must mean something. Leda wished she could be indifferent to Adèle's old scorn and coldness; she was more successful in coming out, she was more beautiful, she had Nicola's admiration; but she could not. She wondered in desperation when this girl would cease to haunt her; why did she care so much?

"They served marvellous champagne at the Hungarian Legation," she said trying to be indifferent. "Supper all night with plover's eggs, and gold braid on the footmen, and a Tsigane orchestra that played in a separate ballroom from the jazz band—Viennese waltzes. It was divine."

"Really?" Adèle stared at her. Although Adèle belonged to a newer family in Boston her establishment was complete; although she belonged to a tradition that had apologized for Boston, anything that was Adèle's was right and desirable; that was to be seen. If Adèle had not been to Washington, then Washington was not worth going to.

"Yes, it really was," Nicola said, laughing her comfortable laugh. She was laughing at Adèle. Leda tried to imagine what it would be like to laugh at Adèle. That would be the way to annihilate her, of course. It was something to remember. She would have to do it artificially, as a technique. She knew how that was done. All that she had accomplished had been done thus: she had vanquished shyness by assuming a surface confidence which had grown nearly real; she had acquired all that was her attraction by manifesting it superficially—and the acting stuck: you became what you pretended to be.

"Nicola, I want you to be on my committee for the Junior League thing," Adèle said. She did not look at Leda.

"Nothing would induce me to get up for anything the Junior League does. It's always at dawn," Leda said. She meant to try the trick. She meant to laugh at Adèle. But Adèle turned her large, contemptuous eyes on Leda.

"I meant Nicola, not you," she said. "I know you never had any school spirit and the same thing goes for the Junior League."

James spoke with his cigarette wagging in his mouth.

"Leda's great charm is her lack of what's called school spirit," he said. "God protect me from militant and school-spirited females." He looked with amusement at Leda beside him.

Adèle closed her mouth. Leda felt a stab of gratitude again to James. He had saved her now. She thought that after all she had better marry James. He would be able to save her always. It wasn't as if she was qualified to choose a man more appealing to her. She needed someone drowned in love for her, who would fight her battles. She was not an ordinary girl. She needed so much help. James could always give it to her. She had better take him while she could. A man who had more attraction for her might not be so valuable. And Leda could not be a free spirit. She must plan her victory as she could. She smiled at James.

"I've got to go," Nicola said. "Mummy's having thirty for dinner and I have to talk French to a fat man."

"I want you to come up and see my portrait," Adèle said. "I'd like to see what you thought of it. I think he's made me sort of strange looking. Lambert Rudd. But he's supposed to be so good. I don't know anything about that sort of thing," she said with pride.

"Leda, will you? I really ought to go home, but I haven't seen you for two days, and I'll go if you will," Nicola said.

"I don't know."

"You come, Leda," Adèle commanded. "You know about those things. I'd like to see if you think it's a good portrait."

It was the ancient shame. The moment Adèle commanded, the moment she wanted you, asked for you, you melted like wax and were all pleasure and vanity that she wanted you.

"I've met Lambert Rudd," Leda said, drawing on her gloves. "He married a girl I knew. . . . He probably wouldn't remember me. I was so high."

"Oh . . . he married one of those Jekyll girls, didn't he," Adèle said with that look of cold amazement. "I believe this one is sort of awful."

"I never really *knew* her," Leda said. "Just used to see her around."

"Yes, you were a great friend of the younger one, weren't you? I remember you were that year she got into Sheraton. Well, come on," Adèle said. She got up; she stood upon her pillar-like legs; she was young and very modern; indescribably attractive.

As soon as she got into the studio Leda saw that Adèle was in love with the young artist. She saw as well that he was not in love with anybody, that he was dark and impatient, laughing with a sort of rage, and intolerant of everything. He was good-looking and magnetic. He walked with confident nervousness about his studio and talked in a low voice with his lips held close together; his beak of a nose stood out in silhouette against the vast dim window; he was tall and spare, with black hair growing in a pointed peak up from his forehead. He joked with Adèle, jollied her as if she were a little girl; but he was not at all in love with her. And she, Adèle suddenly was eager, anxious, forming her remarks to please him, smiling at him, parading her friendship with him and retelling little anecdotes. Leda sat quite still on the low couch in the shadow beside Nicola and stared quietly at him, listened to Adèle chattering.

It was a huge place. Old canvases were stacked against the wall, there was a confusion of tables covered with open boxes of pastels, paint boxes, cigar boxes full of paint-tubes, piles of papers slightly drawn upon. Leda liked it. She had a curious sense of familiarity with the atmosphere of work; she knew, watching him, that she understood Lambert Rudd. He was a painter, and about artists there was never any of the mysterious, baffling potency that so clothed the inhabitants of the world of people. She was not at all surprised when he paused in walking restlessly about the studio and stood in front of her.

"Where have I seen you?" he said abruptly.

He did not smile. He simply looked down at her, and she felt a physical impact from his look.

"In Hampton, at the Jekylls' house," she said coolly. ". . . . I like the portrait of Adèle. I like the composition."

"It's interesting, isn't it. Hell of a portrait. All composition and no Adèle. Hey, fat girl! Next time get a sculptor and not a painter. You've got a noble build but I couldn't fit your legs into the picture. No offense," he said laughing. He reached over and slapped Adèle on the behind.

It was unbelievable. Leda watched Adèle swallow her obvious humiliation. James, in a big chair, laughed.

"The life of an artist," he said. "You're lucky, Rudd. You wouldn't like being a medico."

"What do you mean at the Jekylls'," Lambert Rudd fired at Leda. "Where at the Jekylls'?"

"I was young."

"Oh, young. As opposed. . . ."

"Yes, as opposed to now. I am a lot older than I am," Leda said.

"Yes, you are. Will you sit for me? I want to paint you."

Leda glanced toward Adèle.

"Yes, I'd like to."

"God damn it, I could make something good. Lean over this way," he said, dragging a lamp over to the couch. "The God-damnedest bones in your face. Where the hell did you get those cheekbones?"

Leda shrugged her shoulders. She half shut her eyes and looked at nothing. She had an instinct not to respond with any excitement to this man. She felt him hanging over her, peering at her face, his mouth shut; his vitality carried through the air like a current.

"Smile, can't you?" he said.

"I can when I feel like it."

"You're a tough little thing."

The others were all talking; Nicola was leaning toward James, and Adèle's friend who had been at the Copley-Plaza was sitting on the arm of James's chair. Only Adèle was a little in the shadow; Leda felt her listening to every word, watching them.

"Listen, I'm supposed to turn up at home for dinner," he said. "But I can telephone. . . . You have dinner with me tonight."

"I can't," she said.

"If it's. . . . My wife is used to my not getting home. . . . I work a lot here at night. . . ."

"No, I'm going out to dinner."

"A debutante."

"Yes, why not?"

"All right. What night are you going to have dinner with me? What were you doing at the Jekylls', anyway? You never saw me."

"Perhaps not. I was playing dolls," she said mockingly, without smiling.

"I said what night are you going to dinner with me? Can't you answer me?"

"Yes, I'll have dinner next week."

"Monday."

"Yes, Monday." She wondered why she said that. Perhaps it would be better for what she was doing, with Adèle there listening, not to consent to dine with him at all. That would be the ultimate shame to this girl whom at last, after all those years, she was able to hurt back.

But she thought not; she had better see him, dine with him. The thought crossed her mind that he was a married man, and that she might be criticized. But Adèle could not criticize her; it was written in her face that she would give her eyes to go to dinner with this man.

In a little while they went out into the February twilight. The snow was freezing into points of ice along the ruts. The six of them wandered slowly, talking, up along Ipswich Street, and a street-car rumbled by, full of yellow lights. Dicky Fenton hailed a taxi for Nicola.

"I'm dreadfully late," she said. "Goodbye. Thanks for taking us up here, Adèle. Leda, darling, I'll call you in the morning. Goodbye, James, Ben. . . ." She disappeared into the taxi and for a moment her blonde lovely face was lighted by the cab-light, calm and wise; Dicky jumped in after her and slammed the door.

"He's nice, Dicky Fenton," Adèle said in a low voice. They all paused on the sidewalk and shook hands in front of James's car. "I didn't know he was so nice."

But Leda was not thinking of what she said. She was seeing the pallor of Adèle's face, and feeling the strangest, inner laughter.

"Goodbye, Adèle," she said. For the first time in her life she felt stronger than Adèle. She could hardly keep from laughing out loud. It had all been so easy. Why did she always feel that other people's lives were more fortunate and better arranged than hers? . . . For she was winning, she was a conqueror. She could destroy those whom she hated.

"Goodbye, Leda."

Leda got into the car with James. She was almost unaware of his presence beside her, she was so busy with her own thoughts.

He settled his felt hat down over his head, without speaking.

"Are you going to dinner with Rudd?" he asked Leda, after they had driven out into the Fenway and were on the road to Hampton.

"Next week."

"Listen, darling. I have nothing against the guy. Only you know he's married. And I guess he's crazy, and if you don't mind I'd rather you didn't go out with him."

"But I do mind."

"I don't want the girl I'm going to marry to be seen around with a fellow of his reputation."

". . . What makes you think I'm going to marry you?"

"Why. . . ." His voice was filled with his hurt. "Nothing, Leda. I didn't mean to assume a possessive attitude. Darling, it's just that I love you and I want you always to have the best of everything."

"Thank you."

"Don't be mad at me. Look, I want you to think about this. Realize that I love you, and that I think I understand you, and how much we could get out of life together. You're more of a person than I am, Leda, but you're so young and I'd be so good to you. Think it over. You'll never get anybody who will love you as much as I do," he said gravely. She heard the words dispassionately, doubting them. She believed that a great many men would love her as much, and that they would be better men than James. . . . Lambert Rudd would love her more, she thought. . . . She wondered with a feeling of excitement what he would be like, in love with her.

"I don't think cousins ought to marry," she said.

"I wondered if you'd say that. It's not so, you know; it's all right if the predominant traits are good and . . ."

"Their children are imbeciles," she said.

"Leda, ours wouldn't be. As a doctor I can promise you that."

"We aren't going to have any children," she said. "I really couldn't marry you, James. And I'm never going to have any children. I don't want any."

The car drove on over the freezing ruts, out from Boston towards Hampton, over the old road she knew so well. James was silent beside her, and she had forgotten him. Her mind was drunk with promise.

## CHAPTER XXII

"You see, I got married under false pretences. I shouldn't ever have married anyone. I'm not that kind. Apparently I'm too much for any one woman, too. I can't help it, I've got this damned energy, violence, and I've got to take it out on whoever's around. I don't want to give anyone a beating. But women can't take it—one woman. I suppose I'm a bastard. Only if I am then I think the boys back in the Renaissance were all bastards. I feel that way; all full of violence, stuff that has to come out. The world's different now, and a guy like me is a misfit. The world's fixed for gentle guys now, nice sensible men who go to bed at ten every night. And the women can't take anything that's stronger meat than that. I can't help giving any woman hell, I suppose."

Leda looked at Lambert as he walked up and down in front of her in the big, dim studio. Outside the immense window it was night, and a street light smeared the grimy panes with yellow. She lay relaxed against the pillows of the couch, playing with the pleats of her black dress.

They had had dinner, and he had talked steadily, and then they had come back here to his studio; she did not feel afraid of her unconventional action; she felt self-assured and confident. He was a strange person and she wanted to control his violence; she felt herself capable of understanding him and managing him by making him fall in love with her. She had never felt so strong and decisive. He was an artist, and she understood about that; he would see that she understood his feeling about the things he loved, he would see that she was as strong as he and stronger, he would be enmeshed by her and find himself helpless before her. All this raging violence burst from him because he was married to a woman who was not enough for him, whom he was not in love with. Leda was different; she felt like a magnet that was drawing him; she sat there absolutely still and willed him to her power.

"Your wife's older than you are, isn't she?" she asked. "That must make her less strong than you."

"She can't help it," he said. "She can't help any of it. God knows I'm not crabbing about her, I'm not saying 'My wife doesn't understand me.' You wanted to know why I was so restless and I'm telling you. There's nowhere for me to put all that I've got. There's work, and there's women, and my wife can't take it, and God help me there's something God-damned gone to hell about my work."

"All women aren't weaker than you. There are women who are ten times as strong as you," she said quietly.

"All right. You mean you, I suppose."

"No!" She was thrown a little off balance and spoke sharply. "Not me. But any really vital woman has got ten times as much strength as any man."

"Do you think so?" he looked piercingly at her with his dark, wild eyes. Then he wheeled and went on walking up and down. "Hell no. That's what women always pull on a man—'Oh, I'm strong, I can take care of you, I can take all you can put out, darling. . . .' Jesus. And then you find that after all they're just as weak and whimpering as any other woman, begging to get their sleep, asking for mercy. Christ, I wish what you said was true. I'd look around for one of those women. But I know it isn't so."

"You don't know. You're married to a woman who's older than you and hasn't got your vitality. What do you know about young girls?"

"Young? I know a lot about young girls. I'm crazy mad about youth.

There isn't a girl in the world who's young enough for me, young and strong enough. God damn it, I think I'm going insane. I don't want anything to do with age. I want to fight like hell with a big, strong young girl I can lick the hell out of and who will come right back for more."

Leda laughed. Her eyes sparkled.

"You couldn't lick me," she said. "You couldn't even get started fighting with me." She laughed with her head tipped back, watching his burning dark face, the point of black hair growing sharply back from his forehead.

"Oh, you. It's got around to you. I wondered when."

She went on laughing. It was strange, she had always been so sensitive to insult; what he had said was insolent and yet she liked it. It made it more exciting. She liked saying things that provoked him, and watching him snap back in reply. . . .

"You're adolescent, aren't you," she said. "That was the most adolescent thing to say."

With all the men she had ever known conversation had been a polite thing with no shocks or surprises. This was different. This was like fighting.

"I've always been a lot older than my age," he said. "I've felt like a man as long as I can remember, and I hate it. Nobody can take it."

"You must have known awfully weak people," she said.

"No. They're strong when I meet them, I guess, but I seem to knock them all to pieces. I know I'm a bastard," he said bitterly. "I know I'm an unfeeling brute, and a son-of-a-bitch, with no regard for the delicacy of the female physique and the God-damned female nerves. Christ, why do there have to be women? If there weren't any women I might be able to do some work."

"What's the matter with your work? Why aren't you satisfied with it?"

"You wouldn't know anything about it."

"Oh yes I would."

"Oh no you wouldn't! You're just another woman. What the hell do you care about my work?"

"I'm much more interested in your work than I am in you."

He stared at her, pausing again in his pacing. Then he began to walk again but without speaking, with his head down, his profile dark and as predatory as a hawk's against the gray window. He came towards Leda, abstractedly, and sat down on the couch beside her. She was stiff and ready to start away if he should touch her. But he did not seem to be thinking of her. He propped his chin in his hands and stared into the looming emptiness of the studio.

". . . . I know I'm good," he said. "I've got as much or more talent as any man in the country. I didn't think so for a while. I got to feeling I was just rotten to begin with, but now I see that it's all there, it's just I don't live right. All this talk about naughty artists is bull. An artist ought to be so damned crazy about his work and so busy doing it that he hasn't got any time to pinch girls' knees. He ought to be living a big full life full of his work, giving it the works and expressing all he's capable of to the last drop in him. But he's still a man. That's why painters have wives.

It's his wife's job to take care of that part of him, do a good job on his physical life so that he doesn't think about it, so he can give his guts to his work. But what the hell. The whole thing's such a question of balance. If the wife can't put out what he needs, you'd say he could just sock it to his painting and do all the better for it. But it doesn't work that way. Sex has to be sex, and then you're rested and renewed and have more to give your work. I'm a crazy fool going around with a wild itch that I can't get out in my work. I know the stuff I need to know, I've got my technique where I want it and I'm good as hell on color. But I don't *see* any more. The damned thing's all blurred over with the other thing that's on my mind, and you can't paint what you see if it's got sex all over the top of it. You ought to be boiling inside, rested and satisfied but still howling with energy; you ought to see as coolly as ice, absolutely strictly, analytically. And then having seen it, give the whole of yourself to painting the hell out of it. That's the way. But my Christ, all I do is worry about my wife's health; Jesus, I *do* care how she feels, I want her to get the hell well. But I don't know how to be a nurse, do I? I can't help it if I'm not a gentle, considerate guy. I just don't know how. I know I'm a bastard. I go around ruining people's lives. I ought not to have been born. I don't belong today. There isn't anywhere to put it. Jesus, I've *tried* being quiet and controlled and orderly. It just won't work. I go nuts. Christ, I hate the word order. The word control. The hell with them. Listen, I don't want to be a monster and ruin people's lives. But Jesus Christ, I'm made the way I am!"

His voice rose as he finished, to a kind of agony of impatience. He threw his arms up behind his head restlessly and leaned his head back on them.

"You don't understand a word I'm saying, do you," he said.

"Yes," Leda said. "I understand all about that."

"You're just a little Boston debutante, aren't you? You're shocked to the core at the way I talk, aren't you? Naughty words. That awful artist. Listen, baby, I'm just as Boston as you are. I was brought up on the beautiful yellow sands of Manchester, God help me."

"What makes you think all Boston people are sissies? How do you know it's not all surface control? Bostonians believe in control. But they're pretty hard and tough inside. I think tougher than people from other parts of the country, who don't seem so proper on top."

He stared at her.

"Listen," he said. "Are you like me?"

"No. I'm stronger than you are."

"Like hell you are."

"Much."

"Don't you ever feel fear, agony, craziness?"

"No," she said, and she believed it. She was so surging with energy and confidence that it was actually inconceivable to her that she had ever been afraid of anything in her life.

"Maybe you're right. If you are, I certainly envy you. Maybe there are tough women. But I don't believe it. You're a hard little thing, I can see that," he said, turning his head and staring into her face, not two feet away. She held herself rigid. "I can see you're selfish and self-centered as hell. That's a kind of toughness. But you couldn't be a woman; you couldn't take it from a man, all he wanted. You'd get tired, and your back would ache, and you'd want to go to bed early. You bet. You wouldn't feel equal to producing a child a year, would you? You know, it's funny, it turns out a man wants a woman that can spawn, I mean spawn. It gets to be kind of an obsession. It makes a man feel his maleness if he can keep a woman with child. What a way to talk to a Boston debutante. I wonder why I am talking to you this way, anyhow. Maybe you are tougher. You haven't turned a hair. And you're not excited, either, are you? You probably couldn't be excited. Cold as ice. A modern woman, all face and grab-grab. No brains, but that doesn't matter because I certainly can't use brains in a woman. I apologize for talking the way I have been, baby. You can just put me down as insane. You'll be right. You can tell your little friends about how awful I am. You don't have to see me again, you see. This will be a night to tell your grandchildren about. Except you won't have any grandchildren, will you? You couldn't break down and be a woman, could you?"

"I could if I wanted to," Leda said. "I could do anything I wanted to."

"Maybe you could. Maybe you could. . . . God help me, you may be right." He sighed, and leaned over on the couch against her. His arms pulled her close to him. "Lovely baby. Lovely, dark, beautiful baby. So young. You're so young. I want to eat your mouth. I want to drink your youth out of you. God, it's so good to feel you, all young and cool."

Suddenly she was paralyzed with a terror she had not anticipated. She had not expected to feel his arms around her. She had not had time. . . . His hot, hard lips against her mouth, his heavy, hard chest pushing against her: this was something she had never for a moment dreamt of in all her life, a new and undesired panic. This was not being kissed, being held: this was something that attacked self-confidence and power. She felt that in a second she would cease to be her precious, integral self. She would melt into some vast, writhing sea of humanity, all women. . . . All that she loved, all herself, was being battered, was tottering.

She slipped through his arms and stood up. She shook herself delicately. Lambert let himself slide over and lie still and inert on the couch, staring up at her.

"Just a coldy, of course," he said. "I did tell you so, didn't I?"

The terrible instant was over. Her safety slipped around her again like a garment.

"Why do you say I'm cold?" she asked. She pushed back her heavy, slippery hair with both hands; she stretched.

He held out his hands expressively, without speaking.

"I think it's a little silly to say I'm cold just because I wouldn't let you kiss me," she said. "I only told you I could be anything, if I wanted to be it."

"Yeah, I see. You mean, you have to be in love, before the sanctity of your lips shall be given to the lucky man, etcetera, etcetera. Or rather, I am saving the most precious thing I have for the man I marry, huh?"

"You said that. I didn't."

"No. You didn't. Well then, what? Explain why you aren't cold, for poppa."

She shrugged her shoulders and went over to where her coat lay.

As she lifted it she heard him walk across the floor to her, and she stiffened.

"Look at me," he said, pulling her around by the shoulders. "What would make you want to be a woman?"

"Just wanting to. Just feeling that way about a man, I suppose."

"You suppose. . . . Well. . . ." He looked down into her face with that hard rigidity of face and mouth. "Please tell me whether you are shocked and outraged by the way I have talked."

"I told you I wasn't. I was interested."

"Kind of you. A Boston intellectual. Well. . . . Is it possible that you would dine with me again, or not?"

"I think I would like to."

"You little bitch," he said. "I'll make you want to be a woman for me."

"You won't if you say that to me," she said.

"Shocked."

"No. It just doesn't make me like you."

"You're the hardest, coldest little thing I ever saw," he said. "And you're beautiful as hell, and I'll make you crawl after me on your hands and knees."

She laughed.

When she got home she lay in bed thinking about Lambert Rudd. She forgot that one perilous instant. She had regained her safety, and meant to retain it, now that she perceived where danger lay, forever. She loved the feeling of full occupation of her faculties. She was sure she could make Lambert fall in love with her. There was the most acute pleasure in thinking of his being in love with her, hopelessly in love with her, and being in control of him. Herself would remain as still and impersonal as a ghost; he would not be able to touch her, to approach her; she would be crystal and cloud before him; she would always drift beyond his reach. There was an exciting, difficult time before her; she could not hope for anything more worthy of herself than this combat.

As the tension subsided she stretched her body against the cool, slippery sheets. She felt as young as Spring, and as strong as oceans. "I'm young," she whispered to herself in the dark.


## CHAPTER XXIII

NICOLA did not dislike Lambert. Nicola liked nearly everybody. It was always a puzzle and a marvel to Leda how Nicola, with her calm, polite, prattling conversation, her easy, comfortable laugh, could normalize any-one, reduce them suddenly to conformity. To Leda, alone, people often seemed almost grotesque in their individuality—dangerous, brilliant, or ugly and frightful. These same people, beneath the sun of Nicola's calm regard, suddenly seemed to melt before Leda's eyes and become more of the thousands of pleasant people that surrounded Nicola. Nicola was seldom surprised at anybody; she had small cosy categories for people, to make some distinction between them: there were 'lovely-looking' girls, and 'not-quite' girls and 'mad' young men and 'dreary' ones; but all of them seemed to be just about the same.

Was it that people acted differently for Nicola than for Leda? She never would be sure of that. She was very pleased, about a week after the night she had dined with him, to have tea with Nicola at Lambert Rudd's studio. It would have been even better to take him to Nicola's house, but that, she could see, he would never do. She was aware that something in her own temperament set a pattern behind her that was not conventional enough. What she wanted was to have him in love with her and unable to pry her out of her stable setting. She knew she had not behaved especially conservatively so far; very likely she should not have gone to his studio after dining with him; but all that was going to be changed now.

Nicola pervaded the atmosphere of the studio with fashionable convention. It was not that she was stuffy; she only made it seem normal for two young girls to be having tea with an artist in his studio; pleasant and absolutely unquestionable. She was gay and friendly; the light from the shadeless bulb shone brightly on her fair head as she made the tea; she asked questions about the pictures, questions not stupid, not informed, but simply what an assured person of moderate intelligence and a cosmopolitan background would ask. She immediately called Lambert by his first name, and laughed her comfortable chuckling laughter: and yet the afternoon was as correct, somehow, as if it were presided over by an Episcopal bishop.

It was amazing to see Lambert merge into the frame of an acceptable young man. It reduced her tension with him, her feeling of guardedness. Because obviously Nicola saw nothing in him to be afraid of, Leda was not afraid of him either; they all talked about New York, about Boston debutantes, about people they knew in common. Leda liked being with Nicola. She knew they looked well on the couch beside each other, both with slim silk legs, pearls twisted around their necks, hats like helmets down over their hair. With Nicola she felt irreproachable and conventional, a beautiful and sheltered young girl, and she loved the feeling. Alone, she too often felt that unwelcome wildness creeping out in her like plague; she was repelled by her own stabs of unorthodox restlessness. She did not want to be 'wild.' She did not want to have a bad reputation. She did not want in any way to be considered queer or unconventional. It was all very well to have friendships with unconventional people, like Lambert, but now more than ever in her life she would have to be careful. He was married, and he was a painter, and she knew how easy it would be to make people talk. And yet she was unable to still this desire to make him fall in love with her; she could not, somehow, leave him alone now that she had had this vision; it was all a question of ways and means, how to make him fall in love with her without compromising her own reputation. It had been nice to repay a little of her own hurt to Adèle. But now that was accomplished; now she could leave him alone—only she could not leave him alone.

The portrait of Adèle was in the center of the studio on an easel. Lambert had painted her in a scarlet dress against a background of silver; in her fingers she held the long string of pearls that was looped around her neck. Her head was half turned and her eyes regarded the world with confidence.

"It's just like her," Nicola said. "Our Adèle, all but the legs. I see you've wisely cut them off."

"I kind of admire her legs," Lambert said. "I cut it off at the knees because you girls wear your dresses so short, ugly as hell. Just the most unbeautiful thing you could do to yourselves, from a painter's point of view. That and your belts around the widest parts of your bodies."

Nicola laughed.

"But, Lambert, they're chic."

"A woman ought to wear a dress tight in at the waist to show the shape of her body, with a full skirt ending short enough to show some of her calf. You try to look like boys, and, by God, you even succeed in looking like boys."

Nicola laughed again; comfortably; dismissing the whole of what he had said.

"How amusing," she said. "Painters don't see things as they really are, do they?"

"On the contrary, painters do see things as they damned well are."

Leda had put her teacup down on the floor beside the couch and sat with her chin propped on her hand, looking from the picture to Lambert to Nicola. Somehow she had the feeling that there were two worlds represented here, two ways of life, and suddenly she thought that the portrait belonged more to Nicola's world than to Lambert's. She wondered why.

"But I do like your portrait, Lambert," Nicola said. "It's got style. It's really as good as a Laszlo."

"Oh my dear God," Lambert said. He clapped his hand to the top of his head. "You don't know what you're saying. I hope you don't know what you're saying."

"Come now. Laszlo is an extremely smart painter. Mummy has dozens of friends abroad who've had him do their portraits. He and the Duchess of Rutland do divine portraits."

"Oh my God," Lambert said. "You're killing me. I know this picture stinks but I didn't know it stank that bad. This is the last humiliation. I paint like Laszlo. I paint like Violet, Duchess of Rutland."

Nicola laughed, but Leda looked at Lambert.

"You mean you don't like this portrait of Adèle?"

He leaned forward.

"No. You see, I've done something unforgivable. I've painted her the way she wants to look, not the way I see her. The thing is, I didn't see her at all. I tried, but I've got something the matter with me. I don't see any more. So I did the easiest thing. I should have told her to get the hell out,

I couldn't paint her portrait; and gone back to drawing the antique or something. But I went ahead and used my nice little technique and painted a nice little picture of her looking just the way she wants to look, in that insipid pose. And I wish I could disown it. I wish I could rip it up before people looked at it and said 'Oh! what a—chic—portrait; we must get that clever Mr. Rudd to paint dear Peggy.' Do you know what I am? I'm a prostitute. And I haven't even the excuse of doing it just for money. I'm like a girl who'll sleep with anybody who asks her because she doesn't know how to say no."

Nicola laughed, as ever turning questionable remarks into jokes. Leda kept on looking at Lambert.

"If you feel that way you ought to rip it up," she said. "You ought not to be afraid to. You'll just get worse and worse. You've got to make a stand sometime. While you still care."

"How do you know about it?" Lambert said. "God damn it, how do you know about it? You're a debutante."

"If you really hate it you ought to rip it up," she said.

Lambert got up and went over to the big littered table and picked up a knife.

"All right, I will," he said.

"Lambert! Don't be insane," Nicola said.

"She's right. I'll get worse and worse." He stuck the knife into the middle of the canvas and pulled it down, leaving a long gash.

"I suppose this is the *vie de bohême*," Nicola said.

"I never felt less melodramatic in my life," Lambert said. "I feel as if I'd plucked up enough courage to take a bath after years. Thank you very much, Miss March. I owe you a debt."

"What I'd like to know," Nicola said. "Is how you're going to explain this to Adèle."

"She can get Laszlo to paint her," Lambert said. "She can get the Duchess of Rutland. I hope they make her look very very chic."

"You're absolutely stark, staring mad," Nicola said. "That was a very amusing picture."

"I know," Lambert said. "I could laugh my head off over it. Whee!"

"It wasn't a very good picture," Leda said.

"It was a perfectly frightful picture. And now, when are you going to start posing for me?"

"Any time you like," Leda said.

"Tomorrow morning. Ten."

Leda spent that night at Nicola's. After they came home from a dinner dance at the Somerset they lay in the two beds with the windows open to the late noises of the city and talked.

"Are you in love with him?" Nicola asked.

"I don't know."

Nicola's wise, calm voice said from the other bed, "He's in love with you. Of course there's the wife. But they're said to be not at all happy. I believe she's a bit dreary."

"Do you think I ought not to let him paint me?"

"Good gracious, no. Why on earth shouldn't he paint you? It's just if you were thinking about marrying him we should have to arrange things."

"Nicola!" Leda laughed. Nicola was so unexpected. She was so beautifully neat and orderly and conventional, and yet she could accept and make fit in, things which to other people, to Boston people, would not have seemed conventional at all. It was as if rather than avoiding the unconventional she assimilated it and made it conventional. Nicola made everything in her life seem like herself: calm, elegant. For instance, Dicky. . . . "Nicola, you're such an un-Boston kind of girl."

"So are you, Leda, of course. You couldn't be Bostonian if you tried. Sometimes it seems odd to me that you do try. Why do you bother?"

"I don't want to be criticized."

"You won't be criticized if your life sort of . . . comes off, you know what I mean. It seems to me it's all a question of knowing what you want and then carrying it off. If you behave as if you thought you were unquestionable you won't be questioned."

"Nicola, you know so much."

"No, I don't. I'm very stupid, compared to you, for instance. You know, I think Lambert really suits you. He's your sort of person. He wouldn't bore you the way James does. You're quite a bit alike, both Bostonians irritated with Boston. You remind me of each other."

"You mean you think it would be all right if I did marry him?"

"I must say I don't think you'd be breaking up a great deal. He's very likely at the point of a divorce. The great thing is to make it look all right for a bit."

"Well. . . ."

"I was thinking I could go about with you when you see him. If there were two of us I don't see how anybody could say anything."

"I suppose not."

The winter air blew through the windows and they were silent in the dark a little while.

"What do you think being in love is?" Leda said.

"Everything being very cosy and right."

"I don't feel a bit that way."

"How do you feel?"

"Well. . . . Someone being mad about you and making things exciting and romantic."

"But that's not you being in love."

"Isn't it? . . . Maybe I don't know."

"What do you think you'd feel yourself? What do you think love feels like?"

Leda did not speak for a minute.

"I can't seem to think. I'd like to have someone mad about me that it didn't bore me to *have* mad about me; maybe that's it, feeling in love is being able to have the person mad about you without its boring you—making you feel contemptuous."

"Isn't that funny. You do feel contemptuous of James because he's mad about you, don't you?"

"It's sort of as if it was a battle and I'd won. As if I were the victor."

"Well, how about if you didn't win, I mean if you couldn't win the battle? Then how would you feel?"

"I wouldn't like it."

"Would that make you be in love with them?"

"Maybe it would."

"I do think Lambert would suit you awfully well. I mean I can't imagine your completely conquering him."

"I can't either."

"And you like that, don't you?"

"I suppose I do. There'd be something left to do, trying to win. The thing about James is, there's nothing left to do."

"You're awfully different from me. I don't want there to be anything left to do. I want things to be all understood, and arranged nicely."

"Nicola. Are you in love with Dicky?"

Nicola was always reticent about whatever in her represented emotion. Her emotions moved in a tiny way, and it was as if she felt distasteful about speaking of even that. She never said how she felt, only what she thought. And yet she must feel something about Dicky. She saw him constantly and she had arranged his inclusion in parties all year long. What did she feel about him? Was she excited about him? Impossible to imagine Nicola excited. Perhaps it was only that she would not tell. Leda had suddenly the feeling that she was always telling Nicola her own feelings, spreading them out, while Nicola lived in strictest privacy. There was a dignity about it. There was something almost vulgar about being so affected by emotion as to be compelled to tell about it.

"I suppose so," Nicola said, in her calm voice.

"I mean . . . are you crazy about him?"

"Oh, I don't know. I suppose I'm not very excitable."

"He always seems such a funny beau for you," Leda said. "I mean you're so divine, and somehow he doesn't seem very special."

"I like him."

"It just seems funny that you should."

Nicola laughed in the darkness, her full, chuckling, easy laugh.

"I haven't got the choice you have, you know, darling. I imagine I had just better make do with Dicky."

"Oh, Nicola!"

That was so difficult to imagine.

"Nicola, I don't see how you can feel anything but frustrated if you feel that about Dicky. That he's just around."

"Not at all. I enjoy being with him. It's very nice. We have a great deal of fun."

"I know, but . . ."

"I'm not a bit the way you are, Leda. I don't expect so much. I really don't want great noisy emotions messing things up."

Leda was silent. It was growing late. She was on the edge of sleep when Nicola's pretty, sensible voice spoke again in the darkness.

"Of course Mummy feels just as you do. About Dicky. But I have to be the way I am. I'm not any more like Mummy than I'm like you."

## CHAPTER XXIV

ON A DAY IN LATE MARCH Leda and Nicola were in Lambert's studio, just before lunch. In the past weeks Lambert had made half a dozen starts at a painting of Leda, in half a dozen different poses, different lights, wearing different clothes. In the mornings she would pose and Nicola would sit and read aloud in her unemotional voice with its urbane accent. Lambert would walk around the studio and back and forth from the easel and interrupt when he chose to talk or change the pose. They all got on very well. They used to go out and have lunch together and, with Nicola, Lambert was genial, almost relaxed.

This morning Lambert had made a new start, of Leda curled up in a big faded blue armchair, her arm lying along the curve of the top, her long legs tucked under her, her slender dark face resting on her arm, looking straight ahead.

"God damn it," he said. He put the palette with his brushes stuck into the thumb-hole down on the littered table. "I think I've got it this time. I think I really see something."

"Praise the Lord," Nicola said. "I've never seen such a performance. All the rest of them looked extremely amusing to me."

"Miss Kruger, you belong in the pages of *Vogue*," Lambert said. "All your emotions are by Chanel."

Nicola laughed.

"Yours aren't by anybody. I think mine are rather tidier."

"You drive me perfectly crazy, but I like you. I wonder how your husband will cope with you. Poor devil. I can hear you on your wedding night. . . . 'Don't breathe *quite* so hard, do you mind, darling?'"

"It's so nice for Leda and me," Nicola said. "Learning about life in an artist's studio. Our Harvard beaux don't talk a bit the way you do."

"Let's do something," Lambert said. "Let's celebrate. What are you two doing this afternoon? Tea-dancing? Well, skip it. Let's have a picnic."

"In March?"

"Certainly. You ladies get the food and we'll drive down to the boat-house. At Manchester. My Mamma's boathouse. All madly respectable."

"We have to lunch," Leda said.

"What the hell. So do I have to lunch. I suppose you mean someone's taking you to lunch. Why don't you say so instead of 'We have to lunch.' You're both so damned chic."

"All right," Nicola said. "I think it would be very amusing."

"Oh, my God. Does it have to be amusing? Can't it be gloomy or something?"

"I do hope not."

"Oh, nuts. I'll pick you up at your house at four."

But when Leda and Nicola came out of the front door on Commonwealth Avenue, there was someone sitting beside the driver's seat. Lambert was at the top of the steps waiting.

"My wife is in the car," he said. "She thought she'd like some sea air too. Have you got enough food for four?"

"I'm sure we have," Nicola said. "How nice."

The two young girls climbed into the back seat. They wore tweed country suits and soft beige sweaters and pearl chokers; felt cloches pulled down over their faces, and pearl studs in their ears.

"Miss Kruger, this is my wife," Lambert said. "Maizie, I think you know Leda March."

"Hello, Maizie," Leda said.

The woman in the front seat turned her head and smiled. Her face was thin and haggard. There were round spots of pink rouge on the cheeks. Her eyes were sunken, like the eyes of women in tenements, Leda thought. Her hair stuck out under her hat—bright yellow hair, the only alive note about that whole dead face. It was curly and fluffy, soft and clinging; above it she wore a little blue straw hat with a blue ribbon round it tied in a bow. It looked silly and girlish above that ruined face.

They settled themselves in the back seat, pulling their warm, comfortable coats around them. Everyone lit cigarettes and they started off through the late afternoon traffic out past the East Boston Navy Yard.

Leda and Nicola talked together and in front Maizie kept her face turned toward Lambert. They could hear her voice, with its Southern accent, from the back seat. They saw him nod from time to time, but they could not hear him speak.

When they got to the boathouse it was almost dark. They could hear the roar of the ocean; they could see the shape of the boathouse against the fading light. Lambert carried the hamper across the damp dark sand and up on the porch of the boathouse that was drifted over with sand. He unlocked the door and they all went in. He lit an oil lamp on a table and began to start a fire built of driftwood in the big stone fireplace.

Nicola knelt down on the hearth and held her hands out to the rising flame. She looked decorative in this setting, properly dressed for it, adapted to it, adorning it. Leda stood beside her looking into the fire.

The room was square, compact and pleasant. There were deep chairs and a sofa covered with an Indian rug. The walls were made of logs and three bas-relief ship-models were hung upon them. On the mantel of the fireplace stood a big bottle with a ship in it. The firelight began to fill the corners of the room.

"I'm cold, Lamb," Maizie said.

The irritation that filled his voice was shocking and unmistakable.

"I told you to wear heavy clothes," he said.

He took a folded blanket off the arm of the sofa and wrapped it over Maizie's shoulders. She looked ridiculous, in her little blue unseasonable straw hat, with the heavy blanket draped over her. There was silence for a moment after Lambert's voice.

"What a cosy place," Nicola said, making everything right again.

Lambert was busy filling glasses from a bottle of whisky at the deal table. Maizie slipped out of the blanket without speaking. She took from her purse a compact and began to powder her nose with white powder. She dabbed at the puffs of soft yellow hair over her ears. Then she took off the little blue hat and put it on the sofa beside her.

"I've never seen you in blue," Leda said. "I always remember you in that jade-green you used to wear."

"Yes," Maizie said. "Lamb doesn't like that color."

This Maizie was another person from the pretty girl in the Hampton days. This was a pitiful woman, old and negligible. Leda felt a wave of pity. She had not felt pity for anyone for a long, long time. This was a vague, uncertain feeling, but it was pity.

"You ought to wear black, I think," Nicola said. "It would bring out that marvellous hair of yours."

"Oh, I couldn't wear black. It's so unbecoming. It's so severe. Too old for me."

Nicola, Leda saw, lifted her eyebrows minutely, politely. Lambert came over with the glasses held all four between his hands and they reached up and took them from him.

"This is nice for little Boston girls who don't generally get anything to drink," Nicola said. "We really do need it, after the cold drive. Are you a bit warmer now, Mrs. Rudd?"

"Oh, yes," Maizie said. Leda saw her glance quickly up at Lambert. It was as if she had expected him to strike her.

"What'd you take that blanket off for?" he demanded. "I can't help it when you're cold if you won't dress properly."

"Of course, darling, I'm perfectly warm. I'm nice and warm," Maizie said hurriedly.

Leda stared at them. There was an atmosphere of some fearful and brutal emotion. Leda wondered what Lambert did to Maizie. She looked absolutely destroyed. It was an atmosphere outside anything Leda had ever imagined, and instead of frightening her it was curiously fascinating. What things did Lambert do when he was alone with his wife? What sort of a man was he secretly? The idea that he might be brutal and savage filled Leda with excitement.

Through the past weeks she had been aware of Lambert looking at her. She had never been alone with him again after the night she had dined with him. He had asked her to dine again and she had said that she could not afford to be talked about. He had shut his mouth and said nothing. Nicola was always there. Leda had never wished that she were away. She saw Lambert looking at her and knew that she was disturbing to him and that her aloofness added to her attraction.

And he was attractive to her. Besides the way he looked and the way he spoke there was something in him that she understood, that was quite different from all the Bostonians she knew. She knew the way he felt about his work. She seemed to understand the impatience and restlessness that consumed him. It was, as Nicola had said, as if they were the same kind of person. Lambert knew it too. Once in the studio, with Nicola there, he had said: "Don't you try to fool me with your correctness, Miss March. We're both unregenerate Bostonians and you know it." Leda had laughed. But it was true.

He, like herself, came out of Boston, from Bostonians, and yet like her, he did not belong. He was a changeling, and so was she. But he did not want to belong and she did. The idea seized her now and then, perversely, of what it would be like to·disown Boston and let it disown her, and to be that unknown, unimaginable thing that was her real self—what could it be like? Something like what Lambert was, she thought. Restless, dissatisfied, impatient, and wrapped up in a passion which for Lambert was his painting. For her . . . for her it would be writing. The thought came to her like a fact out of a past life; there was that thing that she could do, that she had loved, that she had stifled out of necessity. What would it be like to give up all this Boston life and be like Lambert?

It was different for a girl. She brushed such thoughts away from her each time they came. And besides there was so much that made it impossible. Lambert was married. No matter what Nicola said, Leda knew her Boston and she had not the confidence to wrestle with it and make it come to her own terms. She would have to play her game its way, Boston's way, and by contriving get what she wanted out of it. No, Lambert was impossible. She thought that after his painting of her was finished she would have to stop seeing him. It was absurd. It would only lead to being talked about, Nicola or no Nicola.

But what would it be like to stop bothering with being a Bostonian? What would it be like to be like Lambert? What would it be like to go back to another kind of life? A life of thinking, the life Norah Hunt had told her of; a life of her own kind of emotion. What would Lambert be like, if she were with him?

They drank their strong drinks in the firelight and talked. Nicola set the tone. It was pleasant, matter-of-fact, and cheerful. After a while Lambert fetched the hamper and Nicola unpacked it and they all sat eating chicken legs and sandwiches. There was a thermos bottle of hot coffee. They finished and Nicola and Leda began to put the things back into the hamper.

"Can't you help a little?" Lambert said to Maizie. "Or are you still cold?"

"Oh, I'm nice and warm!" she cried, and began picking up bits of waxed paper, fumblingly, nervously, not being of any real use. Leda felt pity for her again. She was so awful; grotesque.

"How about a quick run on the beach?" Lambert said, looking at Leda.

"That would be divine," Nicola said promptly. "Just what we all need to drive the city air out of our lungs. And all these cigarettes."

When they went out a strong, cold, salty wind was blowing and they stumbled through soft wet sand down to the harder sand of the beach. In the darkness Lambert's hand reached out and took Leda's.

"Come on," he shouted.

She began to run with him, fast, down the beach in the darkness beside the noisy sea. They ran and ran, and at length Lambert stopped and pulled Leda back beside him. They stood still panting.

"This has been the most God damned awful business," he said. "I don't know why she wanted to come. She didn't enjoy it. I knew she wouldn't. She never does."

"You're rotten to her," Leda said. "I don't see why you can't be nicer."

"Everyone always says that. I know I'm a bastard. I just can't seem to be anything else. You wouldn't understand. It's just too much for me."

"She'd be better off if she were rid of you."

"I know, I know. I know all about that. You don't understand about her. Oh God damn it. . . ."

He reached out his arms and pulled Leda up to him and kissed her hard on her mouth. She started to struggle and then stopped. She began to respond to his kissing. She did not think at all.

"My sweet darling," he said. "My lovely young darling. You're just what I want."

Suddenly she began to run back along the beach in the dark. She could hear him running behind her. She was really running away from him. Things were coming too fast for her. She had had no time to think. In another moment something unimaginable and overwhelming would have happened inside her.

She had the sense of people near her and stopped running. It was Nicola and Maizie, walking along the sand.

"You ought to have some warm, smart country clothes," Nicola was saying. "You'd be so much more comfortable on this sort of expedition."

Leda was struck with amazement. Here was Nicola telling this woman how to dress; fixing everything up. It was so preposterous, it was funny.

"I'm all out of breath," Leda said. She slipped her arm into Maizie's. Lambert came up.

"Come on, Lambert," Nicola's warm, pleasant voice said. "Let's get the things out to the car."

It was as if she knew what had been happening. Perhaps she did. Nicola knew so much more than one could ever understand her knowing. They disappeared into the salty wind and Leda walked slowly back with Maizie.

"It seems such absolute years since I used to have a crush on you in Hampton," she said lightly.

"Yes."

"Do you remember the day Ernest Hamilton was taking you to the Yale game and Betsy and I sat on his knees and you laughed so hard?"

"What?"

"Oh, you remember. When you got home you brought us each a Harvard feather."

"No. I don't remember."

They walked in silence.

"You're trying to get my husband, aren't you?" Maizie said.

"What did you say?"

It was like being struck in the face. Leda had a feeling of outrage. Maizie sounded as if she were talking to a stranger. Her voice was dull, blank. It was as if she had not been hearing anything Leda had said, as if she had begun to talk out of a long, preoccupied train of thought.

"You're after my husband. Girls are always after him. But it won't do any good. I used to think I'd be glad if someone took him away, so I could rest and get well. But I don't any more. I won't let him go till I die. I can't. After I'm dead you'll get him."

"You don't know what you're saying. Lambert's simply been painting my portrait."

Maizie laughed a dreadful laugh.

"I know you're trying to get him. But you won't. I won't let you. No one can ever get him."

This was outrageous. Leda felt smirched by hearing Maizie talk in this horrible way.

"You must be out of your mind," she said.

"Do you think I am?" Maizie said urgently. "Sometimes I think I am too. I know I'm going to die. But I've got to hold on until I die. I've got to hold on. I can't let go. If you got him everything would smash."

They were coming up to the lights of the boathouse. The door stood open and Lambert's figure showed in silhouette, coming out.

"Everything you've said is absurd," Leda said coldly. "I simply don't understand what you're implying."

Maizie laughed again. They went up the steps to the boathouse and the light shone on Maizie's face. Leda shrugged her shoulders and shook her head sharply. Everything was fantasy, this raddled woman and the things she had said, the whole overstrained atmosphere of the last few minutes. What a frightful person.

Nicola was standing before the fire, with her back to it; neat and lovely. It was a joy to look at her. She smiled her lovely smile at Maizie.

"Mrs. Rudd, do you think you'll be quite warm driving back to town? I thought perhaps it might be wiser to take along one of these rugs to put over you. It wouldn't do for you to catch cold."

"Oh . . . I'm all right," Maizie said. It was as though she did not know what she was saying.

Lambert came in and began to smother the fire with ashes. Soon they put out the lamps and went away.

"Wasn't she too awful?" Leda said when she and Nicola were alone back on Commonwealth Avenue. They sat before a little coal fire in the grate of the small downstairs sitting-room and drank hot chocolate. They were drowsy and relaxed after the fresh air.

"I don't think I've ever seen anyone so completely dismal," Nicola said. "I didn't know anybody could dress so badly."

"Poor thing, she simply doesn't understand anything about clothes," Leda said comfortably.

"I think that's inexcusable. The least a woman can do is to dress properly. Nowadays there's no excuse for anyone's not knowing how to dress."

"Oh, I don't know. She comes from the South, originally, you know. I think it's her idea to look pretty, not chic," Leda said.

"If she has such a passion for Lambert she really ought to do something about looking better. She must be a touch half-witted if she can't do better than that. I think her attitude towards him is pathetic. She looks like an adoring dog who expects to be kicked."

"Well, I think that part is absurd," Leda said. "Any woman ought to know better than to be so slavish about a man. What can she expect? I don't feel a bit sorry for her for that part. Of course she'll be kicked if she expects to be kicked."

"No, I'm sorry for her suffering so. It's her dressing that I think is inexcusable."

"He certainly doesn't treat her well, does he?"

"What can you expect, when she looks like that?"

"Oh, I don't know, I think it's more that she acts so ridiculously mad about him."

"Well, anyway, she certainly is a dreary sort of person, isn't she?"

"Completely," Leda said. They drank their chocolate comfortably and went to bed.

After the expedition to the boathouse Leda had a new feeling about Lambert. She felt as if he were not married. Maizie was disposed of in the back of her mind. She had the feeling that she was not interfering with anything at all.

Now that he had found a pose that suited him Lambert worked hard on the portrait of Leda. He was gay and jubilant and filled with an overwhelming energy. He sang songs at the top of his lungs while he was painting, was childishly silly, and poked fun at Nicola for her conventionality. He and Leda joined together to tease Nicola about her views on art.

Now that it was spring in Boston there were not many parties; there were a few dinners, but the big debutante lunches, the crowded teas, the debutante dances and balls were over for that year. Nicola went out with Dicky several times every week, and Leda went tea-dancing at the Colonial and to dine with beaux of hers at Harvard, who belonged to the Fly, the A.D. and the Porcellian, had crew haircuts and seemed curiously alike. She saw James about once a week. She would not allow him to talk to her about Lambert. She told him that he was painting her and that if it made him feel any better Nicola went with her to the sittings, but when he fretted about her having to do with a married man she was biting and cold. She knew he was still in love with her, as much as ever, and it irritated her; his very reticence about it, his pride, gave her shivers of annoyance.

They went to the boathouse on other picnics that spring, but Maizie never went again. Leda did not know how Lambert managed it; perhaps he no longer said where he was going. They had good times as the days grew longer; they ran on the beach and ate their picnic before a blazing fire and laughed and talked and teased Nicola; they always turned to poking fun at her, because she was so imperturbable and good-natured and refused to give way an inch. Lambert and Leda had so many things that they agreed about that Nicola repudiated: her taste was impeccable but bland; she knew what was smart and that was what she admired, and the strange, the disturbing, the bizarre she discarded.

Sometimes the two girls went dancing in the evenings with Lambert and Dicky. Or all four of them would dine and go back to Lambert's studio afterwards and play the tunes of the year on Lambert's gramophone. Leda thought that there could be no more incongruous pair than Lambert and Dicky, though they got on so well. Dicky was stocky, pink, and good-humored; he was no more than five feet nine, and he would stand in front of the fireplace in the studio with his hands in his pockets grinning and looking like the prototype of the young bond-salesman; while Lambert ranged around his studio restlessly with his hair a black point on his forehead, his eyes shifting impatiently, his hard mouth moving hardly at all as he talked. He looked like no one else in the world; he looked dangerous and unhappy.

On those evenings they would split apart, Nicola sitting with Dicky off in the corner beyond the fireplace where they would talk in low tones and at intervals Nicola would laugh her pleasant, chuckling laugh; Leda sat leaning back on the broad couch with Lambert half-lying along it, talking in a nearly inaudible voice and holding her hand. The gramophone near by them ground out its music. . . . "*You were . . . completely sweet so what could I do? I needed phrases . . . to sing your praises.*" Lambert would reach out with one hand and put the needle back to the start and look at Leda's face. They would hear Nicola laugh, and her voice say "Dicky, really . . ." and then the needle would catch and the music begin again. . . . "*That certain feeling . . .*"

The studio was vast; only one or two lights burned in its shadows. The great window was gray from the city lights behind it, and sometimes they would hear the Boston & Albany trains go by.

They joked about their evenings there and Lambert referred to it as "The Bordello." But they were very well-behaved. It would have been impossible to be otherwise with the presence of Nicola. Lambert called her "The Madam." Nicola would say, "I hope you don't expect me to understand what a madam is, you old roué," and Lambert would laugh and Dicky would ha-ha. Lambert called Leda "The Beautiful Circassian." They were all very gay and friendly; once in a while Leda thought that Dicky kissed Nicola. When she asked her, Nicola said,

"Certainly. I do think a kiss can be rather nice, don't you?"

But Leda would not let Lambert kiss her. She would stiffen if he leaned too near her, and glance over to the corner where the others were.

"Oh, God," Lambert said. "You damned little Boston debutante. Don't you think it would be fun to be a little *wild*, for a change, and *neck* a little, with your *boy-friend?*"

"It sounds loathesome," she said.

"You're afraid to let yourself kiss me," he said once.

"Don't be absurd. What is there to be afraid of?" she said. But it was true; she did feel afraid. Things would be unmanageable; out of hand.

She was aware of the power that lay in imperturbability. When Lambert would lean toward her and his hard, dark face came closer, she would be Nicola and laugh. She would keep away the kind of frightening moment that she had had the night she dined with him, by being Nicola. Of course she was not Nicola. She was Leda being Nicola.

Leda had been spending almost every night of the week in town at the Krugers' house. Over the weekends she would go out to Hampton. It was as if all the old pain; the acuteness of the country around the Marches' white house; the almost terrible significance of the house and land where Leda had spent her childhood, were cancelled by her new life. When she was there she moved about the house and slept and ate, and walked in the garden, a new remodelled Leda, not any longer possessed by her surroundings and swayed by them but a young lady who had made her début. A tall, slender, dark young lady whose mind was full of the events of her life, she walked along the path that bordered the garden, thinking of what she would do the next day when she was back in town. She was courteous to her parents; but they might have been new acquaintances, except when it was a matter of something Leda wanted. Then, if they hesitated about granting her the thing, extra money or a new coat for the spring, the mechanics of the relationship sprang up and they were father and mother and daughter.

They made conversation. They had nothing in common. Hampton was a land belonging to a past and unpleasant period of Leda's life, and she did not let her mind re-explore it. Laura and Bernard were left alone again to their little life of which they were fond, with music and the garden and little worries and kisses.

On a Saturday afternoon when she had come back to Hampton in time for lunch and to spend the weekend, Leda was called to the telephone. It was Nicola.

"Leda. . . . I'm going away tonight. Mummy's taking me abroad."

"*What?*"

"Yes. Listen. I wish I could see you. But I'll write. We're going to New York on the five-o'clock and catch a boat that sails at midnight."

"But, *Nicola* . . ."

"It's awful, isn't it? I'll explain later. But it will all be all right. I'll come back and it won't make any difference."

"But Nicola . . ."

And on Monday afternoon in the mail the letter came. It was written in Nicola's extraordinary, characteristic hand. She formed her letters very round and neat, as elegantly as she arranged her person.

"Dearest Leda,

"Isn't it too sickening that I have to go away. Mummy suddenly sprang it on me and I couldn't have been more astonished. You see, she never thought much of my going about with Dicky and now she has decided that I need a bit of travel, and of course it is because she thinks I will get Dicky out of my mind. She doesn't realize that no ambassadors are going to fall for me. The whole thing seems a bit silly.

"I simply hate to go off without seeing you and I will write and tell you about our trip. Of course Mummy is the one who will have a divine time. No doubt it will all be quite fun, but I would much rather stay in Beantown. I will bring you some of that Houbigant *Giroflée* you like from Paris. Is there anything else you'd like? Write, won't you? Care of Morgan & Co., Paris.

Loads of love,

Nicola"

The feeling Leda had was of complete desolation.

She went out of the house in the April afternoon. The garden flower beds were black and dead, with wet straw lying about the roots of the rose-bushes. Rain dripped off the lilac trees on to the grass. The land fell away to the swamp behind the house, that at this season was full of pools and dead reeds. Behind the swamp rose the woods.

She was afraid of being lonely. She had lost or forgotten the pleasure of loneliness. No longer did she have any desire to go to those woods and lose the disappointment of living. She had known talk and lights and the satisfaction of vanity among people. She walked along the garden paths deep in depression. She did not know what to do. With Nicola gone, everything seemed gone. There were other people and things she could plan to do, but these seemed impossible, beyond her. She felt abandoned, and a fear of returning to her old self tormented her.

She went back into the house and up to her bedroom and put on her hat. Her eyes looked back at her from the oval mirror over her bureau, and she put some lipstick on her mouth. She went downstairs again. Laura was sitting before the fire in the living-room, sewing on a pink crepe blouse.

"I'm going out," Leda said.

"All right, sweetheart," Laura said. "You'll be back to dinner, won't you? Or are you going in to Nicola's?"

"Nicola's gone abroad," Leda said.

"Why, Leda! Why, you poor darling. I know you must feel terribly. I'm sorry your little friend has gone away."

"Of course I don't. Why shouldn't Nicola go abroad? She'll have a divine time."

"Of course, darling. Only I know how you'll miss her."

"I don't see why," Leda said coldly.

Laura looked at her helplessly.

"Well," Leda said. "I'll be back for the night. I may have dinner in town with some people."

"Please don't be late. You know we don't like to have you driving after dark."

Leda shrugged her shoulders and went out.

She went around the house and got her car out of the barn. It was a roadster that she had made them get her in the fall. One of the things that she found a private pleasure in was driving her car alone. Now she drove it out into the street. All the country was dead; sad and tired. She felt hopeless too, but in the car it was not so bad.

There was the feeling of being snug within the body of the car; the instruments along the panel before her, her coat wrapped warm about her, the top and sides of the car shutting her in into a little ambulant house that she could direct at will. It felt cosy.

From her little moving box, she could look at the passing country. It made her feel free.

The lights came out while she was driving through the little towns around Boston, in the big groceries, the drugstores on the corners; the traffic-lights stood out bright and succulent in the twilight—red like a raspberry drop, green like a lime drop. There was not yet any feeling of spring in the dusk, and yet it had ceased to be winter. This was the gray time, the wet time, when homecoming commuters dragged along the village streets wearing their galoshes, still in the drab coats and shapeless felt hats that they had worn all winter.

Between two towns Leda stopped and went into a lunch-wagon and ordered a fried-egg sandwich and a cup of coffee. It gave her a feeling of independence, of seeing the world, to sit there on a stool between two workmen drinking coffee and dipping crullers into their cups. Nothing happened in the lunch-room while she was there. It was only that nobody knew where she was; she was alone and in charge of herself; she could sit as a watcher and a listener, anonymous, invisible, her own mistress.

When she got back into the car it was night. Still she had the feeling of being unknown, out of touch with everyone, looking at a private world through private eyes, as though a ghost. She drove slowly into town. Here she had walked as a schoolgirl and later as a debutante, quite another person from this spirit behind the steering-wheel. Down Commonwealth Avenue she had walked in the fine sunny winter mornings arm in arm with Nicola, bound on shopping trips or going out to a debutante luncheon at the Chilton Club. She had come out of the Somerset on early mornings among all the others in evening-dress, under the white arc-lights; she had come out of the Women's Republican Club and out of the Copley-Plaza; she had walked down Boylston Street in the afternoons to go to a theatre.

All that was another life. She drove the dark wet streets as though she were revisiting earth. The feeling she had seemed to take form inside her head in different phrases. "I am a part of nothingness. . . ." "Now I am dead and watch myself alive." Only a few people walked in the bad weather, on Massachusetts Avenue and upper Boylston Street. Through the windows of the drugstores and the all-night lunches the yellow light came in streaks and lay upon the pavement.

It hardly needed to be Boston. Because she was alone, it was anonymous; it might have been London, or Vienna; it was simply the sad after-dark side of a city. She turned the corner from Boylston Street and drove down into Ipswich Street. A train rumbled past, hurrying away to the desolate, fusty towns. Leda looked up and saw on the broad flat face of the studio building two or three great windows lit. One of the windows was Lambert's.

She stopped the car beside the curb in front of the ornate door, lit by two electric torches on iron halberds. She got out and ran up the brick steps and into the hall.

She had not thought of Lambert perhaps for two days, and yet as she stepped into the old creaking elevator she had a flash of knowledge that she had meant to come here all along. It was foolish, it was dangerous, to have come here and she knew that if she stopped for a minute she would not go on; she would turn and go back to the car. But she did not stop. The elevator, groaning in its ropes, took her up. This was where she wanted to go. Something had been removed which had kept her from coming here. She walked down the long corridor. She knocked on the door at the end.

She heard Lambert's steps running up the stairs from the studio to the balcony where the door was. It opened, and she saw his face change from impatience to delight. He wore a long tan cotton painting coat.

"Hello," she said.

He reached out and took her hand and pulled her in. His dark face was all changed with his smiling. He slammed the door shut behind her and put both arms around her and gave a great sigh.

"I've waited so long for this," he said, and kissed her.

They went with his arm around her down the stairs and over to the couch. He pulled her down beside him and began to kiss her. Neither of them spoke. Half of the studio was in deep shadow; a blue bulb shone in one corner over a desk where two copper plates caught the light. The whole building seemed dead except for the tiny corner where they were kissing each other. A train went by outside and the building shook. Then it had passed and there was no sound at all.

"Darling," he said. "Darling. I'm in love with you. I'm really in love with you. You're the only one, the only one."

"Darling," she said. The word felt curious and new-edged passing her own lips.

"Oh, darling, I have to have you," he said. "I really have to have you. Nobody else was ever anything like you. You haven't any of the things that were wrong. You're so beautiful. You'll never spoil. I feel as if I could never leave a mark on you.'"

She did not answer.

"Do you love me?" he asked her.

"I don't know."

"How funny. How wonderful. But you do. You came here. You wanted to come."

After a few minutes she said,

"No. Don't. Really don't. I know I don't want that."

He leaned his head back for a moment and loosened his hold on her.

"All right," he said. "It's all right if you don't want to. I don't know why but I don't want you to do anything you don't want to. Oh, but you've got so much! You're so wonderful! You're going to love me, do you know that, you're going to love me."

"Am I?"

"Yes. We're going to have everything. I know it. Don't think about anything. Everything's going to be wonderful. I never felt like this. You're going to love me, and God knows I'll love you."

He began to kiss her again.

"And I'm going to paint the damnedest pictures," he murmured.

The strange unlikely spring began that night. For the first time in Leda's life she was capable of recklessness, and it gave her an astonishing feeling of confidence. She would not allow Lambert to do more than kiss her; in some part of herself there was a wall of decision against that; there was never any hesitation. Once or twice it made him angry but he always laughed. He seemed almost to like it, that she was so unshakable. They used to kiss; gaily, teasingly, triumphantly, passionately. Sometimes in the daytimes when he was painting he would come across to her, whether she was posing or sitting with paper in her lap writing, and catch her up in his own excitement and they would hold each other laughing and kissing until the laughter drifted away and they were only kissing.

Lambert had set Leda a new pace. She felt natural in it. She had that feeling of remembering something, rather than of learning. She knew how to be this way. It was easier to be like Lambert than it had been to be like Nicola, and furthermore it was just as right, it felt just as strong. She had been Nicola but it had always been a lesson to remember accurately; this was nature. Instead of being uneasy she was brilliantly composed; far happier than she had been in the years of aping a manner and a way of thought that was foreign to her. She loved the life she was living. She loved being like Lambert, making speeches when she felt like making speeches—against Bostonianism, against stupidity—and laughing unrestrainedly, and when she chose, cursing as Lambert did, and kissing him with all her strength, and smelling the paint and etching acid in the studio, and feeling free; freer than she had ever felt in her life except in the lonely days of her childhood in the woods. But this was far superior. She enjoyed being a Lambert kind of person. It felt like being what was, perhaps, after all these years, her own kind of person.

The plan was that he should make another painting of her. That was what she told her family. When they objected and demurred she simply overrode them. For years she had overridden them, and she knew how.

The parties were over, Nicola was gone, and there was no other girl in Boston Leda wanted to see at all. Beginning that night in April she simply dropped the life of the winter and did nothing but see Lambert. Her family thought she posed in the mornings and lunched with other girls later and shopped with them or went to the movies. But she stayed all day at the studio, except when they drove away on trips. The thing that sometimes struck her as odd and even made her laugh out loud as she told Lambert of it, was that instead of feeling wicked, she felt virtuous.

"Oh, but you're not," he said. "You're an awful girl. You're fooling your family and being alone with a Man, and breaking my heart into the bargain. You don't fool me with your talk about virtue. I'm just as Boston as you are. I know what's what."

"No, really," she said. "I have the strangest sort of sense of being good as gold. I guess this is the way I was meant to live."

"I hope not. I sincerely hope not. I'd hate to see you die an old maid."

"I mean it," she said.

He came over and put his arms around her.

"I know. I love to tease you. Of course you were meant to live this way, only more so. Nobody ever intended you to be screwing around with a lot of Boston girls, eating chicken patties. This is where you belong. Only more so."

She would come in to the studio in the morning. Lambert would be there already, setting his palette, shifting things around, whistling. He would run noisily up the stairs to let her in. The mornings were springlike now. She would come down the stairs and they would throw their arms around each other and kiss, and dance around the studio floor.

Then she would pose. They talked all the time that she was posing. It was only once in a while that he would tell her to shut her mouth, he wanted to paint it. And then he would come and kiss it first. They laughed a great deal, and Lambert even made a study of Leda laughing, which he liked particularly.

"God, what a show I could make out of these," he said. "Miss Leda March laughing. Miss Leda March in repose. Miss March as the Tragic Muse. About thirty swell pictures all of you, angel."

"What would Boston have to say to that?"

"God damn it."

"They'd say I was seeing quite a little of you."

"And so you are. And so you are. Jesus, I can't tell you what a model you make. The beautiful Emma was a cook. And I'm a better painter than Romney. Wheee! I'm a better painter than anybody!"

He wanted her to pose for him nude, but even he could see as he spoke that it was out of the question. Leda felt no shock or fear or shrinking when he spoke of it. She would have liked to have him make great paintings of her nude; she felt as though even her nakedness would be invulnerable, as strong as white armor. She said so.

"You're right," he said. "You're so God *damned* unattainable. I wonder if you'd be frigid."

"I don't know."

"I don't shock you a bit, do I? Nothing I ever say or do throws a scare into you. Where do you get all that?"

"I don't know."

It was true, but it was true only with Lambert. With Lambert she felt strong, immortal and fearless.

"But you can't pose nude, anyway. I'm protecting you. What do you think of that? Me protecting someone. Maybe it's love."

"I wouldn't mind."

"I know you wouldn't, and I know you'd be just as clothed in your God damned incredible virginity as if you had a fur coat on, and the wicked artist wouldn't get to first base. Besides I told you I didn't want to do anything you didn't want me to. I don't know why. For some funny reason even if you really would do it I wouldn't let you. On account of people. On account of Boston. On account of everything. I guess it's that funny thing about not wanting people to look at a painting of your wife nude."

"I'm not your wife."

"No, you're not. But you ought to be. What a life we could have."

They looked at each other. Lambert shrugged his shoulders and his face fell into the lines of hardness, from the vitality and animation which changed it so often now.

"I'll tell you about it some day soon. I don't like to talk about it. It's such a mess," he said. "I'm God damned if I know what to do. I don't know anything. Anybody knows more than I do. I'll talk about it now if you want me to. But it's so wonderful not to talk about it and to forget about it and just be here with you and paint and have everything the way it ought to be."

"I don't feel as if you had a wife."

"I don't feel as if I did either. Do you know what we are? We're awful people, hard and tough and selfish. I don't know which of us is tougher. Don't look funny—no, by God, you're not looking funny. Because I love it about you. I love your hardness. I just can't stand pain. I don't want it around me. And I know I couldn't hurt you. I don't want to. But if I could I probably would. There's something about the hurt animal that is so horrible it makes you kick it again. Jesus, how I hate even talking like this. I want everything strong and hard and beautiful and brilliant, and I want to work like hell, *do* something to beauty when it gets unbearably beautiful. You're all of that. You're the most beautiful thing in the world, and the strongest, and I think you're going to live forever. You couldn't possibly die."

He came across the room to where she sat on a chair on the model stand, and mounted it and leaned over and kissed her violently.

"You're stronger than me, too," he said.

In the afternoons Lambert would do other work and Leda would sit curled up on the couch and write verse. The feeling had all come back in a rush, but now it was different and came from different impulses. She felt no longer delicate and tentative about writing as she had in school; she felt a big surge of wanting to write, out of energy, and she wrote stanza after stanza, never revising; chiefly poems about being in love. They did not satisfy her, but she went on writing them; the desire was satisfying if the accomplishment was not. When she read them over she had the feeling that somebody else had written them from a far weaker and more gentle emotion than any she possessed. She was sure now that she was in love with Lambert, but she did not feel tender about him, or sensitive; only strong and vigorous. But the poems came out gentle. She would show them to him in the late afternoons when the great studio window was gray and they turned on the electric light and drank small glasses of Italian vermouth.

She wrote,

> I know that Cerberus and Chiron guard
> The black enamel river-gate to Hell.
> I know its dark rococo portals well;
> But neither man nor baying mastiff barred
> The stream when I dropped naked in its deep
> Fast-flowing currents.
> . . . Only the whirlpools eddying into sleep.
> The little silver fishes hid or darted
> Like water-bubbles rising in a pot. . . .
> . . . But how the steady waters suddenly parted
> And how I came to you, I have forgot.

And,

> My heart, my harried spirit, and my mind
> Have been a triple instrument of pain
> Dealing the same old tortures yet again—
> That heaven is unfair and earth unkind;
> That life's an orange with a bitter rind;
> That love's a grape that leaves a purple stain; . . .
> But now . . .
> Comes soft a secret sound, like poetry
> Sung to a sweet, unearthly, magic tune:
> Like far-off church bells tolling peacefully
> Through a long lovely summer afternoon.

"My God, darling; do you feel that way about me?" Lambert said. He knelt on the floor beside the couch, that was littered with paper she had been writing on.

She shrugged her shoulders. She did not feel like that about him. If the feeling she found coming out in her verses was about anything, she thought, it was about poetry, the feeling for poetry, coming back to her after all this time, after she had disowned and deserted it. About Lambert she felt excitement; they were two people geared the same. About writing again she felt timid and tender and dissatisfied. Sometimes she felt deep remorse that she had ever let it go, and a fear that perhaps she had ruined what she now believed to have been a real talent. Now it was wrongness in her work she minded; herself did not feel wrong at all any longer.

Lambert did not understand what it was she was trying to do. But he

did understand the thing in her that made her want to write, he recognized
it quite naturally and simply as something that moved himself. He did not
realize as she did that what she was doing was inferior to what she had done
more than a year before. What she was doing was exercises in trying to
learn to write poetry again. She felt that her old verses had been really
poetry. These were bad, but she knew that it could be only by trying that
she could get the other thing back. It was Lambert's presence and spirit and
temper that had made her begin to write again; his feeling about his work
had resurrected its counterpart in her; and his proximity made her go on
feeling more and more like writing, and, she thought, the verses did get
better.

She brought in some books of poetry to the studio and kept them there.
Lambert began to buy her others.

"Do you like these?" he would say when she came in in the morning,
and hand her two or three more that he had bought on the way to the
studio. "I hope they're okay. The lady at the bookstore said they were just
wonderful, and I'm sure she knows."

That way she was given a few books that were new and disturbing to
her and that taught her; mostly Lambert gave her new poets. He gave her
Elinor Wylie, and Robinson, and H. D., and Amy Lowell, and Arthur
Davison Ficke, and Genevieve Taggard. She would read them on the couch
in the afternoons, and suddenly a poem would make her want to write another, and she would start to write on the pads of paper that Lambert got
for her.

"Aren't we having fun," he would say, grinning at her with his dark face
across the studio from where he was making a drypoint. "We're a whole
God damned artists' colony."

They seldom saw each other at night. About once a week Lambert took
Leda out to dinner and they came back to the studio and talked and kissed
or else went to the movies, but in general it could not be arranged. There
was Leda's family. Also there was Maizie. They did not talk about Maizie
and she might not have been alive except for that one thing, that Lambert
could not take Leda out at night, even if she had been able to go. One late
afternoon at the end of April, when the light had gone and they had not
turned any lamps on, when Leda was sitting on the couch with her books
piled on the floor, and Lambert half lay beside her, stroking the back of her
neck with one hand, he talked about Maizie a little.

"*I* don't know," he said. "I'm not any good at sympathy or understanding people. It's always been hell for her, I guess. I just go on being myself
and I don't see what I can do if just being me gives her hell. I know I've
messed up her life and ruined her youth and made a wreck of her, but
what can I do? I didn't *do* anything. I just was myself. I've tried to be
kinder, and gentler, and all the rest of it, but then it's as if I was stoppering
myself up and sooner or later the stopper blows off and then it's worse than
ever."

"Do you love her?" Leda said.

"Me? Good God, no. Well, yes, I do in a way. That is, all the mess we've been through together and all the awful times, somehow they make me attached to her, but, no, I don't love her any way you mean. The only thing I could ever think of was just to leave her alone, since not leaving her alone was too much for her, but that's wrong too. If I leave her alone then she gets into some awful state. I guess she loves me, I don't want to sound pompous, but good God, it must be something that drives her like that. She doesn't ever rest. I can't do anything but just be the way I am—I said that —only something about me does something awful to the person she is. We shouldn't ever, ever have gotten married. We're poison to each other, specially me to her. But what can I do?"

"What do you do?"

"Oh, God, I do the best I can. I get the hell out after breakfast and stay away all day, and then I go home and try to be as quiet and unexciting and soothing as I can be, but that's not the answer either. I try to be interested by all the little things she fixes in the daytimes for me to have at night, all the stuff for dinner and the flowers in the vases and her new dress, but I feel as if I was a marionette on a wire. Then after dinner when I've gone through my paces and said all the right things, then if I get back to myself and forget about that stuff, she goes crazy and says I don't love her. Well, God, I suppose I don't, and I've said I don't often enough, but there's something hellish about having hurt anybody so much. You feel so damned guilty. I can't ever look at her and feel natural. I always feel sick with guilt, and embarrassed, and pulled all apart with pity, because she does look like hell and her eyes look like an animal's that's being operated on without anesthetic. But what can I do?"

"I shouldn't think she'd want to stay around if it's so awful for her."

"Well, you wouldn't think so, would you? Neither would I think so. But she does. Don't ask me why. I guess she had some idea at the beginning she was going to make a go of her marriage to me, and although the whole thing has smashed into a million pieces long ago, she just hangs on to it and won't give up. That horrible happy look she gets sometimes when I'm putting on my act of being pleased with the soufflé—and of course I can't hold it more than a little while, and when I quit and go back to being myself she gets the sick look again, whipped. You haven't any idea what hell can be like. I'm sorrier for her than for anybody in the whole world, I'm sick with being sorry for her, and it doesn't do her any good. I don't want even to talk about it any more."

Sometimes they went on trips in the car. In May they drove, one late morning, up on the North Shore toward Cape Ann. The spring was beginning to turn the Northern landscape yellow-green, and as they drove farther north the signs of spring grew fainter and more delicate, the green paler, the sky a stronger, colder blue, the air more wild and sweet.

They stopped and had lunch outside Salem and ate sea-food and drank beer. They laughed a great deal. When they got back into the car and crossed the bridge into Beverly they were quieter. As they drove along the twisting shore road, almost deserted now, they passed spots where the ocean was suddenly stretched out before them for a moment, blindingly

blue in the sunshine. They passed the large, shut houses of the summer
residents; through the sleepy villages; on along the winding road through
Manchester and so to the hill where they looked down over rocks to the
blue semi-circle of Gloucester Harbor laid out below them. There were a
few boats moving slowly across the water. The atmosphere was very white,
bleached, keyed higher than ordinary air. The trees that overhung the
promontory were bare; there was no green anywhere here yet. Everything
was wild, fresh, strong, intoxicating.

They drove across the drawbridge and up into Gloucester town and
parked the car on a back street and walked, arm in arm, down the hill
towards the harbor. The purity of the air was unbelievable. The houses
were the white of bleached bones, the air was white, there was a white
sheen over the water of the harbor. The whole town, houses, lonely
streets, shops, ships, harbor, might have been scrubbed and left to bleach in
the chilly sun.

They wandered down to the docks and watched the fishermen working
on their boats, in a mess of rope and dead fish and nets. The smell here was
of fish, salt, and tar, but through it came the smell of the clean sea.

They walked around, not talking, for a long time. When it turned colder
and the light began to fail they went to a café on one of the harborside
streets and sat at a counter and drank coffee under a dirty yellow light. It
smelled very strong of fish in the café, but it was warm and pleasant.

"Well," Lambert said after a while. "How'd you like that?"

"I loved it," Leda said. There were lines of verse running through her
head, and the beat of a rhythm, and every now and then a few more words
would drop into place in the beat.

> In Gloucester by the border
> The salt is in the sod;
> The boats go out in order
> To catch the silver cod.

She drank her coffee in short sips and listened to the words come in her
head.

> In Gloucester on the tip of Cape Ann
> There's more of winter than summer;
> With autumn over before it began
> And spring a tardy comer. . . .

"Listen," Lambert said. He put his coffee down in the saucer with a
clatter. The yellow light over their heads swayed and cast moving shadows
in the corners of the shop. The counter man was a Portuguese, black, oily
and bright-eyed. Lambert lit a cigarette and leaned his elbows on the
counter. "Listen, we've got to get married."

The words were running like shoals of fish in her head. . . .

> I'd rather be, than anywhere else,
> In Gloucester by the sea.

"What?" she said.

"We make such good sense together. You are the only woman I've ever made sense with. You don't bother me. You just make me happy. I don't seem to bother you. I don't upset you, or worry you, or make you unhappy, or anything. We have a wonderful time. Let's for God's sake get married and us anyway be happy. If we don't I'll be unhappy, and *she'll* be unhappy anyway, and maybe you'll be unhappy. Three unhappy people is worse than two happy ones and one unhappy one, isn't it? And God damn it, maybe she would be happy if she got rid of me, whether she thinks so now or not."

"Yes," Leda said. She felt strangely comfortable; the words swung in her head like ripples slapping on a beach.

> In Gloucester by the ocean
> The sky is harsh and blue;
> The waves are all in motion. . . .

"You would marry me, wouldn't you?" Lambert said.

"Of course," she said.

"Well, then, God damn it, I'm going to make her get a divorce. I don't see why everybody should have to be wretched for years and years and years."

Leda turned her head and smiled at him. She felt happy and rather tired, and warm.

"Jesus, I do love you," he said. "You never talk too much. You don't know how important that is."

"Is it?" she said smiling.

All the way back to town in the car Lambert was jubilant.

"I'm such a damned fool," he said. "I'm such an ass! What the hell! I should have seen what to do long ago. I thought I had to go on as things were. I don't know what I thought. I'm an imbecile. Oh, boy! I haven't felt so good since my grandfather died. Everything's going to be fine. She's going to get a divorce, I'm going to marry you, we're going to have a wonderful life. Just think of my wanting to marry anybody. Maybe that's why I've been so dumb. I just can't get used to it that I'm in love, by God, and I want to get married. Wheee! You're so unbothering, except just the way I like to be bothered."

"Suppose she won't get a divorce?" Leda said.

"I know. I know. She'll just have to. Now is the time for being brutally frank. I'll explain everything. I'll say I don't love her, never did, never could, can't stand being married to her any longer. I'll tell her about you. That I've just got to marry you. If she loves me at all, and I know she must, she'll have to give me something I want more than anything. A clean break, that's what. Everything's been a horrible mess for so long. It'll be like starting fresh. Good God, I'm a young man and I haven't had a young man's life. I don't know what kind of a life I've had. Peculiar. Nasty. Am I going to be young now! With you. You're the youngest thing in the world. You are also the serpent of old Nile, and I love you. Listen, you could stay in town and have dinner tonight, couldn't you? You've got to. I'll call up. You call up. To hell with everybody. We're going to get married. I can't get over how nice it sounds to say that. I always thought getting married was the bell tolling. The end of everything. Nuts. It's the beginning."

Leda telephoned to Hampton and said that she would be home later that evening, and shut off in the middle of Laura's nervous demurrals. Lambert telephoned, and came out of the booth with his face heavy. They got back into the car and drove the rest of the way into town.

"It will be heaven not to be sorry for anyone any more," he said, in a different voice from the jubilant one.

They had dinner at a restaurant on the back of Beacon Hill, and drove on across Boston to the Fenway and went up to the studio in the wheezing elevator. The minute the door was closed behind them Lambert put his arms around Leda. He half-carried her downstairs.

"Oh, God," he said. "Oh, God, I want you so." He put her down on the couch and lay beside her, kissing her face and her neck and pulling her dress away from her shoulders and kissing them. She felt curiously calm and strong and unmoved as she observed his abandon.

"No," she said. "No."

"All right. I won't do anything you don't want. I just want you in my arms. You're beautiful. You know what you do to me, don't you? You just lie there like a beautiful odalisque and watch me. I don't care. I like it. By God, you're the most beautiful wonderful lovely woman and I want you forever and ever and ever. I'll make you want me. Christ, you will want me. We'll have everything. I'll do everything to you. What do you think of that?"

"You can't do anything to me," she said, laughing, and looking at him with part affection and part the excited resistance she felt against him. It was always like a battle.

"Oh, but you'll see how I try," he murmured, laughing too, and burying his face in her neck.

"I'm the boss," she said.

"Oh, are you? We'll fight that out later. Over lots of years, darling. Like a couple of tigers. Won't that be nice? Do you want me to take a bite out of you?" He took the flesh of her neck between his teeth. She jerked away and they began to wrestle together on the sofa, laughing.

The next morning when Leda came to the studio Lambert flung the door wide open at her knock. He must have been waiting for her. He was grinning all over his dark face.

"Everything's set!" he cried. "She's going to give me a God-damned son-of-a-bitch divorce!"

For two weeks they talked about how they were going to get married. In the part of his life that Leda never saw, Lambert arranged matters, and came to the studio and told her of what was planned. Maizie would go to Reno. She would leave shortly, shortly, just as soon as she could get herself and her things together. After the first few days she had moved out to her family's house in Hampton. Lambert went to see her out there and talk things out, and when Leda would ask him about it he would shake his head like a dog with fleas and then grin. Maizie would not tell her family anything about it, Lambert said. She was waiting until just before she left, and then she would tell them. She was supposed simply to be paying them a visit. Lambert said he didn't like it. He wanted to have everything come out and everybody know it.

"But I'm not complaining," he said. "Anything suits me, just so long as she gets off on schedule. Six weeks, darling. And then we get married and life starts being a great big wonderful balloon."

It was just before the beginning of June that Leda came to the studio in the morning and Lambert opened the door with quite a different look on his face. He had the look of being tortured; he slammed the door shut and went down the stairs after Leda.

"What?" she demanded.

"It's too incredible to be true. It's nightmare. She says she's going to have a baby. Another baby. She did this to me before. She got me to marry her this way."

"But how . . ."

"It could be so, all right. You see, the night I told her . . . She said . . . She wanted it. . . . Last time stuff. Well, it doesn't make any difference. Just makes me more of a bastard, as usual. Because I won't have her getting away with it this time. She's got to have it stopped. She damned well will have it stopped. I'm not going to have my life ruined any more than it's been ruined."

"Is it really true? It's so . . . convenient."

"Isn't it? She admits she tried to do it on purpose. She admits she did it to keep me. I didn't see how she could tell. It seems there's something called an Ascheim-Zondek test. It's so, all right. And she's told her family, and everything's dandy, and she's going to have a ba-by. Well, she can just stop having a baby, that's all. I don't care. I simply don't care. I can't go on any more with that. I won't. For a woman who goes through hell twenty-four hours of the day, my wife certainly is a shrewd woman. She certainly goes after what she wants. Oh, the hell with her."

He reached out his arms to Leda, but she stepped back and jerked her head sharply, thinking, I've got to get out of this; I've got to get out.

"We can't do it now," she said. "It's all different."

He followed her, but she kept pushing his hands away.

"Look, you mustn't be sorry for her," he said. "You mustn't be sentimental about the baby business. It may be true, but she's just using it to get what she wants. Just exactly the way she did before. A baby is her weapon. She doesn't seem to be able to think of anything else. She's just using it to keep me. I've stopped being sorry for her. She can get rid of it. It won't hurt her. She doesn't know what's good for her. The best thing that could possibly happen to her would be to be through with me and the whole mess, and maybe sometime meet a nice quiet guy who'd be good to her."

"We can't possibly do it now," Leda said.

Her mind was very busy, running around and looking into corners and putting things together, and giving little cries of alarm. She wished Nicola was here. She had not even thought of Nicola for weeks. Nicola would be able to tell her how to get out of this mess. The only thing left was to try to be Nicola, quickly, to take the point of view of Nicola and work things out. Oh, what a mess! What danger! How had she ever got into this? What foolhardiness! The madness of it; and all that nonsense with writing verse; becoming absorbed to the exclusion of her own interests. If Nicola had not gone away things never would have come to this pass.

Things were smashing right and left inside Leda's head. Oh, this was bad. This was so bad. She had been asleep for two months, and had only this moment waked to find the state that her affairs had got in. If Nicola were only here. . . . Think; think.

Maizie's going to have a baby and she's told her family all about it. She hasn't told them about me, thank God. Not yet. But if Lambert made her get rid of the baby—how could he?—she'd tell them about me, and I'd be the girl who broke up a woman's marriage just when she was going to have a baby. I can just see it all in the Boston *American*. Oh no, that would never, never do; never. Get out of here; get out of this mess just as quick as you can, you fool.

I don't care anything about Lambert, now; I don't care anything about anything except to be out of this messy business and safe; beyond criticism. Oh Lord, things are trembling on a terrible brink. I've got to get out, quick. Get out clean, and neat, and untouched by it.

"I'm going," she said.

"You can't *go*," he said. "What's the matter with you? Look, this can all be fixed, darling. Just sit down and we can straighten it all out. Don't get the wind up like this."

"No," she said. "I want to go, now." She started up the stairs to the balcony, while Lambert stared at her. "I'll talk to you about it some other time. I can't now. I want to get away from you now."

He spread his hands apart and stood looking up at her.

"I don't know what's the matter with you," he said. "I'll call you up tonight. We've got to talk about this."

She went out and closed the door behind her.

She walked up Ipswich Street and down Boylston Street in panic confusion. Everything was swimming around in her mind, but at the core was the absolute resolve to get out of what she had gotten into, and the relief at having left the studio.

It had something to do with the realization of being involved with other people's inner, tortured lives; she did not want to be so near to people as that, as to see their torment. She did not want even to imagine their pain.

She had been drifting in a stupor, with the pleasure and vanity of Lambert's admiration curving around her like light winds. Maizie had never obtruded into this pattern; she had not seemed real. Suddenly out of nothing she and her reality appeared and smashed the design. What was happening was real. Somewhere Lambert's wife was going through some sort of unimaginable suffering, she was crying out, she was protesting, she was asserting her will. And Leda was involved.

It was something dreadful, serious, basic, it was something Leda wanted nothing whatever to do with. She felt dizzy and puzzled that she had drifted with Lambert and supposed that she would marry him, quite pleasantly and as easily as everything else with him had been up to this point. No, she had stuck her head into a nest of passion, people suffering and doing violent things. It was not a story; it was real life.

Maizie was going to have a baby. Leda did not feel pity or sympathy, she felt only an intense revulsion from such naked manifestations of reality. She wanted nothing to do with a man who wanted to marry her and in order to do so, to divorce his wife who was so desperately in love with him that she had carried through a plan to become pregnant in order to keep him. All that it involved—Lambert's fury, Maizie's desperation, Lambert's intention to make her get rid of the child, the conflict that must ensue, the scandal, the talk, the blame, the ostracism—all these were larger than life-size; outside of any world in which Leda wanted to live. They were other people's hells.

Now walking rapidly along she wanted to be clear and free of them. Herself would contain all the emotion that she cared to acknowledge. She wanted most of all to get back to feeling the Nicola way: easy and orderly and unemotional, well-dressed and untroubled. She looked up at the tops of the brick Boston buildings and grasped for their conventionality. She wanted to think of new clothes, and casual admirers, and teas before the fire, and baths in big tubs, and morning sunshine, and luncheon tables. She wanted self-indulgence, and flattery, and peace. She never wanted to hear again of suffering and violence. She felt revulsion to the whole Maizie situation and she felt revulsion to Lambert himself. His face passed across her mind and she shrank from even the look of it: it was too dark, too intense, too real. Maizie's face too appeared to her, as it had been on that picnic weeks ago; the little blue straw hat perched above it. She could remember every anxious line in it, the tension, the strain. She wanted to be quit of these people and their disorderly, racked lives. Oh, they were not what she wanted touching hers at all!

She came to a Western Union office on Boylston Street and turned into it. She took one of the radiogram blanks and wrote out a message to Miss Nicola Kruger in Paris: "WHEN ARE YOU COMING BACK NEED YOU LEDA."

Next day when she was sitting in the garden in Hampton under the flowering lilac tree she got the answer by cable.

"ARRIVE FIFTH WEDDING THIRTIETH YOU HONOR MAID LOVE NICOLA."

## CHAPTER XXV

NICOLA arrived home with a wardrobe trunk full of clothes from Paris. There were crepe-de-chine combinations with her name embroidered in the corner, a dozen nightgowns, a dozen pairs of pajamas, a Fortuny tea-gown and three tea-gowns from Babani's. There were a dozen pairs of shoes made to order for her at Hellstern's; bags from Hermès; hats from Reboux. There was also a trunkful of linen—large damask cloths, small cloths appliqued with colored flowers, napkins, sheets, hemstitched pillow cases—and all with NKF embroidered large or small in corner or center.

Nicola had won her case about Dicky. Somehow, in unimaginable scenes, she had brought Mrs. Kruger over to her side. Leda would never know how. Now there was no faintly perceptible flaw in the front which Nicola's wedding plans presented to the world. Anyone would have thought that Dicky was Mrs. Kruger's own idea. She joked with him, made him fetch and carry for her, was the picture of the smart gay woman of the world with her future son-in-law. The picture was charming. Nicola was perfect, Mrs. Kruger was perfect, and Dicky—Dicky was perfect too and had become part of the Krugers' world and, by some Kruger alchemy, the acceptable young fiancé. The whole picture was delightful and in the best possible taste.

And how were these things done? Leda often wondered, while she gave herself to being part of the preparations and festivities before the wedding. How did people like the Krugers assimilate whatever they decided upon and make it, like themselves, enviable? Other people, like Leda, cavilled at unacceptable newcomers and dared not associate themselves. But the people like the Krugers, once they had decided upon an addition to their lives, brought the addition up to the invulnerability of themselves. How was that done?

Leda herself would never have considered Dicky. He came from the Newtons. His father was an insurance man with a comfortable income; his mother, a Newton housewife. If for one instant Leda had ever considered such a beau, she would have dismissed him immediately after a succession of dreadful little pictures had passed across her mind: Dicky saying the wrong thing; Dicky not knowing how to behave; Dicky looking a fool beside a Porcellian man. And the extraordinary thing about it was that Dicky actually did not say or do the wrong thing; he hit it off to perfection with the Krugers' friends, with the gay Boston bachelors of middle age who came in for cocktails with Mrs. Kruger. He might almost have been a Kruger himself.

It had, Leda thought, something to do with confidence. The Krugers were confident, and Dicky in some amazing way turned out also to be perfectly confident. He teased Mrs. Kruger and criticized Nicola's clothes; smoked cigarettes and fetched a handkerchief for Mrs. Kruger out of her bureau drawer, lit Mr. Kruger's cigar for him after dinner—as though the Newton in his background were no ghost, as if, in fact, he was not worrying about anything whatever.

Such confidence was a talisman that for Leda was always out of reach. Her one aberration, her strange dreamlike two months with Lambert, now sat on her conscience like an incubus. She could not understand how she could have done such a thing; she was still capable, with all she had learned in pain and frustration, of doing something hopelessly wrong. She thought she must have been mad. Nicola went away, and from mere depression and loneliness for Nicola, she must dash off to Lambert and expose herself to frightful possibilities—chief among them that she had gotten herself talked about.

As soon as Nicola returned, they had had a long conference, after dinner in town at the Krugers' when Dicky had been busy and Mr. Kruger in New York; Mrs. Kruger, Nicola, and Leda had had dinner in tea-gowns at a small candle-lit table.

"Darlings, go and straighten out the world," Mrs. Kruger said after coffee. "I have letters to write for my sins. Leda, you look divine in that salmon pink."

They lay on the beds in Nicola's room that looked back over Marlboro and Beacon Streets to the river, one lamp lighted and their nightgowns laid out neatly on the backs of chairs. As of old Nicola's calm and wisdom permeated the atmosphere and made living seem a prudent affair.

"I've done the most imbecile thing," Leda said, and she told Nicola about how she had spent the months when Nicola had been in Paris going to the right shops, drinking chocolate at patisseries, dining with friends of her mother's; while she, Leda, had so much worse than wasted time; had been acting idiotically. "Isn't it absolutely too frightful? Now that you're back I can't understand how I could have been so insane."

Nicola lit another cigarette calmly.

"Well, I don't know," she said, "Of course I suppose you were just the least bit reckless. At least for Beantown. But I wouldn't feel bad. It seems to me the thing for you to do is to let Lambert get a divorce and marry him. I always told you I thought you were right for each other."

"But you don't understand. She's going to have a baby. He wanted to get her to have it stopped. Imagine the sort of story that would make if it got out, and of course she'd make the most of it. It would ruin me. Everyone would think I was a monster."

"There's no use being emotional. I always think it is so absurd to get emotional about things. Personally I think his wife is too dreary for words, and quite wrong for him, and he for her. Obviously he makes her wretched. She'd be better off by far if she got this baby stopped and divorced Lambert and started off fresh."

"I know, but . . ."

"I think you ought to do precisely what you choose about it, and people will come round once it's a *fait accompli*. They always do. You and Lambert would make a frightfully attractive couple. If you're attractive enough, people put up with what you do. To say nothing of the fact that things blow over. Even if there should be a fuss about his making her divorce him, everybody would have forgotten about it in no time. I should do precisely what I chose."

"I know, but . . ." It was easy for Nicola to do precisely as she chose. "I just haven't got the—something—to make people accept what I do," Leda said.

"Nonsense. Of course you have. It's just that you think you haven't. I never knew anybody who was as individual as you, anybody who had so much personality. I can't understand why you always have this lack of assurance. If anybody ought to be assured it's you."

To Leda these were only words. They were all very well for another person to say, but she knew the truth about herself.

"I couldn't. That's all there is to it," she said.

"I just think it's a shame that you should be in love with Lambert and he with you, and so well suited to each other, and then not be married just because of a wretched little horror standing in your way, and the fear of what a few stuffy Boston dowagers might say for a few months until they forgot about it."

"Well, I'm not in love with him. Not any more. Somehow this all turning up just made me stop feeling in love with him at all."

"I don't believe you could really have stopped. It's just because you've gotten the wind up."

"Well, I have stopped. All I'm worrying about now is whether I've gotten myself into any trouble. Whether I'm going to be talked about for going to his studio. It was all right when you were here and went with me. I can't understand what possessed me to go there alone."

"Oh, I can. You probably had a divine time. Of course you wanted to. Naturally it was indiscreet. Obviously one's a bit indiscreet if one's going to marry someone, and you did mean to marry him, didn't you?"

"I don't know. I can't seem to remember. I guess so."

"You're such a funny girl! Of course you meant to marry him. He's mad about you. And if you take my advice you will marry him. Perhaps it will be unpleasant for a bit, but after all. . . . Everyone's indiscreet, you know. And things get unpleasant for everybody at times."

"Not for you," Leda said. It was ludicrous to imagine Nicola being what she called indiscreet; it was impossible to imagine things being unpleasant for her.

"Oh, yes, me too! You can't imagine the absolute rows I had to have with Mummy to get her to see my point about Dicky. I don't know what I should have done if she hadn't come round. Because one way or another I really have got to marry Dicky. But it's all right now."

Imagine for an instant, Leda thought, if she herself had insisted upon marrying Dicky. How odd! How vulgar! An undistinguished young man without background, having done none of the right things nor known any of the right people; how like that awful Leda March. She sighed.

They went on to talk about the clothes for the bridesmaids. Leda was to wear a citron-yellow dress, with a brown turban; the other girls would be in green. There would be six of them, two from school, three from New York and one from Washington. The clothes had been ordered from New York and would be sent to the bridesmaids for fitting, a fitter from the shop coming along to make the alterations. Nicola had bought her wedding dress and veil at Vionnet in Paris. It was absolutely plain. "Absolutely Vionnet," Nicola said.

The preparations for the wedding were like preparations for a theatrical production. Mrs. Kruger had taken a large house out in the country towards Worcester, with extensive grounds, for the purpose of making a beautiful setting for the wedding. The Krugers moved out soon after their return to Boston, and Leda went there and stayed for several days at a time. It was larger than the establishment on Commonwealth Avenue; extra servants had to be engaged—two footmen and additional maids.

During June Leda would awaken to a flood of sunshine coming through her window from the gardens, and hear the low hum of activity all over the house—a vacuum cleaner being used far away, the butler coming up the stairs with boxes of wedding presents to take to Nicola's door, a gardener clipping hedges outside. She would go into Nicola's room and have breakfast off a tray set on a little table by the window—grapefruit with its edges cut in a sawtooth design, thin hard bits of toast, hot coffee. The room was a welter of white paper and ribbons thrown about the floor, while the silver or china objects that had emerged sat about on the furniture—a great silver compote on the bureau, a dozen Spode plates on the mantelpiece, eight antique salt cellars on the seat of a chair.

"Aren't those coffee-cups horrors?" Nicola would say, drinking coffee and letting her eyes wander about the room. "One of Mummy's old school friends sent them. All I can say is, I shall still be writing thank-you notes on our tenth anniversary."

There were just short of a thousand wedding presents. They were carried away each morning after Nicola had gone out, and put in the wedding-present room, on the long tables that had been built to hold them.

Every morning Nicola and Leda would go into town to attend to details about flowers, presents for the bridesmaids, a present for Dicky from Nicola, bits of clothing that had to be assembled to complete Nicola's trousseau. Dicky had given Nicola an engagement ring. It was a very small emerald with square-cut diamonds flanking it on each side. It was charming but unimpressive.

"I think it's rather sweet," Nicola said in her low, comfortable voice. "I'm very fond of it." What did she ever really think? Did she plan to get a larger ring later when they were married? Did she love Dicky with passion? With longing? With what? Leda would never be able to understand the workings of Nicola's untroubled mind. Leda herself, that June, felt often nearly sick with apprehension and anxiety.

Sometimes leaving town to drive out to Nicola's, or to Hampton, Leda would see the back of the Fenway Studios from Boylston Street. It gave her a sick feeling and she would turn her head away to escape the sight of the big brick pile.

She had not answered the telephone on the three occasions, immediately after she had left the studio that day, that Lambert had called. He had not written to her. She preferred to put the thought of him aside; she preferred to conjecture that he was reconciled to his domestic situation, that Maizie would have her baby and in the way that things always happened, at least in books, the baby would fix everything up. She preferred not to doubt whether this were reasonable. She preferred to relegate Lambert to a world of things that had never really happened; dreams, nightmares. She had slipped out from under the hovering catastrophe. She had avoided the awful, thunderous scandal; perhaps no one knew that she had been on all those days to his studio alone, perhaps no one had. ever observed her going in, surely she was safe. Nevertheless there were the moments when dread hung heavy over her head; dread that she pushed feverishly away like a dread left over from a dream.

Shortly before the day of the wedding the bridesmaids began to arrive and were put in pairs in the big bedrooms of the Krugers' house. Leda moved out there for the rest of the time. Dicky had produced eight ushers and they were outstandingly attractive; where had he scared them up? Not only was Dicky metamorphosed into an acceptable bridegroom but all that was his was also acceptable. Leda would never have thought that Dicky would know the right Harvard men to have for ushers; but he did; these were completely right, and not picked up since he had known Nicola, either. It was very puzzling.

The big wedding party rushed in and out from town in a fleet of cars, danced at the Copley-Plaza, drank champagne at preliminary dinners and at the big dinner for the whole wedding party two nights before the wedding. There were luncheons and teas and cocktail parties given for Nicola all about, in town and in Manchester and Nahant. The party tore about the country and back to the Krugers' to change and on again. It was exciting. They were days out of a novel, the life of the privileged living under conditions most ideal for the display of privilege. Leda loved them. She felt that she would like always to live like this.

The talk was of parties, in New York, in Washington; of famous fullbacks getting drunk, of famous debutante successes being 'wild'; of young people in their world who were going to get married, with eight bridesmaids, with twelve bridesmaids, with two orchestras, with sixteen ushers, with a thousand wedding presents, with their trousseaux entirely by Worth, with honeymoons to Paris, to the South of France, with apartments already taken for them on Park Avenue, on Sixteenth Street, with houses taken for them in Hamilton, in Westbury.

All the fortunate young people of Long Island, the North Shore, Lake Forest, were getting married and being given a diamond bracelet by the groom, sapphire studs by the bride, a silver service from Cartier's by the mother of the groom; were taking token jobs with Lee Higginson, with Lehman Brothers; being given Packard roadsters to get to the country over weekends, having the living-rooms of their apartments done in beige and white by a decorator, having a mirror-topped table in their new dining-rooms, were getting their clothes from Hattie Carnegie, their ushers' ascots from London.

Biji, Randy, Hope and Mimi, Petie and Jeff and Lilias and Al, Ogden, Sis, Connie, Diana, were all getting married and it was divine.

Now the days of debuts were over, the balls in the Crystal Room at the Ritz and the dinner-dances at the Somerset; the luncheons where the debutantes snatched the flowers off the center of the table and departed before dessert; the tunes, the debut dresses with tulle skirts, the big man up from Princeton; over forever in the lives of these young people, and the next big splash was this. They were getting married.

They were marrying their old loves left over from Foster's dancing-classes, they were marrying Bones men, and Porcellian men, they were marrying the girl who ate a live goldfish in the lobby of the Ambassador, and the girl who wore green all her year, and the girl who had got to every game for three years, and the boy who was trying for the Diplomatic, and Mrs. Warrender's son, and the man who carried the ball forty yards in the Yale game.

This was a new glamour, different from the coming-out glamour. This had a new jargon: the gift of the groom, the ushers' dinner, the wedding trip, the silver service, the flat silver, the twin beds. They were all just as young and just as strong, and they were still in just as much of a hurry, but now they were getting married. They were going to be married people.

They were getting tea-gowns for their trousseaux from Jessie Franklin Turner to wear before the fire in the evenings in their own homes. Nick was designing the furniture for his own dressing-room. Mr. Elsroad had given Matt and Bettina a house in Virginia where they could go for the hunting. Jeffy Curtis was going to collect first editions. Elvira was going to cooking school. They looked at themselves and at each other and saw, instead of Marna looking heavenly in her coming-out dress, or Munroe playing forward on the winning hockey team, a wife, a husband; but a wife! a husband! It was too divine.

They would all meet at Piping Rock for the dances, at Meadowbrook for the polo. It was all full of new sentiment. *"Sleepy-time girl,"* they sang, softly; *"You'll learn to cook and to sew, what's more . . ."* It was all a new experience and yet they were going to have just as much fun, dance at all the night clubs, play golf at Myopia, and, suddenly, they didn't have to be chaperoned any more. It was getting married; it was divine.

The day of the wedding came and the big house in the country awoke. First the servants, doing a hundred tasks before anyone was awake; then the bridesmaids sleepily sitting up in bed, and the breakfasts being brought up on trays. One bridesmaid went out and played tennis in her bare feet with an usher. There was the dressing, the running in and out of each other's rooms: "We've simply got to tip the hats all the same way or it won't make any *sense*"; the flowers arriving and arriving and arriving, the striped red and white marquee being put up on the lawn by workmen who lived in a world a million miles away; the tables set up, the detectives arriving, and Nicola in her room: calm, unflustered; putting on white satin underclothes with her name written in embroidery.

Faster, faster; the ushers milling about the lawn and being driven away to the stone chapel in the village where the ceremony would be; the cars coming back for the bridesmaids, for Mrs. Kruger, for Mrs. Fenton who had suddenly appeared from somewhere in a purple straw hat; the shiny black limousine into which got Leda, Nicola, and Mr. Kruger; driving along the roads, arrogantly, to the village. There was going up under the awning, treading the red carpet, to the church door, with crowds pressing in from either side; a maid appeared and adjusted Nicola's train in the doorway to the church. The organ wandered on in that sleepy way, that on-the-edge-of-something way; the bridesmaids rushed around the vestibule. "Now . . . Hush, will you? . . . Everybody's ready, aren't they?"—and Mr. Kruger nodded to the chief usher, who nodded to the organist, and . . . the real music began, significant, slow, and the first two ushers stepped out on the aisle. Just behind Leda, alone, came Nicola with her father, her arms full of white orchids; nobody would ever know what she was thinking about. Was she thinking about anything?

And then it was over. Down the aisle, with the festive and triumphant music playing. Outside they all broke up into knots of excitement. . . . "Not now . . . get into that car . . . come on, now . . ." and back they swept through the country roads to the house; and it was all about some people who were now called Mr. and Mrs. Richard Fenton.

The receiving line formed and the first guests began to arrive; the bridesmaids whispered and the ushers brought them glasses of champagne. "My dear, I'm *reeling*. Don't give me another drop. . . ." Mrs. Kruger, Mr. Kruger, then the perfectly presentable Mrs. Fenton, and Mr. Fenton, red-faced; then Nicola and Dicky, then Leda, then all the bridesmaids. The guests came and came. "How do you do . . . how do you do . . . how do you do. . . . I'm so glad. . . . Yes, wasn't it? . . . I'm so glad." Each bridesmaid, with a slight push of the arm, handed each guest on to the next bridesmaid. "I've never seen so many people." "Yes, isn't it divine?" "How long are we going to have to *stand* here?" Mrs. Kruger leaned forward and smiled down at the bridesmaids. "I'll manage now," she said. "You children run along."

Leda moved by degrees through the crowd on the lawn that milled about the champagne table, that simply stood still and talked; the hundreds of people. Small tables were being put up for the breakfast, and to one side there was a table for the bridal party, in the shape of a horseshoe. The sun shone; the grass was bright green; the figures shifted like a kaleidoscope. Leda spoke to people as she passed. They caught at her and chattered. "You look too divine. . . ." "Hello, maid of honor," . . . "When's the bride coming out? . . ." The tallest usher followed her like a mosquito. His name was Anders. "Look," he kept saying. "Look. Listen." She wandered on in a pleasant daze. "Look," Anders said, following her. "Look. Let me get you some champagne and we'll go and drink it somewhere."

"All right," she said.

Quite suddenly in front of her there appeared two figures arm in arm. They were Adèle Macomb and James March. Adèle wore a blue and white printed dress and a big blue hat. Leda felt a sharply unpleasant sensation.

"Hello, there," James said, beaming.

"Hello. Hello, Adèle," Leda said.

"Oh, *hel*-lo," Adèle said. She did not smile. The familiar, scornful, confident face, the face to break dreams. "How funny to see you being maid of honor." She continued to rest her arm on James's and to lean slightly against him.

"Why?" Leda asked.

"Oh, I don't know. I wouldn't have thought you'd have time off from posing for such ordinary things. I wouldn't have thought you'd have time off from your love-life."

"What are you talking about?" James said, laughing. "Leda's got the most enormously complicated love-life. Everybody's in love with her."

"I'm not posing for my portrait any longer," Leda said. She felt weak.

"Don't be absurd," Adèle said coldly. "Everyone knows you're practically living in there at Lambert Rudd's studio. I don't know why I say practically, either."

"Look here," James said.

"How can you imply such a thing," Leda said uncertainly.

"Oh, don't be a fool. If you're living with someone, why not admit it?"

"Now, look here, Adèle," James began. The usher named Anders suddenly appeared. He had a large glass of champagne in each hand and a smile all over his face. Leda turned to him. She snatched the glass from his hand. "Look," he said. "Look. . . . Can't we go somewhere?" She walked away rapidly and he followed her. "Yes, let's," she said. Her heart was beating triple time.

She did not hear anything he said as they sat together on a pair of chairs in the shadow of a copper beech. "Listen," his voice seemed to be repeating over and over. "Listen. I think you're wonderful. Listen. . . ." She could not see anything either. The gaiety and festivity around her was blotted out by a whirling fog.

Everybody knows. . . . Living together . . . and James. James and Adèle arm in arm. Everybody else knows better. Nicola and Dicky. Other people always picked right. Everybody knows . . . everybody knows. . . . Living together. . . . God, oh God. . . . The cloud had fallen. It was all black now. It had happened.

How to get out, how to get out, how to get out. And James too. She saw him walking, arm in arm with Adèle. He was good-looking, and dark, and smiling. Adèle saw him. Adèle thought he was attractive. Adèle knew how to live.

Then Leda was sitting at the horseshoe table eating lobster, and one after another the ushers got up and proposed toasts. Everyone rose and drank them. Nicola was cutting the enormous wedding-cake. She thrust in the big knife, and a caterer stepped forward from behind her and continued cutting the cake. Leda ate some cake. All around her were bridesmaids in green, with blonde hair, with red hair, with dark hair, laughing, laughing, and screaming across the table to the ushers. Did they all know? Had they known right along? James was with Adèle somewhere. Somewhere Adèle had scooped up James, neatly. She knew a good thing when she saw it. Somewhere she was appreciating him. She had come to the wedding with him. She knew how to run her life.

Nicola had left the table, and Dicky too. After a while Leda got up and pushed through the crowds and went upstairs to Nicola's room.

A maid was helping Nicola into her going-away costume. The wedding dress was spread upon the bed, and on top of it the great froth of tulle veil. Nicola sat down on the low chair before the dressing table and stuck her feet into russet leather pumps. There were clocks up the sides of her stockings. Her hair was smooth and neat. Leda stood and stared at her. Nicola looked up.

"What's the matter?" she asked quickly.

"Oh, God, it's happened. Adèle. She said everybody knew I'd been living with Lambert. *Living with him.* I didn't. And she's got James. She was with him."

"Leda," Nicola said, "don't get so excited. You know Adèle's always had a down on you, for some reason. She undoubtedly made it all up, just to say something disagreeable. People don't think any such thing. Don't let her get you upset."

She got up and walked across the room and picked her hat up from a stand on top of the bureau. She put it on carefully in front of a long mirror. It was a beige straw cloche.

"I feel as if the world had come to an end," Leda said. "And she's got James. Oh, I'm such a mess."

"She hasn't got James. That's silly. James is madly in love with you."

"He was, but I let him get away. I've treated him terribly. Oh, I've been such a fool."

Nicola glanced at her sharply. She picked up a russet leather handbag and a pair of beige suede gloves.

"Now, don't be an idiot. James bores you to death and he always has. He always will. For heaven's sake keep your head. I'll be back in August. Let me know if you need any advice or anything, darling. If you ask me, I still think you ought to patch it up with Lambert, although it may be too late now to do anything about the baby. Still, I think even a bad scandal could be managed. You really should marry him. It's the only sensible thing for you."

"Sensible!" Leda cried.

Nicola smiled, and straightened her short skirt, and walked towards the door, and suddenly she was a stranger; a married woman, with a life that no other girl might ever penetrate. Suddenly something was over. All the old days at school, the nights lying and talking about life, the mornings, the afternoons—they were all in the past, a vignetted picture of the friendship of two girls. Leda started forward with her hand out as if she must say something; something she needed was going out of this room and out of her life. But there was not anything to say.

"Come on," Nicola said. She opened the door.

Leda went down the stairs first. People were crowded into the hall, with champagne glasses in their hands, glancing up at the stairs. They caught at Leda's sleeve: "When's she coming?" "Isn't she nearly ready?" But she passed them as if in a dream; a bad dream. She stood near the great open door; she looked at the faces close to her, wondering what they knew; did they know?

Dicky was at the opposite side of the door, having changed from his cutaway; he had a gray felt hat in his hand; he grinned at her. Nicola came downstairs quickly, smiling. Showers of confetti and colored ribbons fell all about her and Dicky as they ran to the car outside; some of it fell on Leda. The crowd pressed out and watched the car go rapidly down the drive; then they were gone, and the party was all at once something different, merely a great number of people gathered together with a great deal to drink.

Leda walked again through the crowds on the lawn, looking into the faces she passed. Did this one know? Had that one been talking? Had this group been discussing her before she passed? People spoke to her, but she was obsessed with the feeling that there was something cold, something critical, in people's manner. Surely it was not her imagination. They were judging her; they knew. But it was not true! But they thought it was.

She passed a monument of purple lace and purple straw; Mrs. Clement Rudd, holding court to half a dozen old Somerset Club members and ladies in Queen Mary hats. Leda hardly dared raise her eyes. She passed on, and saw her aunt, Mrs. Treat March, talking with another March aunt; "Leda . . ." they murmured, and smiled absently, but did not catch at her to join them. The lawn was spotted with old Boston bulwarks. What were they thinking? That March girl . . . the wrong one. . . . Leda . . . you know, of course? . . . But what could you expect. . . . We'll simply have to drop her . . . drop her . . . drop her. . . .

She would be relegated to the limbo of the girls who did not know how to behave themselves and who could not be asked to nice parties. There were always plenty of nice Boston girls, reliable, with sturdy ankles, who could be counted on. It didn't matter if Leda March had misbehaved. Who would miss her?

Suddenly Leda had a sharp little picture of . . . it was Betsy Jekyll, at Leda's coming-out party so long ago, dressed jazzily, laughing too gaily, all out of place; Leda had watched her dancing on the floor with a Harvard senior, tipped back from the waist and laughing up into his face, rouge on her cheeks, earrings dangling. Now, Leda thought, she had thrown herself into the world of cheap girls, the little wrong girls of Boston who went to second-rate parties and either pretended that they were having a lovely time or, mercifully, did not even know the difference.

What sort of a life could she possibly have now? When men took her out they would be set for a big time; taking out that March girl who was good for a whirl any time. Leda had heard that sort of thing said about other girls. There were such awful words for the wrong kind of girl: a necker; a bag; a ginch.

Perhaps she could get out of Boston, go where people would not know. No, she thought, no. She couldn't leave Boston under a cloud; that would help the story. How could she ever have been such a fool, fool, fool, as to risk her precious reputation, for anything at all? Nothing, nobody, was worth being beyond criticism. She hated Lambert bitterly. She hated herself. Of all people she should have known better. She knew all about wrongness and lack of power, she knew well. Oh, she knew this sickness, this wretchedness, this hell.

James was standing under the marquee with a glass in his hand, talking to another man. Adèle was nowhere about. Leda went straight to him. She did not think at all.

"Hello," she said, smiling.

"Leda!" He put down his glass on the long table. "Where have you been?"

"Oh . . . around. Seeing Nicola get off."

"What are you going to do? Are you going back to Hampton? Can I drive you back?"

"Why, yes," she said. "It would be nice. I'll have them get my things together."

They began to walk back to the house, threading through the groups of people in the sunshine.

"Leda," he said in a low voice. "I gave Adèle the devil for talking to you like that. She's an awful little hellion."

"You didn't believe her, did you?"

"Of course I didn't believe her. I won't have anyone talking to you like that. Even Adèle who always says what she pleases. I knew all about your going in to that fellow's studio, and you know I didn't want you to. It really was foolish of you, Leda."

"It was perfectly innocent."

"Of course it was perfectly innocent. But you need somebody to take care of you and keep you from doing crazy things."

"Do I?" she asked. She smiled up into his face. He was very attractive. He didn't look too young. He looked responsible, like what he was, an intelligent young doctor. He was one of the people whose lives came out right. Nothing would ever be wrong about him.

He had the March kind of good looks, pale and large-eyed and dark. He was tall, he wore his clothes forgetfully and well. If the dark moustache he wore had something loathesome about it—she could always make him shave it off. If his voice sometimes made her want to scream at him, because it was so kind, so gently humorous, so Bostonian, that couldn't matter very much. There had to be something wrong with everyone. There was something a little wrong with every husband.

"I'll find the butler and get him to bring my bags down," she said.

"I'll get the car around in front," he said. "I'll meet you there after we've said goodbye to people."

"Listen," she said, hesitating near the door. "You didn't believe what Adèle said, did you?"

"Of course not. If you tell me it's not true I know it's not true. She's jealous of you. Like everybody else."

Leda smiled at him, and went into the house. She would never know how much people did know; how much anybody believed.

## CHAPTER XXVI

JAMES wanted it to be a small wedding; he said he hated a lot of fuss, women gabbling over the presents, rice, all that nonsense. He wanted to have a small family wedding with only a best man and Nicola and a few of their best friends. But that idea never got anywhere. They didn't discuss it.

Leda knew what she wanted. She wanted a big wedding. She didn't want to sneak off after some little ceremony to—what? Whatever was coming next; life with James, what a funny sound it had, how meaningless. But she would see that it was very nice. It would be better than anything she had ever been able to have before.

The wedding would have to be grand too. Things were going to be grand for her, now. No more make-do, no more little pleasures, and specially no more under-cover; everything out in the open, where everybody could admire and envy it.

After a while she had the beginnings of the idea about New York. She realized she had always been dissatisfied with Boston. But she couldn't have gone before, especially after Nicola's wedding; not alone. This would be different. A big wedding, and then going to live in New York; spurning Boston in favor of New York. It would mean something to be somebody in New York.

She put it to James one night when they were sitting in the garden at Hampton in the starlight. James had his arm around Leda's shoulders. When she broke the silence she slipped out from under his hand and faced him.

"I don't want to live in Boston, when we're married," she said. "I'm deathly bored with Boston."

He did not speak for a minute.

"Of course, I've known you were," he said. "What do you want to do? I could see if I could fix it up about that Vienna thing, next year."

"No," she said. She knew that was not what she wanted. It was too vague. They would be alone, they two, a couple abroad in a city where they would be foreigners. Vienna could come later, and so could Paris and London. In the meantime there remained work to be done, friends to be made; the importance to be established that would outweigh anything Boston had to offer; drowning old doubts and old fears.

"No," she said. "I want to go and live in New York. I've always wanted to."

"Well," he said, "I told you long ago I wanted to do anything I could to make you happy. I know you're too big for Boston. I know I'm getting a fascinating woman, darling, and I suppose I shall have a hell of a time with all your admirers. But you do love me, don't you?" He put his arm back around her.

"Of course," she said. He leaned closer and kissed her, pulling her to him, pressing his lips against her face.

"I wish you loved me the way I love you," he said.

"I'm not a very emotional person," she said.

"I know, darling. I'm not criticizing you. It's just I do adore you and you seem so damned unattainable sometimes. But when we're married I'm going to make you love me. I'll be so sweet to you, darling."

She felt a shiver of the uncontrollable disgust she felt sometimes at things he said and ways he said them. But there was no hesitation in her. She had resolved that he was what she wanted, and she never looked backwards.

"But about New York," she said.

"I'll see what can be arranged. I suppose I could practice there, but I don't want to practice. I know a man at Columbia—he wrote me a year or so ago about some research. . . . I'll start working on it tomorrow."

"Good," she said. "I wouldn't want you to practice if it's not the thing you're interested in. You ought to do the work you like." Pictures drifted in her mind; how would a research doctor fit in, what time would he come in in the evening, what would people think of a distinguished research doctor. . . .

"I love to have you care about my work."

"I do."

He kissed her again, drawing her to him, holding her arms in his hands.

"Please love me," he said. "Nobody will ever love you as much as I do."

The answer rose in her mind—What nonsense. Someone had loved her more than this before; and the far and golden future was all superlatives.

But James would be her husband. And a very good husband. He was distinguished and well-bred and good-looking and he had money.

"I know," she said. She kissed him carefully on his mouth, pressing her mouth to it, showing him that she loved him.

"Oh, darling," he said.

The wedding was set for early September. James's mother asked Leda soon after the engagement was announced whether she would like to have the wedding on the North Shore. But Leda had said no. She wanted, she said, to be married in Hampton.

She was sure about this. The house was small, the gardens not extensive, but this was where she wanted the wedding to be. She wanted it to be upon the ground where she had grown up. Upon those long-ago and painful foundations she wanted to erect a wedding—the gaiety, the congratulations, the champagne, rising like fireworks above the place where she had walked a miserable and ignored child. She wanted it big; she wanted it gay. She wanted to make it out of what was her own, and not be given it from outside.

She ran the preparations almost by herself. She told her mother what she must do, and how it must be done. Laura was continually flustered, and Bernard looked frightened and miserable. Leda found in herself an unknown and pleasing gift for organization. She was quite capable of making the plans and giving the orders and keeping it all straight in her mind.

When she encountered opposition from her parents she overrode it. There was the matter of the champagne.

"Kitten," Bernard said feebly. "It isn't just that I can't afford all that champagne. It's that people know I can't afford it. I'm not the sort of chap who buys cases of champagne, I mean."

"Father!" Leda cried. "You don't understand *anything!* Don't be so horribly Bostonian. Weddings are the time for big gestures. I suppose you grudge me a little expense. You've both always grudged me everything I ever wanted."

"Leda, that's not true," Laura said with tears in her eyes. "We've never been able to give you everything the way Nicola's parents can afford to do. I know you've never been satisfied with the childhood we gave you. But we did our best."

"Then you certainly aren't going to spoil my wedding with this business about champagne. Why, you can't *have* a wedding without champagne."

"I thought we could have a nice punch," Bernard said. "I could mix up something, put a little stick into it. . . ."

"Oh no, you couldn't," Leda said. "I just won't have a horrible little wet wedding with some nasty punch. I'd rather not have a wedding at all. You're just trying to ruin everything for me. Trying to keep me from having things right, for once in my whole life."

"I think you've had quite a good many things right," Laura said gravely. "We've given you your own way about everything for years. I don't like to have you putting a false value on things. I don't like to think you put such emphasis on things like champagne. What matters is your love for James and your marrying him, and it doesn't seem to me that you should care so much about the superficial details."

"Oh, mother," Leda said, burning with irritation. "Don't be embarrassing. And don't keep throwing our income at me. I ought to know we never can afford anything. But just this once I think we might have just a little bit of festivity. After all, other people do a little extra when their daughters get married. Don't forget you're getting rid of me, and after the wedding I won't cost you anything at all."

"I can't bear to hear you say things like that," Bernard said. "I don't think you realize how we love you, or you wouldn't hurt us like that."

"We love you so," Laura said, "and sometimes it seems as if you didn't love us at all."

"Of course I love you," Leda said. "And I know you love me. That's why it seems so funny that you don't want me to have a decent wedding."

"All right," Bernard said wearily. "It doesn't really matter. If you want champagne that much you'd better have it."

Leda picked her bridesmaids carefully; she wanted six. Nicola, of course, would be matron of honor. She wrote to Janet Bellingham, in New York, and another New York girl, Cassandra Fellowes, asking them to be bridesmaids; they wrote back notes saying they thought it would be divine.

She asked the Mayson sisters, in Boston, and Jean Harrower, and Marna Elliott; Jean wrote and said she was so sorry, but she would be in Dark Harbor. It gave Leda a brief unpleasant sensation. Jean could have arranged to come down from Dark Harbor if she had really wanted to. But she did not allow herself to be too depressed. She asked Mary Thayer, who accepted. Mary was not attractive, but she was one of the right girls.

She went to one of the most expensive Boylston Street shops and picked out the costumes. She chose dresses and hats that could be worn again, knowing how girls complained about being stuck with a bridal costume that hung in the closet forever. In the July weather in Boston it was pleasant and luxurious to be sitting in the showroom, ordering the dresses and giving directions about them to attentive saleswomen; it gave her the illusion of being very rich. Only she wished that Nicola were not away on her wedding-trip to the Mediterranean. At moments it was lonely, it was a little pathetic, to be attending to everything all alone. It was always she who had to do everything for herself; she was never the one to have things really nice. However, after she was married to James she meant that everything should be really nice.

She went to Shreve Crump & Low's and ordered presents for the brides-maids; narrow gold bracelets with a tag attached like a gold baggage tag, with Leda's name and the name of each bridesmaid engraved on it. They were very pretty bracelets. As she might have expected, her parents made an outcry about the bracelets. But now Leda felt not only irritated but indignant. How could she invite bridesmaids and not give them decent presents, as other brides did? Laura suggested giving each one a little enamel holder for the flowers they would carry. But imagine those girls if one gave them a little enamel holder!

Her own wedding dress Leda designed for herself. Not for her, she thought, the really lovely wedding dress designed by a great couturier; as usual she must substitute wit and ingenuity for the advantages of other girls like Nicola. She went to a dressmaker where Nicola and Mrs. Kruger had had dresses altered, and for many hours on many days worked over plans for a really beautiful dress. Leda thought she could have been a great dress-designer. But she could be greater things than that. All alone she was slaving through the hot summer months while other girls were swimming and playing tennis at Bar Harbor, at Newport. But this would be the last summer that she would have to endure staying in Hampton; from now on life would be different.

She worked very hard.

One day when she returned from town she went down in the orchard behind the house. The midsummer air was stifling. Leda felt tired. She felt a wave of affection for this place, where she had grown up and which she was leaving soon forever; perhaps when she was old she would come back and walk nostalgically over its acres. She wandered through the long, dry, yellow grass. A cicada screamed high and shrill from down toward the swamp, a melancholy, summer sound. In her mind's eye she saw the small, thin figure of long ago, herself, wandering lonely and full of dreams through this orchard. She thought the eyes must have been very large and dark; the mouth sensitive. That child had not known that she was to conquer her loneliness, make a place for herself in the world outside, and these through her own efforts.

Leda ran her hand over the rough, pinkish bark of an old appletree standing deep in orchard grass. On an impulse she climbed the tree and sat upon the horizontal limb, leaning back against the trunk, the smell of half-formed apples sweet in her nostrils. So had she climbed this tree long ago; and sat here on this branch, staring out over the hot meadow lands.

The golden swamp shimmered in the heat. This is a goodbye to youth, Leda thought. I shall probably never climb this tree again. She thought back over the years, mounting them gradually to her self-won success.

Her mind came to Lambert and dwelt upon him. He would have understood about that strange little girl; she could have told him all about her and he would have known. Now she would never tell him. Now the queer sympathy that had existed between them had been smashed—no, not smashed; it had been stolen away from them. But its potentiality was still there forever, and perhaps when I am old, she thought, I shall meet him somewhere, and we shall realize that the sympathy is still there, and then we can talk together. I shall be a slim, distinguished old lady; I will have travelled everywhere and I will be famous for my beauty too.

That short dream was all over, the dream of hers and Lambert's. It was all over, and what was there left of it? Only its existence in their minds. You could not pin down hours, nor cast moments in bronze. Suddenly Leda slipped down out of the tree and walked up toward the house. On the lawn beside the house it was cooler, and the grass was still green there, and fresh. She went into the house and got a pad of paper and a pencil, and came out and lay on her stomach on the cool grass. She started to write.

When she had finished her sonnet she rolled over on her back and read it.

> The way things are, the past lifts off like mist,
> The sun burns through, and in the flash of an eye
> We have forgotten all the mystery
> That filled us . . .
> And memory cheats us, skimping on the gold
> That leafed the hours and made them fabulous;
> The words we said are taken away from us . . .
> And all our pain and passion's stilly cold.
> Of the intangible days I spent with you
> None can you resurrect, nor I relive it;
> No word I ever said can now be true
> Beyond the truth your memory can give it.
> This, then, is all we have of permanency:
> It once was so, and cannot cease to be.

She wondered what Lambert would think of it. He had always been moved by her verses, by her writing of them if nothing more. It was a shame that he could not see this, her epitaph to their days.

Perhaps she owed him something. She would like to show him that she had not been heartless, that underneath it had meant a great deal to her. It was only kind, it was only sensitive, that she should send him these lines, to show him that for her it was all over, yes, but that it had been something precious.

She recopied the poem and went into the house and put it into an envelope and addressed it to him at the studio. Later that afternoon she drove through the village and dropped the letter in the mailbox outside the post office. The evening was dark and breathless. James came for dinner, and afterwards they walked about in the garden, under the dark sky. Leda talked about poetry. He was very humble about his ignorance of literature.

"I'll leave the intellectual pursuits to you, darling," he said. "I'm just an old scientific guy."

"I'm interested in learning about your work."

"I know, but you're so confoundedly bright about picking things up. You seem to have an ear for the jargon. I never was quick at things. You should have seen me plugging through medical school. In college I never could make any sense out of literature courses. I'll just have to leave the artistic side of our life to you."

"Don't say 'artistic'," she said.

"Why not say artistic?"

"It just sounds so wet," she said briefly.

She had no word from Lambert about the poem she had sent him, though for a time she found herself waiting for the mail. She hoped he would not telephone. A letter was what she wanted, something tragic, and beautiful, that would show her, as she had shown him, his state of mind. No letter came. At first she felt resentful, then she shrugged her shoulders. If he couldn't even have the common civility to acknowledge her poem, she was well quit of him. He could stay in the mess he had made of his life. She rather regretted that she had sent him her poem.

In August James went to New York to talk to a man with whom he had been in correspondence about doing research at the Columbia foundation. He would be gone for four days. Leda promised to meet him at Back Bay when he returned. She thought it would be rather nice to have a little vacation from James for a bit. She had seen him every night all summer, and while conversation was not difficult nor unpleasant, since James took such an enthusiastic interest in all that she was doing and thinking and feeling, his love-making sometimes got to be a strain. Sometimes she could not restrain her repugnance.

"Oh, James, *don't!*" she cried suddenly the night before he went to New York, when he was pressing his mouth against her neck, and it was hot.

"I can't help pestering you," he said. "I'm afraid I'm going to be rather an uxorious fellow."

"What do you mean, uxorious?"

"Uxorious means wife-loving, darling."

"I know what it means," she said. "But if you mean wife-loving, why don't you say wife-loving?"

"I sort of like uxorious. It's a nice word."

"You admit you don't know anything about words. You just sound pompous when you try to use long ones. I can't bear pomposity. You'd better stick to saying what you mean."

"Don't get mad at me, darling. I didn't mean anything."

"I'm not mad at you!"

"I know, I know, darling. It's been awfully hot, and of course it is a strain for you."

"*What* is a strain for me?"

"Well, the emotional strain we are both bound to be under while we are engaged."

"Oh, don't be *loathesome!*" she cried.

"Darling, darling. Don't be nervous. Everything's all right. I'll be so sweet to you. Everything will be lovely when we get all this folderol over and are alone together."

"Please don't say 'alone together'."

"I won't say anything," he said mildly, pressing his face against Leda's cheek.

It was the day after James had gone that the letter came from Lambert. Opening it, she realized that she had never seen his handwriting on a full page before.

"Darling," it said.

"Don't be a damned fool. We haven't forgotten all the mystery, not even you, although you're such a tough little thing. Everything is one hell of a mess, isn't it? I want to see you before the world blows up completely, and you're bound to want to see me after the good purgative dose of Boston you have been getting. Before we're all grown up and committed to boredom and Christ knows what, let's see each other anyway once. Let's be young together just one more time. I know you have to think of your God damned reputation. So if you'll be down on the dock at Manchester about three on Friday I'll sail up to it and take you off, and I can't think of any better place to be alone than on a boat. If you're not there, then you're not there.

Lambert."

The letter was like a gust of spring wind in the middle of Leda's summer. She could see Lambert, as she read the letter. She could hear his voice and see his lips speaking.

She told herself that it would be impossible for her to go sailing with him. Friday was the day that James returned, at eight o'clock in the evening, and they might be becalmed and she unable to get to the station to meet him. Besides someone on the dock, someone in another boat, might see them together. It wasn't worth the risk.

But there was one phrase in Lambert's letter that echoed over and over in Leda's head. "Let's be young together just one more time." It seemed to strike a note in her. "Let's be young together just one more time. Let's be young . . ."

On Friday after lunch she got in her car and drove directly to Manchester.

She stood on the end of the dock. After the heavy Boston air the breeze here was strong and fresh, the water and the sky were bright blue, and there was a lift, like singing. The white sails out on the water skimmed along nearly horizontal to the waves, and fled before the wind. She saw a sloop coming up to the dock, and the figure at the tiller raised one arm and saluted, slowly, and she raised her arm and saluted back. The boat swept in closer. Lambert brought it in to the dock and caught the edge of the round logs framing it as he passed them. Leda jumped down into the cockpit and he let go and they swept off again across the broad and rippling water. She sat down on the seat opposite him.

"Trim the jib sheets, will you?" he said.

She shifted the ropes forward on the little deck and made them fast about cleats.

"I haven't been sailing since Islesboro last year," she said, conversationally.

He had on a pair of old khaki pants and a white shirt; it was open at the neck. He was not looking at her, but up at the big sail. His face was brown and hard.

"Who gives a damn when you went sailing last?" he said.

She laughed.

"Have you been sailing a lot?" she said.

"Oh, nuts. I don't know. Come over and sit beside me. You're in the wrong place."

She slipped over to the other side of the cockpit. They were skimming along fast, and the little waves went slap, slap, slap, against the side of the boat. There were no other boats anywhere near them. Lambert kept his left hand crooked over the tiller and put his other arm around Leda. She looked up into his face and smiled and he smiled back at her.

"God bless you," he said. "You don't have to talk everything over, do you?"

"No."

"I suppose you're a bitch, but I'm a bastard, so that makes us two of a kind, doesn't it?"

Somehow she didn't at all resent his saying that. She felt perfectly comfortable and happy, and leaned against him and put her head on his shoulder.

"Our goose is cooked, darling," he said. "Our cake is eaten, or something. The good days are over. I guess it was your fault. But I don't know. I guess it would have been pretty bad anyway. I make trouble anywhere I am, and although you may not know it yet, you'll make trouble anywhere you go too. What the hell. This is nice, isn't it?"

"Yes."

He leaned his head and kissed her on the lips. She did not speak. The cool fresh breeze blew incessantly across their faces. The sun caught in little points all over the blue face of the sea, and far away other white sails dipped in and out of sight. Occasionally they would come about, and shift to the other side of the cockpit together, and Lambert would put his arm back around Leda. It was extraordinarily peaceful. There was a kind of suspension from the hot world, being off alone in a boat on the sea.

Lambert would kiss Leda, and she would look up into his face and smile, and he would smile back. Then she would settle against his arm again, and keep her eyes fixed on the horizon, and more time would go by without either of them speaking. It was only much later in the afternoon when long shadows began to streak the water and the gulls flew low over the waves and shrieked that they began to talk.

"How is Maizie getting along?" Leda said. Her voice was husky from long silence, and she cleared her throat.

"I guess she's all right. The baby will be born in February."

"How do you feel about it?"

"All right. I've sort of made up my mind about it. I guess that things being as they are, it's probably the best thing that could happen to us. It should make Maizie happier. She's excited about it. She wants a boy."

"What do you want?"

"A boy, I guess. I guess it would be nice to have a son. I'd never thought much about it before, about a child itself, I mean. I've thought about the idea of a woman being pregnant, but not. . . . I guess it will be nice to have a boy."

It was curious how unimpassioned their talk was. Their lives had arranged themselves, each of them had a rôle to fill waiting on land, separate paths that they would follow, all marked out and mapped. This afternoon was a dream occurring in the midst of their real lives, that did not disturb nor change anything.

"When's the wedding?" he said.

"September. You'll be asked of course. I hope you'll both come."

"Oh, I don't know. Maybe Maizie will. I'm not much on weddings. There isn't anything to do but get tight. Where are you going to live?"

"We're going to New York. James has got work there. I'm going down next week and pick out an apartment."

"Good," he said. "Good. New York is much more the place for you."

"You too, I should think."

"I don't believe in that, for me. I might like it, I don't know. But places shouldn't make any difference to a painter. And Maizie wouldn't want to live away from her family. Not that she likes Boston. But New York would be worse. She's a Southern girl, you know. I don't think she's ever liked the North."

"I know," Leda said.

They were talking like old friends. They were talking very wisely, very maturely. It was only their senses that were being young together, smelling the salt wind, watching the light fade from the sea and the water turn to purple.

"Do you want me to put you ashore again or will you come along to the mooring and row ashore?"

"Oh, I might as well stay with you. It's all right."

They tied on to the mooring in the late afternoon and rowed ashore in the little dinghy. There was no one about on shore. The land birds were calling in the early twilight. The air was warmer, but there was still the breeze from the sea. They walked in the dusk up the hill to where Leda's car was parked. She got in behind the wheel and he leaned with his arms folded on the side of the door.

"Goodbye," she said.

"It's been a swell afternoon, hasn't it?"

"Swell."

"Let me drive down to the turn in the road with you. I'll walk back," he said.

"All right."

He came around and got in beside her on the other side. She started the car and drove slowly along the road from the sea up the rise to the turn in the road. Then she stopped and pulled on the hand brake. The engine was running, quietly.

Lambert sat beside her looking straight ahead. She turned her head and looked at him.

"Goodbye, my darling," he said. He put both arms around her and kissed her slowly, lightly. "Goodbye, Leda."

Suddenly she began to cry. She had no warning. Suddenly she was crying bitterly, endlessly. Lambert held her tight and said nothing. From time to time he kissed her, gently, on her wet face. She could not stop crying. She had never cried like this before in her life. She did not know exactly what it was that made her tears so urgent, so inexhaustible. It was something about a kind of life being over. It was something about youth being over. It was about something being over that she had never really had, a kind of youth, a kind of simplicity.

It was not that she felt anything must be changed. She simply felt heartbroken. She cried and cried.

"We could always just go off, you know," he said.

"No," she murmured, crying.

"No, I suppose not. I wonder what kind of people we would have been if we hadn't been born in Boston."

She did not answer.

"My sweet," he murmured. "Darling. My sweet love."

She felt his cheek hard and cool against hers.

"It certainly has bitched us," he said. "We stink as people. We might have been perfectly decent if we hadn't always been fighting something ever since we were born. If we'd lived in some normal, easy sort of place. We excrete all the wrong juices. We're all uncoordinated for coping with life on an easy basis."

Nothing he said seemed to matter. His face was unbearably sweet pressed against hers.

"I've got to go," she said. "I've got to meet James."

"Yes," he said. "I suppose so."

He kissed her again, still impersonally almost, on her wet lips, and opened the car door and got out. The dusk had grown deeper. He stood in the half-light looking at her.

"Goodbye," she said. She straightened herself in the seat, took a long breath. "Good luck."

"Don't be silly," he said. "Goodbye."

She did not look at him but threw the clutch in and moved away. When she was almost around the curve she looked back and he was standing in his shirtsleeves in the middle of the road in the twilight. Then she went on around the corner and the car picked up speed.

She walked up and down the long platform downstairs in the Back Bay Station, waiting for the train to come in from New York. The hot city noises came faintly down to the tracks from the South End—the children calling in the evening heat. She had an unformed memory of herself as a schoolgirl standing so many days on the platform on the other side, waiting for the train to Hampton, alone, or, earlier, with Betsy Jekyll. It seemed very long ago, and not especially significant, just unforgettable. She was another person now. She was a tall young lady in a white dress and no hat, in socks and sneakers, walking up and down the platform. She passed a middle-aged man she knew slightly, a Mr. George Ames, also pacing up and down, carrying a stick and swinging it. He bowed, and she bowed gravely back. She was Miss Leda March. She would soon be married.

As the train roared in, the tracks made a shuddering sound and the huge yellow lamp in front of the engine poked blindingly into the station, and then the train was slowing and halting with the sound of brakes put on and off. People stood clustered in the end of each car, and on each end platform was a pile of baggage. When the train stopped the colored porters jumped down and began hurriedly to unload the bags. Then the passengers stepped off. Leda saw James at once. He was two cars away from where she stood; looking around for her. She had no impulse to join him. She watched him with curiosity. He was tall, wearing a thin gray suit and stiff straw hat with his club ribbon round it. He looked prosperous, handsome, and Bostonian.

He saw her, and hurried up to her, beaming. She stood still. When he got near she smiled. He put his arm around her and kissed her.

"Everything's set," he said. "Got a splendid opportunity, working with Mayhill. Looked at a couple of apartments, too. One specially nice, with a river view. How's my sweetheart? Been playing tennis?"

"Yes," she said. "I didn't change."

He took her arm and they began to walk towards the stairs, up into the station, comfortably, with steps that matched.

"Missed me?" he asked.

"Of course," she said.

## CHAPTER XXVII

WHEN IT WAS SEPTEMBER, and the heat broke, and Nicola came back from her honeymoon, everything was different; invigorating. Now Nicola went with Leda on the last shopping expeditions and gave advice. It was nice to be going about Boston, two tall slender well-dressed young women, one dark and one fair, going into shops together and sitting over a table at lunch.

But Nicola could not always go along. She was married now, and arranging her own apartment, and was subtly different from the way she had been in the old days; just as good a friend, as complete a confidante, but with another life no one could share; her married life. It was a strange little feeling. Soon Leda would be married too, and living in New York. She would come back to Boston on visits, and Nicola would of course come to New York for clothes and the theatre, and they would go immediately to each other, and they would lunch together, and all four of them would have evenings. But it would never again be as two free-lances in the world. They would be women, with husbands, with establishments, with lives organized on a different basis.

Nicola and Dicky had an apartment in a made-over house on Commonwealth Avenue, the two top floors. As soon as Nicola moved into it, it took on Nicola's atmosphere. Mrs. Kruger had supervised its decoration while Nicola was away, and now it was a young married couple's apartment that seemed to Leda a sort of criterion for young married couples' apartments. There was silver tea-paper on the walls of the dining-room, the living-room was done in beige and white, there were flowers in the big simple glass vases, looking somehow like Nicola's flowers and nobody else's; the wedding presents were put to use, silver cigarette boxes on the tables and silver dishes for ashtrays, lamps, small tables, and dinner plates. Through her apartment Nicola moved calmly in her trousseau clothes, her hair smooth, moving things a fraction of an inch to achieve perfection. She might always have been Mrs. Richard Fenton.

Leda would go up to the apartment for lunch on a warm, clear September day, or drop in at the end of an afternoon after shopping and be given a cocktail when Dicky came home. The two girls would sit at each end of the large sofa covered in rough white stuff, and reach out their hands for the wedding-present glasses, wet and frosty. Dicky was perfect too. He was the completely right young husband who sold bonds down town and played squash with other young bond-salesmen and came home to mix a drink for his wife and her friends. He teased Nicola and Leda in just the proper vein. The Fentons were an obviously happy, well-suited, and attractive young couple. They spent weekends on the North Shore; they were in demand to dine.

They were not bridal, nor in any way did they give out an aura of emotion. It was more attractive than that. They were calm and joking, they played all games well, they danced well, they dressed well; an addition to society.

Leda observed them minutely. She was learning the rhythm of living of an attractive young couple. She was continually struck with one thing: out of no overwhelming passion, out of what seemed hardly more than liking, the Fentons had made together a successful life. It showed that the novels were wrong; that commonsense was right; that happy marriages were not made from great love. Great love, on the contrary, could not possibly be fitted into such a chic apartment as this; it would knock over all the little tables.

Happy marriages, Leda thought, were made from little things: a nickname for your husband, plenty of money, a good forehand stroke at tennis, your charming mother-in-law dropping in for a cocktail not too often, little dinners with terribly good food and highballs afterwards from expensive crystal glasses.

The fact that Nicola's marriage had turned out so well showed that you did not have to wait around for a man who was everything you could ask for. You chose a man with certain basic requirements and then you constructed around him and yourself a delightful setting. In fact, you had better not wait around for a man you were desperately in love with. You might be hampered by love, you might not do as good a job on making a charming marriage out of it.

James was extremely good material. He was infinitely better material than Dicky had been. She would have nothing much to do to James. And Leda was coming to have considerable confidence in her own talents for organization. Perhaps they were not as unerring and graceful as Nicola's, but Nicola had been born with hers. Leda was not doing so badly for a girl who had been given none of the breaks, who had had to do everything for herself, she thought.

The wedding was going to be lovely. Leda knew better than to attempt things that were beyond her scope, that only really rich people could do properly. It was going to be charming; individual.

Less than a week before the wedding Laura came into Leda's room one evening after she had gone to bed. She was going to bed early for several nights in order to be fresh when the festivities began. She was lying in her bed reading a magazine about decoration, in an old nightgown. All her trousseau nightgowns and other things were already packed, and she was wearing for these last weeks nightgowns and pajamas that would be given away when she was married.

The screens were still on the windows, and the cool late summer air came softly into the room. Laura came in uncertainly and sat down on the old painted wooden chair.

"You look so pretty, sweetheart," Laura offered hesitantly.

Leda smiled and laid down the magazine on the blanket.

"I must, with my face loaded with cold cream. I feel like the ladies in the beauty articles. 'Take every opportunity to cream your face when you are alone, to make yourself beautiful for your husband.'"

Laura smiled vaguely; she did not understand that sort of thing. She had always been puzzled by her daughter, and now her daughter lived in a world whose jargon she did not even understand. She was not sure whether Leda was speaking seriously or whether she was making a joke.

"Precious, I came in because I thought . . . perhaps . . . there are things we ought to talk about before you marry James."

"What?"

"Well, dearest, I don't want you to be frightened about what . . . marriage means. It's nothing dreadful. It's very beautiful, and lovely, and it can be a sort of sacrament between you and your husband."

"Oh, my God!" Leda said. "Look, I know about the facts of life. I've known about them for years. Everybody does."

She was strangely revolted by the idea of her mother coming in to her to talk seriously and embarrassingly. She obviously wanted to say things of a sentimentality that made Leda's flesh crawl. It was incredible the way her parents always did everything wrong. Imagine Mrs. Kruger coming in to tell Nicola about sex. If she had ever done such a thing, she would have put it intelligently, attractively; not slimed it over with this cast of revolting emotion.

Leda picked up her magazine.

But Laura stayed.

"I know," she said. "I know your generation knows all sorts of things. It wasn't just to tell you what . . . sexual relations are, that I came in. It's something else. It's rather hard for me to put into words to you, Leda."

"I think I know everything I need to know," Leda said.

"No. It's this. I love you and I want you to be happy and have a full, beautiful marriage such as your father and I have had. I know you aren't satisfied with the way we brought you up. I know you are impatient of us. But we did our best. And we want to see you happy. We don't want to see you missing the most precious things in life."

"I don't intend to," Leda said briefly.

"I think perhaps you're a little hard, sweetheart. Not kind. Not outgiving. Perhaps it is our fault that you had an unhappy childhood, and it made you grow hard. But you aren't really hard. You're the dearest little girl in the world. I remember what a sweet, gentle, dreamy little girl you used to be before you went out in the world and it changed you."

Laura's eyes filled with tears.

"James loves you with all his heart," she said, "and I want him to get the little girl that we know. You can trust him, you know. He would never hurt you. I want you to be happy with him. What I wanted to tell you tonight was how beautiful, how exalting, relations with your husband can be. I don't want you to think there's anything unpleasant about it. It can be the loveliest thing in two lives, if you love and trust each other."

"Oh, mother!" Leda cried violently. "Please go away. I know all this. It's so . . . wet, talking about it with you."

Laura looked at her reproachfully but humbly, with tear-filled eyes. Her face was white in the light. Her hands were folded on her lap.

"I just want you to be happy with James," she said.

"I will be. Honestly, mother, I will be. Everything's fine. Everything's grand. I just don't want to talk about it."

"I wish I could have been closer to my daughter," Laura said. "We will miss you so when you are gone, but we haven't really had you for a long, long time. You left us long ago."

"I'm sorry, mother," Leda muttered. "I love you both very much, of course."

"I hope you do. I hope you really do, underneath. Because we love you with all our hearts, and we will always be here whenever you want us. You are our baby, and I want you to remember that we are always here for you, as long as we live."

She got up and came over to the bed and bent over Leda. Leda held herself still and lifted her cheek to Laura's kiss. Laura rested her face for a moment on Leda's cheek.

"My precious," she said. "My little baby. Grown up, and going out in the world with her husband. I'm so glad it is James you love. I trust him so. Oh, my baby!"

When she had gone out and shut the door behind her, Leda drew a long breath. But she could not go back in peace to her magazine and the pictures of dining-room arrangements.

She was haunted by an image which had not come to her for years, since the time when she had first learned about sex and imagined her parents in the act of sex. It was a picture charged with disgust for Leda; those two together made a picture shudderingly revolting. What a frightful thing sex could be that way, all cuddly and somehow filthy!

The only way that sex was decent was the way it must be for the people like Nicola and Dicky; Mr. and Mrs. Kruger. Somehow Leda could not imagine them in the act at all, and that was the attractive thing about it. They would always be in control of themselves. They would say, 'Darling, you're too divine.' It would be clean. It would be attractive.

She let herself think of something that she rarely did think of: herself with James. There was something potentially disgusting in James, his ardor and his moustache and the thought of his loving body. But it would be up to her to control that situation, and as in the other departments of her marriage, shape it to something attractive and acceptable. It wasn't as if James looked like her father. He was well-built and well-groomed. She would say, "Darling, you're too divine," and be gay, and look lovely in a well-cut nightgown with her hair spread on the pillow.

Three days before the wedding, things began to move with festive precision, the reward of the time Leda had given to organizing. She felt herself relaxing, at the same time that she was stimulated; everything was coming off right. It was almost as if it were someone else's wedding; she could not help admiring it.

Parties were given—a big dinner the first night by Mrs. Kruger, a luncheon on the North Shore by James's mother, lunches and teas by girls Leda knew, the Mayson sisters and Marna Elliott, who were bridesmaids. Two nights before the wedding was the ushers' dinner at the Club; Leda took the bridesmaids to dinner at a restaurant in town that night, and they all sat together laughing at a round table, watched by the other diners, wearing the round bouquets Leda had sent them. The night before the wedding the wedding party was given a dinner by Bernard and Laura—though of course it was Leda who had done everything about it—back at the Club.

Leda looked up and down the long table. Even Laura looked fairly decent at one end, in a pink lace dress Leda had chosen. Bernard was at the other end, talking to Nicola, calm and lovely in honey-colored satin from Chanel with a red glass buckle. And up and down the table were bridesmaids chattering with the ushers; the ushers were all a little tight, but making the most of the evening and of the bridesmaids. Up and down the table ushers rose and toasted the bride in champagne.

Even Bernard had the wit to make quite an amusing little speech.

After dinner more people came in to dance; a small orchestra from Boston arrived and began to play in the little ballroom. Leda was very happy. Everything was going on schedule, even better than she had hoped. She laughed and joked and knew that she was looking well in a cherry-red chiffon dress. James cut in between every other usher; she was pleased with him and smiled as he danced her into the corners. The usher from Richmond made a great show of falling in love with the bride at the last moment.

"Beatin' your time, boy," he said to James, cutting in. "Not going to let this charming little Yankee girl get away from me. Aiming to let you wait for her at the church."

"Don't pay any attention to these Southern devils," James said over his shoulder as he walked away. "With their Southern lines. Professional heart-breakers, that's what they are."

"Don't you pay him no heed," the Richmond usher said, dancing her off in a complicated pattern of steps. "It's always my luck to find the real girl just on the eve of her weddin'."

Leda laughed.

The Richmond usher was very tall, very thin, with a face like a boy's, clear-cut and bony. He was a doctor; acting like a Freshman in his few days of liberty from work.

"Always thought Yankee girls were homely and cold as ice—brrrr!" he said. "Never knew they were hiding anything like you back up here in the land of ice and snow. It would take old James to find you lurkin' like a violet among the leaves. You're his cousin?"

"Yes," Leda said, laughing.

"Honey, you can't go and marry kin. Old Dr. Merriman's telling you, terrible mistake to marry kin. Old James must be forgettin' his eugenics. Never marry kissin' cousins. Marry me. This is such a charming wedding party, let's throw a little excitement into it and elope. Leave a note for old James. Just say, 'Can't marry kin.'"

Another usher cut in, and Treat cut in, and then James again; then Merriman was back again, scuffling with James and pushing him out of the way.

"Warning this lovely girl against you, boy. Nice girls shouldn't marry their cousins. You know that, Doctor. Think of all those squalling brats; not one of 'em'll have good sense. How can you do that to a nice girl, James, boy?"

"Dominant traits magnificent in both of us, Doctor," James said, pushing Merriman.

"Don't give me that. I know all about your dominant traits, Doctor. You haven't got a dominant trait that's fit to print."

"How about your own dominant traits, Doctor?"

"Doin' fine, Doctor, just doin' fine. Besides, I ain't kin to this lovely girl. Thank my stars."

He whirled Leda off.

"Where do you keep your moonlight up here, beautiful?" he murmured. "Got to have the proper light on my work. Isn't there a little door leadin' out, somewhere in this delightful club?"

Leda laughed and nodded towards the French windows that led out on the terrace. How many times as a child had she not thought with envy of this club, where all the rich and powerful people played and danced! Then she had been a wretched little forgotten nobody. Now this club and everything else was hers. They were all here in celebration of her, the whole thing revolved about her. She liked being with this Southern boy who probably thought she was rich and had always been powerful and had what she wanted. From now on her life would be among people who took her on her face value of beauty and power.

They walked out on the terrace under the bright sky full of stars, and down the slope of the grass toward the golf course, arm in arm. It was exciting; it was romantic; Leda knew nothing about this man nor he about her; he was strange material that she did not understand, but he was a man and presumably responsive to the same stimuli as men of Boston. It was fun to flirt with him. It was especially fun because it was the night before her wedding; just because she was being married she would not cease to be attractive to men.

"Honey," he murmured, and stopped still in walking. She stopped too.

He took hold of her firmly and kissed her on the mouth.

"You beautiful thing," he said. "What in the world you getting married for?"

She pulled away from him sharply and started back to the clubhouse that stood lighted like a ship upon the hill. She heard him coming after her.

"Wait," he said. "Don't be in such a tearin' hurry. You being a cold

old Yankee girl on me? Listen, you know you're interested in a little moonlight."

"I'm being married," she said without turning her head.

"Oh, listen, honey."

"In the North we don't go around kissing people the night before our weddings."

"Don't hand me that, honey. Don't try to fool old Merriman. I know all about Yankee girls. Don't pretend like you're some little old Southern girl."

Leda did not answer. She hurried across the terrace and into the club. James was by the door, looking out. She caught at his arm and pulled him to dance with her. When his arm was around her she looked up at his face.

"That man," she said. "The Southern one. He tried to kiss me outside."

"Huh?" James laughed. "He did? Why, the son of a gun. Listen, sweet, don't be disturbed about it. Those Southern boys are different. Merriman's a bit high. He didn't mean anything."

"Aren't you mad at him?"

"Me? Oh, furious. I'll knock his block off. No, darling, don't let it disturb you. It doesn't mean a thing."

Leda looked sharply away from James's face. She felt annoyed, but at the same time she felt relief. There had been a moment when she had been frightened. That was why she had told James at once. For they might have been seen, or Merriman might have made something out of it. And she was not prepared to have anything happen to her beautiful plans now that they were running so magically.

Nevertheless, James was annoying. Merriman's kissing her had meant something to him. She was sure it did. Nobody ever kissed Leda and meant nothing by it.

The wedding was at four o'clock in the afternoon.

At six o'clock the matron of honor was in the bride's room; she sat on the edge of the bed watching the bride putting on pale beige crepe-de-chine underclothes. They were both very calm; they were both very beautiful.

"I hope you make a go of it," the matron of honor said. "James is a darling, really."

"Of course I'll make a go of it," the bride said, smoothing her stockings up her long slim legs.

"The only thing I worry about is that you don't seem madly in love enough."

The bride shrugged her shoulders.

"I think that's silly. You and Dicky aren't madly, madly in love either, and look at you."

"We're different. Besides, we . . . we sort of have so much fun together. Do you have any fun with James?"

"Certainly I have fun with James," the bride said after a minute.

The door opened and the bride's mother came in. The matron of honor stood up, politely. The bride glanced up and went on adjusting the skirt of her beige suit.

"My precious baby . . ." the bride's mother began. There were tears in her eyes. But the bride was very calm.

The bride and groom got away in a big car. The people crowded around the front of the house, waving and laughing. When the car passed around the corner they all went back to the champagne and to their little groups. People began to leave, taking the white boxes of cake that were neatly piled on a table by the front door. The wedding was over and the bride had gone away. The party would last on a little longer, the bridesmaids and ushers going on a last dancing party in town that night, and the out-of-town ushers would be put on the midnight train.

The bride and groom had a drawing-room on the train.

"Well, *that's* over," the groom said, smiling at the bride.

"They're all going dancing tonight," the bride said. "It's too bad, isn't it, we have to miss part of our own party? I feel sort of left out." She laughed.

The groom laughed too, comfortably.

"You look perfectly beautiful," he said. "Marriage agrees with you, Mrs. March."

"Do I? Good," the bride said abstractedly.

It was strange to have all the excitement over. The bride drummed with her fingers on the clouded window-pane of the train. The wedding party would be having dinner now, somewhere in town. Nicola would be there, calm and shining, and Dicky, and Janet would be carrying on her flirtation with the Baltimore usher, and the older Mayson girl with one of the New York ushers, and the Richmond usher, the one called Merriman, he would be flirting with somebody. Bernard and Laura would be at home alone, messing around, picking up the debris. The presents would still be spread out on the tables, to be packed in a day or two and sent on to New York by Laura. All the guests would have gone home, gone to what came next in their day, to dinners or parties or the country or a quiet evening alone. Maybe they were still talking, a little bit, about the wedding. But it was all over.

"Don't let's forget," the bride said, "to get the papers when we get to New York."

"Read all about the big doings," the groom said. "March marries March. Excited, darling?"

"Not exactly excited," she said. "It all seems over, doesn't it?"

"All that fuss, and then it's over," he said. "Maybe it would have been simpler to have a little tiny wedding, after all."

"Really!" the bride said. "This was the only possible kind of wedding. I mean, parents like to have a big do when their only daughter gets married. And all the rest of it."

"Naturally. I know, darling. Well, it's over, isn't it?"

"Yes," she said. "It's all over now."

### CHAPTER XXVIII

On the *Conte Grande* the James Marches had a large stateroom on A Deck
with two beds. The boat turned out to be not very gay at that season, but
there were a few attractive passengers with whom they talked in the mornings sitting in their deckchairs and had a cocktail before dinner. The hon-
orary purser was the most attractive man on the boat, an Italian nobleman
with a cocked eye and great charm, who had them into his rooms for drinks
and entertained them with the facility which had made him one of the
chief assets of the Italian Line.

He was enchanted with young Mrs. March, who had such night-dark
hair and such dark eyes and such a lovely figure. He flirted with her, smiling at her husband and saying,

"You Americans find yourselves these charming ladies and then you do
nothing about them. I tell you I am an Italian, and I would like to steal her
from you."

He laughed and James March laughed and Leda March laughed.

The third evening out there were movies after dinner and when the lights
went up Count Ruggiero came over to where young Mrs. March sat.

"Where is the bridegroom?" he asked.

"He went down to get some cigarettes," she said, smiling up into his intelligent face.

"Ah! This is my opportunity. Will you take a little walk with me round
the deck, and perhaps every time the bridegroom comes looking for you
we will be on the farther side of the deck?"

She laughed and got up, in her slim dark red tube of a dress, that stopped
at the knees and showed her pretty legs. She took his arm and they began
to walk. Perhaps it was as Count Ruggiero had prophesied, for they did not
meet James.

Now that they were alone together the Count did not flirt with her. He
talked to her about Italy.

"You are well read," he said. "It is not every American young girl who
has read Symonds. You will adore Italy. I wish I could be with you when
you see Florence first. You will feel emotion."

"I know. I have a feeling about wanting to see it first at night, the lights
shining on the Arno and all the palaces making big dark shapes."

"And you will walk into the Piazza della Signoria and it will all be so
beautiful, so still, and you will see the David in the moonlight, and the
peasants' carts will go by over the cobblestones as they did five hundred
years ago."

She sighed.

"You are so intelligent," he said, "but you have not been in the world
nor lived among grown-up people at all, have you? It is always so surprising to me that you wonderful American girls will marry yourselves to your

nice American husbands before you have seen anything at all, before you know what there is in the world."

She looked at him in the quiet light of the deck. The sea was very calm and the ship drove through it steadily with a low, rushing sound. Very few other people passed them.

"But then," Count Ruggiero said, "I suppose you know what you want. It only seems odd to an Italian, that all you want, you, so beautiful and dazzling, is a nice husband and a nice house and children and nothing at all more for the rest of your lives. For Italian women, yes; they are brought up for that life. But for you it is different. You are intelligent, you are restless, you are like a man, except that you are so beautiful. I should think you would want to have had a great career, worldwide, with admirers, fame, applause, adulation."

"I do want that," she said suddenly. "I do want that. It's what I want to have."

"I am sure you have talent. Perhaps you sing?"

"No." She took a long breath. "I write poetry."

"Ah! A poetess! Of course. I can see it in your eyes. You will write great poetry,.and it is true, the world will come to your feet—if you do not allow the house and the babies and the husband to make you forget. But of course, perhaps I am very wicked, perhaps such a life is far wiser for you and perhaps you would be happier."

"I could never be happy with just that," she said with the same intensity. "I want everything. I want everything there is. I don't want to miss anything."

"That is so American. And so charming. I am sure you will have it all. It only seems curious to an Italian that you should begin your career as you have done—the husband first, instead of at the end. But you perhaps know best. Your American husband will allow you to do as you choose and to make this career for yourself. To an Italian that would be impossible. If an Italian had a wife like you, Mrs. March, he would not permit her to go out of his sight. He would come home for lunch every day, and he would be insanely jealous. He would occupy every minute of your time."

"I wouldn't stand for that," she said. "I'd go away."

"Ah, yes, you would. But you are not an Italian wife. That makes it so nice for all of us, that you are not an Italian wife, for you and for everyone else also." He laughed lightly.

"Nothing's going to get in my way," she said.

"I know. I am quite sure. It is not true at all that human nature is constant over the world. Perhaps it is some sort of arrangement of Nature, fitting the species to their environment. Certainly an American wife—the type, I mean—could not endure an Italian husband for a moment. They would eat each other up. He would beat her with a stick and she would leave him directly. It would be impossible and Nature sees that it shall not occur."

"All I want is to live, really live, and be happy."

"Yes, yes. I feel sure you will be happy in Italy. Italy was made for you, Mrs. March. And you will also live. I am a prophet for a moment, I assure you that you will live, and beautifully. Do you speak Italian? *Parla Italiano?*"

"No, I don't. I wish I did."

"Perhaps you will permit me to give you a few lessons as we are crossing the ocean. I am sure you will have an ear for it. It is a beautiful language."

"I'd love it."

James came out of a doorway directly in front of them. He saw them and came towards them, smiling.

"Where have you been?" he demanded. "Count, have you been stealing my bride?"

"I have had no success," the Count said smiling. "I return her to you with a thousand thanks for these few moments of pleasure. Until tomorrow, then, Signora. *A rivederla.*"

"Well," James said, as they walked on alone along the deck. "The old boy's been doing his stuff on you, I guess. Making another steady customer for the Italian Line."

Leda glanced at him. She had the oddest feeling that he was a stranger to her, that she had never seen him before. At the same time there was a familiarity about him, a familiarity as of old clothes, of a room one knows and hardly sees, of scenes so well-known that there is nothing left in them to view.

"We've been talking about Italy," she said coldly.

"It's a swell country. I'm dying to show it to you, darling. I'll show you the Colosseum by moonlight."

"I don't feel," she said, "as if I could stand the Colosseum by moonlight."

But that night when she had gone to bed and the lights were out and somewhere across the room in the darkness James was lying quiet, Leda felt a strange, overwhelming rush of remorse. It was remorse for everything. It extended beyond James. It was like a terrible revelation.

She was desperately, achingly sorry for James. He was so kind. He was so patient. He was so in love with her, and uncomplaining that his love-making had hitherto been repulsive to her and she had not allowed him to approach her but once or twice. He believed in her and he adored her and trusted her, and he did not know—the revelation came in blinding shocks—that she was bored with him and revolted by him and that she had married him to suit her own purposes. For this strange moment she looked at herself with loathing. She had never felt this way. She saw herself as hard, relentless, and scheming, selfish and cold. She had not treated James like a human being. She had used him. He might not have been flesh and blood.

And her parents. She thought of them, little and timid and frightened, dominated by her and forced to her will, apologetic and always bullied, never receiving any of the love or gentleness that they longed for. She had extracted everything she wanted from them; by hard force, without ever responding to their love even by tolerance. She had made them miserable for years. She was a monster.

She felt that it was more than she could bear. She could not fight off the self-accusation that came in waves, making images before her closed eyes

of unkind things she had done, of harsh things she had said. She was the
most inhuman person in the whole world. She seemed to herself to loom
like a symbol of grasping cruelty. It was unbearable to be herself.

She slipped out of her bed and felt her way across the stateroom in the
dark. She held her hand before her; it touched James's face.

"What, darling?" he said quickly. "Is something the matter? Are you
sick?"

He switched on the light beside him. He sat up in bed and Leda sank
down on the edge with her face in her hands.

"What, my darling? What, my sweet darling?"

"I'm so awful. I've always been so awful. I've treated you so badly. I'm
a monster. You're good and kind and I've been rotten to you. To everybody."

He put his arm around her and pressed his face against her cheek.

"No, no, darling, no, you haven't. You're the sweetest thing in the world."

"You don't know. You don't know. I'm horrible. I hurt everybody that
gets near me, ruin everybody's life, just hurt everybody."

Through her mind flickered a memory, faint and soon blotted out. Somebody had talked to her about hurting everybody, somebody else had said
that of themselves . . . Lambert. . . .

"I'm a beast," she said. "I want to be better so much. I will be good to
you, darling, you'll see. Honestly I will."

It felt good to say it.

"Darling," he said, "you're lovely to me. You're the sweetest thing I ever
dreamed of happening to me. Don't feel bad. It's just reaction, darling. It's
after the excitement of the wedding. Everything's going to be lovely. You
make me so happy. I'll make you happy too."

"I don't deserve you," she said.

"You deserve better than me. You're wonderful and lovely. How can
you say something as silly as that a beautiful creature like you doesn't deserve a boring old guy like me?"

"But I don't," she said.

She could never tell him, even in such a moment as this, the reasons why
she had married him. She could not admit that she had never loved him.
Besides, now she loved him. She would do anything to make up for the
way she had been.

"Darling . . . darling . . . put your arms around me, too. I love you so,
my darling. Darling . . . kiss me. . . ."

In July of the following year Betsy Jekyll, who was living in New York,
saw the announcement of the birth of a son to Mr. and Mrs. James March
of 440 East 57th Street, at Miss Lippincott's Hospital. She cut it out and
glued it in her scrapbook.

## CHAPTER XXIX

AUTUMN was the high time of madly blue skies and flaming leaves, the smell of fire in the air; the time of football games and tea-dancing and driving at night through back roads that smelled of grapes and dead leaves, to park in the darkness and kiss. And now for Betsy there was no school any more to interrupt the absolute joy of being alive. The year that Leda was coming out, Betsy had finished school at the Hampton Country Day and was living at home waiting for romance to happen to her.

Every morning she would wake up in her tower room and jump out of bed and run across to shut the window. Before she shut it, even when the mornings were cold, she would hang in her nightgown out of the window and gulp down the morning air. She would slam down the window and turn to the bureau where she would peer at her face, that looked like a boy's face with curly light brown hair cut very short around it, and big eyes that stared back at her. She ran the comb through her hair and wrapped her old pink corduroy dressing gown tight around her hips, stuck her feet into a pair of ratty pink satin mules and clattered down the two flights of stairs to the dining-room.

Minnie May would be sitting at the end of the table with a cigarette stuck in the corner of her mouth. She was reading letters or the paper through a cloud of blue smoke. In a dish that had held eggs half a dozen cigarette butts smoldered. The coffee pot was within arm's length and as Minnie May read, she would absent-mindedly fill her cup again. Whorls and streaks of blue smoke drifted along the sunbeams and hurried over to the window. Tom's place was cluttered with the remains of his toast and eggs; he had left some time before, and so had the Brats, whose places had not been cleared either.

As she came into the dining-room and surveyed the breakfast table Betsy would for a moment think of Maizie; Maizie was gone away and she was wretched; there was something terrible the matter with her life.

But the sunshine and life itself were too brilliant and wonderful for sad thoughts. "I'm the Maizie now," Betsy would think sometimes; "I'm the young daughter of the house now, I go to the parties and I have the beaux." She would hug herself and grin all over her face and go and kiss her mother.

If there was a maid Betsy would shout to her to bring some breakfast; if there was no maid she would go out into the kitchen and cook herself something and carry it back into the sunshine. She would sit in the middle of the morning and eat and smoke cigarettes and drink coffee, feeling luxurious, talking with her mother about clothes and dates and boys and clothes again. There was Bob and Petie and Mac and Kipper, and there was always Sam; good old Sam. "Old Faithful," Minnie May called him. "Except he doesn't gush," Betsy would say. "I do the gushing. I'm going to try to talk less. I think it gets them if you're mysterious." "Reckon it does," Minnie May would say. "I thought you looked right mysterious in your new beaded red."

There was the new beaded red, and the purple satin for tea-dancing, with a purple felt cloche picked up at Filene's basement, and the purple shoes! "I might just kind of take purple as my color," Betsy said. "Write in purple ink and always wear purple, and I'd be known as the Purple Girl. That would be intriguing, wouldn't it, don't you think?"

Minnie May agreed. But sometimes with all her interest Minnie May's eyes seemed to Betsy to grow abstracted, and that was a moment she dreaded. It meant that Minnie May's back was hurting her again, or, far more likely, that she was thinking about Maizie. Something had broken the Jekyll charm of happiness; in their lives now was this shadow. It was almost but not quite the same happy-go-lucky, whooping family as in the old days.

Betsy would raise her voice and hurry on, about the fur coat—the real fur coat, bunny, bought for only $45.98 at Hovey's, and the patent leather pumps with three-inch heels, and the chiffon stockings, and the intriguing new perfume. Minnie May's eyes would gradually clear and she would sparkle back at Betsy through the cloud of smoke. "Seems to me you've got a real feelin' for clothes, honey," she said.

"Do you really think so, Ma'am? I do adore clothes so. Maybe I could get a job doing something about clothes, sometime. Maybe I could be a— a buyer."

"You know what's snappy."

"Maybe I could pick people's clothes out for them. Tell them how to fix their hair and what to wear. I just know I could. I always want to fix people up to be snappier."

"Reckon you could. You might try to get a job for yourself like that. You just go ahead and have fun for yourself this year, though. There's time enough for a career. Maybe you'll meet The Man."

In the old days Minnie May and Maizie had talked about The Man. Now it was Betsy they were talking about. Betsy drew a long, quivering breath. The sky was blue outside the window. The red leaves slapped against the panes.

Later if Betsy was going anywhere she would dress, but usually in the late mornings she lay on her unmade bed and read. What she loved best was *The Green Hat*. She read it over and over. That green hat, worn gallantly, that long low foreign car—going to a man's room; all Iris's lovers, taken gallantly, the great emerald worn—loosely—on the finger. The Marches are never let off anything. For Purity! Oh, that green hat, worn bravely, *Pour le sport!*

Betsy rolled over on her back and drew a sigh of purest delight. She knew just how Iris March looked—like Leda March, she was sure. But sometimes the face, so pale, so enchanting, beneath the green hat was Betsy's own—gallant, desperate. And often when she was going out with a boy she felt herself wear a spiritual Green Hat, and her eyes would grow large and her mouth would droop and she would flick the ash from her cigarette in a gesture of disillusion. Blasé.

She bought a ring at the ten-cent store on Washington Street in Boston, with a large green stone in it, much too loose. She would sit with her hand dropping over the arm of a chair, and the emerald would hang loose on her finger. And sometimes a boy knew enough to cock a sophisticated eye and say, "Ah . . . the fall of the emerald. . . ."

She went to a few debutante parties herself, and put the invitations in the rim of her mirror. She had a Memory Book in which she fastened mementos—a red usher's ribbon, dance cards from the boys' prep schools to which she went even now; with comments written on them by herself—Divine! or, The Night.

She went tea-dancing at Shepard's Colonial in her purple satin. She danced extremely well. She would watch Boston girls dance by, separated from their partners and half walking as they talked. Betsy liked to dance too much for that fashionable trick. Her partners held her tight and did hot steps to the music. "You've got rhythm," they would say, and she would open her eyes and smile mysteriously.

She went to football games in Cambridge. There was something about them, the cheering, the coonskin coats, the beautiful, tall, smooth young men, the crimson banners waving, that stirred her. It was cold, and the boy with her would bring a flask. All around, Harvard men were cheering, the beautiful young men of Harvard, all handsome, all broad-shouldered, their felt hats battered, their socks falling down, all smooth, terribly smooth. She wore her bunny jacket and bright little red hats, for Harvard. Any day, any night, you might meet a Harvard man who would look at you mysteriously and say, "You're smooth." Later, when she had been tea-dancing after the game and out to dinner and dancing again, had parked somewhere on the road back to Hampton, she would get undressed in her tower room with her eyes still entranced by the magic of Harvard. She would sing to herself as she dropped her teddy, her stockings: *"Ten thousand men of Harvard. . . ."*

In November Minnie May gave a dance for Betsy.

She was going to make her debut, and the word was magic, like the air. It was going to be at the Hampton Club. She bought a dress, bright scarlet, straight as a tube to the knees, with a silver flower on one hip. New silver slippers. A silver evening bag. They got a good orchestra. It was not one of the expensive fashionable ones, but it played in one of the Boston hotels uptown; Betsy had danced to it, and she knew a good orchestra when she heard it. It was a real bargain, five pieces. The leader was called Dave; Betsy had often talked to him. Minnie May herself would supervise the punch for the dance. "I'll put a real stick in it," she declared. "I'll make the punch your grandmother always made for our parties down home."

There were the invitations to be sent. The Junior League kept a list of Harvard men which people applied for in giving dances in Boston, but Betsy did not belong to the Junior League. She did not know just why not. How did girls join the Junior League, and that Vincent Club thing? She supposed you must have had to graduate from Miss Sheraton's, or belong to one of the big Boston families. It didn't matter. She was going to have a dance!

She made out a list of girls she had known at Sheraton's the year she went there, and of girls she knew at Hampton Country Day. She knew plenty of boys; the list went over page after page. They got the invitations engraved: Mr. and Mrs. Thomas Jekyll request the pleasure of your company at a small dance. . . .

And they were going to have an ushers' dinner before it! The dinner was at the Hampton Club too; creamed chicken in patty shells, and peas, and ice cream and petits fours. There were sixteen ushers, and Betsy asked fifteen of the girls she had liked best last year at Country Day to dinner.

When Betsy came downstairs to drive to the Club with her father and mother, it was like the nights long ago when Maizie had whirled off to dances; but now it was Betsy who was the heroine. The Brats hung over the banisters and shrieked at her; it was her party she was going to! They went out into the wine-cold night and climbed into the Ford touring car that they now had, and drove to the Club.

The other girls at the dinner were lumpish, with the vague stare and girlish speech which Betsy thought of as typical of Boston girls. Actually these were not Boston girls, though cast in their mold, but Hampton girls who had not gone away to school. They wore taffeta dresses in light colors. "Gosh," they said. "She's got a peachy forehand." And the boys drank the punch that was served at dinner, the old Green punch, and said "Gosh! Look at old Hump! He's getting stewed. Some punch!"

Minnie May, at the end of the table, talked and laughed and called down the table. Betsy went at her dinner partners with the peppiness that she had labored to master. She threw arch glances at them and cried, "You're awful! I think you're terrible!" and stuck into their buttonholes the carnations beside their plates.

When they all went into the ballroom of the Club to begin dancing, the orchestra sounded loud and echoing. Betsy kept dancing up to the orchestra and talking to the leader, a thin, young man with patent-leather hair. She grinned at all the other men in the band. Minnie May had punch sent to them between dances. "This is a swell little dance, Betsy," the leader said. "Your mother's a lovely woman. I don't know when I've seen such a lovely woman."

Betsy had the feeling that they were playing with extra energy for her party. They played her favorite tunes, *Who* and *Half a Moon* and an old tune she loved, *Mighty Blue*.

There was no receiving line. Minnie May or Betsy would spot someone coming in, and dash up to him, smiling and sparkling. "I'm so glad you've come! It's wonderful to see you! Have some punch. It's over there." A stag-line began to form, loosely, in the middle of the room. It was becoming a real party. It was almost too delirious to be true. Occasionally Betsy would remember to be mysterious. She would suddenly cease talking and look at her partner through half-closed eyes. Then she would forget again; it was too exciting; all she could do was laugh and laugh and chatter; she could not remember about herself for more than a minute.

Lots of Hampton people came. They were all people the Jekylls knew at church and of course they had been asked. But lots of Harvard men came too, beaux of Betsy's. Once or twice she was baffled by seeing young men whom she did not know at all entering the ballroom. She quickly understood. "They're crashing my party," she thought. "It's a good party, so people are crashing it!" She was more flattered than anything else.

All her schoolmates at Country Day came. And she was delighted to greet several girls whom she had known at Miss Sheraton's. She realized that they were not the girls who had been leaders; they were the quiet or the pilly ones; but it was so nice of them to have come. She ran to them with beaming smiles. "Lilian! Betty! Joan! How simply darling of you to come! Isn't it a lovely party?" These too were lumpish girls, who met her greetings with embarrassed smiles, and looked anxiously about the crowded room. But the ushers were doing their duty, dragging men out of the stagline and taking them up to be introduced to girls who had danced too long with one partner.

Some really popular girls had come, girls that Betsy had met not at school but on dates, at football games, girls that she knew through boys. These girls were dressed, Betsy thought, smoothly; in black and in red and in bright green; they danced with their arms hooked behind their partners' necks, and tilted their fluffy heads back and murmured as they danced, something surely intriguing, for the men bent over them, dancing with their chins thrust out, and looking down into the girls' faces with the look that Betsy thought of as snaky.

She was dancing near the entrance to the ballroom when she saw Corinne Taylor come in with two men she had never seen. She broke away from her partner and hurried up to Corinne.

Corinne was a girl she had known at Miss Sheraton's, a girl who had never been important there but who to Betsy had always seemed more attractive than the others. She was a thin girl with beautiful red hair who giggled a great deal. Betsy had seen her often since the Sheraton days, out dancing with boys and at football games. She was quite popular. Her family came from Texas and her father was now in business in Boston; they were rich, and had a big house in Brookline.

"Corinne, I'm *so* glad you came! Isn't it marvellous?"

Corinne giggled.

"Looks like a wonderful party," she said. "I see you've got Dave to play. He's hot."

Corinne was one of the very best dancers in Boston. Betsy had often watched her on the floor. She had heard from boys that Corinne danced like a streak.

Betsy glanced at the two men standing just behind. Corinne giggled again.

"Oh, Betsy, I brought a couple of men, I thought you wouldn't mind. This is Oren Garth, Betsy Jekyll, and Peter De Laney. They come from New York!"

They were both tall, and well-dressed, and very smooth looking. The one called Peter had sleek black hair and a dark skin darkened further with freckles. Betsy liked the way he kept his chin stuck out; it looked smooth. The taller one, Oren, had brown curly hair; his face was long and restless, with narrow blue eyes, and when he smiled his mouth went up only on one side.

As he stood there, almost unnoticeably he did a tap step with his feet. He had a vague, wandering look. He put his arm around Corinne and they danced off; Betsy noticed that they were doing incredibly complicated steps. The one called Peter grinned at her.

"Dance?" he said. Betsy's partner had disappeared. She started off with Peter. His dancing was smooth; not complicated, but with perfect rhythm, without a jerk.

"Do you go to Harvard?" she asked, tipping her head back and sparkling at him.

"Yep. Orey and I room together in Westmoreland."

"Oh! Do you know Barky Harrison?"

"See him around."

"What do you go out for?"

"Me? Oh, I play some tennis on the indoor courts. Orey doesn't go out for anything. He's a musician. He's mad about the piano. And he plays the banjo like a streak. You ought to hear him."

"I haven't seen you anywhere around, have I?"

"No, we don't go to these Boston dances much. Orey can't stand Boston girls. None of them can dance. Some of the games, we've gotten girls over from New York, though."

Betsy was abashed. It was terribly impressive.

"You can dance, though," Peter offered. "I'll have to tell Orey."

"Corinne can dance."

"You bet she can."

"And—oh, there are other girls in Boston who can dance. One of those Wolcott twins is supposed to be a marvellous dancer."

"Well. . . ." Peter said. "You see, Orey is sort of a strange guy. Sort of a socialist, maybe you'd call it. He can't stand big social stuff and girls from big social families. He's had a stomach-full of that in New York."

Betsy looked at Peter with large eyes.

"You know who the Garths are, don't you?" he said. "Of course you've heard of the Garths. Well, Orey got terribly fed up with all that stuff long ago. I went to St. Paul's with him and even then he couldn't stand it. He's been through hell with his family, his old man getting married all those times and everything. You know about all that Garth stuff, all the divorces and the money and all the scandals there've been. Orey will inherit a couple of million anyway, I guess."

Scraps from the social pages of New York papers that she had scanned in search of glamour began to fuse in Betsy's mind. Garth . . . Garth . . . of course. They were something like the Vanderbilts . . . weren't they cousins or something? They had a château in Newport and there was one ex-Mrs. Garth who was always arriving from or leaving for Paris, and one of the boxes in the Golden Horseshoe at the Metropolitan Opera was held by Mortimer Garth—that must be Oren's father.

"How intriguing," Betsy breathed.

Somebody cut in on Peter and he wandered off to join the stagline. Betsy danced on, and people kept cutting in, and she would smile and sparkle and tip her head back and pull a line. She felt almost drunk, and the faces that appeared before her one after another seemed faces in a dream. Suddenly Oren Garth cut in.

"Hello, baby," he said in a melancholy, husky voice.

Dancing with him was not smooth, like dancing with Peter. It was a fantasy of rhythm, of imaginative, creative interpretation of the music. You found yourself doing things with your feet that you had not known they could do. You did not even want to talk. You wanted to dance.

"Peter was right. You can dance," Oren said. His voice was as strange as everything about him, his narrow eyes and his one-sided smile; his voice was husky but not deep; melancholy and teasing. Everything about him was elusive, the smile, the voice, the glance, as if in a second he would be gone.

Somebody cut in, and somebody else, and Betsy chattered on and laughed gaily, but now something had happened to her. She kept looking out of the corner of her eyes to see where Oren was. She saw him dancing with Corinne, and she saw him wandering back to the stagline; standing there, alone, tall and individual, with his shoulders hunched a little, and his knees moving slightly; he was doing a tap step by himself. Then she saw him start to walk on to the floor. She fixed her eyes on her partner's face and talked rapidly, and prayed inside. It was all right. She felt her partner's arms drop away from her, and different arms come around her, and looked up and saw that one-sided smile.

"Hello, baby," he said as before; and they danced.

They danced, and it was magical, but this time Betsy felt glad that dancing with Oren was so absorbing, and that he did not seem to want to talk, for suddenly for the first time in her life she felt at a loss for something to say. Her throat felt choked.

Peter cut in on Oren, and Betsy watched Oren stroll off, back to the stagline, and look around the room vaguely.

"You've made a hit with Orey," Peter said. "He says you're the best dancer in Boston. It takes quite a lot to make him say anything like that."

"Really?" Betsy breathed.

"Yep. Orey's danced with some of the best dancers in the world, I guess. He danced with Lenore Hughes last year. You know, Maurice's partner."

"Honestly?"

"Yep. He's practically a professional. But of course his family wouldn't let him do it. That's something else he's got against them. He's really good at tap, too. And he wanted to play the banjo in a band last year, but they wouldn't let him. I guess what he wants most is to play the piano. Play classical music, I mean. Concerts. He's written some music, too."

"You're terribly good friends, aren't you?"

"Well, you see, I've always kind of taken care of Orey, since we were in school. He's a crazy guy, always having to be got out of trouble. Absolutely impractical. I have to look after him."

"It must be . . . kind of wonderful, I mean it isn't like just looking after anybody, is it?"

"That's so. I guess I love that guy," Peter said. Somebody cut in on him.

Betsy was in a daze. The way Peter had said "I love that guy" had a kind of fascination about it. These were new and exciting people with mystery about them. Betsy's chatter and laughter were automatic now. She kept watching Oren. There was something so wonderful about him, and his strangeness, and the roommate that adored him.

After far too long Oren cut back again.

This time he did not speak at all. He danced her rapidly off into a corner and there began to do those complicated, fantastic steps with her. Suddenly he dropped his arm from her and smiled. It was a queer smile, one-sided and sweet and almost shy, but not that exactly. . . .

"Let's have some punch," he said.

Betsy led the way over to the table where the punch-bowl stood; she was hardly conscious of taking the steps that moved her forward. Everything was like a dream; everything was drawn up into a knot of concentration on the young man with her.

He got two cups and handed her one.

"Good," he said, sipping his.

"It's a family recipe," Betsy said eagerly. "Mother's mother used to make it down South where they lived."

"Really? It's awfully good." He filled his cup again from the big ladle.

"Want to sit out?" he asked.

"Oh, yes!"

She smiled with all her heart up into his face and he smiled back at her. They walked through the crowded room carrying their drinks, and out of the door into the hall, where couples were sitting on the stairs. Betsy started toward the stairs. Oren took her arm and pulled her gently. She felt his fingers on her skin.

"No, somewhere else," he said. "I want to talk to you."

They opened a door off the hall and it led into a back hall, lighted with a dim bulb in the ceiling; cartons stood piled against the wall, and there was a high stool. Betsy sat on the stool. Oren let his back slip down the wall so that he was resting against one hip, his legs bent. The door into the main hall swung slowly to on a spring; the sound of music and of laughter was suddenly shut out. It was perfectly quiet.

But now that they were alone Oren did not talk. He seemed unaware of Betsy. He sipped his drink and drummed with his fingers against the wall. Betsy realized that it was a tap rhythm he was beating out.

She felt stifled; choking. She sought about desperately for something to say but for the first time in her life she could not talk. It was terrible. Now, when she wanted so wildly to be attractive, to be peppy and make this strange, wonderful man like her, she was dumb and felt like a shy child.

He seemed to feel no embarrassment whatever. He seemed unaware of
the silence. Betsy tried to feel natural too. But she could not. She felt that
she was at her worst at the most important moment in her life.

Oren leaned down with his strange grace that was almost awkward, and
set the cup down on the floor. He straightened up again and put the heel
of his hand on the edge of the stool. He looked down into Betsy's face,
smiling his tipped-up smile. Her heart was beating frantically.

She looked back up into his face and everything in her life seemed to
stand still. She forgot everything except the way he looked. She had forgotten herself; she was all eagerness, all wonder. It was a moment like no
other in life, and it seemed to last a long time.

Then he bent over and kissed her lightly on the lips.

His lips were soft and sensitive; they rested on hers for only a moment.
She felt as if all the exaltation and eagerness and concentration inside her
were flowing into her own lips. All of her seemed to be coming together
and going out of her through her lips into him.

He stood up again and stood looking down at her, smiling.

"Sweet baby," he said in his husky voice.

Then suddenly it was as if he had forgotten that he had ever kissed her.
The smile on one side of his mouth broadened, and his eyes sparkled, and
he caught hold of her hand and pulled her off the stool.

"Come on," he said. "Let's do some dancing."

She did not want to go back, she wanted to stay and be kissed by him
again. But she could not show him that. She tried, by laughing too and
jumping down from the stool, to fit herself to his mood. But it was so difficult to assess his mood. He was strange, like a wild creature, a deer.

When they walked together back on the floor the orchestra leader caught
Betsy's eye and grinned. They were just finishing a tune, and now they began again, one of Betsy's tunes. Oren put his arm around Betsy and they
began to dance.

> Oh Gee . . . I'm mighty blue . . . for you . . .
> I've . . . been mighty true . . . to you . . .

Forcing herself to do something, say something, Betsy tipped her head
back and sparkled her eyes at Oren.

"That's your initials, isn't it? O. G.? 'O. G., I'm mighty blue for you!' "

He smiled and said nothing. Betsy had a feeling new to her; a feeling
that what she had said might not have been amusing. She was surging with
excitement, dazzlement—and with lack of confidence. . . . Somebody cut
in. Oren wandered away; she watched him go. He was so different from
anybody else in the world. She danced on.

> While you whisper . . . nighty-nighty to
> somebody else. . . . I'm mighty blue . . .

When she woke up late the next morning in her tower room full of
November sunshine, the whole of life was made of joy and glamour and
excitement.

Instead of jumping out of bed she lay still and stared at the bright window. Her feet hurt pleasantly from dancing until five. Her head was full of snatches of music, and out of them emerged that tune, the tune—"Oh Gee I'm mighty blue for you. . . ." She sang it aloud, softly. But she thought of it now as "O.G.—I'm mighty blue . . ." It was a tune about Oren. Last night came back to her in flashes and she saw him again, and saw Peter, and then Oren again, Oren's tall, loose frame and his feet doing tap steps, and his one-sided smile, tantalizing and sweet, and his husky voice. "Baby . . . Sweet baby . . ."

I'm in love, she thought. Oh, I'm in love!

She leapt out of bed and clacked down the stairs in her old mules. Minnie May was still at the breakfast table, as usual, smoking. She looked up and smiled as Betsy clattered in.

"Ma'am! Good morning! Isn't it a heavenly day!"

"Well darlin', did you like your party? I thought everybody had a right good time."

"Oh, it was wonderful, Ma'am, wonderful! I had the most wonderful time I've ever had in my life!"

Minnie May poured a cup of coffee for her.

"Somebody fell, I reckon."

"I don't know . . . I don't know . . . but I did! I met the most wonderful man . . ."

Suddenly Betsy felt curiously. She did not want to talk about Oren. Not talk about a beau to Minnie May! She swallowed a big gulp of coffee and grinned desperately.

"Why don't you have him out to supper," Minnie May said. "We've got a ham, hasn't been cut yet."

"Oh, no!" Betsy said, to her own surprise. "I couldn't. I've got to wait. I've got to see. . . ."

"Don't see anything the matter with havin' a beau to supper," Minnie May said. "If you want to see more of him.—Betsy, I'm real worried about Maizie."

Betsy looked at Minnie May and saw that the look had come into her face, the strained look that was no part of the Minnie May Betsy had worshipped all her life. It was all wrong. But today even that look could not disturb the sunshine, the music that sang in Betsy's head; she could not seem to keep her mind on anything except the picture of a long face with narrow blue eyes and a one-sided smile.

"What?" she murmured.

"Well, she didn't come last night. Course that man never does take her anywhere, but yesterday on the phone she did say he'd agreed to come, bring her. Just like him to go back on it. Betsy, I'd like to see that man boiling in oil. I declare I would. I'd like to have him catch leprosy and beri-beri and plague and pneumonia and be able to stand by and watch him suffer."

"Mmmmh," Betsy nodded.

"I *am* so worried about Maizie, honey. What's going to happen to her if she goes on looking the way she does? If I just could get to the bottom of it. If I could just get her to tell me what he does to her, what's troublin' her so terribly. I know I could fix things better. I'd give him a piece of my mind. If I could only make her leave him. But she won't. She certainly has got it bad. If it just wasn't that man. He doesn't seem like he's human. I don't understand any man lettin' his wife look the way Maizie does—like a ghost, that's the way she looks. I don't know if you even remember what your sister used to be like, Betsy. Why, she was the most beautiful, gayest, most popular. . . ."

"I remember," Betsy said. But nothing could cloud the sunshine.

The telephone rang.

Before the first ring had stopped Betsy was out of her chair and clattering into the hall, stumbling all over her dressing-gown cord. She heard Minnie May laughing behind her. She snatched the receiver off the hook.

"Hello?" she said casually.

"Is Miss Betsy Jekyll there?"

It was. It was the husky voice on which life hung.

"This is Miss Betsy Jekyll."

"This is Oren Garth."

"Oh, *hello!* Uh . . . how are you?"

He made no answer to that.

"Will you be in if I come to see you this afternoon?"

"Oh, uh, yes, I will. I'll be in this afternoon."

"Fine. Goodbye." He hung up.

Somehow Betsy got back into the dining-room and into her chair; a coffee cup was somehow in her hand. The sunshine came waving in ribbons and banners into the room, and the smoke of cigarettes danced upon the beams. The world was sunshine and music. The world was dancing and strange, one-sided smiles and a kiss, the first kiss in life that mattered, the only kiss; "Baby. . . ."

"I'm goin' in to see this doctor in the afternoon," her mother was saying. "Tell me he's a miracle man. Hope he can do something about this devilish back of mine. If he's any good, I declare I'm going to make Maizie see him. I won't have her lookin' like that, I won't have it."

"Oh, Ma'am, you'll get back, won't you? I need you. . . . This boy . . . he's coming out to see me this afternoon. That was him that called up. His name is Oren Garth. He's . . ."

Minnie May smiled and the cigarette on her lower lip waggled.

"Oh? I'll get back real early, honey."

But now suddenly Betsy hoped she would not get back. Everything was topsy-turvy. Not wanting Minnie May to help her entertain a beau! Everything was different.

She was dressed, in an orange silk dress, and ready by three o'clock, and from then on she seemed to wait for hours and hours, sitting for a little while in the living-room and then hurrying to a mirror to see if her hair was still right, and going to the window and counting up to five hundred to see if he would come before she had finished, and running upstairs to

put on fresh lipstick and run a comb through her hair. Once she opened
the front door, and the sweet cold air of late November came in against
her face, but she shut the door quickly and ran upstairs again to rearrange
her hair. She was keyed to the sound of a car driving up.

It was nearly five and dark when the doorbell rang. She ran to the door
and opened it and Oren stood outside. He was very tall and narrow in a
black overcoat with a velvet collar. He stood in the twilight on the thresh-
old and smiled his one-sided, shy smile. He had a big case in one hand, a
banjo case. The light from the hall shone on his brown, rough curly hair.
There was no car in the drive behind him.

"How'd you get out?" Betsy asked. It was the only thing in the world she
could think of to say.

"I took some street cars. . . ." His voice was vague. He came into the
house and took off the long tubular overcoat, setting the case down on the
floor. He kept smiling at her; that smile, bashful but also self-assured, ingratiating.

She led him into the living-room. He brought his banjo in with him. He
was not like the smooth, decorous Harvard boys. He was not like anybody. He sat on a low chair and Betsy watched the way he sat down;
almost awkwardly, but at the same time gracefully and with a loose-hung
individuality. He seemed always to be conscious of his feet. He wore a pair
of black patent leather dancing shoes with his gray daytime suit, and they
looked wet; he must have walked up from Hampton Square.

She felt tongue-tied and ill at ease. He came from a different world. She
stared at him with big eyes, trying to think of something gay and intriguing
to say. There was nothing. Perhaps, she thought, she had better try to be
mysterious and say nothing on purpose. But she could not feel that way.
She was centered on him, reaching out to him, enchanted by him.

He took his banjo out of its case and let it lie on his lap.

"Peter says you're a real musician," she said finally.

"Hmmmm?" His voice was husky, low and endearing. "God, I'm not
good. I've played this thing since school, that's what Peter's talking about.
Banjo! I want to be a pianist. But it's so late. You have to begin young to
get a concert technique. I've never been let to do anything I really cared
about."

"Are your family very mean about things?"

"Oh . . . the family," he said. "Nobody has any idea. I'll tell you all
about them some time."

That meant he intended to see her again.

"Don't you like your father?"

"I hate him," he said. "He's hurt everybody so much. My mother. I don't
know her very well. I've never been allowed to know her. She married
Clyde Vanderkirk afterwards. They live in St. Jean, I've seen the château
and visited her there, but I'll never really know her now. She's beautiful.
She's the most beautiful woman I ever saw."

"How beautiful?" Betsy said in a faint voice. It was like a Michael Arlen
novel.

"She paints. But she'll never be any good, it's too late. Vanderkirk is a painter, but he'll never be any good either. They've been ruined by money, and never being allowed to do things till too late, and people like my father, and, oh, all the stuff you get into. I want to get out of it before it's too late."

He looked wretched.

"Couldn't you just leave, I mean run away or something?"

"My father. . . . You don't know. All this stuff about being a Garth. God! He'd disown me. It's all very difficult, you see. . . . There's more to it. . . . He wants me to be an international banker."

The words were in capitals in Betsy's mind. International Banker.

"He ruins people," Oren said bitterly. "After my mother he married a woman and then got rid of her later. When I was in school he married a beautiful woman. Peter knows all about that. I was in love with her. God! You can imagine what that was. In love with my father's wife. I can't talk about it. Now he's married to somebody else. They travel a lot. God knows what's happened to Elena. Lovely Elena."

He picked up the banjo and held it with his long nervous hands, and began to play very softly the tune *San* and to sing in his husky, ingratiating, melancholy voice:

> I had a sweet Mamma
> I had a sweet Mamma
> But she's turned sour now. . . .

It seemed to Betsy incredibly skillful, professional; never in her life had she heard any voice or music so teasing and provocative.

> Gee. . . . She handed me one grand surprise
> Because I thought I had her pasteurized. . . .
> I had a sweet Mamma. . . .

"We made up the words," he said, laying down the banjo again. "Peter and I. Back at school. Like it?"

"I think it's wonderful."

He got up and walked around the room with light, nervous steps, as though he were dancing. He glanced out of the windows into the dark. He picked things up off tables and looked at them and put them back. Betsy felt panicky. What could she say to interest someone like this?

Suddenly he broke his wandering with a sharp, loud tap-step on the floor. Ta-cla! He looked at her and laughed, and did it again. He was like a child, unique and unself-conscious.

"I've got a room in Boston on Newbury Street," he said. "Where I can get away from all that noise out in Cambridge. I've got a piano in there where I can practice. It's rather nice. You must come in some time and see it and I'll play for you."

"I'd love to."

It was at that moment that Minnie May came in in a flurry from her trip to town. She had picked up the Brats at the house where they had been playing, and all of them burst into the living-room laughing, talking, rushing around. Betsy introduced Oren to Minnie May. Jane and Glory stared at him for a moment and then began edging closer to him, still staring, and grinning. How was he going to like this, Betsy thought; for the first time feeling uncertainty about her wonderful family. He was used to things so different from this, beautiful, strange women, great houses, butlers. . . .

But everything seemed to be all right. Everything was fine. Oren was sitting on a chair playing the banjo very fast and loud and the Brats were hanging over watching, and Oren was talking above the music to Minnie May, who was laughing and chattering back. He seemed to love it. Betsy slowly relaxed inside. Oren's face had lightened from its melancholy and he kept laughing at things Minnie May said, and acting pleased and excited and much more like other boys. How wonderful Minnie May was! She wasn't stricken speechless by this strange young man. She took him in her stride, as she did everything else.

"Now, you must stay to supper," she said.

"May I?" Oren murmured with one of his shy smiles.

"You've got to. You don't look as if you ate enough, either," Minnie May said vigorously.

He smiled again at her, and Betsy felt as if she could not bear it, he was so wonderful, so enchanting. She went out with Minnie May to get the supper and heard Oren singing in his husky voice to the Brats, the low, nervous thrum of his banjo behind it . . .

> Often a bridesmaid but never a bride
> It was a slam to her personal pride . . .

"*Isn't he wonderful?*" she asked Minnie May breathlessly. Minnie May was slicing bread. The ham was on a platter ready to go into the dining-room.

"Right nice. Right pathetic. Doesn't look like he ever had the proper care. Nobody to keep him in order. So he's The One," she said, smiling at Betsy.

"Oh, Ma'am, I'm crazy about him. He's so wonderful, I mean different. All his family and everything, in New York. His roommate told me he'd inherit millions. I'm so afraid he won't like me."

"Betsy, don't be stupid. You're a Green, child. Take a lot to beat that. And money! You ought to know better than to talk like that. I think he's a right nice boy. I wish Maizie had ever got a chance with somebody like that instead of . . ." She sighed and her mind went away from Betsy.

Oren acted surprised and delighted and like a child during supper, fetching and carrying at Minnie May's orders and doing tap steps under the table, which delighted the children. In the middle of supper Tom came in from town and Oren was introduced.

"Good evening, sir," Oren said in his husky New York voice.

" 'Evenin'," Tom said in his tired voice, looking at him uncertainly.

Oren stayed late. It was midnight when he said he must go. Betsy drew a long breath. It was awful to have him go, but it was a relief too. The strain of the adoration and wonder she felt, the eagerness and the tongue-tied feeling, were terrible.

"How you going back to Cambridge, boy?" Minnie May demanded.

"I guess the same way I got out, on a street car," he said.

"Street cars stop running from here at eleven," Tom said.

"Well, I can walk."

"Walk to Cambridge? Nonsense," Minnie May declared. "I'll call up and get you a taxi."

Oren smiled, one-sidedly, ingratiatingly.

"You'll have to lend me some money, then, I'm afraid. I haven't got but fifty cents."

Tom reached in his inside pocket and took out his bill fold and drew out a ten dollar bill and handed it to Oren. Betsy saw him to the door, when the taxi came. He ran down the steps without looking back, that tall, narrow figure with its fidgety feet, and jumped into the cab. Betsy closed the door and came back into the living-room. Minnie May was turning out lights.

"I never thought," Tom said, "that I'd be lending money to anybody named Garth. It's right funny, come to think of it."

He smiled at his wife across the room, and stuck his hands into his trousers pockets; tall, rangy, his bullet-head turning gray, his face simple and with no light behind it.

## CHAPTER XXX

Betsy used to go out with Oren and Peter almost every night. They would go to some place where there was music; to strange downtown places where Betsy had never been before, with tough customers and a down-at-heels air, the St. Regis and the American House below Scollay Square. They sat in a booth and drank orangeades into which Peter put a spike from a bottle of gin that he carried in his pocket. They danced with Betsy by turns, and with Peter it was smooth and rhythmic and with Oren it was inspired. Oren knew all the men in all the orchestras and he would stop and talk to them, not as the college boys Betsy knew did, but seriously; about music; on a basis of equality. Sometimes when the music stopped and Oren and Betsy would be standing in the middle of the floor, he would break suddenly into a wild short burst of tap, and one of the men in the orchestra would grin at him and improvise a short strip on his instrument to accompany him.

Those were strange nights. Betsy could not take her eyes off Oren. Peter looked at him all the time too. She had the feeling that they were both adoring him, both taking care of him, and that he was wild and beyond either of them. Every night she knew more that she was terribly, finally in love with him, but not in any way that was solid or secure, for he never said anything to her about love. He called her baby, and they had these three-cornered dates nearly every night, but it was as if she gave him something he needed and he had drawn her into his orbit, along with Peter. She wondered whether she would ever be able to make him fall in love with her.

He filled the centre of the stage and she and Peter revolved around him and she felt that although he needed both of them he hardly noticed them. Sitting at the table he would suddenly begin to beat out a meter, with his fingers, looking around the room with his narrow blue eyes, a melancholy smile on his lips.

In the early morning they would come out of whatever place they had been and get into the car, Peter's car, a tiny old green Italian Bugatti.

"Button your coat up, Oren," Peter would say in a worried voice. "It's cold as hell. You can't go around with your coat flapping like that."

Oren would sling himself behind the wheel of Peter's car and Peter and Betsy would slide in beside him. The motor made a deafening roar in the dark silence of the downtown streets. They tore through the empty city and out under the cold stars toward Hampton.

The three of them were always together. Except for that first time, Oren brought Peter with him when he came out to the Jekylls. Peter was smooth and neat, with his dark, freckled face, the jaw thrust out; he was extremely polite to Minnie May and to Tom, and carried food in from the pantry, and joked with the children, and absolutely fitted in. But it was Oren who was the focus of it all. He looked as wild as a buck.

He spoke abruptly or not at all, but it was he whom everybody adored, Brats and Minnie May and all. Everybody felt the instinct to take care of him. Betsy ached with love and longing to hold his restless hands in hers, to pull his head down to her cheek. Often he looked thin and white, and it would turn out that he had forgotten to eat all day.

It came as a great shock when the Christmas vacation began. Oren and Peter were going home to New York; they were driving down in the Bugatti. Betsy and Oren sat on the circular window-seat in the living-room the night before they left. Peter sat at the old piano, playing in his neat, civilized way. The dance tune he played sounded orderly and pleasant, like Peter himself.

> Sweet child . . . you're driving me wild;
> I'm putting it mild . . . sweet child . . . I'm wild about you!
> Say when . . . you're gonna say when . . .
> Then say it again . . . sweet child. . . .

Betsy was tense and concentrated on the expressions that slid over Oren's eyes and mouth. He sat staring ahead of him; his strong, long fingers beat time on the windowsill beside him. Sometimes he would smile at something inside his mind, but his face was in the main melancholy and restless. He never seemed to feel the need to talk. Suddenly he spoke.

"You ought to come over to New York during the holidays," he said. "We'd take you to some parties. I'm going to miss you."

"I'm going to miss you!" Betsy cried.

He turned his sweet and sidewise smile upon her.

"Sweet baby," he said in his husky voice. "You better come over. Try to, will you?"

"Yes, I will. I will," she said.

"God!" he cried, jumping up with one of his sudden movements. "Peter, will you stop that?"

Peter slid off the piano stool, smiling. Oren dropped down and began to play in his strange, untethered way. He pulled the tune all to pieces and put it together again. Peter came over and sat down beside Betsy.

"Make him wear enough clothes driving down tomorrow," she said, in a low voice. "It's getting so cold."

"I'm going to do my best," he said, and their eyes met and smiled. As suddenly as he had gone to the piano Oren got up and walked away from it.

"God," he said. "I'm so terribly, terrible lousy. God, I'll *never* be any good."

"You were going to town on that tune, Oren," Peter said.

"That! Jazz. God! Make me work, will you, Peter? Or I'll *never* be any good."

"You haven't been in to the room enough lately."

"Well, make me."

They always spoke of 'the room.' Betsy had never yet seen it.

Now, as if in fury and irritation, Oren broke into a tap step in the middle of the room, his whole body liquid and mechanically accurate. After a second he stopped and stood still. He smiled across at Betsy and Peter on the window-seat; his sudden, sweet, crooked smile that stole the heart out of Betsy's body.

Minnie May was all for taking a trip to New York.

"I'd love to, honey," she declared. "We'll have a real good time. We'll go to a good hotel and enjoy luxury."

So they went. They took the one o'clock train from Boston, and lunched on the train, and Betsy felt the excitement and glamour coming on: the busy, rich-looking people lunching around her, the atmosphere of everybody going to New York.

In New York they drove in a taxi through the early darkness to the hotel. Minnie May had decided on it from an advertisement in *Vogue*. The place smelt of expensive perfume, and of flowers from the florist's shop; beautiful women in furs were hurrying through the lobby, and well-dressed men, and there was string music playing at one end where people were finishing tea. Waiters hurried through in white coats, and bellboys, and on the desk stood vases of roses.

They took a room, and it cost ten dollars a day. A bellboy carried their bags up in the elevator. Their room was square; it had rose-colored covers on the twin beds, and low, comfortable little armchairs, and a dressing table with a triple mirror. Betsy went over to the window and looked out.

Below on Park Avenue the cars moved and stopped, moved and stopped, their lights like diamonds in the early evening; the red and green lights went on and off, like jewels too. Across Park Avenue there were lights in the apartment houses. Betsy drew a long, quivering breath.

"Aren't you going to call the boys up, tell them you're here?" Minnie

May said. She lay on the rose-colored chaise longue, smoking a cigarette. "My, I love luxury," she said. "I haven't been at a hotel for years. I'd forgotten how I love it."

Betsy curled up on a bed. She reached for the telephone book and began leafing through it to the G's. "Garth, Mortimer." There were three numbers listed, office, residence, and garage. Betsy's heart was pounding as she picked up the telephone and asked for the residence number. A man's voice answered the telephone—the butler's—and she asked for Mr. Oren Garth.

"Yes, madam. Will you hold on, madam?"

In a minute Oren's voice was on the other end.

"Hello, baby," he said. "God, I'm glad you could make it."

"It's wonderful to be here," she said.

"Your mother bring you?"

"Yes. She's here."

"Good," he said, and his voice trailed off in its characteristic way. There was a silence. It was agonizing.

"Well," Betsy said. "I just wanted to let you know I'd come over."

"Yeah. What time shall I come?"

"What?"

"Oh. This aunt of mine's giving some sort of party tonight. It won't be any good. I have to go. We won't have to stay long. We can go dancing somewhere else, or something. It'll be horrible. Do you mind? My aunt's Mrs. Horatio Starr, she's an awful woman."

"Oh!" Mrs. Horatio Starr was a name like New York itself.

"Suppose I pick you up at ten," he said.

"All right."

"So long, baby."

Betsy lay flat on her back for a moment, and then jumped up and began to unpack her bag, shaking out the evening dresses and inspecting them. She sang under her breath, the song that so often now ran through her mind for hours. . . .

> O.G. . . . I'm mighty blue for you,
> I've . . . been mighty true . . . to you. . . .

Minnie May lay on the chaise longue in a cloud of blue smoke.

"Let's have a marvellous dinner," she said. "Let's spend all our money quick and enjoy ourselves. Let's go out and buy some clothes tomorrow."

It was all like a dream of glamour.

Oren came at eleven. Betsy could never remember that he was always late and count on it. She had been dressed for an hour and a half and sitting in their room rigid with tension waiting for the desk to ring up and say that Mr. Garth was waiting. She wore the red dress that she had worn for her party; she felt that it brought her good luck. At last the telephone rang and the words that Betsy had been hearing in her head were actually spoken. She shivered with excitement.

She met Oren in the lobby and they went out onto the sidewalk. The

New York air was high and rare, and long dark cars swept past; people came hurrying into the hotel in evening dress, and the atmosphere was purest magic. Oren had Peter's Bugatti at the curb, and they climbed into the little front seat. The engine started with a roar.

"Oh, I *adore* New York so!" Betsy cried.

"It's the only place," Oren said. "It's got everything."

Not knowing the city she was confused as to where they went, but it was not far. They drew up in front of an. enormous brownstone house on what Betsy knew was Fifth Avenue; there were lighted windows of great shops all up and down the street. A red carpet was laid down a broad flight of steps and across the sidewalk. A footman ran down and pulled open the door of the Bugatti. Betsy got out. Behind the Bugatti other cars, great limousines and town cars, were halted, and she caught a glimpse of white shirtfronts and jewels within.

"Stick this somewhere, will you?" Oren said to the footman.

"Yes, Mr. Garth."

They went up the red carpet and through the huge glass door which was opened for them, into a marble hall with palms standing in pots. There seemed to be dozens of footmen. One of them indicated to Betsy where to leave her wrap. She went into the dressing-room. It was filled with women, young ones both plain and pretty, and older ones. Betsy peered anxiously at herself in the mirror. She thought she looked rather well. She had more snap to her than most of the girls in the room. Her head looked like a boy's, and her slim figure was as straight as a boy's in the tubular red dress. She smiled at herself in the mirror: a melancholy smile, that tipped up only one side of her mouth. It was her new smile. She had a long ostrich feather fan, and she swept it slowly across her shoulders and cast a backwards glance at herself.

Oren was waiting in the hall. They went into a circular room where dark paintings were hung on the walls. They stood in line, and came at last to their hostess, whose photograph Betsy had seen many times in rotogravure sections, in fashion magazines and on society pages—Mrs. Horatio Starr. She was an old woman, in a blazing silver dress, with a wide silver bandeau holding her white hair; her shoulders were powdered, soft and plump; around her neck were blazing stones; Betsy realized that she was looking at a diamond necklace. She shook Mrs. Starr's hand.

"Oren," Mrs. Starr said, "it's about time you came to one of my parties. Where's your father?"

"They went down to Palm Beach yesterday."

"Didn't tell me. How are you, dear? Harvard. . . . Nice to see you . . . Miss Jerkkblf." Her head turned to the next in line.

In another room beyond people were dancing. Oren and Betsy went in and began to dance too. It was a funny kind of a party. There was no stag-line. A few men stood gathered in the doorway, but they did not do any cutting in. The orchestra, although this was New York, was staid and played strictly on beat. Oren paid no attention to the orchestra men. The walls of this room, too, were hung with paintings—misty landscapes with a great many olive green leaves and blue-green distances. Betsy spoke of them to Oren.

"Those are the old boy's Corots," he said. "General Horatio's Corots. God!"

He executed a difficult bit with his feet and Betsy followed easily. They were outstanding on that floor, she thought. The house, the footmen, the atmosphere were impressive, but the other women were not impressive, they were merely rich. They did not look as though they were vamping anybody. They had no pep.

This was the world of old New York families, of family butlers, of Newport villas, of all the things you read about in the society pages. The hostess came in and began to circle the floor slowly within the embrace of an old gentleman with a bay-window. "I'm actually looking at Mrs. Horatio Starr," Betsy thought. It was as if she were looking at the Taj Mahal, only much more so, for the Taj Mahal was on view to the public.

They danced, and had some champagne, and danced again. Nobody asked to be introduced. But then, there were no ushers, as at Boston dances. And anyway, this was all different. It didn't seem to matter whether you were popular or not. Betsy tipped her head back and chattered animatedly at Oren, making herself the picture of pep and popularity. He smiled his one-sided smile at her and hardly spoke.

Suddenly he said, "Come on. Let's get out of this now."

They said goodbye to Mrs. Horatio Starr and got their wraps and went out into the black crystal night. They got into the Bugatti and the footman slammed the little door after them.

"Let's go up to the family's," Oren said. "There won't be anyone there." Betsy's eyes were enormous like those of a young puppy.

They drove up Fifth Avenue, among the colored lights and the low, thrilling hoots of motor horns. Betsy had the feeling that her heart was too big for her body. All her life she had dreamed of glamour, but now glamour was around her. It was more wonderful than anything she had imagined.

They drew up in front of an apartment house and a doorman came out and took the Bugatti. They went up in an elevator lined with mirrors, to a floor high in the building. Betsy had always thought of apartments as little places with small rooms. But now Oren opened the door onto a great hall.

"Servants all gone to bed, I *hope*," he said.

They passed through to a long drawing-room. One light was lit in a corner, rosy and dim. There was a deep sofa before the white stone fireplace and Oren dropped down in it. He held out his arm.

"Come sit by Papa," he said in his husky voice.

The room was full of the smell of lilies, tall and white in vases on tables and on the grand piano at the end of the drawing-room. She sat down beside him and he put his arm close around her. Her heart was pounding. He had not kissed her since the first night she had met him. Now he kissed her. His skin felt curious; tough and a little moist.

"I love you so!" The words simply came out of her.

"Sweet baby," he murmured. "Do you? Love you too, baby."

"Do you? Do you really?"

"I really do. Really love my sweet baby."

He kissed her. Then he lifted his head sharply and began to hum a snatch of a tune in his husky voice, stressing the off-beat and moving his head slightly as if he were working out some problem about it in his mind. Then he laughed out loud and bent his head again and kissed her.

This room might have been in a dream; none of it seemed real, the smell of lilies, and far away the sound of the cars passing on Fifth Avenue; the silence and dimness here.

"Oh, darling," she murmured. "I adore you. All I want is to do things for you. I love you so. I don't think of anything but you."

He went on kissing her. She did not know how long they stayed there in the mysterious room, kissing on the velvet sofa.

"Baby," he said once, "I love you to love me. You don't know how horrible everything gets. God, my family! And the kind of life they want me to live. You don't know anything about what hell can be. I'm glad you love me. I need you to love me, baby."

"I love you with all my heart. I'll always love you."

"I hope to God it's not going to hurt you," he said in his melancholy voice. "I can't stand the idea I might hurt somebody."

"Oh, no! It makes me happy just to look at you."

"I'm not an ordinary sort of guy. I'm always getting in the most awful jams."

"It's all right. I love you. Anything you do is all right." She felt both exalted and humble; she had the feeling of vocation; Oren was the beginning and the end of everything. Of course he was different from everyone else. But he wouldn't hurt her. What might hurt another girl would only exalt her; anything that was him she wanted.

"God, I don't know. Sometimes I think I'm going crazy. Love me, will you? Hold on to me and don't let go."

"I do love you. I do. I adore you." She clung to him.

"It isn't any fun for anybody who's near me. I put them through hell. Like poor Peter. I can't promise you any fun or any happiness."

"Oh, darling, I have everything just being with you!"

He kissed her rapidly and held her to him.

"I guess I ought to go," she said after a long time. "Ma'am might get worried if I stayed out too long."

Oren jumped up. Suddenly he was galvanized. He began to laugh, his almost hysterical laughter that she never understood but always joined in. He began to dance around the room, on the deep carpet that made no sound. He drew out a long-stemmed lily from one of the vases. They walked out of the front door to the elevator, Oren holding the lily in front of him and laughing.

When they got out of the elevator Oren was still laughing. He turned to the elevator man and thrust the lily into his hand.

"For purity!" he cried, laughing harder than ever. Betsy laughed too, eagerly. It was a line from *The Green Hat*. It sounded glamorous to hear

Oren say it, but she did not know what he meant nor why he was laughing. They went into the cold, late night.

Betsy and Minnie May went back to Boston four days later. Betsy leaned her face against the cold, damp train window and looked out at the snow falling slowly over the New England landscape. She was tired from excitement, from being up very late every night. But her fatigue exalted her mind into a state where music and the thought of Oren floated like the flakes of snow outside. Close to the train windows the flakes flurried in eddies, but beyond out over the fields they fell in a great peace. "O.G., I'm mighty blue for you. . . ."

Minnie May had a pile of magazines they had bought in the Grand Central; she looked through them, her yellow, homely monkey's face alert and curious, and she moved about restlessly and at last got up and walked swaying down the aisle to go into the lounge car to smoke. Betsy felt wonderfully alone.

The early dusk was beginning to tinge the white landscape with blue, and the snow kept falling, slow, slow, over the Connecticut fields. The train stopped at New London. Then it started again and went racketing on over the country, breaking the silent fall of the snow.

Something in her seemed to have awakened and she knew with a feeling of predestination that she loved Oren and that she would always love him. The only necessity was that she should always be near him. This was worlds different from 'crushes' and 'yens.' This enveloped her, calmly, deeply, like the snow covering the fields outside the train.

She prayed that she could be worthy of him and good enough for him to want to marry. She would wait till he got out of college, she would wait any time necessary, but she must have him. It was breathtaking to think of being married to Oren Garth. She would be so good; so gay; she would take such care of him; he would not be able to get along without her. Nobody, she thought with a deep absolute assurance, nobody would ever love Oren as much as she did.

Minnie May came staggering back up the aisle of the lurching train, sat down and grinned at Betsy. The train was slowing for Providence.

"*Didn't* we have a good time?" Minnie May said.

"I had the most wonderful time I've ever had in my life."

"Certainly do like New York. Got so much going on all the time. I declare sometimes I wish we lived in New York. Every other place seems tame in comparison."

Betsy stared at her mother with dreaming eyes. Some day she would live in New York. She would live in New York, and her name would be Mrs. Oren Garth. Betsy Garth. She would meet all sorts of wonderful people and she would be quite a different person from the old Betsy Jekyll. The world felt huge and glorious, with snow falling over it and lights shining through the snow and music playing, and vistas opening beyond and beyond and beyond. All through the world she heard a voice whispering, and singing softly.

"Wonder how Dad's been," Minnie May said. "I hope he hasn't got all balled up without me here. Thing I really do worry about is Maizie, though. Everywhere I go I can't forget about her. It most ruins things for me. If I could just do something . . . I'm her mother and I'm perfectly helpless. She won't even *tell* me. . . ."

Betsy heard her voice going on. She loved her sister, but there was no room in her for trouble. Even her mother did not seem quite real any more. She lived in a private world where there was no other person except Oren. She was on the edge of another life; the old life was half sloughed off. The only reality was the future.

## CHAPTER XXXI

AFTER THE NEW YEAR a great deal of snow fell, and the young men came back from the holidays and began to cram for midyears, at the Widow's or other tutoring schools in Harvard Square. It was very cold and the snow made high mounds between the street and sidewalks in Boston, so that the street could only be crossed at intervals. Out in the country in Hampton the snow clogged everything and the ruts in the roads were very deep and everyone put chains on.

Betsy began in January going in to the room. It was in a brownstone house on Newbury Street. The lower floors had been made over into shops and offices. In the evenings Newbury Street would be very still, the streetlights winking, the flakes falling quietly down over the city; beyond Arlington Street lay the Public Gardens and there it was an open stretch of deep snow, with the wooden walks cleared, under the calm, winking lights.

They would park the loud Bugatti at the curb. They would go up the dark steps to the unlit vestibule; it seemed mysterious, like an underworld lodging house. Oren turned the key and they would go into the building, and up one narrow flight; two flights; three flights. There was a door toward the front, painted gray, that Oren also unlocked, and then they were in the room.

It was a high-ceilinged room of medium size, obviously a one-time bedroom from the days of the house's private life; a door led to a passage with closets, and a bathroom with a hanging, glaring light and gray marble washbasin. Oren had furnished the room out of his allowance to suit his tastes. There was a large Oriental rug on the floor. Heavy dark blue curtains hung at the three long windows overlooking Newbury Street. There was a dark blue velvet cover fitted to the broad couch, and dark blue velvet cushions. The grand piano stood filling much of the room. Everything that Oren did had a charm over it; but Betsy wondered sometimes when she saw that room why it seemed to look like her idea of a haunt of dope fiends. Betsy would stand between the curtains looking out over Newbury Street and the still and orderly city; behind her Oren played the piano. She felt suspended above the world, shut away in the tower of an enchanted castle.

He played Mozart, Bach, Brahms, Chopin, Debussy, and to Betsy, who knew nothing about music, they all sounded like variations on the same deep, surging theme—the room, and their being together there. The music was part of the loveliest thing that had ever happened to her. She could not help believing that more and more he loved and needed her.

For Peter did not come to the room too. It meant that it was she that Oren needed for this most important part of his life. When he was playing music he was bound up in inner processes and urgencies that she did not understand, but still he wanted her there; she half lay on the wide, dark blue, sinister-looking couch, letting the torrents and tricklings of the music flow over her mute mind, letting them become a part of what the room with Oren meant to her. She was always waiting for the time when he would get through playing and it would be he and she together, kissing.

There were two ways in which he might stop. If he had been satisfied with his own playing, which was seldom, the notes would trickle clearly like drops falling slower and slower from the edge of a cliff, and stop, and he would be coming toward her, smiling, ready to kiss her and make jokes that she did not understand, and laugh wildly.

But if he did not like his music, and generally he did not like it, it broke off sharply and turned into hectic rendering of some piece of jazz, and then that would stop too and she would hear his voice say "God!"

He would look as if he hated everything, as if he hated her too, and it was no use touching him or trying to be comforting because he hated that; he hated the air around him.

"God!" he would say. "God!" The only thing was to try to get him to talk it out, and that way bring him slowly round to where he would begin to make jokes and laugh and burrow his head in her neck.

He was taking lessons now, in spite of impending midyears, from a young musician in Boston, for whom Oren had the most tremendous respect.

"He's absolutely contemptuous," Oren would say. "God, that guy can be contemptuous! And he's right. I haven't got a thing. I was ruined years ago. It's too late. The only thing I've got to respect in myself is that I will try; I will try. . . . Fernald knows I'm a lazy bum, a rich man's son; he's so right. How am I ever going to get anywhere with it? My father wants me to be an international banker." He laughed hysterically. "Nobody else cares a good God damn what I am."

"I care," Betsy would say, with the desperate hope that it would make some difference to him.

But he sat in silence on the edge of the couch with his hands dropping between his knees, the light from the lamp beside the piano gilding his brown curly hair.

"What am I?" he would begin again. "I'm a product of a system that's dead. I'm an end result of what the capitalist system can really produce when it's given a chance. God! I see myself, all the time. I see myself at school in a sweater with a letter on it. I could shoot my lunch. I'm a Harvard boy, a rich Harvard boy. I'm Oren Garth. I've had it rammed into me all my life. I'll never get away from it. I'm a Garth and I've got to go to hell on account of it."

"Listen," she said one evening. "I know how you hate Harvard, so why don't you leave it? Why don't you write your father that you want to study music, and then you could just move in here and work hard all the time at it. If you said that was what you were going to do, I don't see what he could do about it."

"Oh, no," he said in his melancholy voice. "You don't know my father. You don't get the picture. Nobody ever understands. . . . He'd cut off my allowance and then how could I live? He'd—God knows what he'd do. He's a terrible man. I think I admire him more than any man alive. Can you understand that? He's like God, or the Devil. He does absolutely what he wants, and makes other people obey. Women. He takes women and owns them and takes everything out of them until he's ready to take another one. Do you know that my father pays out nearly a million dollars a year in alimony?"

And then Betsy would think of the ex-wife named Elena, that Oren had been in love with. He spoke of her sometimes with a wistful, tortured look. Perhaps he would always be most in love with Elena.

But Betsy was willing to fill any niche, however inferior. Perhaps she could be the comforter, the essential presence . . . that was enough. . . .

"Well, why couldn't you get a job and make enough money to support yourself and pay for lessons?" she asked.

"Oh, no. Oh, no. Don't you see, my hands are tied. They've been tied since birth. I couldn't take a job. I don't know how to do anything. And then there wouldn't be enough time to practice, and it would be bad for my hands. And can't you see the papers, God, they'd get hold of it and there'd be one of those big stories in the Sunday paper over two pages, like about my mother, about how Oren Garth was working in a factory for twelve dollars a week. I'm lost. I can't do anything. I can't even have fun."

"It wouldn't have to be a factory. . . ."

He shrugged his shoulders as though it were an anonymous voice that was cross-questioning and heckling him. He spread his hands before him as though he had never seen them, and moved the fingers one by one. They were beautiful hands, strong and nervous· with blunt-ended fingers. Suddenly the movements took rhythm and he was beating out a meter with his fingers on his knees.

"Ta-ta, ta-ta-cla, t-t-t-t-t-*cla!*" he cried aloud, and suddenly his face broke into a gay, child's smile.

"Baby . . ." he sang in a husky voice, a jazz voice, "When my baby, *my baby*, smiles at me twa twa twa twa," he sang, imitating Ted Lewis but at the same time being himself, always himself. He snatched up the banjo that lay at the foot of the sofa and began to play a fast accompaniment. He kept his eyes fixed steadily on Betsy's, and sang in that exaggerated style, with a look of ecstasy. "I sigh—ah-hah! I cry—ah-hah! It's just a bit of heaven, when my baby—smiles—at me. . . . —Is ev'rybody . . . *heppy?*"

"Honestly, Oren, you ought to go on the stage. You're terribly good. You're absolutely professional. Peter says you could any day, and Peter knows all about that kind of thing," she said.

"Poor Peter," Oren said, dropping the banjo. "I've ruined his life. I ruin everyone's life. I'll ruin yours too. You better get away while the going's good.—I couldn't go in the theatre. I can see my father. I've tried, oh, I've tried . . . I wanted to go on the Keith Circuit with a sweet little girl who could dance like mad. We would have been good. Gretchen. Sweet Gretchen. She'll be in the big time before you know it. She came from the West. We used to work out some pretty hot routines together. But then my father heard about it. That's when I went to St. Jean two years ago, and saw my mother. God, she looked unhappy."

He sat, his eyes brooding, his fingers moving on his knees. Betsy watched him, respecting his grief, burning with jealousy of "sweet Gretchen"; her head spinning with that incomprehensible, desperate, rich, frustrated world that made Oren so unhappy.

"Ah, baby," he said suddenly in his sweetest voice, and put his arms around her. "Do you know what's the difference between a cynic and a stoic?"

"What?"

"A cynic's vere you vash de dishes, and a stoic's vat brings de babies."

He laughed crazily.

He pushed her back on the couch and lay beside her, tickling her.

"Baby . . . my sweet little virgin. . . . She was pure as snow, boy, but she drifted. Wouldn't you drift, just the least little bit, for Papa?"

But this was never even so much as a problem. Betsy had a streak of pugdog obstinacy in her. She knew that she was not going to lose her virginity. She did not think it over, she did not think about it at all. It was as if there was one corner of her that was different from all the rest that loved glamour and intrigue and Michael Arlen atmosphere. The fall of the emerald was one thing, but this was here and now and on the fourth floor of a brownstone house on Newbury Street, and she simply never considered giving up her virginity.

She was willing to do everything else. She had done nearly everything else for a couple of years now, in parked cars, on beaches at night.

She herself had never got much pleasure out of necking, and she did not now. The loveliest moment in her whole life had been when Oren kissed her that night she first met him. And the beginning was always the best part, the first, fresh kisses before things got hot and sticky. She liked necking less and less as it got further and further. But she had always had a feeling that this was something she must render. It seemed to matter so much to boys. Many of them had told her that it was extremely harmful for a man to stop. . . . It didn't hurt her.

With Oren, because she loved him, she had a feeling of happiness in knowing that he was finding what he wanted. But she was happy because he was happy. She was always rather glad when he was through with active necking. There was a feeling that during the last of it she, as a person, was almost forgotten. Later they could lie still together and kiss softly, and say pet-names, and play like children.

When they left the room it would be late, and they came out into the deserted street and shut the door behind them. The street-lights blinked solemnly at the white sky. The Bugatti stood beyond the massed ridge of snow at the edge of the shovelled sidewalks. It started with a deafening roar, and shot around the corner to Arlington Street, into Boylston Street, and out into the country toward Hampton. The lights in the houses were out, and the country lay white and still beyond their leaping headlights.

Minnie May always called out, softly, as Betsy tiptoed up the stairs to the tower. She would open the door of her parents' bedroom, softly, and Minnie May would whisper, "Have a good time?" Tom was always fast asleep.

"I had the most wonderful time I ever had!" Betsy would hiss. It was a kind of formula.

"Where'd you go?"

"Just dancing."

"Well . . . 'Night, Bets."

"Good night," she would whisper, and then go on up the other flight of stairs to her tower room. She never gave any thought to lying about what she did in the evenings. It was just a necessity. She couldn't say where she'd been.

One afternoon in late February, after the lights had been lit in the Jekylls' house, Tom Jekyll got home from the office. They were all sitting around in the big living-room. The Brats were doing homework and sucking lollipops at the round table at the end. Minnie May was in the most comfortable chair, looking through a fashion magazine, in her customary cloud of smoke. Betsy sat in the window-seat putting silver paint on an old pair of silver slippers; she had got some of the silver on to the window-seat cushion.

The front door opened and swung back and banged against the hall wall. Tom Jekyll walked in. He took hold of the door and slammed it closed again. Then he walked into the living-room.

He looked around. They all looked at him. Was he drunk? He had never been drunk in the afternoon on days when he went to the office. His pug-dog face was set. He did not take off his hat or coat. His hands were in his trousers pockets, and there was the sound of money sharply jingling.

"You," he said, jerking his head at the Brats. "You children get upstairs and stay there."

Jane and Glory edged out of the room to the stairs, staring at him. Tom Jekyll stood without speaking, jingling his money, until the sound of the children's feet going upstairs had ceased.

"Tom, honey, what in the name of . . ."

"I'm goin' to talk," he said. "You all keep still till I get through. I put up with a lot. I put up with this God damned place and these God damned Yankees, trash goin' through my house night and day. . . . But there's one thing I'm not going to put up with, by God. I'm not going to have my daughter a common prostitute. I'm not going to have a common Yankee bastard on a train telling me my daughter is a prostitute and laughing at me, the Yankee bastard. . . ."

Minnie May glanced sharply at Betsy and back at her husband.

"Honey, you're so mad you don't talk sense. Try not to be so mad. Calm down and say exactly what's happened."

"I will get mad," he said. "I'm going to get so God damned mad something'll happen round here to make things different. Get mad! Nobody gets mad up here, that's just what's the matter, those God damned, pawky, smooth-talking bastards that never get mad. What this place *needs* is for somebody to get mad. Maybe if I'd been man enough to get mad long ago I wouldn't be standing here looking at my daughter who's a common prostitute and my wife who lets her be and lets my other daughter get married to the God damnedest son-of-a-bitch in God's creation, and my children grow up in this God damned place along with these God damned Yankees, so they'll be prostitutes too, and bastards'll get hold of them and all the time those bastards, those Yankees, standing there laughing. Never getting mad at anything, just standing there laughing. . . . All right, I'll tell you.

"I get on the train tonight to come on home after work. There's nobody on that train but a lot of stuffed Yankee frozen-faced bastards, and generally I say to hell with them and read my paper. Tonight one of them comes up and says can he sit down, so I say sure and move over to give him room. But he wants to talk. He wants to tell me something, he says, that he thinks I ought to know."

Tom's voice went up into a bitter imitation of a Boston accent.

"He's a member of the Copley Club, he says, and that's on Newbury Street, right next to some houses. And in one of these houses, he says he happens to know that young Garth, the son of Mortimer Garth of New York, he says, has an apartment. He doesn't know what he has it for, he says, since he's going to Harvard out in Cambridge, but he supposes, he says, for the usual thing. Young men, he says. And sitting in his God damned son-of-a-bitch Copley Club he says he has often seen young Garth coming out with a young girl, late at night. Very late at night, he says, oh, two or three. And the thing I ought to know, he says, is that the young girl is my daughter.

"He hopes I'll understand his motive in telling me, he says. He says he took an unpleasant duty upon himself to tell me because he was sure I'd want to know. And then he looks at me. Jesus Christ in Heaven, what it's like when a Yankee looks at you! Figuring out how I'm taking it. Figuring how his own daughters wouldn't do such a thing. Laughing at me. And looking at me. Me sitting there in the seat with my pants down before a Yankee. What the hell could I say? What did I know? I told him thank him for his interest in my business. He said he was sorry if I wanted to take it that way, that he thought fathers ought to know what their daughters were up to. I said thank you very much, Sir, again, and acted like I was reading the paper."

"That wasn't the way to act to him," Minnie May said. She looked concentrated, abstracted.

"I know. I know. I don't know how the hell to act to a Yankee. You should have been there. You can do everything. Well, you can have every last Yankee in Yankeeland and act to them like you please as long as I don't have to see them. I know I didn't act right. I'm not a God damned Green. I'm just a country boy and I don't know how to behave, and I don't get along with Yankees and I'm nothing much. But I do know a couple of things. All right.

"First. Betsy, have you got anything to say about this? Have you been going to Garth's room, or haven't you?"

"Yes, I have," she said slowly. If somebody had seen her, there wasn't any point in trying to lie. Besides, for the first time in her life she felt frightened of her father. "Only you don't understand. What we did was different from what you think. . . ."

"I don't want to know what you did. If I know any more than I know now I'll vomit. Now you look here."

"Yes, sir," she said. Years ago, back down in Annestown, when she had been naughty and he was going to tell her what her punishment would be, he would say, "Now you look here," and she would say, "Yes, sir." Then he would take her across his thigh and spank her hard. But that hadn't happened very many times; not in the Jekyll family.

"We're going to get out of this God damned place, hear? Right away. We're going to get out just as soon as I can get someone to take over my work at the office. We're going back down where we belong, where we should have gone long ago. We're going back to Annestown so quick you can't count it, and we're not coming back. We're going to live down there where we should have been living all the time. I hate this place, do you hear?" he cried to his wife and his daughter. "I've always hated it. Life's not worth the living up here when you haven't got friends and you haven't got peace and your daughters are out prostituting themselves with Yankee bastards. I want to get out, and I'm going to get out, and you all are coming too, and we're going home.

"But first I'm going to have a talk with this young Garth man of yours. I'm going to tell him what a Southerner has to say about Yankees. I'm going to tell him enough so he'll keep his hands off a daughter of the South next time he's looking for a fancy woman. I'm not going to make him marry you. I can't stand another Yankee son-of-a-bitch in this family. Maybe I ought to. But I won't. If you want to get married you can marry some decent Southern boy—if any of them'll marry you being what you are."

"Tom, you're talking crazy," Minnie May said firmly. She looked ready to take the situation in hand. "Betsy, go upstairs to your room, hear? I'll come up later after I've talked to your father. Go on, now."

Betsy got up and went out of the room and up the stairs. Her heart was thumping heavily. Out of the tail of her eye she saw her father slump down into a chair facing Minnie May, and let his head drop back against the upholstery. He had stopped talking. As she went upstairs Betsy heard her mother's voice going on, steadily, intensely.

She was lying flat on her face on the bed when she heard her mother's footsteps coming into the room. It was entirely dark. She turned over quickly and switched on the light.

"Ma'am, I *can't* go away, I don't *want* to go away, Ma'am, I'm in love, I'm so in love. . . ."

"Now hush." Minnie May sat down on a chair. "You let me talk for a while. You've been a sillier girl than I thought any daughter of mine was capable of being, but we'll go into that later.

"We're not going away. Your father is half crazy with the humiliation you've put him to, the having a man he hardly knows come up to him and tell him a thing like that. . . . I don't want to leave Hampton any more than you do, and we're not going to. He sees that now. He'll see it better in the morning, when I can talk to him some more. Poor Dad. You've done a dreadful thing to your father, Betsy; I've never seen him like this before in his life. I hope he can get good and drunk and feel a little better.

"We're not going away. I've got him to agree to that. I'm not going back down to Annestown and moulder away, and that's all there is to it. We're just beginning to get started up here, because it does take a right long time in the North before they realize you're there. We're not going away, but it's on condition. That's no more than fair. You've been a silly, silly girl, and a fool, and you've got to expect to pay for it."

"What?"

"You've got to promise me solemnly that you won't see this boy, Oren, again, ever. Your father makes that an absolute condition. He's going to see him tomorrow—he's talked to him on the telephone already and he's coming to your father's office—and he's going to get him to give his solemn promise too. That's the conditions on which we can stay here and not have to go on back to Annestown. Your father does handle the money, you know. Reckon in the last analysis it's him that can decide. And I've never seen him this way. He means what he says. And don't forget you've brought it on yourself. And all of us."

"I can't, Ma'am! Oh, that's horrible! You mean can't see him again *ever?* I'm in love with him—I want to marry him. . . ." Betsy threw herself around on the bed.

"He ask you to marry him?"

"No. No, not yet, but he's in college, Ma'am; he can't; how could he?" Suddenly Betsy sat up straight. "Ma'am, what Dad said about me is not true. I never did . . . honestly. I never have."

"I didn't think you had," Minnie May retorted. "Now look here to me. Dad's had an awful shock. He's got ideals about his daughters—men have. It doesn't take the top off my head that you've been to a man's room, but I know it doesn't have to mean what he means. And it does take the top off Dad's head. Now look here to me. Dad's going to see to it that you don't see any more of Oren in any case. You can make up your mind to that. You're not going to be allowed to see him. It's a question of whether you want us all to have to go on back down home with our tails between our legs and be buried for the rest of our lives in that poky old town. Or whether you've got enough sense to see that if we stay up here everything'll keep happening, and you'll meet a lot of other interesting men, and Jane and Glory will have a chance. To say nothing of me. Maizie and Dad's the only

ones who have any homesickness for Annestown and I'm sure I don't understand why. Poor darlin' Maizie, I suppose anything would have been better
for her than what she got. But Dad—I can just see him if he'd stayed down
there in a two-by-four office on Courthouse Square. You don't want to go
back to Annestown, do you?"

"No," Betsy said dully.

"Well, then. You give me your promise you won't see Oren again, and
I'll tell your father you have, and pretty soon this will blow over and your
father will forget about it and everything will be all right."

"I feel as if I'd die if I couldn't ever see him again. It's giving up my
whole life."

"Well, you're not going to get to see him anyway, either way. You might
think of the rest of us."

"All right. All right."

"You promise?"

"Yes, I promise."

Minnie May got up briskly.

"That's sensible. I'll go and tell your father, and try and get him to calm
down."

"Ma'am!"

"What?"

"I'm so terribly unhappy. . . ."

"Well, Betsy, you deserve to be unhappy. You've certainly been a silly
girl. You've made your father plenty unhappy, I can tell you that. Bets, you
ought to get one thing through your head. Southern men, anyway, have
ideals about their women. More ideals than you could shake a stick at. There
isn't anything a woman does that they haven't got an ideal about. I don't
know about Northern men. But Southern men don't want to know about
what you may be feeling really or your reasons for things. They just want
you to be ideal. I would have thought you'd know that."

"Ma'am, do you hate me?"

"Of course I don't hate you. I'm amazed at how little sense you've got.
I reckon practically any girl on earth knows better than to let herself be
seen going to a man's apartment. That's just sense. You can't imagine any
Boston girl doing such a thing. Leda March. You can't imagine her."

"I'm so unhappy. I feel as if you hated me."

"No, I don't, but I hope you've learned a lesson." Minnie May bent and
patted Betsy briefly on the shoulder. "You'll get over it. Plenty of other
boys, goodness knows."

She went out, and Betsy reached up and switched off the light again. She
lay there quite still in the darkness, staring at a star that had appeared in the
window. She felt so empty, so bereft, that she could not yet begin to cry.
She did not know where to begin thinking about what had happened to
her. She wished there were someone in the whole world who could understand and sympathize. But her mother did not sympathize.—She would have
sympathized with Maizie, Betsy thought, in one of the stabs of inferiority.
But Maizie would not have done it.

But Maizie would be able to understand about doing it—wouldn't she?

There was no romance left any more in the tower room. It was just a room. Betsy lay on the bed and big, heavy tears began to roll down her face. Oh, Oren, she thought. Oh my love. Never to see your face again. . . .

Two days later Betsy went to see Maizie in town, in the afternoon.

It was awful at home. Her father would not speak to her, and her mother seemed irritated and impatient, and the Brats knew perfectly well that something was the matter and that Betsy had done something wicked.

The idea of the meeting between Oren and her father haunted her mind, and she had the most strange and differing pictures of what the interview could have been like. Her father shouting at Oren as he had shouted at Betsy. . . . Oren championing her innocence and—perhaps?—asking for her hand in marriage. . . . She did not dare to ask her father anything about it. She asked her mother, the following morning, and Minnie May said merely that Oren had given Tom his promise not to see Betsy again.

She felt she would die if she could not tell someone the way she felt about Oren. The thought of Maizie had seemed to her the solution. Maizie would sympathize.

The young Rudds lived in an apartment at the back of Beacon Hill. A middle-aged, slatternly Irish maid opened the door to Betsy's ring and eyed her.

"Yeah, she's in," the maid allowed. "She's been in bed all day. They was out to a pahty late last night. You can cmin."

Betsy went in to Maizie's bedroom.

Maizie lay on one side of the very large double bed, in a nightgown and an old pink crocheted bedjacket. She just lay there; there were no books or papers around her. Her face was white and slack; deadly tired. Her brilliant yellow hair lay uncombed on the pillow behind her.

A lamp was turned on beside the bed, and the Venetian blinds of the windows were slanted shut, although it was three o'clock in the afternoon and the sun was bright outside. An evening dress and underclothes lay across the back of a chair, with slippers kicked at angles underneath it. A pair of men's evening trousers, with braces attached, lay across another chair. Maizie had been smoking all day, for the air smelled dead and smoky; there was a pile of butts on the table beside the bed. A tray that might have held lunch and was now a confusion of dirty dishes had been pushed down to the foot of the bed.

"Maizie! You sick?"

Maizie smiled; her stiff face broke at the mouth.

"No, just restin'," she said. "We were out late last night and we didn't get to sleep till the sun was up. I'm getting rested for when Lamb gets home tonight," she said, and the smile went away and the anxious leaden look came back.

Betsy put the evening trousers on the same chair with the dress and sat down.

"How's Lambert?"

"Oh, he's fine. He's fine. . . . He's doing a portrait, did you know it, of your old friend Leda March. . . ."

"Oh, really?" Betsy blinked. "Are you—are you getting along all right with him, Maizie? And everything?"

"Yes," Maizie said. "We're terribly happy, terribly happy. . . . I love him terribly, Betsy. I love him with my whole soul."

Betsy stared at her sister. She did not look happy. She looked wretched. What was it? . . . The voice she talked in, the things she said. . . .

"Maizie, you look so tired I hate to bother you, but I wanted to talk to you so much. . . . I'm in the most awful trouble. . . . I just wanted to tell somebody about it, nobody understands. . . ."

Maizie sat up part way on one elbow and looked at Betsy and nodded.

"Dad won't speak to me. Ma'am's furious. It's because I went to a boy's room on Newbury Street, and somebody saw us coming out. . . . But it's not what Dad thinks. I never did it. I'm just terribly in love with him, that's all, and now they've made me promise I'll never see him again, never, never." Betsy stared at Maizie with stricken eyes.

"Yes," Maizie said vaguely. "Ma'am told me about it over the telephone when she called me this morning. . . ."

"She *did?* Did she tell you Dad was so furious, he wanted us all to pack up and go home to Annestown?"

"No!" Maizie sat up straight, her eyes suddenly bright. "She didn't tell me that! Annestown! When are you going? Oh, you'll all go home to Annestown and leave me here in the North and I'll die here. . . ."

"No, no, we're not going, it was just Dad wanted to. . . ."

"And you don't want to?"

"No, I don't want to go down there."

Maizie shook the tangled hair away from her face.

"Listen to me," she said. "You're unhappy, aren't you, and you wanted to talk to me about it, and I love you, Betsy; you're my sister and I'd like to have you happy and not go through torment. Go back to Annestown, go on, go. Everything that's terrible comes because of this place up here. Go on back down South where you can be happy. You can rest there, and nothing ever frightens you. It's not like this. Do you see how I keep the blinds drawn down like this in the daytime?" Maizie asked. Betsy nodded.

"It's because I can't bear to look out and see this place when I look out of the window. I keep the curtains drawn so I can't see. The buildings look like bare bones there in the cold wind. Oh Betsy!" she cried, and tears began to fall down her exhausted face. "I know you think I sound perfectly crazy, and maybe I am. But it's this place. It's the North. I can't bear it. I can't *bear* it! I can feel it killing me. You say I look tired. It's just this place. If I was at home I would get well. But never, never. . . . You know," she said, and her voice sank to a whisper, and she looked quickly at the door as if she were afraid someone might be standing there, "when I was in South America when I was first married I had some trouble with my insides. I had an operation, Betsy. And it was so queer and awful down there that things went wrong, I didn't get well. . . . One of my tubes—Fallopian tubes—got enlarged, and it used to burn and burn, all night. They say it's all well now, but it isn't. I feel it burning. I feel it right now, burning."

"Why don't you go to a doctor? . . ."

"I go to doctors all the time. I've been to five different doctors this winter. Lamb hates me because I go to so many doctors—no he doesn't; Betsy, don't pay any attention to that, *please;* I didn't mean it. Lamb wants me to be well and strong, and I will be. I'm going to get very strong and be able to stay up all night. . . . But I'm just telling you, in private, about that burning. Don't tell anyone I complained, will you? Don't tell Ma'am. . . . She's so impetuous, she might tell Lamb I'd complained. Doctors don't do any good. It's too much for them. They can't find what it is. I've had every kind of test there is, I keep having tests and they can't find out why I have that burning and they can't find out why I feel so sick. . . . I've got bad blood, that's what it is. Our family isn't strong enough. Up North everybody is so strong; they take exercises and they never get tired at night. Southerners are weak. You'll find you'll be weak too, like me. You'd better go on down home while you can, Betsy. Then you can do things and it won't be too much for you."

Betsy was squinting in her effort to understand.

"He doesn't treat you right, does he?" she said. "He doesn't take good care of you."

"Oh, yes! Oh yes he does! Betsy, don't think that for a minute. He's the wisest, greatest man in the world. I worship him, do you know that, I worship him. It's me that's wrong, I'm weak, I get tired too easily, I haven't any intelligence. . . . Oh, no, it isn't his fault. *It's the fault of this place*," she whispered.

"But, look, I don't understand. You could make him take you away from here if you hate it so. He couldn't want you to be living in a place that you were wretched in. If *that's* all it is," Betsy said, drawing a breath, "why don't you just get him to live somewhere else where you like it? Annestown. He doesn't have to live in Boston, does he? He hasn't any business. He can paint anywhere."

"Oh, no, no, no. You don't understand. You don't understand what it is to be really married. You want to submit to your husband in all ways. You want to worship him. You don't ask for things. You don't want your own way. You live for him to get what he wants. I wouldn't ask him for anything for me. He would be angry—no he wouldn't, Betsy, I didn't mean that; but I only want to obey him. . . ."

"I don't believe there can be many wives who do that much for their husbands."

"No. There're not. Most women don't understand marriage. Most women are bitches. Lamb says they are bitches. They don't understand about obeying."

Betsy stared at Maizie, and they were both still.

"Maizie," Betsy said, feeling awkward about changing the subject, "what am I going to do about Oren? The boy, I mean? You see, I really am terrifically in love—I mean, of course, I know it's not what you mean, but, gee, it certainly feels like a lot to me, Maizie. What'm I going to do? I want to marry him! And I know he would have asked me. But he's still in college. Do you suppose he would be true to me and wait until he could ask me . . . only I don't believe that could happen . . . oh dear. . . ."

"You don't know what love is, yet," Maizie said. Her head was back in the pillows and her eyes were shut. "You don't know what love is until you have given yourself, utterly, and you belong every pore of your being to a man."

"Well, I know, but I couldn't do that, nobody would want me to do that until I was married. You should have heard Dad. He thinks I did do it. But I love him all I can, with everything I've got."

"You don't know what love is," Maizie said again. "Nobody knows what love is till they have given their whole selves away."

Betsy felt frustrated and helpless. There was nothing she could say. It was not at all the way she had thought it would be. Maizie had changed so. Five years ago she would have understood all about it.

"I guess I better go and let you rest," she said, hesitantly.

"Is it late?" Maizie opened her eyes abruptly and sat up. "What time is it? Five? I've got to get up. I should have gotten up half an hour ago. Why didn't you tell me? Lord, I'll have to hurry. . . . I'm a wreck. . . ."

She leapt out of bed, and snatching a brush from the top of the littered bureau, began to brush her hair with long, vigorous strokes. "Do you think my hair's got darker, Bets?"

"No. It looks beautiful."

"Here, hand me that jar. I want to slather cold cream on my face while I finish brushing, it sinks in. . . . Throw me my mules, will you? My feet are freezing. No circulation. I've lost five pounds in the last three months, do you think it's becoming?"

The change in Maizie was bewildering. Betsy felt a little hurt. Maizie had shown practically no interest in Betsy's affairs, which were so urgent. She seemed wrapped up in herself and her own concerns.

But the change in her in the last few minutes was at least reassuring. She seemed normal now, she talked quite reasonably; not like that frightening murmur that had come from the bed. Very likely she had been half asleep, to talk that way. She looked much better now that she was up. Her eyes sparkled, her skin looked more alive. It must mean that she needed to make a little effort, to pull herself together. Now she was hurrying around the room like any girl getting dressed in a rush. Betsy felt in the way.

"Goodbye, Maizie," she said. "I hope you'll feel better."

"Oh, goodbye!" Maizie smiled and sparkled through the mesh of her hair. Betsy went to the door.

"Wait a minute, Bets. . . . Don't pay any attention to anything I said this afternoon, will you?" The look of strain was back on Maizie's face as she stood in the center of the room. "You didn't think I sounded disloyal to Lamb, did you? Did you?"

"I thought you sounded terrifically loyal. Goodness . . ."

"All right. That's all I meant. Just I wouldn't want anyone to misunderstand when I sometimes feel rotten. Lamb is a wonderful husband. He's perfect."

Betsy smiled at Maizie. There was nothing to say. She wished she could get back to the old love between them. She thought, I've lost her. She's been lost for a long time. I haven't got my sister any more. She went down the narrow dark passage and let herself out of the front door and went away.

The days of early March were loud and windy. Sam called up, Old Faithful, and asked as usual for a date and sounded almost incoherent when Betsy said he could come round in the evening. They stayed in the living room. Tom and Minnie May were in the study. The Brats had gone to bed. Sam kept talking, eagerly, in his Boston accent; he was such a fool in his brown tweed suit and his brown shoes, with his big brown eyes and his serious expression. Betsy was torn between irritation and an almost pleasant melancholy; romantic, bereft. She sang under her breath while Sam talked; not listening to what he said. "O.G.—I'm mighty blue . . . for you, I've . . . been mighty true . . . to you. . . ."

Suddenly she wanted to cry. It wasn't romantic at all. It was true. She got up and stood in front of the fireplace, leaning against the mantel. "I've . . . been mighty true . . . to you. . . ." she sang softly, wretchedly. How true she had been! She would love Oren all her life; she could carry him in her heart, as Iris March had Napier, and the things she did, the hearts she broke, would mean nothing to her. Nothing would matter but that long face seen in dreams, with a crooked smile.

Sam came and stood looking down at her with his large brown eyes.

"Gosh, I've loved you a long time, Bets," he said. "Isn't there any chance for me?"

She smiled at him, bitterly, putting a provocative look into her eyes.

"Can I kiss you?" he said in a low voice. "I haven't kissed you for such a long time."

She did not move. He leaned forward and kissed her gently on the lips.

"Gosh, I love you," he said.

She still smiled at him, mysteriously. She was probably ruining his life, she thought. It was always the one you couldn't get that you loved. . . . Her life had been ruined, and she was here, unhappy, without a heart, ruining Sam's life too. Well, it would probably do him good to have it ruined, she thought irritably; maybe he would stop looking so much like a spaniel dog.

The telephone rang. There was no reason any more to dash when the telephone rang. She heard her mother's footsteps in the hall. Sam lit a cigarette.

"Betsy!" Minnie May called. "Some girl wants to speak to you." Betsy crossed the living-room, a doomed, romantic figure.

It was Corinne Taylor. Betsy heard her giggling when she picked up the receiver. She said, "Hello, Betsy?"

"Hello, Corinne. How are you?"

"Oh, *I'm* fine. I wanted to know if you could come for the weekend next weekend. Come Friday in time for dinner."

"Why . . . yes, I guess so. I'd love to."

"It won't be exactly a house-party," Corinne said, giggling. "Just a couple of kids. There's one person who wants to see you *very much*, though."

"Who," Betsy began, and then she knew. Her heart pounded. Now she did not want to ask who, because if she didn't know it wouldn't be her fault. "I'd love to come," she said hurriedly. "Thanks for asking me." She hung up.

"What'd they want?" Minnie May called.

"It was Corinne Taylor. She's having a house-party this weekend. I can go, can't I? I said I could."

"That's nice," Minnie May called. Betsy floated into the living-room. Sam was sitting smoking the same cigarette. She gave him a blinding smile.

## CHAPTER XXXII

FRIDAY NIGHT they had all driven far down toward Providence to a roadhouse for dinner. Nobody, Corinne said, that they could possibly know could possibly see them there. They had had the duck dinner sitting round a table under dim lights, and every time anyone arrived at the roadhouse they would all look, quickly, to see who it was. Nobody came that they had ever seen before. But they were all tense about it, and keyed up, and excited. Peter had a bottle of gin that he kept under the table, where the white cloth covered it, and from time to time he made them drinks with ginger ale and ice. There was a small, inferior orchestra playing and they got up and danced sometimes, indifferently; they were all too good for the music. Betsy and Corinne wore bright-colored crepe day dresses; the boys had on dark suits and Oren, as usual, wore patent leather dancing shoes. The snow was deep outside.

When they left, around midnight, Peter drove Corinne back to Brookline in her roadster and Oren and Betsy got into the Bugatti. That was the way they had come.

It was all strange, and special. Betsy was a suffering, wronged romantic heroine. From the moment that she had seen him late that afternoon Oren had been attentive and hanging over her as he had never been before. Peter had squeezed her hand and said, "God, Bets. Oren's been through hell about this." Corinne had lent her a fur coat for the cold drive, and they had got dressed together in Betsy's room at the Taylors' big house, and Corinne talked to her in a new admiring way. The whole evening had been charged with significance, and the significance was the frustrated love between Betsy and Oren. She had never been quite so happy in her life.

The Bugatti started up and the grinding wheels sent up a spray of hard powdered snow. They followed the other car for a little way, and then lost it. Oren was driving with his left arm—the car had a righthand drive

—around Betsy, and she sat deep down in the seat with her head leaning against his arm, her short curly hair snapping against her face in the cold, dry wind.

"Baby," he said, turning his face and pressing it against the top of her head. The lights of the car bobbed up and down over the white night-veiled landscape as they tore down the long road.

"Darling," she said.

"It's so divine to have you in my arms," he said.

"Oh, darling, yes."

"You don't know what I've been through," he said, slowing down so that his voice was clearer above the engine noise. "I thought I'd go out of my mind. My little sweetheart taken away from me. I nearly cut my throat. Peter had to stay up all night with me for a couple of nights."

"Oh, Oren," she said, feeling anguish for his anguish. Still, it was over now; now it was wonderful. "Listen, tell me. Was it awful seeing Dad? I mean, was he awful?"

"It was pretty grim. God, yes. It was grim, all right. I hope he didn't do anything frightful to you."

"It was horrible," she admitted. "He called me all the most terrible names."

"If he only knew!" Oren said, laughing shortly and bitterly. "We hadn't even had that."

She felt so happy. Now, instead of his long silences, his queer laughter, his ignoring her sometimes for periods of time, Oren was adoring; he was all she had ever dreamt of his being. They went roaring through the little New England towns in the night, alone together, exalted. He turned the car off on to a back road and stopped, in from the road on a bare patch where a sweep of the wind had driven the snow away.

"Kiss me, my sweet," he said. She put her arms around his neck and they clung together, their mouths soft and warm pressed together with the cold sharp wind around them. He put his hand gently inside Corinne's beautiful fur coat and held Betsy closer.

"I'll love you all my life," she murmured.

"You're my sweet baby. You're my sweet baby," he said, and shook her softly with his hand. "Don't leave me again. I want my baby with me."

"Oh darling, I thought I'd die when I didn't think I was ever going to see you again. Do you really, really love me?"

"I love you," he said. "I love you. I'm so hot for you I could die. Let's get married."

"Oh, darling. . . ." At first she hardly realized what he had said.

"Let's drive somewhere, let's go to New York tonight, and get married. Connecticut," he said. "I think you can get married quick in Connecticut. I want to get married. Let's do it."

"Darling, we *can't!*" She sat up straight. "Oh, Oren, how could we? It would ruin your career."

"I don't care," he said. "I can't go through any more of the hell I've been going through without you. What does it matter? Let's get married and go somewhere together. I'll leave college. All I want is a lot of loving with you."

"What would your father do?"

"God. He'd do plenty, I can promise you that. He'll probably cut me off out of his will with a shilling; he's threatened to do it often enough. He'd do that all right. I could get a job in an orchestra. I could get a job playing banjo any day."

"Darling, I can't let you ruin your life," she said. In the dark her forehead was all puckered up. "I want to marry you more than anything in the whole world. But if we did it right now it would just make such trouble for you. Wouldn't it be better to wait, and you could tell your father and kind of get him prepared. . . . Or something. You know I'll wait till you finish Harvard. I'd wait forever."

He reached inside his overcoat and got out a cigarette and matches. He took a long time lighting it, and she watched his queer, rocky profile in the small red glow. She felt desperate with indecision, and yet inside her the impulse grew and grew that she must take care of him, at the expense of her own desire; she had always wanted most to take care of him. She felt as if her heart were breaking, and yet she felt noble, too; she loved him so terribly she could not let him wreck that glorious career that everybody knew lay ahead of him. Later, when they did get married he would love her more for her heroism; besides, he might argue her out of it now. She was prepared to be argued out of it.

"I want you to get everything there is out of life," she said, as the glow died and the cigarette tip was the only stab of red. "I can't let you ruin your career. That's what would happen if we got married tonight."

He put his head down on her shoulder with a gesture that wrenched her heart.

"You've got my life in your hands," he said. "Take care of me, won't you? Be good to me."

"I'll be so good to you. . . ."

"I guess I'm a crazy fool to want to get married tonight. I'm always a crazy fool. You'll have to take care of me. I'm just so crazy hot about you, I want to drive this old wreck as fast as it will go in the night till we get somewhere where we can get married. Oh, baby, baby, do I want to get married tonight! But you know best."

She felt beloved and happy—but disappointed.

"Just wait a little . . . kind of arrange things . . ." she said.

"I know," he said in his melancholy voice. "That's right. God, it's got to be all right. I'll tell my father about you when we drive down next week for the Easter. He's got to let me do what I want. He's got to let me be happy just once in my life."

"What are you going to tell your father about me?" she said. "Don't tell him about there being this mess with Daddy."

"No. I'll tell him you're the most beautiful little girl in the whole world and I want you for my baby. Oh, God, he'll want to know about your family. Your family isn't Boston, is it?"

How strange he was. He knew about, he had discussed, her family coming from the South.

"No. We come from Virginia. My mother was a Green," she said, with a feeling of pride.

"I'll tell him that. Maybe he'll know. He's got to let me marry you. He can't always crucify me. Oh . . . oh . . . oh"—he put his arms back around her, under her coat, and pressed her to him, moaning in an ecstasy of tenderness—"such a sweet, soft, cuddly, cute, hot little baby for Papa!"

Saturday they all drove up, with Mr. and Mrs. Taylor, to their winter camp in the south of New Hampshire to spend Saturday night. None of them knew how to ski except the Taylors, and Corinne, who had always seemed so languid and lazy at school, turned out to ski beautifully. There were skis enough for everybody, and they spent the short, sunny afternoon falling into snowdrifts and taking turns letting the lumbering farm horse pull them on their skis until they fell down.

The mountain shadows fell in luminous blue across the snow fields, and in the twilight they ploughed home through the snow carrying their skis. Mr. and Mrs. Taylor had gone before. Peter and Corinne went ahead, as was only proper, and the lovers, Betsy and Oren, stumbled together with their arms entwined, their skis clashing; now and then they would fall down and in the dusk, in the cold fresh snow, they would cling together and kiss. Their mouths felt very warm. When at last they climbed the hill to the camp the others were inside having tea.

It was like a dream, after so little sleep the night before, to be sitting before the big log fire beside Oren, drinking hot, hot tea and eating, and turning to see his eyes on her, Betsy, with their melancholy, shy, ingratiating smile. For all Mr. and Mrs. Taylor knew they were only two more of Corinne's friends; but Peter and Corinne knew; they realized the romance. Betsy felt more than ever like a heroine now; she had made such a sacrifice last night. If she had not been so devoted to Oren's truest interests, she would be married to him now. They were engaged; what else could you call it?

They were all so sleepy from the fresh air that they went to bed early. The sleeping arrangements were open porches; one for women, one for men; Mrs. Taylor slept out with Corinne and Betsy. She was a comfortable, middle-aged woman who had a pleasant acceptance of young people and let Corinne do what she pleased; as different from Boston people as anyone could be, Betsy thought.

In the morning they skied some more, and Corinne tried to show them a little about it. Oren was by far the quickest at it; he learned to do a Christy in an hour, and practiced and practiced with a look of ecstasy on his face.

"God, it's beautiful!" he cried. "Corinne, I'm mad about it; I'd give my eyes to do it like you. God, you're beautiful! You look like a dark angel swooping down like that."

Betsy worked hard at it too, gritting her teeth and setting her pug-dog face.

"You look more like a boy than any girl I know," Peter said, as they climbed the slope together. His voice had a husk in it, the New York sound. "In those pants you really could be a boy."

"Do you like me that way?" Betsy said, laughing and sparkling her eyes at him. "Do you think it's smooth?"

"It seems to get away with Oren, all right," he said. He came nearer to her and let his voice sink confidentially. "Oren told me about the other night. I mean, Oren tells me everything. I want to tell you you did a fine thing, saving Oren from himself like that."

"What?" she said, wrinkling up her nose.

"He's such a madman. If you two had got married the other night there would have been hell to pay. I don't know what Mr. Garth might not have done. Oren's damned near a genius, but he hasn't any sense about himself."

"I didn't want him to ruin his career," Betsy said, slowly.

"That's what I mean. God, what I've been through with Oren. I know you understand."

Betsy started to say something about their plans for getting married later, but somehow the impulse died in her. After all, Peter didn't have to know everything. He smiled his dark, smooth smile at her, sticking out his jaw as he smiled, and took her mittened hand and squeezed it.

"Good girl," he said.

That night they were back at the Taylors' house in Brookline. Mr. and Mrs. Taylor went out to dinner and the young people changed and had supper and went into the drawing-room and turned on the gramophone. They were silly and playful after the day in the snow. Oren did a dance, half tap and half ridiculous contortions, his face split in a broad, one-sided smile; he looked wistfully and pleadingly at them as he convulsed his body.

Suddenly he came out of it and snatched at Corinne who leaned against the wall. He danced her off with wild and incredible steps which she followed with precision. Gertrude Lawrence's tempting voice sang . . . "*My heart begins to sigh . . . Di-de-di, de-di-di-di!*" Oren sang with the record, his voice husky and sweet.

Betsy wanted to be alone with Oren. She wanted to talk to him, to resume their long, caressing dialogue about love; to discuss marrying, and especially to talk about what they were going to do about seeing each other now. Now that the prohibition had been broken it was out of the question not to see each other. It was right. It was the other that was wrong. There was a law much stronger than obeying your parents or keeping promises or telling the truth; the law was love. Betsy felt stalwart and virtuous with it behind her.

But Peter and Corinne didn't clear out. Time went on. They kept the gramophone going. They played all the tunes of that year and the year before—the Taylors had hundreds of records; the Gershwin tunes, and the new, crazy tunes by Cole Porter, all the rest. Sometimes Oren pulled Betsy to him and danced with her, but she couldn't get him to be anything but wild and unrestrained. He was laughing out loud half the time. His dancing didn't have any love in it, it was almost acrobatics.

She didn't enjoy it. But she laughed and sparkled, and pretended to feel the same way herself. Oren and Corinne were working up an adagio dance together. She held her lovely slim body rigid and with one hand on each of her hips he lifted her high above his head—and then let go; he caught her again as she fell, leaning her body backwards, just before her head hit the floor.

It was hard for Betsy to feel admiration. She wanted it to be herself Oren was dancing with. She knew he loved her. But why did he dance so much more with Corinne? It was because he was wild tonight; he was in one of his mad moods. It would pass. But there was so much to talk about, and when would they talk? The boys had to leave early the next morning to get to a nine o'clock class in Cambridge.

Sometime after midnight Corinne said they would all have to go to bed or the boys wouldn't get any sleep at all. Suddenly a kind of lassitude struck them. They were tired, after all. There was nothing to say. They trailed up the broad slippery stairs. The boys' rooms were on the floor above Betsy's and Corinne's rooms. They drawled out good night and continued up the stairs. Corinne came in and wandered around Betsy's room for a while; she yawned again and went away. Betsy sat on the edge of her bed in the dark, her finger on the switch of the lamp. She didn't feel at all sleepy. She wanted to see Oren. As she sat there she heard Mr. and Mrs. Taylor come in and go to their room beyond hers and shut the door. Then everything was still.

After a while she opened her door softly and went out into the dark hall. There was a light burning on the floor above. Perhaps they hadn't gone to bed yet. Or perhaps it was only that the light had been left burning. She decided to go downstairs and get something to eat from the dishes of sandwiches and fruit that had been in the study when they came upstairs. She started down in her bare feet, feeling her way.

Something soft hit her in the head. It dropped to the step below and she bent over and picked it up by feel, fumbling at it. It was a man's undershirt. She looked up, and Oren was leaning over the stair-rail on the upper landing. Her heart jumped. She whispered, "Hello!" He began to run down the stairs, without noise. In a moment he was beside her.

He did not speak. He kissed her quickly, and picked her up in his arms and ran with her down the rest of the stairs. She held her breath; it was absolutely dark. But he tossed her to her feet at the bottom, and then he was gone; in a minute a light went on, and they stood and looked at each other.

He looked wild, and bad, and wistful, and teasing. He went into the study, and she followed him. They turned on a lamp and sat down on the broad deep leather sofa. It was cold, to Betsy who had on a nightgown and a thin wrapper. Oren wore a dark red dressing-gown.

"How are you, baby," he whispered. "How's this? Just a little Mr. and Mrs., huh? Who's going to change the baby's diapers?"

She laughed. Perhaps soon he would begin to be nice.

"Mama love Papa?" he whispered. "Ooooooh, sweet Mama. Give Papa lots of lovin', hmmm?"

He liked to talk in the language of popular songs. It was part of what Peter called his socialism. He hated the upper-class talk he was too used to. But she liked it so much better when he talked as if he were not thinking of the words at all, just of her.

"Oh, Oren, I love you so," she said.

He ran his hands down her upper arms and held them tight at the elbows and shook her, gently, persistently. She shook all over.

"Oren, when am I going to see you again?" she whispered.

"Will you see me in your dreams, baby?" he murmured. "Will you? Because you'll be in mine. My sweet baby's goin' to give Papa a lot of hot dreams, oooh!"

"I think of you every minute," she said. "Awake and asleep."

He put his head in her neck and burrowed, crooning wordlessly. She put her arms tight around his back and held him.

"I don't see how I'm going to live without you till you get back," she said. "Oren, will you write to me? Will you tell me what your father says?"

"Hmm?"

"About us? About getting married?"

"Mmmmh. I'll write to you. Let's pretend we're married now. Let's put the sofa cushions down on the floor and pretend we're in our little bed, in our little home."

"I wish we were," she said.

"We will be," he said. "Honestly, we will be. I'll get what I want this time. God, I will. He's got to let me live my life."

This was better. Betsy clung to him.

"I want to so much," she said.

"So do I, baby, sweet baby. Let's pretend we're married. I want to eat you all up."

He jumped to his feet and threw all the sofa cushions on the floor and pulled her down with him. He could not seem to keep still an instant. He hugged her, nuzzled her, shook her. The light was very dim. This was the way she never liked it, this was when it had got beyond being thrilling.

"Sweet baby," he breathed against her skin. "My cute hot baby. . . . Let's have a little love. Hmm?"

"No," she said. "No. I don't want to do that. No." She sat up.

He sat up too, in a moment.

"You're not giving anything away, are you, baby?"

"Oh, darling! It's not like that. It's just I never am going to, till I get married."

"I know. I know about that. That's why hot babies come so high. God! And when you count the alimony in, why, it's higher."

"Oren! How can you hurt me like that?"

"All right," he said. "I take it all back. We'll get married, baby. Don't worry. I'm going to have to have you, sweet. I'll fix everything."

He got up and stood, quite still, staring out of the window at the starlit snow outside. Suddenly he did a sharp, exaggerated tap step. It sounded muffled on the carpet.

"Let's go to bed," he said. "Nighty-night, baby."

"Let's talk a little while," she said.

"What is there to talk about?" he asked. His voice was blank.

She felt wretched.

"Good night," she said.

Suddenly he hugged her, kissed her, and it was all right. They went up the staircase in the dark with their arms around each other's waists. He kissed her on each step, and at the top.

"Don't forget all about me," he said.

"Oh, darling! How could I?" she whispered desperately, and could have begun a long, explaining conversation, but he was going up the second flight silently, two steps at a time. He waved down from the top. She went slowly into her room.

## CHAPTER XXXIII

Two weeks later the long waiting was broken. A telephone call came for Betsy in the evening, and it was Peter. Nobody had ever said anything about not talking to Peter. . . . But why did he sound so funny?

"Listen," he said, in his metallic New York voice. "Listen, Orey's in the hospital. He's very sick."

"*What?* What . . . Tell me what . . ."

"Well, look, you see, it was like this. I haven't got much time. Got to get back and talk to the doctor. But I thought you'd want to know. Driving back Sunday—you know how cold it was, it was snowing part of the way . . . he wouldn't button up his coat, *you* know, I kept telling him . . . Anyway, that night back in Cambridge he was tossing around all night and in the morning he couldn't get out of bed. It's his lungs. He's had a spot on one of them ever since St. Paul's; he had it there. . . . He's got pneumonia."

"Oh, Peter. . . . Where is he?"

"They've got him up at Stillman Infirmary. He's very sick. Of course his family is off somewhere, California, they left while we were in New York. I've been telegraphing everybody. I've got to go now. I just wanted to tell you. . . ."

"Peter—Peter, isn't there anything I can do?"

"Nothing anybody can do right now. You can't see him. They only let me. He doesn't know it."

"Peter, you'll let me know, won't you? Call me up?"

"All right, all right. I'll keep letting you know. . . . It's double." His voice faded off and there was a click, but Betsy could hear his voice, still murmuring . . . it's double. . . . She hung up the receiver and sat still in the empty, brightly lit hall at home, with her mind beating in thumps, it's double . . . Oren . . . my Oren . . . my love . . . It's double . . . they've got him in Stillman Infirmary; and a sour little strain began to run feverishly in her head, So young, so sweet, so fair. I went up to . . . I've got those St. James Infirmary Blues. . . . Those Stillman Infirmary Blues. . . . So young, so sweet, so fair.

She walked back into the living-room. The lights were all full on and there was nobody there. She went into the window-seat and pressed her face against one of the large panes, staring out, seeing darkness and from the corner of her eyes the lights of the room reflected blankly on the pane. Outside the snow of the winter was beginning to melt and she could hear the torrents rushing in the gutters of the street. The street-light in front of the house twinkled and as she stared at it, grew larger, yellower, the shape of a huge four-pointed star with rays running far, far out from its heart; then it shrank again to a point of light in the darkness. She watched it swell and contract for a long time; her chest hurt her where her heart was.

After four more days of it Peter telephoned her again in the morning.

"He's going to be all right," he said. "It's just nursing now, the doctor says. It'll take a long time. He'll have to stay perfectly still in bed, and God, it's going to be a job to make him. As soon as he begins to feel better. . . . You know."

"Oh, Peter, Peter, is he really all right, really?"

"Sure."

"Are his family here or anything?"

"God, no. They wouldn't come. They did a lot of telephoning. I've been run ragged. Now it's all right, they're going to stay in California."

"Peter, can't I see him? I wouldn't talk."

"He can't see people yet. I'll let you know as soon as they say it's all right. Honestly. I'll give you a ring. I'll keep you posted."

She hung up. If she had married him that night when he wanted to marry her, she would be at his bedside now. She would be his family. She would be Mrs. Oren Garth. But if she had married him he would never have got pneumonia. She would have cared for him like a child, so dearly . . . Here in my arms. He was her child, her love, her father. She had read that somewhere and now suddenly she understood it. He was all there was to be to a woman, he filled her life. Here in my arms. It's deplorable, that you are never there. . . . What had happened in New York, what had he said to his father, what had his father said to him, what had he been coming back to tell her when he was stricken down, his mercurial body struck still? Would they get married when he got well? Was it all right for them to get married if she waited till he had finished college? But she couldn't even see him. He couldn't tell her. Did he think about it? Or was he too sick? She couldn't even *see* him! Here in my arms. It's deplorable, you never *will be there*. Hush, that was only a song. You mustn't let yourself think songs and phrases were omens. But they seemed like omens. This was the spring of the year. The snows gushed freely into rivers in the streets and the fields shook themselves free of the snow. This was the season for love beginning. But she couldn't even see him. Oh, God, I love you so, she thought, over and over.

Peter kept his word and telephoned her every day, giving her bulletins on Oren's progress, in his New York voice, in his New York phrases. "It's too lousy for him," he said, and, "Anyway, they're taking nifty care of him, I must say." He said, "The whole thing's absolutely too grim. He looks like a shadow." Every word he said cut her heart and the metallic accents were ground into her and she would never be able to forget them, entangled with her suffering.

After a week he telephoned her and said,

"I've got the doctor to say you can see him. I explained about your being an actual girl of his. Don't stay more than ten minutes."

"I won't. Oh, Peter, I'm so glad I can see him!"

"Yes, but listen. How about your family? Are they going to let you see him? I mean, after all . . ."

"I don't care," she said.

She had given no thought whatever to whether her parents knew what was happening, whether they had heard what she had said on the telephone on different days, what they thought of Peter's voice asking to speak to her. It simply seemed too unimportant to matter. The only thing in the whole world that mattered was Oren, and now that she might see him she was going to see him and nothing was going to stop her. She simply said, "Can I have the car this afternoon?" Nobody said she could not. If anyone had, she would have done something else about getting there. She had to get there.

She drove in the swishing slush, the gray April air, to Cambridge and along the curving, melancholy drive, out to the Infirmary. When she got out of the Ford, the gutters were running with noisy water. She went into the stiff, brick building. She wondered whether the nurse who led her to Oren's room was thinking, This is Mr. Garth's girl. This is the girl he has been talking of in his delirium. Did they all know? She felt special, sacrosanct. She was the beloved of Oren Garth.

Peter was there. He was sitting in an armchair by the window. Oren lay, a narrow, flat strip in the middle of the bed; his face was thin and white. But his eyes were bright blue, and his smile, when she came in, went up the side; irresistibly.

"It's the red-hot Mama," he murmured.

She felt as if she were drowning in relief, in emotion, in the sheer over-whelmingness of seeing him at last. He stole the heart out of her body. She wanted to go down on her knees beside the bed and press his hand to her cheek and tell him she adored him and would never leave him. Why didn't Peter go away?

He sat there, his dark, freckled face serious, his black hair brushed sleek, his jaw thrust out a little importantly, seriously. He was the one who was taking care of Oren. He had made all the arrangements, sen telegrams, been on the inside of everything. No mother could have done more.

But it could have been Betsy. If she had just said yes instead of no she would be sitting in that armchair now, looking serious and important, belonging there. No, Oren wouldn't be here at all, if she had said yes. They would have been together somewhere. And she heard his old, strong, husky voice say "Little Mr. and Mrs. . . ."

"I'd ask you to kiss the invalid," Oren murmured, "but you'd get bugs. And my temperature would go up, ooooh. . . ."

"Oren, don't try to talk," Peter said.

A nurse came in and put a glass down on the table beside the bed. She was a pretty, red-haired girl with a neat figure. Oren smiled up at her.

"This is the fair Elaine," he breathed. "Elaine the fair, Elaine the lovable, Elaine the lily-maid. . . . Meet your rival, baby. She gives me baths, don't you, beautiful? Baby over there never gave me a bath." He laughed, a ghost laugh, with the echo of the old teasing, the wistfulness in it. He was unbearably the same, though faint and diminished. Betsy grinned at the nurse, hating her.

When the nurse had gone they all sat there. There was nothing to talk about except Oren's illness, how it had come, what it had been in suffering; about his recovery. Betsy did not know what to say. But suddenly something burst from her.

"I'm so terribly glad you're getting better," she said. "You don't know what I've been through, thinking of you sick. I haven't thought of anything else."

"He's going to be all right," Peter said. "He just has to take it slow."

Why did he have to speak for Oren? Why didn't he go away?

Oren looked at them both with his sick-looking, but still provocative eyes.

"Lucky me," he sighed. "Got two Mamas. Got Peter. Got you, baby. Got lots of Mamas. Everywhere I go, there's a sweet Mama."

"Don't talk so much," Peter said.

"Got Hope, lovely Hope. Got Elaine, the lily-maid. She gives me baths. You ought to take a bath," he said to Betsy. "You look as if your arm-pits smelled. Do they?"

"I . . . hope not," she stammered.

She was bitterly hurt. Perhaps he didn't know what he was saying. Perhaps having been ill did this to him. She had heard of patients being irritable. She could only smile, feebly, foolishly, at him.

"I think you'd better go now," Peter said in a low, important voice. "He's only supposed to see people for ten minutes. You're the first person he's been allowed to see," he said, smiling as if he were giving her a present. "Don't pay any attention to what he says. You know Oren," he continued, as they walked toward the door. "He just goes crazy if he has to keep still. I'm going to have a hell of a time with him before he'll be well."

She felt dispossessed. At the door she turned and smiled at Oren; she felt that her heart, her soul, all her humble longing and adoration were in her smile; they burst from her.

"Goodbye," she said.

Now he looked gentle and sweet.

"Bye, Bets," he whispered. "You were an angel to come to see me. Will you come again, hmm? Please come again."

"I will," she gasped. "Just as often as they'll let me."

Peter went along the corridor with her, and then left her to go back to the room. How long was he allowed to stay there?

She felt wretched and unattractive picking her way through the slush across the road to the car. She had no right there, with the one person in all the world that she worshipped. Out of her love and her unselfishness she had refused to elope with him and become his wife with more rights than anyone else; and this was what the reward for love was: she was barely permitted into his room; an outsider, a tolerated visitor.

She tried not to think of the thing he had said to her that had hurt her so. Peter was right, he was a wild creature, and if he were confined he probably really did go crazy and say things to wound out of what was pent up inside him. He was really so sweet, like a beautiful child. . . .

But who was Hope? Or did he mean hope? Surely he had meant hope. Yes, that made perfectly good sense. He meant, I've always got hope. That was a perfectly reasonable thing to say. But why did he put it in the middle of talking about real girls? He had only been teasing about the nurse. It was like Oren to be persuasive and wistful with any pretty nurse. It was to be expected.

She knew it would be horrible, often, when he played and smiled with other women. But she was willing, eager, to put up with anything at all, if she could just have him. It was her dream. It had to come true.

As she drove along, she let herself drift into the mood of the dream. Herself and Oren, together for always, Mr. and Mrs. Oren Garth; with sweet music playing, and dancing, and the shy, wild smile; and she caring for him, being everything to him; his necessity. She did not see herself in the dream, specifically; she had no picture of how she would look; she was just Oren's attendant spirit, laughing with him, being crazy with him, taking charge in case of trouble. . . .

But who was Hope? Surely it was only hope. But how about New York? Had he *met somebody?* He went to New York to talk to his father about Betsy. Soon he would be able to tell her what had happened; if Peter would only get out of the room. He was in New York more than a week. Had he *met somebody?* Named Hope?

Betsy went to Cambridge every day. Sometimes she got the car to drive over. Sometimes she made the long trip by train or street-car to Boston, by subway from Park Street to Harvard Square, and then the long, wet gray walk out to the Infirmary. The Square was full of boys; their overcoats open and flapping in the warm wind; in old gray battered felt hats. Ten thousand men of Harvard. She hardly noticed them, she never even gave a provocative glance up under her felt cloche. She was through with all that. It was only Oren now.

She got there to see him. every single day. She made no special effort to keep from being found out. She simply did not mention where she had been, and made up careless stories of other occupations, shopping. The prohibition against seeing Oren did not seem real any more. There was no law but love.

They were unhappy, desperate weeks. It was nothing but agony when she got to Oren's room. He was sweet to her only in snatches. He was cruel, and teasing, and unrestrained. But she had to go, as she had to breathe.

He got stronger steadily. When she came he would be sitting up in the big armchair in a dressing-gown. His face was thin, his hair was ruffled, there was a wild look in his eyes. It was from having to keep still so long, she knew. When he was able to get out of here and do things and get back to his piano and dance, he would be himself again; kind and loving to her. The doctor said that the warm weather would be coming at just the right time for his recuperation; he would be able to get outdoors. Betsy met the doctor two or three times. The only happiness she got for herself out of these trips was the feeling that, as she passed along the corridor to and from Oren's room, the nurses and doctors knew who she was: Mr. Garth's girl.

He sat up for longer and longer periods during the day. At last a day was set when he could go home to Westmoreland with Peter. Betsy went to Cambridge by street-car the day before his dismissal from the hospital. It was May. Hampton was green and soft-aired now, and even here along the drive in Cambridge the distant trees were furred over with green and the air was sweet and on the Charles the shells swept by like water-beetles, all the oars moving together. She walked along with her head bent; this was the last time that she would have to walk this dismal walk. To the Stillman Infirmary. The St. James Infirmary.

They could go on picnics soon, perhaps; spring picnics, and sit on a coat in some meadow and kiss. They could go dancing at roadhouses, and drive back in the night through the spring air, and hear the frogs singing in the swamps, and stop the car and kiss. The old prohibition, that she was not to see Oren, simply did not exist any more. She was going to see him all it was possible for her to see him, and they could do what they liked. She had to see him.

When she came into the hospital room there were three people there: Oren, Peter, and a girl. They were all sitting in chairs and drinking out of tall glasses and laughing. Betsy stood still in the doorway. Peter got up.

"Hope, this is Miss Jekyll," he said, with his correct, metallic accent. "Betsy, Miss Bayne. She came over from New York to see Oren last night."

"How do you do," Betsy said.

"Have a glass of ginger ale," Oren cried. "We're drinking ginger ale. Funny ginger ale, with tickles in it. Peter, fix up some funny ginger ale for Miss Betsy Jekyll." He turned his full face on her and gave her a smile that made her choke: wry, wistful, teasing.

The girl from New York had the ineffable New York look. She was thin as a rail, with hips as narrow as a boy's. She had a head of dark yellow ruffled curls, and long green eyes, and a big scarlet mouth. She had a cigarette between her fingers. Her legs were long and thin and the ankle-bones stood out sharply. She wore a beige jersey dress with pleats all round the brief skirt, and a choker necklace made of big blobs of red glass: New York clothes. When she talked it was with the New York voice: husky, metallic, slurring; an important voice. She paid no attention to Betsy, and instead of feeling resentful Betsy found that she was admiring; just admiring. That was the only feeling in her beside the huge, threatening despair.

Hope talked, and Peter talked, and Oren made his strange, hysterical jokes; they all had a sound in common in their voices; they were all being New York together.

"But darling, I said to him, it's simply too lousy," Hope said, with that magic rasp in her voice. "After all, I mean, a thing can be just so lousy. Darling, can you *imagine* a speak run like that? I mean it's simply too much, honestly, darling."

Betsy could not understand half the words they were using in this conversation, this bitter hell.

"Darling, get me some more of that lousy ginger ale," Hope said to Peter. "I mean, haven't you got *anything* to put in it?"

"Oren's not meant to drink anything yet," Peter said. Peter was just the same as ever. But now you saw where it came from, where he fitted in; he was with his own kind. "I can't exactly bring anything in to the hospital, I mean, can I? But we can tonight."

"Tonight I'm gonna be in Heaven," Oren said. "I'm going away from this little hell," he continued conversationally, across the room to Betsy.

"I know . . ." she said desperately.

"I'm gonna walk all over God's heaven," he said. "Ta-ta-cla. They're gonna have angels in that heaven and their name's gonna be Hope. Sweet Hope," he said, giving the girl his sad, wild smile.

So they were all going to do something tonight and nobody had said anything to her. She hadn't been asked. Betsy looked at the floor.

Perhaps they had to entertain this girl over from New York, she thought faintly, this girl named Hope; perhaps when she had gone Oren would call up and everything would be all right. . . . Oh, no. Oh, no.

Hope's voice went on and on. Darling, she said, darling, I mean. If you were like that, you had everything. You understood how to treat Oren, you made him play up to you.

But he used to play up to me. But all the time I was weak as water inside, and it was only God's Providence. The New York thing. They talked, and they knew so well what they were saying; they had assurance, and everything was lousy, and they were not impressed. If you had that you could get what you wanted. If you had that you could not be hurt. It was New York.

Betsy got up. She wanted to go away. But she could not go away like this. She set her small pug-dog face.

"Oren," she said. "Look. I've got to go. But I just stopped by, uh, to know if you could go dancing next week, if you'd be well enough, you and Peter go dancing with Corinne. And me. Corinne wanted me to ask you. She didn't know whether you'd be well enough. . . ." She heard her voice go on and on. She could always fix it with Corinne. Perhaps, perhaps, by this route, perhaps everything would be all right.

Oren's face twisted in one of his rare frowns. He looked cross; like a tired child.

"No, I don't want to," he said loudly. "I don't want to go dancing with old giggling Corinne. I don't want to go dancing with you. You're too hot." Suddenly his frown broke into a laugh and he bent his head and vibrated his hand as if he were playing a banjo. "'I had a sweet Mama . . . But she's turned sour, now.' You're too hot, but you're not hot enough." He laughed a high, hysterical laugh, and then smiled his sweetest, shyest smile straight at her. "You don't mind, do you, baby?"

"No, naturally, I just was asking for Corinne . . ." she mumbled, and somehow got to the door.

"I'd hate it if you minded," she heard Oren say, differently, anxiously. But she kept on going.

"Goodbye, darling, it's been divine meeting you," Hope's voice said.

Peter came to the door with her. He opened it, and she went out along the corridor. He was beside her.

"Don't let it get you," he was saying. "Orey doesn't mean half he says. You know that. He's sort of had this girl, Hope Bayne, on his mind lately. . . . You know how Orey is. Listen," he said. "Listen. I'll call you up. Orey's completely vague. I'll call you up."

Then she was alone and walking along the barren, springlike drive. She kept her shoulders hunched.

## CHAPTER XXXIV

ON AN EVENING IN MAY Betsy walked out into the yard after supper. The yard faced west and the light was failing down the streaky sky. The Brats were playing Prisoner's Base, farther over, near the house. Where Betsy stood it was bare and flat, looking off towards the distant woods at the back of Hampton, and the sky. It was like a frontier. At her feet lay the remains of a flower bed attempted by her mother the summer before: there were old stems, and seed-pods, flat to the damp earth. Far away in the marshes beyond the town, near the woods, the frogs sang loud and sweet in their springtime chorus. The voices of the children screamed. The air was sweet with the things beginning to come out of the earth, the buds swelling on the twigs. The light faded from the soft late afternoon into the spring night.

Betsy felt the torrent of tears behind her eyes, but she could not cry. Here was the spring, and here the mild weather, the sweet smells and the country all around in the dusk; the beautiful time had come. And she was alone, and she smelled it all alone and felt the little chill of the air on her skin, her neck, her cheeks. The high days of autumn were long ago gone, and the winter was over, and the spring had come at last and she was alone.

She stood for a long time looking over the country toward the woods, listening to the sad, sweet music of the frogs.

After a while she turned and walked back to the house. The children were running in the deepening twilight. She went in the back door and through the unlighted rooms to the hall. There were lights in the study where her parents sat. She went up the stairs, and up the second flight, to her own room where it was dark and the windows were open. She took her clothes off slowly and felt the blowing air on her body. She went into the bathroom and switched on the strong white light and ran a bath. She stood and watched the water run, pale green in the white tub. The room was white and bare and clean. When it was full she got into the tub and let the hot water go on running. There was the faint sucking gurgle of the water running out of the overflow pipe.

The hot water soaked through her and she lay in the bath staring at the faucets. The heat made her feel better; not so rigid, not so aching. She began to cry, without noise; the tears fell from her eyes, off her cheeks, and dropped into the water. She began to sing, under her breath, in the tub, as she cried. "O. G., I'm mighty blue . . . for you, I've been mighty true . . . to you, I've decided, Something I did, made . . . you go away. . . ." She sang it with her voice catching on her sobs, listening with a sort of satisfaction to the sound of her broken voice, and felt better.

But when one afternoon Peter called her up everything inside her took hold and she thought Maybe, Maybe, Maybe, like a heartbeat.

"Will you go out with me tonight?" he said.

But the sound of his voice meant so much more, it was like an echo or a promise of a world she thought she had lost. Maybe, maybe. Maybe Oren was sorry and this was the way. . . . Maybe.

She had been going around for days in old dresses, but now she spent a long time dressing. She put on her newest bright green crepe dress, with a gold belt around her hips. She leaned forward across the bureau and stared into her own face.

Peter came alone. He was driving the Bugatti.

"How about the Brunswick?" he said. "How about dancing a little?"

"Marvellous," she said.

The worst was getting into the Bugatti and seeing the familiar instrument panel, feeling Peter to the right of her, and fitting into the seat so. She talked as fast as she could, and laughed; let Peter mention Oren first.

But she could not keep to it. After they were at the table near the floor, drinking gin and ginger ale, she said,

"How's Oren?" She tried to say it as if it had just occurred to her to ask.

Peter sat beside her in his dark gray suit. His hair was black and shining, his freckled face was smooth and worldly. He kept his feet and hands quiet. When he picked up his glass he drank from it and then set it down and let go of it.

"He's fine," Peter said, looking out over the floor. "Working like the devil to try to make up some of what he lost. He wants to go to summer school to make up some credits. His family want him to go abroad, though. Dance?"

Is he . . . is he. . . . She almost asked a dozen things that cried out inside her. Is he still in love with Hope? Is he much more in love than he was with me? Does he ever say anything about me? Does he *laugh at me?* But she didn't ask any of them. All the answers, she thought, were right here; in her being here at this table, out dancing with Peter. She wondered why he had bothered. Maybe he felt some kind of loyalty; maybe he remembered all the times when they had sat together and watched Oren. She got up and led the way out on to the floor. Peter put his arm around her and they glided off. It was very smooth, dancing with Peter. He held her beautifully, and danced in perfect rhythm. It was inconspicuous, correct dancing. And because it was she felt her heart wrenched and chewed inside her.

Driving home the spring night was all that she had ever looked forward to. Even above the noise of the Bugatti she could hear the frogs in the swamps. She didn't try to keep up the conversation any more. She put her head back against the leather seat and let her hair blow sharp against her face. The sky was blazing with spring stars, the Milky Way was crowded, and she saw the Big Dipper, filled with night, spilling down the west. She forgot that Peter was behind the wheel, at her right. She did not precisely pretend that it was Oren. It was more that she was alone, in this car in which so much of her life had happened, rushing through such a night as she had dreamed about.

She lifted her head from the seat-back as Peter stopped the car. He had turned up a side road and they were under a row of willow trees, beside a marsh; the frogs were very loud. She lifted her head and turned it and looked at him in the dark in surprise. He was lighting a cigarette.

He put his arm around her.

"Hello, Honey," he said. "What a night!"

So that was what Peter said, she thought. He said Honey. So he wanted to neck her. She didn't care. It was the most ironic, the bitterest thing that had ever happened to her, to be sitting here beside Oren's roommate, waiting for him to begin to neck her. But why not?

He put his mouth on hers and she caught his smell, rather dry and musty. So that was how Peter smelled.

"Does Oren send you around to do his repair work after he's through?" she asked.

"Now listen, Bets. Don't be like that," he said, moving away. "What a thing to say. Naturally not. I've always thought you were swell. But naturally before . . . you weren't in circulation."

"I see," she said mildly.

He moved back.

"You're a wonderful little girl, Honey," he said. "You've always appealed to me."

And with that to hold her, she thought—he started kissing her. It was like his dancing, smooth and technically correct. It was impossible not to feel that he had necked girls for years, expertly. Why did he want to? He didn't seem especially excited, or only in an expert way. It was interesting to watch. His necking progressed in technically correct stages; this, no doubt, was how they did it in New York. At intervals he breathed, "Honey" or "You're wonderful."

"Ah, Honey, let me," he murmured. "You're so wonderful."

She said nothing and made no resistance. This was what she had never done before; this was what she had thought she would never do. Perhaps if she had, things would have been different; she had thought that a great deal lately. Perhaps that was what she had done wrong—*What did I do or say?* She had never done it and she had lost everything she ever wanted.

Why hadn't she done it? She could not seem to think why, now. Why not do it? Suddenly she wanted to laugh, because it struck her as horribly funny, that this was what Oren, whom she loved with her whole heart, had wanted, and she had never given it to him; and now she was giving it to Peter, for whom she cared nothing.

Peter lay with his head pressed against her neck; his arms slowly relaxing from around her.

Oh Oren, Oren, something cried out suddenly inside her. Oh my darling, my love. Oh Oren, Oren!

He was with her so vividly, that she could see the texture of his skin, the color of his brown eyelashes, the edges of his large, flexible mouth as it began to curve up one side. Every look of his was stamped upon her memory. She began to ache, inside, in heavy throbs. Oh Oren, darling, my darling. . . .

Peter moved away.

"Look," he said. "I promise you I had absolutely no idea. . . . Honestly, I didn't know at all. . . . Look, do you know what to do?"

"No."

"God."

They drove back into town and stopped at an all-night drugstore. Then he drove her home to the house in Hampton. There was nothing to say. At the door, when he went up the steps with her, it was too much effort even to say goodbye. She smiled mechanically and went in.

Nothing untoward came of that night. But he did not call her up again. She was glad he did not. She did not know what she would have said. She did not have any prejudice for or against him.

In late May during a visit from Maizie, the Jekylls had a glider swing put out under the maple tree in the yard, and a couple of rickety canvas deck chairs, and sat out there most of the time. Minnie May liked to sit there, while the blue smoke of her cigarettes floated away on the air, and look at the spring coming to the grass, the miniature maple leaves, the elm trees that hung over the roof of the house. Every now and then she would sit up straight and put her hands on top of her head and start to lift first one side, then the other, of her chest, pulling up hard. It was one of the exercises Dr. Cunningham had given her. He said her back trouble was all bad posture. Then she would place her hands on her hips and stiffen her abdominal muscles. She had become an addict of Dr. Cunningham's. Posture was the answer to everything. All illness came from things being out of place, muscles being improperly used, organs pressed down. She went in to his office every fortnight and was gone over by the doctor, then sent upstairs where his technicians gave her new exercises, to be repeated morning and night, ten times each. But Minnie May did them many more times, during the day, whenever she remembered.

"I declare I feel ten years younger already," she said. "People get old before their time, lettin' their stomachs sag. Guts, that's what you have to have. Physical guts. All that sag I had is moving up, turnin' into muscle around my chest." She laughed. "My Lord! Maybe I'll acquire a bosom, at my time of life!"

Betsy sat in one of the deck chairs, fitting her body to its curve. Minnie May was after her all the time, now, to stand correctly, chest up, stomach in, buttocks down. But Betsy had no wish nor intention of standing like that. She could not conceive of ever being anything but thin and hard all over. She stood with her shoulders forward, her chest flat, her hips thrust frontwards, but her stomach was hard as a corset. She listened to her mother, only half hearing. There was nothing to do but sit out here under the tiny leaves of the maple, in the sunny, sweet air.

"Now, I'm just countin' on its doing Maizie some good," Minnie May said. "I've made her go to Dr. Cunningham twice. I'm just as positive that it would solve all her troubles for her, make her feel well again. I don't think she takes it seriously enough. . . . Bets, I've got a feeling that things are worse than usual. I thought I'd seen my daughter look like Death before, Heaven help me, but this time is the worst. Betsy, things can't *go on* like that. Human nature can't stand it. She's got to leave him or I don't know what will happen."

Poor Maizie. Poor Minnie May. Poor everybody. Everyone was sad, everyone was beset. There used to be joy everywhere, gaiety, laughter. But not now, in this place. This was the place where everything happened. This was the place where it had all begun and where it had all ended.

"Ma'am," Betsy said. "I want to go away."

"Away, honey? Where?"

"I want to go to New York and get a job. I don't want to hang around here any longer. I'm not having a good time. I'm not getting anywhere. My life is just kind of marking time. I don't want to go out on dates any more with the boys here, and have Sam hanging around, or even meet any new boys, around here." And always compare them, she thought, always see how dull and flat they are. "I want to get out and have a job. I want to go to New York. I've thought it all over."

Minnie May put her head on one side and considered, blowing vast clouds of smoke from her slightly separated lips; her upper lip was yellow.

"Well," she said. "I don't know why not. I see what you're talkin' about. For a minute I thought you maybe meant go on back down to Annestown, I get so much of that from your father and Maizie, I don't know what gets into them to make them talk so crazy. But, of course, you never did want that. New York. Unh-hunh. It would be excitin'. Everything's going on there, always something moving. Remember what a good time we had Christmas?"

"I remember," Betsy said.

"What kind of a job would you get, honey?"

"Something to do with clothes, I guess. That's what I'd like."

"You've always had a knack. Well. I don't see why not, Bets. I'll talk to your father. He ought to be glad that you've got some get up and git. Yes. Yes, I always thought of it that way. Maizie the one who would make a brilliant marriage and have beautiful children. You the clever one. My poor darlin' Maizie; she certainly hasn't got what I've wanted for her. She's got nothing."

You always loved her more than me, Betsy thought quietly. Perhaps I can't make people love me very much. I wonder what are the ways, I wonder how you make someone really love you, best of all.

"Will Daddy mind?" she said.

"Don't worry, darlin'. I'll take care of your father. He's mostly got over what happened last winter, but I think it kind of hurts him still. Might heal up better if you went away. Course I'll miss you, darlin'. Terribly. But I do have the feeling, this is what you were meant to do. The clever one."

"I'm not clever," Betsy said. But a tiny nerve jumped in her. Could I be the clever one? Clever?

Betsy left for New York the first of June. The untidy lilacs were all in bloom in the yard the day she left, the road was shimmering black with tar, a bobwhite called from the fields behind the house. Minnie May drove her in to the Back Bay Station to take the one o'clock. The Brats said goodbye at the house and climbed all over her and squealed with excitement. She had said goodbye to Tom Jekyll earlier, before he left to catch his train. After all the months when, she realized, he had tried not to have to look at her, he put his arms around her and kissed her and when she put her head back she saw that there were tears in his eyes.

"Goodbye, Bets," he said. "I still feel as if you were just a little tike, you know. Going off like this."

"Daddy," she said, and kissed him again.

But more than anything she wanted to get away. She couldn't begin to think, begin anything, till she was clear away and could start fresh. All the way in to the station Minnie May talked steadily. For they had just heard the great news. Maizie, who had just gone home, was going to have a baby. It overshadowed everything else. Betsy realized that her mother was hardly conscious that her second daughter was leaving home.

"Maybe this will fix everything up for Maizie," Betsy said.

"Bets, that's what I'm prayin' for. It's bound to make a big difference. The only thing disturbs me, Maizie looks so poorly. It takes a lot out of a woman to go through nine months of having a baby. I dread it for her. But if it'll bring that man around. . . . She's going to have to go to Dr. Cunningham. I'm going to make her. I just know he can do wonders for her. She's got to do it, for her own sake and my sake and the baby's sake. All of our sakes."

They kissed goodbye on the gritty, windy platform of the station as the train came roaring into the cave of the Back Bay. Betsy remembered how the engine used to rush in like this when she and Leda March took the train home from school. That was long, long ago, in a different life. The porter put her bags up on the car platform and she climbed the steps, and turned at the top to wave to her mother. Minnie May waved back, with both hands, and then she walked away.

She was going directly from the station to Maizie's.


## CHAPTER XXXV

THAT OCTOBER Betsy used to walk from the Barrington Hotel, where she lived, to catch the Lexington Avenue street car to work, with the highest sense of jubilation. She was in a new world. There would never be anything again like those New York mornings before nine. The sun was bright and the air was sharp, brilliant and gay. The people hurried along the sidewalks on the way to work. In the florists' shops they were setting out pots of bronze chrysanthemums. There were also orchids on display, crammed lavishly into glass vases. But they belonged to the night world, the same New York as the drawn, shirred curtains in the big apartment houses where the rich women were still asleep.

In the mornings, although she might not have got but three or four hours' sleep, Betsy felt as strong as ten men and her heart was as high as the air, and of all the places in the world there were to be in, she was glad to be here. She walked with long, vigorous steps on her high heels across the freshly watered streets, in her new, smart little tweed dresses and her little hats. She knew she looked like a boy and she was glad; she felt like a boy. To be a young girl in New York in those days was to be like a young boy: as free, as unshackled, as adventurous.

She had got a job on a fashion magazine at twenty-five dollars a week. She would stride in to the big office where her desk was. There were about ten desks in this room. Some of them belonged to older women, wheel-horses who did the work of copy-reading, proof correction, who were constantly on the telephone to the press. At the other desks sat girls like Betsy, young women starting out in New York, with alive faces and minds quick to imitate the way things were done. They worked here for small wages and were glad to get them for the experience, the prestige, that a job on *Lady* gave them. Many of the most important women in New York had started out on *Lady*. The advertising manager of one of the biggest department stores, a famous woman writer, countless stylists and buyers of the first rank, to say nothing of several women now married to great New York fortunes—had begun their careers just this way, as a little girl on *Lady*; a caption-writer, an assistant to the fashion editor.

Betsy was one of the assistants to the fashion editor. Shortly after she had come in in the morning she would get a summons on the telephone, and march in to Mrs. Edison's office, where everything was babel and chaos and sunshine.

The offices of the editors were quite different from the big, bare cowpasture where the young women's desks were. The editors' offices were decorated along *Lady* standards, since this was where visitors were shown. Mrs. Edison's office, on the south side of the twenty-fifth floor, was as chic as a rich woman's sitting-room. The chairs were covered in a chintz with huge lilies, there were baroque mirrors and framed originals of covers painted for *Lady* by French artists, the carpet was soft deep beige, and Mrs. Edison sat behind a frail, beautiful little fruit-wood desk.

Mrs. Edison had a clever, red mouth, cold eyes, long red fingernails, and exquisite clothes that she bought in Paris on her two yearly trips abroad. When Betsy came into Mrs. Edison's office in the morning, incredible numbers of things would be getting attended to at the same time. On one telephone Mrs. Edison's voice, low, husky, assured: "Mr. Goldstein? Mr. Goldstein. We thought that a very amusing little pajama and we hope so much to get it into a page of . . ." On another telephone her skinny little secretary, nerves worn ragged but voice poised and social: "Mrs. Edison hopes so much you will lunch with her at the Colony at one, Friday." On a third telephone another of the assistants, young and tall, looking like an illustration for *Lady* on a total of $19.85, speaking in imitation of Mrs. Edison's voice, but more eager, younger: "Could you have the bracelets and the clips at Schumann's studio for a sitting at three? . . ." And all over the chintz-covered armchairs, clothes: dresses, furs, a box full of hats spilling out on the sofa. On Mrs. Edison's desk, a dizzying clutter of papers, photographs, photostats, cables, big first-draft drawings, and among these a pair of bright red gloves, two pigskin purses. There were fresh flowers in vases. The cool, yellow, October sunshine came in and lay upon everything. In a corner cringed a little Jewish messenger who had brought the box of hats and was to wait for them. Every woman in the room except the secretary had her hat on.

"Jekyll, I want you and Symonds to go into the market this morning. Hammerstein and Koven's showing, it won't be any good but talk to them nicely. Miss Grindle will give you the address. . . ." Now she was off on another tangent, the telephone again: "Is that Mrs. Lovell? Oh, Mrs. Lovell, this is Clare Edison. About what we were saying last night at dinner. I am hoping so much you will let us photograph your two little girls. . . ." But now her voice was soft, disarming, husky, in merely a well-bred way. The secretary was talking on the telephone too: "This is Mrs. Edison's secretary. Will you have a round bunch of red camellias here by half-past twelve? Mrs. Edison wants to wear them out to lunch. . . ."

Betsy might be sent on any one of a dozen different sorts of jobs out into the Seventh Avenue garment district. She might be sent to help at a fashion sitting where professional models with beautiful, expressionless faces and tall, curveless bodies would wear the clothes. She might be sent out into the country to help a photographer to take pictures of the interior of some fashionable woman's Long Island house, or of some children in riding habits. In a pinch she might be sent to fill in at a sitting herself, as a model. All the fashion assistants were chosen with an eye to their ability to pinch-hit as models; they received nothing extra for doing it, but it increased their value if they photographed well, their faces were recognized in the trade; it was just another little wedge. Betsy photographed well. With her boy-like, stubborn, tilted face and her thin boy's body, she looked the way young girls were supposed to look in the pages of *Lady*.

It was exciting to be a model occasionally, and try to make friends with the strange, mute, beautiful professionals, and have her picture appear in photostat, in proof, in the finished issue. She sent the pictures home to Minnie May, before the issue had appeared on the stands, to show her how successful she was being, how she was getting the very best out of New York life.

She worked very hard all day. She was on her feet most of the time. It was quicker to walk to Seventh Avenue than to get there any other way except by taxi, and taxis could not be put on expense accounts; the assistants rode in them occasionally when they were accompanying one of the editors, who took taxis everywhere. Sometimes, when lunch came in the middle of an important job, an editor would take an assistant along to one of the fashionable restaurants where the editors always lunched: the Colony, Voisin's. The luncheon would be of a professional nature: everything was professional; it would be with a head buyer, or a publicity head, or a man who owned a great shop. "This is my little assistant, Miss Jekyll, Miss Weinkopf. How chic you're looking!" They would eat the most delicious food, which the editor would put on her expense account, and Betsy would keep perfectly quiet except when spoken to; but copying her important companions she would look wisely around the restaurant, recognizing faces; there was Mrs. Addison Fiske at her regular corner table, there was Curtis Bright, there was a table of debutantes (Fisher, de Haviland, Hayden, Perkins). When she was spoken to she tried to be as intelligent as possible about the things these women were so terribly intelligent about: fashion trends, the market.

The rest of the time the assistants lunched, alone if they were out on a job, on a sandwich and a cup of coffee picked up somewhere; in bunches of two or three if they were in the office and could arrange to go out together, to Schrafft's or to little Italian speakeasies they discovered where it was possible to get a cocktail and a meal served in a kitchen for seventy-five cents. They trooped in and out of these places, looking like debutantes, as fresh and smart, and the sum they had all spent for their collective clothes would not equal the price of one debutante's dress.

And they would not have changed with a debutante. They were going somewhere. New York was a germ in their bones and in their blood. They were embarking on a hard, exciting trip to the top. They were learning fast, faster than they had ever learned in school. Their eyes were sharp, their memories were like steel traps. They were getting their New York values. They were learning to keep an eye to the main chance.

Betsy's principal friend was a girl named Elizabeth too, but called Liz: Liz Symonds. She was taller than Betsy, with short tight red curls all over her head, a long, beautiful, strong neck, and shoulders as broad as a man's; she dressed in tweeds and bright-colored knitted caps, and she was always used, when they needed somebody quick for a sitting, for the outdoor girls;

the girls in riding-habits or wearing skiing clothes presumably in St. Moritz or Davos. She had brilliant high color and great energy and although she was as ambitious as the others she talked with wild irreverence of her superiors behind their backs. At their lunches in cheap speakeasies she referred to *Lady* as the old prostitute. At all times her language was colorful and unrestrained. Nevertheless she seemed to be the favorite among the assistants with Mrs. Edison. Liz got the only really indulgent smiles Mrs. Edison ever dealt out. She would stride into the beautiful little cluttered office and sit down and put her feet up on the arm of a chair.

"Mrs. E., darling, you have me hanging on the ropes. I'm worn to the bone. You're a hard, merciless woman. Can't I have the afternoon off?"

Then would appear, miraculously, the indulgent smile. But the indulgence went no further than the smile.

"Liz, you're a dreadful girl. I'm positive you only want to meet a beau. Get out of that chair and go to work."

"Naturally you're absolutely right," Liz would say cheerfully, and hoist her long legs and body up from the deep cushions.

Liz had worked on *Lady* for nearly two years and made thirty-five dollars a week. Up until now she had lived in an apartment with two other girls, one a model in a Fifty-seventh Street shop and the other in an advertising agency. But the lease ran out the first of that October and the model married a wholesale manufacturer and the advertising girl decided to move back to her family in East Orange and commute. Liz moved into the Barrington with Betsy. By that time they were on good, easy, free-speaking terms, like two young men. Neither trespassed on the other's privacy.

In the Barrington the rooms were tiny cubicles; there was one bathroom to every two rooms. Betsy and Liz occupied two such rooms. The hotel was for women only. There were other young girls, and women ranging up to elderly spinsters. They were all working women. By nine o'clock in the morning the hotel was virtually deserted. It was a very inexpensive place to live, and very respectable; men were not permitted above the mezzanine. Betsy hoped that made her father feel comfortably about her. Liz called the place the Baboonery.

It was a gay, confident life; the smell of success, in different, dissolving scents, was over everything. It was over the whole of New York for them in those days, it was over the working days and the sparkling nights and it was in the way they lived. In the cubicle just beyond Liz's lived a girl they saw sometimes going out to the elevator: tall and hawk-faced with black hair; she worked in the daytimes, somewhere, and at night, sometimes even when they came in very late from dancing, they could hear the sound of her typewriter, steadily; she must be going to be a writer. The muffled clatter of her persistence was one more note in the rising crescendo around them.

At half past eight the women came out of the Barrington on their ways to work, and all the young ones had the same look: of pursuing something, cleverly, wisely, shrewdly, looking their best, dressing their best, using everything a hand could be laid upon to aid them in their pursuit, and there was no need to ask what it was they pursued. It was success. Success was scattered all over New York like specks of glittering mica fluttering in the city wind, settling on everything: in the interiors of town cars at night, halted for an instant in traffic; on the lapels of doormen at nightclubs; on a florist's boy as he ran up the steps of a private house to deliver a square, white box; on Mrs. Edison's silver foxes as she hurried out of her office on the way to the Colony to lunch, on her chauffeur's uniform as he followed her bearing packages; on taxis and the awnings that led up to apartment entrances and people having tea in the lounge of a hotel, on men's bowler hats as they waited outside the grill of a speakeasy. The golden dust settled on the tops of the drinks that were being drunk all over New York, on the Side Cars and the Martinis and the Manhattans and the Bronxes. The gold twinkled down the bars of sunshine, making New York sunshine different from other sunshine.

Liz knew quantities of men and introduced them to Betsy, and through each man they met a dozen more. They each had a little book in which they wrote down names and telephone numbers, of men in the Federal Reserve Bank, men in art galleries on Fifty-seventh Street, the office telephone numbers of men with families in the Seventies, of men in business offices, and dozens and dozens of customers' men. The girls were on as confident a footing as the men. The men had unlimited money; but they had unlimited youth, and were equals. They said what they pleased and did what they pleased, knowing that if one man did not like it there was another who would. With their long, boylike stride they walked into the Embassy Club, the Lido, the Broadway nightclubs with a floor the size of a handkerchief, the theatres, along the side-streets towards a taxi, into a hundred speakeasies on all the West and East streets near Fifth Avenue; hailing the bartenders, joking with the waiters, dancing, listening, talking: with their cropped heads held high on their long necks, their broad shoulders hunched as they leaned on a speakeasy table, their hair bare when they pulled their hats off with a careless gesture in a restaurant; their hips narrow, their legs long.

On Sundays Liz and Betsy would get up around noon. One of them would take her breakfast, which was left outside the door in a box, to the other's room, and in pajamas they would sprawl on the bed and one chair and talk, or lie on their stomachs on the floor like children and read the Sunday paper. They spent this one day loafing, smoking cigarettes, discussing people, mending clothes, drinking milk that they kept on their windowsills, until the street turned dark and the lights went on and they separated to get dressed to go out to dinner.

One Sunday, lying on the floor in a flood of autumn afternoon sunshine, Liz said "Look." Betsy leaned over her shoulder from the bed, where she was curled doing her nails. Liz was looking at the front page of the society section of the New York *Times*. She pointed to a photograph of a man in tweeds leaning on a shooting stick. "Mr. William Fellowes at Green Run, Virginia," the caption said.

"That's Eddy's beau," Liz said. Eddy was what she called Mrs. Edison in private. "Ain't he beautiful?" It was a very handsome man, with a heavy, vain face.

"Madly," Betsy said. "But I thought she was married?"

"Oh, absolutely; she's got a baby. You should have seen her last year when she was pregnant, just as dynamic as ever, dashing to the hospital at the last minute shrieking back to poor little Porky—'Get those hat pages redone!' But if you could see what she's married to you'd see why the poor darling really rates a lover."

"Mr. Edison? Doesn't she like him?"

"Nobody could possibly like him. He's just the least bit hunchbacked, for one thing."

"What on earth did she marry him for?"

"To get into the Social Register," Liz said simply. "That was the only thing she couldn't get for herself. He is frightfully good family."

"That seems perfectly silly."

"It works very well. They give dinners. . . . This boy, Fellowes, is the love of her life. It's very romantic. She's been in love with him since she was about our age. But he's always been married to some horror with lots of do-do-deo-do who wouldn't divorce him. He goes abroad every year just when Eddy does the Paris collections. Terribly coincidental. Everybody fixes it on those big Long Island weekends so as they'll have adjoining rooms."

"Doesn't Mr. Edison mind? Don't people get shocked?"

"No, my precious. That's one of the reasons we all love New York so. I'm sure Mr. E. is rather relieved. I don't believe he functions so good. And as far as everybody goes—don't *you* think it's nice, and romantic? She's got to have *some* fun, poor darling. After all, tolerance is the most important thing you can have. Intolerant people really are the last straw. I mean, what's life for except to be happy in? I think you ought to be just as happy as you can get yourself without hurting anybody," Liz said.

Betsy listened intently. Never in all the casual years of school had she studied as carefully as she did all the time now. She was learning about New York, the greatest place in the world. She was learning how to become a New Yorker. As Liz finished, however, she spotted another picture on the same page, and snatched it up from the floor.

"Look!" she cried. "That's a picture of Leda March. She used to be my best friend. She married my cousin last September. Look."

The picture showed Leda and James standing at the rail of a liner, and the caption said they were returning from their honeymoon in Europe. Liz viewed the picture critically.

"Terribly good-looking," she said.

"She's old Boston family, and so's he," Betsy said proudly. "I think he's got loads of money. Don't you think he's attractive, too?"

"Yep." Liz dropped the newspaper as if she had thought of something else. "But *why* do these divine girls our age want to get married, that's what I want to know?"

Betsy pulled her knees up under her chin.

"But wouldn't you get married *if* you fell madly in love with somebody? Somebody divine, with lots of money, and everything?"

"I'm damned if I would. Some day, but why now? I suppose you had to years ago if you wanted to stop being a *jeune fille* and have any fun at all, but it's different now. What could I possibly get out of marriage that would be worth the things I'd have to give up? I mean if I did it while I'm still young?"

"Mmmm," Betsy murmured. She was watching Liz, who was lying now on her back on the floor, smoking; she wore a pair of dark blue polka-dotted pajamas and her short red curls were rough.

"This interests me very much," Liz said. "I think about it. I mean, the question is always coming up and I think, well, how about it? But I think it's this way. We've stopped being women, in the old sense of women. Girls like you and me. We can't make the regular calculations. It's more as if we were men. I mean, to figure on. We work, and we have a big time, and if we don't like what goes on we can do something else. I guess it spoils us. I know I wouldn't like being married to just one man and having to make all the compromises and adjustments and bothering with all that, no matter how much I was in love. I mean, love is divine, but why marriage? Well, money, yes. But what a lot to give up to get money. Maybe I'll be making a lot of money some day. Or maybe somebody will be foolish enough to give me some. But to give up my independence and the ability to do just what I please when I please, and being accountable to nobody—for any love-nest I don't care how cosy and warm—I think it's crazy."

"How about wanting to be loved?"

"Oh, pooh! I mean, that's absurd. God knows I'll be loved a lot more by somebody who doesn't feel he's tied to me. Like poor Tubby, or Pete, or Tom Hawkins. Or even the beautiful Mr. Starr, I think his resistance is wearing down, Betsy. . . . No, if it was wanting to feel I was loved that I wanted, I'd certainly stay out of marriage. If you're not married to them they have to keep showing you how much they love you to remind you, and that's the divine part. But actually I don't think I'm much interested in being loved, the way you mean it. All I want is to have F-U-N." She spelled out the word.

"No, but I mean the thing about having somebody love you and you love them back, terrifically, more than anything in the world, so that you want to be together all the time."

"Oh, pooh! I think that's absolutely abnormal. It makes my flesh crawl. I know what you mean. And maybe when I'm absolutely doddering with false teeth I'll be all for it. But not now. The thing is, I love to feel free, and strong, and I have the feeling that that love business absolutely incapacitates people; they get all weak and logy and want to go to bed all the time in the most completely loathsome way. I mean, I think going to bed with somebody fascinating is one thing, but you ought to do it gaily, and for Heaven's sake have a little *fun* doing it."

"Were you ever really—in love?" Betsy asked.

"Millions of times. Sometimes shatteringly. But thank God I never completely went ga-ga enough to get married. All the girls I've ever known who have gotten married are leading the most vomitous lives, with their husbands either pawing them or refusing to speak, and the whole house reeking of babies' diapers.—Have you?"

"Once," Betsy said. "Last year. It almost killed me. I was played for a complete sucker, I guess. I would have cleaned his shoes. He came from New York."

"Did you want to marry him?"

"Terribly."

"You ought to thank God you didn't, if you felt that way. The only possible way I can imagine a marriage being any fun would be if you ran things your own way. Are you still crazy about him?"

"Not really. I mean I'm glad I'm out of that hell. But I get a funny feeling sometimes. Sort of like homesickness. Sort of sad, because it's all over and I did put everything I had into it."

"D'you go to bed with him?"

"No."

"Maybe if you had you would have pulled out of it better. I mean, I wouldn't ever dream of marrying anybody I'd never been to bed with to find out if I really liked them. I think it's madness not to. I mean, you might simply loathe everything about it, and then just think if you'd married them. Betsy, I've sometimes wanted to ask you, haven't you ever done it with anybody?"

"Yes. I did. Afterwards. With his roommate."

"You don't look as if you'd thought much of it."

"I didn't. It just wasn't anything at all."

"I know what you mean," Liz said thoughtfully.

"The only thing about it is," Betsy said, hesitantly, "I don't like the feeling that they think they've conquered you. That you've surrendered to them."

"Me surrender!" Liz gave a loud laugh, a hoot. "I'd like to see anybody conquer me. Look, if I should do that with anybody I'd conquer them every bit as much as they'd conquer me. That's the way I feel. I go out for what I please and I turn down what I don't like. I'm in command of what I do with my life. I mean, for instance, I don't consider that I'm what people call promiscuous. Not a bit. I'm good and choosy. Anything I do, I do because I've decided I want to do it. Nobody's going to 'have their way' with this girl. If anybody gets conquered it's going to be some poor shrinking little man I've decided I like."

Betsy nodded thoughtfully, and ran her fingers through her short curly hair.

"That was the thing," she said. "It just seemed so empty and nothing. And as if I was licked, somehow."

Liz shook her head.

"You went about it all the wrong way, then," she said. "You want to be triumphant. Maybe you were trying to get even with your real beau, or something. I know how it would feel. But that doesn't count, it's madness.

Do what *you* want to do. March in and conquer. Have fun. Be on top of everything, running things. Or at least act as if you were. The great thing in life is to put on a good act. Do *I* look like a miserable wage-slave making thirty-five bucks a week?"

"You certainly don't. You look as if you were a millionairess."

"Whoops! And so maybe I will be. If you act as if you were something somehow you always get to be it. That's the way I see it. Look at Eddy. It's all a great, big, beautiful act. Actually she comes from Ohio or somewhere and never had a dime, and look at her, the wonderful Mrs. Edison, editor of *Lady*, minks, silver foxes, Social Register, Long Island, Paris, what have you. Don't you adore her? Hard as nails, but underneath she's such a cutie."

"I'd love to be rich, and famous," Betsy said.

"And you will be, Innocent, if you stick to it and just listen to the words of wisdom I drop you. I can give you lots of the best quality advice on where and when and how. Symonds on Success. Symonds on Sex. And you ask me to dinner when you've got your own château at Newport, dearie. Well, got to pull the carcass together and get dressed," she said.

Liz began to pull things out of the small closet that the Barrington provided: hats, dresses, jackets; putting things together, discarding things, making combinations, evolving the costume in which she would emerge this evening, tall, beautiful, and chic.

"Who are you going out with?" Betsy asked. She picked up her cigarettes and prepared to depart.

"Mr. Starr. Again. He totters, Betsy; he seems to feel the thrill of life along his keel. Even if he is the son of Mrs. Horatio Starr."

Betsy laughed.

"That man I told you about took me to a party of Mrs. Horatio Starr's. She was his aunt."

"Honestly? You ought to be able to use that somewhere. Heegleef, dear. *Per aspera ad astra*, meaning the Starrs. I could just eat the Starrs. I'd like to wriggle my bare toes in them. They're *so* rich. We never eat anywhere mangier than the Colony when Mr. Starr takes me out, the sweetie-pants. Where are you going?"

"Speakeasying. With Basey."

"What would we do without our customers' men?"

As Betsy got up to go she caught Liz's eyes, and suddenly they both grinned hard at each other. Standing in the middle of the little room, Liz threw her arms straight up in a long stretch, on tiptoe, her head bent back in a yawn, the muscles of her neck standing out, her waist hard and flat, her thighs lean. Then abruptly she relaxed and grinned at Betsy again: a smile full of sweetness, gaiety, and forthrightness. Betsy went out through the bathroom to her own room.

Before she turned on the light she stood at the window looking over the square of New York that could be seen outside. The lights were going on over the city, twinkling and merry. She put her hands around her upper arms and hugged herself hard. It was a new world. There was no reason why anything at all that it contained should not belong to her. She was young, and strong, and charged with ambition. New York was like the slot-machines in the speakeasies where you stood and put in quarters; somebody had to get the jack-pot, and she felt in her bones that it would be she.

She used to write her mother long letters about the famous places she went to at night and the famous faces she saw there. Minnie May wrote back that she was thrilled. "Vincent Astor, Dorothy Parker, Heywood Broun and the Marchioness of Queensberry all in one evening really is too much riches to be true, Bets. What bliss! Now you have an inkling of how I used to feel when, as a young girl, I visited your dear Aunt Glory and her husband in Rome. I was presented to the King and Queen and we used to see the Duke of Aosta frequently. Such a handsome man.

"I have news about Maizie for you, good, thank Heaven. Her doctor has put her to bed for the remainder of her time, until the baby is born the end of February. I feel so relieved about it and I keep thinking that that man can't get at her now she is safely in bed. It seems that several times she started to miscarry and since she is so set on having this child it would have been too heart-breaking if the poor child had had that to endure too. I wanted her to move right out here into her own room where we could all take the best of care of her. I can tell you if that man had started any of his monkeyshines whatever they are with her under my care I would have got some oil boiling in the kitchen and popped him in. It would have given me the greatest of pleasure. But I must say he seems to be behaving better. She chose to go to his mother's for her long ordeal of being bed-ridden—she's not allowed to get up out of bed at all—because I think she felt apprehensive about being even as far as Hampton from the doctor. And she is so wonderful about loyalty to that man and his whole family. Personally the baby will always be a Green and a Jekyll to me, I hate the very sound of the name Rudd. But anyway, Bets, she's at Mrs. Rudd's house on Commonwealth Avenue, all established in a very comfortable, sunny bedroom, and I must say I feel the greatest relief. They have engaged a maid especially to look after her and make her bed with her in it, since she doesn't actually need a nurse. I go in every day to see her, of course, and take her little things. She seems so much calmer. I am sure all will come out well for her now at last that she is being allowed a little rest. That blessed doctor is right around to see that she is as she should be, and he orders early hours and long times of quiet rest in the daytime, and I am so grateful to him I could spit. Now she can rest and be in good shape to have the darling baby—my first grandchild—and when he comes there'll be that to make her happy and take her mind off that monster, and if he begins making her wretched and unhappy and exhausted again *then*—well, then, I really will carry out my threats and attend to him myself with a good big knife or gun.

"We all long to see you, Bets dear, and the first chance you get try to come up and pay us a flying visit even though I know your position on *Lady* keeps you tied down. I'm so proud of my daughters. Maizie to become a mother and you having such a gay time in New York and making a name for yourself. I have decided to send Jane to Miss Sheraton's next year. I have made great friends with Anita Cunningham—Dr. Cunningham's wife—and she will do all that is necessary about Jane. Both the Brats are making so many friends around here. Jane hits it off splendidly with the little Cunningham girl, Sara, and I am so glad, for the Cunninghams are such nice people, so entertaining and yet thoroughly solid and Bostonian. Your father doesn't get on with Dr. Cunningham worth a hoot, I'm sorry to say, but he has so many prejudices about Boston people. I do my best to break him of them. Everything of that kind just takes time. The Brats really are turning right into little Boston beans. So much happier for them. We are having dinner at the Cunninghams' tonight and going to the Symphony. All I hope is that your father won't go to sleep. I am willing to grant that classical music can be mighty soporific. Anita Cunningham wants me to serve on her Welfare Committee with her, and I welcome the prospect. I'd like to get my teeth into something I can really work at and put some life into."

## CHAPTER XXXVI

OF ALL HER NEW BEAUX Betsy thought Basey McKean was the nicest. He was in love with her, and she thought that probably she was in love with him. Being in love, she had found, was not the complicated, do-or-die business she had once thought it; she even found it was possible to be in love with more than one person at a time, for she was quite a lot in love with Basey, and also with a young Englishman who worked in Wall Street, named Dudley Forsythe, and a little in love with Max Wilkes, who was an assistant in an uptown art gallery and knew everybody and never stopped talking. He was enchanted with Betsy and kept exclaiming over the tilted-back poise of her head, which he declared was the lost head of the Victory of Samothrace. "Not the least Greek, you understand, but of our time, neo-Graeco-Manhattan. Divine. Darling, you must let me take you round to Benson Levy's studio. He'd go mad. He could do such marvels in terra-cotta with you. He'd make you famous overnight in New York as a beauty. Betsy, darling, I do adore you so. You make me think of the ocean, the wine-dark sea. Always in motion, but divinely. You really have got to let me take you to Benson's."

It was all so thrilling. Betsy thought it would be a wonderful thing to be made a beauty overnight, and one afternoon a date was fixed for her to come to Levy's studio. She could not get off from work till late, and she rode uptown in a taxi to Fifty-eighth Street as the lights were coming on in the shops; free from the day's work she felt exhilarated, as if she had had a drink already. She ran up the stairs of the building and knocked at the door marked "Benson Levy." Max threw open the door and smiled at her and took both her hands.

"This is my angel baby beauty," he cried over his shoulder. "Benson, do come here and simply look."

She stood there laughing, a little out of breath from running upstairs, with her head back. A thin, dark man came forward out of the shadows of the big room and he was smiling too. He had an aquiline face.

"Max talks my ear off about you," he said, very gently, as if he did not want to frighten her, she thought. It was so absurd to think that anything could ever frighten her.

"Max, angel," she said. "I've got a taxi waiting downstairs and not a dime to pay it with. Would you? I wanted to get here as quick as I could."

Max ran down the stairs. It was a trick Betsy had learned from Liz, of going to meet beaux in a taxi and getting them to pay for it at the other end. They appeared to love doing it. It was convenient. But more than this, to Betsy it had an air about it, a cosmopolitanism, a dash. To arrive glowing, breathless, brimming over with chatter, exuding youth, and waving a hand over a shoulder to a waiting cab. . . .

"I didn't realize you were so young," Benson Levy said. He was not a bit like Max. "Sit down, won't you, and I'll give you some sherry, not very good. Better than bath-tub gin."

She hated to sit down, even, and sat on the edge of her chair, tense with sheer vitality. She could not erase the smile of her delight from her face. She looked around her in the shadowy room. On high stands were objects covered with wet cloths. It was a sculptor's studio!

Max came back, talking steadily as he entered, and they all sat and Max did most of the talking. Betsy was conscious of Levy looking at her, and when she got up to go with Max, he said,

"I hope you are going to let me do a head of you."

"This awful work I have to do . . ." she said.

"How about your lunch hours? You could stretch them out a little, couldn't you?"

"I guess so."

They arranged for her to come the next day at one, and she left, running down the stairs again with Max hand in hand. In the cab he kissed her gaily. The kind of being in love Betsy had with Max was gay and unbothering.

"Darling, you were superb," he said. "I do adore you."

For a while from that day Betsy's life was more hectic than ever. She would get to Levy's studio at one and stay for an hour and a half, while he worked on her head in clay. He did not need to have her stand still, and so she walked around the studio, with her head tipped back triumphantly, smoking cigarettes.

It was funny. In the old days she had tipped her head back because she was little and wanted to look up, and later she had tipped it back to look at boys she was dancing with, and to these had been added an imitation of Liz's glorious poise of the head. Now Levy was doing her head and she would be a famous beauty some day. She wasn't really beautiful at all—she never had been in other places. But she had the New York thing, the thing they liked to look at.

Levy smoked too and talked, and they had nice, companionable times together. One day when he was almost through with the head, he kissed her, suddenly, as she was going away. She laughed and kissed him back.

"You're a lovely child," he said. "So terribly young and so sweet. You move me very much."

After that he began to ask her to go out to dinner with him; he became one more beau. There were far more invitations for Betsy than there were nights to divide up. Sometimes she made late dates and met some man after she had dined with another, and went dancing or to a midnight show. She felt rich. All these men were in different stages of being in love with her, and she was in different, pleasant, untroubling stages of being in love with them.

It was very different from the other love, the being in love with Oren. She shrank from remembering that more than she could help, the agony, the longing, the humiliation. She did not ever want to be in love like that again. She thought that she never would be. Nobody could be in love like that, so terribly, but once in their lives. It was something she had lived through and passed beyond.

Sometimes in a taxi, late at night, by chance she would look out and see that apartment house where she had gone once with Oren, where his family lived. She always looked away quickly. The sight of it, the number on the apartment awning, were too stabbing still. She did not want to remember suffering. There was nothing but pleasure in the life she was learning to live.

The head, cast in plaster and terra-cottaed, was a success. Levy declared that he was satisfied with it and that he would put it in his spring show at the Rangoon Galleries. Betsy could hardly take her eyes off it. It looked so coppery and triumphant. That was her neck, long and muscular, her lifted chin, her nose, the sockets of her eyes. Max Wilkes said it was just what he knew it would be, and it was marvellous, and Benson was marvellous, and Betsy was the most marvellous of all. And from Max that must be praise, for he went out to dinner at famous houses and spent weekends on Long Island.

Betsy looked forward to the summer that lay far ahead, beyond this winter, for by that time she would know even more people and be asked on weekends on Long Island. They seemed to her to represent something. Dudley Forsythe went away on weekends constantly, but that was principally because he was English, and as Liz said, "They can't eat enough of the British." He was very young too, younger than any man Betsy knew in New York, and had brilliant color, and an accent that was sometimes almost incomprehensible. He was mad about New York and never seemed to grow used to it; he said the air affected him like champagne and that furthermore there must be a great difference in the climate because, whereas in England he could drink a good four whisky-sodas without disaster, here in America two did for him nicely. He gave cocktail parties in his flat uptown, which was filled with signed photographs of English beauties, all fair and with their heads tipped down slantingly, taken by Cecil Beaton. He was like a child at its own party, rushing round the room with an immense shaker in the shape of the Statue of Liberty that someone had given him, shrieking with delight at each new arrival.

Afterwards, when everybody had left around ten, he would take Betsy out to dinner.

"Darling, did you ever see such absolute masses of people?" he would say. "I am so glad to be alone with you, my sweet."

They would hold hands across the speakeasy table and it was all rather sweet and affectionate. Sometimes Dudley would say,

"I really do love you so very much, darling. D'you mind?"

And she would laugh.

"Of course I don't mind. I love you too, Dudley. You're so sweet."

He was kind, and in a way protective; not that she needed anyone's protection. But she liked the feeling that he wanted to look out for her.

"Betsy, d'you know I think you *scatter* yourself. Rather badly. You shouldn't, you know. I mean I know you're frightfully young, but after all. Why don't you concentrate for a bit? On me, as a matter of fact?"

She laughed, for he was so very young-looking too, and one of the things she loved best about this new life in New York was that very thing, scattering herself. It was possible to be in an amazing number of places in one day. Dudley didn't understand the magic of that. And besides, he himself got around to all sorts of places when he wasn't seeing Betsy. Men always had at the back of their minds an idea that it would be nice to reserve a girl for their exclusive use, and of course the whole fun was not being reserved, but being, as they said, in circulation. It was probably English of Dudley to talk so much about it. He was very English, or at least not New Yorkish, about a number of things, much as he loved the city. He was, for example, not tolerant. Although he said American girls were glorious, Betsy had noticed that he sometimes said hard and biting things about girls, called them tarts and old hags when they were not in the least. His intolerance showed in the way he criticized the way people lived, pointed to flaws in their morals. It was not his business, Betsy reminded him; it was not tolerant.

That was one of Basey McKean's greatest virtues, his tolerance. It was impossible not to realize that actually he saw through everybody in his wry, mocking way, but it was not in him to judge them; let them hang themselves in their own time with their own rope.

He was rather older than the other customers' men; big and lazy and saturnine. He had narrow blue eyes in a face that remained healthy and brown in New York. He dressed carelessly, in Brooks suits with plain white collars and knitted black ties. He knew everybody, and never seemed to put himself out to be pleasant, but Betsy could tell by the way women called to him from tables in speakeasies that they thought he was wonderful. He was never impressed with anything, he walked with a slouch, he knew all the places of yore, and yet Betsy was sure that in his way he loved New York too. She wondered why he had so little ambition; why he was content to remain a customers' man.

"Why should I do anything else?" he would say, smiling at her. "I make

enough money to make out. The one thing I want to avoid is responsibility.
I've been around. I'm not so excited about being alive as you are, kitten."

"But you could be the head of something. You know so much. I never
heard of anybody who could repeat so much poetry by heart."

"I might explain that to Mr. Rothstein. I'm sure he would get your point
and make me the head of something. Only I don't want to be the head of
something, see, baby? I want to be all free and unworried and no stomach
ulcers."

She grinned at him and he put his hand out palm up on the speakeasy
table for her to put her hand in.

"How do you like being my best girl?" he said. "Millions are screaming,
but you're elected. I love you. I love you because you look like a baby
puppy and because you're so absurd and because you don't bother me."

"Why should I bother you?"

"You shouldn't. I like your kind of girl, only it's so hard to find one.
You ought to hear how the other kind call you up. At the office. You don't.
You're busy, and you have the hard heart of a child. Quote. That's why
we can have such fun together, and why I'm quite a lot in love with you,
pet."

"Me too," Betsy said. It was just before dinner, and she had come in a
taxi to meet Basey at this speakeasy on West Forty-ninth Street, and they
were drinking Side Cars. She looked happily round the bar they sat in. It
was one of Basey's favorites. Interesting looking men and girls were sitting
at the other tables and at the bar. Betsy stuffed a handful of potato chips
into her mouth; they tasted salty and delicious. The little red-shaded lights
were on at all the tables. It was gay, and cosy, and exciting. She squeezed
Basey's hand and wriggled with pleasure.

"I love you because you have such a good time," Basey said. "And here's
a present for a good girl."

He leaned over and gave her a light kiss on the cheek. Then he ordered
another Side Car for himself. Betsy was not halfway through hers. She
always forgot to finish her drinks. She felt intoxicated enough without a
drop. But Basey drank a lot; he was a really heavy drinker. He was never
unpleasant when he was drunk; he was just more like himself, more lazy,
wry, tolerant.

The fashion assistants on *Lady* had another value to their superiors, and
that was as fillers-in at dinner parties. It was always convenient to have on
call a number of charming, lively young women who on no account would
ever decline such an invitation although it came at the last minute. It was
an unofficial part of their jobs. For them it was worth it, since they had
there the opportunity to meet all sorts of famous people, and every introduction counted in the climb up. Liz Symonds often filled in at Mrs.
Edison's dinner parties. She had met Horatio Starr at one of them, and he
had become the heaviest of her beaux. Betsy had her first such invitation
early in December. When she was dressed she went through the bathroom
into Liz's room to show herself.

Liz had finished dressing to go out on a date; she was just putting on a jacket made of tawny red foxes that matched her hair.

"For Heaven's sake," Betsy said. "Where'd you get that?"

"At Jaeckel's, precious, and it cost precisely eight hundred dollars."

"Liz! How divine you look! Do you mind telling me where on earth you got eight hundred dollars?"

"In the nicest possible way. What you do is this. Mr. Starr is going to buy some wonderful stock, and he imagines, just makes up in his head, some money which he invests in your name. It's all on margin anyway, so what's the difference? Imaginary money anyway. So when the stock goes up ten points, as of course it does, he sells the imaginary stock which by that time has made something over eight hundred bucks. And you take it in your little hot hand and walk into Jaeckel's and say, 'Mr. Jaeckel, have you got a nice fur coat . . .'"

"But the eight hundred dollars aren't imaginary."

"You bet they aren't. But the principle is there, the high principle. Mr. Starr never gave you no money, see. All you're spending is the profits of some money that never existed anyway, so he isn't giving you anything. Your Aunt Sophronisba couldn't see anything wrong with that."

"You certainly look marvellous. I wish I had a fur coat. Just one really good thing makes such a difference. If you've got one good thing you can wear cheap other things and it makes them all look expensive."

"You're telling me." Liz put on a tiny felt hat the same orangey-red as her hair and the coat.

"Do I look all right?" Betsy revolved slowly and the skirt of her pale blue chiffon dress stood out like a morning-glory; it had silver beads making a girdle round the hips.

"Like the nicest possible *jeune fille*. I hope you make a big killing at Eddy's tonight."

"I'm scared pink."

"Don't be crazy. Get in there and fight. Give all you've got for dear old You."

"What'll I talk about?"

"What do you generally talk about? Talk about you. That's what the boys will ask you to talk about anyway. Tell 'em you come from Virginia."

"Well, I don't, really. I mean, it was such a long time ago. I really come from Boston."

"Well, then you can all have a good laugh at poor old Boston. But I think you ought to try Virginia sometime. See how it works."

Betsy nodded thoughtfully. It did not really matter much what place you said you came from, since the only point of bringing it up was to declare how divine it was to have gotten away from it. Everybody here seemed to come from somewhere else; there was hardly a living native New Yorker; all were loud in relief at being in New York.

Nevertheless, she was shy as she walked into Mrs. Edison's beige and white drawing-room. It was so completely the top of everything. It represented the pinnacle of the success that everybody was working for. It was far more enviable than the drawing-room of Mrs. Horatio Starr, where Betsy had once been. For the Starrs and the others like them were the backwater, rather dull. Mrs. Edison's surroundings spelt the acme of everything that was most of the moment in the 'twenties. They held the works of the most fashionable artists, dead and alive, the most talked-about people of the day, the atmosphere of absolute, dead-center chic.

But it would never do to show her shyness. It would be all too easy to be swamped in a party like this where every single person was what Liz called "in there fighting." The faces of the women were beautiful and clever and animated; there was no help to be expected from them, since to them another woman represented just one thing, competition. Mrs. Edison was the last person to expect a helping hand from: she respected you if you could do well and make a showing on your own, but if you couldn't you had forfeited her respect, in work or socially. Now was the time for all Betsy's technique, for everything she had learned in New York. She lifted her head, remembering that the tilt of it was her great specialty, smiled brilliantly, and sailed in, knowing that she was younger than anybody in this room, as she might have known that she had money in her pocket.

At dinner she found that she was seated next to Curtis Bright, who was unquestionably the most famous bachelor in New York. He was about forty, with a small, clipped moustache and sad, restless eyes. His name was at the top of the lists published in the social pages of the guests at every important party in New York. In the summer there were pictures of him at the helm of a racing sailboat; he was a famous yachtsman, the owner of the *Campaspe*. It was frightening to be sitting next to this man who was hardly a man at all, rather a printed name, a legend.

On Betsy's other side was sitting, she read by his place-card, Mr. William Fellowes. In an instinctive flash she grasped what that meant, for beyond him was Mrs. Edison. She had put Betsy next to him because, as an assistant to Mrs. Edison, Betsy could not possibly be competition with this man Mrs. Edison loved. She stole one good look at him as he settled himself in his place: a big, ruddy-faced man with a well-fed, sleek look; she could smell his hair-tonic from where she sat. Then Betsy turned her shoulder firmly and began to talk to Curtis Bright.

By the middle of dinner his sad, drifting look had been dispelled and he was being exceedingly charming to her. He talked to her as if she were a little girl, but the expression of his eyes showed that he admired her as a woman.

"And you work on *Lady*," he said. "That curious publication. It must be very stupid. Once in France some misguided organization sent the men a great package of magazines, and when they were opened it was found that they were all copies of *Lady*. Hardly the thing to send men that, one hoped, were going to kill Germans the next day."

Betsy blinked.

"You mean you were in the war?" she said, breathlessly.

He smiled sadly.

"I was indeed. I suppose that makes me an antique to you. It seems so very odd to me, on the other hand, that you undoubtedly remember nothing about that show. Odd and delightful. Perhaps if I remembered just a little less of it I should be better off."

"Does it sort of haunt you, you mean?"

"Something like that. Some things you can forget, but some you can't. I can't talk about it at a table like this; the incongruity of it would be insane. It's just that it was so bloody awful for my generation. None of us will amount to a row of pins, ever, of course. We might as well never have been born—far better never. We're a vacuum, as far as counting goes—a missing generation."

Betsy felt tears rise into her eyes. She was putting herself in his place as hard as she could. She hadn't realized how empty men of his age who were in the war felt. It was something she had never given any thought to. He was so tragic. Instead of being frightening he had turned out to be pathetic. She wished there were something she could do to make him feel happier. All the time, all these years, at all those parties, he had been going about with this awful despair.

She smiled gaily. She thought she could do this at least for him, be terribly gay, and terribly young, and yet terribly sympathetic and understanding.

"Will you come to tea with me one day?" he asked. "I shan't ask you to go to one of these rotten noisy speakeasies. I can give you a good cup of tea or a decent cocktail if you prefer. My man makes excellent cocktails, and I thank God I still have a bit of drinkable whisky left from the deluge."

"I'd love to," she said. Into her eyes she tried to put sympathy, trust, youth, enthusiasm, freshness. The effort made her blink.

He laughed.

"Or should I be corrupting the young?" he said lightly. "Snatching from the cradle, and all that sort of abominable thing?"

"I'm quite old," she said. "I'm practically twenty."

"Practically twenty," he repeated, and looked at her as he wiped his moustache with his big, white napkin. "An antique," he said.

## CHAPTER XXXVII

THE WEEKEND AFTER CHRISTMAS, Betsy got Saturday morning off, and went up to Boston to spend the weekend with her family. She took the train after work, Friday. She could not help thinking, as she sat in the club car smoking and looking at the people, how different a person she was than when she had taken the train for New York last June. Then she had known nothing, her heart had been broken, and she had nothing but hope. Now she was a true New Yorker. She had an enviable job. She had got herself a whole string of beaux and kept getting more. Quite a lot of people knew who she was. Although in New York she felt young and breathless, now, on the train, she felt sophisticated. She knocked the coal off the butt of her cigarette and lit another.

It was fun to be at home with the Brats squealing and hanging on her, and Minnie May asking all about her New York times. She slept deliciously late in the mornings and went down to breakfast in her old corduroy wrapper that she had left at home. She and Minnie May drank coffee and smoked together in the sunny dining-room. But now she was an important person. Outside in the snow in the yard the Brats played with their friends. They had grown, Betsy thought, just since she had been away. Jane especially was a young girl, not a child, who wanted to examine every article of clothing in Betsy's bags and exclaim over the dresses, the junk jewelry. Glory was a child still, but a very wise-looking one. She stood and stared silently, and seemed to have her own thoughts. She picked up a long string of huge imitation pearls that lay on Betsy's bureau.

"They're not real, are they?" she asked. "I think real are nicer."

"Honestly," Betsy had said, turning to Minnie May, "she sounds like an old Boston dowager, doesn't she? You stuffy old lady!" she cried, hugging Glory's thin, straight little shoulders.

The Christmas tree stood, as in those other years now far away, filling the bay window in the living-room. Betsy cried out and admired it, not patronizingly but as a grown woman recapturing a moment of her lost youth. It seemed very long since she had lived in this house. It seemed much more than a year since the last Christmas tree. Then she had been in a fever to get to New York and see Oren. A stab of the old agony struck her as she looked at the mantelpiece where he had stood so many times, leaning on his elbow, suddenly to break out into a wild tap step. She could almost hear the *ta-cla*. She had a sad feeling of the waste of it; she had given her whole heart, and been hurt so, and all for nothing. She was glad she would never be able to love anybody again like that, and at the same time a little melancholy. She would never have a whole heart to give anybody again, only pieces. But it was happier, to have only pieces to give. It was nice to be appreciated. It was nice to be in love with people and have them in love with you without there being any hurt in it at all.

She opened the presents that had been saved for her from Christmas. She liked best a pigskin purse, from Maizie, and her father's present, a check for twenty-five dollars. She could use those. Her mother's present, a small fitch fur, was, she thought, a measly little thing and she could not wear it by itself; however, in the spring she could have a suit made by one of those inexpensive little tailors that you had to work with, and have the fur incorporated as a collar. A year ago she would have been enchanted at owning a real piece of fur, she thought amusedly. A year ago she knew nothing.

"How'd Maizie get me this?" she asked. "I mean, in bed. Did you get it for her?"

"Lambert got it," Minnie May said. "I have to admit, he's behaved real well. Seems to me having a baby and all Maizie's been through's done him a lot of good. He got all the presents she wanted to give people. A man doesn't enjoy that kind of shopping. I'm so happy about it. Reckon things are going to come out right, after all. I feel like I could relax and enjoy life if Maizie was all fixed up."

She still loves Maizie, best of all of us, Betsy thought. But now she did not feel the pang of jealousy that she used to feel.

On Sunday afternoon they went in town to see Maizie. A neat middle-aged Irish maid opened the door of the big house on Commonwealth Avenue, and they stepped into an interior that Betsy viewed with amusement. She had forgotten that such modes of decoration existed, she said to herself. The dark walnut woodwork, the wide, curving old-fashioned stairs, the rubber-plants in pots at the bottom of the stairs and on the landing, the heavy, dark-red velvet portieres—it had its own kind of chic, of the mouldering old aristocracy in the cities like Boston and Philadelphia.

Mrs. Rudd received them. She was tall and upholstered in handsome brown cloth.

"I think your house is charming," Betsy said with the frank look that was always so successful. "There aren't many houses left like it. I wish you'd let us photograph it for *Lady* some day. I work on *Lady*, you know."

Mrs. Rudd turned her large gaze on Betsy.

"My dear Betsy," she said. "I shouldn't dream of such a thing. This is not New York, you know."

Betsy almost laughed. They went up the deeply-carpeted stairs to Maizie's room. Maizie was lying with her head on two pillows; her brilliant hair was spread out; she wore a satin nightgown with a bedjacket to match. She looked ecstatically happy. She held out both hands to them, and Betsy went over and kissed her. She was very thin, but that was no doubt from lying in bed for so long. There was no mistaking the look of radiant happiness in her face.

"Isn't it wonderful about the baby?" she cried. "Mrs. Rudd, show Betsy the layette.—It's all in those drawers over there." She waved her hand toward a small bureau at the other side of the big, comfortable bedroom.

Lambert came in while they were exclaiming over the pretty baby's clothes. He shook hands with Betsy and stood at the foot of his wife's bed. Betsy thought he looked much older than the last time she had seen him. His dark face was much more serious; he did not have such a wild look. Having babies changed people all round, she thought; made them get serious about whatever it all was; they stopped being young people.

"How do you like our heroine, Betsy?" he said. "Maizie's being a real little soldier about having to stay in bed all these months. We're hoping it will be twins to pay her for all her trouble."

Mrs. Rudd lifted her eyebrows, but indulgently. Maizie smiled at Lambert and he smiled back. Betsy saw Minnie May look from Maizie's face to Lambert's and back again. Minnie May did not look worried any more. Babies certainly had their uses, bringing people together.

All of them, Maizie and Lambert and Mrs. Rudd and Minnie May, talked about only one thing: the baby. Everything was plans for the baby, little jokes about what to call the baby, more clothes they were ordering for the baby; plans for Maizie to go to Manchester for the sea air as soon as the baby was born and she had stayed three weeks at the hospital, which would bring them to the end of March. They talked about the nurse that had been engaged already for the baby, the nurse that had been engaged to take care of Maizie at the hospital, about exactly what Dr. Forbes had said yesterday and last week and the week before that. No wonder Maizie was happy. The world of this house revolved around her and the miracle that she was about to perform.

"My wife is a born mother," Lambert announced. "Darling, you should have thought of this before. We're going to have an extensive family and they will all look like their mother, Betsy."

"No, like their father," Maizie said, smiling at him.

"You'll be like the old woman in the shoe," Betsy said, playing up. "Don't you remember. . . .

> There was an old woman who lived in a shoe
> And had so many children she didn't know what to do.
> But there was a young woman who lived in a shoe,
> And she didn't have any children, for she knew what to do.

—that'll be me, if I ever get married!" Betsy said.

But her little joke, so well meant, was not a success. Mrs. Rudd's eyebrows went up, and there was a silence.

"Youth, youth, what won't you think up to say next?" Lambert murmured. That relieved the atmosphere, but Betsy felt annoyed with all of them. Even Lambert could have been less stuffy. Youth indeed. Anybody would laugh at that, except a Bostonian. They had no tolerance, that was the thing; no tolerance at all.

"We must all leave Maizie now," Mrs. Rudd said after a while. "Dr. Forbes wants her to be very quiet most of the time. Have a little nap if you can, dear."

Betsy kissed Maizie goodbye.

"Make Lambert wire me the minute it arrives," she said. "And I'll do my damnedest to come up and see my nephew. Or niece."

"It's going to be a nephew," Maizie said radiantly. Her face was flushed. How awful it must be just to stay in bed all the time and never see anybody but just these same people over and over, Betsy thought.

"Lamb, kiss me goodbye, darling," Maizie said. He bent over her and Betsy saw the white, very thin arms go around his neck.

When Betsy and Minnie May said goodbye in the big dark hall downstairs, Mrs. Rudd barely touched Betsy's fingers with hers.

"Goodbye," she said.

She must still be stuffy about that rhyme, Betsy thought. She was silly if she thought Betsy cared; for Mrs. Rudd meant a little bit less than nothing to her. She could be stuffy all she wanted to.

She seemed to be on the best of terms with Minnie May; they took a long time saying goodbye, discussing matters about the baby and both saying over and over how wonderful Maizie was being. Minnie May was so different from Bostonians, Betsy thought, watching them; but she always managed to make everybody like her, no matter how different they were. If she wanted to be liked in Boston, she would be; you could trust her. It might

take her time; it had taken her time; but now look at her; you could trust
her to get where she wanted to.

Minnie May took Betsy to the station and they stood talking on the cold
platform, waiting for the six o'clock train.

"Give Dad lots of love and say goodbye to him," Betsy said. "I feel as if
I'd hardly seen him. I'm sorry he had to work all day Saturday. I wish he'd
come with us to see Maizie."

"He hardly ever goes. I try to get him to go oftener. I'm afraid it will
hurt darlin' Maizie's feelings. But it seems to do something to him, I don't
know how to explain it, to see her lyin' in bed there so good and patient. I
keep tellin' him she's just as happy as a bee, lookin' forward to her baby
and all, but he gets a look on his face. Sick. Men don't understand how
happy women can be about their babies coming. I was always healthy as a
buck. . . . All he seems to see is his daughter lyin' there in bed. Poor Dad.
It'll be all right as soon as the baby's born and Maizie's strong again. He'll
forget she ever was in bed."

"She's all right, isn't she? I thought she looked thin."

"Maybe just a little. But Dr. Forbes holds out assurance all will go well.
Says she's as able to have a healthy baby and recover as any woman. And
it's my belief the rest is doing her good. Just what she needed. She was
complainin' about so many pains—in her feet, and her side, and her back.
. . . Course, if she'd done everything Dr. Cunningham told her, like I told
her to do . . ."

The engine roared into the underground station and the red of its fires
cast a murky glow on the ceiling. They kissed goodbye hurriedly and Betsy
got on the train. She left her gloves on the seat and went back to the club
car as the train pulled out of Boston, past the Arena, through the confusion
of tracks—the old scenes, so familiar to Betsy from days now long ago and
discarded.

Just past Providence she got up and walked, balancing herself against the
lurch of the train, to the ladies' toilet at the end of her own car. The door
sank slowly shut behind her and she stood in the brightly lighted little place
looking at her full-length reflection. She looked very smart—not a Boston
girl at all; a New York girl. She wore a beige knitted jersey dress with a
leather belt around her hips, a string of big pearls looped once round her
neck and hanging, and a small beige hat. She smiled at herself in the long
mirror, an assured, gay, important smile. She did not see how people could
be such fools as to stay in Boston when there was New York to live in. In
New York it was possible to learn how to live, to act, to speak, to dress.
After New York other places were faintly ridiculous, contemptible. She
gave herself another fleeting, wise smile. She was a New Yorker.

New York was waiting for her at the other end of the long tracks; its
lights and people, its streets, its apartment houses, its smart women, its men.
It was her city. She felt her heart beating faster for it. She loved it and she
had the feeling that it loved her. It had made her one of its own and like all
of its own beyond ridicule, beyond contempt. She was one of the wise ones,
the assured ones, the lucky ones, now.

## CHAPTER XXXVIII

"You make me so terribly happy, darling," Maizie said.

Lambert uncrossed his legs and slowly crossed them again the other way. Then he spoke, with careful gentleness.

"I'm glad, darling. You know I want you to be happy, don't you?"

"Oh, yes, I do! I know you do. Everything's going to be lovely from now on, isn't it?"

"Lovely," he said.

He hoped that his voice carried the calm and assurance that he wanted it to. He did hope everything would be lovely from now on: for Maizie, and for the baby they would have, and for himself. No more hell, no more anguish, no more dangerous ecstasy for anybody. It was January now and for some time he had dedicated himself to making things be happy; to defeating that subterranean, eruptive spring in himself that was opposed to happiness, opposed to Maizie, opposed to calm and comfort. Perhaps it was drying up, for he had had no overflows of it; he had been gentle, considerate, quiet, and even found that one of his tasks was to restrain Maizie's emotion, calm her, try to make her, like himself, controlled. That was a funny thing.

It was after dinner and he was sitting in Maizie's room beside her bed, holding her hand. He had finished the after-dinner cup of coffee that he had brought upstairs, and it stood on the bedside table, with little Chinese figures walking round it. He let his eyes rest on it; it was a charming cup, thin, of old design, scarlet and black and gold. There had been good coffee in it, very strong, the way he liked it. Such things gave him comfort now. He thought perhaps these were substitutes that had to be made as a man got older, as he found himself a husband, a father; responsible, necessary. Hell, you couldn't be young forever. Sometime you had to be what people wanted you to be.—But if you had something else, something invaluable that had to be sacrificed?

With the habit he was learning he put the cover down hard on that. There was time for everything later. As Maizie kept saying, everything would be lovely. If you were a painter, if you were any good, wouldn't you keep on being a good painter without necessarily having an utter absorption that everyone else had to pay for? You couldn't kill talent . . . could you?

He jerked his head to put a stop to treadmill speculation. There was a job to get done first. That was the thing to remember. It was only a question of a month or so more.

He put his other hand up to the new moustache that he had begun to grow soon after Christmas. It was amazing how fond he was of this moustache. He turned his eyes away from the coffee cup and smiled at Maizie.

She smiled back, eagerly; over-eagerly, perhaps. He hoped his smile

hadn't been a frightening smile. It was a hell of a thing to know that you
scared another person out of her wits; your smile, your voice, just your face.
He said everything very softly, smiled cautiously, hoping that he wouldn't
get her all upset; that she'd stay calm and relaxed the way she was supposed
to.

"Hello, old lady," he said, squeezing her hand. "How is old Clem this
evening?"

Their son's name would be Clement, after his grandfather. He was there,
with them in this room, already alive. He was the thing that they had made
together, he was why Lambert was here at all, he was why Maizie was in
bed, he was why two people plucked from opposite worlds, two people
who had brought each other only anguish, were here together in a warm,
curtained room holding hands and talking in low, controlled voices and
smiling at each other.

"He's been cutting up all day," Maizie said lightly, without moving her
eyes from Lambert's face. "Kicked me practically out of bed this afternoon."

"The little tough. I'll give him a licking for it as soon as I can get at him."

They laughed. Maizie's hair was bright against the pillows, her eyes were
bright and blue. It seemed to Lambert that they were like an animal's eyes,
fixed on him; bright and frightened and secret. All at once he was swept
with an awful wave of feeling: they did not know each other at all, they
never had and perhaps they never would. They were going to have a child
together and they would be that child's parents and perhaps the parents of
other children, and live together all their long lives without knowing each
other; congenital strangers. They had been married now for several years
and their juxtaposition had meant to them agony, frustration, suffering.
From now on, because he was bound it would be so, there would be no
more suffering, but they would still be two stranger beings.

He smiled at her again. All these years she had been wretched, hurling
herself against his difference to penetrate him and possess him when it was
impossible because they were of opposed species. Poor Maizie. He was
desperately sorry for her. Perhaps it was out of that pity that something
would come that would make everything possible; what she called lovely.
He was sorry for her, and now, besides that, he did feel protective, shelter-
ing, to this strange racked being with whom he had lived so long in violence.
The violence in him was over like a storm that had blown itself out. Now
there was the tired calm, the pity, the quiet.

"Darling," she said eagerly, "Dr. Forbes says I'm going to be as strong as
I ever was in my life, when it's over and I'm back on my feet. I haven't got
a thing wrong, just not being able to hold on to Clem."

"Slippery customer," he said.

"Won't it be wonderful?" she pressed. "Oh, darling, I'll make you so
happy! I just know I'm going to be as strong as an ox. We'll go dancing."

He almost said, "Oh, don't!"

It was all so pitiful, so pointless; something heard and heard again, a
thousand times before. She wouldn't seem to change, no matter how he
tried. He thought in some ways she was the strongest, the most relentless

person he had ever known. She never gave up. She beat at him as she had beaten for years, she did not know hopelessness, the tension mounted in her and she said, "I'll make you so happy," with that eagerness, that lack of comprehension he had heard in her voice and her words before, so many times. She wanted something that had never existed and never could, and what he was trying to do was to offer her something else that he had to give; something furthermore that would not hurt her or frighten her. But still with this tension, this perverseness, she clawed for the other thing. She wanted his violence, his passionate love, all the things that he realized now she couldn't take and that he was bound he would not flog her with. Besides it was too late. Those were things of youth and he and she were grown-up now.

"I'm so sick of bed," she said intensely. "I don't mean to complain."

"Of course you are, darling. You're a soldier. If it was me I'd be crabbing steadily."

"Would you mind terribly," she said, "would you be terribly angry if it was a girl?"

He uncrossed and crossed his legs. He did that to give himself time to summon the essential patience. And yet it was fair enough. All she had ever known of him was anger.

"Of course I wouldn't be angry, pink-face," he said carefully. "I'd think it was cute. I hope it would be a dead ringer for its Ma."

"It won't be," she said eagerly. "I just know I'm going to have a boy. I feel it. No girl could kick as hard as Clem does." She laughed, and to his ears her laugh sounded hectic.

"Either way I'll be the original proud father."

She kept smiling at him, and his gorge rose at the things he recognized in her smile, the longing, the frantic possessiveness, the passion.

"Nobody ever had a husband as good to them as you are to me," she said.

"Nonsense, my good woman."

"I just hope . . ." she said.

"What do you hope, my pretty?"

"I just hope," she said in a low voice, "you don't hate me. For being in bed and all the things I know you hate."

He felt his fingers clench.

"No. No. No," he said.

"You do hate me, some, don't you? You wish I could have a baby like other women, without going to bed. I know you hate invalids."

"I love you very much," he said, and his lips felt stiff.

In a moment she would say that she knew he hated her for having this baby at all, and then he did not know what he would do. Control was everything. It was like a raft to the drowning. He clung to it.

He would not be trapped into losing control. He leaned over and kissed her mouth to stop it quickly.

"You hush," he said. "You're supposed to rest, don't you know that? Not work yourself all up about something that isn't so. Now you be quiet. Everything's lovely," he said. "I'm right here beside you and Clem's right there planning how he can make trouble for his old man as soon as he gets born, and Forbes is sitting on his ass waiting for a chance to work on you; Mamma's in a ferment to get her grandson, and you're a heroine with beautiful golden curls and no sense. Darling," he said, stroking her hair.

She looked up at him with her wild, animal's eyes.

"You're so good to me," she said. "You're so wonderful. Do you *really* love me, underneath, inside?"

"I really love you. Underneath. Inside."

They were both silent. This was the best that could be done. The surface must be calm, like a lake.

Underneath lay the past. The thing was never to go back to it, to keep it covered. The terrible old years of South America, of Boston, of agony and tears and shouting and hate and fury and exhaustion, lay behind everything. Maizie kept scratching at the surface to get at the past; like picking the scab off a sore. If he hung on to control long enough she was bound to stop, and then the past could die. This was, he thought, his ordeal; a sort of test. This way he was paying for what he had done to her. He would continue to speak calmly, gently, softly, until the crust over the past was too thick to pick off, until the new life was established on another basis. And what kind of a life would that be? Well, calm; quiet. And would it be worth living, he thought suddenly.

He jerked his head, and put his hand up to his stiff, short moustache.

"I'm going to let you rest now, so you'll have a good sleep tonight," he said, getting up and releasing her hand.

"Where are you going?"

"I thought I'd run up to the studio for a while. I'd like to get some fresh air and do some work there. I'll be back early. You just go to sleep."

"Darling," she said, "you know I'd understand if you . . ."

Everything screamed inside him suddenly.

". . . If you felt you had to have a woman," she said.

Very slowly, very carefully, he bent over her and kissed her. When he had straightened up again he spoke.

"Don't you be a silly," he said. "I wouldn't know what to do with a woman if I saw one. I'm an old, respectable married man about to be a father and I've got quite enough on my mind without strange women scaring me to death. Now, don't give me any more of your lip."

"I'd understand," she said again, watching him with that awful eagerness.

But he was far too wise to be trapped. He knew all about this. He knew from long ago. He knew from South America and from last year and from the year before. Oh no.

"Darling," he said. "Get this through your pretty head. I'm going to be absolutely faithful to you. That's a fact. I want you to get your teeth into it. If I find you're stewing about any such thing I'll give you hell," he said with great gentleness and care. "I want you to be happy. I'm not going to do anything to disturb that. I swear it."

"Truly?"

"Truly."

"Oh! But I'd understand . . . you know that, don't you?" The anxiety came back into her voice.

"I know that," he said. He kissed her again. "You got everything? Water? Sleeping pills? Your bell?"

"Yes, darling."

He went very softly out of the room, leaving the door ajar.

The air outdoors on Commonwealth Avenue was very cold, and smelled of snow. The street-lights seemed to snap, white and small, all up and down either way. Lambert ran across the street and began to walk fast uptown on the shovelled path in the middle of the Mall. The big bare trees on either side creaked in the winter wind and cars went by at intervals, downtown and up. At Massachusetts Avenue he turned left and walked along the broad sidewalks that were skimmed over with ice and had sand thrown on them, past the big dark buildings, past the lighted windows of the drugstores and the all-night restaurants. Up Boylston Street a block, and then he turned the corner into Ipswich Street and ran against the hard wind, and up the steps into the studios. Inside it was hushed and overheated and only one light burned; the old elevator stood empty and lighted at the back. He ran up the staircase and went along the dark hallway with the boards creaking under his step to the end, and climbed the concrete fire-escape at the back to the second floor and crossed the corridor and unlocked his studio door with a key. He went into the darkness and closed the door behind him and stood still. It was warm and smelled of paint and dust and turpentine and nitric acid. He went down the stairs from the balcony in the dark. The great north window was luminous gray against the lights outside. The shapes of things stood out dimly in the room: the two tall heavy easels, the model stand, the high table before the window. It seemed to him to breathe as he stood in it in the dark, as if his things had been alive there while he was away and still drew their long, quiet breath. He felt relief, as if he had returned to a place that held his shape suspended on all sides—like floating in water—that gave way and filled in smoothly, silently, to all his motions; warm, soundless, enveloping.

He switched on a blue light beside the high table and began to wander around the studio doing little things. He scraped the palette he had used and transferred the blobs of paint to a sheet of glass and went into the bathroom and put the glass into the bottom of a soup plate that he filled with water. He cleaned a bunch of brushes with water against a cake of soap.

He stood in front of the biggest easel and stared at the painting he had been working on that day, a nude leaning back in the blue upholstered chair with her head turned aside so that the sterno-cleido-mastoid muscle of the throat stood out like a long, taut cord. He stood in front of it and stared at it trying not to think, trying to look at it with his eyes and see it without thinking about it. But his thoughts kept forming in little gusts and making sentences about it, that he pushed away. He kept thinking that it was painted well, the construction able, the values intelligent; there was nothing that he could find with his conscious mind that was the matter with it. But he knew it was not any good. The thing that was the matter with it had nothing to do with thought, with technique or knowledge or conscious criticism. The thing it lacked was something that had been missing in his eyes when he looked at it in painting it and looked at the model he was working from. His eye had looked at her and seen what she was, a nude with certain forms, values, planes, and had transferred these things to the canvas. But the picture was no good because he had not seen it or the model with an innocent eye.

He threw a stack of old newspapers into the fireplace and set a match to them. The fire roared up and he tossed on two logs. He went and sat down on the old couch beside the fire, still staring sidewise at the canvas.

The innocent eye, he thought. The innocent eye saw things as they were: without association, without literary values, without their meaning anything except what their shapes and colors meant privately to the painter's dissociated mind. A tree must never be a tree, that word with its associations, to a painter; he must see it innocently as a shape without an associated meaning; to him it should have equal interest whether right side up, upside down, or sideways. It was certain form with certain colors, upon which the light fell in certain ways. Its interest to the painter lay not in that it was a tree; it would be better if he did not know its name; it lay in the pattern it made with other things around it, its design, its *notan*.

Seen innocently and with delight, a tree, a nude, a box, an egg, became something beautiful and essential and significant for the first time; as fresh and unknown as dawn on the first day of creation. Painters had painted trees, nudes, boxes, eggs, since the beginning of art. If a painter today saw them for what they were known as, he would only be painting another tree, another nude. But if his eye were innocent, if he was an artist, he saw these things and they were as new as if they had never before existed, because the lights could never fall upon them twice the same way, because they were always in a new relationship to their surroundings, because the painter's own eye was fresh and curious and amazed and innocent.

Pictures could always be painted that were new, undiscovered, a revelation. In those paintings was the only glory of art, its unassailable glory: the world born again and greeted with joy and wonder. The innocent eye encountered the world and rendered what it saw, the world with a new light cast upon it making new shapes, new shadows. That was the only art that was art. It could only be seen and made by the eye that was innocent.

He put his head in his arms and shut out the picture that shivered with the shivering red light from the fire. He felt bound; tied up with the long black and white tape of thought, and each new thought tied him tighter and he was further away from freedom and his proper alignment, that of his nature bearing directly upon what he saw. Thinking was an evil to a painter, this sort of thinking: this analysis and explanation.

His eye was sick. The symptom of the painter's illness was this long tortuous train of thought. It was not a healthy symptom that worked toward recovery. It drew a thicker and thicker skein, a mesh, before the eye. With his hands he felt the muscles of his upper arms through his clothes, his deltoid muscles; they were hard. He was a healthy strong human animal but as a painter he was sick. His eye had lost its innocence. The picture out there in the room could have been painted by anyone with a sound technique. It was one of a hundred thousand studies of nudes, displaying what was known about the form, the color, the action of nudes. It was not seen for the first time. It had no delight.

Lambert dropped over sidewise and lay on his back at full length, looking up at the high shadowy ceiling of the studio where a faint light shifted. What am I going to do, he thought. What am I going to do?

He stood up abruptly and went into the bathroom and turned on the light. He looked for his face in the small, paint-smeared mirror over the washstand, and there it was, no different, as far as he could remember, from always; except for the new, small, dark moustache. He opened the door to the cabinet behind the mirror and from among a mess of turpentine bottles and old squeezed-out tubes took a pair of barber's scissors, with a metal curl protruding from one ring, and began to trim his moustache.

He might look just the same but he was not himself. All that mattered in himself was not there.

He trimmed the bottom edge of his moustache, along the edge of his upper lip, and wondered what cure he would employ, if he was free to cure himself at once.

"Oh, Christ," he said out loud to the mirror, and suddenly felt like a nostalgic child, longing for the hoot of a steamer's whistle moving out to sea, for the long sound of a train whistle.

"Hey," he said to the mirror, and put the scissors away. "Got to think this out."

He went back into the studio and sat down on the couch and began to try one more time to think it all out again, so that he would see how he had got here, and why he couldn't go anywhere else.

All right. For God's sake, don't begin any further back than Leda. Everything before that has been digested and redigested and regurgitated until it doesn't mean anything. All right, begin with Leda. Leda was wonderful. Don't go into why. All right. That stopped. She went away. Why did she go away? She went away because Maizie started to have a baby, because she wanted to put a stop to Leda. So she put a stop to Leda. But, Christ, that needn't have been so, there were a hundred things that could have been done, a thousand things. I could have. Leda could have. Maizie could have. All right, but *they didn't*. Get to something else. It could have been wonderful with Leda, it could have been right; suppose it was the last chance for something, it's lost and I've got all over thinking about that, for itself, months ago. Months ago. It's just the last chance aspect. . . .

So Maizie started the baby. Hate and rage and more tears and all the old stuff, the old, old stuff. Then it was August. Then there was that early morning. Waking up. How long had she been awake? Sitting up in bed, and lying down again when the pains came, and sitting up again, watching the clock; too scared to wake me up because I always get mad when I'm waked up. She said, "Oh darling. . . . I didn't want to wake you up. You

would have been so angry." Oh, for Christ's sake, for Christ, Christ, Christ.
Telephoning, and carrying her down in blankets, and racing to the hospital,
and Forbes waiting. Your wife's going to miscarry in a few hours. Sitting in
the waiting-room and thinking that Leda wasn't married, not yet, when
Maizie was somewhere waiting to miscarry. She said, "Oh darling. . . . It's
the end of everything. You and this baby are all there is. I won't want to
live." And she meant it. She means everything. She's on the opposite side
of the universe, but she means it. She really does feel all these things. I did
it all to her.

All right, so she didn't miscarry. Forbes said: "I don't understand it." She
said, "Oh, darling. . . ."

All right, here we are. After that, you couldn't. It meant a miracle to her,
being rescued from some kind of hell in the nick of time, and her face like
a God damned Madonna. Nobody ever looked so radiant. And frightened.
You couldn't. You had to stay.

Because it's like this. The miracle happened to her and she's going to have
the baby. She's going to have it anyway, now, and she's put to bed so she
can't miscarry it. There aren't going to be any more miracles. She can
either have it and it can be awful for her, some strange unimaginable kind of
awful that you've just got to take on faith after watching it all these years.
Or else she can have it and be happy, and the way she does that is if she
gets the kind of things that in her world mean heaven. A kind husband. A
kind, gentle, considerate, unfrightening husband. That's you.

Don't throw out your arm. Move slowly. Smile. Speak quietly. Smile.
Stick to safe subjects. Stick to the baby. Keep remembering she's going to
have a baby. Everything's for that. It's all about the baby. Hush. Don't.

Everything's going to be lovely. Yes, yes. Everything's going to be lovely.
Well, everything is going to be lovely, isn't it?

Naturally you'll still know how to get to work. Don't be an ass. If you
can forget how to paint in a few months you never knew how to paint. If
it's your eye that's the matter, then why won't your eye get well when
there's no trouble any more? What makes you think it won't get well? And
you can quit looking for trouble ahead because that's then and now's now
and you've got a job to do first.

Everything's going to be lovely.

God damn it, stop saying that. Or say it some other way. Everything's
going to be . . . all right. I swear to you it is. Look, fellow, everything is
going to be all right.

Everything's going to be lovely.

He stood up and jerked his head, and put his hand up for an instant to
touch his new moustache.

He picked up his hat from the paint table. He switched out the blue light
and in the darkness went up the creaking steps to the balcony. His hands
felt for the spring lock on the door and turned the little knob, and he went
out into the long, empty, dim corridor of the studio building, smelling of
dust and old paint.

He had a latchkey to the house on Commonwealth Avenue and let himself in quietly, but the lights were still on full in the hall and upstairs on the drawing-room floor. He walked lightly up the stairs, thinking how his footsteps sounded like all men's footsteps he had heard going upstairs all his life. He looked into the library and his mother was still up, sitting beside the fire that died slowly in the grate, reading. She had her glasses on her nose, and held the *Atlantic* out in front of her, rather far away, to bring it into focus.

"You still up, Mamma?"

"Why, Lambert." She laid down her magazine and looked over the top of her glasses at him. Her small feet in satin slippers were set side by side on a footstool. She wore the black satin and lace tea gown in which she dined at home. Her hair, that did not resemble hair but a dense pile of some substance, curled and twisted and massed and gray, capped her head and below its edges at the side there glittered in the light the small diamonds in her ears.

"May I come in and warm my feet?"

"Of course, my dear." She leaned forward and pulled symbolically at the arm of a chair to draw it nearer to the fire. He sat down slowly and thrust his legs at full length towards the small, hot coal fire, and lit a cigarette.

"Maizie all right?"

"I went up to see her for a little while after you went out. I think she must be asleep by now. She hasn't rung."

He nodded. The fire, of briquets, was silent. Its red glow was moment by moment dimmed by gray ash, but the heat given off was intense. His mother had gone back to the *Atlantic*. He turned his head and looked at her.

She had always been a perfectly satisfactory mother because she had never interfered with him. She was dignified, conservative, occupied with many things; a great lady. When he was a child he got from her anything it ever occurred to him to want from her—affection, help, money—but it had never been in him to turn to his parents for much. He had always had what he wanted most inside himself. If his father, who had been one of the last Boston gentlemen politicians, had lived, there might have been trouble, Lambert thought; objection to the way he had chosen to live and the career he had desired. But his mother had been able to assimilate the idea of an artist into her scheme of things; at least she had never said a word in objection, never insisted upon Harvard because it was traditional for Rudds and Lawrences, taken his art education in her stride. Now he was thinking that really he had no idea what she thought of him.

She had looked a little dizzy that night long ago when he brought Maizie home as his wife just before they left for South America. She had rocked on her heels a little, but that was all. Maizie was, he thought, the utter antithesis of his mother as a type of woman: emotional, demonstrative, passionate, possessive. But they seemed, now, at close quarters this winter, to get along as though it were the natural, ordinary thing. As soon as the doctor had said Maizie must go to bed for the rest of her time, his mother had stepped in and proposed the present arrangement, which solved everything. Lambert wondered what his mother, really, thought of Maizie.

He threw his cigarette on to the dying coals and watched a flame spurt for an instant.

"Well, she's almost through it," he remarked. He wanted to talk; that was a curious thing to feel, for him, whose conversation with his mother had always been a reflex thing, but no more curious than anything else these days, he thought. It all stemmed from not being satisfied with his work, and that stemmed from Maizie having a baby. . . . Wanting to talk to people; feeling lonely. It was a hell of a way to be feeling. He grinned, thinking: *Never lost a father yet.* His mother would think the grin went with what he had said.

"Only a little longer," she said. She took off her glasses. "I think everything has gone extremely well—under the circumstances. Maizie is remarkable; she never complains, I've never heard her." She looked directly at him. "And I think you have behaved beautifully."

He wondered what she meant by that. He would probably never know. And in a little while he wouldn't care. He bowed.

"Thank you, madam, I'm sure."

"Men hate sickness," she remarked. "They can never accept it. Your father was that way. Sickness seemed to him an outrage."

"But you've never been sick a day."

"No, I haven't. But there were times when I could see what his attitude was."

"We've never been much of a family for getting sick, have we?" he said.

"We've had remarkably good health on both sides. Though of course there was your uncle Gaspar."

"My uncle Gaspar. . . . Was he the one that died of drink?" His eyes sparkled to see his mother's eyebrows lift minutely.

"He had a very unfortunate love-affair when he was a young man. A Miss Hemingway. She treated him very badly. He didn't have your father's stamina. He was never able to put it out of his mind."

"Did I ever see him?"

"He died before you were born. It was very sad to see so much ability wasted. Your father said he had twice the political sense he had himself. But he never displayed any interest. He wasted himself. He spent a good deal of time in Paris in the 'nineties. Dear me, I haven't thought of Gaspar for years."

"Another black sheep like your son."

"My dear boy, I can't permit you to call yourself a black sheep, even in fun. I've always known you were fundamentally solid."

"Mamma, you overwhelm me.—What was Uncle Gaspar doing all the time in Paris? Raising hell?"

"I believe he was writing some kind of poetry," she said.

"He was writing poetry. . . . I never knew that, Mamma. How amazing. You never told me that. Was it any good?"

"I believe not."

"Haven't we got any of it?"

"There was a book . . . somewhere . . . privately printed, I believe. . . . It may be somewhere in the house. I don't know."

There was a silence between them for some minutes.

"Well," he said, "I expect I'll be hitting the hay. Don't you ever get tired, Mamma?"

"No. But you look tired."

"I can't imagine why. I don't do a thing to get tired about, these days. Maybe I've got weakling blood, after all." He laughed, but in a second he stopped laughing.

"I expect your painting can be fatiguing," she said. He stared at her.

"On my feet, you mean?"

"Perhaps. I have noticed that things like that can often be more tiring to people than work."

He started to say something, but there was nothing to say. It should not be surprising that his mother didn't consider painting work. There was no reason why he should find her words slightly unpleasant; why should he care? She didn't know anything about it, and he had always taken that for granted.

He smiled gently and said nothing.

"After the baby is born," she said, "you'll be going on with your painting?"

His eyes sought her face in a moment of bewilderment and then he got up, not too quickly.

"Oh yes," he said. "I expect so. Yes."

"You're going up now? Good night, dear."

"Good night, Mamma," he said.

But he stumbled on the edge of an Oriental rug, going out of the room. He went up the stairs. He had the remains of a smile fixed on his lips. He went along the upper hall to the staircase that led up to his room.

"Lamb. . . ."

Maizie's voice. He turned and went back to her door, just ajar, and put his head in. A light was switched on within, and he saw Maizie raising herself on her elbow, her eyes dazed with light.

"Why aren't you asleep?" he said softly.

"Come in and say good night to me."

He went and sat on the edge of the bed without putting too much of his weight on it, and looked down into her face.

"You must go to sleep."

"When I close my eyes," she said, "all I can see is spinach. It's like that. All spinach, all chopped up and sort of surging, everywhere, masses of it. And I can't go to sleep."

Like chaos, he thought. But it might not seem like that to her, and it might frighten her to hear the word. He stroked her hand.

"You take a pill," he said. "Here."

He shook out one of the yellow capsules into her open palm and held the glass of water for her while she put the capsule in her mouth. He wondered what it could be like to have your life confined to one bed, in one room, for a long time. He thought of his father. *"Sickness seemed to him an outrage. . . ."* He wondered what Uncle Gaspar had thought of sickness. He himself, he used to know the feeling of outrage. So many, many times, in so many places. But he was getting quite used to it. It seemed the normal thing. What would life even be like, without sickness in it? He bent down and kissed Maizie.

"I love you," she said. "You know you're my whole life, don't you?"

"Yes," he said, "I do."

"I love to know you're here. It makes me feel so together with you."

"We are together," he said.

"And I stop seeing the spinach."

"Go to sleep, and you won't see any more spinach."

"All right." She sighed and turned her head into the pillow. "We are together, aren't we?"

"We are together."

Again he crossed the upper hall, and went upstairs where, in the upper regions, a gas jet wavered against the wall. He went into his room and switched on a light. The old furniture stood around, the desk, the bed, the bookcases holding Latin grammars and Henty. He stood in the middle of the room. This was the room of one part of his life, even as the studio was the room of a later part of his life. He tried to imagine how he had felt as the boy whose room this was, the boy who was not yet a painter. How could it feel not to be a painter?

"Are you planning to go on with your painting?" he said out loud.

"What makes you think I'm not?" he said out loud.

It was funny how he had got this trick, lately, of speaking to himself out loud.

## CHAPTER XXXIX

IN FEBRUARY Dr. Forbes said that Maizie might get up for a little while each day in order to strengthen her muscles; there was now no further hazard of miscarriage. The day predicted for the baby's arrival was less than two weeks ahead. The first day, Dr. Forbes was there when Maizie took the steps from her bed to the big armchair. He took one arm and Lambert the other and Maizie, in a voluminous pink dressing-gown, took the steps slowly and sank into the chair. There was an atmosphere of triumph, of progress. Dusk had fallen and the lights were on in the room. Dr. Forbes stood and looked at her. He was a man with an immense beaked nose and small blue eyes behind thick glasses; his reddish-brown hair fell in a lock across his forehead.

"There you are," he said. "Do that every day, now. A little longer each time."

"The baby won't come too soon?" Maizie said.

"He can come any time he likes now. We'll be ready for him. But if you take it easy and don't trip or anything, you'll be able to get a little muscle there. It'll help. Not necessary, though," he added.

"Can I do the getting up late like this? Then Lambert can be here to help me."

"Any time."

"You don't mind, do you, darling?"

"Of course not."

He wished so she would get over being afraid of him. He wished it so.

"Well," Dr. Forbes said. "I'll be going along. You're doing fine."

"Just one thing. I can't seem to sleep. . . ."

"One of the yellow capsules at bedtime," he said briskly. "Another if you awaken. But it is my thought that getting up, moving around, will make it easier for you to sleep."

"Oh, good."

"Well, keep your fingers crossed," the doctor said, and left. Every time he left, he said that. Keep your fingers crossed.

In two or three days Maizie was walking out into the hall, and on the fifth day she went downstairs, on Lambert's arm. It was shortly before dinner time. They paced into the drawing-room, where a big log fire was snapping. The lights were not on, and Lambert reached out to the switch.

"Don't," she said. "It's lovely like this, with just the firelight."

The red light flickered and sprang up the walls of the long, high-ceilinged room. They sat by the fire. Maizie drew a breath. She sat turned slightly away from the blaze, facing the space of the room and the reflected light and the shadows.

Lambert lit a cigarette.

"It's like a cave," Maizie said in a whisper. "Isn't it? It's so queer. It doesn't seem like any place I've ever seen. It's as if I were with you in a great cave with a fire at the end of it."

"You've had to be in bed so long it wouldn't be strange if you didn't recognize this room," he said lightly.

"No, but Lamb; look. Isn't it like a cave? Somewhere far away. And we're alone in it. Everything else has disappeared. I've just waked up and here we are in a cave. Just me, with you."

"And the baby."

"It's as if this was different. I've forgotten about the baby." She stared at the long, high shadows that stalked and raced across the walls. "It's just us and nothing else in the world. In a cave. I've loved you such a long time, and now I'm here."

He smoked and looked at her, wondering what she meant, wondering what Maizie's thoughts felt like to have.

She laughed suddenly.

"I feel happy," she said. "Everything seems so simple. I just keep on and keep on and keep on loving you, and that's the answer, it all comes out and it's happy. I just keep on. Oh, now it's going to seem simple."

"Of course it will," he said. "It's going to be lovely. I haven't said boo to you for a long time, have I?"

She didn't answer.

"Nothing matters any more," she said. "You can do anything to me. All I have to do is just keep on, and on, and on. It seemed so big, and complicated, and frightening, but it isn't really. It's little. It's tiny. All I have to remember is just to keep on."

"Don't work too hard," he said. "I think you'd better be taking the trek back to bed, darling."

"All right. I hate to leave it here. I love it. I feel so happy. I wish it would just stay like this, all simple and in one little place."

"Don't you worry. Everything's going to be as easy as pie."

He helped her to her feet and side by side, his arm around her waist, they paced out of the firelit place into the brightly lighted hall outside, and climbed the stairs, slowly, laboriously.

All the lights went on in the house, upstairs and downstairs, in the middle of the night, near the end of February. It might have been Christmas, or a burglar; along the dark, melancholy stretches of Commonwealth Avenue, above the lonely snow, into the before-dawn emptiness—suddenly the lights blazed out, upstairs and downstairs.

Inside the house all was purposeful. The telephone calls were made by Mrs. Rudd, sitting in the upstairs hall in a mulberry-colored dressing-gown with her curious hair hanging in a tail down her back. Lambert had dressed in a hurry when Maizie's bell rang: the long-awaited, the fateful ring. He had put her suitcase, packed long ago, by the bedroom door ready to go down. Maizie sat up in bed, smiling, her hair tossed back, holding Lambert's watch in her hand to time the pains. "Now take it easy," he said, cheerfully. "Wait till the nurse comes. No use your wasting strength dressing."

Mrs. Rudd dressed, in the large chamber that was hers, in a black suit and a white shirtwaist with a jabot, and put up her hair and crowned it with a hat made of black broadcloth and feathers. She put on her rings. The front doorbell rang, and Lambert ran downstairs to open it. The nurse came up to Maizie's room, with a small case in her hand. She took off her hat and her coat and stood forth a strong young woman with short black hair, in a starched white dress. She had been engaged months before. She took Maizie's pulse and then laid her hand on Maizie's abdomen and looked abstractedly at Lambert, standing there.

"Dr. Forbes said as soon as they were coming every fifteen minutes, Miss Percy," Mrs. Rudd said, coming into the room with a black fur coat over her arm. The nurse smiled.

"I think we might be getting dressed and ready to go," Miss Percy said. "Mr. Rudd, if you would . . ." Lambert went out and shut the door. He went slowly, step by step, down the broad stairway. He found that he was smiling.

He peered out of the window beside the front door and saw his mother's car standing there at the curb. He opened the door against the February wind and called to Peterson. The chauffeur came up the steps, grinning.

"Come in and keep warm. Have a butt?"

They stood smoking in the brightly lighted hall. Lambert forgot to talk and lit another cigarette off the first one.

After a while there were footsteps on the stairs and side by side his wife, his mother, and the nurse came down, with Maizie in the middle. She had Mrs. Rudd's fur coat wrapped around her. The chauffeur stabbed out his cigarette quickly in the hall-table ashtray and came forward to the foot of the stairs with Lambert. The women stood aside and let the two men help Maizie down the front steps to the car. Then they all got in.

Through the empty lonely streets the car drove, fast, to the hospital. Maizie smoked a cigarette Lambert gave her. He sat beside her and held her hand. Mrs. Rudd, on Maizie's other side, talked. The nurse sat on a jump-seat and looked out. There was nothing personal or emotional in the atmosphere. It was objective and charged with a significance that had to do with time and speed and efficiency. The car drew up at the big doorway of the hospital where all the lights shone out in a blaze, and an orderly came out with a wheel-chair. The night was just turning to dawn.

"Good luck, Mrs. Lambert," Peterson said. Maizie got into the wheel-chair.

"Thank you, Peterson."

Everybody was fine. Everybody knew his rôle and played it. The wheel-chair rolled along the hushed corridors, and the nurse and the husband and the mother-in-law followed it; up in an elevator, along more corridors, and into a room, where they were joined by a floor nurse. There was a tap on the door and Dr. Forbes came in smiling. Lambert and his mother went out and came back again, and Dr. Forbes went away. Nurses came and went, carrying piles of linen, and basins covered with a towel. Maizie was in bed, in a cotton hospital shirt; she made a big mass in the narrow, strict white bed. Lambert gave her another cigarette and she smoked it, knocking the ashes off into a kidney-shaped basin. There was a round top bulb in the ceiling of the room that cast a hard, white light. Outside the dawn was coming and above the sounds inside, sparrows could be heard chirping loudly. Lambert went to the window and drew up the shade. Outside the light was dirty and gray. He drew the shade down again.

"Now," Maizie said, glancing at the nurse.

"I think we'll have to ask you to go out now," Miss Percy said.

Mrs. Rudd and Lambert walked down the corridor past the desk where two nurses were and went into the waiting-room. They sat and talked in low tones.

Maizie's mother and father came in. Everyone shook hands. Mrs. Jekyll was chattering and gesticulating; she held Mrs. Rudd's hand in hers and they looked into each other's faces.

"Maizie's wonderful," her mother said. "She's just bein' so wonderful. . . ."

Mr. Jekyll stood off, to one side. He did not speak. Lambert held out his pack of cigarettes. Mr. Jekyll shook his head. He made a sucking sound with his mouth, and went and looked out of the long windows at the end of the room. Tom Jekyll's back was tall and narrow and he held his hands clasped behind him.

The floor nurse who had first met them came to the door. She looked from one to another of them.

"Mrs. Rudd is going up now," she said. "She wants to see Mr. Rudd before she goes."

He started toward the door. Tom Jekyll turned from the windows and looked at him. Lambert saw him looking at him, all the way to the door.

The stretcher was coming out of Maizie's room, with a nurse and an orderly easing it around the turn. Miss Percy walked beside the stretcher as it came down the corridor.

"Hello," Lambert said.

"Hello, darling."

Maizie smiled. He had never liked her so much as now. She was behaving beautifully. She was perfect. There was nothing to ask.

The nurses moved away and left the stretcher pushed up against the wall in the corridor.

"Keep your chin up, sweet," he said. "I'm cheering for you."

"Things are really happening," she said.

"Does it hurt too much?"

"I like it. It feels all right. There's nothing frightening about it at all."

"You're a wonderful, strong, beautiful girl. And I love you."

The nurses and the orderly came back and Lambert watched them steer her down the corridor to the hall, and on to the elevator. Then the green door slid shut and she had gone up to another floor.

At eleven-thirty that morning Lambert was in the middle of a game of checkers with Tom Jekyll. They had been playing for hours. They sat in Maizie's room, before the wide window; Lambert sat in the low armchair. The checker-board was on the hassock that made his chair into a chaise longue; opposite him Jekyll sat on a straight chair, his elbows on his knees, his head nearly a foot higher than Lambert's. They stared at the counters on the board, the red and the white, but sometimes Lambert would look up and find Tom Jekyll staring at him.

About once an hour the nurse would put her head in. "Everything's going well," she would say. "The doctor says it won't be much longer." They would look up at the nurse, and watch the door close behind her. The ladies were out in the waiting-room. They had all had breakfast on trays in the hospital, at seven. Once in a while, after a game, Lambert would lean back and light a cigarette and try to start a conversation. Jekyll would look at him. "I'll play you another," he would say, and they would set the counters up in double rows again. They had played dozens of games, and Jekyll had won all of them. He played a quick, tricky, unbeatable game. Once he said, "I learned to play this game in the Army. In the War." A picture came into Lambert's mind, of Jekyll in khaki, playing checkers, and somehow he felt as if he had actually seen it. Jekyll was the type for a uniform, he thought. He was just the kind of man who had been in the War.

Lambert's mind seemed to be functioning on three separate and unrelated planes. The first was concerned with Jekyll. Like a jeering little boy this part of his mind kept figuring Jekyll out, realizing that his father-in-law disliked him and was jealous of him today. It realized that Jekyll was trying to prove something to himself by winning again and again from him at checkers, and got malicious pleasure out of the private knowledge that such victory counted for nothing because he, Lambert, didn't give a damn who won the games. The old bastard thought he was a bastard. Maizie was his darling daughter and Lambert was the bastard who had taken her and got her with child and put her where she was now, writhing in labor. Jekyll was the one to whom this meant the abuse of something he loved and probably wanted to keep for himself—his little girl under glass. Jekyll hated him, and he thought "Yah!" at Jekyll, because this was life and reality; for him Maizie was not under glass but in childbed.

The second level of his mind was sad and sorry for this. This level comprehended the older man gravely and realized the futility of his position on this day. It saw Maizie up on another floor of the hospital, going through what must be gone through, in suffering but also ordered, measured, controlled, like a ceremony with unchanging rites. It saw himself, the man, who had set this machinery in motion, sitting still, playing checkers, in a hospital room; his part played; his rôle to wait until he was shown the fruit of the whole long process, the child at length brought forth.

He found that he loved Maizie. More than ever before in their life she seemed his partner, carrying out her end of a complicated bargain between them. She was up there going through the rites and he was grateful to her. She was his wife and it was a bargain that would stick now. After all the violence, and unhappiness, and conflict, they had put themselves into a machinery of parenthood that took hold of them and moved them along; they had to do it together and they had done it. It was the only time they had done anything together toward the same end.

The third level of his mind sailed like a cloud up from the top of the second. Like a cloud it floated without thought. But his eyes felt tired and oddly clear. It was like waking up, and he had not expected it. The counters on the checker-board looked beautiful to him, round polished discs of blood-red and ivory white; he almost wanted to put one of them to his mouth and touch it with his tongue. The fabric of the upholstered chair, rough, of striped blue, was as surprising as if he had been blind until this moment. He turned his head and looked out of the window. The angle of the hospital, in white stone, stood pure and dazzling in the winter sunshine, and a long stretch of ground was covered with snow, criss-crossed this way and that with footsteps; its surface glittered in points like mica. A nurse crossed the snow along a path, in a blue cape that blew up sharply and showed her white dress beneath. The blue and the white and the figure walking were full of surprise and delight.

Jekyll spoke and he turned back and moved a counter promptly. Jekyll jumped three of Lambert's men. Lambert laughed. Jekyll pressed his lips together.

The door opened again and the nurse stood there, smiling at them.

"Mr. Rudd, you've got a beautiful little daughter," she said. "Born ten minutes ago."

The father and the grandfather looked across at each other.

"Congratulate you," Jekyll said in his Southern voice.

Lambert bowed.

". . . You," he said. He felt extraordinarily excited.

"If you'll just come now, and go to the waiting-room. She'll be coming down in a little while."

The men got up and Jekyll folded up the board with the counters inside it. They clattered as he put the game that he had won again and again on the hospital bureau. Lambert stood back and let Jekyll walk first out of the door to the corridor.

Mrs. Jekyll kissed Lambert on both cheeks. Mrs. Rudd was smiling. All of them sat in a circle and smiled at each other; Jekyll's smile kept coming and going. Mrs. Jekyll pressed her husband's knee with her hand.

"All over, Tom," she said. "All over and just lovely. Wish that nurse would come back and tell us some more. Why, I don't even know how much the little darlin' weighs. Declare, I can't *wait* to see my precious little granddaughter. Oh, I do just love new babies. Tom, honey, the first grandchild! Think of that. Us. I'm so excited! My, I'm goin' to have such fun spoilin' that baby to death."

Lambert, watching, saw his mother put out her hand and put it over Mrs. Jekyll's and smile. It was extraordinary how well the two women got on, when they might have come from separate hemispheres. But they had something all fixed up between them. They were one about something. It was a baby in the family. He wondered if it ever did that to men. He glanced over at Jekyll's face on which the smile came and went, and knew that he would always be an enemy in Jekyll's mind. He felt sorry.

The nurse came back and beamed at them.

"She's down from the delivery room. Getting along fine. We want her to sleep for a while, now, but she wants to see you, Mr. Rudd, for a minute. Just a minute, now."

Lambert got up and walked to the door once more. Once more he saw Jekyll's eyes follow him, and the sound he made, sucking his lips in.

Maizie was back in bed, flat and narrow under the covers. Her face was white, framed with her metallic hair. Lambert put his hand over hers, and she opened her eyes. They looked drugged. But she smiled and her face bore a look of absolute joy, of triumph.

"Darling," he said. He felt a tide of great happiness and relief and loyalty. "I'm so proud of you."

Her lips moved.

"Do you mind that it isn't Clem?" she murmured.

He felt a queer stab that that anxiety should follow her into the deep pit of unconsciousness.

"I'd rather have a girl," he said. "I'd much rather have a girl."

She shook her head slightly.

"Say it again . . . that . . ."

"I'd much rather have a girl."

"No . . . the other . . ."

"—I'm so proud of you, my darling."

"Say it . . ."

"I'm so proud of you."

He tiptoed out of the darkened room. He could have cried.


## CHAPTER XL

ON A MARCH DAY nearly three weeks afterwards they drove out to the house in Manchester from the hospital. Lambert sat in front with Peterson, and Maizie, Mrs. Rudd, Miss Percy, and the baby were in back. The baby lay wrapped in a pink knitted blanket in Miss Percy's lap. It slept.

Maizie sat in the middle, her eyes wide with happiness. She felt like a little girl going on a journey. Ever since that strange, half-conscious time in the delivery room when a voice had said to her out of the darkness, out of the corners: "You have a little girl. Perfect. A little girl, Mrs. Rudd," the happiness had risen, day by day. Everything was lovely. All the trouble was over and dead. This life was a life of joy and perfection; everything, everything was happy. The smiling nurses, the trays of things to eat, the doctor's visits like visits of daily congratulation. The vases and vases of flowers, the telegrams, the letters, the presents for the baby. The lovely nightgowns on her new flat body, and the pretty bedjackets, and the nurses admiring everything, admiring her, admiring the baby, the presents, the nightgowns, the masses of flowers. Her mother and her mother-in-law, adoring her for the thing that she had done. Her father, looking down at her silently as if she, and the baby in her arms, broke his heart; she reached out from her heaven and patted his hand that hung by his side. "Smile, Dad! I'm just as happy as a queen."

And the baby; that treasure, that little miracle, whose name was Honora. It had been the name of one of Lambert's aunts, long dead, and once, a few days after the event, when they were talking of family names he had mentioned it, and Maizie snatched at it.

"I want to name it after your family, darling. It's your baby. I'm yours. I want everything to be your things." She smiled at him and could not smile hard enough. It was impossible to tell him, to show him, how she loved him and how happy she was. She held the tiny baby at her breast, giving it milk; the room was shaded from the afternoon sun. She loved to have Lambert sit with her while she nursed the baby. And he liked it too. He loved her and he loved his baby and he sat beside her bed stroking her hand. She lay there, the center of the universe. Sometimes she cried from pure happiness.

This afternoon, when she was dressed and ready to start, and sitting in the big armchair in the window, Miss Percy had brought the baby in, dressed for the first time in its own clothes. Maizie had never seen it except in the hospital shirt and blanket.

She looked at it, lying in Miss Percy's arms; Miss Percy, beaming, leaned over and laid the baby in her lap. The little cap, the little pink coat. Suddenly tears rolled down Maizie's face and she looked up at Lambert; she smiled and the tears rolled into her mouth and tasted salt.

"Oh, look!" she said. "Just look."

Lambert smiled and laid his hand on her shoulder. She couldn't say what she meant. It was the little face, so new, wearing the pink cap. . . . It was the little coat, to go home in. She wept. "It's just that I'm so happy."

All the nurses on the floor gathered to say goodbye as she rolled along in her wheel-chair to the elevator. She loved them all; they were part of her triumph. "Goodbye, Mrs. Rudd," they cried. "Be good, now." They leaned over the baby Miss Percy held in her arms. "Goodbye, Honora," they said. "The best baby in the nursery. Get fat, now!" Maizie rolled through the hospital with her little entourage, saying goodbye, goodbye; goodbye to the orderlies, to the desk nurse, to the elevator man.

The car drove smoothly and fast along the roads to the North Shore; Lynn, Salem, Beverly, around the curves of the black road, past the great summer places that were closed now. She looked at all they passed with pleasure, as though she were a child. The baby slept in Miss Percy's lap. It was extraordinary how much she loved Miss Percy. Miss Percy had been there with her through all of it. In the hour of delivery; with the first tray, the next morning, smiling in the sunshine—"How does it feel to be a mother?" Maizie felt as if, really, she loved Miss Percy more than any woman alive, more than her mother.

"How delicious the salt air smells," Mrs. Rudd said. She ran the window down a little and ran it up again.

"We'll get strong in no time in this grand air, won't we, Mrs. Rudd?" Miss Percy said.

The car rolled up the crackling gravel of the drive. The front door flew open and three maids ran down the steps to the car. "Ah, look at the little darlin'!" Maizie stepped out, Lambert helping her; her face was covered with smiles. The little procession moved into the house, up the stairs, into the big bedroom.

"Oh, how lovely!"

The wall-paper was blooming with pink roses. There was a fire crackling in the fireplace, bright and tiny and gay. There were flowers in vases on the table by the fire and on the white bureau. The bed had been opened; the smooth sheet turned over on the pink blanket, soft and inviting.

"Now the first thing for us to do is to get into bed," Miss Percy said, coming into the room.

"Oh, no!"

Maizie went to the window, running away from her nurse, and pressed her face against the cold pane.

There was a white gate, leading into a pasture. Beyond stood a big red barn. And far away, making the edge of the earth, lay a gray line that was the ocean. The scene was suffused with afternoon sunshine. It was as beautiful as a dream. The moments while she stared at it seemed to form themselves into a flower; this was the happiest moment in her whole life, the happiest of all.

"Let me help you to undress."

"Oh, no, I want to look!" But she turned.

She sat by the little fire while Miss Percy on her knees drew off her stockings. She put on the dear blue nightgown; she had worn it the day after Honora was born. Her feet slid into the white fur slippers and she got up and went to the window again.

"This is the happiest—the very happiest—day in my whole life," Maizie told the nurse. For the nurse would understand.

"Of course it is, dear. But you must come to bed now."

"Must I?" Of course she must. She climbed into bed and lay with her hands smoothing the cool sheet. She watched the nurse picking up her clothes and hanging them in the closet.

"Where's my baby?" she said. "I want to see my baby."

"We mustn't wake her up now. She's having such a sweet sleep, in her beautiful new crib."

"Oh, I want to see her beautiful new crib!"

"Tomorrow. We can have a little tour of inspection tomorrow. And pretty soon we'll be going for real hikes. Down to the beach and everything."

Maizie hugged her arms close to her inside the warm bed.

There was a sound. Was it the sound of the world revolving, going comfortably round and round? She listened.

It was the sound of the ocean. A low roar, a deep, ceaseless sound. It was there behind everything; the sound that went with this new world. She lay still with her eyes shut and listened.

When the baby was just under five weeks old Miss Percy left. The day before, the nurse that Mrs. Rudd had engaged to take care of the baby had arrived. She was an elderly Irish woman with black hair; her name was Katie Moran, but she wished to be called Nana. She and Miss Percy had spent the day together in conferences over the baby. "Still on the breast?" Katie Moran asked. "Gaining well, too." Miss Percy said. "We've cut out the two o'clock, of course. If she wakes up in the night I just change her and she goes off again. . . ." For the ten o'clock feeding the night before Miss Percy left, Nana brought the baby to its mother, marched into the rosy bedroom with the little blue woollen bundle held upright against her shoulder and laid it down by its mother's side.

Nana laid back the flap of the blanket. The minute lips were beginning to move, Maizie looked up at the lined, leathery, respectable Irish face.

"Oh, but the boric acid . . ." she said.

"It's right by you, madam."

Maizie reached clumsily for the cotton in the jar and the other jar of solution, on the table by the bed. Miss Percy had always wiped off the nipple for the feedings.

The car came round to take Miss Percy to town soon after breakfast. Maizie had breakfast in bed.

"Be good now," Miss Percy said. "And come and see us some day at the hospital."

She stood by the bedside in her coat and hat.

A maid came in and took the tray off Maizie's knees and carried it out of the room. The sun was shining outside. The fire was lit in the little fireplace. On the walls the roses climbed up the trellises.

"I can't realize you're going!"

"You won't miss me a bit. Nana's going to be fine."

Maizie reached up her arms. The nurse bent down and kissed her affectionately.

"I feel as if you'd always been here," Maizie said.

"We've had a lovely time. Now, you call me up when you have little brother, won't you? I'd just love to nurse you when you have little brother."

"I'll never have anybody else."

"Well, goodbye, dear."

"Goodbye. . . ."

Maizie was alone in the pretty bedroom. Miss Percy had gone. Who would rub her back in the afternoon? She must stop thinking about things like that. She was going to get stronger every day, and back to where she had been—years ago. Was it three years? Winter—summer—winter—summer . . . South America. . . . She tried to grasp the feeling of well-being she had known back in the days before she ever met Lambert. Anyway, that was the way she would feel again now, now that all pain was past.

In the meantime the day stretched out empty before her, and today she must live it through alone.

But she had her routine. Miss Percy had left the routine, established, behind her, and there was that to cling to. All she had to do was to follow it. She got quickly out of bed.

She went immediately to the window. She went to it every day when she got up, and so it, too, was part of the routine. It was, she thought, a magic window. The world was beautiful through it as through no other window. She would never forget the day she came home, when she had first looked out, at the white gate, the empty pasture, the red barn, the sea-bound horizon.

"It's all sunny," she whispered aloud. "And there's the white gate. And there's a barn. They're so beautiful and sunny."

There it was, but somehow she could not let go to it, it did not give her the stab of happiness. She pointed it out to herself, again.

Surely it was only that she was missing Miss Percy. That would pass.

When she had dressed before the fire, that bit of ritual that had held so much pleasure, she made her trip into the nursery to look at Honora in her crib.

Nana was sitting in the window in the sunshine folding clean diapers. She looked up and nodded silently, with a glance toward the crib. Maizie tiptoed across the room. Honora lay there under the blue blanket, with her tiny pink face pressed against the sheet, asleep. Maizie looked down at her for a long time.

It's my baby.

But it was as if something behind her were pushing her; hurrying her on to do something else, so that she had no time. She made herself stand still and look at the baby. She tried to think about what a beautiful baby she had.

But she must hurry. She must go downstairs.

Mrs. Rudd was at her desk in the little morning-room, writing letters. She glanced up.

"Going for a walk, dear? It's a lovely morning. Warmer every day." She went back to her letters.

The house seemed big and strange. She must do something quickly so as not to think about how strange and large the house seemed.

She went into the hall and Lambert came out of the dining-room.

"Aren't you going in to the studio?"

"I thought I'd stay home today and play Miss Percy for you, darling. In case you missed her."

"Why, Lamb! What a sweet thing to think of!"

Tears came to her eyes. It was true: he was a new, wonderful Lambert who did love her and was good to her. That was something she must remember to hang on to, until everything slowed down again inside her and she could think again.

"How would you like to take a walk?"

"I'd love to."

They put on tweed coats that hung in the hall closet and went out into the sharp, salty spring morning.

The lawns were brown, the garden was full of bare shrubbery. They walked along the paths, and Maizie drew in long breaths of cold air. For Miss Percy had said, "Fill your lungs, dear. It's good for you." They crossed the drive to a wide, flat lawn that stretched back of the house toward the farm.

"I'm going to put out the croquet set this afternoon," Lambert said. "Don't you think that might be fun? A little mild exercise for the nursing mother."

Croquet? That was something new; not included in the routine. . . . But she must gradually increase her activities.

"Do a little more every day, dear," Miss Percy had said.

"Lovely," Maizie said, and thrust her arm through Lambert's.

Everything was perfectly all right. Here she was, walking with her husband in the sunny spring morning. The thing to do was to think about what a lovely day it was and how spring was coming.

They stood at the foot of the lawn looking over the farm toward the ocean. Through the high, clear air came the ocean's sound, the long, deep roar.

"I love the sound of the ocean," she said, loudly.

"So do I," he said, and squeezed her arm.

She looked down and poked with the toe of her shoe in the dead grass, the dead leaves.

And there was a spike of green.

"Oh, look! It's flowers!"

"Some kind of bulbs. Crocuses, I suppose. Mamma has them all over the place. They look fine when they're all out."

Spring was coming. Spring was strength. Think of it that way, she thought. It can be a symbol for me. As the spring comes I'll get better, and better, and better. . . .

"I'm going to get better, and better, and better," she said to Lambert. "You're fine now."

He put his arm round her and pulled her facing him.

"I want to kiss you, God damn it," he said. "Do you know I haven't had a good kiss for I don't know how long? Without nurses and my dear Mamma superintending."

He put his mouth down over hers.

It was a new kind of kiss—a very old kind of kiss; the other kind. She strained herself against him, pressing her mouth to his. This was the beginning. It had to begin again. She was his wife again. Now she was getting strong, so that the old life could begin as it had once been—but different now, because now everything was lovely. It wasn't going to be agony this time. He wasn't going to hurt her any more. This would be something happy. She was going to show him—she had thought of it so many times—how passionate, how strong she could.be. Now it had come. It had begun. She was going to be all he ever wanted. Now that everything was lovely she wouldn't fail him any more.

"Hey, whoa!" he said, laughing. "You don't want me to rape you in the farmyard, do you? Because if you don't, you're riding for an awful fall."

She stood back, breathing fast.

"Come on, let's go down and look at the cows. Mamma loves to be told how handsome her cows are."

But she hung back.

"I've never walked that far."

"Huh? Oh, are you tired?"

"I just . . . I don't want to overdo . . ." She tried to explain.

"You're still nurse's darling, aren't you?"

But he said it good-naturedly, and turned to walk back to the house.

"You don't hate me, Lamb, do you?"

"Quit that, baby. I don't want any more of that stuff. See?" He held her hand and swung it, smiling down at her.

"It's just that I do want to get terribly strong, and I don't want to get set back by overdoing, and—oh, darling, you understand, don't you?"

"Of course. Stop acting as if I was an ogre." He squeezed her hand. "It doesn't matter. I don't want to see the God damned cows. You're all the cow I want, baby. You're a lovely cow, aren't you? I couldn't very well say it in front of Miss Percy, but now that we're on the subject I don't mind telling you that it makes me horny as hell to see you giving Honora her dinner. God damn it, it's quite a sight." He drew her nearer to him. "Sweet, do you know I love you? Do you know I want the hell out of you? Do you?"

Her legs felt weak and her head spun.

"Darling . . ." she muttered.

"You do, don't you? You want me too. God, it will be so fine getting you back again after so many months. It's not much fun leading a celibate life, did you know that, baby? I've been celibate as all hell for you, you know. We'll make up for lost time, won't we," he whispered. "Listen. How would you like to go upstairs now and make up a little lost time? Think that would be fun?"

"Oh! . . . I couldn't!"

"Why, you little virgin. I didn't realize how you'd retrogressed. Listen, dear, you got married, remember? To me?"

What was it that was so impossible? This was her husband, and she had thought so many times of how it was going to be. But she couldn't. No, she couldn't.

"Not now, Lamb. . . . It's the middle of the morning."

"And a damned fine time too. Don't tell me you don't want to. I know all the signs. What *do* you want to do?"

"Well . . . before lunch we always played Canfield."

He stared at her, and then put back his head and roared with laughter. He stopped to look at her and then roared again.

"I love you," he said. "I think you're wonderful. All right, baby, we'll go back to the house and play Canfield and I'll let you win. But don't forget I won't be here tomorrow morning. Maybe you'll be sorry then, when you begin lusting after me."

"Oh, darling, I didn't mean to make you mad. It's all right. Let's . . . let's go upstairs now. . . ."

"Don't be an ass. I'm just kidding. There's lots and lots of time. And for God's sake stop thinking I'm mad at you. I'm not going to get mad at you. That's all over and done with."

She smiled anxiously. The thing about his being mad had just slipped out. She must stop. Of course it was not true. It was just today that the feeling about it had come back. Perhaps if he didn't swear so much— maybe that was what made her feel that in a moment he would slip over the edge and they would be in hell again. But that was silly. He swore naturally.

They went into the house and set up a double Canfield game on the table before the living-room fire. Just so and in this place had Maizie and Miss Percy played cards every morning since they had been home. But it was not the same. How could it be? This was Lambert, not Miss Percy. But it was different beyond that. The cards . . .

The cards were unpleasant.

She played faster than she had ever played. She did not mean to, but something was hurrying her. Faster, faster . . .

At lunch, in the white dining-room, they ate minced chicken on toast and drank raspberry shrub out of big engraved glass goblets.

"Don't bolt your food," Lambert said. "For Heaven's sake, where's the fire? Honora can wait."

"I don't know," she said, helplessly. "I just keep feeling as if I had to hurry."

"You're tired," Mrs. Rudd said. "Go up and take a nice nap after lunch."

After Honora had finished and been carried away by the silent Irish nurse, Maizie lay stiff in the bed and could not sleep. It was as if she could not put her head down into the pillow, as if her head was lifted an inch above it.

It must be simply that Miss Percy had gone, and she had not got used to it yet. It must be simply that she was tired.

She wanted to comfort herself. She put her hand up to her cheek.

"There, there," she whispered. "Just tired, that's all."

Maizie came down to dinner in a new pale-blue pajama costume that her mother had given her. Its silk crepe clung to her thighs, and flared around her ankles. It had a black diamond-shaped plastron on one hip, and a draped neck that emphasized the breadth of her shoulders and chest. Her hair was beautifully arranged; it glittered in waves and the curly tendrils over her ears and in her neck. Her cheeks were brilliant and her eyes shining.

She talked all through dinner; about Honora, and the six o'clock feeding; how much the baby weighed today, the competence of Nana, and about the coming of spring. She turned her face from Lambert to Mrs. Rudd and back to Lambert, emphasizing her words and looking into their eyes eagerly. Lambert sat eating his fish, his beef, his dessert. He smiled and looked at her vivid face appreciatively.

After coffee she glanced across the living-room at Lambert.

"Now our breath of air," she said.

They had made this custom, since they had been here, of going out after dinner to take the air and look at the dark sky together. It was a step in the routine.

"My wife is becoming as much a creature of habit as you, Mamma," Lambert said, getting up. Mrs. Rudd smiled comfortably and picked up the *Transcript*.

They walked over the brittle grass in the cold spring night. His arm was around her, and she leaned against him, but it was more as though she were leading him faster and faster. There was no wind. The wide sky above the land was crowded with great white stars.

"A damned fine skyful tonight," he said.

"I feel them," she said; "don't you? I feel them sort of pushing me."

"That's nice." He laughed in the darkness.

"Isn't it funny how everything seems to mean that for us . . . I mean all the stars and that sound all the time, the ocean off there. . . . Everything means we have to do it."

"That is a very satisfactory way to respond to nature."

She stopped short and threw her arms wildly around him. She lifted her face and kissed him again and again. She was trembling.

"Come on, let's go in," he said.

"Just a minute . . . wait . . . I want to kiss you . . . I can't let go."

After a while he disengaged her rigid arms and began to lead her toward the house. The light shone from the windows on either side of the front door.

"Children . . ." Mrs. Rudd's voice called from the living-room.

Lambert glanced down, making a rueful grimace, and shrugged his shoulders as they dropped their coats in the hall. Maizie looked back at him with that fixed brilliance in her eyes.

They went into the living-room.

"I wanted you to look at this editorial," Mrs. Rudd said to Lambert. "After all I've said to Donald Higginson. . . ."

He picked up the *Transcript*. Maizie sat down in a chair opposite Mrs. Rudd. Her arms were crossed, and her hands gripped her shoulders. Lambert's eyes moved down the column of type.

Mrs. Rudd made an exclamation. She got up and put her hand on Maizie's forehead. Lambert let the paper drop, and saw that Maizie was shaking all over.

"She's had a chill. Lambert, she's burning with fever."

Lambert said nothing. They both stared at her speculatively. Her face was raised to them blindly.

"Get her right upstairs and into bed. I'll call Dr. Forbes."

When Maizie was lying under the covers, with Lambert walking around the bedroom smoking, Mrs. Rudd came in.

"He said stay in bed till we see what this is. And to give her plenty of fluids. He can't come out himself. He said to call the local man to find out about whether there's some infection, so I called little Dr. Walker and he's on his way. Put this thermometer in your mouth, dear."

With the tube between her teeth Maizie lay still, her eyes following Lambert around the room. It was almost pleasant to feel her body burning like this. It felt rich and flowing. But her mind still shivered. There was still that pressure in it, that insistence; something was there that must be done . . . Lambert. . . . And then a tune began in her head and went round and round, brassily, getting louder. It was a tinny tune, for fifes to play. In spite of its strange symbolic quality, she did not at first recognize what the tune was.

The doctor was shown upstairs and came into the room. Maizie turned her eyes eagerly on him. He was a small round man with a head as bald as an egg and a face like a bank clerk. It was inconceivable that he could be a doctor. She had seen so many doctors—and none of them looked like this one. He sat down on a chair by the bedside. Lambert went out of the room. Mrs. Rudd was explaining everything, and Dr. Walker kept nodding and blinking his eyes. He had no eyelashes or eyebrows. He kept his eyes on Mrs. Rudd's face.

"And I took my daughter-in-law's temperature. One hundred and three.

Dr. Forbes asked if you would call him when you have made an examination."

"Ayah, Ayah," the doctor said in a nasal, New England country accent. He might have been a teller in a little country bank, she thought, or sold dry-goods over the counter. "Surely," he said. "Well now, let's see."

He turned the covers back gently and took a stethoscope from his bag.

"Still nursing your baby?" he asked, with the instrument in his ears. She nodded.

Then he took out a blood-pressure device. Maizie watched as he wound it round her arm. She wondered how many different types of device for taking blood pressure she had seen in the last few years. But the tune filled almost all of her mind. Round and round it went, round and round. 'Hinky-dinky, parlez-vous. . . .'

"Nothing there . . ." He sat back in his chair and regarded her.

"Anything on your mind, trouble you? Been having enough milk for the baby?"

"Oh, yes . . ."

"Nothing else troubling you?"

"No . . ."

"Feel happy, contented? Not distressed about anything?"

"Oh, I'm terribly happy," she said, eagerly. She wanted to go on, to explain about how happy she was, but then she stopped. It would take too much time. She had to listen to the tune.

Mrs. Rudd was telling more of her medical history, about the threatened miscarriage, the months in bed.

"Ayah; ayah. . . ."

"But the delivery was perfectly normal."

"Ayah."

Maizie raised her head from the pillow.

"It couldn't be the tube again, could it?" she asked. Her eyes glittered with fever.

"The tube . . . ?"

"The Fallopian tube. It was enlarged. Oh, long ago. When I was first married. Long ago . . ."

"Well, now . . . I don't want to examine you, you know; now. Maybe when I call Dr. Forbes. See what he says. Ayah."

The talk between the doctor and her mother-in-law went on and on. She lay now with her eyes closed. Her mind was divided, neatly, in two parts, like the halves of an orange. In one the tune went round and round: Hinky-dinky, parlez-vous' played on shrill, squealing fifes. In the other there was a pulse-beat, a throb: tube, tube, tube. She was convinced. It was something corrupt in her, that was making her sick, that had made her feel so queer all day. It was that tube, from long ago. Take that out, and she would be whole and well. Once she had fought against the idea of losing that tube. Once long ago. Now she knew that was the root of everything. This was the way cancers were. She had a tube of corruption poisoning her. She could feel the poison moving along her veins.

She opened her eyes. The doctor stood at the door with his bag in his hand.

"Plenty of fluids, before she goes to sleep. I'll call Dr. Forbes right away. And I'll be here in the morning."

Maizie closed her eyes again. The tune went round, louder and louder, merry and ghastly.

Somebody put a glass to her lips, and she raised her head. It was Lambert, holding a tall glass of orange-juice. Mrs. Rudd had gone. Maizie drank.

"Poor old baby," Lambert said. "Sick again."

She sat up abruptly in bed.

"Oh God," she said. She began to cry, and the tears stung her hot eyes.

"Please don't cry. Please rest."

"Oh, God. Oh, God. It's all back."

"What, darling?" Lambert sat down on the edge of the bed.

"All of it. I'm sick again, and you'll go off . . ."

"Hush . . . hush . . . I promise you I'm not going off, anywhere. I'm staying right beside you, right here . . ."

"It's all back. The old days."

"No, no. Nothing's back. Everything's lovely. Don't forget, everything's lovely. You've got Honora, and you've got me . . ."

"I forgot Honora. Listen. I know what the trouble is. It's my old tube. The burning. I can feel it. It's coming back. Lambert. I want to have it taken out. Right away. Then I can get well and then I can sleep with you and you'll love me and you won't leave me."

"Darling, don't get upset. I know you feel like hell. But please stop worrying. I can wait, you know. I'm not an ogre. There's no hurry. I'm not going to leave you."

"Not ever?"

"Not ever."

"Lambert. Make them take that tube out. Right away. So I can get well."

He looked at her uncertainly.

"You really feel it again? What makes you think that's it?"

"I know that's it. It's all the same, again. You see, I keep hearing that tune. That tune they played on the deck before they ducked us. 'Hinky-dinky parlez-vous.' Don't you remember?"

"No."

"And the next day was Guayaquil. And then it happened. That was when the tube began. And I hear the tune now, and I know it's the tube again. Don't you see, it's all together. The tune came first, and now it's come back."

"Did you tell this guy about your tube?"

"Yes. But he doesn't know anything. Oh, Lambert, make sure Dr. Forbes knows about it, won't you? Tell him. Just in case anything happens and I can't."

"What do you mean, something happens?"

"I don't know."

"Look. You've got to stop worrying now, and rest. Just put all this

business out of your head and try to go to sleep. Everything's going to
be all right."

"And you won't leave me? You won't . . . go off, somewhere, with
some girl?"

"Look. What can I do to convince you? I swear to you by everything
that I never think of such a thing. I swear to you I'll never leave you."

She closed her eyes.

"Now rest. Everything will be all right."

"But I can't sleep with you. I've got to sleep with you."

"It'll all come. There's no hurry about anything."

"I keep hearing that awful tune," she said. "It's so awful. It means it's
all going to happen again."

"No. Listen, darling. Listen to the ocean. Keep listening to the ocean.
Hear it?"

"Yes."

"Has the tune gone away?"

"It's going," she cried. She opened her eyes and looked at him apologetically. "I can't help it. I'm sorry, darling."

"Quit being sorry!" he exclaimed. "There. I'm sorry, too."

Mrs. Rudd came into the room.

"Better, dear? Dr. Walker thinks you'd better not nurse the baby until
we see how you are tomorrow. It just might be something contagious,
and the baby might catch it through the milk. He's left a formula to try.
Nana's down in the kitchen making it."

After a while they went away and turned out the lights. Maizie lay
with her eyes open in the dark. Her mind was bursting. Everything in it
was terrible.

Lambert said to listen to the ocean. He had told her to do that, and so
that was what she must do. Listen, listen, she thought. She strained out
of herself, to pass by and beyond the contents of her mind, to hear the
ocean. And it was there; booming deeply on the distant shore.

## CHAPTER XLI

DR. WALKER came the next morning and Maizie's temperature had dropped
to normal.

"Better spend the rest of the day in bed. Ayah. And now about the
nursing."

"Did you tell Dr. Forbes about the tube?"

She felt cool and quiet this morning.

"Ayah . . . He's pretty sure there's no pathology . . . Certainly if the
fever stays down like this. . . ."

"But there wasn't any fever . . . before . . ."

"Well, well. Don't worry about it. You say you feel it burning? Well
. . . But about the nursing. Dr. Forbes agrees, we think it might be a little

wiser, ayah, just in case there might be something . . . Hard to tell right
now. Formula seemed to stay down pretty well last night and this morning, the nurse says. Have you got a strong piece of cloth, unbleached
muslin, use for a binder?"

Mrs. Rudd, standing by, nodded.

"Don't feel badly about it, you know. Got to wean the baby some time.
You've nursed her five weeks, haven't you? Ayah. Plenty to give her
a good start."

"You mean I can't nurse my baby any more?"

"Well, just to play safe, you know. It's just minor discomfort. We can
relieve you if it hardens up much, ayah, a breast-pump. Hand one. Get it
at any drugstore."

He looked up at Mrs. Rudd as though for corroboration.

"Isn't Dr. Forbes coming to see me?"

"Well, now, you haven't got fever today. Let's bet that you're going to
be all right by tomorrow."

"But what made me sick?"

"Well, these things just happen, sometimes, you know. Can't always tell.
Go away too quick. Forget about it. Chances are tomorrow you'll be
chipper again."

After he had gone Mrs. Rudd came with a long strip of heavy cotton
and a paper of large safety pins. She bound it tightly around Maizie's chest.

"The tighter it is the quicker the milk will disappear."

Maizie's breasts already ached and burned, from the missed feedings.

"Can't I see Honora?"

"Yes, dear, of course you can. Nana will bring her in. Dr. Walker doesn't
think it could be anything she could catch except through the milk. He
just doesn't want to take any chances. I wouldn't kiss her, though."

At half-past ten the nurse entered, carrying the little blanketed bundle
over her shoulder. She laid the baby beside its mother and turned the
blanket down.

Maizie had forgotten. Why, here was her baby, her precious. Like a
tiny flower: so sweet, so small, so tender.

"She took her bottle ever so nicely," the nurse said primly.

The tears poured down Maizie's face. It was too cruel. Here was her
darling beside her. Mother and baby, side by side, who had been so close,
so secret, joined together.

"Oh, my darling," she whispered, and the tears dropped on the blue
wool blanket. The nurse turned and went over to the window. "Oh, my
darling. They took you away."

There was no fever that day, nor the next.

"Now look, darling." Lambert sat on the edge of the bed. He spoke in
a gentle voice; he spoke slowly and carefully. "I talked to Forbes for a
long time. He says it couldn't be the tube. It couldn't be. You're to stop
thinking about it. What you had was some little flare-up, and it's gone.
You'd have fever if there was anything the matter. If it was anything about

the tube, it would bother you again later and there'd be plenty of time to do something about it then. It can't do you any harm. I asked him what you said, and he said it is impossible for a tube, even if there was something the matter, to send poison through your system. It doesn't work that way. But there's nothing the matter.

"He wants you to get up and begin going around again. 'Resume your routine,' as he would say. He does not want you to stay in bed. He wants you to move around and get your strength back. He thinks seeing you've started weaning Honora it's probably a good thing. Help you to get strong quicker. See? Now, you just get up and we'll take a little walk. It's a swell day."

Maizie stared at him.

"Did you ask him about sleeping together?"

He laughed.

"I must confess I did, sweetie. He says that's okay too, now, any time you feel like it. But for God's sake don't think you have to. I can wait. I know you want to. I'm perfectly prepared to wait."

She shook her head slightly.

"You mustn't stay out here," she murmured. "I know you want to go to the studio."

"You quit stewing about what I want. What I want is for you to get the hell well again. Now you just hoist yourself up out of bed. I'll wait for you downstairs."

That evening, in the middle of dinner, at the long oval table lighted by white candles in silver candle-sticks, Maizie broke into tears.

It was loud, brutal, uncontrollable sobbing. Through the tears her eyes, like the eyes of an animal, flickered in terror back and forth from the faces of her husband and her mother-in-law.

Lambert got up and dropped his dinner napkin beside his plate. He put his arm round Maizie's shoulders and raised her from her chair.

"I'll take care of her, Mamma," he said. Without speaking he led her out of the room and upstairs. He laid her down on her bed and stood looking at her for a moment. Then he drew up a chair and lit a cigarette.

"Now," he said gently. "How about telling me what's the matter? What are you crying about?"

"I don't know!"

"You don't know what's the matter?"

"No!"

"Can't you think?"

"I'm frightened!"

"What of?"

"I don't know!"

He went on smoking his cigarette, flicking the ashes aside, drawing neatly upon it so that beneath his dark moustache the coal brightened at the end. He did not take his eyes from Maizie's face. Her crying slowed, and she gasped.

"You know what I think?" he said.

"What?" she whispered.

"I think what you need is to snap out of it. I think you've been babied so long you don't know how to act like a grown-up woman. Look. We all know you had a bad time. But it's all over now and you're perfectly all right. I don't think there's a thing the matter with you but being sorry for yourself. You've got to quit. God knows I've been patient as all hell, we all have. But the time's come when you've got to snap out of it. Quit babying yourself."

"Oh, Lambert . . . Oh, please don't be angry with me . . ."

"For Christ's sweet sake, will you stop saying that? I'm not angry with you. I'm telling you to stop being a damned little quitter and get some guts into yourself."

And indeed he did not look angry. He looked strong and remote; a judge, dark and muscular and cold, of the creature that lay upon the bed and stared at him.

"I'll die," she whispered. "I'll die if it all begins again. If you're going to hate me again. It's all come back. Oh God! Lambert . . . kiss me."

He drew upon a fresh cigarette, and looked down at her with his calm, dark face.

"Don't be hysterical," he said. "The thing for you to do is to get a grip on yourself. You won't get anywhere by hurling yourself around."

Mrs. Rudd tapped at the door and came in. In the dim light of the bedroom she looked large and reassuring.

"Feeling better, dear? Good. After you went upstairs I thought about you a little bit and I came to the conclusion that you might very well be lonely for your mother. Most natural, and with having to wean Honora . . . And so I telephoned her and she is coming out tomorrow to spend a few days. Does that make you happier, dear?"

"Yes."

"And one other thing. You may think me very silly," Mrs. Rudd said, with calm assurance. "But I telephoned Miss Percy and found that she is free. She's coming tomorrow too. Just for a day or two. You see, I decided that perhaps it is too quiet for you just now, out here. With your mother, and Miss Percy, it will be busier for you. Are you pleased?"

Maizie sat up straight on the bed.

"Oh! I know everything will be all right now!" she cried.

But Lambert started to his feet and jammed his cigarette out in a dish.

"For Christ's sake," he said, and walked out of the room.

Maizie put her hands up over her wide, staring eyes.

When Mrs. Jekyll and Miss Percy had come, Lambert began driving in to the studio again every day. He went into town each morning before Maizie was up, and returned in the late afternoon before dinner. Maizie was now surrounded by women again. She would look across the room at him, apologetically, pleadingly, but if he caught her eye he would smile and look away. He took the evening stroll with her after dinner each day, but he would not talk; he looked at the stars. When she threw her arms around him in the darkness he would disengage her fingers without violence, carefully, and turn his mouth from her hot face that reached up to him.

"I don't want to get you all upset," he said. "When will you learn I'm not an ogre? Apparently I upset you. I'm sorry. Naturally I want you to get well, when you get ready to. I hope you're feeling better, with all your nurses and mothers."

"But I'm not," she whispered. "It doesn't work . . . It's getting worse . . . I keep going faster and faster."

"Well, go slower then," he said.

Maizie threw her head back and looked at the skyful of stars. She thought, Oh stars, save me. Oh stars . . . stars over my love and me, calm, cold, lovely stars. . . .

But the stars were too big. Far too big. They were hideous and huge.

Now the routine had been re-established, Miss Percy was there, her mother was close, talking gaily and thrilled with the baby. Maizie strained to hear what they said; the baby was beautiful, unique; she tried to think what the words meant and to feel it too. She hung over the crib with her mother. There was a little face there, against the blanket. It was her baby. She tried to enjoy the things that, such a little while ago, had been happy and comforting: the breakfast tray, the walks, the coming spring.

Why was it all horrible?

One afternoon she was lying on her bed, for her daily nap. But now she never slept. The contents of her mind surged round and round; voices, and scraps of a hideous tune. She kept her eyes closed and with them the world outside seemed to close and she was alone in a red place where everything burned and whirled.

She opened her eyes and the world was there again, and she looked at the clock beside her bed. It was time to get up now. She got out of bed and went across to the window. Each time, she went to it with hope. Perhaps, one of these times, she would look out and the magic would have come back.

She saw the gate, the pasture beyond; the red barn, and far away the line of ocean.

They were loathsome. They were phlegm-gray. They were so menacing and full of evil that she could not take her eyes from them, but went on staring. It was the most frightful scene she had ever looked at. She wrenched her eyes away and began to dress, faster, faster, faster. . . . There wasn't anywhere to get away to. There wasn't anything else to think of. The door of her bedroom opened with a harsh, screaming squeak.

Miss Percy stood there.

"We're going to have a nice little game of croquet," she said, from far away. "We're all waiting."

"Oh, yes!"

Hurry down the stairs, hurry into the garden, hurry out to the lawn, where Mrs. Rudd and her mother waited, in thin spring coats, talking. . . . It took too long to decide who would play with whom; it took too long to pick out the colors on the mallets; oh, hurry, hurry, hurry.

The grass was turning green and the wickets were painted white. The leaves were in bud on the trees that bordered the lawns, and a bird sang. There was no time to look or listen. Quick, quick, the first and second wickets, the third, across to the fourth, hurry.

"My, look at her," the nurse said. "She's half way through before we've begun."

"Didn't know you were such a whiz at croquet, honey."

"Now, I'm going to catch her," Mrs. Rudd said, striking her ball precisely. She moved majestically down the lawn.

They played and played, and Maizie won each round.

"Such an athlete," the nurse's voice said, somewhere.

"I declare I'm worn out. Let's all go and sit down somewhere!"

Then they were in the glassed-in sun porch off the living-room, drinking tea. There was no time to drink the tea.

The ocean was outside. It never went away. On and on and on, the roaring rolled.

"How about our favorite game?" the nurse said. "Your luck is so grand today I'm sure you'll beat me hollow."

They laid the cards out on a wicker table. The two older women talked at the other end of the porch. The western sunshine came at an angle into the room; the red western sunset of New England, sad and strange; and the ocean of the North beat rhythmically upon that phlegm-gray shore. Maizie turned to the spread-out game.

But the faces on the cards looked at her. They looked at her; the kings, the queens, the knaves, with little shrewd ferret-faces. Like animals in the roots of trees they peered at her as she hurried, hurried through the darkening forest, and there was a whispering of animal voices and all the bright little eyes peered at her passing.

When Lambert came in the sun was just sinking and the light was crimson.

"Lambert," his mother said. "I think it would be a nice idea if we all had a drink. Could you make us a cocktail? A Martini, perhaps."

He came back with a tray of filled glasses. Maizie drank hers eagerly; liquor made people feel better, she thought. Lambert went to the gramophone in the corner and began turning over records.

"Lamb, honey, play us something nice and gay."

"I wish I saw what you do in this awful caterwauling," Mrs. Rudd said to Mrs. Jekyll, raising her voice as the first long notes began; the St. Louis Blues.

"St. Louis woman, with her diamond rings," Minnie May sang, smiling brightly at her daughter.

But this was living hell. This was more frightful than flesh could bear. Through the twilight of the room Maizie looked toward her husband. He stood before the gramophone, smoking. She had to stand it. It must be endured. It could not be endured. '*That evening sun go down* . . .' But this was ultimate evil; this meant the end, louder and louder to the end . . .

"Oh, stop that!" she cried.

Lambert turned around very slowly; in the dusk his face was a dark shape.

"No," he said. "You can't run everything, you know. Your mother and I like it."

"Oh, honey, I don't care one bit. Turn it off, if it bothers Maizie."

"If you don't mind, I won't. She's got to learn she can't have everything her own way."

Nobody spoke.

*'I hate to see . . . that evening sun go down, I hate to see . . . that evening sun go down . . .'*

It was evil, threatening her, driving her, closing, closing in on her.

After a while the lights were turned on, and soon after that they all went in to dinner.

Maizie sat at the table in a chair with a plate before her. The candles in the centre blinded her, but all around the table were her friends. She must remember that. They all loved her. She was lost in hell but they were there, quite close, and they were her friends. It was herself that was evil. She was drowning in a sea, a moaning sea. It filled her ears so that she could hear nothing that was said at the table. That was her evilness. They were there and she must hear what they said. The world was getting smaller and smaller around her and these people who loved her were outside the circle. What she must do was push with all her strength to keep the circle from closing. She must look out of it, look up from it; not in and down. She must not stop hearing the words spoken outside of it.

"Oh, I love you all!" she cried.

Mrs. Rudd and Lambert looked up but did not speak. The nurse smiled. Minnie May stared at her daughter and her yellow, dry monkey-face puckered.

"Dad called up this afternoon while you were restin'," she said. "I forgot to tell you. He sent you lots and lots of love."

Maizie wished that she could cry. She tried to see her father's face, to hold it still upon the chaos. But that could not be done, any more than she could cry. Her heart beat in her: bang, bang, bang, bang, bang.

That night she could not sleep. The mounting hours went by like elephants marching. She was alone. She was fighting to keep above the rising tide, to keep the circle open. She did not dare to close her eyes. Something was hurrying her, and in bed, under the blankets, her legs were tensed as though in running. She was evil. She had done an irreparable wrong. She tried and tried to find what it was that she might undo it.

She heard the clock downstairs strike twelve, and then strike one. She sat up and turned on the light. In the night the ocean was booming forever far away. The room seemed striped with falling rain, long gray lines slanting down across the walls. And up the walls crawled little shapes, rodents or cockroaches, colored pink. She put her feet out of bed and put on her wrapper and went to the door.

She crossed the hall, the lights from her room lighting her. Directly opposite was the closed door to Lambert's room. She opened it and crept into the darkness there. Her hand struck the post of his bed. She felt her way along the edge, and touched his solid body lying warm under the covers. She got into bed beside him.

He opened his arms and received her, and did not speak in the darkness.

Her lips kept moving and making little sounds, trying to explain that this was what must be done. His mouth came down hard over them and stopped them. His arms held her and his body was heavy, big, and very warm.

She pressed herself against him with all her strength and it was not hard enough. If she pressed herself hard enough she would escape. Now she could not seem to feel him there at all. It was only herself in the bed, pressing harder, harder; straining for the opening that would let her out. Everything seemed to give way before her. Everything sank back. She must press harder and find a resistance which she could break through. But it went away.

At last he sighed.

His arms fell away from her in his sleep.

After a long time she got up and out of the bed. She was as cold as stone. Her hands were clenched. She went out of the dark room and across the hall and got back into her own bed. The light still burned. It threw liquid yellow streaks through the strange, gray, striped, humming atmosphere. She went queerly to sleep.

She woke up hearing, from far away, the downstairs clock strike six and the ocean; the ocean, still roaring, on and on. She opened her sick eyes and saw the glutinous light. She shut them again. Inside her, chaos was small and round and filled with chopped-up, surging stuff. Faster and faster, and closer and closer.

It would have been easiest to stay drowning and suffocating in horror. But there was a strange morality involved. While she could she had to get up and find help. If she stayed even a little longer the space would close down to a pinpoint of existence, and then she could never, never tell any more and she could not call for help. That was the way of evil. The way of good was wrenchingly difficult; she dragged herself out of the bed and crawled along the long corridor down to her mother's room. All the air now, gray with hideous dawn, was streaked with those long lines of rain. She had to push through the rain.

Her mother lay asleep in bed. Maizie could not see her through the rain, but it was her mother. She knelt down by the side of the bed and stretched her arms over upon her mother's shoulders.

"Mother . . . Mother . . . Mother . . . Mother . . ."

In an instant her mother was there.

"Maizie! Darlin'! What on earth's the matter? Tell Mother what's the matter."

She drew her daughter up on the bed and held her in her arms. Maizie was rigid.

"Mother . . ."

"Mother's right here. Tell me, darlin'. Are you sick?"

"Yes, I'm sick. Mother . . . Mother . . . I want to go home. I've got to go home or I'll . . ."

"Home, darlin'?"

"I've got to go home to Virginia. Make them let me go home. They'll all try to keep me away from home. Oh! I'm so frightened, Mother. Mother . . ."

She muttered her words. Her eyes were dry.

Minnie May held Maizie's wrist in her fingers.

"It's too fast to count," she said. "Darlin', you're sick. I'm going right and call Lambert this minute and he'll drive you in town to your own doctor. We're going to get to the bottom of why you don't get well."

"Oh, no!" Maizie's voice rose shrilly. "Don't call him. Don't tell him. Please don't. It makes him so angry to be waked. . . . Promise me you won't call him."

"Maizie, you're shakin'. Tell Mother what you're scared of, darlin'. Did you have nightmares?"

She held her daughter close to her as if she were still a little girl, and rocked slightly.

"No . . . Oh, no . . . I've got to see Dr. Forbes. I've got to get to him before it's too late."

"Don't talk that way. You're goin' to be all right, yes, you are, Mother's baby. Now, you stay warm here under the covers and I'll go call Lambert."

"Oh, don't, Mother! Please, please . . . Just take me away and don't tell anyone. Don't leave me. I'm so frightened. I can't stand it any longer."

"Can't you tell Mother about it?"

"It's raining everywhere . . ."

Minnie May did not speak.

"Oh, please, please, Mother, take me away and get the doctor and make him let me go home. If I could just go home it would stop. . . . I could get out . . . Please, Mother . . ."

Minnie May began to get out of bed.

"I'm goin' down and phone to Dr. Forbes right this minute," she said. "I'm going to ask him what's right to do. You just stay here, darlin', and keep covered up, and I'll be right back and everything will be fine."

Maizie stared while her mother got into her dressing gown.

"You won't tell Lambert?"

"Honey, he's the first who'd want to know if you're sick. He'd want to drive you in, if that's to be done."

Maizie bit the knuckles of her fist.

"Ma'am. Ask the doctor . . . ask him now . . . ask him to let me go home. Oh please, Ma'am . . ."

"Maizie, darlin', you're in an awful state. I don't know what's the matter. But Dr. Forbes will be able to get you all straight. He'll do what's right. Now, don't you worry."

"Dad will," Maizie mumbled. Her heart hammered faster and faster and faster. "Dad will. He'll let me go home. Even if none of you will. Dad will."

She shook her head and her eyes were dry and bright like an animal's. Her mother was hurrying out of the door. Maizie could see her, through the gray and fast-falling rain. If she could just last out till she got to the doctor's office, she thought. . . . If she could hang on until she got home, back to Virginia, the world would clear.

They would try to stop her. She did not trust even her mother. Her father was there; she knew now that he had always been there. He would try to get her home. But could he? They were all lined up to stop her, all of them, and everywhere, shadowing them all, the tall dark figure, the hard dark face, Lambert, Lambert . . .

Why would he never die? Why could he not be killed? Why must he be in the world, making it gray and hideous and streaked with evil? Lambert, whom she loved; and her love was like . . .

Her love was hate, her love was hate, she hated him, she hated him murderously, for he had killed her and killed her again, she hated him. . . .

And in the silent house Maizie began to scream. It made no sound.


## CHAPTER XLII

ON AN AFTERNOON IN JUNE Betsy Jekyll Jayne stood on a curb on Park Avenue waiting for the lights to turn. She was going home from a day spent lying in a bathing-suit on a truckload of sea sand in a photographer's studio, posing for a color picture to be used in advertising.

In the five years since she had come to live in New York she had changed little. In particular, she had not changed inside; she felt the same about things; she was still governed by enthusiasm, by admiration untempered with criticism; she was still directed in her behavior by the behavior of those she admired. She had never judged anything that seemed attractive as other than attractive.

She would have said, if a reporter had interviewed her standing there at that instant on the curb, that she was a New Yorker. She liked feeling that she was a New Yorker. She dilated pleasurably to the song, *The Broadway Melody*, and to the line, "it's a fake, it's a phony, but it's my town. . . ." But she did not think it was a fake or a phony. She thought it was wonderful. She considered herself outstandingly lucky to be what she was, where she was. Anything that had gone wrong in five years, and things had gone wrong from time to time, she laid to her own unworthiness or stupidity. For she was vain without being self-confident. Her vanity was a youthful thing concerned with her person. She had no conviction of inner worth. The self-assurance which her appearance indicated was based purely on knowing that she was a good imitation of a model pieced together from New York types. She had no feeling of inferiority, but that was because she had confidence in the model in whose image she had formed herself.

She was not, however, conscious of this. She had no instinct for self-analysis. She could use the catch-words of Freudianism in conversation only because they were among the things she had picked up to use in making the New Yorker named Betsy Jayne. She collected and employed phrases, expressions, styles, accents, manners, like a magpie.

She was charming.

She stood quite still, in a red print dress and jacket and a white straw hat with a red ribbon. She looked like a picture in a fashion magazine, all except for one heel which showed a hole above the shoe. With all her talent for imitation she could never go far enough as to keep herself in real order. It was the Jekyll in her. There was always, if you looked for it, a little flaw somewhere; a hole, a run, a ripped seam; the edge of a pique collar, not soiled but not first-day fresh. She could never believe in her heart that such little things would ever be noticed.

She was now, in the early 'Thirties, the gallant manly type of girl instead of the pert boyish type that she had been in the 'Twenties. But that was fashion, and the times, which were late Prohibition. In just such a way, what she had now was glamour instead of "it". She admired Marlene Dietrich instead of Clara Bow. Her supply of energy and youth was undiminished. The surface, from the outside, was different; but the girl, inside, felt the same. She was still looking for something that she had not found; but she was still absolutely sure that she would find it. She had never been afraid. She had never visualized defeat or despair or shame. She was like a shining, brown, uncracked nut.

Nearly five years ago her sister Maizie had entered a sanitarium in Annestown, Virginia, where she still was. Various euphemisms were employed by the Jekyll family in speaking of the cause of Maizie's confinement. It was generally spoken of as a nervous breakdown. Betsy had never been able to grasp the cause or the reality; she thought of a nervous breakdown in terms of a tall, white-faced woman with streaming black hair, who pressed her hand to her bosom and was exhausted, too exhausted to lift her head from the pillow.

This image had nothing in common with her sister Maizie. She had seen changes in Maizie the year before little Honora had been born, but those changes were now blotted out in her mind; Maizie, when she thought of her, was a laughing, golden-haired young girl surrounded by beaux. What was this Maizie doing in the Annestown Retreat, which Betsy faintly remembered from her childhood, a brick building covered with ivy, set a little way back from the street?

Once, on a visit home to Hampton, Betsy had said, "I should think she'd get so *bored*, poor Maizie, cooped up there in that old sanitarium." Her mother glanced across the room at her father, who dropped his eyes; he looked sick. "Dr. Ellyot said," her mother murmured, "that Maizie's was a mighty small world. He said it was getting smaller. I don't like to think about it." Tom Jekyll got up and walked out of the room. "But why does it take so long to get over a nervous breakdown?" Betsy asked. "Takes time, honey. Everything takes right much time, things like that."

It was mysterious and unsatisfactory. They said "a mental condition," but what did that mean? Did it mean Maizie was crazy? She couldn't be crazy, not in the Jekyll family, and besides the Annestown Retreat wasn't an insane asylum; it was a place for people with nervous breakdowns.

Honora, who looked like Maizie, spent half her time with the Jekylls and half with Mrs. Rudd. She had a nurse who went with her from one house to the other to take care of her. She did not seem one of the family, but someone far more exciting. Jane and Glory played with her as if she had been some very superior form of doll. But Jane and Glory were far beyond the doll age now. Jane had come out in Boston last year at a dance Mrs. Rudd gave her at the Somerset, and Glory was in her last year at Miss Sheraton's and was going to have a dance at Mrs. Rudd's house in Manchester the summer after she graduated.

The Brats had changed. They were terribly Boston. There was a chasm between them and Betsy. They were like rather stiff strangers. When they came to New York for clothes they came to Betsy's apartment, but they looked at everything in a supercilious, Boston way. That was absurd, because everybody knew Bostonians would give their eyeteeth to be New Yorkers. There was no question in Betsy's mind but what her life was enviable. It was simply that her little sisters had turned out rather stuffy. No doubt they would learn better with age.

Everything was somehow different. The whole family was different. Everything was all shaken up. Jane was a member of the Junior League and the Vincent Club, and Glory was thick with all those healthy Sheraton girls. In Betsy's day it hadn't been like that. She thought of the family as a Southern family, transplanted to the North, but still Southern. They used to be that. But now they were a Boston family. Minnie May had done it, because it was what she had wanted and she always got what she wanted. There was nothing to do but admire her. But it made a difference. Betsy still would have sworn that her family was the gayest, the most marvellous family in the world, but perhaps, inside, she did not wholly feel it any more. Once the family had been there, a heart, a core, a whole. Now it was pieces. Maizie was gone and cancelled out from life, her child that she had left a doll, and Lambert gone away to live in Italy, because—this was one more thing that Minnie May had dropped—it made Maizie worse to see him. Dad was cancelled out too. He never talked when Betsy was at home; he sat behind his paper and Minnie May said he was tired; he looked old; he was some way withdrawn from what had been the family, so that he too was a minus quantity. The Brats were Boston debutantes; they talked with a Boston accent. They might have been daughters of another, a Boston family.

Minnie May was the same; tremendously the same while she was being quite different. She seemed to have conquered Boston, without ever striking her colors. She was still slapdash, exhilarated, and garrulous, and she went everywhere, knew everyone, was asked to serve on committees and be a patroness. Betsy said something about it once; that Minnie May had the stiff Bostonians eating out of her hand. "Pshaw, child," her mother said. "They're just people. They're just real shy, and real scared, and if you take 'em by surprise and make 'em laugh and hurry them along, why, they love it. They'd like to be like Southerners but they don't know how."

But the family was broken into bits. After all, and in the end, it seemed to be she, Betsy, who was the luckiest and the most spectacular of them.

Who would have thought it? It made her feel quite wide-eyed and thrilled. She was a New Yorker. She was seen at all the places. As a professional model, a Powers girl, her face was seen in advertisements in magazines. She was just not quite somebody. But there was lots of time. It took you a lot of quarters to hit the jackpot.

Betsy had been fired from her job on *Lady* nearly two years; she had worked in an advertising agency for a year and lost that job too; since then she had made her living posing for photographers and, occasionally, commercial artists; she was given five dollars an hour and her popularity ranked in the middle of the Powers models. By one means or another she had saved about five thousand dollars, which she had put in a savings bank. She felt shrewd about having done this, since most of her friends had lost their money in 1929. Actually it had not been intelligence that had protected her from the market, but the fact that she knew so many customers' men that she had never been able to decide which to intrust with her money. But she had forgotten that.

In her first year in New York she had married a young photographer named Wilson Jayne, in the middle of the night, over a weekend, in Maryland. This fact seemed vague and dreamlike to her now. She had not seen Willy for two years, since he had left for the promise of a job in California, and she had not lived with him for some time before that. Willy was a drunk. He was a thin, endearing, childlike character and she was very fond of him; their marriage seemed a dream partly because with him she had never felt quite grown-up, and there had been nothing grown-up about him or their relationship.

She had seldom seen him when he was not drunk. He was not a bad drunk, he was gentle and melancholy, and inclined to nostalgia. He was sweet; she had sat in numberless speakeasies with him holding his hand. He was so much sweeter than anybody else she knew that she had had an idea, that night she married him, that this was perhaps the right kind of way to be in love. But it was obvious to her in a day or two that she was not in love with him; the feeling she had about him did not change in the least the interest other men had for her. Nor was he any less fond of all sorts of other girls he knew. Neither of them minded. They lived for a while in an apartment hotel in West Fifty-fifth Street. Then Willy got involved with an Austrian girl who called herself a Countess, and after a while they simply stopped living in the same place. Neither of them ever got mad at the other; they loved each other very much, but it didn't matter.

The only thing that had ever happened to them that made them feel in the least married, was when Betsy discovered when they were in Fifty-fifth Street, that she was going to have a baby. Willy found out the name of a doctor, and one cold morning in January they had driven through the snowy stretches of Central Park, in a taxi, to an address far up in Manhattan, where the doctor had operated on Betsy. It was nothing very bad; she felt quite well the moment she came out of the gas they had given her; but Willy put his head in his arms, out in the waiting-room, and cried with fear and pity; the doctor's nurse had given him a drink of bonded whisky.

That was the only thing that they had ever done together. When she thought of him at all, now, Betsy thought of Willy with affection and amusement and a little worry for fear he might be in trouble out there on the Coast. There had never been the time or the desire to think about getting a divorce.

Betsy had had, in five years, a few colds, a case of trench-mouth, and influenza twice. She had lived in the Barrington, the Fifty-fifth Street place, and an apartment with another girl on Lexington Avenue; an apartment alone on Fifty-sixth Street, and now she lived on Forty-eighth Street in the top floor of a walk-up. She had been to Florida for two weeks on a posing job for a magazine, to race meets in Maryland with a horsy beau she had had at one time, to Martha's Vineyard to visit a girl, to Long Island on weekends of many widely varying kinds. She had picked up some French, and a smattering of German and Italian phrases.

She stood on the curb in her white hat with the red ribbon, sweating little beads on each side of her short nose. At this hour the day was limp and dusty, waiting, she always felt, to turn triumphantly into evening. She was on her way home and she had no engagement that night. She meant to spend the evening mending clothes and pressing the pleats of her dresses. But she also meant to, and knew self-indulgently that she would, make it a night off; a sybaritic evening, in bed reading magazines with cold cream on her face; shameful if you were the kind of girl who had nothing better to do, but luxurious if you knew you had only to pick up the telephone and call one of half a dozen men to spend the evening out instead.

The afternoon traffic swept by up Park Avenue: limousines with Wall Street men in back reading the paper, taxis, and cars with their tops down bound for Queensboro Bridge and Long Island. The hot, late sunshine climbed the buildings on the east side; the people walking north and south hurried across the street with an eye out for swooping cabs. Out of the traffic a funny little town-car bobbed, and pulled up directly at Betsy's feet; a Ford parody of elegance; the chauffeur jumped out and ran round like a mechanical doll to open the door. Somebody cool and lovely like a flower in a box leaned out and called.

"Betsy! Betsy! Get in."

It was Elizabeth Starr, the rich and well-known New York beauty who had once been Liz Symonds. Betsy had seen her only once since her marriage, when they had had lunch together; but she was one of the people Betsy read about.

Betsy jumped into the car as though she were jumping into a perfumed bath. It started uptown again.

They kissed each other lightly on the cheek and cried,

"Darling!"

Liz was noticeably the same; conspicuously without affectation or the grand manner. Betsy felt almost completely at home with her. With her bright eyes she took in all the delights: the thin black dress, the big black hat thrown on the floor, the big chunky ruby ring and the enchanting disarrangement of red curls. Among them was a wide streak of short gray hair also erect and curly, and all at once that was amazing and enviable. Here was perfection. Here was Mrs. Horatio Starr, Jr. It was all so attractive.

"What are you doing in town? I should think you'd be in the country."

Those pictures of Liz in shorts playing tennis in Southampton; laughing in a bathing suit at Newport.

"Horatio has had an attack of being indispensable and I am just the little woman. So here we are quietly melting away. How are you, *darling?* I'll take you home. Where?"

Betsy gave the address and Liz repeated it through the speaking tube.

"Please come up and have a drink. You've never seen this apartment. I've missed you terribly."

"Darling, it makes me *sick.* I never see anybody I want to see. Such boring people. I never have a minute."

This was of course nonsense. But Betsy appreciated her being so polite. Betsy had never borne a grudge in her life. She accepted changes cheerfully as inevitable. Being a New Yorker she knew you had to fight for what you got.

"Just come up a minute."

"Darling, I can't. I'd give anything to. But look! I have a brilliant idea. What are you doing tonight that you can't get out of?"

"I'm not doing anything," Betsy said, eagerly.

"You're dining with us then. Lord, what a load off my mind. We're living in the town house for a day or two and we've got this man. Horatio said we had to have him. A newspaperman or something like that," Liz said with a wonderful innocence, an utter ignorance of the ways in which people made their living. "Anyway he's writing a book about the Starrs. You know, the whole blush-making story. Horatio thought perhaps if we were nice to him he wouldn't rake so much muck. I don't agree. If we give him a heavenly dinner he'll just go away and make us more Bourbon than ever. So here we are saddled with this great *lump,* and I was terrified. I wouldn't know how to cope. Thank you so much, darling, for stepping in and saving me. I know you'll handle everything too beautifully. I can just relax."

It was done so gracefully. Liz was a clumsy, terrified little thing and Betsy was conferring a real favor. It wasn't at all that Betsy had been asked to fill in a four at the last minute chiefly to pacify her hostess' conscience at neglecting her old friend.

"I'd love to!"

When the little car pulled up smartly in front of the brownstone house made into apartments, Betsy jumped out laughing and nodding.

It was a lovely world where things like this popped up, quite unexpectedly.

The house of the younger Starrs, on a street near the river, was small and gay. Like the Ford town-car it was a sort of joke. Everything in it was cheerful and unimportant and pretty; there were surprises round every corner, little tricks of decoration that were all wit and no grandeur. It was a toy house arranged by a child having fun. As in all houses, there was an atmosphere here that had its speech to make: 'Isn't it silly to have so much money? And besides we lost most of it in that '29 business. For goodness' sake, we're not *rich!* We just want to have fun. There's nothing here that could scare anybody. We are rather divine, aren't we?'

The living-room had one dark-gray wall, one light-gray wall, one white wall and one pink wall. The cocktails were on a fat little table made entirely of glass, and Horatio Starr, a red-faced young man in his forties wearing a white dinner coat, mixed them himself. Liz sat on the pink buttoned sofa in a long pink and white striped cotton dress like a dairymaid's, with her feet drawn up and tucked under her. It was hard to see how anybody could be angry with such disarming people.

"Do you love rum, Mr. Connolly? I do."

The rather grim-faced young man sat on a tufted chair with a Daiquiri in one hand and a cigarette in the other.

Betsy smiled her childish smile at him. She had stepped into this atmosphere in her yellow dress and hugged it to her. Her eyes were very wide open.

"Have another, Connolly." Horatio Starr shook the glass shaker, with a swishing, tempting sound, and lifted his eyebrows towards his guest.

"Let's all get just the tiniest bit pie-eyed," Liz whispered, suggesting conspiracy.

Hector Connolly held out his glass and half-lifted himself from the chair in a compromise between two possible behaviors. Then he sat back. He had not quite caught hold of the atmosphere. He was much more serious than the other people in the room. He kept looking from one to the other of them and it was obvious that he was trying to catch on.

He had a big, heavy build like a football player's, under his black dinner-coat. It was quite a good dinner-coat, but a very serious one.

His face was big and long and pale. It would have been handsome if it had not been so big. He had thick, colorless hair brushed very smooth and straight to the side. He had a way of thrusting out his chin suddenly, but he seemed to realize that he was doing it and that there was nothing to do it for, and then he would retract it.

A man in a white pea-jacket came to the door and bowed.

"Yes, Jean," Liz murmured.

"Shall we let ourselves be buffaloed?" Horatio Starr said, looking at his wife.

"They treat us like dirt," Liz whispered to the others. "They absolutely *run* us, Mr. Connolly. They're so stern. I'm going to *assert* myself, by golly. I'm going to have another drink. Darling, give me another drink. We'll all have another drink and *show* them."

She was so very pretty. The red curls and the white one stood straight on end in defiance. She set her jaw.

Mr. Connolly laughed.

After a while they all got up and went down the little staircase to the dining-room.

One side was all glass and looked out over the garden, which was now illuminated like a little stage. Instead of being placed round the table, the chairs with their violet and white striped seats were one at each end and the other two behind the table facing the scene, as children might rearrange their seats so as to look at what they pleased. Liz and Horatio sat at either end. Liz bounced up and down twice and then kept as still as a mouse while the butler brought in the soup.

"Black bean!" Liz cried. "Oh, I love it so. I don't see why I can't ever have just soup for my dinner when I love it so."

Hector Connolly gave just one, instantaneous glance at the big spoon in his hostess's hand and picked up his and began to eat.

"You been many years on the *Dispatch?*" Horatio asked his guest, quite shyly.

"No. I've only been in New York a couple of months. I was on the Pittsburgh *Progress.*"

"Was it awfully smoky?" Liz asked.

"Pretty smoky." Hector Connolly laughed.

Betsy leaned both elbows on the table like a child and gazed at the man beside her.

"I love to hear newspapermen talk," she said. "So sort of experienced sounding."

"Out of the corner of my mouth?" Hector Connolly glanced at her.

"Oh, no!"

"Do you *come* from Pittsburgh, Mr. Connolly?" Liz asked, blinking very seriously and taking an intelligent interest.

"Well, no. I'm sort of a Southerner. You probably never heard of it. Annestown, Virginia."

"*Not* Annestown, *Virginia!*"

Betsy put down her fork and switched entirely around in her chair so that she was sitting sidewise facing Hector Connolly. She put her elbows on her knees and her chin on her fists and beamed.

"But I don't believe it! It's not true! Look, I come from Annestown, Virginia, my whole family, I lived on Pinckney Street for centuries, all my entire childhood. . . . Don't look so calm about it!"

He smiled uneasily, but he stopped eating and looked at the flushed and shining face that leaned toward him. He almost turned around in his chair too. His voice held no trace of Southern accent. It was part Irish, part city; hard and truculent and defensive.

"You wouldn't have known me," he said. "I was on the other side of the railroad tracks."

"But there's nobody on the other side of the railroad tracks but the negroes. Didn't you ever know my sister, anyway? My name used to be Jekyll. She was Maizie Jekyll."

"Oh, yes, the Jekyll family," he said. "Oh, yes. I saw you all. In fact I lived right down the street from you. But you wouldn't have known me. We didn't know anybody but Catholics and there aren't many Catholics there. And hell, I haven't been there since I was fifteen," he added roughly.

Betsy stared at him without moving. The plates were changed again but she didn't turn back to the table. Horatio Starr talked, and Liz winked at him.

"I remember," Betsy said. "I haven't been back since I was terribly young, either, but I remember where you lived. You had that house behind the fence. On the corner. And there were always fires burning in the yard. And a lot of children."

"And, spit it out, you weren't allowed to associate with them."

"Wasn't I?"

She looked like a young angel, rosy and healthy in her clean yellow dress. Nobody could be angry with her, or suspect her. Hector Connolly's heavy white face smiled reluctantly.

"Okay," he said. "I'm Irish. I've got a chip on my shoulder. You're not responsible for the way your people were. Skip it. I didn't say you looked down on me."

Betsy shuddered and squinted up her eyes.

"What an embarrassing idea. God. I can't *believe* it, that you lived in Annestown. Why, do you know I never met anyone before that came from Annestown. I mean, nobody comes from Annestown. Except us," she added cosily. "Do you remember Miss Addie Lane? The one with the red parasol who had fits sometimes when she was downtown? She had one in Williston's drugstore once when I was a child."

He laughed out loud, a harsh, eager laugh, and this time, glancing first at Liz, who was paying no attention to him, and moving self-consciously, he too turned around in his seat and faced Betsy. In a few moments he had forgotten himself and was laughing and talking without taking his eyes from her face. He seemed almost like the others.

"This is a divine dessert," Liz shouted plaintively. "I worked my fingers to the bone making it. I wish somebody would pay me some compliments."

Hector Connolly turned back to his plate and his face turned heavy and conscious again.

"You never did a stroke of work in your life, Mrs. Starr," he said. "You're joking, of course."

"Well, I didn't make this dessert, except in spirit, but by golly I've done plenty of work. Haven't I, Bets? Didn't we two stoke coal side by side for years in the stinkhole of *Lady?*"

"We certainly did."

Hector Connolly raised his eyebrows. It was the expression of a diplomat in a movie.

"No kid," he said.

"I wish you'd let *me* find who you know that I know. Pittsburgh. . . . Did you ever know Evelyn Swift?"

"Yes. I knew that piece."

Liz never flinched. It was true enough that she had worked for years before she met Horatio Starr and some time before he married her. But she had shed whatever was unnecessary from those years. She had an air of charming and befuddled innocence, a cockeyed irresponsibility, the childishness of one who had always had a great deal of money.

"Tell me, did you see much of her?"

"Not too much. She was a friend. . . ."

"A good friend? Spill the beans, do. I always thought she was a naughty girl."

"I was going to say, she was a friend of my wife's."

"Oh. I wonder if I ever knew your wife."

"You probably do. Her name was Cornelius. Baby Cornelius. She divorced me last year."

"I'm frightfully sorry." A variety of expressions drifted quickly across Liz's face. "I'm frightfully sorry I brought it up," she repeated.

"It's okay."

Connolly's face was heavy and defiant, and at the same time proud.

Liz jumped up from the table and swung her wide striped skirts around her and began to chatter.

"Let's have coffee outside. They *hate* to give it to us outside. The French. Outdoors. But I don't see why I can't sit in my own garden, do you, darling," she said, hooking her arm through her husband's.

Beyond the glass wall was a little fairyland. The bluish floodlights lit up the curly white iron chairs, the rows of geraniums in pots, the star-shaped stepping stones, the little iron version of a Madame Recamier sofa. Outside and above and beyond and all around, the city roared, but this was like a private kingdom fixed just so within the walls. The grown-up world howled outside, its radios blared, its children cried in the tenements across the street, its traffic rushed and screamed and hooted, but this was the garden of two children playing house.

"Do you like my rose tree? I raised it from seed."

"You're an awful liar, darling."

"Aren't I?"

Furthermore it was impossible not to feel friendly and confiding, in this blue artificial moonlight where faces were only partly seen, where cigarettes glowed for an instant. The coffee cups made a cosy chinking noise as they were set down in their saucers. A tray of drinks was brought out and for a time the lights in the dining-room shone and then they were extinguished. The ice rattled in the glasses.

"Mr. Connolly, I bet you hate me for making a break at dinner," Liz said sadly much later in the middle of something her husband was saying. "It makes me so unhappy."

Connolly cleared his throat.

"No. I love you, Mrs. Starr."

"I love you too, Mr. Connolly. What a relief."

She gave a loud sigh. Connolly cleared his throat again in the darkness.

The butler in the white coat came to the glass door and spoke in French. Horatio Starr got up.

"Do you want me too, darling? Look, will you excuse us just a very few minutes? It's about this horrible little boat of Horatio's. If I don't stand at his elbow the man who runs it will skin him. You go on talking about your childhoods, will you, darlings?"

They were silent in the garden. Betsy's dress was like a beam of yellow light across the blue-white chair. Connolly got up to make himself another drink.

"I suppose you speak French too, Mrs. Jayne," he said in his angry voice.

"Hardly any. The man said the captain of the boat wanted to speak to him."

"Jesus Christ. I suppose the horrible little boat of Horatio's," he said, in a shrill falsetto, "is the god damned *Andromeda*. Just a few thousand tons, that's all. Just a lousy little rowboat, something to get around in."

Betsy giggled.

"You've got to admit they're divine."

"What do you mean, divine? Oh, all right. I admit they're not like what I thought they'd be. I suppose it's an act. But Mrs. Starr seems like a good kid. All right."

"It isn't an act," Betsy said earnestly. "Honestly. I've known her a long time and she's sweet and natural and *everything*. She never put on an act in her life."

He had filled his glass; he walked across the garden in the clear, synthetic moonlight and stood in front of Betsy, looking down at her. She tipped her head back. She looked up at him.

"Hello," she whispered.

"Hello, kid."

He bent down very slowly and kissed her on the lips. Then he stood up. She reached out and took his hand and pulled him down on the iron sofa beside her. Then she simply went on staring at him, with her mouth breaking into little smiles.

"I knew something wonderful was going to happen to me tonight," she said in a small, breathless voice. "I knew it. I had a kind of a feeling."

He went on drinking from his glass and looking at her.

"Don't kid me," he said, and cleared his throat. "I'm not the boy to kid."

"I don't want to kid you. I don't expect you to feel the same way. It's just me. I just feel about seventeen."

"Like to go dancing, later?" he asked abruptly.

"Yes. Let's!"

"I guess we can get away."

"Yes. I didn't expect to meet you."

"All right, I didn't expect to meet you either. I didn't expect a lot. These Starrs—are they really on the up-and-up?"

"They're just people like anybody else, only more attractive."

"She is. They're just capitalists. No matter how thin you slice it. She's quite a girl for pulling the wool over your eyes, isn't she?"

"But she isn't pulling any wool. She's always been just the same. We used to room together when she made thirty-five dollars a week."

"Well. . . . Look, you say when you're ready to go, and I'll say I'll take you home, see?"

"Yes," she whispered. She squeezed his hand and looked at him shyly in the blue light and took her hand away. The Starrs came back, talking about their boatman.

When Betsy went to get her wrap to go, Liz went with her to the upstairs room. She sprawled on the bed while Betsy did her face. For a moment it was almost like the old days in the Barrington.

"He's kind of a rough diamond, isn't he? Queer. I'm always scared to death of those kind of men. They'd like to put a bomb under Horatio, I can see it in their eye. But you did marvels, darling, marvels. Thank God for dear old where's-it, whatever the place is you both came from."

"I think he's divine."

"You do? That's nice, dear. You know who he makes me think of?"

"Who?"

"Horatio's cousin Oren. Golly, weren't you in love with him once or something? Maybe you run true to form. The same kind of queer business, kind of abrupt business, unpredictable; they've got the same *thing*. You can have it."

"What's Oren doing now?" Betsy was putting on lipstick. She looked wide-eyed at herself in the glass.

"Oh, you know. Funny places, Brioni in summer and Sestrières in winter, but still always well within the pale. He isn't a *real* rebel. I bet you this man downstairs isn't either. You know why?"

"Why?"

"His wife. Pittsburgh Cornelius. Lots and lots of money. It's all very well a newspaper and books about wicked tycoons, but that was a perfectly respectable dinner coat. I'd say he was the class-conscious thing, dead set against the rich and marrying them at the drop of a hat, trying to be chic and saying he hates it because he doesn't think he's doing it right. Don't let me put you off. He's probably divine."

Betsy stood up. She put on a short yellow jacket that matched her dress. In the doorway of the bedroom Liz put her arms around Betsy. Liz smelled of some far-away delicious perfume; for an instant a snatch of something forgotten, sweet and nostalgic, and in an instant lost. They kissed each other affectionately. They might have been nearest and dearest friends.

There was no formality about departing. The butler did not even appear. Starr got Connolly's hat himself. "Can't I get you a taxi?" he asked anxiously.

"Let's walk!" Betsy cried. Connolly shook hands.

Starr opened the little red front door, and Liz stood waving as they climbed the steps to the brightly-lighted, still hot street.

"*Amusez-vous bien, mes enfants!*"

"What the hell does that mean?" Connolly said as they started to walk west.

" 'Have a good time.' But I didn't tell her we were going dancing!"

"Why not say, *have a good time?*"

"Isn't it funny how people know what you're going to do?" she said.

At four o'clock in the morning they came walking slowly down Forty-eighth Street arm in arm. The city was quieter, closed up. It seemed very calm. In the empty, dark street a policeman tried an areaway door, singing to himself . . . *"No more money in de bank. . . ."* Across the still city came the hoarse sound of a boat-whistle on the North River.

Betsy unlocked the downstairs door of the brownstone house and they went up the three narrow, dimly lighted flights to the top, and she unlocked the second door. The keys she took from her evening purse were attached with a chain that ended in a huge, hard pearl. He put out a finger and touched it. "They were giving them away at the opening of a new speakeasy," she said. "Nice," he said. They went directly into a square room that was faintly lighted from outdoors, through windows giving on the back. She began groping towards a light. He followed her and pulled her outstretched arm under his. "Let's look out of the window."

It was not yet dawn. The sky was dull whitish dark and the shapes of a few high buildings stood out, their edges blurred; in some of the towers an occasional light burned far away, single and remote; who was there, in this lonely hour, and what did they do? Whoever they were, they too were awake and living, across the air. His arm was round her shoulders and after a while he turned her to face him and stood looking down at her in the darkness.

"I don't just love you, I'm in love with you," she whispered.

He made a sound, not quite words.

"I've never been able to be in love, but it's what I've always wanted," she said.

They began to move away from the window, with their arms entwined. They went slowly through the obscurity before them, into the next room. In that unseen place they leaned down, separately, bent and turned, and at intervals each reached out a hand in a caress to still the qualms of the other.

They lay smoking cigarettes side by side in the dawn that had come.

"I suppose you won't believe me," she said at last, "that this is the only time in my life it's ever been right."

"How about your husband?"

"That wasn't even anything at all. This way."

He turned his head and looked at her in the early light.

"I believe you if you tell me it's so," he said.

"I feel as if it was the first time. The first time that ever counted."

"But it's not the first time. . . ."

"I've done it with two men," she said. "A lawyer, and a broker."

"I don't want to know who they were. I've never been exactly celibate myself. I've gotten over a lot of ideas about women I used to have. I mean about chastity."

"But they don't seem real. Nothing happened. They don't count, do they, when they didn't mean anything?"

"I don't know. . . . I guess anybody gets a part of you if you give it away."

"But I never gave anything away."

He pressed her hand gently. They smoked in the silence.

"No, three," she said suddenly. "Another broker."

"You don't have to tell me."

"But I want to tell you. I want everything to be clear and right."

"Everything will be all right. If you just tell me the truth."

"Oh, I want to! I want to tell you the truth."

"Good," he said softly.

There was another silence.

"Does it feel at all different to you?" she whispered. "Isn't it a little bit new for you too?"

"You're a sweet kid," he said. "I love you."

"Was it . . . was it better with your wife?"

"I don't know. It was different."

"I'm jealous of her," she whispered.

"You needn't be. It's dead as hell. I was a bastard to her and it's all washed up long ago."

"I wouldn't care if you were a bastard to me. I want you to be any way you want to me."

"I don't want to bitch anyone ever any more."

"You wouldn't. You couldn't hurt me. I love you."

He turned on his elbow and looked down on her, and his hand picked up a lock of her brown hair and twisted it.

"You want to stick around with me?" he murmured.

"I want to stick around with you all the time."

"You've got lovely hair. I wish you'd grow it out long. You don't look like a woman, you look like a boy. Do you want to be a woman?"

"I want to be a woman. . . ."

## CHAPTER XLIII

IN JULY they were living together. Everything about life had been changed. Hector worked at the *Dispatch* rewrite desk from two till ten in the evening; he didn't want to go to bed for a few hours after that, and he slept all morning. On Betsy's appointment pad in the Powers' office a card was pinned that said, "Will not take appointments in A.M." Only a few of the most popular models could afford to be choosy without suffering for it, and Betsy's demand noticeably fell off. Her long, curly hair was not in fashion, either, and it was not quite long enough to do up. Mr. Powers said, pleasantly, "Mrs. Jayne, are you *crazy?* The other hair-do just suited your type." But Betsy did not care. Nothing mattered. She was keyed to highest tension, her thoughts were possessed, she was a new self. It was exactly as if all of this new feeling had been there all the time, waiting; it felt that way; as though this was the way she was meant to feel. Passionate, obsessed, insatiable; voracious for the love that was the staff of her life and nourished on it; giving herself from her depths, from her bone and her blood, and receiving it again from the man that she must have. She fed upon his virility; this was the way that women felt, and now she wanted more than anything in life to live as a woman.

After Hector had left the apartment she would get ready to go to any posing appointment she might have, or if there was none, she would move about the rooms absently, cleaning, straightening, bathing herself, dusting. If Hector had time to eat dinner comfortably he would telephone to her and she would walk over west in the long twilight of daylight saving time to eat with him at some restaurant off Broadway. The time seemed very empty when she was apart from him; it was time to kill. At ten in the evening she would arrive at the *Dispatch* building and wait upstairs in the waiting-room by the elevators, outside the city-room, until he came out to meet her.

On a July night she was walking on West Forty-eighth Street looking in the windows of the restaurants, filled with hand-painted menu signs and live lobsters, dawdling to use up the extra minutes. She felt lonely and happy; her loneliness was a kind little thing, an imitation of what she would feel if she were not going to see Hector in a quarter of an hour. She sang under her breath as she strolled; a month ago she would have been interested in watching the people passing; but now she lived in her dream and her heart sang all the time . . . "I can't live without you. . . ." A man hurrying by in a blue suit looked back over his shoulder at her, and then turned round and went back. He had no hat on his thick, curly hair.

"Bets! Hello, how are you?"

"Hello, Laudy," she said. They shook hands. He was a young theatrical producer named Lauder Beam.

"What on earth are you walking along here for at this time of night? Not batty, are you, darling? I never see you anywhere any more. You've deserted us," he said.

"I'm on my way to meet my beau," she said, looking at him with a face bemused and happy.

"Beau, hm?"

"I'm in love," she said. She wanted to tell him, to tell anyone. "I'm really in love. That's why I never go anywhere any more. I don't want to see anyone else."

He looked disconcerted.

"Well," he said. "Happy, hm?"

"I'm terribly, terribly, divinely happy."

He looked embarrassed but kindly too.

"I've never felt like that. Retiring from the world stuff. The world forgetting, by the world forgot."

"That's it," she said. "That's how it feels."

"That was a quote. Betsy. . . . Can I take you anywhere?"

"Oh, no. Thank you."

"Good luck," he said. "I hope it all turns out fine."

She gave him an absent-minded, dazzling smile and he turned and hurried down the street again.

She continued on, and around the corner and down Broadway, crowded and noisy and full of flashing lights. She crossed.

Hector came out with a reporter named John Hannon and they all went down in the elevator together. Hannon was a short, stocky man who talked a lot, and they all walked up Broadway and up Fifty-second Street to a speakeasy, where Hannon was meeting his girl. She was a blue-eyed brunette who looked gentle and domestic; she and Hannon held hands on top of the table. They ordered four whiskies. The brunette was with Hannon and Betsy was with Hector. The two men talked about Walker and told the girls cracks that had been got off in the city-room and about the new man on the desk from Cincinnati. The brunette had a very soft, low voice and Betsy saw she loved Hannon and it made her like the girl. It was nice, relaxed and kind, unlike any New York life Betsy had ever known before.

Betsy had her back to the smoky room. Somebody put a hand on her shoulder and said, "Hello, beautiful." She looked up at a man named Jock Hamilton, whom she had seen several times at parties on Long Island. He looked tight. He bent over and kissed her. "You beautiful thing," he said. "How's Catherine?" Hector and Hannon stood up. They stood with grave shut faces looking Jock Hamilton up and down.

"Oh . . ." she said. "Mr. Hamilton. Mr. Connolly, Mr. Hannon."

"Let me tell you you've got one of the most beautiful girls in New York with you," Jock exclaimed. His large handsome eyes shone.

The two men stood still and did not speak. Jock Hamilton looked at all their faces.

"Got to be running along," he cried. "Got the night before me!" He went out through the curtained doorway.

"Who was that son-of-a-bitch?" Hector asked. The two men sat down slowly, warily.

"A man I used to see around. An actor."

"You seem to have known some of the God damnedest bastards," Hector said. His big, white, Irish face glanced angrily from left to right. "I'd like to paste that son-of-a-bitch."

"He *looks* like a ham," Hannon said.

"I wish I'd taken a crack at that fat face while I had a chance." Hector was restless; he did not seem to be sitting all the way down in his chair.

Betsy looked at him pleadingly.

"He didn't do anything to you," the brunette said softly. She laughed, a reasonable, womanly, healing laugh.

"What in hell did he mean kissing you?"

"Darling, everybody does things like that in New York. Don't they?" she appealed to Hannon.

"Yeah, they do."

"I don't like it. I don't like to sit here with my finger up my nose taking it."

"It doesn't mean anything."

The brunette talked softly, soothingly; Hannon was practical and dismissed matters; Betsy kept looking at the large, pale, furious face she loved.

"Okay," he said at last. "You boys win. I'm a hick and I can't take it." He put one hand on his hip and ogled Hannon. "I think it's just too wonderful, your New York. Do you suppose anyone will take a fancy to me?"

"You don't have to see people you don't like," the brunette said gently. "You can just stay around with the people you like."

She looked at Hannon and smiled. Her dark blue eyes were beautiful.

"You tired, sweet?" Hannon asked her. "Want to go home?"

"Not unless you want to. It's only midnight."

They were such nice people and Betsy liked them. They were like people in a small town, Annestown or Hampton. There was something about being in love with Hector that made her like people like Hannon and the brunette. They got up in a little while and said good-bye and left. Hector was on his fourth drink. She put out her hand palm up on the table-cloth. He put his hand over it, but bent, so that the fingers tapped her palm restlessly.

"What's the matter, my darling?"

"Son-of-a-bitch drove me nuts. Sorry." His fingers tapped her palm as if it had been the top of a desk. "Let's go somewhere else."

When he was tired from work, and when he was a little tight, he never wanted to rest. They went out and walked fast up Fifth Avenue. Betsy held his arm. They did not linger to look in the shop-windows as they often did. Hector did not even glance at the displays of expensive men's clothes. Generally he liked to stand and look over each item and talk about them; clothes were one of his obsessions and he liked to talk for hours about good leather and good tweed and the right cut for lapels. His interest went oddly with his tough manner and his bold, pale face.

At Fifty-eighth Street they boarded a bus and climbed on top and rode uptown. Although he did not talk, he put his arm around Betsy and she leaned her head back on it, feeling faint with love for him and a longing that she did not quite understand. They got out and walked again, and went to a Cuban speakeasy in lower Harlem. Hector knew how to drink tequila with salt and lemon and he was proud of his technique. They danced to the rowdy rumba band.

"You really can dance," he said finally, looking down at her and smiling. The relief she felt was so strong that her heart skipped a beat.

"So can you."

"We're hot. Look at that little piece over there. Look at her shake. I bet you the tarbrush did a good half of the work there."

They sat in the noisy smoky place and looked at all the flamboyant, screaming, dark-eyed dancers, who drew apart and shook their hips, then snatched back to each other.

"What filth," he said. "What foulness. They oughtn't to allow stuff like that."

She looked at him in surprise.

"I thought you liked Cuban music. I thought you liked this kind of thing. How do you mean, filth?"

He shook the salt-shaker, making a little pile of salt before him on the table.

"I get funny sometimes," he said. "Don't mind me. You've got a pure mind, haven't you? I've got a dirty mind. Don't forget I was a Catholic once. I've got a lot of it in me. Not that I've been to confession for years and years."

He rested his head on his hand.

"Let's go home," she said. "Don't feel bad."

"I've bitched everything I ever did," he said. "My mother considers me as dead, you know. Because of the Church. To say nothing of some of the other pretty things I've done. I'll tell you this much," he said, raising his voice roughly. "You don't know anything. You think the world is kind and decent and good, because you were sheltered. I've seen everything. Did you know I came damned near being a Party member once? Me, that was once a Catholic. Oh, yes, I've been around and I know all about that stuff. You better go away and give me a wide berth. I'm bad. No wonder the society people spit on me. I'd spit on me. I've done everything. Do you want me to tell you something I've done?"

"If you want to."

"I've slept with a Negress. Why don't you get up and walk off? What are you sitting here for?"

Her eyes were full of tears.

"All I know is that I love you with all my heart," she said.

He lifted his other hand and buried his whole face.

"And furthermore I can't take it," he said, sitting up straighter. "Come on, let's get out of here."

He was very assiduous in holding the doors open for her as they passed out of the place.

They walked downtown from Harlem through Central Park in the night. The towers rose from the south and hung the sky with spangles. They walked arm in arm, and near Seventy-second Street, alone on the dark blank path, Hector pulled Betsy around to him and kissed her.

"I don't mean to make you unhappy," he said. "Jesus knows I don't mean that."

"You don't. You don't."

"Let's sit down here. I want to sit on a park bench with my girl. Like this?"

"I love it."

"We might be sitting on a park bench in Paris," he said. "I feel like this is the way it would be. The air smelling nice and dirty at the same time. I've always wanted to go to Paris. Would you like to go to Paris, sweet? Crap," he said roughly. He sounded embarrassed.

"You're always so ashamed of feeling sentimental."

"You're getting me over it, I'll say that. Well, I'll settle for New York. I'm getting to like this place."

"I love it. Don't you think it's wonderful? It's got everything."

"Maybe it has, maybe it has. I'm a suspicious bastard. Sometimes I think I've got paranoia."

"I thought that was insane."

"I'm not any too sensible sometimes. Sometimes I've suspected my own mother of things. . . . Make me have some sense, will you? Make me keep on enjoying life the way I do now."

She rubbed her cheek against his.

"You're true to me, aren't you?" he asked.

"I've never looked at one person since I met you."

"You haven't had time, baby. You be true to me."

"I'll be true to you all my life. I swear it. I belong to you."

"That's what I want."

"Don't you know I belong to you?"

"I guess maybe I do. If you say so. You just keep telling me the truth, will you? It's the only thing I still believe in, telling the truth."

Her head pressed against his coat.

"I never met anybody before like you," she said.


Week after week through the summer passed and they were happy discovering about each other and making new habits together. A sort of cult grew up with them; he was man, she was woman; he was to dominate, she was to give way. Part of the time it was a little game that they played. When they shopped for food she would carry the packages. "Woman's work," they called it, smiling at each other. Part of the time it was something passionate, a deep obbligato to their lovemaking, played on the bass strings of their senses; male and female. As a basis for living it grew along with the piling days in which they had lived together.

Hector had Wednesday off each week. They had a special way of living on Wednesdays. He used to lie in bed after they woke up, and doze while she got their breakfast in the little kitchen. They ate the things they liked best, and like married people they had their little habits: English muffins, and orange marmalade, and black Guatemala coffee. Betsy had introduced Hector to Guatemala coffee. He had an odd manner when anything new was introduced to him: he was curious and learned all about it in a few minutes, he seemed to master it and make it part of his information; at the same time he was somehow truculent, as though he did not like it that there was anything new for another person to show him. And afterwards he did not like to be reminded that he had not always known about it.

It was after one o'clock one afternoon when he came out of the bedroom in his thin, brown silk dressing-gown. She had the breakfast spread on a table before the sofa that faced the windows. The windows were open and the yellow curtains blew inward on a breeze that was hot and carried the sounds of the sunny city, the sound of hammering and the sound of radios. The terra-cotta head of Betsy stood on the top of the bookcase, the chin tilted back, the hair swept from the ears; against the pale gray walls it looked adventurous and triumphant. They drank their orange juice curled up on the sofa side by side, and lit cigarettes to finish their coffee with.

"I love the way the first cigarette *knocks* you, don't you?" She put her legs up over the arm of the sofa and leaned back against his shoulder and watched the smoke rise from her cigarette and run out of the window.

"How would you like to go to the movies?"

"No."

"How would you like to stay right here?"

"Yes!"

"You're such a nice, inexpensive, easily pleased girl." He turned his head and kissed her cheek.

"We'll just sit around, and we can get dinner here, and drink some of the brandy."

"Are you ashamed of me?"

She sat up and twisted around to look at him.

"Well, are you? Or am I kind of a gigolo you keep hidden. A fancy man you keep in his place."

"Are you insane? You're being funny."

"Partly. . . . You never write your mother anything about me, do you?"

"How could I? Dear Mother, I am living in sin with a man. His name is Hector Connolly."

"All right, all right, all right. Skip it."

"I don't want to skip it. Don't you know I feel like saying my prayers out of thankfulness every time I look at you?"

"Did you write your mother about the other men you lived in sin with?"

"Hector, don't be this way. I told you, I never *lived* with any of them."

"One night stands, eh?"

"Hector, don't."

"How many of them did you say there were?"

"Three."

"How am I compared with them? How do you rate me?"

"Hector, don't spoil everything. Nobody ever meant anything to me at all until I met you. I can't remember anything about them."

"Suppose I went away a couple of nights? Suppose you could remember anything about me?"

"If I can't have you I don't want anything, ever."

He pulled her into his lap and held her.

"I'm sorry," he said. "I don't know why I have to hurt you. To show myself you really do love me, I suppose. The itch to dominate. Like I had to practically kill my wife."

"Don't say 'my wife'," she whispered. "It makes me jealous. She's not your wife now. I'm your wife."

"I used to get so drunk. Christ, how drunk. I'll tell you something. I threw her down a flight of stairs once. It broke one of her teeth. Like something a drunken Irishman in a tenement would do, isn't it? Well, I'm Irish. We don't like feeling anybody's out to destroy us. You'd better clear out. You want me to throw you down some stairs?"

"She must have done something wrong. You couldn't hurt somebody unless they hurt you. You couldn't hurt me. I love you too much."

"She didn't do anything wrong. She was just being her. Just Baby Cornelius, the sweet little blonde thing with a lot of money and been to the best schools. She went to school in Switzerland, too. She just trudged along after me, picking me up when I got drunk, and once in a while I'd paste her. Then she'd give me something. She couldn't think of anything else to do. She gave me this dressing-gown. Got it at Sulka's."

"She should have known better than just to buy things."

"Don't criticize her, God damn it. I feel loyal as hell to her. She got God's dirtiest deal. I don't see how she stuck as long as she did."

Betsy was silent.

"She was just as good family as you are, you know that? Not only rich. She was a beautiful girl before I went to work on her. She got kind of battered. But they'll fix her up, now they've got her back, Elizabeth Arden and a trip to Paris."

"Why didn't she stick?"

"Oh . . . I told you she took a beating. She wasn't brought up to live in a tenement with a drunken Irishman. No, that's not it. I'll tell you. She found me with a girl she knew. We were lying on Baby's bed. What the hell."

"I'd take it if you were untrue to me. It would kill me, but I wouldn't leave you."

"I wasn't untrue to her. Only that one time. But I wanted to be. I used to want to be; all those damned smooth babes; loose, too; loose. But I never was, just that once. But that mattered to her. She never looked at anybody, even after I'd paste her one and go off drunk, maybe. She got thin, and her eyes got bigger and bigger. It wasn't any good with her any more. But I didn't. I only wanted to. I'm not trying to justify myself. I did do it, and I'll tell you who it was. That bitch Evelyn Swift your friend Mrs. Starr asked me about. She was quite a job; tall. But then everything started to end and it never was any good anyway and nobody was happy ever. Poor little Baby Cornelius, that married that big no-good of a mucker. Poor Baby."

He got up and lit himself another cigarette and went over to the window. The sill came to his hips and he leaned out on his elbows; his shoulders made a big dark shape against the light. The quality of the day had imperceptibly changed to afternoon; it was afternoon sunshine and the sound of hammering was an afternoon sound.

After a while he turned on his elbow and leaned there, looking at Betsy. He was smiling now.

"What's the matter with you?"

"It makes me unhappy when you're so unhappy."

"I don't want any more unhappy women around."

"All right, darling."

"You are a good girl, aren't you? Do just what I tell you to. You know what I want?"

"What?"

"I want a happy home. I want a nice, cheerful place and a nice, cheerful girl, and not to be the way I've always been any more. I want a girl that's a fine hearty piece, begorra, and causes me no whit of worry in the world."

"That's me. You've got me tied up and delivered."

"Have I so?"

"I want that too," she said. "A happy home. I want something solid. I've never had anything . . . solid. We've got it, haven't we?"

"Let's see," he said, coming to her. "Let's experiment around and see how solid."

She got up and put her arms around him. They left the breakfast dishes on the table and walked through the room entwined. Hector stopped in front of the head of Betsy. It was now in full sun.

"I don't like that girl," he said.

"You don't? Why not?"

"She looks too damned cocky. She doesn't look like a woman. I like this girl better. She's getting awfully big and beautiful," he murmured. "Her hair is getting awfully long. She's growing up to be a woman."

"You're a man and I'm a woman."

In the evening he stood in the doorway and watched her cook their dinner; the pots on the little stove steaming, the yellow lights falling on her flushed, concentrated face. They had soup and chicken and salad and cheese, and a bottle of red Italian wine. Afterwards she washed the dishes and he stood in the doorway again and made personal remarks in a teasing voice. They went into the living-room and sat on the sofa together again and Betsy brought out a portfolio of pictures of her family and showed them all to him. He asked questions intently and seemed fascinated by the smallest autobiographical facts concerning them; but he also seemed angry that she was telling him anything that he did not already know.

He took his billfold out of his inside pocket.

"Want to see my mother?"

"I'd love to! I didn't know you had a picture."

He passed over a small snapshot of a woman standing in the doorway of a frame house. Her arms were folded and her hair pulled back. Her face was thin and serious.

"She's a beautiful, good woman," he said defensively. "She's had a lot to endure."

"I think she's lovely. I wish I could meet her."

"She's not speaking to her oldest son. But she'd like you."

All at once it seemed as if her heart would break.

"Oh, darling, darling. I love you so."

But the day after, when Betsy met Hector in a restaurant off Broadway for dinner, he came in hurriedly and did not look directly at her; he tapped with his fingers on the table and kept looking around the room.

"What's the matter?"

"Nothing."

They had clams first.

"What's the matter?"

"Nothing, I say. . . . Why did you say you liked the way newspaper-men talked?"

*"What?"*

"At Mrs. Starr's," he said impatiently. He still would not look at her. "You said you just loved the way newspapermen talked." It was his shrill, bitter falsetto.

Her heart was beating thickly, heavily. She was glad he could not see it, pounding there inside her.

"I don't know why. I just said it. . . ."

"Did you mean you liked the way Don Garrett talked?"

"What are you talking about?" she said.

Now he turned his eyes and looked directly at her. He leaned forward on the table.

"All I want is for you to tell me the truth, baby," he said. "God help me, I wouldn't do anything to you. I just want the truth. If you really love me you'll tell me the truth. Christ, you've sworn you'd tell me the truth."

The moment was hideously threatening. She had the feeling that in another second he would get up and walk out of the restaurant, away from her, and she would never, never see him again.

"There's a girl up on the seventh floor who works for Lemmon. She comes down sometimes and sits around and bulls. She told me she'd seen me with you, did I know you very well? . . ." His voice went into falsetto again. Then it dropped. "I said I saw a lot of you, and she said you must be quite a girl. She'd understood you were a girl of Don Garrett's. Sure, quite a heavy girl, Don Garrett was supposed to be sleeping with you."

They both stared silent and stricken at each other.

"All I want is the truth. I can take it. You don't think I'm a sissy, do you? Do you think you have to feed me crap? Tell me the truth."

"I swear to you," she said. "I swear to you it's not true."

"You do?"

"People say such things," she cried. "That's one thing about New York. If you're seen with anyone you're supposed to be sleeping with them. People say it about everyone. When they don't know anything about it."

"Do they know anything about you?"

"I swear I didn't. Oh, God. . . ."

"What's the matter?"

"You don't know what it does to me to see you looking at me that way."

He looked down, and picked up a clam on the little fork. Then he let the fork drop.

"I can't eat," he said. "Let's go somewhere and get a drink."

They walked miserably along the sidewalk in the deepening city twilight. After a few blocks she took his arm. He clipped hers to him with his elbow.

"I knew that girl was a bitch," he said. "I'll tell you one thing, my friend. I'm in love with you. It's got to be love if it makes you feel like shooting your lunch."

"Don't let people take you away from me. Everybody tries to get people for themselves. Everybody's got a knife in everybody else."

"I thought you liked this place."

"I guess people would try to get you anywhere."

He squeezed her arm.

"I wish we could go home now," he said. "I don't know what's the matter with me. I feel lousy. Come on in here, let's get a drink."

They sat, between seven and eight, at a little table in a cellar crowded with noisy people, and drank from glasses of whisky and soda. Across the table their fingers held each other's. His face was very white and hers was flushed. She cried a little, but no one paid any attention. "Don't feel bad," they whispered to each other.

In September they went to their first party together. It was a big party given in a penthouse by a rich, elderly art collector, and Betsy received an engraved invitation. Over Hector's uncertain protests she telephoned the collector's secretary and asked if she might bring Mr. Connolly. A pause. "Yes, Mrs. Jayne, Mr. Schwartschild says he would be very glad. . . ."

"Is this some kind of a kike party?"

"Oh, no. He's a non-Jew Jew. A Hellenized Jew."

"Where do you learn words like that?"

"It will be very big and all sorts of famous people."

"How do you know all these damned people? Do you know a lot of Jews? It seems so queer that you were going around living before this summer. I can't ever catch up with your life," he said, complaining.

They got all dressed up for the first time in the secret, hidden-away summer that they had lived together. She put on a dress made of white lace with a little frill that stood out around her hips like a lace paper. Her hair was curly from the hot bath and she pinned it into a roll around the back of her neck. She stood up from the dressing-table and looked at Hector in his dinner-jacket. They moved forward and embraced each other to cover their faces. "You look beautiful," she whispered in his ear.

They went in a taxicab; they had never been to a party before. The separation to the dressing-rooms, the meeting in the long hallway, the receiving line and the introduction to the white-haired little man with a ribbon in his lapel; dancing together to the smooth, swooping music: these were all new and entirely different from anything in the past.

"That was the Legion of Honor," he said. "In the old boy's buttonhole."

"He's *nice*. He's a dear old man."

Hector kept smiling and he did not look angry. Somebody cut in, and she watched Hector standing with the other men beside the orchestra, so unlike them, so big, so powerful and so defenseless. He came back to her in a minute.

"You don't mind if I can't leave you alone, do you?"

But she knew he was shy, and it wrenched her heart that he should be liking the music, and wearing that pleased, vulnerable look. When she was alone with him he was bigger than she, and tougher and stronger and harder; but here he was not so sure as she.

They walked along a terrace that looked out over the southern stretch of Manhattan, the whole great splash of night and lights. The terrace was lined with little tables where people sat and drank and chattered, in their beautiful clothes, their jewels; their faces catching the light as they turned to say a word, their hair smooth and shining.

A girl with yellow hair reached out and caught the frill of Betsy's dress. "Hello, darling. Where have you been?"

It was another of Powers' girls, a tiny creature not over five feet tall, with the hips of a doll and a doll's pretty face. Her name was Judy Elliott, and she introduced the man that she was with as Henry Hunter and said that he was an architect. He was a big man as tall as Hector; they shook hands with each other and all sat down. There was champagne to drink, brought around constantly on trays. Everyone at the party seemed to Betsy to look pleased. It was the end of the summer; the beginning of the New York winter.

Hector danced with Judy, and Betsy with Hunter, and then they exchanged again, and then Hector and Betsy talked to some other people in a small panelled room with French furniture, and then they danced. By half past two they were with Judy and Hunter again on the terrace.

Hunter was a serious young man. He leaned on his elbows and talked to Hector about Frank Lloyd Wright, pausing to sip champagne. Hector wore the face that meant that he was interested and absorbed: set, alert, and a little angry, but Betsy could see that he liked Hunter and it gave her a strange, fond pleasure.

"I've had all the champagne I can drink," Judy said. She laid her hand flat on her little waist. "If I eat anything, if I drink anything, you can *see* it. Everything makes a bulge."

"Why don't you come back and sit around?" Betsy said. "Let's sit around and talk at home."

They all drove downtown together in a taxi; they were like old friends. It was all taken for granted. Hector unlocked the door to the apartment with his key; it seemed quite natural. He switched on the lamps while Betsy got the glasses and the whisky. They sat on the sofa and on the neighboring chairs and talked.

Only Betsy sat back peacefully in the corner of the sofa and looked at Hector, in his dress-shirt, as he listened and then spoke; she had the oddest sense of completion. She felt calm and satisfied; she felt in absolute pitch with her life. It was a peak, ultimate and happy, of contentment.

He was talking about the Chrysler Building, and then quite suddenly he finished what he was saying and his eyes met Betsy's.

They smiled across at each other.

When the others had departed, Hector closed the door and walked back to Betsy, who stood at the window watching him. They took each other's hands and stood face to face.

"This is the best of all," he said.

"This is the happiest in my whole life."

"I looked at you and there you were."

"You looked so absolutely right, as if you belonged there."

"I do belong here."

"I want to be your wife," she said.

"Don't you say it. I'm the one to say it. Will you marry me?"

"It's the only thing in the world I want."

They stood together looking out of the window at the night fading from the city.

"That little girl was so jealous," he said. "Anybody would be jealous of you, the way you look. Proud, and sure, and strong."

"They knew we have everything."

"You looked like a wife. You looked like my wife."

"I love to have people see that I belong to you. I never felt like that before. I always wanted to feel that I just belonged to myself. When I was living with Willy it always felt uncomfortable. I was his wife and I didn't feel like his wife and it irritated me to realize people thought of me as his wife."

"Because it wasn't right."

"Nothing was ever right. You are the only one."

"When are you going to get a divorce?"

"When shall I?"

"Right away, darling. Quick. Go to Reno."

"Six whole weeks."

"What am I going to do for six whole weeks?"

## CHAPTER XLIV

THE LEASE on Betsy's apartment ran out the first of October and they decided that she would leave for Nevada then. There was not much time before the first. The furniture would have to be stored, and things had to be packed. She wrote to her mother that she was going to Reno—although she had been separated so long that her marriage seemed unreal, now she felt an instinct to declare her plans—and she told Mr. Powers that she was going away. She wrote a letter to Willy at the last address she had for him, and told him that she was going to get the divorce now.

The apartment became a confusion of packing boxes; she took down the curtains to pack them and the windows stood bare and rectangular at the end of the room.

She was busy packing her clothes the night before the movers were to come. Hector got home a few minutes after ten. It was a chilly evening and Betsy had thrown a lot of trash into the little fireplace and lit a fire. They had never had a fire there during the summer. Hector came in and threw his gray hat down on the littered table and went over to the blaze, holding his hands out to it.

"I'll make a drink for you."

"Cosy home life."

"What's the matter?"

"Oh, nothing. I'm tired."

"Tell me what's the matter."

Everything was ending, everything was beginning; everything was on a hair-trigger.

"Oh, crap. Just let me alone. I'll get over it."

"I can't do anything till I know."

"Every time that bitch passes me she has a gleam in her eye. She thinks she's got something on me."

Betsy sat down on the armchair, stripped of its slipcover, by the side of the fire. She looked into the blaze.

"Has she got something on me?" he asked.

"People are so cruel. People can't let anyone alone. They can't stand seeing anyone be happy."

"Has she got anything on me?"

Betsy pushed her hair back from her forehead. She looked tired.

"Don't you know I'm all yours?"

"Answer me."

Quite suddenly she put her head down in her hands and began to cry. He did not touch her.

"Quit bawling. It's true about Don Garrett, isn't it?"

"Nobody ever took anything from me. I never gave any of myself away."

"It's true, isn't it?"

"You don't understand. I was a different person then. It didn't mean anything, any more than if I'd kissed him. . . ."

"You don't need to go into that. So it's true."

"Don't you see I couldn't tell you?"

"Why did you lie to me?"

"I couldn't tell you. I couldn't lose you. I'd put everything I had into us. It's the only thing in my life that's ever mattered."

"Didn't I tell you all I wanted was the truth?"

"I know. Don't think I haven't gone through hell. Sometimes I felt I couldn't stand it. I wanted you to know. But I couldn't lose you."

"Now, let's keep this very, very clear. You started off lying to me the night you met me. Remember?"

"I wish you could understand. . . . It felt true. I didn't feel as if that were anything but the truth. I felt so young, and in love for the first time, and kind of untouched. I didn't say anything that didn't feel true. I swear it."

"Let's omit about how you felt." He sat down in the chair opposite her and leaned forward with his elbows on his knees. "I think we'll stick to the truth for a change. There's a lot we've got to clean up."

"Besides," she cried frantically, "I didn't know it to tell you, the night I met you. I swear to you I'd forgotten it. It was only that horrible night in the restaurant when you mentioned his name that I remembered, and then I couldn't tell you."

"I can see how convenient such a short memory would be. I think you're going to have to give your memory a little exercise. Now. You get to work. Who else?"

He did not look especially angry. He had the intent look that he wore when he was bent on gathering information. His big face was dead white. He did not take his eyes from her face. She glanced wildly around the room.

"That head. The man who did it of me. It was a long time ago, before I married Willy . . . long, long ago."

"What was his name?"

"You shouldn't make me tell names. It isn't nice."

"We aren't going to spend much time on what's nice. You're going to make a clean breast of it if I have to spend a year making you do it. I'm going to have the truth out of you. What was his name?"

"Benson Levy. . . ."

"Who else?"

"I can't think of anybody else. That's all. I swear it."

"You're good at swearing to the truth, aren't you? Who else? Think."

"You're torturing me!"

He lit a cigarette quietly. His hand shook. But his voice was not angry. He leaned forward again.

"What do you think you're doing to me? . . . Think, now. This isn't going to stop until you've told me the whole truth, about everything. You'd better start remembering."

"Oh darling!" She leaned across and held out her hands to him. He did not stir. "What does it matter? I love you with all my heart and I could never look at another man but you. I did those things in the past when I didn't know anything, and they didn't mean anything to me, anything at all. I know I was horrible and it was wrong and I could kill myself for it now. But I didn't mean anything then. That's true. Everybody I knew did that way. Can't we just put it behind us and forget it, both of us? I didn't know you then. If I'd known there would ever be you I couldn't have."

"I was ready to take a blanket statement about your past once. I would have accepted anything you said, I was so in love with you. But it's too late now. Even you must see that. You've lied to me, and lied, and lied, and now you've got to go back and tell me every single thing."

"Aren't you in love with me *any more*? Don't you . . . want to marry me any more?"

He looked at her.

"Who are you to talk about marriage?" he said.

"You don't understand! I didn't think I was ever going to be in love like this. You see . . . oh God, it's so long ago. . . . I was in love when I was about eighteen and . . ."

"We'll skip the reasons till later, *if* you please. We're getting facts right now. Who else?"

"I can't remember."

"Well, remember. We've got all night. We've got forever, if it takes you that long. I'm going to get the truth."

At six o'clock in the morning they were still sitting there, on either side of the dead, the ruined fire. The hearth was scattered with cigarette butts. The whisky bottle stood on the floor beside the glass, by Hector's chair.

He was not drunk. He was still calm; intent, with his face as white as paper. Betsy drooped sidewise in her chair and her face was congested with weeping.

"You don't even remember this guy's name," he remarked. The lamp behind Betsy's chair still burned in the gray daylight of the room.

"I told you."

"Not him. The one we're talking about. *Did you ever know his name?*"

"Of course! But it was so long ago. . . . I met him at a cocktail party at a girl's, Mary Dawson's, and he asked me up for a drink a little while afterwards, and I went and there were some other people. And they went away, and he played the piano, and——"

"We'll come to the case-histories another time; later. Another one of these instructive evenings we're going to have. Unfortunately I have to take time off to work. I'm going to bed as soon as you decide to tell me this man's name."

"I don't remember."

He waited, smoking a cigarette from his third pack. Outside the noises of traffic began to take hold; the New York day was beginning.

After a while he got up and threw his butt into the fireplace. She lifted her face.

"Where are you going?"

"To bed. What's it to you?"

"Oh, my darling. . . . You look so tired. I love you so terribly and I'm going through hell. . . ."

"Are you? Personally, the only thing I want to do is puke."

She followed him into the bedroom. He would not look at her. He flung himself into bed. She knelt down by the side of the bed, looking at his face, his closed eyes.

"Darling . . . may I come to bed too?"

He did not open his eyes.

"If you don't mind," he said, "I wish you'd stay out of this room. You make it smell bad."

She still knelt there.

"Tell me just one thing," she whispered. "What do you want me to do? The movers are coming at noon. What do you want me to do?"

Now he looked at her, coldly.

"Want you to do? Why, just keep on going. Keep on remembering, if you will, please."

"But I'm not to go to Reno?"

"Naturally not."

"What do you want me to do? Go away?"

"Oh, no. Oh, no. None of that. You're not going sneaking back to mother. You're not going to get to whitewash your memory so the holes don't show. You're not quitting till you've finished."

"What are we going to do?"

"Do? We'll have to go somewhere. Somewhere where we can continue our researches. Go to a hotel."

He shut his eyes and turned over, away from her. When she touched
him, once, laying her hand lightly on his warm shoulder, he wrenched it
away. She got up and went into the living-room and lay down on the sofa
in her clothes.

When he got up the movers were in the apartment. She had not let them
go into the bedroom, and she had cooked a breakfast for Hector and saved
out china for him to eat it from. He walked into the living-room, dressed.
She looked desperately at him but he avoided her face. A mover was packing glass in a barrel.

"Here's your breakfast. . . ."

"No, thank you. I'm going out for my breakfast."

He looked round the apartment as if he had never seen it before. His
eye rested on the terra-cotta head. He walked over and picked it up, balancing the heavy thing in his hand as if it were a paper-weight.

"This anything you want?"

"No. Oh, no. . . ."

He crossed the room and tossed the head into the fireplace. It struck with
a thud and lay among the ashes and the old cigarette-butts.

"If you don't mind," he said.

"Of course not. . . ."

"It was a pretty thought of yours to keep it here all this time," he said.
"Nice for me."

He went over and opened the door.

"You can call me around ten," he said. "Maybe I'll know where to tell
you to go."


"That's all," she said. "That really is all."

It was three o'clock in the morning.

They sat in the large, high-ceilinged, hotel bedroom. A door stood open
into a smaller bedroom. The rooms were old-fashioned, with brass double
bedsteads and big pink armchairs with lace antimacassars. The bath to each
room was up a step, with marble washstands and tubs that stood on legs.
Here there was no fireplace to sit by, so they sat facing each other across
the room; all the ashtrays were choked with butts and ashes. Now and then
Betsy got up and emptied them in the bathroom. Then she would come
back and sit down again in her chair, and look at him with her tear-streaked
face, steadily. He held a glass in his hand, filled with whisky and water and
ice, and most of the time he regarded the glass and jingled it gently.

"Now think. That really is all?"

"That really is all."

He sighed and took a sip from the glass.

"Now. We enter another phase of our research. You're a very interesting
case, did you know that? I should like very, very much to understand you.
The inquiring mind, you know. Now. Could you explain to me in what
way you are any different from an ordinary pushover?"

"Oh, God. . . . Can't we rest?"

"I'm afraid rest is a stranger to me just at present. We have a lot of work to do. Answer my question."

She put both hands to her forehead and pushed back the hair.

"It didn't feel like that. . . . I wasn't a pushover. Can't you see? I always felt like a boy. Liz used to say. . . . It's so hard to make you see. I wasn't being pushed around. Anything I did I did because *I* wanted to."

"Interesting. I thought you said you didn't want to do . . . all that."

"I meant it didn't mean anything to me. It didn't take anything away from me. Young men go around and have different girls. . . . I felt like a young man."

"Morals didn't enter into it, of course?"

"But don't you see? Everyone I knew did it. Morals about that were supposed to be old-fashioned. Besides it was supposed to be bad for you not to. People get inhibitions. . . ."

"Ah, yes. The Freudian angle. Your husband, of course, didn't constitute a barrier?"

"He didn't care. He had lots of girls himself. I mean, he wasn't grim about that kind of thing. It didn't mean much to him either."

"You've known such nice people. You mentioned Mrs. Starr a minute ago. I am to understand that your kind of life was not much different from what she was used to. Right?"

"Oh, yes! She lived with Starr for ages before they were married."

"I wasn't speaking of living together, exactly."

"Well, yes, I know she had a lot of beaux."

"You say it meant nothing to you and you had no sense of immorality, and yet I notice you are fond of euphemisms in referring to the past. Now. Did anybody, ever—besides this saintlike character you seem to have married—did anybody ever ask you to marry them?"

She stared at him.

"Yes. Lots of people."

"Who?"

"Why, a whole lot of people." She mentioned four or five names.

"They were all people who were—as you put it—beaux?"

"No. Some of them were and some of them weren't."

"Why didn't you snap up one of them instead of working on me?"

"But, don't you see. . . . I didn't want to be married. I wanted to be free."

"What made you set your cap for me? Were you getting scared by that time?"

"No! No! You've got it all wrong. I fell in love with you. I'd never felt anything like it in my life. I felt all reborn. It was like being a young girl."

He drank from his glass.

"I wonder how long it's going to take me to break down that story."

"You can't break it down because it's true. Don't you know it? Don't you know you're the only thing in my whole life?"

"I wonder why I couldn't realize you were a pushover on the basis of our own history," he said.

"But I'm not a pushover!"

"What are you?"

"I wish I could make you see. I always wanted to be glamorous. I used to want to be kind of like Iris March in *The Green Hat*. I wanted to be a *grande amoureuse*. Everybody thought it was divine to be like that. Nobody thought it was awful."

"Go on."

"It didn't keep people from getting married if they wanted to. That was all Victorian, that about marrying virgins. Willy didn't care a bit. Liz married Horatio Starr. People asked me to marry them. I never heard anybody criticize anybody for having lots of beaux."

"Think what you're saying. *Anybody?*"

"Well, not the kind of people that were . . . smooth. Glamorous. Kind of New Yorkers."

"You know what I make out of all this?"

"What?" she whispered, trembling.

"I used to think New York was a cesspool. You got in your licks and got me believing maybe I was wrong, maybe it was a good clean place like anywhere else. I've been an easy pupil, haven't I? A quick study. It's quite interesting to find I was right on my own observations. And you know what I think of you?"

"What . . ."

"I think you are a cretin, to put it kindly; the sort of poor half-witted girl who does it for a quarter. Hell, no; I take that back. Those girls are earning their living. You haven't even got that."

"You hate me so. . . ."

"Or have you? How about that? Have you taken money for it?"

"Of course not!"

"Now you think. All that money you've got salted away in the savings bank. You make it all?"

"Certainly. Except . . ."

"Go on."

"Except some money that was made for me in the market."

"Now what would 'made for you' mean?"

She pressed her fingers into her eyeballs. She told him of the system Liz had explained to her years ago; the imaginary capital that earned real money. "Only one man ever did it for me, though."

"What was his name?"

"Curtis Bright."

"Couldn't you ever get anyone else to do it for you?"

"I never tried. I didn't ask him to; he just gave it to me for a present."

He got up and went over to the bureau where the whisky bottle and the pitcher of water and the ice bowl stood. The bowl was full of water now; he fished in it with his fingers and put the slivers of ice that floated on the surface into his glass. The whisky gurgled as he poured it out. There was only a little water left in the bottom of the pitcher, and he dashed it into his drink and went into the bathroom and filled up the glass. Then he came back and sat down and put the glass on the floor beside him.

"Why did you lie to me?"

"I told you! I couldn't lose you, and you were different from anyone I'd ever known. I saw you cared about things like that. It meant something terribly important to you."

"You were right about that. Why did you bother to lie to me the first night you met me? You didn't know anything about me then."

"I didn't feel as if I was lying. It felt true. I felt so young, and untouched. I couldn't have told you everything then. It wouldn't have been true. I didn't feel as if . . ."

"You told me three. Remember? Why did you tell me anything if you felt so untouched?"

"I don't know."

There were some things beyond explanation. And she felt so confused. It was like the life of another person, that she was trying to explain without understanding. That first night, had it been a sort of token confession? Falling in love with him so overwhelmingly, had she had an instinct that he would want to know what other men never bothered to ask? She didn't know. She could not remember. It was long ago. She had never been able to live except in the moment.

He sighed.

"And you didn't feel like a prostitute?"

"No! I never did. I felt . . . young, and adventurous."

"You thought of yourself as a perfectly good woman?"

"I wasn't a woman at all. I never thought of myself as a woman."

"You were able to feel perfectly self-respecting."

"Yes."

"And you were going to let me go on and marry you like a poor little sucker, and never tell me."

"No . . . no . . ."

"What were you going to do?"

She put her face in her hands.

"Tell me why you wanted to marry me? Were you getting scared?"

"I told you that wasn't true!" She threw her head back. "I was married already. I'm married now. It wasn't marriage I wanted."

"What did you want? What was in the back of your mind that first night?"

"Nothing was in the back of my mind! I fell in love. Completely. It was the *coup de foudre.*"

"If you don't mind," he said, "I'd rather you didn't speak French. It makes me think about where you probably picked it up."

She began to cry again, softly.

Already the steam was pounding in the radiators. The light came in around the drawn shades. Someone went down the hotel corridor outside, and a door slammed; there was the sound of water being run in a tub.

"Go away," he said. "Go to bed. I don't want to look at your lying face."

"I've told you everything. Don't you believe me?"

He gave her a long look.

"Go away," he said, sighing.

Near noon she crept into his room again. The bed was empty, and the shades were up. It was a beautiful, clear, brilliant October day; the sky above the low downtown buildings was blazing blue.

He stood in front of the mirror in the bathroom brushing his pale, thick hair, fully dressed. She looked at his big shoulders in the warm, brown worsted suit; his clean white shirt and the necktie knotted snugly under the flesh of his chin; the scrubbed, shiny look of his white cheeks, freshly shaved.

He laid down the brushes and came out into the bedroom. He went to the bureau and put the money that lay there into his pockets, the watch with its chain and small gold knife, the billfold; he folded a clean white handkerchief and stuck it in his breast-pocket, glancing into the mirror. He ignored Betsy.

The remains of breakfast stood on a table by the window. A newspaper lay, open, on the floor. He picked it up and folded it and thrust it into his outer coat pocket. He took his felt hat from the top of the chiffonier and put it on the back of his head. He looked around the room as if seeing whether he had forgotten anything.

Then he walked over to Betsy, near the doorway to her room. She put out her hand and touched the woollen stuff of his sleeve. He smelled of shaving-soap and orange-juice.

"I've got to leave you," he said, gently.

"Can I . . . can I meet you tonight?"

"You don't understand. I'm leaving you. For good."

She began to cry, and stretched out her arms blindly to him. He did not shake her off; he stood still, and her hands moved over his arms, his shoulders, the smooth shaved sides of his neck.

"Don't you see that I've got to leave you?"

"I love you so. . . ."

"It's no good."

"I haven't got any life. If you go everything's gone."

"You can just go on where you left off when you met me."

"No!" The tears streamed from her wide-open eyes. "Never, I'll never go back. I never could."

He patted her shoulder gently.

"I hope you don't," he said. "But it's none of my business any more."

She watched him cross the room and go out; the door closed.

She began to walk rapidly around the room. She touched the things lying on the bureau; she passed the closet and went back and put her hand on the sleeves of the suits that hung there; she went into the bathroom where the light still burned, and stood breathing the warm, soap-scented air, moist from the bath that had been taken there. Then she went back and looked at the suits hanging side by side: the gray, the blue, the dinner-jacket, the bright brown tweed that made him look so very pale.

His things were all here. He would have to come to take them away.

She sat down in the armchair by the window in front of the ruins of his breakfast. She sat up straight, rigid, and looked out of the window at the brilliant midday.

At half-past six the telephone rang on the stand beside the bed. The room was full of evening. She was lying on the bed, and stretched out one hand and took up the receiver.

"Do you want to meet me in about an hour for dinner?" His voice was very far away. "I'll wait for you at Luigi's."

"Hector! Yes, darling, of course. I'll be there in an hour. . . ."

She leapt up and ran into her room and switched the lights full on.

They sat at their old corner table in the bar, in the reddish half-light, close together, holding each other's hands tightly. There were very few other people. The bartender moved about behind the bar, against a background of rows of polished glasses and bottles of liquor: many kinds of whisky and gin, and strangely shaped bottles of things like Strega, Kümmel, and Fiori d'Alpini.

"I couldn't leave you," he said. "I couldn't do it. I kept feeling as if I was going to die. Larkin asked me if I was sick. I said I was sick. He let me take the night off."

"I thought I was going to die too."

Two generous glasses, Martini cocktails, stood side by side before them. A glass bowl was filled with peanuts, and they both kept reaching for them. The salt stuck to their fingers.

"When I thought I'd never have a cocktail with you again . . . I kept thinking, My heart's broken. I kept thinking there must be something that could be done. I kept thinking how young you are. I kept thinking of all the ghastly people you've known. I kept thinking about the way your face looks; you look innocent, did you know it, darling? And then I kept thinking about . . . everything else. It went round and round. But I think I got everything straightened out. I think there's just a chance."

Their fingers pressed and pressed. Their white faces looked at each other with longing, with agony, with tenderness.

"Do you really love me?" he said.

"I really love you."

"I figured it out. . . . I don't have to leave you, on one condition. Can you take it? Can you make yourself over? How do you feel about it? Do you want to regenerate yourself?"

"I'd do anything. Anything."

"Could you live for three years without anybody, without me? Could you make yourself into the woman I want? Could you make yourself a new past that would be good? It wouldn't be easy, you know. It would be hell, for both of us."

"I could do anything. If you were at the end of it."

"It would have to be without any promises, even. All I can say, is that I want the real you with all my heart and all my mind. I want the good you.

I want a strong, pure woman that loves me and has gone through hell to get me. I wouldn't even promise to be true to you. I wouldn't belong to you, nor you to me. Whatever way you lived would be because you wanted to live that way, for its own sake."

"Couldn't we ever be together?"

"No."

"I could do it. I will do it. I want to. I want to be good."

Life and the cold bitter years floated through her mind and she felt aspiring and purified. Her face was lifted. She would live somewhere, alone, up bare flights of stairs: strictly, strongly, sustained by a great faith. There would be nothing soft. Life would be like pure cold water and plain meat. Life would be like climbing a high bare hill to the top where a light burned and great music would begin to play.

"I kept thinking about my wife. I know it hurts you for me to call her tnat, but she is my wife. I kept thinking of all I've done to her. I've got such a load of guilt. I'm not a Catholic any more; you know there's no divorce. You'd have to be better than she was. You'd have to make me feel I wasn't descending to anyone less good than she was. You'd have to be better, and finer, than she. Is it worth it to you?"

"Yes."

"You could be the finest woman I ever dreamed of. But it would be hell. There can't be any promises. But if you cared enough, and if you were strong enough—there could be something great. Do you feel it? There could be a marriage so great that it would be greater than anything, than any wrong."

Their faces, side by side, looked through the dim atmosphere of the place they were in, and beyond it.

A man came in and hurried through the bar to the door that went into the dining-room. He glanced at them as he passed; a small, blond man.

"Hector. . . ."

"What?"

They looked at each other aghast.

"That man?"

"No. Somebody that looked like him."

"Who?"

"An Englishman. Stephen Ebery."

"You didn't remember?"

"I didn't remember. I can't understand why I didn't remember. Oh, God, it's so horrible. It was just buried. I've tried so . . . I swear I thought I'd found everything. You've got to believe me. I don't know what's the matter with me."

He held her hand tightly.

"I believe you," he said. "I believe you're sincere. It's all buried. In a way it makes me believe you never were that kind of woman. It was just the people you've always known, and you were so young. In a way it makes me trust you. You couldn't have wanted to produce that, just now, after everything. I believe you really want to tell me truth."

"I want to tell the truth. I want to be good. I will be."

The bartender came around the bar with two more Martinis and set them down, big and dripping, in front of them.

"We can't begin the new life yet," Hector said. He looked down into his drink. "We've got to get everything out first. You've got to think, and think, and find everything there is to tell me. We've got to work, before anything else."

"How will I know," she whispered. "How will I ever know that I've got it all out?"

"I don't know," he said helplessly. "I can't tell you. You'll just have to know."

After they had eaten a little they walked downtown through the October night, arm in arm, from uptown to far downtown where the hotel was. They walked very fast; the traffic swept past them and the lights on the avenue changed from red to green and to red, but they were deaf and blind. Their faces were white and tired and exalted.

Now, again, they had dinner together every night, and every night they met at ten and walked downtown to the hotel for another night like the others. Betsy did not report back for work. She paid for her hotel room out of the money she began to take from her savings, and she spent every day indoors or sitting on a bench in Washington Square, reliving the past that was like a nightmare to her, trying to recall it month by month and combing her memory for voices, faces, scenes. She was tortured by self-distrust. It was agony to lift herself back out of the present into days that had once seemed so bright and were now made hideous.

For dinner they went to all the places that were now so dear, so nostalgic of their summer, and tried to laugh and talk of other things, but their eyes would meet and their fingers would reach for each other's and they would look at each other in silence, in misery and sadness. Once on a Wednesday they ran into John Hannon and his girl, the brunette, having dinner, and joined them. There sat the others, so comfortable and contented together; happy lovers. They all joked and smiled, and after dinner they went back to the apartment where Hannon and the girl lived. They drank highballs and talked, and it was like being allowed into somebody else's Heaven. They left about eleven and began their long walk downtown.

"I was proud of you, darling," he said. "You kept your chin up. You didn't let them see anything was wrong. That's the way I love you. You're a strong, good woman."

She looked up at him speechlessly. Her eyes were full of tears.

They would sit all night in Hector's room with the whisky and the cigarettes, doing what they called "working."

That strange October went slowly by, and near the end a night came when Hector said, in the early hours,

"I think you've got it all."

"How can I know . . ."

"I guess you couldn't know. You can't trust yourself any more. I'll do it

for you. I believe you've got it all out. And if you haven't, you can tell me.
I don't think there's any use going on like this. There's something more important you've got to get done."

"What?"

"You've got to go out to Reno and divorce Jayne. That's got to be done
so you can start clean. There mustn't be any leftovers. There's something
else too. You've got to send Bright back his money."

"He'll think I'm crazy. I haven't seen him for two or three years."

"You've got to do it."

"I will. I'll do it tomorrow. I'll get a ticket and leave right away. Oh, I
want to start fresh!"

He set down the drink he held and leaned forward on his elbows.

"Or do you?" he said. "Maybe you'd rather hang on to that dough.
Maybe you don't like to disturb Bright's fond memories of you."

"Hector . . . that's not true!"

"Maybe you hate to destroy that nice, sordid, slimy little episode."

"It wasn't sordid. . . . You don't understand. It was perfectly clean and
friendly and decent."

"Oh, it was, was it?"

"You make everything filthy!" she cried. "When lots of the times were
perfectly self-respecting and . . . fun—I mean they seemed so then."

His face was heavy and contemptuous.

"Don't you criticize me. Don't you dare. Who are you to judge anyone?
You bitch."

He got up and came to her in one step. He struck her across the face as
she sat there, and struck her again, knocking the chair over; she fell inside
its arms. He walked away to the window and ran up the shade on the night.

She got up and righted the chair and sat down in it. Her face was turned
towards his back framed in the window. She waited.

"You can't take it, can you?" he said without turning around.

"I can take anything you give me," she said in a low voice.

He whirled around on his heel and looked at her.

"That's just a taste," he said. "Of what you've got coming to you. My
wife had to take a hell of a lot worse than that. And she didn't deserve any
of it. I'd have to break your head to show you what I think of you."

She waited.

"Stop looking saintly," he said. "You bitch. You ought to be down on
your knees."

She slipped out of the chair and knelt by it without taking her eyes from
his face.

"Please forgive me. . . ."

"Oh for Christ's sake get up."

She got back into the chair.

"If you knew what it's like to look at that lying, half-witted face." He
walked with hard, quick steps to the place on the floor where he had left
his full drink, picked it up, and threw the contents in her face. Slowly she
took a handkerchief from the pocket of her suit and wiped the water and

the whisky away. He came to her and struck her. All at once he turned away and went and lay down on the bed, face down, silent.

"Darling . . . poor darling. . . . Forgive me . . ." she murmured.

She sat on the edge of the bed and laid her hand on his shoulder. He reached out and pulled her down beside him.

"Christ . . . I can't bear to hurt you. . . . And I hurt her again and again and it wasn't like this. Why can't I hurt you without hurting myself?"

"I swear to you I can take it."

"I know you can. Oh, Betsy. . . ." He groaned. "I love you so much." He held her to him and kissed her eyes and her mouth.

"We mustn't do this. . . . You said we mustn't do this."

"You let me be the judge," he murmured. "You let me say what we can do."

"Yes."

The day she left they had breakfast together in a small, dark, oak-panelled tearoom near the hotel, full of middle-aged women having lunch. They ate their eggs and drank their coffee, and reached for each other's hands. They would look up from the food and smile encouragingly at each other.

"How are you going to spend the time?" he asked.

"Writing to you, and—working, and trying to be what you want."

"You're such a good woman."

"Don't say that yet. How are you going to spend the time?"

"I've got to work on that book. Our summer put the quietus on that."

"I'm sorry, darling."

"Don't be. I wouldn't swap our summer for anything in the world.—I'm going to miss you so."

"Is it all right for you to write to me, too?"

"I'm not going to be able to help it."

They went out into the clear sunshine of late October, and arm in arm they walked back to the hotel. Children were zig-zagging and whizzing down the sidewalk on roller-skates. Women pushed baby-carriages peacefully in the sunshine.

They stopped, in front of the hotel, and he took his hat off.

"Goodbye."

"Goodbye."

"Come back to me, darling."

"I'll come back to you soon."

He kissed her with his hat in his hand, and then they turned the fine sightless exaltation of their faces in opposite directions. At her back she could hear the sound of his heels striking the pavement as he walked away from her towards his work.

## CHAPTER XLV

TOWARDS NIGHT, in upper New York State, it came on to snow. The train rushed pell-mell, streaming through the strange, darkening country, and from time to time a dash of its smoke would whirl past. In the small, isolated farmhouses lights were turned on as the train went by. The land was black, bleak; against this background the sparse snow tumbled down softly. It was only the first of November; to have snow fall now was a kind of miracle, an act of blessing the world. Close to the train the snow whirled in eddies and clung for a moment in soft clods to the windowpanes. It was almost like Christmas.

Leda sat curled up on the seat in the compartment, pressing her face to the unclouded double window. She had turned out the light. She was clothed in invisibility, a being enclosed in a small, warm place, a disembodied heart, a mind, a pair of eyes. Above the deep and steady roar of the train she seemed to hear music: over the simple bare country, falling with the snow from the dark sky, like the sound of pealing bells. The lights in the little houses seemed to go on in a great silence, as though of themselves; the snow fell silently from heaven.

In her invisibility Leda was smiling, with a child's surprise and delight. She stretched out her hand to feel for the light switch, withdrew it and looked again at the scene beyond the window. Then she reached again and turned on the light. She rummaged in her leather purse for a silver pencil and a shagreen notebook.

She looked all around the little room. Why did it give her such joy and such release to be here in this box that moved? The fixtures of the room— the mirror, the cloth of the chairs, the shining artificial woodwork that reflected light—seemed so comfortable, so secret and snug. She kept her legs tucked under her. From the notebook she tore a page that listed New York engagements, and tossed the crumpled ball into the metal spittoon. Then she began to write.

> The wind sweeps slowly, like a long curved knife,
> Along the darkened edges of the hills.

She drew a line through the words. It was beginning again, the secret, unique pleasure that came with being alone. Alone in the compartment she sang under her breath.

> *Le ciel est noir, la terre est blanche.*
> *Cloches, carrillonez gaiement!*

If she could only write something that held the peace, the lovely hush of that . . . She had not felt like poetry for a long, long time; almost never in all the years since she had been married. Too many people, too much to learn, to possess, to win; and underneath, the fundamental premise of her position all wrong. Now the lessons, she thought, were long ago learned, the battles won, and with mastery came the shrinking to absolute unimportance of what had been mastered. Now she was free. She was moving fast through space to the freedom that was what she wanted.

Marriage to James March had been worse than stupid, worse than empty. It had been not merely his stolidity, his monotony, his unassailable basic conventionality, the other unbearable characteristics that were his, that had made marriage to him seem impossible to Leda. What alarmed her, what made her act, was what she saw happening to herself placed in relation to him; his character was altering hers, her own special private nature. With horror she observed herself as she screamed at him sometimes when his heavy good nature was unbearable. He made her irritable, angry, bitter, caustic; she would not let herself become those things. She would not let him change Leda March.

It was all very well to know that she was stronger than he. Living with him subtly altered her; she would not be altered. She seemed to feel herself becoming, not only the things in reaction to him, but like him; stolid, monotonous, conventional. The life they lived, so correct, so the model of well-to-do young married people of position in New York, was not good enough. There was no time to waste on such a life. Where had her special nature gone? Where was the sensitivity, the awareness, the strange delicate life lived alone that once she had had? Those were the real Leda March. They were her pure spirit, undissolved, uncorrupted. She had felt panic for fear that she had lost them and had become entirely Mrs. James March and all that Mrs. James March meant.

It was so thankful, it was like a vindication, to find that the secret waters still ran underneath. This was her true self, and it had not been dried up. With the beginning of freedom, already, now, there had come the old and precious tremor; the chiming of words in her head like little bells; the appearance of things laid bare from their material aspect to a kind of purity, clear and breath-taking. Words meant more than their meaning, they could be tasted and smelt, a snowflake melting on the tongue, the smell of snow in the night.

> *Il tremble dans la paille fraiche*
> *Ce pauvre petit enfant Jésus;*
> *Et, pour l'echauffer dans sa crèche,*
> *L'âne et le boeuf soufflent dessus.*

Christmas was more than six weeks away, but Christmas was in the air she breathed. The peace, the joyfulness, and that knowledge that the world was reborn in the snow to the pealing of bells: they were Christmas and they were in this moment.

The door that connected the two compartments opened and Miss Lovejoy looked in.

"Am I disturbing you, Mrs. March?"

"No . . ."

"Treat is all tucked in his bed."

It was an actual shock to realize that she had a child. For a little while she had been disembodied; no tie had held her to a living human. She got up and went into the other compartment; Miss Lovejoy held the door open for her and then passed into Leda's compartment and closed the door.

The little boy lay in the lower of the two made-up berths. His cheeks were red and his dark hair lay flat on his forehead in a bang. Along the two window-sills ran a line of small automobiles.

"Mummy, read me the farm book."

Leda sat down on the plush chair pulled up beside the bed.

"You must be sick of the farm book. It's an awfully stupid book, darling."

"Read me the farm book."

"No. I'll tell you about when I was a little girl in Hampton and it would snow. Did you see the snow falling outside? It's coming down very slowly. Big fat flakes. Do you know what they are? Mother Goose is shaking out her feather comfortable for the winter."

"I saw it."

"When I was a little girl, there would be lots and lots of snow, and I would go out in the morning and the snow would be drifted all over the tops of the fences so that I could walk right over them on snowshoes. They were snowshoes like what the Indians used to wear. I would walk on them back into the woods and it was all quiet and you could see the tiny tracks that animals had made over the top of the snow."

"What kind of animals?"

"Rabbits. And mice. And birds like quail and grouse. And all the big spruce trees were loaded down with the snow, their big dark green branches bent way down, and suddenly, with everything all quiet, the snow would drop off one of the trees into the snow underneath. It made a thud. And then it would all be quiet again. And I would walk in the woods in my snowshoes and it made a track behind me zig-zagging like this."

Leda spread her hands and moved them one before the other.

"Mummy."

"What, darling?"

"Mummy, I don't want to hear about the snow."

"Darling, you must think about it and try to hear how the snow sounded falling off the trees. Don't you remember the snow last winter—how beautiful it was at Grandma March's? How you and I went out in the morning and made a picture on the front lawn where it was all untouched, by walking on it with our feet?"

"I went coasting on a sled. Can I go coasting on a sled out West, Mummy?"

"I don't think there'll be any snow out West, darling. But you can ride a pony."

"Can I have a cowboy suit?"

"Yes, darling."

"Yip-peeeee! Mummy," he said in a small, pleading voice. "Mummy, read me the farm book."

She looked at his eyes, that were shaped so much like hers; he blinked and wriggled under the covers. She picked up the large, flat book that lay, waiting, on the foot of the bed.

She began to read.

" 'We put our seven puppies in a big basket. They wanted to get out. They were too small to climb over the top of the basket. They wanted to run and play. Would you like to play with them? They——' "

"Yes," whispered the little boy.

" '—They would climb all over you if you would lie on the grass. They would lick your face and hands. The picture shows one of the puppies when he got older. His master is holding him. See how happy the boy is. See how happy the puppy is. They like to play together. The boy runs. The puppy runs after him. Then the puppy runs and the boy tries to catch him.' "

Treat lay quite still with his face turned to her and his eyes shining.

When Miss Lovejoy came back into the compartment, Leda put down the book and kissed Treat's cheek and stood up.

"Come along, Treat," the governess said. "Bedlington."

"I'm going into the lounge car," Leda said. "You may sit in my room in just a minute."

"Thank you very much."

"Good night, darling."

"Good night, Mummy."

Leda closed the door between the rooms and stood still in hers, her head thrown back, trying to recapture the thing she had felt before. But people had gotten between her and the feeling. Miss Lovejoy had to sit somewhere while Treat went to sleep.

She drew a long breath of the warm, close air. She picked up her mink coat and flung it over her shoulders and went out. She walked, balancing against the rocking of the train, down several cars to the lounge. Between the cars the air was very cold. She glanced at the men and the one or two women in the lounge car and went and sat in an empty booth near the far end. A steward came and she ordered a glass of 3.2 beer and lit a cigarette.

Treat was a disappointment to her. When he was a little baby she had envisioned a secret, delicate understanding that would be between them. The perceptions of her own childhood were still clear and separate to her. She would never be practical and grown-up with him. She would be able to feel the things that he was feeling and they would communicate instinctively. The things in his world that nobody else would understand she would understand. He would gain by it and she would gain—regain the thinking of a child.

But it had never been at all like that. He was the practical one. He liked animals, and running and shouting, and his supper. He didn't like fairy stories and he didn't like to play alone and when she spoke about the feelings about nature that had been so acute to her and still were, he stared at her uncomfortably and was bored. He did not seem to her to be her own child. He was James's child.

She had not given up. Treat might change. What she wanted was a sympathy between them that was neither mother-love on her part nor dependence on his, but a kind of sharing of experience . . . and that might still come. He was James's child and he seemed to respond naturally to James, but now James would not come often into his life. In the separation agreement arranging the disposal of property, she had kept the custody of Treat. '—the said party of the second part shall have the right to visit the said child at the home or other place of abode of the said party of the first part . . .' Her own child . . . she wanted a sensitive, thoughtful boy, who read, and saw, and listened. She sighed and looked around the car.

At the writing-desk at the end sat a young woman, writing. Leda's eyes came back to her again. Her brown hair was parted in the middle and made into a small knot behind. She wore a dark suit and her face was tired and composed. The desk in front of her was strewn with sheets of written-over paper. At that instant she looked up from her letter and their eyes met. They looked steadily at each other.

"Hello."

"Isn't it Betsy Jekyll? Yes," Leda said, leaning forward across the table and smiling.

Betsy gathered up her papers, took an envelope, and came over to the booth. They shook hands and Betsy slipped into the seat facing Leda. Leda was struck by the smile that came over Betsy's face; it was calm and radiant, and seemed sent out of private depths.

"How extraordinary to see you again! Have a beer."

They continued to smile, looking curiously into each other's faces.

"You've changed."

"So have you."

"Where are you going?"

"To Reno . . ."

"So am I . . ."

Betsy folded the sheets of paper and stuck them into the envelope, licked the flap and sealed it. She put the envelope into her handbag.

It was a queer experience, thus to be confronted in limbo with a face from long ago, Leda thought. It had a quality of significance and unreality, here, rushing through strange country in the night; from different worlds they had come to the same microcosmic rocket-world and met. Ordinary circumstances were not present. Anything could be said. There need be no adjustment for either of them to the other's surroundings. In more ways than one they had sloughed off their lives, being here. They were back, face to face, as they had been so long ago; but behind their faces was all that had occurred in the meantime, and it would be interesting to know what that was.

As the steward brought the second beer, Leda wondered if Betsy's altered face meant that she had had, in her way, triumphs over life comparable to Leda's triumphs. They were no longer the raw girls they had been. When she thought of her own past shyness, her old frustrations, what she had had to go through to conquer them and come to what she was now . . . ! She remembered the way Betsy had looked, eager, puppyish, undiscriminating. Now she looked as if she knew a secret, an answer.

"Tell me, where have you been living?"

"In New York."

"So have I, isn't it strange? You must tell me all about your family, and what you've been doing, and your marriage. Don't think I'm inquisitive. After all, this is a sort of vacuum, isn't it? Between two lives."

"I suppose it is. . . ."

They talked, not attending so much to what was said as to each other's new voice, new face; clothes and gestures and little things that showed the women they had become. They kept smiling. Leda leaned forward on her elbows.

"You mustn't think me rude. But it's all so interesting. Don't answer if you'd rather. . . . What are you going back to?"

"It's all right. I'd love to talk about it. I'm going back to being in love."

"In love!"

Betsy smiled that strange, radiant smile.

"It's the only thing that matters in the world," she said. "It's like seeing a light. I guess religion is a substitute for it."

How strange that she should be saying this to me, Leda thought. Betsy was always one for spilling out her heart. She gives away all she knows. She's really just the same.

"For years I've led a very messy life," Betsy said. "I never knew anything. Now it's all changed. I feel as if I'd been saved. I can sort of see things and what they mean."

It was the way people must talk in 'experience meetings.' Impossible to imagine making a confession like that. Humbling oneself. . . . Although Betsy did not look humble. She looked almost transfigured. This was a most extraordinary meeting.

A conversation in a comet.

"It must be wonderful to find something like that."

"Yes. It's funny, I feel as if I must talk about it. I feel like telling people. I feel like telling them to keep the door open for it, no matter if they've never believed they'd be really in love. Because you never know when it may come. I didn't. I thought I'd never be really in love. I didn't understand anything."

Is she saying this to me, Leda thought. It's so inspirational it's very nearly funny. Not quite. She does look as if she had a light burning in her. Have I a light burning in me? When I was alone in the compartment looking out of the window—I had a light then. I wonder if I could ever really be in love.

They stared at each other, faintly smiling.

"How is Maizie?"

"I think she's a little better."

"I didn't know she'd been ill."

"She had a nervous breakdown."

"I'm so sorry."

"Lambert's been living abroad."

Why does she say that, Leda thought.

"Do you remember what fun we used to have watching Maizie dress to go out with one of her beaux?"

Or does that sound condescending?

"Oh, yes."

"You know," Leda said, putting a cigarette into her holder and lighting it, "I was an awfully shy child, and your family was the first thing that ever took me out of myself."

But what was lost, she wondered suddenly. Was it a kindness, after all? I wonder what I should have been if I had stayed the way I was.

I should have been a poet.

"I was a horrid child," she said. "I hated everyone because I thought everyone hated me. It takes a long time to prove to yourself that the bear behind the cellar door really isn't there. Once you've learned it isn't, it's easy enough to be quite a decent person."

Now *I'm* talking extraordinarily, she thought. I wonder if she has the faintest idea what I mean. She's so wrapped up in herself.

"What are *you* going back to?" Betsy said.

Leda was surprised. She laughed.

"Oh, nothing so dramatic," she said. "I'm not going to marry anybody. But I've been wanting to do some writing. . . ."

She hasn't really changed much, Betsy thought. She's terribly important, and rich, and she knows everybody, and she's beautiful, but she wishes she had what I've got. Everybody wants that really. She used to look like that when she stood in the doorway at home and Ma'am was playing the piano. How strange that I should turn out to be somebody that women like this envy . . . because of the thing I have.

*Blessed art thou among women.*

They came to Reno in the middle of a morning. The city was very low and all around the desert lay broad and flat in the strong Western sunshine. The March luggage was stowed in a taxi and the governess got in. Leda stood smiling on the platform. Treat, in a blue coat and a little round blue cap with a visor, was hugging Betsy round the knees.

"You come with us!"

"I can't, now, Treat."

"Will you come this afternoon?"

"You will come and see me often, won't you?" Leda said, holding out her hand. "And don't forget, we must have Thanksgiving dinner together."

"I'll come and play with you soon," Betsy said. Leda took the child's hand and let him jump, before her, into the taxi. He sat very small between the two women, leaning forward and peering anxiously through the window.

"Goodbye Betsy, goodbye Betsy, goodbye Betsy," he called.

"Goodbye Treat, goodbye Treat, goodbye Treat!"

## CHAPTER XLVI

Parkway Hotel
Reno, Nev.
November —

My darling darling darling,

I'm all established and I have a big calendar I bought at the five and ten up over the desk and I have already crossed out the days I've got through with big black crosses. And I've got a circle around the Day in December when I get the divorce. And then three days on the train and I'll be there. My stomach turns upside down when I think of the moment when I walk up the ramp in Grand Central and see your face. Oh, *darling.* . . .

My lawyer looks like a gambler in a Western. Skinny and round-shouldered and a big moustache. But very nice and helpful, he owns this hotel and told me about it because I said I had to find somewhere cheap, and he's going to charge me the minimum divorce rate. $250. His office was all lined with framed photographs of celebrities, movie stars and people. He said, "Some night you must let me show you the sights of Reno, little lady." But I said I was here to rest. I hope I didn't hurt his feelings. But I don't want to go out with anybody, I don't want to see anybody. I'm going to build my whole life out here around you, darling. *Because I want to.* I don't want to be interrupted from thinking about you for one minute. Even when I'm talking to people I keep right on thinking of you.

This is a funny little hotel. The washstand is right in the room. The room goes around a corner. But I like it. The minute the porter shut the door after him I *hung* out of the window (which looks all over the top of Reno) and ran the water, and opened all the bureau drawers, and jumped into the middle of the bed. With your letter. I called for it at the post office before I even went to the lawyer's. Then I read it. I know it by heart. This is where I am going to live for six weeks, all alone, and make myself good, good, *good*. Oh, my darling, I want to be worthy of you so hard it hurts. . . .

Parkway Hotel
November —

. . . How can you think that for one moment of the day I forget that I am out here *to do a job on myself?* If you could see me you'd know my life is just one thing, trying to make myself deserve you. I mean people don't exist for me any more, just you. I don't believe in their having important things happen to them. I *know* none of them has anything like the thing I've got. Oh, Hector! Of course I don't forget the past. But I know that I couldn't ever be that girl again. I can't imagine myself ever having *done* any of those horrible things, even. They make me feel sick and weak. But it's not wrong to think in the other direction, is it? I mean I can't help living in the future. How wonderful everything will be *some* day, when it is all over and I have made myself worthy of you and . . .

I've made a routine for myself and I do it just the same way every day. It's all I can do to sort of express something. I never lived in a routine before. My life has been so messy! Now I want to do the same things every day, thinking of you hard all the time, because I feel as if that way they would all mount up to mean something.

I get up late after I have thought everything out every morning. It's like saying my prayers. I go all through the past to *make sure*, and then I think about last summer, and then I think about making myself good.

Then.I go out and get my breakfast-lunch at the nice drugstore on the corner. It's all full of sun, like every place here. I have the same thing to eat every day because that's *part of it*. First I have a bowl of soup and then I have boiled eggs and toast, and then I have vanilla ice cream with hot chocolate sauce.

They give you a whole little pitcher of chocolate sauce to yourself.

Then I come back here and sit down and write my letter to you. That's where I am now. And this is the time when I check the day off on the calendar. There's just gallons of sunshine in the room and it dances all over the paper.

Then I go out to mail my letter. I walk up to the post-office and put it in the airmail chute. Then I take a long walk.

Lots of times that little boy I told you about goes for a walk with me. His mother rides out at a ranch but she has to ride alone because she is writing and has to think. *You* know. If you knew her you might fall in love with her, she's terribly fascinating. Oh, darling, don't forget that nobody could love you as much as I do. . . .

I have an awfully good time with Treat. We go way out on the roads towards the desert and run. It must be fun riding out here but it's pretty expensive so I don't.

You think it's all right for me to play with the little boy, don't you? I thought about it a long time. I had such a sort of sick feeling that maybe it would be corrupting him to be with me. But I'm *not* that girl now, I'm good, I know I'm good.

When I take him back to the Riverside his mother is generally back. She wears brick red jodhpurs and the most divine printed foulard stocks. She bought them in England at the *same place* your evening scarf with the monogram came from. She always offers me a cocktail but I never take one. I'm not going to drink one drop of anything until the moment when we are sitting looking at each other across a table and we lift our glasses.

When I go out I have to go past the bar in the Riverside and it is always jam packed and a man singing cowboy ballads. You see movie actresses going in. I feel so *thankful* I am not in there.

It's wonderful at night here. It's very clear and cold and the stars are white and *enormous*. I run from the Riverside to here, because that is the time when I can look for your letter in my pigeonhole. If you knew the way it makes me feel to come up here to my room with your letter in my hand! I put it right in the center of the bed and then I take my hat and coat off and light a cigarette, and then I climb on to the bed, and then!!!!!

Do you think it is all right if I go to a movie once a week? I won't if you think I ought not to. Mostly I use the evenings for beauty culture, and that's for you, darling, and I *think* hard, about you, all the time I'm brushing my hair or manicuring my nails or anything, so it isn't just vanity *at all*, it's part of my routine, because when I come back I want to be my best inside and outside. And I turn out the light exactly at eleven o'clock. It makes me think about how I only have to turn out the light so many more times before I'm back, my darling. . . .

Parkway Hotel
November——

I had Thanksgiving dinner with Leda March and the little boy. That was all right, wasn't it? I *hated* to break my routine. But I thought it would look too funny if I didn't. She knows I don't know anybody here.

She has a great big suite in the Riverside with a dining-room and a piano in the living-room. It looks right over the Truckee River that the women throw their wedding rings in when they get their decrees. I don't see how I'm going to *stand* it when I get mine. I feel as if it was going to be a paper that said that I was a good woman now and worthy of you.

She had a terribly good special Thanksgiving dinner and the little boy was so cunning and got the wishbone.

Parkway Hotel
November——

. . . I *don't* think it's easy! Oh, I swear to you I don't! I know that it will take a long time to make myself *really* good. Honestly, I don't forget about the past. But I can do it. I can do anything.

You see such *terrible* faces here in Reno, all along the streets. Some of the women look as hard as rocks and you can just see they're getting hunks of alimony. But lots of them have the most tragic faces. Something awful has happened in their lives, and they haven't got *anything*. Today before I started your letter I couldn't help crying. There are so many ruined women. And I might have been one of them, if you had really gone away and left me that day. I kept thinking how I wouldn't have *anything*. But I would have changed anyway, darling, because I had known you. I would have come out here anyway and my face would have been like that, wrecked, and all the rest of my life I would have had *nothing*. But I would have been good and done things for poor people, and things. But it makes me feel like dying, thinking about it. . . .

Early in December the streets of Reno were decorated for Christmas. The telegraph poles along Virginia Street were twined with red and green. At every street corner rose the jingle of a Salvation Army bell. At night garlands of lights sparkled red and blue and green and yellow, making a holiday pergola of Virginia Street from the courthouse down to the other end where the sign arched across the street, "The Biggest Little City in the World."

Betsy and Treat dawdled along on the way back to the hotel, swinging

hands and looking into the lighted windows. It was almost full dark. The
bells all down the street rang rhythmically and the shopping crowds hurried past. Betsy and Treat played a game of choosing from the windows
what they would buy and whom they would give it to.

"I'd give that to Daddy and that to Mummy and that to Miss Lovejoy
and that to Bridie," Treat jabbered very fast, pointing with his finger from
object to object in a window full of luggage.

"Who's Bridie?"

"The cook. Will Bridie be there when we get back?"

"I guess she will. Wouldn't you give the big brown bag to anybody? I
think that's the nicest of all."

"I don't know ·ny more people," he said.

"I'd give that to my mother and that to Maizie and that to Dad and that
to Jane and that to Glory. And the brown bag to Hector."

"You've given the most things to Hector."

"I like Hector the best."

"I know who I would give the brown bag to."

"Who?"

"I'd give it to you," he said in a small voice.

"Thank you very much. And I'd pack my clothes in it to come to see
you."

They wandered on up the street and past the shops to the bridge and into
the hotel. Betsy left Treat at the elevators. He stepped in the lighted cage
in his small blue coat and cap and the door swung shut.

In the bar they were playing Christmas carols in jazz time. A burst of
loud laughter and talk rushed out as somebody opened the door. Betsy went
out into the early evening. The air smelled of snow. She hugged her elbows
to her sides and took a long breath of cold desert air and began to run along
the sidewalk towards home, singing to herself.

> *God rest you mer-ry, gentlemen*
> *Let nothing—you dismay. . . .*

She flung herself against the door of the Parkway and came up to the
desk with her face tingling. The clerk reached up for the long, airmail envelope in her box and handed it to her. It was a thick one. The smile seemed
to burst out of her face at the man. She turned and ran up the stairs as fast
as she could go.

Inside her own warm lighted room she stood still and shivered with joy.
Then she went through the exact preliminaries that ended with her climb-
ing on to the middle of the bed, and very slowly, very neatly, opened
Hector's letter.

Dearest baby,

I hope you feel full of guts. I'm afraid there's something for you to take.
Now is the time to see if this thing really is what we feel it is—if you really
are the big, strong woman I think you are and that you say you are.

I want you to do a job of understanding me, sweet. I get so God damned tied up in my own knots. What we've got to do is to get them untied so we can live the life we want—straight and honest and big and strong as all hell. I want to be a good man for you, darling.

I've always been haunted by so many things. And, I'm not trying to be mean, but that fine October we spent didn't help much to straighten me out. There are so many ghosts.

Most of the time I can believe in you and believe in *us*—that you're a fine girl who's going through hell to be what I want, and that not too far in the future we're going to live together in a way that will knock most marriages into a cocked hat. Most of the time I know it's true.

And then the demon tightens up on me. The ghosts begin to walk. When that begins it's hell. Those are the nights I can't sleep. Those are the nights I sit here in the room alone and drink whisky and try to remember your face as I saw it last—beautiful and strong and good. But you're not here and as I look your face changes and turns into something slimy—you've got to take this, baby—and I close my eyes and try to shut it out but it keeps looking at me. It's a bad, lying face.

That's the kind of nights I spend, not all the time, but plenty. I haven't got any work done on my book. I wish I had your convenient capacity for concentrating on the future. I'm not giving you hell, baby, I know you're seeing things straight now. But the past doesn't haunt you the way it does me. I wouldn't wish it on a murderer. I've got to lay a few ghosts before I can have any peace.

I've been doing a lot of thinking. How do you lay a ghost? Every man his own ghost remedy. All I know is that to have any peace at all I've got to know what I'm doing justifies itself. I've got to know you're as good a woman as my mother was, so I can tell her and know I'm telling the truth when she gets talking to me. As far as your past goes, I keep saying to myself that you'll be all the better woman for having licked that and gone on. Maybe that makes you a better woman even than my mother. That's what I want.

I want the best woman I've ever known. You've got to be a better woman than my wife. And you can be. I've got it all figured out, and it's all up to you, baby, whether you love me enough to be everything I ever dreamed of. You see, my wife gave me everything, she damned near killed herself trying to be a good wife. It wasn't her fault if the thing just never was right, the way, God damn it, with everything you've done, the thing is right between you and me.

There was just one thing my wife couldn't give me. God knows I don't hold it against her, there's not one woman in a million that could. But I'm betting on your being that one woman. Don't you see, if you can give me that one thing then you're a better woman than she and we've licked the ghosts.

She couldn't take it when I went to bed with that Swift number. That ended everything between us. The medicine's coming now, baby.

Last night the ghosts began to walk and it was just one night too many and I called up Jerry Firth on the copy desk and he said to come over. It was just a regular New York drinking party, you'd never have known that there'd been a Repeal—the place blue with smoke and people screaming and liquor spilled all over the place and somebody being sick in the can.

Hell, I'm just stalling around. I hate to hurt you, baby. Why is it so much harder to hurt you than it was to hurt my mother and my wife?

Here it is. I sat and talked to this woman named Drew. We had a lot of drinks together. She was one of those tall, handsome, big jobs that I wouldn't be married to on a bet but are fun to talk to. Anyway she said she had to go home and I said I'd take her. I took her home in a cab, somewhere up in the Nineties, and she asked me in and I went. After a while I went to bed with her. Now you've got it. Can you take it?

But you've got to get it exactly as it was. You mustn't think she took anything from me that belonged to you, because she didn't. She was nice. It was on a purely carnal basis, good animal fun. She got what she wanted and I got what I wanted. She wasn't asking for love or making any claims to being anything she wasn't.

I'm not throwing that at you, darling.

I want you to try to understand and be glad about it, darling. Because you should be. All the time I was with her I had the damnedest feeling that I was getting rid of something—something bad, that had been poisoning me. I'm yours, now, more than I ever was before. You needn't worry for fear I'll see her again; that's over, it's served its purpose.

It did more for me than I even meant it to do. You see, I've been untrue to you now—technically—and you've never been untrue to me and so in one more way I can't look down on you from any superior virtue.

I feel clean, somehow. If you'll understand you'll be glad too. You'll be glad and you'll take it, as no one ever took it before. You are taking it, aren't you? I know you are. And we can tell the ghosts and everybody else to go to hell.

Betsy had no memory of how she got to the drugstore. She was sitting in a booth, on schedule, as on every other Reno night. A cup of coffee stood in front of her, with steam rising from it. Her face was burning hot. The clock on the wall said seven.

She was staring at a large glass case full of bottles of whisky. Her mind was tight and clenched and could not let go. Tall bottles, round bottles, pinch bottles. Suddenly she had a formed thought: she would buy one of those bottles and take it back to the hotel and drink it all; she would be unconscious then and out of reach of the dreadful voice that was beginning to speak in her mind.

But instead she took a sip of the scalding coffee. She looked all around her in the drugstore, and saw nothing; carefully she looked again and made herself see the white soda fountain with the boys in white coats behind it, the prescription counter, the piles of cough medicine in yellow boxes, the wall lined with shelves of glass pharmacy bottles, with labels in gold-leaf.

She drank up the rest of her coffee, paid for it at the cage, and went out into the street.

She walked uptown, over the bridge, past the mass of the Riverside Hotel with its square lights burning in rows. Her eyes, in her thrown-back face, found the row of lights where Leda was. Leda was reading, or writing, or sitting, with her child asleep nearby and comfortable things around her. Leda, Leda, do you remember me? You used to be my friend. Leda was up there, beyond the dark.

Leda, do you hear me? I'm in torment.

Faces passed her in the lighted darkness, glanced at her and walked on. She looked into each face, looking for something there to which she could speak. The eyes, the mouths, lighted by rays of red and green colored lights, were private; they did not know her.

Do you see me? I'm looking for you. He put his arms around another woman—somebody I have never seen—and his shoulders that I know sank down and his mouth kissed hers.

Beyond the hotel, beyond the courthouse, the dark grew deep and broad and there were no people. Out there was the desert with nobody in it, only houses far apart closed for the night with lights in the windows and people inside, together; living lives together. She turned around distracted in the road and walked back through the town.

The faces passed her. She looked into them searching for something and she spoke to them in silence in the street. A man came out of a gambling joint and drew his hand across his eyes. He carried his big felt hat in the other hand. As she went by he gave her a blank look and began to walk the other way.

Isn't there anywhere to go? Isn't there somewhere else for people to go? I want a place where people are together, being friends.

Two girls came out of a drugstore farther down the street with their hands in their purses, rummaging round and stuffing things back. Their shoulders bumped each other's as they moved slowly forward. Betsy looked from one face to the other.

We were going to be true to each other. We were in love. I was so true. There never was anybody else but just one person. I never did anything to hurt him.

All down Virginia Street she walked and across the railroad tracks and into the quieter, tree-lined streets on the other side of town. Here were the ugly, comfortable houses of families.

You're all kind to each other. You're families, like my family was. You are sorry if you do anything by mistake and find it has hurt. You're all in your houses being friendly and saying, "Don't move. I'll run upstairs and get it." He doesn't care. He went to somebody else. He didn't care if he hurt me.

She passed the Catholic hospital with the lights shining courageously from the rooms. The nurses and the nuns were there awake all night to bring the patients through the hours.

Can't you help me? I've been hurt. I don't know where to go. Can't you tell me where to go?

She wandered around for a long time among the quiet streets and here the faces in the yellow street-lights looked peaceful and benign. She might have spoken to any one of them and they would have answered.

What do you do when you find you didn't understand? I thought he loved me. I thought there wouldn't ever be anyone but me. I wanted to be so good, and work so hard, to be worthy. I never looked at any faces. And he didn't care. He looked at the woman's face and came closer to it and then he kissed her. Then he was with her. Not me.

By midnight she had come back into the center of Reno and turned up the street to the Parkway. The lights inside had all been turned out but one behind the desk, and there was no one there. All the people had gone to their rooms, all the people had retired into their own lives. She climbed the stairs to her floor and went along the corridor and unlocked her door. The lights flew on and she was in her own private place again, but it was impossible to sink down into it because here all was agony and shock. She moved about the room opening and shutting drawers, staring into the closet where her dresses hung. She looked at the small table-desk with hotel stationery stacked along the back in two piles.

But I wrote my soul out to him every day, I gave him everything so that I shouldn't have anything left that wasn't shared. I wrote it all down and I was so afraid I would forget something, the trip to the shoe store for my bedroom slippers. And then he wrote to me and told me. But did he ask her? Or did she ask him? And what did they say as they walked into the room? Did he have his arm round her waist? I'll never know. It belongs to them. There is that, all that, that he has outside me and he doesn't want me there. I don't belong there. I'm all alone.

She looked all around her, wildly. Everything stood quite still. Baby Ben on the bureau ticked. She went into the bathroom and turned on the taps full force. Then she began to tear off her clothes.

She lay in the hot bath and looked at her long body wavering under the green water.

It's the same old me. I'm me, going on through everything year after year, this is the same body I had when I was a little girl. All the things pass over it and I'm still here. When I'm an old woman I shall lie in a bath and look at my legs in the water and they will be withered but they'll still be the same old legs. I could drown it if I wanted to, but it would still be my body that would be found dead. Nothing I do *shows*. This is the same body I was born with.

In a short time she was in bed, with the window thrown wide open on the large Western night. Sometimes a car would dash down the street full of people laughing and shouting, and turn the corner out of hearing.

She felt exhausted and unavailing. What she was, she was. Hector was somebody else, and no matter how she strained herself towards him she could never enter him, nor he be surrounded with her.

She turned over in bed and pulled the pillow up on each side over her ears. She wanted to melt, to fuse; to become and to be converted into more. She wanted movement, and the sliding of change. It was not enough to be herself alone; it was like a block of uncut stone. She wanted to alter, somehow.

In the morning when she woke she lay flat on her back with her eyes closed. She saw Hector directly before her: large, hard, pale face and muscular neck, thick hair brushed down; his shoulders, his chest, his arms. She felt something like anger. She felt impatience with her own long fear and shame. There was his face, and his body, that she must have.

When she came back from having lunch at the drugstore, she went at once to her desk. It stood in the centre of a huge yellow pool of sunshine quivering like half-jellied liquid on the floor. She picked up the pen and wrote with decision.

> Parkway Hotel
> December ——

My darling Hector:

Of course I can take it. I hope you see now that what I've told you is true, I can take anything at all ever. I am glad it did the thing for you you wanted it to.

I'll be back in a few days. I won't ever leave you.

Last night I thought it had killed me. . . .

She paused in her letter and stared at the blinding square of the window. She bit the end of the pen lightly with the tips of her teeth. She wanted to say—I was far away and while I was gone you did this to me.

But now she knew that she could never write in a letter and never say the things she felt. There was no way to communicate them. There was nothing to do and nothing to say, except the things that were necessary to make events move as she felt they must. It was no use to try to put herself into letters to him because she loved him. She would go on writing the same kind of letters, but that was because that kind of letters were needed.

She loved him with all her heart. But that was not what he wanted. What he wanted was acts. Acts, such as letters, could be given and received, but the heart stayed in the body.

## CHAPTER XLVII

IT WAS A CHRISTMAS TRAIN. Girls in printed travelling robes popped their heads out of compartment doors and squealed with laughter and popped them in again. And all along the sleeping cars, half made up, half green curtains and half sunshine, people were chattering and laying their hands on another's arm to command attention. "And I'm going to *say* to her. . . ." On top of the luggage, the bags and cases, were piled boxes for Christmas. The train hurled itself towards home, along the border of the Hudson River, and outside the country lay under morning snow that reflected the sun.

It was snow for the schoolboys to go skiing on and the husbands and wives to take walks in to get up an appetite, snow to add to the gaiety of shopping; people would turn from the breakfast table and look out of the windows and say with satisfaction, "Look! There must be six inches of it!" All down the dining-car people sat at the square sunny tables and as they waited for their grapefruit and their ham-and-eggs, gazed, already filled with comfort, over the landscape.

The black waiters swayed sidewise from the hips to let each other pass, holding the metal trays above their heads; the freshly unfolded napkins seemed to fly through the air and land like snowbirds in the breakfasters' laps. Now was the time to say it, whatever it was; the train would soon be there, the sunny hour shortened. The breakfasters leaned across the table; the words trembled on the tips of their tongues. There was something left to be said, before the train should draw to a stop. "But listen, there was something I wanted to say to you before——" The journey was almost over. Soon they would all be turned loose to scatter through the city like whirling flakes; when would they ever find one another again? Something remained to be told. "Let me finish telling you about what happened. . . ." But their eyes kept wandering to the window. "Look at all that snow!"

Leda, Betsy, the little boy, and the governess sat together at one of the tables. The waiter set down the loaded tray on the edge of the white cloth and began to deal out the plates like cards, the thick glasses, the silver. There was barely room to put it all down; the oval platters of eggs, the toast stacked under a battered silver cover, the salt, the pepper, the coffee cups and the coffee pots, with steam trickling up from the spouts. The waiter took off the cap of the milk bottle with a flourish. Over all of it, in and out of it, the sunshine twinkled.

"Come along, Treat, let's see what a good trencherman you can be."

But Leda and Betsy looked at each other over the tops of the dishes, smiling.

"Well. . . ."

Betsy ate a little and laid down her fork.

"Won't it be funny to be back in New York?"

"It seems more than six weeks."

"I wonder what New York will be like with Repeal."

"I got all my shopping done in Reno."

They said these things, but the minutes were clicking past and there was all the rest that had not been said. As they talked their eyes searched each other's. Where will you go, and then what will you say? In both of them there was the question that hid, and popped out for a second, and was buried again: Have you got it all solved, now? Do you see, now, where you are going? Is it all quite clear to you?

"I'm going to get a two-wheel bicycle for my Christmas," Treat said firmly. The governess wiped his mouth.

"Then you must be quite, quite good from now until Christmas," she said.

"Are you coming to see us on Christmas?" he asked Betsy.

"I hope so. Where will you be?"

Treat could only look at his mother.

"Where will we be, Mummy?"

"We'll be in New York, darling. Maybe we will have found a new apartment to live in."

"Where will we be if we haven't found a new apartment?"

"In the hotel, darling. Looking all over New York."

"But where will I ride my bicycle?"

All four of them looked helpless.

Treat finished his milk, looking at them over the rim of the glass.

"Where will you be, Betsy?"

She took a long breath.

"I don't know!"

"You're not going back to Hampton for Christmas?" Leda asked, conversationally.

"My plans aren't definite."

All that remained to be said danced in the sunlight before them. The train was rushing through the suburbs. New York was getting bigger and bigger, nearer and nearer, and realer. "My plans are not definite."

The governess and the child left the table, but Betsy and Leda sat on, smoking.

"I haven't seen half enough of you," Leda said suddenly.

"I haven't seen you, either. I hate to say goodbye to you."

But that was not it; there was much more than that, that would not now be said.

"It makes me feel different, to be with you," Leda went on, making circles in the air with her cigarette. "It brings back the way it used to be, a little bit. I mean, sometimes I can't remember how I used to feel. I want to remember, to get back to the way it used to be. . . ."

Out there, they had never reached for each other; only once Betsy had felt a need for Leda, and nothing had come of it. Now they remembered the years long ago when they had been closest friends, and wondered why they had not tried to bring that back.

Each of them was like a key to the other's past.

Betsy thought: that was the way I used to be, before I got going all wrong. She is a part of my good past. I'd like Hector to see her.

Leda thought: if I could only catch hold of the smells, the sights, the sounds that were there in those days when we walked along the Hampton streets together. If I could catch hold of them—and then move back, back. I want to go all the way back and begin again from the beginning. That's what I must do. I don't want it to be the same. I want to make it what it would have been if I hadn't had those impulses, those compulsions, if I hadn't had to fight so hard . . . Now there's nothing I need to fight. I want to live. I never enjoyed being young because I had to fight so hard. I'm afraid that I'll go back to New York and it will all take hold again and I'll be busy and important and in demand and all the things I worked for and got. But I want to be free. I want to feel. It can't be too late. I would have been a poet. Those old dreams . . .

"Did you ever hear that line of Schiller," she said, " 'Keep true to the dream of thy youth'?"

"No."

But that says it, Betsy thought; that's what I want. The thing I want with

Hector is the thing I always really wanted. I always wanted love. Why did I have to do all the other things? They're all finished with now. If he will only forget them.

I need her, Leda thought. I haven't anything to remind me. It won't always come back by itself. All those rides I took in Nevada, and nothing came, I stayed on the surface; worldly. I can't do it alone. I want to be reminded.

"I didn't want to say it in front of Treat," she said, leaning forward. "But of course we shan't be able to get out of the hotel until after the New Year. There'll be too much to do, and besides . . . I don't know exactly what I shall be doing."

"I'd like to send Treat a Christmas present. Where will you be?"

"We'll be at the Waldorf Towers. I want to see you again, Betsy. I'm going to give a party on New Year's Eve and I wish you'd come. Come and bring your young man."

"I'd love to."

The train stopped short and they were in the One Hundred Twenty-fifth Street station. In a hurry they got up. Leda pulled her coat around her shoulders. The dark rich fur lay against her darker, shining hair. Shall I ever find out, Betsy thought, what makes her so untouchable looking; how does she do it?

Their cars were at opposite ends of the dining-car. Leda walked balancing herself past the deserted tables towards the mirror at the end. She glanced back over her shoulder at Betsy's back. She's in such a hurry, she thought; she's going to be met by this man. I never saw anybody look quite so illumined. I wish I could find out how you make yourself as alive as that. How do you keep happiness from turning to water in your hand. . . .

But it was not quite the end, they felt. They would meet again. Something might still be done with what was left of the past.

## CHAPTER XLVIII

BETSY AND HECTOR were married at once, at City Hall. No reason seemed any more to remain, no scruple, no unmended ideal, to delay it. It seemed to them both that they had been through an ordeal and deserved their reward without waiting. Each looked at the other with adoration and relief. "Why should we suffer any more? I love you so. Let's have the happiness we know is there. . . ." The weeks that they had been apart seemed quite as long as the three years that they had once, in their sober anguish, spoken of as a separation.

They went back to the hotel feeling a kind of triumph; they had won. In those same rooms where such confessions had been made and such recriminations, so many frantic tears had been shed, they now lived at a high pitch of joy. The reassuring words could not be spoken often enough— "I love you, darling. I'll love you all my life." At night they went dancing, or to midnight movies, or walked hand in hand among the holiday crowds on Broadway, and all of it was magic because at the end they would go home together, and they would always go home together. In the daytimes Betsy looked for an apartment where they would live the strong, true, mutual life that they had envisioned and won. But they were in no hurry; they felt so much sentiment for the hotel; after the New Year would be soon enough to move.

The telegram to Hampton announcing their marriage brought an answering wire insisting that they come there for Christmas and signed by the whole family. Hector was able to get Christmas Day off, and they went up to Boston on the midnight, Christmas Eve. To Betsy it was a triumphal progress. After her years alone in New York—that had once seemed sparkling, that now she saw as sordid—she was coming home to display the prize she had won, her miracle, her husband; it was as if she could say to them: "Look at what I've found in life! I've got the man I want, the man I have to have." More than her mother, far more than poor Maizie, she had triumphed in love. If they only knew. . . . She looked at Hector beside her as they drove in a taxi from the Back Bay Station out to Hampton in the early morning, and he seemed to her unique: powerful, mysterious.

The drama of their arrival was diminished by Glory's engagement, a surprise which the Jekylls were announcing that Christmas Day. The fiancé, Matthew Bradford, came out in the morning to join in the opening of presents around the Christmas tree. He was the pattern of Boston desirability: from an old Boston family, in his last year of Harvard Law School, he had a pleasing face, good manners, and a crew haircut. Betsy was not surprised to see Hector looking at him as if he were a specimen. The splash of her own marriage might be lessened by this new alliance in the family, but it was only heightened for her privately. Hector was so much more of a man than this nice young Grotonian. Her pleasure and pride mounted through the day.

She kept observing how her family, who had once been so exciting and fantastic, had fallen away somehow from the remarkable to something approaching the Boston mould. It was most apparent in what she could no longer think of as the Brats. Glory was charmingly pretty and gay and calm and it was easy to see how acceptable a daughter-in-law she would appear to the Bradfords. She wore a tweed skirt and Scotch sweater. She was a new mould of Jekyll daughter; nothing of Annestown, nothing of the old Jekyll unconventionality, clung anywhere to her; she was a Jekyll of the later, the Boston period. Jane was just such another; it appeared that she was engrossed in Junior League work.

Only Minnie May remained garrulous and vital. Looking her same, nervous, restless self, although now her clothes were less eccentric—Jane or Glory must buy them for her—she still pulled the whole houseful of people together by the power of her personality. In her alone Betsy could find the atmosphere, large, reckless, and indomitable, that had once surrounded her whole family.

Her father had diminished to a presence who sat by and watched, who stood up and shook hands, whose words, when he spoke, somehow could not be heard. Betsy watched him eagerly when he first shook hands and spoke to Hector. She remembered the long-ago Oren Garth episode: now, if Dad only knew it, she had been redeemed from all in her life that belonged in that category; Hector had been able to do what Tom's ancient rage had never done; Hector was her saviour and she wished that her father might know it. But as she watched, Tom, after congratulating his new son-in-law in a low, Southern voice, shut his mouth; his eyes searched Hector's face in a tired, uneasy way; then he gave a jerk to the corner of his mouth. Hector was looking at the floor.

She wanted to tell her father that Hector knew Annestown, that Tom loved so; that he had lived there when he was a child. She had wanted to tell all of them that. But before they came Hector had asked her not to. He was always so queer about his childhood there. He was sure that families like the Jekylls had looked down on his. Betsy could only protest without effect that it was no such thing, they just hadn't happened to know the Connollys. It was one of Hector's peculiarities, that made him dearer to her; it made her feel protective.

But it came out anyway. And sure enough it didn't amount to a thing. Late in the morning, when they were all drinking egg-nog in the sun-filled bay window, Minnie May looked at Hector in her piercing way and asked if he was one of the Connollys that used to live in Annestown. Goodness knew how such a connection had occurred to her, Betsy thought. But Minnie May was almost psychic.

Hector looked full at Minnie May with his big, pale face, and said truculently, that he was.

"Just think of that! Real romantic, you and Betsy meeting in New York. I remember your mother. A fine woman."

Hector did not speak.

"Ma'am, how did it occur to you?" Betsy asked, beaming. "Think of all the other Connollys there are."

"Why, Bets, you wrote it to me yourself in a letter. Last summer sometime. I remember just as well, you saying you'd met such a divine man, that used to live in Annestown. When I heard the name Connolly, I knew it must be the same man." She smiled all over her gay, yellow monkey-face at Hector. But Hector was not looking at her.

"I *did*?" Betsy had no faintest recollection of it. She could not remember anything of the preceding summer except herself and Hector and their life together. It now seemed preposterous that she should have even written any letter at all to her mother. Her picture of her summer was just of them two, alone, without another soul existing in the world.

But what did it matter?

For Hector did not seem angry. He went out of his way to be agreeable to the Jekyll gathering, and Betsy overheard him kidding Glory in his heavy, tough-voiced way. She could imagine how Glory would amuse him: a regular little sheltered Boston debutante. Such a type stimulated him like red pepper under the skin. It was as if he could not believe there really were such people. He teased her, but at the same time he was being very polite; in the way he had he was almost courtly, paying compliments to Minnie May and calling Tom "Sir." It was a manner he had learned before Betsy ever met him, that was not a part of him but which he assumed sometimes. His big, powerful body hastened across the room to open a door when Minnie May went out to the kitchen for a moment.

In the afternoon a great many people came in. It was a big party—Christmas, and Glory's engagement, and Betsy's marriage. The long living-room and the dining-room and Tom's study were crowded with people drinking Minnie May's Virginia egg-nog. All sorts of people turned up—good old Sam, who was now beauing Jane, and Mrs. Rudd with Lambert, who Betsy had thought was abroad, and Dr. Cunningham who, it appeared, was now a widower and kept hanging around Minnie May and laughing at everything she said; and Boston people Betsy had never even met before. She kept hugging herself with pleasure because it was a party and because she was married to Hector and he was there, right across the room. Everybody was very gay. People kept stopping and saying to Betsy, "Your mother's so wonderful!" Obviously Minnie May had been accepted as a character and an indispensable personality by these Bostonians. She was having a success like a debutante, complete with Dr. Cunningham for a beau. Betsy wondered whether Tom minded having this white-haired Boston doctor hanging around his wife like a college boy; but she decided that Tom did not care; he looked drawn and tired. Betsy spared a pang of regret that he should have grown so old, that he should care so little about anything any more. He walked through the crowd, his hair grown all gray, with the gait of an old man: passing egg-nog. When he spoke it was as if he had to prepare himself to bring out words: they came forth few and low, in his slurred Southern accent. He was Minnie May's age, but he had withered and she had grown younger. It seemed as if she had all her own fire and had taken from him all his too. Betsy wondered whether he still longed to go home to Annestown or whether now he didn't care any more.

There was no proper supper. Most of the people stayed, and a Virginia ham, turkey, and salad were set out in the dining-room. The time flew past in chatter and laughter, people pushing past to find others, in blue smoke and the smell of egg-nog and the smell of ham. Betsy and Hector were to leave in time for the eleven o'clock night train back to New York. Before calling a taxi from Hampton village Betsy went around saying goodbye to all these people towards whom she felt so warmly because of her own good fortune; she loved everybody.

When she came to Hector she found him talking to Lambert Rudd. They were both somewhat drunk, and swayed back and forth gently as they talked in a fraternal manner.

"This is my God damned brother-in-law," Hector said to Betsy.

"How the hell did you get to be my brother-in-law?" Lambert asked.

"There are ways, boy. There are ways."

"There are ways within ways, brother."

"True. Are we getting the hell out of here, my good wife?" Hector asked. Betsy felt delight that he should be having such a good time and getting along with members of her family.

"I'll drive you to the station," Lambert announced. "My Mamma went away long hours ago. I am at your command."

Betsy said goodbye to Tom and the girls and heard Hector speaking with elaborate gratefulness. Minnie May went to the door with them, and Dr. Cunningham tagged along.

"Goodbye, honey," her mother said. "And goodbye, Hector, dear. Now, you all come back real soon. Make my daughter pay some attention to her old mother, hear?"

"Yes ma'am!" Hector said, suddenly using a Southern accent himself. "But if I may say so, you look as young as your daughters."

Minnie May laughed.

"It's all due to this kind gentleman right here. I was turning into an old bent-over crone, yes I was, but he's a miracle doctor and he made me stand up straight. It's all posture, you know that, Hector?"

"It's a good thing to know about," Hector said.

Lambert drove them at breakneck speed into town. He and Hector seemed to have hit it off. Betsy sat quite still smiling in the dark and let them talk crazily to each other. On the platform waiting for the train they did football starts using Lambert's felt hat. When the train came in Lambert stood and waved.

In the car, hung with green curtains, they threw their coats into their made-up berths.

"Isn't Lambert nice?" Betsy said.

"Seems vaguely human."

"Darling . . . it's so nice to be alone with you again." She came and rubbed her face against his coat sleeve.

"Come on, let's see if we can get a drink," he said.

"Don't you want to go to bed?"

"No. I want to get drunk."

"Did you have a good time, darling?" she asked as they stumbled through the silent cars on the way to the lounge car. He went before her, and she had to raise her voice.

"Oh, wonderful, wonderful."

For an instant she did not quite like the way he said it. But she was supersensitive to his moods, she thought. And by the time they had found the lounge car and sat down, he was all she could want; he leaned over against her and kept whispering in her ear.

## CHAPTER XLIX

ON NEW YEAR'S EVE Hector came home in a taxi from the newspaper to dress for Leda's party. Betsy had finished bathing and was putting on her stockings. He came into the room and went over to her and pulled off the stockings she had halfway on. She reached her arms up around his neck.

"How's for not going to any party?" he mumbled in her hair. "I know an awfully good way to spend New Year's Eve."

She shook her head and pulled away from him.

"No, sir. I want to show off my husband to my friends. I want you to see Leda too. I want you to see what swell friends I do have. She used to be my best friend in Hampton."

He moved his hands along her leg and did not speak.

"Guess who called up?" she asked.

"Who."

"Lambert Rudd. You know. I told him to come and go with us to Leda's. He used to know her. He painted her portrait once. I think Maizie used to be jealous of her—but that was just before she—had her nervous breakdown, you know. He said he'd like to go a lot."

"You're a funny girl," he said. His hands dropped away.

"Darling! Don't you love me?"

"Yep. I love you."

He went into the bathroom and started a bath.

Lambert arrived and was sent up to the room as Hector was finishing dressing. They all had a drink before leaving.

Lambert was sober, smiling, pleasant; his eyes were shining. He looked very dark, with the black peak of his hair, next to Hector.

"I'm looking for a studio in New York," he announced. "I can't paint in Boston. Place gives me acute colic. I should have come here long ago."

"I thought you were painting abroad," Betsy said.

"I don't want to get to be an expatriate," he said. He moved restlessly in his chair. "I've got to be an American painter."

"You got anything on the ball, fellow?" Hector asked, tying his black tie.

"Damn right, fellow."

"How is Maizie now?" Betsy asked.

Hector sat down in a chair with his drink and looked from Betsy to Lambert and back with his attentive air.

"About the same." Lambert's smile vanished. He looked into his glass.

"It's so awful for us all, but it must be worst for you."

"It's worst for her," he said.

"Have you seen her?"

"Not for a long time. It's not good for her to see me," he said.

"It must be awful to have to think of her all the time there and not be able to do anything. I should think it would be hard to work."

Lambert shrugged his shoulders.

"Betsy," Hector said suddenly in a voice that made her stare at him, "go get your coat on. It's time to go."

His face was entirely changed. Now it was as hard, as closed, as she had ever seen it. She went into the other room and picked up her coat from the bed. He followed her in in a minute and shut the door.

"Darling! What's the matter? What have I done?"

"You have to ask me that. . . . You cretin. . . . For Christ's sake, haven't you got any feeling for anyone but yourself?"

"Yes! I have!"

"The hell you have. That you could talk to that poor guy like that about his wife. It was a lot worse than half-witted. It was vicious."

His face was filled with an angry tenderness. In the midst of her pain realization took shape in Betsy's mind: Hector had a deep tenderness and compassion for men; for women, for her, he had hatred and suspicion.

"You don't understand," she said. "All that's been going on a long time. And she's my own sister."

As she spoke, her moment's understanding of him vanished; she had forgotten it. All she had, once more, was love for him, eagerness and humility and a crying anxiety to be what this man wanted her to be.

"Sure," he said. "Everything is yours. *My, my, my.* Now shut your face and come on and try to behave a little better."

At the party the people came and went, to and fro in the large, clean, brilliant rooms of Leda March's hotel apartment. It was the first Repeal New Year's Eve, and everyone was a little stately. Like snakes they had shed their old skins and were bright and shining. The word *elegant* insinuated itself into the rippling chatter. Everyone was tired of his Prohibition past, disowned it. The men wore white tie and tails, and the women chiffon, satin, and jewels. It was not they who had sat holding hands with some forgotten stranger along dimly-lighted banquettes, ripped a felt hat off their rumpled curls or talked French to an Italian waiter.

People were now discussing wines, gravely. It mattered, to know the different Châteaux. In the minds of these people for an instant, like a will-o'-the-wisp lantern flickering through the rooms, was envisioned the sort of restaurants they meant to dine in from now on; the graceful dancing to a sweet orchestra, the delicious pressed duck, the bottle of Yquem.

The hotel waiters passed large trays of champagne, legal, French champagne. There was a consciousness that they were making history on this New Year's Eve.

Midnight struck. There was a jangle of church bells in churches far below the party, floors and floors below on another level. Someone threw up a window and in from the lively winter night came the hooting of horns, the shrill whistling from all over New York.

A group of people that included Betsy and Hector was sitting in a circle playing a game that someone had invented. Each was assigned an imaginary profession, and then had to spell out his real name, as though over a telephone, in terms of the profession.

"C for Christ," said Hector, who had been made a minister. "O for organ, N for Nativity, N for nave, O for ordain, L for Lamb, L for Lot's wife, Y for Yahveh."

Betsy had been made a dressmaker.

"C for crinoline," she said.

"Darling, a modern dressmaker," somebody said.

Betsy glanced desperately at the speaker. Then she looked back again
to Hector's pale, impassive face.

Her heart was beating far too fast. He would not look at her. The fear
that had been evolved in the past months for her, out of her blood and her
flesh and her bones, awoke like a germ of disease. A pulse throbbed in the
back of her head. She was unable to think.

"C for . . ."

Hector would not look at her. She was a woman married to a man she
worshipped. What life lay ahead of her? What sort of years had she chosen
for herself? All she knew about herself was the tenacity that pounded
along with fear in her veins; she would never leave him, she would see it
out. If she had been able to think, it might have been better. But the nature
of her love—and of herself—was unthinking, stubborn, dogged. All she knew
was that she was in for fear and love and confusion, and never giving up.

"C for. . . ."

"You're not taking our lovely game seriously," the voice complained.

"C for cambric," she said. "O for organdie, L for linen, L for lin-
gerie. . . ."

"Betsy, my dearest child."

She whirled around in her chair, and behind her stood Curtis Bright. She
stared at that face with its sad, worldly smile and the clipped little moustache; there he stood, the type of bon vivant bachelor.

"My dearest child," he said. "Our hostess has just told me you are married. Won't you introduce me? It's perfectly lovely to see you again."

Now she knew that this moment was what she had been waiting for.
She had known something awful was going to happen, and this was it.

"Hector," she said clearly. "This is Mr. Bright. This is my husband."

But that was the most that she could do. She could not wait for any more.
She jumped up without glancing at either of the men's faces that must now
be confronting each other, and started blindly away.

Behind her a voice wailed,

"You don't like our *game!* You mental giant. . . ."

She made for the hall and pushed open a door and found herself in a
passage with several doors. One light burned. There was a straight chair
and she sat down in it and put her cold hands up on her hot cheeks. She
was listening for some sort of catastrophic noise. Hector would knock
Bright down. Or there would be a cry, a shout. . . . In a moment someone
would come and say, "You must go home. . . ." Or Hector would be
standing before her, looking down at her, saying—"You brought me here
to come up against your lovers. New York is full of your lovers. You're a
mass of corruption." Or would he not speak at all, but only strike her? Or
would it be Leda who would come. . . . "I asked you to my party out of
old friendship. Go away."

She waited and waited and nobody came, there was no loud sound at all.

But she could not go back. How could she go back now? She must wait,
an hour or more, and perhaps everything would be different then. She
wanted to wash her face with cold water and forget her life. It seemed to

her that she had spent all her years building a trap for herself, a trap that had sprung and caught her. And she had never known what she was doing. It was only as if she had awakened one morning and found herself disgraced. But there was no use thinking about that. She could never keep her mind on the past. With her heart pounding, she must simply continue to push forward.

She began opening doors softly, looking for a bathroom. The first door was a broom closet. She opened the next on the dark, and an open window with gently blowing curtains.

"Who's that?" a child's voice said.

"Hello, Treat," she whispered. "Is that you?"

A light went on beside the bed, and Treat was sitting up in bed in a pair of flannel pajamas with puppy-dogs printed on them. His dark eyes were squinted up against the light.

"Betsy!" he cried. "You didn't come to see me on Christmas."

"I couldn't come. I went home to Hampton."

"Don't go away," he said. "Were you at the party? Do you have to go back to the party?"

"No. I'll stay and talk to you. But you ought to go to sleep."

"I'll go to sleep if you'll stay."

She lay down on his bed with her head at the foot, propped against the post, looking at him. He had a fur cat and a giraffe in bed with him. She pulled up the quilt from where it had fallen on the floor and wrapped it around her shoulders. Treat slid down under the covers again.

"Tell me about Hampton."

"Well, my sister has a new dog. He's an Irish setter. His name is Patrick. . . ."

Word by word, her heart slowed down into a temporary, a truce-like peace.

But there had been no scene, nor the beginning of one, outside.

At an antique, fruitwood backgammon table close to a window, Leda and Hector Connolly sat. The curtains brushing them were full and billowing and made of gray taffeta, hanging to the floor and crumpled upon it. The rattle of the dice and the clack of them as they were thrown on to the board, the snapping of a pair of counters back into a corner point, went on steadily, but in between they spoke. Their conversation was strange and difficult, and they looked strangely facing each other. Leda was dressed and arranged to perfection, all in water-green satin; her dark eyes and her mouth were beautiful shapes in her white face. Hector's large, pale face, with its straight nose, was like a Greek pugilist's, but bleached to whiteness and fair hair.

"I'm not a capitalist!" she said.

"Do you think I'm crazy?" he said. "What the hell. I suppose they give you this apartment. Manager a friend of yours?"

"I have alimony," she said. "But I don't see why I should explain my affairs to you."

"Don't. I don't give a damn about your affairs. You're just another rich New York woman, with nothing beyond your clothes and your baths and the men you want."

"It's a shame we shouldn't be friends," she said indifferently. "I'd like to, on account of Betsy."

"You and I couldn't ever be friends."

"I don't see how you could be a friend of anybody," she said. "I can tell you don't like anybody. You're intolerant of everybody. You imagine things against them. You think you love 'the worker,' but what you mean by the worker is just you."

"For you to say that," he said furiously. "You never loved anybody in your life. All you do is paint a fancier and fancier picture of yourself in a fancy world. Get this, I hate your world. I spit on your world."

"Oh, but it isn't my world."

"Nuts."

She set down the dice cup and spread out both her hands, gently, and said nothing.

"All right, I beg your pardon," he said, pronouncing the words in an artificial voice. "The world I believe in is something you wouldn't even understand. There'd be simplicity, and innocence, and a voice from your beginnings that told you what to do."

She rested both her bare elbows on the frame of the table and leaned forward with her eyes fixed on him. Her eyes were dark and wide. On her wrists the aquamarine bracelets swung back. She was about to speak.

An undersized brown hand was laid on the edge of the backgammon table, and they both looked up, startled. A small man stood smiling down. He was dapper, like a little bridegroom on a wedding cake. He wore glasses attached to a black ribbon that hung slantwise across his starched white shirt.

"Lovely Mrs. March, I haven't spoken to you," he said.

She held out her hand.

"Mr. Connolly—Mr. Levy."

Hector got up. His big face looked down at the little man's.

"How's your work?" he asked roughly.

"I beg your pardon?"

"Mr. Levy is the head of Chameaux Frères. . . ."

Hector looked from one face to the other as though he thought he were being gulled.

"You're a banker?"

"I am, sir."

"My mistake. I'll give you the game," he said to Leda. He pulled out his wallet and laid two bills down on the table and walked away.

Mr. Levy slipped into the vacated chair.

"What an extraordinary friend for you to have."

"I've barely met him."

"Odd . . . you appeared heart to heart. Do you know, I thought he was going to knock me down. Anti-Semitic, I thought to myself."

As they sat talking, a conversation as formal and experienced as a dance, Lambert Rudd came up to the table and laid his hand on the edge of it. It was a square hand with blunt fingers, rather large. Leda turned away from Levy and looked up into Lambert's eyes.

"Are you going to show me your view?" he asked.

Leda walked between the little man and the tall man to the long windows at the end of the drawing-room that gave on a small glassed-in balcony.

"This *is* an old friend," she said. "I haven't seen him for years."

"You'll want to talk," Levy said and, bowing as Lambert opened the long window, left them.

On this New Year's Eve, although it was now late, the city that lay below them had not even begun to fade. It twinkled up a hundred streets and its colored lights winked. But no sounds penetrated the glass walls. They had closed the window behind them on the party.

Lambert's voice had changed since the old days in the studio on Ipswich Street. He sounded more hurried, more impatient.

"All this horsing around for years like a fancy dance when what I wanted was to see you. It's so *ridiculous*. Now here you are. It's perfectly simple. Nobody can see if I kiss you."

"Oh, no, no, no, no! Don't be absurd. It's wonderful to see you, but you can't be like that. We've got to go way back and catch up with each other before we can even be friends."

"*Why?* I'm just the same. You're just the same. Stop being so damned cerebral. I *hate* brains. They're at the bottom of all the trouble. Come on, kiss me, my darling."

"Do you want me to go in? I won't have it. You're crazy and I won't be treated that way. I've got to know all about you and I want you to know all about me."

But the coincidence of meeting hung like doom around them; it must mean something. They were both thinking of the last time, when she had wept and he leaned over the car door, so long ago. There was significance to that; this re-encounter years afterwards took on a balancing significance. They both assumed it at once. There was no attempt at acting casually or pretending they had forgotten anything. A coincidence had occurred and something was beginning.

Lambert reached for her; he shook his head as if driving away flies; he tried to kiss her.

"Stop it. This is a wrestling match. It's too degrading."

He let his arms hang by his sides and his face was betrayed and baffled.

"All right. But I've always imagined it being different with you. All this *talk*. Jesus Christ! All right."

Having won, she leaned on one bare shoulder against the glass, a cigarette in her fingers, looking at him gravely, and began to talk.

"Well, for one thing, you're still married, aren't you? And your wife is sick, isn't she?"

Although he did not touch her now he still looked eager and hurried; his eyes were fixed on her with an intent impatience.

"Yes. That's true. One thing I've always known is that I should have been married to you. But I'm married, and my wife is insane."

Leda took a long breath.

"Tell me one thing," he said. "Don't you know that you should have been married to me all this time?"

"Yes."

"That was the mistake."

"Yes, that was the mistake. That was the beginning. Everything since then has been a waste of time."

He started to reach out to touch her, but let his hand drop.

"Well, tell me one other thing. Do you want love?"

"Yes. I want love. If I can."

"You can, if you will."

"That's what I don't know. I've felt for a long time that I couldn't love anybody—the way other people seem to love—a person. I can love feelings, and places, and ideas, but I keep thinking I can't love a person."

"You loved me, though."

"Yes, that's what I'm thinking about. I think I loved you. I want to explain to you. Are you listening?"

He nodded.

"I've come to a sort of a crossroads, since I went to Reno. My life has all been going in one direction, and I don't like it, it's been getting less and less what I want. I started that way a long time ago when I was young and insecure and took other people's ideas of what was success. Now I know it's not me, and I don't feel afraid any more. I can do what I please. But I wasted all that time. Now I want to go back and start over."

She turned and looked down at New York and spoke over her shoulder.

"I don't want to go on with *that* any more, in that direction. I want to find my own way back to *me*. I haven't been me for years—oh, years. Since I got back I've been marking time, living in a hotel, not wanting to start anything till I could decide what point in the past I want to aim back to. I want to find the right place, way back, when I was still myself, and then go on from there in my own direction, the one I would have taken if I hadn't been so afraid and self-distrustful. I want to be myself. I *hate* being this person I made myself into. I want to live in—I want to live in a simple, innocent world inside myself, where I do what a voice out of my own beginnings tells me to do."

She looked out through the glass wall in silence. Then she went on.

"It's bad, it frightens me, not to think my own thoughts. For years I've thought thoughts that went with the way I was dressed. I want to be my own nature, the way it was born. Do you remember how I used to write poetry in the studio? Well, I haven't written poetry for years, because the pipe-line between my nature and my mind was all stopped up. You can't write poetry about what you think somebody else would feel about something. All these things I've done, the person I made myself into to give myself confidence—they get in the way like spots before the eyes. It's such a waste of time—and all because I was afraid and didn't believe my own self was any good. I wanted to be like the successful people."

"If you hadn't gone off from me. If you'd kept on the way you were going then, you would have been yourself, wouldn't you?"

"Yes," she said. "I think I would. I think that was the right way."

"What shall we do?" he said. "Shall we stay here in New York, or shall we go away somewhere together?"

"Oh, wait," she said. "We haven't come to where we can discuss that yet. We've got to talk. I have to find out about you. And I haven't really made it clear about me, either. It's so hard to say. It goes away when you try to say it."

He groaned.

"Why do we have to talk so much? Why can't we just walk out of here now and start living? Why do we have to talk?"

"We have to. It's got to be clear. I don't want to move in a fog, and have things come up afterward. I want to get everything straight before we decide anything."

"I don't like it. It kills life. Emotion's like a wave, and if you don't catch it at the crest, it breaks."

"If it breaks then it wasn't worth anything. I want to be sure."

"What I want to know is, when we can kiss each other."

She laughed.

"Tell me. Did you feel you had gone wrong, too?"

"Of course. Everything was as wrong as hell."

"Did it get in your way? Did it hurt your painting?"

He gave her a queer, wild look.

"Yes, it did at first," he said rapidly. "But I've learned a lot about painting I didn't know. Oh, Christ, yes, I nearly went nuts stewing about it for a while, it seemed as if I couldn't see right. . . . But I've learned a lot. I didn't know a damned thing. I worked with Kahn in Florence. He's got something, but I've made it into more, for myself. I'll tell you about it. The form must have an *aura*, that makes it luminous. It's kind of an old thing painters knew once but it got forgotten. It's the whole answer. Auras. . . ."

The glass door into the room was flung open.

"Mrs. March. . . ." One of the hotel butlers stood at the door, with downcast eyes, self-effacing. Leda stepped inside.

Hector Connolly stood before the dwarfed marble fireplace, his felt hat on the back of his head and his overcoat hanging from his shoulders. He looked as though he had just knocked someone down. His white face looked truculently from side to side. But no one seemed to be hurt. All around him the well-dressed people talked with heads averted, and he was all alone. Something must have happened only the second before. Something had just finished happening. Leda took a step forward. Hector's gaze fastened on her.

"You're all full of——"

His voice came loud and harsh in the murmuring room, and then he flung away from the mantelpiece and ploughed through the rooms. The butler followed him, and there was the loud slam of the outer apartment door.

Mr. Levy appeared out of nowhere at Leda's elbow, little and Levantine with his clever, ugly face full of humiliation.

"I was the cause," he said. "The Jew and the Irishman. I must apologize and go. I have caused all this unpleasantness. The usual thing. He said I was a kike, a sheeny, a cherrypicker, he said I killed Christ. . . ."

"As drunk as a monkey," a voice said nearby.

"Dear Mr. Levy," Leda said. "Please don't go. You are my honored guest. It is I who must apologize. I beg your pardon with all my heart."

The little man looked up and saw that there were tears in her eyes. They were real tears.

"I can't bear that this should have happened to you in my house," she said. "I can't bear it."

All around the party was declining from tension into pleasantness again. Already the incident was forgotten. It was an ugly, anachronistic vulgarity from what was already the past—the age of violence. In all the heads of all the people at the party was the cloudy, but settled resolve: we must make New York, our world, very clear and neat now. No violence any more. We must make it attractive.

Leda began to walk forward, to join other guests. The hour was growing late. Soon they would leave, decorously.

"But what became of his wife?"

Mrs. Hector Connolly had not been seen for a long time.

She was not found until seven o'clock in the morning, when the governess came in to get Treat up. The governess shut the window down and turned. There lay the little boy, in his bed, and on top of it, her head at the foot, lay Mrs. Connolly, all curled up with the quilt and the extra blanket over her. They were both asleep. There was no question in Miss Lovejoy's mind of what sort of performance this was—drunken guests of Mrs. March's coming into Treat's room and falling asleep. She shook the young woman's shoulder briskly. She herself had slept soundly since midnight the night before.

"I think you'd best be getting home," she said, with a rising inflection.

Treat was not allowed to go with Betsy to the door. She went alone through the hotel rooms and found her wrap in the deserted dressing room. Alone, in evening clothes, she went down in the elevator and took a cab outside the hotel. The streets were freshly washed, and empty. The taxi dashed unblocked downtown. She went in and borrowed the fare from the sleepy clerk behind the desk, paid the taxi, and took the elevator up to the room.

Hector lay on the bed, still in his evening clothes, with his stiff shirt pulled open. His eyes were closed. The curtains were drawn and only a little of the clear morning light came around the edges; the room was gray and close and smelled of cigarettes. Betsy turned and shut the door softly.

When she turned back Hector's eyes were open.

"Where have you been?" he said. He did not stir.

"I couldn't help it!"

She had too much to explain and too much anxiety, and no idea of where to begin or how to make him understand about it.

"It was so awful . . . I knew how you felt . . . I didn't know what you would do, darling . . . I couldn't bear it. I know you hate me for running away. I went into the little boy's room. I fell asleep, and I only just woke up. Have you been here all this time? What did you do? I didn't hear anything. I came the minute I waked up. . . ."

Hector closed his eyes.

"*Don't you believe me?*"

He sighed, a long sound.

"Don't you believe what I'm telling you?"

"Do you have to talk so much?" he said under his breath.

She tiptoed around the room, undressing, putting on a bathrobe. She kept glancing at him, but his eyes were closed and she did not dare to speak. At last she said,

"Shall I order breakfast?"

"Why not? We've got to eat."

She ordered over the telephone, and then went in and took a bath. But she stayed tense in the hot water. When she came out of the bathroom Hector had not moved. The breakfast came and she pulled up the shades and the waiter put the table in the window.

"Do you want to eat?"

"Why not?"

He drank three cups of coffee opposite her in the sunshine. His face was almost green in the strong light. She could not imagine what he was thinking. There was nothing to do but brace herself and wait. He said nothing at all.

He set down his cup in the sloppy saucer and pushed back his chair.

"Well, when are you going to get a divorce?"

"Oh, Hector!"

She began to cry, staring at him through the tears that magnified his face.

"Don't give me that. You don't want to be married to me. You don't know any more about being married than the first bag out on University Place."

"But what have I done?"

Now he had started. Now he was talking.

"You haven't done a damn thing. Not a thing. You never will do a thing. Go on, sit there and bawl. It's so useful. A good wife. My God, when I think of all the talk you gave me about being a good wife I could laugh. It's my own damn fault. I've always been a sucker. I thought you knew what you were .talking about. Now for God's sake go away and get a divorce and go back to your men and leave me alone."

"Oh, Hector . . . I don't want anything but you. You don't believe me."

He got up and lit a cigarette and began to walk around the room, talking.

"Yes, I believe you. I believe you've been faithful to me. But that's not it. You're a cretin. A half-wit, I can't trust you. You do what I tell you to but you don't get anything straight by yourself. I have to cross-question you to get anything. You have no understanding by yourself of what I want. Oh Christ, it isn't just sex. You're so one-tracked! You haven't any integrity. Look at the way you lived. I come along and you want me so you cut it out because I don't like it. But you didn't do it yourself. You can't figure anything out for yourself. How can I trust you? How could you ever be a wife?"

"But I want to be just what you want."

"I can't take care of you as if you were an imbecile child. I want a wife who sees things for herself and understands how I feel. Sure, you do everything I say. If I said, 'Jump out the window,' you'd probably do it. But I don't want a woman to jump just because I say jump. I want someone who's got a big view of life, who's a fine woman, and I can trust her."

"I will be. I will be. I'm trying. I will be strong and good."

He gave her a brief, distracted glance, as if she only interrupted him.

"Quit trying to get me into society!" he cried. "Even you ought to know enough not to do the things you do. I know I'm a mucker. I know what I did. I'm glad I did it."

"What?"

"Oh, skip it. You wouldn't understand it if I told you. You were asleep in the nursery, weren't you? Yes, I believe you. You ought to be in a home for the feeble-minded. If anybody tried to sleep with you, they probably could, because you wouldn't know how not to."

"That's not true! I've never been unfaithful to you! I never will be! You're the only unfaithful one."

"I wondered when that would start coming up. You did quite well. Holding in so long. I knew you didn't have the faintest understanding of that. I shouldn't have ever told you. You can't see beyond your own little low-grade mind where everything is simple as ABC. I didn't expect you to understand—yes, I did, but I was a sucker."

"I'm not reproaching you. I never reproached you."

"No, you're a saint. You are a genius at whitewashing yourself. You're all pure, aren't you? Well, I can tell you you're not. The way you lived is still there and you still haven't explained to my satisfaction why you lived like that. I incline to the opinion it was because you're a cretin.

"You thought I was happy, didn't you? I've been in hell. But you wouldn't see that. If there's a lot of sex you think everything's fine. It never occurred to you a man would want to drown what he was feeling, did it? I won't go on living here with you any longer. I won't see your lovers everywhere I go, grinning at me. I won't have you pretending you're a good girl, taking me to your God damned friends' houses. I won't go on being your tame crow."

"Oh, Hector!"

"If you want to be my wife you've got to be my wife. You've got to live my way. I won't live here any more, I'll go crazy in this filthy place. I can't work. You didn't think about that, did you? All you want is a tame crow to follow you around and butter you up and go where you say and make you his whole life. Well, I'm not that kind of a bird. I want to write a book, and you know it. Well, I'm going where I can write it. If you want to come too you can, but you've got to work. You've got to be a good wife. Or you can get out. I'm leaving. I'm quitting work tomorrow. I'm going somewhere where nobody ever heard of you and where I won't see your lovers everywhere I look. When I get there I'm going to work. If you come, you'll be second to that—if you even get to be second. God, when I think of my marriage and how I used to want to be unfaithful and wasn't, and when I think of how you went about being married to that poor cuckold of yours—I could vomit. I'll give you a chance to be a good wife, on my terms, my way, in a place I'll pick out. But God knows you don't have to take the chance."

"I'll go anywhere you go."

"Oh, don't be melodramatic."

He sat down on the edge of the bed with his back to her. The room was perfectly still, and full of sunshine. There was a long silence.

"I'm sorry," he said. "I'm sorry. But I felt like I was going nuts. I know you can take it. I'm sorry."

"Do we always have to have crises like this?"

"I don't know."

"I think we ought to go away," she said. "I think we both would be happier somewhere else."

"That's what I said."

"I've got some money left," she said. "Enough for a while. How long would it take you to write your book?"

"Not long. Not if I just could work. I've got all the stuff. If we could just get a house somewhere, just a shack, and get out of this hell, I could work. I've got it all planned out up to a point. Look. The thing has to balance, this way. At the start you've got the old boy, his life, old Horatio and his time. And then at the end you build up to a parallel, see, with a different kind of piracy and . . ."

He got up and began to walk up and down the room, talking rapidly, while Betsy sat quite still in her chair and listened and nodded.

## CHAPTER L

ONCE SHE HAD LET GO, Leda had the feeling that she had become a different person. Not a strange person, but the person she always might have been, that had been there all the time waiting to be allowed to live. It was quite extraordinary how this new person who was herself had popped right out, become a whole character; it was like a discovery. You stripped away the surface, that long-built-up, careful coating, and there was the real picture underneath. She wanted to laugh. Carelessness, ease, were part of her discovery. One day at lunch in a little Italian place uptown nearby Lambert's studio, for example, she had suddenly realized—"I can be shy if I want to!" It was so amazing. For all those years she had felt that compulsion to be self-assured, poised: now it came to her like a flash of light, simple, amazing: if she felt like being shy, why, she could simply be shy!

It was a snowy winter. Lambert's studio was on the top of a house in the Nineties, a warm, bare garret with skylights through which stared the pale blue winter sky. Leda used to walk up there every morning, all the way from her hotel, in a fur coat and high overshoes through the cold bright streets that were skimmed with ice and filled with shovellers, and come into the heated place with her face cold and tingling. Lambert would already be working in his shirtsleeves; he would throw his arms around her when she came, with his thumb still holding his palette out and away from her coat, and kiss her. She posed for him all day, and they talked and Lambert sang, and at noon they would go out into the cold and run up the street to the little restaurant to eat hot minestrone and gnocchi. It was like the old days in the studio in Boston, but different too, and for Leda, better; because in those days there was always something pushing at her, she had not ever been wholly sure of her choices, and now she had lived through a number of years that had left her as she was now: with a feeling of assurance, of impatience with all she had learned. The hell with it! She was not bothered any longer by the outside world. She was herself. Let them go about their business and she would go about hers. She had played their game, and won at it, and found her victory meaningless; very well. Now she could do what she wanted to do, and this was it.

It was like having the light of the sun come into a place which had been lit by lamps. She saw things, and now it came to her that that was really what she wanted in her life, to see things. It was impossible to see things when she was occupied with a life whose execution was like the planned strategies of a campaign. Away with all that! She would never plan anything again. The air was cold as icicles, the sky was the color of icy water, the snow fell at intervals, softly, silently, over the gray city. Everything was magic. She seemed to drink up the warm air of the studio that smelled of paint and turpentine, and now every single thing had a lovely significance: Lambert's blue shirt, the pools of mixed and unmixed color on his palette, the sky through the skylight, the crackling of the old radiators, the dash out into the street at noon, the winter sunshine, the smell of food cooking in the Italian place and the taste of hard breadsticks and red wine and cheese. This was being alive. To be alive it was necessary to be free. And she was free. There was not a thing out of her carefully constructed past life that she cared for, that she would bother for.

When she went home in the late afternoon, in the cold twilight, to her hotel, she would stop by Treat's room to kiss him good night. She smiled with friendly good will at the face of her child looking up at her. She wanted him to be happy, and inquired as to his day that was spent in Central Park with Miss Lovejoy; he had children in to supper and the governess was instructed to order special ice cream in moulds. No longer did Leda feel the dissatisfaction and disappointment she had felt about her son; that was an enslaved, involved feeling that she was rid of. She was free of possessiveness and she wanted him to be free too. She told herself that this was by far the best way; she didn't want her child to have a mother complex. This way she was a gay and friendly adjunct to his life, who read to him and saw that he had what he wanted, but did not try to make him a different boy from what he was. Let him like the machinery of his toy trucks, and food, and other children. He had a right to be the person he was, just as now she was being the person she had really been meant to be.

When James wrote to her in late February and asked her if she would not reconsider her custodianship, if she would not let him have the child for half the year, she was able to write back freely and generously and say that she would. Before the New Year she would not have considered such a thing. Now it seemed to her fair. James had gone back to Boston before she even left for Reno, and she supposed he was building up a practice there, or working in some laboratory. She wished him well. She wished everybody well. James and Treat had always got along, and it was right that they should have half the year together; they were father and son. The old wild irritation and exasperation that James had always caused her was buried now, and she hoped he would be happy in his way. It had been her own fault for marrying him for reasons unconcerned with love. She was sorry for the years he had wasted on her—almost as sorry as she was for the years she had spent for nothing out of her own life.

She meant to be happy now, now that she had learned the way and owned the confidence. It would be nice for James to be happy too, and Treat. The boy still was her own child, and she wanted him to grow up loving her and admiring her; she would see to it that he did. But six months she could spare. She would enjoy being free for six months. A half-and-half arrangement would be just right. And much fairer.

She had her lawyer draw up another agreement giving Treat to James for the six winter months, but leaving the legal custody in her own hands. 'The party of the second part shall have the right to have the aforementioned child with him at his home or place of residence for a period not to exceed six (6) months commencing November 1st. . . .' The agreement would go into effect the winter following this.

The ties and troubles of the workaday world seemed to have lost their weight. Even the fact of Maizie's sickness and confinement, which troubled and harassed Lambert, since it appeared to make it impossible for them to be married, seemed unreal and unimportant. The new Leda was not any longer obsessed with such things as the strategical importance of marriages. Occasionally it occurred to her that people might be talking about her and Lambert—people always knew things; she realized that now. But she did not care. The panic that had attacked her long ago in Boston at the thought of scandal touching her name seemed now interred. She was interested in being the magic individual whom she had cheated and suppressed too long. Let anyone talk. Lambert would marry her if he ever could, and in the meantime, and forever, there was the world, rediscovered and beautiful, to be lived in and seen and enjoyed in freedom and delight. She had never really needed people, only their good opinion. Now she was able to laugh at that. She wanted to explore all the sensations and reactions of the person she had so recently released; there was enough for a lifetime there, and too much time had been lost already.

Something kept her from agreeing to live in the same place with Lambert in New York. It had, of course, to do with her child. Treat liked Lambert, who drew him long strips of pictures giving the history of a truck named America; he grew entirely used to having Lambert in the apartment drinking cocktails with his mother every late afternoon. But after they had dined, and gone perhaps to a theatre, or more likely sat and talked, Lambert was always sent home. Not that he did not make love to her. But in New York she could not even now conceive of anything further than their days together in the studio, their evenings when they were so gay and when she laughed so much with her new freedom, and understood and agreed now when Lambert made fun of people. She felt a surging, astonished pleasure in laughing at people, being rid of them, seeing how preposterous they were.

In March, however, they went to Bermuda. Lambert wanted to paint landscape. The high tension Leda felt in him all the time seemed to center on his work. Not that he was as impatient with it or as critical as he had used to be. On the contrary he was on a new track, one that he believed in fanatically, and which he kept wanting reassurance on. It was concerned with a theory of auras, the surrounding of objects with a halo of other color which was intended to give luminosity to the object. Leda herself could not feel enthusiasm for his new manner. She preferred the way he had painted back in the old Boston days. But her feeling was that everyone, surely, must be able to see his own way through things and must be allowed to see it through alone. She listened with some care and sympathy while Lambert walked restlessly around the New York studio expounding again and again the superiority, the absolute uniqueness, essentialness, of this way of painting. All other ways were up the wrong street; this way only could the thing be done right. After a winter of painting Leda after his new tenets, Lambert, although he expressed himself as satisfied with the work he had done, said that he wanted to apply the method to outdoor painting. He wanted to paint water, and green trees, and they went to Bermuda in the middle of the month and took Treat and Miss Lovejoy.

The morning when they all went ashore in Hamilton and drove in a carriage to the hotel was one Leda would not forget. On that morning all her new freedom and her joy in living seemed to culminate. She felt bursting with delight. The harbor lay vivid green, streaked with brilliant blue, and the trees were green and overflowing with cascades of flowering vines, scarlet, yellow, and orange. The air was sweet and mild and smelled of lilies. After the New York cold, it was like escaping to an ultimate South Sea island of beauty and warmth and freedom. Treat bounced up and down on the seat and yelled to the horse, and Lambert, sitting facing them in the carriage, looked sharply from side to side, his face bemused.

Leda took a house far out on the island towards Somerset, a pink block with a broad terrace looking over the bay and a stepped roof of purest white coral. There was a one-room guest-house at the foot of the hill where Lambert lived. That was surely sufficient concession to propriety, especially since she was not alone; Treat and Miss Lovejoy lived there in the house with her. "Mr. Rudd is renting the little house from me," she said to the governess the day they moved in. "Yes, Mrs. March?" That was all there was to it.

Every morning he came up to the main house in his dressing-gown and they had breakfast out in the early flower-sweet sunshine on the terrace. A little later Lambert would ride away on a bicycle with bathing-trunks under his trousers, a paint-box slung by a strap over his shoulder, the wire basket on his handle-bars filled with small wooden panels to paint on. He would tell her where he was going, and later in the morning she would join him on her bicycle, with their lunch in a box in the basket. He liked to have her with him when he painted, he liked to be able to talk and to sing and not to be alone. She would lie on the beaches where he painted, scribbling on a pad of paper, and before lunch they would go swimming in the mild water.

There was really no more to be asked of life. In the evenings they would go out in a boat on the bay in the starlight, or ride into Hamilton and sit in the bars for a while, or go dancing at a hotel. They drove all over the island, and dined at the country restaurants; they explored the old town of St. George's, read the obituary inscriptions in the church there, rode their bicycles for miles in the pure sunshine between the hedges of flowers, and went down in diving-bells and walked along the sea-bottom. One day, driving through St. George's in a carriage they were so happy, they were so gay, that they began to bow to the passers-by, as though they were a king and queen passing.

They would go home in the sweet dusk and make drinks of rum and lime-juice and falernum and drink them out on the twilit terrace.

"You're so perfect," he said, insistently, reaching for her hand in the darkness. "You're so lovely in strange places like Bermuda. I'd rather travel with you than anyone, man or woman, I ever saw."

The tenseness of his nature seemed nowadays to take the form of insisting on things, over and over. He never said a thing once. He repeated it, varied his statement of it, said it again and again.

This was a place, she felt, where anyone would be bound to be happy. There was no question but what Lambert was happy; he said so every day, as though he expected to be contradicted; he almost shouted it. Treat played all day on the little beach behind the house with some children who came down in bathing-suits from the house up the road, with their nurse. And for Miss Lovejoy this was a little England; she found a number of women with whom to make friends. Everyone was happy.

It was in the middle of May that Leda took the morning's mail along in the basket when she rode down to the beach beyond the bay to join Lambert, around eleven o'clock. It was an especially warm day. She leaned her bicycle against a tree at the top of the dune and walked down the path in her bathing-suit with towels over her arm, carrying lunch and the mail.

Lambert was painting on the beach up under an overhanging coral cliff. He stood with his legs planted apart, in his bathing-suit, in front of the slender folding easel he had set up. When she called to him he turned. His face was burned dark mahogany brown. He held his palette in one hand and the brush in the other. A bunch of brushes was stuck into the hole of the palette with his thumb.

Leda dropped down into the fine, hot, silky sand.

"Here's your mail," she said. She began to tear open her own letters.

He set the palette down carefully on the sand and squatted down on his heels and stuck the brush between his teeth. He sorted through the letters and ripped one open. Then there was silence while they read.

"Listen," he said in a low voice.

She turned her face from the letter she was reading. The sun was in her eyes, and she squinted at Lambert. The sun burned her sunburned shoulders. The air smelled of the salt sea.

"'Dear Mr. Rudd,

Since my last letter to you in January I am glad to report that Mrs. Rudd has been making considerable progress. I may say that we have come to feel extremely hopeful about her case. Dr. Birdsong, who has recently become associated with our staff, has become interested in Mrs. Rudd's case and has been having daily periods of talk with her which have proved helpful beyond anything we expected. These talks, which serve the double function of a relief to Mrs. Rudd's agitated depression and something we call re-education, were undertaken on Dr. Birdsong's own initiative since as I wrote you we have never had much success in inducing Mrs. Rudd to tell us about the mental content which troubled her.

I am writing to you to suggest that you come to Virginia if that is possible, for a few months at least. Dr. Birdsong, who has assumed the management of Mrs. Rudd's case, feels that part of her readjustment must include a successful reassumption of her position in the world as a wife and a mother. He feels that very shortly she will be well enough to see you and her child, and that it will be most valuable if this can be arranged. I shall look forward to hearing from you of what plans you can make, and am delighted to be able to assure you of this change for the better in the condition of . . .'"

Out on the grass-green and sapphire water rode a white yacht, long, pointed, and shining in the full sunshine. The little waves came up on the coral shore of Bermuda, and slapped lightly against the yellow sands.

Leda ran her fingers up into her thick, dark hair, and simply looked at Lambert. He lay back on his elbows, squinting into the sun.

"Fantastic," he said. "The God damned most fantastic . . . Always."

"What are you going to do?"

"I'll have to go, of course. I couldn't refuse to help to get her well. And if she gets well . . . After all, I couldn't marry you before because she was sick. The great thing's to get her well. I'm responsible for the whole thing. I'm responsible for everything."

She stared at him. That other side of his life, his life with Maizie, had always seemed strange, unimaginable; full of a vague, exciting menace. She knew it was brutal, that it was full of suffering. But she had never tasted any of that side of him. To her he was always someone she was able to love, who suited her; she tried to make herself imagine being afraid of him.

"I'll have to go," he said. "Break up all this here. But you've got to come too. You could take a house. Take Treat. Live there. I don't see why I should have to give up everything. You want to, don't you? I could live in another house. You aren't going to get funny about it, are you? After we've found how life can be together? And as soon as she gets well, why, we can start. . . ."

"I don't see why not," she said calmly. Her eyes and her skin and her body were full of sun. She began to think about Virginia. Virginia was a new, a beautiful place to live in. She would ride through the summer fields on a horse, seeing it and feeling it, with new thoughts forming inside of her, living.

## CHAPTER LI

IN A MONTH the life they had lived in Bermuda was transferred, in large measure, to a place outside Annestown in Virginia, called Andorra. Lambert had gone ahead, leaving Leda in Bermuda, and he had taken this house for her. It was a house built in the early nineteenth century, up a long avenue lined with black cedars, at whose end the square brick house with its white doorway stood, flanked with box, with mimosa trees and crape myrtle. It was let furnished with early Victorian things, all jumbled together in the dim rooms with their long shuttered windows. Inside it was always very cool and dark. But on the front porch the smells of flowers and of the box floated up, hot and sweet, and through the gap in the center of the avenue could be seen the misty purple peaks of the Blue Ridge, far away and strange in this lonely land.

The place had a small tenant cabin, and it was here that Lambert lived, in two rooms. A colored man named Davis went down from the big house to clean and cook breakfast for him. He came up to the house for dinner.

Leda had arrived with her son and his governess. She had been met by Lambert at the station in the hot little town and been driven out through the increasingly strange and romantic country. Next the little girl, Honora, arrived. They had settled that the practical thing was for her to stay at the big house, where she could play with Treat; there was no room for her anyway at the cabin. The thing was, she was actually in her father's care, as she was supposed to be.

The evening after Honora arrived, Lambert and Leda sat on the porch of Andorra drinking their coffee. The night was soft, like thick black velvet, and noisy with the frogs and crickets in the wide fields all around.

"You know, people are going to talk," she said, into the darkness.

"Now look," Lambert said. There was the sound of his cup being put down in its saucer. "Let's get it all clear."

He sounded nervous and impatient. In the darkness Leda smiled. Lambert got so wound up about things. He was as tense as a spring drawn out. She knew without seeing how he looked now: his shoulders hunched, his dark face darker, his body twisted and rigid. It was an odd thing how he, who appeared so hounded, could set her free.

He was far more tense than he had been in the old days in Boston. He had always been violent, but this was more than violence. It was as if he could not endure the slightest stop put in his way, as if he were driven to frenzy by a person, an argument, a point of view that blocked him. He had developed a mania for clear sailing. The obstacle of Maizie was always there, and he was always hurling himself at it, and over and over trying to remove it by his calculations about the future, trying to make it seem gone because some day it would be gone, and then sinking back before the fact of its present existence.

"Let's clarify it all," he said rapidly. "I'm here to help in getting Maizie well. Honora's here for that too. I'm not actually living with you, I'm living in a separate house. You're being kind enough to keep an eye on the little girl. It wouldn't do for her to live down there with me. I wouldn't have the faintest idea of how to take care of her. You needn't be here on account of me, if that's what you mean. You're a free woman; you wanted to come to Virginia so you took a house. Maybe I interested you in coming to Virginia. But why not? You have to live somewhere; you're fed up with New York. You like Virginia. I live in a cabin on your place. That's the story. Sure, people can always make another story. But they can't get hold of anything to matter."

"It wouldn't do Maizie much good to know, I suppose."

"Now, look. Be clear about it. Maizie doesn't have to know. And the whole thing is, the point is—when she gets well I'm going to explain to her that I want to marry you. God damn it! Don't you see?"

"Yes, I see. Does that doctor you talk to know about me?"

"No, of course not," he said in a hasty, muffled voice. "He knows I'm living out here in the country in a cabin. . . ."

In the dark she heard his chair scraping, and he came and put his arms around her.

"Leda, Leda. Don't let's go on stewing about it. I love you. I always want you. You're the answer to everything. You're beautiful. You're strong, I love you. . . ."

The soft, deep night was all around, far and lonely in this southern country; a whippoorwill called at intervals from the lower fields. Far away in the night the late freight trains could be heard hastening across the countryside, and the sound of their lonely whistles crying in the far darkness.

"I love you too," she said. In the darkness she rose and with his arm around her they began to walk down the lane to the cabin.

In the mornings it was growing daily hotter and the doves moaned in the eaves of Andorra. The sweet-smelling air came in the open window and a colored woman named William, who had come with the house, brought Leda's breakfast to her on a tray. There was also a cook, and the man Davis who served dinner at night.

When Leda got up to dress she could see across the green wheatfields the house half a mile away which was Andorra's nearest neighbor, Porto Bello. It rode on the top of a swell like a ship. It belonged to some people named Rickett. Mrs. Rickett had left cards one afternoon when Leda was out, over at the cabin.

But Leda did not plan to return the call. She did not want people any more. She no longer depended upon them. She wanted to be with Lambert, or alone, feeling and seeing privately, and people always broke in upon the deep, delicate pleasure which this was. She had, she felt, learned this much: people were no good to her. The beautiful, secret, privately experienced life she had now was too lovely to allow people—people—to interrupt.

When she came out of the wide front door into the hot sunshine, in a linen dress, the two children would be playing on the lawn under the cedar trees, with the governess sitting on the porch watching them. Leda and Miss Lovejoy exchanged good mornings. Leda would stare abstractedly at the children for a few minutes, smiling, but there was nothing there to hold her. She would walk down the drive to the side of the house, down the red clay road past the barns, along the track that led through the fields and the patch of woods to the cabin.

It was a small whitewashed shack at the edge of a field. Davis would be in the lean-to kitchen behind, washing up Lambert's breakfast dishes; he sang loudly in a high tenor voice. Lambert wore a pair of trousers and a shirt with the sleeves rolled up; he would be smoking on the little porch or sometimes painting in the yard. Generally he took his folding easel and paint-box farther away, looking for new scenes. But he always waited till Leda came in the mornings. This was where their real life was lived, in this cabin. The big house was a front. This was where they really lived.

"Hello, darling," he would call when he saw her coming down the path in her white dress.

"Hello."

She would come up on the porch and kiss him. The cloth of his shirt felt thin and fine over the muscles of his upper arms. They smiled at each other. She would sit down and light a cigarette, and they would look together over the green fields, already hazy with heat. Never had Leda felt such calm, such large country; it had a kind of strangeness from its size to her, and she felt her heart expand in the early summer heat, and beat with a slow, full beat. Her mind surged with ideas; she had a feeling of being deeply occupied.

"Are you happy?" he said.

"I'm terribly happy. Are you?"

"Yes, yes. I won't be perfectly happy till we get this all straightened out. . . ."

His forehead knotted into strings. She looked at him and smiled. She wondered if it was because he was a Bostonian that he had to have everything tied up and completed before he could consent to be happy. As for herself, she thought she had never been a Bostonian, really. She had been born with other channels of reaction. For a long time she had tried to be a Bostonian. But now, she thought, she did not have to bother with anything any more.

"I'm happy being with you," she said. "You give me all this peace."

After he had gone to painting she would go into the small dim living-room of the cabin. She had sent boxes full of books down here from the big house when she first came. She would lie on the dark red couch inside and read, Matthew Arnold, Byron and Shelley, Dickens, Dostoievsky, and Tolstoi, picking from among the dark, musty-smelling books.

The stream always flowed here, in this place. She would read, and the current of her mind would turn into its private channel and she would be lost; she would put the books down on the floor and pick up the pad of paper and the pencil and begin to write down what flowed into her mind, and it seemed as if now, in these days, everything was made clear and articulate. All that in ordinary life was matter of fact, obscure, and complicated was now resolved; she seemed to know the answer to things which in life she did not know the answer to. The people she had known, the events which she had observed, from being meaningless became significant and she could express them in a pattern. From this shell of comprehension where she was curled she could view her own and other people's confusion and express it. All the years in New York which she had cast off now took on their value. She wrote:

> Chary of trust
> And afraid of love
> We believe in dust
> Below and above. . . .
> Until we are shown
> We cannot believe.
> We have never known
> What it is to grieve
> For someone else.
> We are racked with sorrow
> Because today melts
> Into tomorrow. . . .

And as in the old days, she wrote to Lambert:

> Because you are
> Somewhere alive
> The bumble bee
> Within the hive
> Shall suck his honey
> In content. . . .

When Lambert came back to the cabin around one Leda would be flushed and vague and smiling, and she would read him what she had written. They would sit out on the porch that the sun left shady after eleven, and eat the sandwiches Davis left on a plate in the kitchen, and drink beer.

Lambert always said he liked her verses. It was all she needed. She was so bemused from the daze she had been in that his voice praising her was enough. She would sit with a sandwich in one hand and read:

Your tears and mine augment the natural rain,
Dissolving salt in its imperfect virtue;
Whether for worse or better, in the main,
You will not know until the breath desert you.
If it be sensible to be so sorry
You will not know, nor shall I, in a hurry. . . .

O weep for the ill, and you are no more wise.
A speck upon the sun, and it no matter,
Had parted woeful oceans from your eyes;
Perceive this wrong, and you are none the better. . . .

Thus should you wilfully avert your eyes,
Dash down those tears, deny the apparent death,
Swear there's no thunder in the ominous skies,
Bite careless on the maggot in the truth— . . .

Lambert sat with his dark face in the shadow, eating. His morning's painting would be leaning, face hidden, against the cabin wall. After a time Leda would come out of her daze and ask to see it. He would turn it around. In gratitude for all he did for her, Leda would praise it. But actually, in these days, she seldom felt any emotion in looking at Lambert's work. It seemed strained, to her.

He would talk about what he was trying to do, with rising excitement. Sometimes he almost shouted.

He had this theory which he felt was the answer to art. In July he sent one of his new pictures to the North Shore Exhibition but it was not accepted. It was the jury that was all wrong, he shouted—not his theory.

Leda thought that perhaps he had not mastered his theory, and that when he had, his work might be all that now he insisted it was. In the old days he had been far more pessimistic about his work, and she had liked the work much better. He had never been satisfied with any of it, then. Now he said over and over and over that he had got it in some picture. But nothing came from the picture to move Leda.

She did not know what to say. So she praised him.

After lunch Lambert would drive in to Annestown to the hospital. He had rented an old Ford. He would drive off in the blazing sunshine, with the top down, and she waved goodbye to him as the Ford went down the lane jerking from side to side in the sun-baked ruts of red clay.

All afternoon the sun inched down the white summer sky and a thousand

insects sang from the summer fields, and the jar-fly squealed its shrill contented note. Often Leda sat on the rickety porch doing nothing at all,
staring without thought at the lizards and scorpions that darted out of holes,
across the boards, back into other holes. Their triangular reptilian heads
looked from side to side as quick as a flash and they were gone. Sometimes
a rabbit bounded past through the high dry grass and often a long thick
brown snake passed the front of the cabin with a rustling sound, moving
with the regular curves of waves upon a beach.

If Leda lifted her head she looked across long flat fields to a longer stretch,
a long flat sweep blue and misty like the sea, toward Richmond far away.
Far away trains would pass, and the sound of their sad long whistles came
through the late afternoon. Ah-aaaah, cried the whistles of the freight
trains, going down the miles and miles of track lost in the country, going
to towns with Southern names, Lynchburg, Staunton, Waynesboro. She
thought of the trains and the towns, and they seemed melancholy and
mysterious; Waynesboro; Waynesboro; it was a name like the sound of a
train whistle, long and sad.

She did not wonder why she was here nor what for, she had no plans,
she did not think of time at all. She let herself sink, sink, float upon the humming golden sea of the Virginia afternoon. All fears, all hopes and projects,
were gone away and her mind rested; she had a drowsy feeling of nourish-
ment and well-being. But herself was lost. She was part of the afternoon,
part of the world, the land, and went with them slowly toward the night.
It was beyond happiness; it was living peace. It was love.

## CHAPTER LII

Maizie sat in the big wooden-armed chair beside her window, with the
shade drawn against the sinking sun.

Outside beyond the shrubbery the people passed with sharp footsteps up
and down along the sidewalk. She could take a glance out now and then,
when she needed to, and examine their faces as they passed the entrance,
and see that they were all right; they had normal faces, of people, Annestown people, good people. On the lawn within the shrubbery the nurses
in white came and went from the nurses' home at the back. She knew them
all, Miss Bakewell, Miss Petersen, Miss Oliphant, Miss Dirk. . . . They
were her friends now, and so were the strangers on the street her friends.
There were no hideous menacing faces any more, elephants' faces, dogs'
faces.

The world, every day, became fuller and fuller of reassurance. She could
look at the black and white checked linoleum floor in the corridor and it
lay flat. Dr. Birdsong said, Think black for night, just as well, night when
you sleep. And so now she could look at the black checks, and they lay
flat, and she thought: they are black; not black for death; black for nice,
quiet night.

The bathtub was no longer full of phlegm, nor the moonlight long thin rays of cold poison as it had been once. Better and better and better and better and better, she murmured now to herself, allowing herself a little confidence, not too much, not enough to frighten the good away too suddenly, just a little more and a little more . . . better'n better'n better'n better. . . . The nurses' mouths did not open too wide, too wide, like animals' mouths; they had become kind mouths.

Even Lambert. . . . Yes. . . . But not to think about yet with too much freedom; it was not like the floor, the nurses' faces. . . . Lambert was the root; the root of all evil. . . . Dr. Birdsong said, Yes, and when you can see him and talk to him quite freely, then the root is good too, don't you see? Yes, I see, she thought, but cautiously. Take care. Everything whispered, Take care.

Maizie sat at the window, and there was a tap at the wide, golden oak door made out of one solid slab of wood, with a brass handle and no lock. She turned her head as she had turned her head so many times—for nearly six years—and said "Come in," as she had said, or not said, for nearly six years; and the door opened, as it had opened for so many years now, although sometimes it did not seem years; it seemed sometimes like a dream, a long evil night's dream . . . as it had opened on monsters, wavering shapes that leered at her so she shrank back into the chair; women's figures with dogs' faces; evil men with white coats; but now no longer.

But now no more, no more. Now she waited for the tap to come, because of him who in these days tapped; she longed for it, she watched the handle on the door to see it move; she was happy, yes, happy! She had come up out of the evil sea, and above it was the light after all, it had been there all the time; there really was happiness, and there was the sun. The sun was the source of all good, all rightness; its coming made the day, its going made the good night; the sun; and the door opened this afternoon and he came in, as he came every afternoon late like this: Dr. Birdsong.

He peered around the edge of the door—just his brown eyes—and said, "How de do."

"Oh, come in!" she cried, almost laughing, all of her pulled together inside into a knot of pleasure. She held out her hand and lifted her face.

As he always entered, every afternoon since the good things had begun, since the crawling ocean had shrunk bit by bit away, he pushed open the door, and sauntered in, limp, loose-limbed, smiling that half-smile, reassuring, tired.

He stood at the foot of the bed regarding her in the chair, and took a long breath and let it out in a sigh, and took off his long white hospital coat and tossed it over the foot of the bed. "Hot," he said. "Phew." His face was white and there was sweat on his forehead. He dropped down (as he always did) into the straight chair that faced her, pulled up his trousers at the knees, and stuck his legs out in front of him. He took a mashed package of cigarettes out of the pocket of his shirt and offered it. She took one, trembling with happiness, and he lit hers and his own.

Of course it was in the hospital, and he was her doctor, and this was his afternoon call, his daily visit. But it wasn't really a bit like that. It was her own room; she had fixed her hair only a few minutes beforehand, specially; he was calling on her, really. She smiled and smiled.

"Hot as Tophet," he said in his deep voice. "Well! How you been making out?"

"Oh, just fine!"

"Heard one just now downstairs," he said. "Dr. Parsons had it up his sleeve. Heard the story about the two bald men?"

"No . . . !"

He told her the joke and they both laughed. Every afternoon. He had a new story for her every afternoon.

"Well. Have your drive this afternoon? Get along all right?"

Her smile vanished. This was her doctor.

"Yes. It didn't bother me at all."

"You have fun with him? Pleasant time?"

"Oh . . . yes. . . ."

He stuck his long legs out farther in front of him, passed a handkerchief across his forehead. He worked so hard . . . his face was so pale . . .

"Had a talk with Mr. Rudd earlier this afternoon," he said. "Now, you know, it seems to me that he understands mighty well. He knows the ways he hurt you. We've been all over it. He seems to have the right desire to get hold of the thing properly. You haven't anything to be afraid of from him."

There was a short silence.

"Why do I have to?" she burst out. "I don't see why I have to go back to him. I don't want to! I'm happy now at last. Without him. I just want to stay as I am. If I go back to him . . . it'll just all begin again. . . ."

Two tears forced themselves from her eyes. Even in her distress she noted them, was glad of them; tears, from her eyes that had for so long, long, long, been dry, that had stared dry at horror.

"No, no," he said softly. "No. It won't begin again. If it begins again you can just quit, you know. We've been all over that. You would have been all right if you'd quit him the other time."

"But why do I have to go back to him at all? I don't *want* to!"

"Well," he said. "You know. We've talked it over. Must be something mighty strong there that held you two together through all you went through. I'm just saying you ought to give it a try. If you don't like it, when you have given it a try, all right. You don't have to stay married to him. I'm just saying, it wouldn't be fair not to give it a try."

"I can leave him if I don't like it?"

"Unh-hunh. Don't look like that, though." He looked at her smiling. "I think you're going to like it. That's the way you must try to think about it —it's going to be all right. I'm pretty sure it's going to work out. He's not the same fellow you were married to before, you know. He's older. Knows more. I've found him very cooperative," he said, twisting his face around in a way he had; resting it, perhaps.

"I know . . . but you don't realize. The way it was . . . the things he did. . . . Oh God!"

Dr. Birdsong sat still and watched his patient cry. He was a tall young man with light hair and a long square face. His hands lay limp over his knees. From time to time he twisted his face, pulling the mouth around to one side, making deep vertical furrows in his thick, pale skin.

"You've got all those things off your chest to me, haven't you?" he asked when she was quiet. "All those things he did to you?"

"Yes." She nodded.

"Well, I think it would help if you got them off your chest to him. Make a list tonight. Tomorrow you just tell him all the things he did that still bother you. All the things that would have to be different. How do you feel about doing that?"

She nodded again. She smiled a little. The light from the sunset came through the lower part of the window and made her yellow hair burn.

"But he'd be so mad," she said suddenly. "Oh, no, I couldn't. He'd be so mad! I never could tell him anything, you see. He always got so mad . . ."

"It's different now," he said patiently. "He understands better now. I've explained everything to him. He understands about controlling himself. You just try it."

She looked at the doctor's face with obedience and devotion.

"All right. I will."

"That's right. Got any questions?" he asked, smiling, his eyes moving towards the bed table.

She got up and went over and pulled open the drawer to the table. Inside was a mass of papers, written on in her handwriting, long lists of things to tell the doctor about. . . . Sometimes by mistake she would turn over one of the early ones and feel a sharp little stab of terror,—because the handwriting then was so huge, so sprawling, illegible. Now she took a paper from the top and came back to her chair and began to read off the thoughts that were listed.

"Fear that Lambert will fail me . . . conscious or unconscious? . . . Feeling I failed and afraid to fail again . . . afraid of myself, what I might do, get in a panic. . . . *Would it happen to me again,* would I break? . . . He doesn't seem real. . . . Will this go away? . . . I don't want him to be real. . . . I feel content but I don't want to go ahead. . . . I talked to Miss Williams for some time listening to what *she* said. . . . Is it true you have to be yourself and then give yourself away? . . . I feel myself being like Lambert. I want to be myself. . . . I can't love him, that's the past. . . . I want all new things. . . ."

Her voice read the questions written in the night, and his voice answered as it always answered, easy, logical; pushing things away, making little maxims of reason. This method they had followed now for months. The welter of old notes in the drawer told the story. Those earliest notes, in the inchoate hand—they sprawled hopeless words: "Dr. Birdsong . . . help me, help me . . ." the words scrambling, tumbling down the page—"crawling feeling down my legs, oh help me. . . ."

But now she spoke and he answered, question and answer, pushing away the doubt, the fear, the horror, further and further back; out into the sun they moved together, he leading her, to where feet moved step by step soberly and the heart beat quietly and the brain made thoughts; no longer cries of terror, no longer screams.

An hour went by and the doctor rose to go. He slung his white coat over his shoulders. Far away in Annestown fields, far away outside the town the crickets were singing for evening, and their song came sweet and tender through the window.

"Good night now. Have a good sleep."

She rose and held out her hand. They always shook hands, gravely. His hand was large and square and dry. He smiled down at her with his wry easy smile and she caught her breath . . .

Then he went out of the door. The door swung silently shut.

She let out her breath sharply and let her hand fall, her smile go.

She sat down again, alone by her window, and looked out at the twilight. She had the feeling of safety and comfort that he always left with her, like a daily present. Now that she was alone her mind found its new embryonic world shaped from old chaos; a kind world full of growing assurance.

Lambert was nowhere in this proper world at all. He was behind; back; blocked by the years of horror and causing them. She only thought of him out of duty, because Dr. Birdsong told her to. She would do anything he told her to, she always would, she thought, always; she would think of Lambert later because he wanted her to.

But now there was only pleasure, this flower of surprise and wonder, the slow miracle of recovery. Across the street in the dusk some evening birds flew low over the road twittering, and she thought of what they had once been to her—little lumps of filth—little frightful lumps singing a doom song. Now they were summer evening birds.

Next day when Lambert came after lunch she had her list all made.

He came to her room in his way.

First the hard, quick footsteps down the hall. She had to tell herself, following Dr. Birdsong's instructions, to shrug her shoulders at the sound of those footsteps. They couldn't do her any harm. They were just footsteps. But she had heard them long ago, in other places, when her heart had tightened and her fingers clenched. . . . But now it was different and he couldn't hurt her.

Dr. Birdsong wouldn't let him hurt her.

So then the door opened and Lambert stood in the doorway. Tall, dark, sunburned—nothing had ever happened to him. Nothing had ever touched his health. He'd never had to pay for anything. She looked at his big form with tightened lips and let him speak first.

Never again would she be eager, impatient. "Oh, darling . . . !" She knew better now. She knew what happened. Out of the hell that had come to her, the fire, the brimstone, and a thousand evil demons, she had wrested, with the help of God and one other, this flower of peace she held now in her mind. She looked at the man in the door with cool eyes. Not for anything in this dangerous world would she forget to hold her flower tight. The days of forgetting were long over. Now was the day of remembering. Let him speak first.

He came into the room, struck against the foot of the bed as he always did, and stood in front of the bureau with his brown hand lying on the white cover. He cleared his throat.

"Hello, baby! Feeling pretty good? You're looking fine. . . ."

She pressed her lips together again. Let him be uncomfortable, let him reach for words, for an easy manner. She would never help him. She knew about helping him, and what came of it. He could do very well. Nothing ever hurt him.

"I'm all right," she said. A token answer. For he did not know, he never would know, what she had been through nor of what it meant. She could never tell him. These years were incommunicable. No one would ever know, no one but herself and Dr. Birdsong.

"Like to take a drive?"

She pursed her lips, tipped her head, considered. Dr. Birdsong said it was good for them to go off, be alone together where they could talk without restraint. So she was going to do it, going to take a drive. But Lambert was not to get a false idea of her acceptance. She was not leaping, any longer, at his slightest wish. Oh, no. She was making up her own mind, having her own way.

"I'd just as soon," she said.

They walked through the corridors of the hospital that were so known to her, that were her home—both horribly and fondly; full of fearful memories and of the slow, calm rising tide of recovery. There were nurses at the corners of the corridors. They smiled, they all knew her; they all knew who Lambert was, too. Her affairs were a matter of interest to them, she belonged to them; they were her mothers, all watching her go out from home with this tall, dark man.

"Hi, Miz Rudd. . . . Hi, dear. . . . How do, Mr. Rudd. . . . Goin' out in all that heat? . . . Hi, Miz Rudd. Certainly are lookin' pretty."

The heat met them at the door; it was everywhere, huge, shimmering, buoyant. The little Ford was at the curb beyond the shrubbery. They got in and it started with a clatter and they drove away down the street, out towards the country and the mountains.

There was always this moment of realizing she was alone with him. She was at his mercy. Her heart beat faster in a reminder of the old panic when all buildings tottered, when all automobiles dashed for disaster, all mountains were huge, horrible, threatening.

But now she had a saviour and a gospel; she was safe, girded round. 'I will lift up mine eyes unto the hills whence cometh my help.' These hills. I will lift up mine eyes unto Dr. Birdsong. He said, "If you think he's driving too fast, why just say 'I'd like to take it a little slower.' He's anxious to do all he can to give you a feeling of security with him."

"I'd like to take it a little slower," she said now. Not that she meant it; they were not really going too fast. But to test this formula, to see.

"Okay, baby," he said, and sure enough the car slackened speed and they were driving along the Mountain Road rather slowly. There was the Watkins cabin, where old Aunt Frissy had lived, who did their washing when she was a little girl. Oh, lovely, sweet Virginia! But she wasn't going to tell Lambert about it. She wasn't going to pour her new, precious pleasure out to him, waste it, throw it away. What had he ever done to cherish anything of hers?

She must remember to tell Dr. Birdsong: "As we drove along Mountain Road I had the most wonderful feeling. Real happiness. As good as I ever had in my life."

"Where'll we go?" Lambert asked.

"Oh, *I* don't care. Drive over the mountain to Ranlet." Then she remembered about the lists in her purse. "Oh. Somewhere you might stop the car. There's some things I have to say to you. Dr. Birdsong wants me to."

"All right. As soon as there's a spot of shade."

In a few minutes they stopped under a row of sycamores beside the road that cast a flickering, dappled shadow on the red clay road. Lambert took out a cigarette. She reached in her purse for the pages of lists. He twisted around in the seat behind the wheel to face her. He left his free hand on the back of the seat, and his fingers touched her shoulder, lightly. But when she moved her shoulder he took his fingers away instantly.

"Shoot, darling," he said. "What's coming?"

"Well," she said, coolly, "Dr. Birdsong thought it would be a good idea if I told you some of the things that bother me out of the past. Things you did to me that still stick in my mind and make me unhappy. He thinks we ought to get them straight between us before we go any further."

"Grudges," he said.

Instantly she folded the paper and thrust it back in her purse.

"If you want to talk like that," she said, "all right. Let's go back to the hospital. We can't get anywhere. *I* don't care. I don't get any pleasure out of sitting here with you in the hot sun."

And quite unexpectedly two tears jumped out from the corners of her eyes. God forbid they were tears for Lambert. They were tears because of all this she was doing, seeing this man who had wrecked her, going through this, because . . . because Dr. Birdsong wanted her to. . . .

But Lambert snatched out his handkerchief and wiped away the tears as they lay on her cheeks. His dark big face was close to her. She shrank back.

"Darling," he said. "I swear I didn't mean anything. I'm terribly sorry," he said with deepest humility. "I'm so God damned thoughtless. Forgive me. I do understand how sensitive you are."

"I don't bear any grudges. You don't know . . . you have no idea . . ."

You don't know what it is to see slime running down the walls of your room, you don't know what it is to be surrounded with the screams of those in hell.

"I know I'm an ass. Let's forget it and go ahead. I *do* want not to hurt you, darling. I want you to get well—Jesus—more than you can possibly have any idea of."

"Well," she said, sniffling a little. She reached for the lists again. Then she glanced at him in apprehension. She was alone with him. The things she was going to say. . . . He could kill her, here, if he wanted to. He used to threaten to kill her. . . .

"You're going to get terribly mad," she said, uncertainly.

"No. I swear to you I'm not. I swear by everything. Nothing you could say would ever make me mad. I give you my solemn word," he said, his dark red face glistening with sweat. "This guy Birdsong knows. You ask him. I'm not going to hurt you."

"Well. I'll read them off. If you want to say anything, just break in."

But he said nothing. Her voice went on and on, in the heavy heat, under the sycamore trees, and he said nothing. Sometimes he looked at her for a moment, but then he would look back at the mountains, blue, misty against the sky.

". . . I hate you. . . . You were unfaithful to me when I couldn't do anything to keep you from it. . . . I hate your face. . . . I was so afraid of you I began to feel queer as soon as the time came to see you. . . . I jumped with fear when your name was mentioned. . . . You took me away from a whole lot of lovely lives I could have lived, because I loved you, and then you kicked me in the teeth and hurt me and hurt me and made me live in that awful horrible Boston. . . . I gave in to you on everything always. . . . You broke me all to pieces. . . . You were unfaithful to me over and over. . . . You made me jealous all the time. . . . You made me take a picture of you and that Spanish girl on the boat. . . ."

"*What?*" he said suddenly.

"Coming back . . . from South America," she said defiantly. "Are you pretending you didn't?"

"Oh. Fire ahead."

". . . You kissed that girl outside my stateroom window right where I could see you and you didn't care if I was in agony. . . . You never went anywhere I wanted to. . . . I went everywhere you wanted to and never got any sleep and got sicker and sicker. . . . You wrecked my whole life. . . . I hate you. . . . I hate your mouth because it makes me think of how you have snarled at me and cursed at me. . . . You just gave me hell all the time. . . . You didn't appreciate how desperately hard I was trying. . . . You hit me. . . . You said you'd sock my God damned jaw. . . . I hate the name Rudd. . . ."

The words went on and on, in the hot, melting Virginia afternoon. After a while the words stopped.

Maizie looked down. The glaring paper was shaking in her hands. There was no sound or movement from Lambert beside her. Her heart was beating hard. Let him speak first.

Her hand lay on the burning black leather of the seat between them. She felt his hand come down and cover hers. Then she looked at him. He was looking across at her; his dark face grave, gentle, oppressed. She saw that there were lines in his forehead running vertically from his eyebrows.

His hand pressed hers. But he did not speak.

She meant to make him speak first, but she was not strong enough. She had to say something.

"Well, do you want to say anything?"

"No," he said. "I always was a son of a bitch to you."

"You always loved violence," she said. "You know you did. You worshipped it. You're made that way."

"I was. I was once. I'm not any more."

There was nothing to say. She wished she were back at the hospital. She wished, now, that he would say the wrong thing, fly into a rage, do anything that would give her cause for ending this. If he would be his old self, violent, intolerant, she could go back and say that it was impossible, he was the same, he frightened her. Then she would not have to go on with this.

But he only sat still. He was doing everything he could, he was being everything he should. Dr. Birdsong said he understood; that he would be different. It was true.

His fingers curled tighter around hers and he looked into her face.

"You're not afraid of me now, are you?" he said. "Are you afraid of my face now? Don't you see I couldn't hurt you? I wouldn't do anything. Ever. I'm not going to hurt you. Do you feel afraid?"

"No. . . ."

"Christ, I hope you aren't," he said.

He leaned nearer and kissed her cheek gently.

"There. That didn't hurt, did it? Does it make you hate me? Was it awful?"

"No. . . ." She felt nothing; nothing but a strange, weary curiosity at feeling nothing when Lambert kissed her.

He sighed. He put his arm that lay upon the seat back around her lightly.

"Do you mind being my wife? Does it make you feel horribly?"

"No."

She felt nothing. He hardly seemed real. What was real was only little snatches of pictures—her room at the hospital, and a glass of iced tea waiting for her, and the hour, coming nearer, when she would be sitting in her chair and the door would open a little as it always did, every afternoon. . . .

He sighed again.

"I'll do anything," he said. "Anything I can to make it up to you. I know what I did to you."

He kissed her again, very lightly.

"That doesn't frighten you?"

"No, it doesn't."

"I'm glad. Everything will be all right, you know," he said. "Really it will. Nothing's going to hurt you."

After a while he started the motor and turned the noisy little Ford around in the road and drove back in the late afternoon sunshine to the hospital. They drove along the shaded streets of Annestown. She kept her face bent down so as not to see the people who walked along the streets of her town. She had always done this since she had come back. She did not want to speak to anyone, she did not want to recognize anyone until she had begun to live again. If she saw no one's face she would not have to speak. She was not yet a human being like them. She was still, partly, that awful branded outcast that she had been so long, behind the shrubbery.

He left her at the door and she went straight in without looking back.

She was sitting in her chair, waiting, the shade drawn, when the moment came and the door opened a crack and Dr. Birdsong's head looked in round it. "How de do," he said.

Her face flooded with smiles.

"Come in!"

"How'd it go?" he asked, as he slouched into the room, took off his hospital coat, and threw it over the foot of the bed.

"All right."

"It didn't disturb you to accuse him of things—didn't agitate you?"

"Not a bit."

"Fine!"

He looked at her, she thought, with pride and approval, and her heart lifted.

But that night the weather changed and there was a thunderstorm in the early hours that woke everyone up, and next morning Maizie woke to a day that streamed with rain, hot rain. She ached all over and her eyes burned. There could be no walk this morning with the nurse. She sat all morning by the window looking out at the hopeless, weeping weather, and the frightful images of the past did not seem so far away, but crouching just back of yesterday.

She wept. This was what had come of all her life. Once she had been a young girl, pretty and happy. Now she was here, and there was nothing. Her memories were of horror, symbols and hallucinations. If there was a God he had cut her out of her birthright. And all because of a day long, long ago when she had met a man in Boston and fallen in love with him. And all because she had not stayed here in the good land, the kind land; because she had gone away to live in a cold and evil country.

When Lambert came to see her after lunch she told the nurse she could not see him. She could not be persuaded. The nurse looked uncertain. Maizie began to cry, and at last the nurse turned and went away, and nobody came.

Between weeping and staring at the rain the afternoon passed until it was time to comb her hair, powder her face, get ready. She sat in the chair and waited. Finally the door opened a crack, and the face she waited for looked round it. "How de do."

He dropped down into the chair facing her, stuck his long legs out.

"What's this about you today?" he asked, smiling. "Feel kinda puny?"

Now all she could do was smile. But she tried to bring it all back, to tell him.

"I've felt so awful . . . awful. . . ."

"Depressed?"

"Yes. Not the old way. I didn't see anything awful. Just—oh God, my life is all smashed to pieces and I haven't anything." She began to cry, the tears rolling down her cheeks without sobs.

"I hear you didn't want to see your old man."

"I couldn't. I couldn't. I didn't want to. I'm sorry! I will tomorrow. To-day's been so awful."

He held out a cigarette to her, took one himself, and lighted both. Then he leaned back, tipping the chair on its back legs against the bureau, blowing out a cloud of smoke.

"Tell me about it."

She got her notes and read them; she tried to tell him the way the day had been.

". . . Don't you see, I just keep feeling, I haven't anything. I could have had a good life and been happy. I could have been happily married and had nice children. He did it to me. He smashed my whole life so I've never had any. . . ."

"Yes. . . ."

"I've spent all these years of my life being . . . sick, and now I'm not young any more and I'll never have anything. It's too late to begin anything, I can't start over, even if I wasn't too frightened anyway. My life ended long ago when I met him. I've never once been happy since. Oh! People are supposed to be happy, aren't they? I haven't had any happiness. Just hell, hell. Nobody else has to have hell. Other people can be happy. Other people have happy lives and love someone who loves them, and they aren't smashed so they're no good any more. . . ."

Her eyes clung to his square white face. He was so good, so wise, so God-like.

"I'll just have to go on living till I die, without anything. Always afraid of everything. You don't know how awful it is not to be like other people. It's so shameful. I'll never, never have anything. . . ."

"Well, now, it's not quite that bad," he said.

Now he would talk. She wiped her eyes.

"You know, I think you're just about a cured customer," he said. "You're running in the same old ruts, playing the same record over, you know? I think you need to get out and leave us. I think you need a real life again. I think you're ready for it."

She started to speak, but he lifted his hand with easy authority.

"Take it easy. We're not kicking you out, you know. You will need help for some time, and I'm right here. There's no problem there. But you don't need to live here any more. In fact, you mustn't. You're ready to start living."

"I don't *feel* ready—I don't want to go! . . ."

"Well, you know the little birds have to be kicked out of the nest. . . . I think you're ready. Everything's ready for you to be ready. You're all set. Got a husband all ready and waiting—don't have to go out and catch one. Got a little girl all ready—don't have to go to work and have one!

You'll be all right. You'll be a lot better. You don't need institutional life —it's bad for you at the stage you've reached. You need living a life, husband, child, plenty to keep you occupied."

She kept one hand pressed over her mouth, and watched him as he talked.

"I talked to Mr. Rudd about it this afternoon—when you stood him up he dropped in to see me. He's more than eager to see that the change is made easy for you. Naturally he wants to get you back in life again. I told him I thought it would be as well if you stuck around Annestown for a while anyway . . . not too much change all at once . . . so that we're here if you should happen to need us. . . . I told him I thought you'd probably like to live right in town for a while—see some of your old friends. Gradually, I want you to look up some of the people you used to know. You could take one of those new little houses along LaCroix Street."

Almost against her will the vision of a neat little house came before her eyes. Sunshine in the morning . . . a nice breakfast . . . a fire in the fireplace in the living-room. . . .

"Maybe you'll ask my sister and myself for dinner some night in your new house."

"Oh, yes!"

Now it was becoming clearer, realer. The table set in the dining-room, with candles. Friends, kind and laughing. The Birdsongs to dinner—she would never ask for more than that, his head shining in the light of her lamp, in her house—the Birdsongs for friends.

"There's only one thing. . . ."

"What's that?"

"Lambert—I can imagine all of it except him. He'd never be content to live the only way I want to live. Oh, do I have to have him?"

"You don't have to do anything. Only I think you're going to find it's all a lot of different from what it used to be. From what I've seen of him he'll do a lot to make up for the mess you all got your life in before. I don't think you need to worry about that."

"I just wish I could leave him out of everything."

"You won't get over your uneasiness until you've seen just what his performance is. The thing you mustn't forget is that you two stuck together through a lot most people would have split up over. I want you to see if there isn't something worth salvaging out of it. If there isn't—if it doesn't work—then it doesn't."

"And he really won't—do anything awful to me?"

"He really won't do a thing to you you don't want."

"He's really different?"

"He's really different. He really wants to rehabilitate himself. He was pretty bad husband material when you had him on your hands, but I am convinced he wants to make a better showing."

After he had shaken her hand, made the little bow of the head from the neck, smiled, whisked out of the door in his long hospital coat—she sat by the window until supper should be brought. The rain had stopped. The shrubbery, burned yellow all summer by the sun, dripped water that formed rivers and ran downhill towards the hospital, making trenches in the red clay. But in the sky the sun had come through, above the horizon; it was clear red along the west.

It seemed to Maizie—and it was familiar to her now to form images; she had been a wretch screaming in hell, she had been a creature of incarnate evil walking upon the earth—it seemed now to her that her life was a clearing in a great dark forest. It was a small space with a house, a garden, a path, the equipment of existence, while all around stood the great trees, pressing to the border of the clearing. Once the forest had been too much for the little seed of reason that kept the clearing orderly; the trees and all the ghastly scrambling underbrush had come into the space, grown over everything so that all was forest, all was dark and possessed, nothing was left but the crumbling house. Inside the terrified besieged creature cowered while the trees marched nearer, the branches reached into the windows, the vines could be heard creeping into the cracks between the boards and forcing them apart. For a time only a few boards, a few beams, stood to stop the forest from being the whole; covering; silent.

Now with time and pain and toil the forest had been pushed back again, the awful trees cut down, the brambles pulled away, until now there was a clearing again; almost as big a clearing, almost as clean a clearing as ever. The house had been repaired until it was almost as good a house. The forest was pushed back. The panic was stilled and it was possible for the creature to come out of its house and see a round of sky above, circled by the treetops.

The time for terror was over. But there would never be a time, she thought, when vigilance could be forgotten. She knew now the way of the forest and how trees could march and how vines could race. Nothing, nothing in life would ever be distracting enough to make her forget the forest waiting to move in.

One eye must always be on the roots of the trees to catch the moment when they began to reach; be fixed warily on the cut-back brambles. Vigilance came first forever.

That was the difference. That lay between her and the rest of the human race. She knew now that she would walk and talk and live in all appearances like other people. She would seem the same. But she would never be the same.

Those that had lost their foothold in the world, cowered in the last extremity, could never forget. Such as these could never forget to guard their home.

## CHAPTER LIII

IT WAS EARLY SEPTEMBER. Already the sweet and spicy smell of autumn came faintly, mixed in the summer air, and the lawns around Andorra were reviving from the summer drought.

Leda sat on the front porch in the twilight, in a white dress, waiting for Lambert to come up from the cabin for a drink before dinner. The tray with glasses, whisky, water and ice stood on the table behind her and now and then as she listened to the crickets' chorus rise from all the fields she would hear the cool chink as the ice settled in the silver bowl.

She sat resting in a long chair and her eyes drifted along the line of the purple-blue mountains far away beyond the cedars. The country seemed to her to drown in lovely melancholy. It was wide and misty, without boundaries, stretching over miles without a human dwelling, down into secret semi-tropic marshes where the frogs sang and chuckled in the early dark, along the deserted fields and up into the mysterious blue foothills.

She saw Lambert as he came out of the thicket that hid the cabin and started up the red clay track to the house. His white shape in the last light came slowly up through the slanting fields of dusk, threading through the cornfields, past the farm buildings, past the garden where under the twilight the pumpkins lay upon the earth and the beans hung in clusters on the poles. Then he came through the gap in the box hedge that hid the garden from the drive, and waved, and up the driveway to the steps to her.

He bent down and kissed her. It was a long kiss and there was something about the way he kissed her, something almost frantic. When he stood up she looked up at his face, but he turned away immediately and began to make their drinks.

"Is anything the matter?" she asked as he handed her a glass.

"No." He slung himself into the chair beside hers.

"Is she doing all right?"

"Oh, yes. She's doing fine. Children gone to bed?"

"They must have. It's late. They rode their ponies after Honora got home from the hospital."

In the last weeks Honora had gone along with her father when he went into Annestown in the afternoons.

"Good."

Something was the matter.

Leda turned her glass around in her fingers. The twilight was deepening so that although she could see his face she could not find what his expression was. But he sounded the way he always did when something came up about Maizie—repressed, wretched, confused.

"Isn't she nearly well by now?" Leda asked tentatively. "It's been all summer."

"Yes. Yeah. I guess she is. Look."

He set his glass down hard on the wooden rail of the porch.

"Go ahead. I knew there was something up."

"Jesus Christ in Heaven. Sometimes I think I'm going insane myself. Look. Do you know I love you? Do you know you're the only perfect woman I've ever known?"

"Yes, darling, I know you love me."

She did know it. She had never doubted it. The doubts of all her life had been concerned, always, with her own confusions and one thing she had

never needed to worry about was the loss of any man's love. Besides there
was, and always had been, a kind of ease between her and Lambert that was
absolute; they got along; they met in their emotion. There was never any
conflict or disturbance to throw them out of balance when they were together. The confusion she had seen in him had always been connected with
Maizie, and it had always gone away after they had been alone for a
while.

"Then try to understand the spot I'm in, the thing I'm trying to tell you
about. This guy Birdsong . . ."

"The doctor."

"Yeah. See, it's his job to get Maizie well. I see that. That's what he's concerned with. He doesn't give a hoot in hell about me. Why should he?
I'm not his God damned patient."

"Go ahead. What's happened?"

"He wants me to start living with Maizie. Take a house. Have Honora
with us. See, he says the thing she's got to have to get her back to normal
is a normal life, husband, child, house, so on. What in the name of God
Almighty did I ever do to get myself into this, Jesus, God. . . ."

"Well, you aren't going to do it, are you?"

"Don't you get it, I've got to! I can't refuse to get her well. Christ, I got
her sick! Did you ever for one moment think to yourself what it would be
like to know you'd driven someone insane? It rides me all day and all night,
I'll tell you that. I drove my wife out of her mind. She's been insane for six
years. I don't know what insane is. You don't. It's something beyond any
. . . She's a totally different person than the woman I was married to. As
though she'd been through some Christ-awful course of torture. I'm responsible for entirely changing the course of her life, wrecking it, I suppose.
Sometimes I wake up down there in that cabin and I'm soaking wet with
sweat."

"So you're going to go and start living with her?"

Her voice was as sane and unemotional as a man's; nothing untoward
made its way into her voice at all.

"I've got to. For God's sake understand, Leda, darling. I'm not leaving
you. I'm asking you to put up with a ghastly situation a little longer. You
know damned well I can't do without you. You're not a foolish woman,
you've got a man's mind. You ought to be able to see it as a man would."

"What do you want me to do?"

"I want you to go on loving me. I want you to try and get this. This situation is unparalleled." He laughed queerly. "There's the set-up of the married man having an affair with another woman. That's what this would look
like. Because God knows I can't give you up. But it wouldn't be that. You
know we should have married each other, years and years ago. You're my
wife. I'd be living with another woman and having an affair with my wife.
Christ."

"You want to go on with me."

"What the hell did you think? Just remember this. It's not permanent.
It won't be any longer than I can possibly help it. As soon as I can get the

damned thing straightened out . . . I mean, Birdsong seems to think with this kind of a life she'll get well fast, really well, strong. As soon as I can —as soon as I can do it without feeling I'm throwing the woman back into the insane asylum—I'll explain to her. I'll tell her I love you and I've got to marry you, and when she's well she's bound to see that. She can have Honora. She can have anything I've got. But I can't tell her now. I've got enough on my conscience to drive anyone nuts. Birdsong says she needs a normal life—this business. I can't say to her doctor, can I, I can't say the hell with that; the hell with what she needs. If I could only make you see. . . . We spent so many years together. Jesus, what years. I drove her out of her mind. Literally. I know about each separate hellish time that haunts her, it's as if she and I'd been in hell together. If I can drag her up out of it I've got to."

His voice fell away as if exhausted. He got up and made himself another drink. It was almost dark now.

"Have you told the doctor anything about us?"

"No."

"Wouldn't it solve things if you did tell him—he'd see why you couldn't go ahead with Maizie."

He sat down again. When he spoke his voice was high and tortured.

"Don't you ride me too, darling. I just can't take it. No, I can't tell him. Not what you mean. I know, and he knows, that it was, oh Christ, other women that were the worst thing, that got her started. . . . I can't tell him I'm just going ahead doing the same thing that drove her mad, can I? I did tell him . . ."

"What did you tell him?"

"Well . . . I had to say something about the set-up out here, in case he heard anything." His voice now was muffled. "I mean, I told him I'd been in love with you, and that I had a cabin on your place, and that he wasn't to make anything out of it. . . ."

"You mean you said it was all over, finished, hm? Oh. You have quite amazing conversations with this doctor, don't you?"

"Ah, darling, don't be like that, will you? I expect so much more from you than anybody could from an ordinary woman. Don't get female on me, will you? Look, Leda, sweet, I'm trying to get Maizie the hell well. I'm trying to get a load like sin off my conscience. I can't sleep till I get that straight. You see that, don't you?"

"Why don't you tell me the whole thing, straight?"

"But I am telling you straight, I'm telling you like I'd tell another man and expecting you to understand, have compassion. . . . All right, I told Birdsong there was nothing going on between us. I had to tell him that. He said Maizie's getting well depended. . . . And the thing I can't do is give you up. Christ, if it *works*—if it serves the purpose—what the hell. . . ."

"I have to admit I don't like being discussed, made a lay figure of, you and the doctor . . ."

"Ah, now, sweet. You're just a name to him—not even a name. Look at it this way . . ."

The colored man Davis's voice spoke from within the screened front door, softly, sweetly.

"Dinner served, ma'am. . . ."

They both got up abruptly and went into the house.

Anyone observing them at dinner that night might have concluded that whatever news Leda had heard was good, not bad.

Throughout the long, hot summer they had dined together easily, like the old married couple they might have been. For months now the heat had laid a patina of sweat upon the silver on the sideboard; the four candle-flames on the table had swayed and trembled in the breeze coming in from the summer evening. Leda had sat at the end of the table, drooping over her plate in the candle-light, sometimes smiling at nothing; often they had hardly talked at all. They had eaten cold beef, peach ice cream, drunk iced white wine, and murmured casually the length of the table about their day, the weather, painting, poetry. Now all was changed.

Leda sat upright; she was gay. Her dark eyes sparkled, her beautiful hands picked up the silver goblet with a kind of formality. This might have been a dinner-party, though there was only Lambert, who sat heavily at the other end, eating chicken and laying his fork down again. Leda was very gay; she was galvanized.

". . . I went to the Russie, in Rome. The manager was very obliging. He was a little sleek man like a rat and he couldn't do enough. I was given an overwhelming suite with windows looking over the gardens. And Rome was packed, just then. The first night after I'd gone to bed, suddenly, there was a little tap at the door. I was half asleep and called out asking who was there. This dreadful little voice hissed, 'It's Asssss-ti . . .' The manager. I said 'Go away, I've gone to bed.' I got up and double-locked the door. Next night, late, same little tap. The night after that I was dining at the Excelsior with friends and I told the story. Of course the little horror thought he was making himself agreeable—Italians!—everything at the service of the American lady. George Cameron was in a rage. When I left he came back to the Russie with me and we sat in the little salon and he smoked an enormous cigar. Pretty soon—quite late it was—a tap at the door. 'Come in!' George called in that big, official-sounding voice and went to the door and threw it open himself. George is about six feet four and weighs well over two hundred pounds. A definitely imposing apparition. There stood the little rat with his hair slicked down. He obviously itched to run away down the corridor full speed. 'Come in, come in,' George said. 'What did you want?' The rat gasped out something about seeing if I had all I needed. George took a long, conspicuous look at his wrist-watch. 'Oh, I'm sure Mrs. March is most comfortable,' he said. 'And if she shouldn't be comfortable for any reason she can count on me to repair the trouble.' Then he simply stood staring, and the rat slunk down the corridor making obsequious gestures. After that, no more taps."

Lambert grunted. He was not playing up. But it did not seem to matter.

Leda's oval face was illumined, she spoke her words precisely, and laughed an enchanting laugh.

"But did you ever meet any of the Bespoli in Rome? They had, that is to say Gabrielle de' Bespoli had, an extraordinary anti-Fascist salon, people talking right out against Mussolini when ordinarily one went around speaking of Mr. Smith. Nobody did anything about it. I suppose the aristocracy wasn't supposed to be sufficiently dangerous. Gabrielle had been an intimate friend, an intimate friend, an adorer, of Lauro di Bosis. I went there one evening rather late after a dinner and there they all were, rocking with laughter. . . ."

Coffee was served to them at the table, and after they had finished they went out on to the porch in the almost cool, sweet-smelling evening. Leda stood at the rail looking out across the darkness towards the invisible mountains. The sky was filling with white stars. Lambert came behind her and laid his hand on her shoulder.

"Let's go down to the cabin."

With the most delicate of gestures she slipped out from under his hand.

"Oh, no, I don't think so," she said in her clear, gay voice. "Do let's simply sit here and I'll give you a drink if you'd like. I'm rather tired. I shall go to bed early."

"Oh, quit it," he groaned in the darkness. "For God's sake. Let's for the love of Christ go down to the cabin and stop this."

They stood in silence.

"Well!" she exclaimed. "I shall have to get a wrap at least, it's turning cool for the first time, isn't it?"

He did not answer and she went back into the house and up the staircase. The upstairs hall was lighted by a single shaded bulb far down near the door to Treat's room, and she walked down and opened the door softly and went in to the darkness where a breeze blew faintly. She tiptoed over to the bed and sat down on the edge. Her hands were clenched.

In a moment she could see the round head lying on the pillow, on its side, and even in this dimness the look of infancy, the round cheek, the innocent closed mouth.

She leaned nearer to hear the regular breathing and she could smell the smell of childhood, soap and fresh air and sweet breath and still the faint smell of a baby.

It seemed to her in her confusion, the alarm which she had controlled all evening, that here, in her child, was the right: the simple, the true emotion. She forgot him, she forgot her child for months on end, and dashed off after the satisfaction of old vanities, old selfish demands. What she wanted—it pounded in her head—was purity; simplicity; deep amazed emotion. And it was here, in her child, the thing that could have been between them and that she was so quick to abandon: her love for him, his love for her, that she forgot to feed.

Lambert was people. Lambert, for all he suited her, for all they got along in that strangely easy way, was of the world of people and, having given herself to him and to being with him, she had exposed herself once more

to the wounds she knew so well that came from the world of people. She
was a fool. It was what she could never remember: people will hurt you:
safety lies in solitude.

She pressed her mouth against the warm, firm cheek of her child. I love
you, she thought; really I love you. You are my own, you are me, between
us can come no harm. Everyone else is the world. And the world always
meant me harm. You are me, and I am you. I make my life so wrong, so
complex, so grown-up, and it is wrong to be grown-up, I know it is. I always
knew. I don't want to forget you. I want to remember you all the time. Do
you love me? Or do you forget me too because I leave you? I have wasted
so much. . . .

A step came into the room behind her and she sat up abruptly.

"Is that you, Mrs. March? I saw the door open."

The prim, correct, eternally controlled British voice. It seemed to represent something to Leda, something in opposition to the delicate precious
thing, the distilled drop of purity, simplicity, left still to her from her beginnings—beauty, emotion.

All that she was going through suddenly fused into a core of hatred; the
old hate of the powerful world, the old feeling of being a child wandering
in an alien country; the feeling of herself forever against *them*.

Not that the woman mattered. But the woman represented the world,
which had always been her enemy.

"Can't I ever be alone with my own child?"

At her raised voice the child stirred in his sleep and threw his arm up
from under the sheet.

Both women pressed their lips together, and tiptoed 'from the sleeping
room. Out in the hall Leda started to walk on to her own room.

"Mrs. March. I must say that I consider your remark unjustified. I don't
deserve to be spoken to like that. I have done my duty faithfully. I have
never been aware of any *opportunity* for coming between you and your
child."

"Oh, I'm sorry," Leda said irritably.

She turned and faced the thin, sallow, fair-haired face of the governess.
The woman appeared to be on the verge of tears.

"I have never been one to make complaints, but I really must point out
to you that I am a human being too," she said in a shaking voice.

"You have nothing to complain of," Leda said.

It was an old reaction. It might have been her mother, long ago. Something had struck at her vulnerability from the outside world, when her
guards were down, and now there was nothing she could do, there was
nothing but the unbearable feeling of being helpless, a victim. There was
nothing to do but strike out desperately at the solid surrounding things, the
dull people who never helped.

"But indeed I have a great deal to complain of!" cried the governess. "I
would like to point out to you that I have been in sole charge of the two
children all summer without any relief. No one has seen to my having a day
off."

"I'm very busy now," Leda said. "There is a great deal on my mind. Of course you can have a day out at once. You should have asked for one. You can have tomorrow."

"I was never one to ask for my due. Some things must be given. I don't mind caring for the poor little things. Somebody has to love them. It's more than a duty. But I am a human being too. I have my feelings."

"Aren't you being a little impertinent?"

"Mrs. March, no one has ever complained of my deportment before!" cried the woman, her face working. "I have never criticized anything myself in this position and I don't feel I have done anything to warrant criticism. I must really give notice."

"Perhaps you'd better. You may have a month's notice."

Tingling with irritation Leda went on to her room and shut the door. She snatched a light coat from the closet and dropped down into the chair before the dressing table. She picked up a lipstick and began to fill in the dark shape of her mouth.

She was surging with despair, rage, guilt, and a frantic helplessness. The desire to protect herself came boiling to the surface as it had not needed to do for years. It had been years since she had felt the old terror of failure and defeat.

She felt a sickish stab of shame about the governess, but it was pushed aside by more pushing, throbbing emotions. She felt her mind running round and round an ancient, dreadful, familiar treadmill. It was unbearable. She was being made to suffer by the world again, after she had thought she had conquered the world. After the trusting delight of letting down the bars at last, finding herself, dropping her mask, ceasing to play a part, she had once more been caught naked and helpless and she felt as though she heard the raucous laughter of Nemesis.

It was unbearable that she should be left empty-handed, a fool. Everything that she had done with Lambert made her into a fool, if in the end she should lose. Lambert! He was the one human being she had always trusted, whom she had counted on, that she could find her old true self with. He had been her own, of her kind, not of the ordinary run who were —who always must be—her enemies.

But in the end he was one of the world too. He was an enemy. She had been half-witted to trust him. Even after all these years she had not, she thought, learned the old, old lesson thoroughly: trust nobody.

No one in the world could be trusted. Trusting was the instinct of an idiot; there was something that should always be put in its place, conquest. You could not trust people, but you could conquer them. You could make them do what you wanted. Leda had spent half of her life in learning how to make them. She had that power in reserve. It was all that could save her now. She felt her heart beating double with the urgency she felt.

She must not lose. She had not lost for years. Defeat was inconceivable.

She stood up and stared at herself in the long mirror; her face was in shadow, the light was behind her. There were the long dark eyes, the shape of the mouth, the pale oval that was her face. These she had always had.

But she had grown older and learned more in the world—she knew how to talk, to interest, to amuse. She was no helpless half-grown girl. She was no girl in an impotent position in the world, trying to make power out of nothing. She had money and position and beauty and intelligence and experience in the world. With all these it was incredible that she should be beaten as she had been when a girl. She had ultimately won then; surely she could win now.

She felt her hands clench. She would not be defeated! She would not be made a fool of! She would not be left, abandoned, deserted, the figure of a woman who in the eyes of the world had tried to break up a marriage and failed!

It was not fair! A combination of circumstances had lulled her into false security, allowed her to feel safe, happy, relaxed, newborn in self.

Enough of that, too much. She shook all over with her dreadful vision of herself a fool. She had thought she could be free. She had thought that she was safe. She had been wrong. Now she would pick up her weapons. Now she would go back into the world.

She slung the wrap over her shoulders and walked slowly, firmly, down the hall and downstairs.

Lambert was standing on the porch in the darkness.

"Hello," she said in a low voice.

"Hello, darling," he said hurriedly. "Come on."

They walked in the dark along the rutty track and through the woods to the cabin where a light was burning. In the little sitting-room some books and papers of Leda's were lying on the couch. She looked at them as if she had never seen them before; as though they belonged to another person. Lambert swept them off in both hands on to the floor. He reached for Leda's hands and pulled her down beside him on the couch, looking pleadingly, coaxingly, into her face.

"Now. . . . You're all right now, aren't you? You're not mad at me? That would be just too much to bear. You will be sweet, won't you?"

She laughed and rubbed her face against his shoulder.

"Oh, Leda," he said. "I love you. I love you. I love you."

She raised her face and looked at him smiling. She spoke quite gently, naturally.

"Lambert. Are you trying to conceal something from me?"

"No. I swear I'm not. I love you. You're the only woman I've ever loved with all my heart."

"I only wanted to be sure."

He went on kissing her lovely face, her cool lips.

Before she left they stood in the sitting-room before the fire they had lit, looking down into it. Leda's head leaned against his shoulder. The mass of books and papers lay at Lambert's feet. He nudged it with his toe and a book tumbled over.

"Did you write anything this afternoon, darling?" he said.

"Oh! . . . Yes, I did."

It was a hundred years ago in someone else's life.

"Read me, darling."

She shook her head, for it was all forgotten and meaningless, but then she leaned down and picked up a marked, scored sheet of paper. She began to read. Her voice sounded disdainful of the words.

> See, I can span its middle, thumb to thumb,
>> Small finger to small finger, and you'd reason
>> I have the world here, between a pair of palms:
> Asia in little, Africa become
>> A concentrate for the mind; a trick to wizen
>> Europe into linear theorems.

> See, where the checkered line marks the equator,
>> A yellow cloud arise! You don't observe it?
>> A monstrous column sucks up from the sea;
> An unnatural mountain from the heart of nature.
>> Do you suppose my pencil-point can swerve it,
>> Marching like prehistoric beasts of prey?

> Here, where a lack of cities leaves a desert
>> A sky-high wall of sand moves like an army
>> Upon the screaming living, and the dead.
> Is this a phenomenon? Is this a hazard?
>> But then, the night is cool, the air is balmy.
>> Time the geographer was in his bed.

> —I would rather drink myself to death in London;
>> I would rather choke for air on Everest;
>> I would rather have my head dried to a pea,
> Than argue how a flood might have been undone;
>> Than prove an earthquake happened for the best
>> I would rather founder in the Sargasso Sea.

"I like the way it sounds," Lambert said. "I don't know what it means, though."

"Neither do I," she said. "I've forgotten."

"Work hard while I'm gone," he said. "Won't you? Get lots done. Lots to show me when I come out to see you."

"You're coming out to see me?"

"Why do you ask me that? Of course. I'm coming out every chance I get. You'll stay here, won't you? You won't get ideas?"

"I'm going to stay."

"I'll think of you all the time. I'll wish to God—I'll wish I could be here living the way we've been, painting, having peace—I'll wish it, only better, without the other thing hanging over all the time."

"Will you be painting now?"

"I'm a painter!" His whole body stiffened and she lifted her head from his shoulder. "Oh, God. I don't know. I guess so."

The morning was superb. The grass was cool and sparkling with dew, the birds flew in long curving swoops, the sun shone pure pale yellow out of a sea-blue sky. The air smelled freshly washed. Leda stood out in the full sunshine and watched Lambert sling his bags into the back of the Ford. Honora's bags were already stowed. The little girl played on the cabin porch with Treat. They had not hitherto been allowed down at the cabin. The governess sat in a chair on the porch, her eyes downcast, darning socks of Treat's. She and Leda had greeted each other quite calmly this morning. Nothing more was said. But Leda was glad that Miss Lovejoy would be going. She had been with Treat long enough.

Lambert climbed into the topless driving seat, behind the wheel. He sat there bareheaded in the sun. Leda stared at him, smiling. His hair was receding on either side, leaving the point in the center more pronounced than ever. His face was burned copper-red. His black hair which had not recently been cut stuck out bushily from his red, strong neck. He looked healthy, well-fed, and powerful. But his heavy shoulders sagged slightly. He was smoking a cigarette that was one of a chain. And this morning in his right eye had appeared a tic, a tiny nerve that jerked the flesh of the lid instantaneously. The lines from his nostrils to the corners of his mouth were deeper; he looked unhappy.

He patted the shabby black leather seat beside him.

"Come on, Nora," he called. The little girl came switching through the long grass in her short pink dress. Her hair was glittering gold in the sun.

"Are we going to Mother's now?"

"Yep."

"Are we going to the hospital?" she asked, climbing up the step.

"Nope. We're going to Mother's house."

He stuck his arm in its thin white shirtsleeve out toward Leda. She took a few steps forward and caught hold of his hand.

"Well, Mrs. March dear. God be with us till we meet again."

She smiled and squinted calmly into the sun.

"Goodbye. Good luck."

The Ford drove off into the morning, jerking sharply from side to side in the crooked ruts of the red clay track.

Leda walked back to the big house with Miss Lovejoy and Treat. The morning was still superb and full of purpose. She played tag with Treat along the double path, in and out of the shadow of the thicket. He ran into the barnyard and she ran after him, and when they returned to the track Miss Lovejoy was still walking along, the complete English governess, sallow, lemon-haired, expressionless, alert. She reached out and pulled Treat's sailor tie, which had slipped behind his ear, around to the front.

How odd, Leda thought; how extraordinary about the governess; imagine her keeping all that intensity stoppered up. She might almost have dreamed last evening. It might almost have been a part of her own nightmare. Now Leda was full of her new resolve. She was going back to the conquest of people. She had been a fool ever to risk leaving them.

In the afternoon Leda dressed in a fresh red-and-white print dress and a large red straw hat, and put on a pair of short white gloves. She got into her own car and drove the half mile to Porto Bello.

Mrs. Rickett and another woman were sitting on the broad stone steps of the house, a tray of drinks beside them. Leda walked across the grass toward them smiling. Mrs. Rickett rose to meet her.

"I'm Leda March."

"Miz March! I'm delighted to see you. How nice! This is Miz Hanover from Portland, down the road."

They all sat down again on the steps. Mrs. Rickett handed Leda a drink. They sat facing across the fields, yellow with corn; the country looked unbelievably cool and kind and restful. Here was comfort. The ice tinkled in the drinks, and there was a quail in the hedge at the foot of the lawn.

"You've been right withdrawn all summer. I'd hoped to make your acquaintance long before now."

"I've been doing some writing," Leda murmured.

"How interesting," Mrs. Hanover cried. "My Bessie told me you were a poetess. My Bessie's married to your Davis, you know."

"I didn't know." How complete was the information carried thus below stairs? What else did they know?

"Well, I hope now you've come out of retirement we're going to see a lot of our new neighbor. You've taken the house for a year, I hear. It's a sweet place, isn't it? My grandfather built the wing on to Andorra. I used to play there as a child with my Clapham cousins."

"I've fallen in love with the whole country," Leda said.

"There's something about it," Mrs. Rickett agreed. But there was something beyond smugness or provincialism in her voice. There was a kind of stability, of contentment; something that hinted of the full life lived in a pleasing place, the life lived in the round, not strung out episode after episode horizontally like the sawing line of a fever chart.

"I'm looking for six-year-olds," Leda declared. "I'm looking for children for my child to play with."

"My two are five and eight, but they'd love to have your little boy come over to Portland any time."

"He's had a little playmate staying with us all summer, but now she's gone."

"Somebody said something about the little girl being kin to the Jekylls, used to live in Annestown," Mrs. Rickett said vaguely. "I used to go to school with Minnie May Green."

They seemed to know everything. But apparently it was all right. These were kind people. She would be safe with them. The ice tinkled in the glasses, and slowly, slowly, the pale blue dusk came like a veil between their eyes and the Virginia countryside. Far away across the fields Leda could see the roof of her own house, a spot of red in the long green swells.

"This may seem right last-minute, but couldn't you come over to supper this evening, Mrs. March?" asked Mrs. Hanover. "We're having a little buffet party out on the lawn now the weather's cool. Just love to have you.

There's a moon tonight, you know, and I'd like to have you see Portland by moonlight, it's real pretty."

"The people passin' over the lawn in their white clothes in the dark," Mrs. Rickett agreed.

"I should love to come," Leda said. She began to feel protected. No matter what happened, she would not be alone. She would not be outcast. She needed to surround herself with the reassurance of people and their approval.

## CHAPTER LIV

DURING THE AUTUMN WEEKS Maizie used to think about the meaning of home. Since her recovery her mind strained for significances, for broad reassuring generalities.

Dr. Birdsong had given her comfort in the form of what she thought of as rules for life. She used to make lists of them, like joining links in a chain to save her in the bad moments that came. She had become a great one for lists. The doctor had taught her the device. Lists seemed to order things, to put things down positively one after another, 1, 2, 3, 4. She re-listed the laws she had learned in the hospital; in particular there was a group of three questions Birdsong had given her with which to try the power of the panic anxiety that at times assailed her. She would go, perhaps, to the bookcase of the living-room in the house on LaCroix Street where she and Lambert and Honora now lived. Her hand stretched out in the ordinary room to touch an ordinary book; but suddenly the book was redolent of doom, shivering with it under her hand: death, death; evil, said the book.

Put your fears up against this yardstick, Birdsong said. Is the fear real or imaginary? Is it present or future? Is it important or unimportant? If it is neither real, nor present, nor important, bid it go.

None of her anxieties, none of the apprehensions of this new life, were real nor present nor important. She checked off her fears against the rule and cancelled them painstakingly.

Don't sit and work things out, Birdsong said. Keep going. Get up as soon as you wake up. Everything will be all right.

Everything Birdsong said she believed as revealed doctrine. She believed that this life (which he had ordered) would slowly blossom out in peace, in security and a slowly beating heart (as he promised). She would not fall into the abysmal pit of horror again. She knew the danger signals. She would not endure what was too great for her to endure. She would apply the laws. And—behind all laws, deepest of all, sweet and ultimate in the core of her mind—Birdsong was there in his office, ready to advise, to comfort, to dictate new rules, to meet the new fear and annihilate it; he was there, omniscient, guarding the gate to hell so that she should never fall past him through it.

In her new mind all things had their solemn meaning; the good meaning, as opposed to the fearful, grinning meaning the sick mind gave it. Even while she kept going her mind pondered the matter of life, looking for virtue and expelling the persistent itch that said evil was true. She spent her mornings marketing, meeting, now, old friends and making with them the beginnings of her future life here; playing with Honora in the small fenced-in garden, talking over the back wall with Mrs. Dunn, who was a great gardener and had beds overflowing with chrysanthemums; but all the time, as she walked, as she spoke and listened and smiled, her mind pondered, pushed evil away, looking for meanings. By her bed she kept a diary. She would stop in passing and write down these things she thought that seemed like steps going up. "I am really quite brave. I am only afraid of fear, and anybody would be afraid of that if they had really experienced it." "I must keep thinking beautiful and exalted thoughts when not occupied. Try hard to think of the beautiful side of things that might be frightening if thought of from the wrong point of view. It must come with practice. One side should be as easy to think of as the other, and one is constructive and the other is destructive."

The thought of home and its meaning kept flooding her mind.

It seemed to her, in her generalizings, that all men must keep a home base that could be touched in direst need. There must be a home base in the world, even as a bed was the core and base of a bedroom. There must be for everyone somewhere that was rockbottom. All travels started from there and to there returned and in sickness and in sleep the mind returned to that home base for reassurance and renewal.

Home, she thought, is where the heart is. How strangely, prophetically true. Such old sayings, when they returned to her, seemed now invested with a grave poignant significance. Maizie's heart had always been based on the rock of Annestown. In the wild and anguished travels of past years her heart had always yearned for its home.

She had come home. And home had brought her back to health. Home was where the heart had always been, home was Annestown. And deeper yet, the deep core of Annestown itself was one entity, one face, one voice, that had saved her, lifted her.

In the meantime, today, in those autumn weeks home was a new tidy brown-shingled house on LaCroix Street. There was a new development out this road. Maizie remembered it as a dirt track that wound out into the country past the Galt's old crumbling house. Now this had been repaired and made into apartments, and LaCroix Street had been paved and these small, pretty, architected houses built side by side each with its little lawn. It was all so new that the patina of ordinary easy Southern living had hardly begun to blur the surface—here and there spilled trash, here and there rusty lines down a white housefront from an unrepaired gutter, and the swing sets and tricycles and toy trucks of all the LaCroix Street children.

Downstairs there was a southside living-room, a dining-room, a kitchen, and a small room where odds and ends were pushed. Upstairs was Maizie's room over the living-room, Honora's room, and the small room above the junkroom where, beyond the connecting bathroom, Lambert slept. "I think you will sleep better in a room by yourself," Dr. Birdsong said.

A colored maid named Jeannie came early in the morning and got breakfast and stayed until after dinner, taking care of Honora in the afternoons while Maizie took her nap. Jeannie had Thursday and Sunday afternoons off, and was paid on Saturdays to meet the expenses of her Saturday nights down in the black Washington Street quarter of town. Maizie took Honora marketing with her, looked after her on Jeannie's out afternoons, and came in and said good night when the little girl had gone to bed. "It will be valuable to take care of the child yourself," Dr. Birdsong said. "I wouldn't advise a fulltime nurse."

In the mornings Maizie had her breakfast on a tray in bed. Lambert carried it up. "You're so good to me," she would say with a lifted face and a smile of enthusiasm. "Nonsense, my good woman," he said, as he had said so many times, so long ago; another world, two other people. He had his breakfast in the dining-room with Honora, and later when she was dressed and came downstairs Maizie would find him on the front porch gathering up his sketch-box and folding easel. "Can I do anything for you, my pretty?" he would ask.

She shook her head, smiling, and watched him as he walked alone out LaCroix Street towards the country, his tall burdened figure growing smaller and at last passing out of sight in a grove of cedars. He was gone. He would not be back before lunch. Maizie let her eyes lift and rest upon the blue hazy mountains far away. Then she would go back into the kitchen and begin her list for marketing. "Leg of lamb, snaps, pound of butter ..." Writing, she would take another sheet of paper and jot down another list.

1. Get up as soon as I wake up. (Exercises.)

For she had lain for a while this morning after waking, and a procession of dwarflike and grotesque figures had appeared on her mind's horizon and begun to march nearer. She had heard the sound of a freight train's whistle as it passed from town out into the country. That long, sad sound ... All at once there had come the strong, full memory of hearing such a whistle in the hospital when she was very sick; the walls streaked with dripping phlegm, the sun outside hot and evil; and through her hell a long sound, a cry that promised utter death; a train of cars passing in the outside, awful world, bearing her life away. . . .

2. Eat a good breakfast.
3. Bathe and dress with care always.

Lambert called her "my pretty," and "beautiful." Her face looked as it always had to her in the mirror—always except in the days when it had grinned and mouthed like the terrible shape of a tragic mask—and she did not worry about her looks. The pang that had once gone with the anxious doing of her face to greet Lambert in hope and terror was now something of evil memory, to be pushed away. She would not endure that pang again upon this earth for any living being. But Dr. Birdsong said, "It's important, you know, for a woman to be very particular about her appearance. Bolsters the morale, for a woman. Make yourself attractive for your husband." Between herself and Lambert the thing was unthinkable, of the old, bad past. But beyond that—now—her hair was still lovely. She could not concentrate on differences in her face. Dr. Birdsong. . . . Dr. Birdsong thought her attractive. He could not, of course, say so to her face. But surely he implied it. "Make yourself attractive . . ." He was there, always; any morning she might pass his car along the street. *Bathe and dress with care always* . . .

4. Try to plan one new thing to do during day.
5. Arrange to see people outside family. (Birdsongs to dinner?)
6. Eat a good lunch.
7. Take a rest after lunch but *not too long*.
8. Have a cocktail with Lambert before dinner.
9. Go to bed in good time but *not too early*.

The autumn evenings came mild and starry and Maizie and Lambert had dinner together in the square dining-room with the white candles dripping and the kitchen door squeaking gently as Jeannie passed to and fro. Sometimes Maizie would notice Lambert, how his dark face looked down the passage between the candle-flames. They had had their cocktail, and the strong almost neat whisky seemed in Maizie to clear away the uneasinesses of the day and make her comfortable and confident. Now she could feel her life revolve around her, taking pleasure in the vision of it—the house's walls around her and her child asleep upstairs, the maid in the kitchen pursuing her duties and a husband in his place down the table.

Sometimes they left the front door standing open part of the evening while they sat reading in the living-room. Towards ten the chill would reach them and one of them would go quietly and close the door on the sharpening Virginia night. When it was half-past ten Maizie would get up and go looking around the house in a vague housewifeliness before going to bed. The wandering, the looking into the warm stuffy kitchen for a moment, the glancing into the refrigerator, covered a difficult moment in the evening: going up the stairs to bed.

She could kiss Lambert with a quiet finality and retire; or she could stand talking at the stairs, beginning to climb as she spoke; but there was always the probability that he would slip his hand through her arm and climb the stairs with her, and this was right and not to be objected to. "It is important for you to resume normal sexual relations." But there was always the possibility that he would not join her, and then she could go to her own room alone and throw off her clothes in something approaching relaxation and enjoy the calm routine of going to bed. Without exactly cheating, without ever denying the hand once it was thrust under her arm, by ways and means and perfectly ordinary bits of behavior the possibility of leaving Lambert reading or drawing by the living-room lamp might be achieved.

If he joined her, there would be known, accepted passages between them and she never failed to make the gesture of response. "Don't be afraid of your own impulses—letting yourself go won't hurt you." Eventually they would lie side by side again, once more, as long ago they had lain but now peacefully, with nothing joining them, even hate, Maizie thought. The light beside the bed burned steadily and threw a round blurred circle on the ceiling. She would fall to thinking how life must get better day by day, herself stronger and surer, the meanings of things righter.

It was abruptly that she would remember that she was not alone. A man lay beside her, to whom she was married; who had once been her stars and moon; who had once been the arch-demon of hell with a thousand faces; who now lay here quietly beside her. She turned her head on the pillow and looked curiously at him. She always looked at him with a sort of caution, as though at first she were keeping her eyes half closed and only slowly let them open.

It was always a relief to find that after all his face could not hurt her. It stayed where it was and did not swell or shrink or take hideous shapes. It was after all simply a man's face, dark, with a beaked nose and strong pointed chin and black hair receding from the sides of the pronounced peak in the center of the forehead. She found that she could look at him and feel nothing, absolutely nothing, aside from the small complacent throb of confidence in her safety. She could see that he was older; there were a good many lines in his face and now, in these days, after all, he looked tired. There was nothing to fear. At the first faintest tremor of fear she knew what to do, she would take action. . . .

But in the meantime no fear of him as he was today came to her. "You've got to forget the past. Try to make a new life with your husband, think of him as a new person." This advice had been possible to follow as it concerned forgetting Lambert as her persecutor; day by day she saw he was not going to hurt her; he could not hurt her.

After a while he would get up and lean over and kiss her good night and go out through the bathroom and she could be alone.

She heard the light go on in his room and heard him brush his teeth; she heard his footsteps in the hall as he crossed it and opened Honora's door softly; he was going in to look at her as she lay asleep. After that sometimes she would hear him go downstairs, and she did not know what he did then. Perhaps he went on reading or drawing, because he did not like to go to bed early, but now there was no threat or terror in that. "Let him follow his routine and you just do what is right for you." No more was there the stab of panic, the passion to be with him. He went downstairs and after a while she went to sleep and did not hear or care when he came upstairs again, or whether he went out to smell the night, or whether he took a drive as he sometimes told her in the morning he had. "Don't forget you are your own mistress; you don't have to be anyone's slave; he doesn't want you to be his slave; that's all in the past."

Thus she had her own private bedroom in which to meditate and ponder the meanings of the elements of living. Here her heart could return to its home. Day by day there were more little comforts, little satisfactions, to soothe her and make her know that after the long wreck of years there was still pleasure, small and snug, to be got from what was left of her life.

And there was the new power to daydream—broken at times by the old sudden habit of anxiety, but growing—the power to lie on the way to sleep and relive lovely moments instead of quivering under the recollections of terrible ones; she had her little treasury of good memories; as when, for example, the door to her hospital room would open in the afternoon and a face would look around it and a voice begin by saying, "How de do . . ." And even more precious, there was the power to daydream into the future; people to dinner, herself the hostess; everything calm, ordered: "Will you have a cocktail?" "What a pretty house, Mrs. Rudd!" "I hope you'll come again. We must have some more evenings like this." Friends to dinner; a circle of friends to entertain and be entertained by: "We see quite a lot of the Birdsongs. . . ."

Some of the evenings she could be alone like this from the moment she left the living-room to climb the stairs. Sometimes Lambert did not join her. "Good night, baby," he said quietly as she bent beside the lamp and kissed him. He put his hand on her shoulder. "Get a good sleep. Sleep like a log." She had an instant's feeling of utter separation from him; he was a stranger. He could say, "Sleep like a log" to her, not knowing anything of what she had lived through, not realizing a phrase like that belonged to another world from hers, who had seen whole nights through as marches of the damned, the doomed; who never, never, even in spite of the growing assurance, would live again in the world of "sleep like a log." But she said, "Yes, darling," because none of it could be explained to a stranger.

"What are you going to do, darling?" she said. "Oh, I thought I might nip out for a drive around. Get some air. I feel sort of restless . . ." "Do," she said, sympathetically, and in return patted his shoulder, and with this exchange of affection she would leave the room and go alone to bed.

One October afternoon toward four she was walking home down LaCroix Street with Honora's hand in hers. It was bright blue, sunny weather. Lambert had gone off to paint far down beyond the railroad track toward the mountains. Maizie and Honora had walked together down to Williston's Drugstore and had a dish of ice cream each. The little girl wore a dark green plaid woollen dress and carried a small red leather purse that her father had given her. Her hair had the same texture as Maizie's, soft, clinging, and tendrilled; it was a pale brassy yellow, the color Maizie's had been at her age. Maizie wore her dark blue suit with a fresh white blouse. They would talk for a while and then Maizie would forget to answer and her eyes would lift from the road and the child's face and find the mountains.

On the way home they walked slowly past the thick green shrubbery in front of the Annestown Retreat. "That's where you lived before we got our house, isn't it, Mother?" Honora asked. They walked along in silence. "Isn't it, Mother?" she said, raising her voice. "Yes, darling, oh yes. Mother lived there for a while." Maizie swung Honora's hand back and forth. They passed down the street and around a curve. A little farther and they turned into LaCroix Street. Mrs. Bessborough came out of her house, the first in the row on the Rudd's side of the street. She was a stout woman with a muddy, smiling face. "Hi, Miz Rudd!" she called. "Hi, Nora, honey! You all want to go out to Edgefield with me and see my sister? It's a real nice day for a drive."

"I don't guess we will today," Maizie said smiling. "Thank you anyway just loads. Nora told the Withers child she'd play with her soon as we got home. But thanks."

They passed on down the concrete sidewalk. Farther down the street an orange taxi-cab from town stood at the curb, waiting. It faced away from them and the taxi driver's elbow could be seen sticking out of the window. As they came nearer they could see that the cab stood before their own house.

The taxi door opened and a thin middle-aged woman with a sallow face and fair hair under a brown felt hat began to step out as they drew abreast. "Mrs. Rudd . . ." the woman said. Honora broke away from Maizie and ran to the taxi. "Hello, Miss Lovejoy! Did you come to see me? How's Treaty?" The woman bent over and kissed Honora and looked up at Maizie again. Maizie stood still at the gate to the front yard.

"My name is Doris Lovejoy, Mrs. Rudd. Might I talk to you for a few moments—alone?"

"Why . . . yes," Maizie said. She felt suddenly uncertain and afraid. It was something she did not understand. If she took this woman into the house would the woman murder her? attack her? She did not want Honora to leave her. She felt all at once dependent on the child. But there was the instinct to conform, not to let anyone see her fear. The thing was to behave as people did behave. Honora was already backing away, smiling, toward Cissie Withers' house down the row. Maizie put on the face of the young matron, a little perplexed, confident, cool, but polite.

"Will you come in?"

They walked through the gate and up the steps of the porch. Maizie opened the door.

"I took care of Honora in the country. A sweet child."

"You took care of Honora . . . ?"

They passed into the living-room. Maizie sat down in the big chair by the fireplace and indicated with an easy wave of the hand the straight arm-chair at the desk. Inside she was rigid with tension; she was like an animal, keyed up, watching, listening, alert. The encounter was beyond her comprehension. There was alarm in the atmosphere.

Miss Doris Lovejoy sat down beside the desk and folded her hands in their gloves over her black pinseal pocketbook. She leaned forward slightly, her back very straight. Her pale, bluish eyes were fixed on Maizie's face. What was it? Maizie heard her own heart beating.

"I have been in Mrs. March's employ. Mrs. March March. Both the children were in my charge before Honora came to live with you."

"At Mrs. March's . . . where was Mrs. March?" The thing to display was mere perplexity, patience, until the thing was made clear.

"Oh dear," the woman said with a sort of social primness, "you didn't know at all. I was sure you couldn't really know. But I couldn't be sure the whole disgraceful," her voice began to rise, "outrageous, shameful business had been concealed from you. . . . I have always been employed in respectable situations, Mrs. Rudd. Yes, indeed, at the very least. I am not one to take upon myself matters which are none of my affair. But some things can go too far. Some things stick in my crop, that is. I do like to see fair play. And I know," she said oddly, "I know what it is to be taken advantage of, I know what it is to suffer. Mrs. Rudd, I should say first of all that I have left Mrs. March's employ. What will become of the poor little boy I'm sure I can't say."

"What are you talking about?" Maizie said. The fixed, gracious smile remained on her mouth.

"Mrs. Rudd. Your husband and Mrs. March are in love with each other." She shrugged her shoulders. "They have been carrying on an affair for months. For months and months. I have had to stand by and countenance such a thing and try to keep my little charge from . . . I felt it my duty. I felt you ought to know. I put myself in your place, Mrs. Rudd. We are both women."

The very first reaction that took place in Maizie's mind was the thought of what expression to assume, how she must behave. She leaned forward and looked gravely into the woman's face. Or should she give a cry? Or should she tell the woman to leave her house? She was not sure.

But she must find out the rest of this . . . this that suddenly plucked at her violently, with a kind of wild excitement. Before the woman could speak her second reaction came. Was this going to hurt her? Could she endure it? Quickly her mind like a little hurrying rat found a refuge; she began to plan: as soon as she goes I shall go straight to the telephone. . . .

"When did all this occur?" she asked.

"Oh, dear, Mrs. Rudd, it's still in progress. I might not have been able to be presumptuous enough to come to you if I hadn't been there, all this while, knowing Mr. Rudd had come in town and joined you, and seeing him come out in the evenings and the two of them go off down to that cabin. . . . Mrs. Rudd, this is extremely painful for me, to be the one to tell you what must cause you such . . . But how could I go away and be the one who might have let you know? . . . I don't like to think of a woman, a good woman, being made a fool of by any man and that—I must say, Mrs. Rudd, now, that Mrs. March is a bad, vicious, selfish, unspeakable woman. I have never been placed in contact with anyone of her sort. Naturally, I know how rich, spoiled women can be. But this is something quite beyond all that. She cares nothing about any human being except herself. She doesn't care who she hurts, who she wounds. She doesn't know other people have feelings."

"Perhaps you had better tell me all about it. Now that you have told me I must know exactly what you mean."

The woman began to pluck slowly at the tips of her glove fingers as she started her story. She talked, in her brisk, cold British voice, telling the story that began in New York and moved to Bermuda and came to Virginia, but now and then her voice would rise and she would interpolate comments of her own, shocked, condemnatory, and emotional. A deep, pulsing force seemed to push the story out of her; she shook her head sharply at times as though ridding herself of old hoarded grievances. But she herself, as a character, hardly entered the story. She had seen, heard, understood everything; nobody had considered her, there all the time, putting the situation together in her mind.

"But when I realized, Mrs. Rudd, that you had been in hospital for a long time, that all this had been carried on with you unable to know or do anything about it, then my blood began to boil. I saw everything then, I can tell you. I saw what was going on. All my sympathies went out to you, Mrs. Rudd. . . ."

The bluish, faintly swimming eyes fixed Maizie's.

With another part of her mind than the part that was listening sharply, Maizie had a strange thought that came down and clamped her.

That's why she is doing this, she thought. She knows. She was one too. Somehow she knows. She knows about me, and she was too, so it is like a sisterhood. She came to me because we are bound together in a secret union beyond other people's comprehension. We know.

She leaned a little farther forward. She wanted to ask the woman. But it could not be asked. Surely, surely. . . . She knew she was right, she was sure of it. Somehow, somewhere, perhaps years and years ago. Nobody knew. The woman had got jobs as a governess.

It must be so. It was as though there was a blood tie between them, unguessed-at, stronger forever than any other ties with the other people, the rest of the unguessing world.

"Well, now you know, Mrs. Rudd. I shan't stay longer, as I know you will want to be alone. I must say I feel I have done my duty and I'm sure you don't think me presumptuous."

"No, I don't." Maizie smiled, smiled faintly, into the bluish eyes. We know, she thought. We are not alone. There are others of us. . . .

Miss Lovejoy stood up.

"Goodbye, Mrs. Rudd. I dislike having been the one to upset you with this but I felt. . . . From someone with your interests in mind. . . . It wouldn't be nice hearing it in some other ways. . . ."

"Yes . . . yes. . . ."

"I don't know what you will do, of course."

"No. . . ."

"Goodbye."

"Goodbye."

Maizie stood still in the middle of the living-room while the figure in its brown suit went out into the hall, out of the door, down the walk; Maizie heard her footsteps quick and sharp on the asphalt. She heard the taxi door slam and the cab start. She had been waiting for the sound. The cab drove away and she was alone with the enormous pounding of her heart. Bang bang bang bang, it went, but not in fear.

She went to the telephone in the hall. The front door was shut. Jeannie was out. She rang the hospital, the number she knew so well.

Dr. Birdsong's voice:

"Hello?"

She was in the middle of things, she could not begin. She burst out:

"I've found out all about him. The woman came and told me. I know all about it. What am I going to do? Can I see you?"

"Now," he said quickly, firmly. "You come on down here right away. I can see you right away."

Once she had told the doctor all of it, once she had handed possession of the facts over to him like a pair of reins, she felt released abruptly from all control and all responsibility.

It was not frightening, it was almost luxurious; she almost . . . almost . . . enjoyed herself. She sat in the small bare square office with the doctor, and the sunshine from the west came in and lay on the floor. He sat behind his desk, young, grave, calm, efficient, taking all upon himself; with his long legs stretched out under the desk, his hands folded on the blotter, leaning slightly forward, his square face pale; with serious, responsible eyes.

"Certainly you're not carrying on about it," he said. "This is a real problem. A real strain. I would have given a great deal to have spared you this."

But she had not really meant what she said. In a way she had never felt so confident and unafraid. She knew she was not carrying on about nothing. She had a clear conscience. Lambert and Leda had done something that anybody could recognize as an injustice to her and none of the fault was on her side. She was—anybody would admit it—the injured party. If she should be hysterical nobody could blame her.

Now she would be utterly taken care of. She was the one whose feelings must be considered. She felt young, irresponsible, happy. It was something she could not explain. Even the doctor, who knew everything about her, everything, thought that she was suffering. This was a strange, funny secret. She was not suffering. For once in so many years, she was not the one who would have to suffer.

"You did know about it all this time, didn't you?" she asked, gazing straight at that white, grave face.

"No. I knew, he told me, of their connection, but he gave me to understand some time ago that it had terminated. He deceived me as to that. I did not know that they were continuing the relation. I am right put out with Mr. Rudd," he said.

The situation was so important, she thought, that even his language had altered as though in deference to it. Generally he was easy, slangy. Now he was portentous.

"You never told me anything."

"I wanted to spare you anxiety. He gave me to understand he recognized the importance of your peace of mind, and was willing to make any adjustments necessary for it."

"You got me well on the whole basis that he had changed. That he wasn't going to be the way he used to be any more. The whole getting me well was based on not having anything to fear from him any more."

She felt on such firm ground. There were no fantasies nor hallucinations here. There was a whole series of sound, reasonable complaints.

"I know. I recognize that. You have been very badly treated. I might go as far as to say outrageously. You must not feel that you are reacting too strongly to all of this. I think you are handling it very well," he said.

She felt a wave of pride and pleasure. Life had been a hard thing at best since she left the hospital, a matter to be got through with courage and rules, to be filled with manufactured occupations. Now there was plenty to do. And none of it would be hard for her. She had only to sit back and be taken care of. Her interests would be protected.

"I can't just go on the way I've done," she said. "How can I just go on with him knowing about this?"

Playing a part. . . .

"There's no question of that," the doctor said. He lit a cigarette and straightened himself in his chair. "The first thing that will be necessary is to find out where everybody stands. It seems to me," he said, "that the only individual in this situation who knows where he stands is Mr. Rudd."

Lambert's going to catch it, she thought.

"Will Mr. Rudd be at home by now?"

"I think so. . . ." The sun was sinking. "I *can't* see him right now. . . ."

"I am going to telephone him, if you agree, and get him down here for a preliminary talk. You needn't be alarmed. I shan't leave you alone with him."

Nothing for her to do . . . nothing at all.

"All right," she said gently.

Dr. Birdsong held the telephone receiver and spoke into it in his deep, professional voice.

"Mr. Rudd? Dr. Birdsong. I'd be much obliged if you could come down here to my office at once. Mrs. Rudd is here."

She could hear the crackling voice at the other end. Outside the window the trees were golden and cool in the late afternoon.

"Then you must arrange to leave her with a neighbor," Dr. Birdsong said firmly.

Honora. . . ? Maizie had forgotten all about her. But nobody could blame her for anything, now.

Dr. Birdsong hung up and leaned back in his chair.

"This is real, and present, and important, isn't it?" Maizie asked, assuming a small, pleading voice.

"Yes, it is. This is a situation you have every reason to find disturbing."

But it wasn't disturbing, only rather exciting. It was like slowly building up to some kind of triumph.

When Lambert arrived he came into the office hesitantly and Maizie saw with a slight shock how unalarming he appeared. The hair on his temples was turning gray. His waistline had thickened. She saw him objectively, as though after a long passage of time. He sat down in a chair, glancing at the doctor and then at Maizie, and lit a cigarette.

Maizie watched him sitting there, perfectly still, while Dr. Birdsong talked; his head was bent, his hands, one holding a cigarette, hung between his knees; he did not look at either of them; and she noticed a tic in one of his eyelids, that jerked the skin minutely. His dark face seemed yellowish, and that, she supposed, meant that he was pale; she had never seen him pale before.

"Among other things," the doctor said finally, "there are a lot of questions that nobody knows the answer to but yourself, Mr. Rudd. You've been practicing a rather elaborate deception with everyone concerned including myself, and before anything can be done I feel that it is absolutely necessary for you to clarify your position. Just before you came in Mrs. Rudd and I were discussing the matter of a divorce between you. I think perhaps Mrs. Rudd had better put the question about that to you herself."

He turned to Maizie and nodded.

"Lambert," she said. Her voice was very clear. "I'd like to know if you want me to divorce you."

He did not look up at all. His voice was deep and thick.

"Good God, no."

"It is not your wish that there should be a divorce between you and Mrs. Rudd?"

"No, I said. No."

"I see. As far as I am concerned, as Mrs. Rudd's physician, your wishes are not of any importance except so far as knowing them helps her to see what to do. You understand that I am completely concerned with Mrs. Rudd's welfare. In the face of what appears to have been your total lack of a desire to cooperate, I must ask you whether you will now comply with what I consider necessary steps toward protecting her."

"I'll do anything," he said. His eyes did not move from his limp hands.

"Perhaps. It is my thought that a meeting between all those involved will be essential to clear up exactly how each one stands. It is the only way I can see which precludes the sort of deception and telling of different stories to different people that has been the case. I should like to be present, of course, to protect Mrs. Rudd's interests. I mean I want you to arrange for Mrs. March to come in to this meeting here in my office so that there can be no question of misrepresentation toward any of the persons involved. Can you arrange that?"

"I'll try. A sort of trial, you mean."

"A meeting," said the doctor crisply. "If you are not sure you can persuade Mrs. March to come perhaps I had better talk to her on the telephone myself."

"I'll get her." Lambert's voice was a flat monotone.

"Will tomorrow afternoon be convenient? I wish to avoid any unnecessary delay for my patient."

"All right. Okay."

There was a silence. After a while Lambert stepped his cigarette out on the floor and lifted his face and looked at Maizie.

"Shall we go home, Maizie?" he said.

"No," said Dr. Birdsong. "I think it most unadvisable for you to stay in the house with Mrs. Rudd as though nothing had happened. You had better go to a hotel. Or wherever you choose," he added.

Lambert turned his face from side to side nervously.

"All right."

Nobody said anything. Lambert looked at their faces, and then got up. He waited, and nobody spoke, and he walked out of the door. For a moment they could hear his heavy footsteps going down the hall.

"You're going to be all right," the doctor said. He bent over the desk, writing. "Here's a prescription for something to make you sleep. You'd better take it, in any case. You're going to be all right. Don't forget, you're not to do anything you don't want to do. You're to have what you want. You're not to feel you ought to stay married to this fellow if you don't want to. You do what you want to do."

She had, suddenly, a feeling that she had been calm for too long. She spoke, letting her voice rise.

"I never get what I want!" she cried. "I only wanted a few things in my whole life and I couldn't have them. He's had everything he ever wanted. He's broken my whole life and had everything else and never had anything to suffer ever. I never get anything I want."

"You are going to get what you want this time. I shall see to it you're not victimized.—I don't want you to be vindictive about him. I can understand it. But I want you to try hard to see what exactly you do want, calmly, and to take action based on that. Not punitive action."

She looked at him with obedient, adoring eyes. What she wanted was to do whatever he told her to.

"You don't think I *ought* to take him back?"

"Certainly not. You've given him his chance—to rehabilitate himself. The only conceivable cause for taking him back would be that you wanted to, after hearing him talk tomorrow—and for sound reasons."


The meeting was held not in Dr. Birdsong's small office but in the office of the director of the Retreat. At an hour late in the afternoon of the following day Dr. Birdsong and Maizie sat in his office, Dr. Birdsong behind the large ornate mahogany desk and Maizie in an upholstered armchair near his side. The door stood open on the corridor. The wan familiar smell of the hospital was in all the air, sad and sanitary. The office was very dim inside half-closed Venetian blinds. They talked in low voices.

When Lambert appeared in the doorway they raised their heads and looked at him. He had not shaved.

"You may sit over there," Dr. Birdsong said, nodding his head at a chair.

As Lambert passed Maizie he put out his hand and pressed her shoulder as though, she thought, in reassurance. She made no response. He took away his hand and dropped into the chair and lit a cigarette.

In a minute more Leda stood in the doorway. She stood there tall, dark, shining, beautiful, in a green tweed suit with no hat over her dark brown glistening hair; cool, removed. Her appearance brought with it the atmosphere of other places, far from Annestown; the cut of her suit, the arrangement of her hair, the expression of her eyes and mouth, were of another world. Dr. Birdsong rose and bowed to her.

"I appreciate your coming, Mrs. March," he said in his Southern voice. "Will you sit over there?" As Leda crossed the room he went and closed the door upon the corridor. Leda sat down and crossed her ankles. Her eyes met Maizie's and after a moment, faintly, they both smiled in a sort of recognition. Lambert turned his head without lifting it and stared at Leda; she nodded to him as though he had been a person in the next pew in church. Dr. Birdsong returned to his chair behind the desk.

"You all understand that I planned this meeting in the interests of my patient," Dr. Birdsong stated. His voice was dry and efficient. "She has been exposed to considerable stress following the revelation of the situation existing, and I have felt it wise, as her physician, to try to bring about a complete clarification of the attitudes involved. I am glad you saw fit to come, Mrs. March. It was an understanding thing to do."

"I could hardly refuse," Leda said in her clear voice.

"What is said in this meeting is, I need hardly say, completely confidential. It seems to me valuable that we should all of us say what we mean. It is important that each one should state his position and try to make clear to the others how the situation has been made to appear to him. Any complaints or, shall I say, grudges had better be brought to light now. I repeat that I am asking for your cards to be put on the table in the interests of my patient. Incidentally I should think it would be of value to—the others, to have the opportunity to see the whole picture.

"My patient is in a position where she must decide her future course of action. She will decide it on the basis of a more complete understanding of the situation which has been revealed to her. You are all prepared and willing to speak frankly?"

Leda nodded slightly. Lambert wrenched himself to one side in his chair and lit another cigarette.

"I shall state the outline of the situation in brief," the doctor continued. "And then each of you may say what you wish in modification or explanation of it. As I understand it, it may be put thus. Mrs. Rudd has for the past several years been in a condition requiring medical care and necessitating absence from her husband. I may add that a major cause of her condition was anxiety concerning her husband's relations with other women. In the past few months she has become much stronger up to a point where I was able to consider her as, shall I say, cured. An important factor of her cure we held to be the cooperation of Mr. Rudd in giving Mrs. Rudd a feeling of security. She was helped by being led to suppose that such episodes as had distressed her in her former married life would not recur. These assurances were given her in good faith with the complete knowledge of Mr. Rudd.

"Mr. Rudd on many occasions reaffirmed to me his willingness to cooperate and his word that there was nothing currently in his life of a nature to cause Mrs. Rudd distress. By my advice Mrs. Rudd resumed married life with Mr. Rudd. She had my assurance and his that it was his desire to resume such a life. It was not until yesterday that someone, I believe a governess formerly in your employ, Mrs. March, came to her and rightly or wrongly took it upon herself to give her information proving that what she had supposed to be her position, her husband's position, and their mutual relationship, was in fact unfounded on facts. The facts were quite otherwise. As I understand them, they were that Mr. Rudd had formed an attachment to you, Mrs. March, which he had at no time intended to terminate. I may add, since the purpose of this meeting is to make everything quite clear, that Mr. Rudd had told me earlier that such an attachment had existed previous to Mrs. Rudd's improvement, but that he had terminated it. As I told Mrs. Rudd yesterday, it appears to me that Mr. Rudd is the only one of us who, shall we say, knows what he has been doing. I need not say that for my patient it is out of the question that the existing state of affairs should continue. There must be some resolution of them.

"Now, Mrs. March, if you are quite willing, I think it would be of value if you would add to or amend what I have said. You have seen my position and the extent of my knowledge as Mrs. Rudd's doctor. Will you give us your position, Mrs. March?"

Leda gazed with her clear, beautiful eyes back at the doctor. She looked exquisite, immaculate, and untouchable. She drew off the gloves she had been wearing. Then she began to speak.

"I'd be glad to be perfectly frank. I haven't been given a true picture of things either. It would be a relief to see exactly what is what. I first knew Mr. Rudd a good many years ago, Dr. Birdsong, in Boston, before I was married. He was married to Mrs. Rudd at that time. I was—very young. Mr. Rudd said that he was in love with me, and I fell in love with him. He said that his marriage was very unhappy, completely unsuccessful, and that he could not go on with it. He asked me repeatedly to marry him. He made me believe that it would be perfectly easy for him to get a divorce. He said Mrs. Rudd would be quite willing. I believed him. I had known Mrs. Rudd—slightly—but only as a child, and my paths did not cross hers and I took his word for it that the marriage was unpleasant to both of them. He—said he only made her suffer. I said I would marry him when he was divorced. Then he told me that she was going to have a baby. He said he would get the divorce anyway. But everything seemed quite different to me. I couldn't go on with it. I broke off with him. Soon afterwards I was married."

Leda paused and cleared her throat delicately. Her eyes met Maizie's across the room again.

"I did not see Mr. Rudd again until last winter," Leda continued. "I met him again at a party I was giving, to which he had had himself brought. He told me that he was still in love with me. He said that his marriage had really come to an end, since his wife was hopelessly ill. He said she would not recover.

"He said," Leda murmured after a pause, "that he was in an impossible position.

"When I saw him again all the feeling that I had had for him revived and

I felt that now, according to his statements, there was nothing that stood between us morally. That is, he said his marriage could never begin again because of Mrs. Rudd's condition. No doubt I acted rashly but it was with the belief that I was not interfering in anything. At any rate I fell in love with him again, and I went to Bermuda with him in the spring. In Bermuda he had a letter from here. It said that Mrs. Rudd was beginning to recover. It was the first I had known that there was any possibility of her recovering. I felt that our relationship must come to an end. But he convinced me otherwise. He said that he would never be willing to be married to Mrs. Rudd again and that as soon as she was well he would be able to ask her for a divorce so that we could be married. I believed him that this was what he wanted and that marriage between Mr. and Mrs. Rudd was out of the question. He had been asked to come to Annestown to assist in Mrs. Rudd's recovery.

"He said he couldn't in decency refuse," Leda said. "He said it was a duty that would have to be got through. He begged me to come to Virginia to live while he was—cooperating with the doctors—because he said he couldn't go through it if I didn't come. He said just as soon as Mrs. Rudd was well enough he would ask for a divorce.

"It was a shock to me when Mr. Rudd said that he was going to begin living in a house with Mrs. Rudd. I felt extremely uneasy and considered breaking off our relation as I had done before. But Mr. Rudd said he was only doing it on the insistence of Mrs. Rudd's doctors, and that it would hasten Mrs. Rudd's recovery and in the end our marriage. I seem to have been awfully credulous, but I believed him again. I stayed in Virginia, out in the country, because he said he couldn't go through with it if he couldn't see me sometimes. He came out to see me in the evenings frequently. He said Mrs. Rudd was much better and it wouldn't be long before we could be married. He said he didn't think Mrs. Rudd cared anything about him any more, and she wouldn't mind getting a divorce. I took everything he said on its face value. He kept insisting I wasn't hurting anyone else by continuing our connection.

"I only knew what he told me. Naturally I couldn't have gone on as I did if I'd had any idea I was hurting anybody. It makes me feel dreadfully to realize I have been the cause of distress to Mrs. Rudd. I wish there was anything I could do to make amends."

Leda's voice stopped, in the room, where the light was steadily failing. There was a silence. Then suddenly Maizie leaned forward and stretched out her hand. Leda reached and took it. For a moment they clasped one another.

"I think you have been caused considerable distress yourself, Mrs. March," Dr. Birdsong said. He cleared his throat.

Lambert, in the shadows, did not speak or move. There was the sound of a match scratching as he lit another cigarette.

"Mrs. Rudd, would you like to say anything now, after hearing Mrs. March?" the doctor asked.

"Well," Maizie said, "it seems like I don't know what to say. I don't blame Mrs. March, not a bit. I know how fascinating he can be, and I know the way he makes you believe everything he says. I reckon he just fooled Mrs. March like he fooled me, making me believe he wanted me to be happy and wanted to be married to me and how he was going to be different and wouldn't ever hurt me any more. Do you mind if I call you Leda?" she asked.

"Of course not. We were friends long ago, weren't we?"

"Way back."

There was a sharp sound, a sort of cough or laugh, from Lambert. Maizie turned slowly in her chair and faced towards him.

"I wouldn't have believed it even of you," she said. Her voice was perfectly controlled, confident, biting. "Telling any story you liked so you could get what you wanted. You just said what you wanted about me, didn't you? Said you were in *an impossible situation*. I was the one it was impossible for. You were so sorry for yourself, weren't you? Why didn't you get out? I didn't want you. If you'd gotten out I might have had a little peace. I've just tried to do what was right. You had to *go through with it*, did you? What do you suppose it was like for me to go through with it? And all this time you told her you wanted a divorce, and telling me you were happy. . . . And going out to see her all those nights. And telling her I didn't care any more. After I've just sacrificed everything for you, always, and you've taken everything I had, you think I can just shrug my shoulders. . . ."

The doctor broke in, smoothly.

"Mr. Rudd, if you have things you would like to say I think now is the time for you to say them. If there is any way in which you think you have been misunderstood, or if you have any explanation to make, we are waiting. I want Mrs. Rudd to hear all there is to hear before she makes up her mind what to do. Perhaps you know this," he said, turning to Leda, "but perhaps not. Mr. Rudd told Mrs. Rudd yesterday that he did not wish a divorce from her. This was after Mrs. Rudd had learned of the situation. His statement does not seem to agree with what he has told you."

"No," Leda said.

"I am sure we will all be helped by a little clarification from Mr. Rudd. Have you anything to say, Mr. Rudd?"

"You're God damned right," Lambert said. His voice struck into the silky air of the room like a violent, loud blow.

The doctor leaned forward abruptly and seemed about to speak. But instead he switched the desk light on. The room was flooded with low yellow rays of light. Lambert sat in the armchair at the back, his hands grasping the tops of his thighs. His face was so dark it appeared almost black. He spoke with his lips held stiffly, so that the hard line of his mouth scarcely moved with his words.

"You're out to get me, aren't you? You feel fine because you've been able to gang up and get me. You want to destroy me. You always did. Both of you did. You wanted to get hold of me and smash me. In your God damned sneaky clinging womany way. You couldn't play it my way. Neither of you could. So God damned scared you'd get hurt. Jesus, the sky would fall if you got hurt. You couldn't play it my way. Oh no, I had to play it your way.

"All right, I made it easy for you. You got so much on me. You got yourself hurt so much, so everybody had to be careful and not speak in a loud voice. You fixed it so you could break me down and get me where you wanted me. Good for you.

"Listen. Now we're being so God damned frank, I'll tell you something. I never wanted to marry you. I never wanted to marry anybody. Not either of you. You know that God damned well. That was just something you could hold out for, to get me where you wanted me so you could destroy me. It does something to you, doesn't it, to see a man being himself, being a man? You can't stand it. Oh, no, you've got to get yourself married, and safe, so you can begin breaking him down. You know God damned well how you got me to marry you. You know how you kept me married to you. You know, all right. But that doesn't come out. Not when we're all being frank.

"All right, you too. You had to have marriage promised to you before you'd give up one drop of your precious self. You knew you were putting me through hell. That was what you were after. It's a God damned sneaky fight, no holds barred, so the women can win. The men get destroyed. You wouldn't know about that, you damned emasculated bastard. You're not a man. You're playing on the women's side.

"Christ, I'm not going to sit here and spout my grievances. But I'll tell you I've got plenty. Take my word for it. The hell with it. How much do you think I've been getting out of life, playing it your way? Did you ever give it a thought? Why the hell should you? You were busy destroying me like a pack of little stinging ants.

"You've done fine. You've gotten me to play it your way for years and years, tiptoeing and eating milk toast, a God damned wet nurse for your God damned egoes. You did a good job. You can flatter yourselves you did damned well, right up to the point where you could gang up and get me in here and finish off the job. A God damned fine job of destroying a man. But I'm getting up and walking out on you. I bet that's a shock. You didn't think you'd left me enough guts to walk out, did you?

"Both of you can go to hell. I'm getting out of this God damned stinking place," he said, and with a wrench got himself up out of the armchair and without looking at any of them threw the door open and walked out. The door swung slowly shut behind him. They could hear his footsteps for a long time, going down the corridor, hard, sharp, and heavy. There was no other sound. There was only the sound of Lambert's footsteps, like no other footsteps, going away.

They sat in the lighted office.

The doctor lit a cigarette.

"A good deal of that was melodramatics," he said. "He hadn't any rational explanation to make of his behavior. This was a sort of refuge."

But neither woman seemed to be listening.

Leda got up and drew on her gloves.

"I must go," she said. The distaste of her expression had vanished. Her face had flushed slightly.

"Thank you, Mrs. March, for coming here today."

Maizie did not speak. But when Leda held out her hand Maizie shook it.

"I know this has been trying for you, Mrs. March."

"Do you know where he is staying?" Leda asked.

"I think he went to a hotel," Maizie said.

"Well . . . goodbye."

When the door closed after Leda, Dr. Birdsong, who had risen, sat down again. He flicked his ashes into a large bronze ashtray.

"He's gone," Maizie said.

The doctor glanced at her.

"If he has gone, you're well rid of him," he said. "It would simplify your problem. I believe now that even if none of this had happened it would have presented difficult problems of adjustment for you to continue living with him. I suppose you've made up your mind what you want to do about him, after this?"

"I don't know. . . . It's queer. . . ."

"Tell me how you feel about it."

"Why, when he walked out," Maizie said. "When I heard his footsteps going down the corridor—I had the strangest feeling. I remembered all the times I've heard his footsteps, everywhere . . . in South America. . . . I don't know, I had the strangest kind of feeling. I wanted to run after him and throw my arms around him. It's so queer. I seemed to realize suddenly —I guess I'm still in love with him. The way I felt about his footsteps. . . ."

"Hm," the doctor said. "I don't think you're seeing this problem straight."

"I just feel . . . this sort of wave, the old way. . . ."

"My advice to you is on no account to consider going on with Rudd. If you felt love for him just now that clinches it in my mind. You can't go on with him," he said, earnestly, leaning forward on the desk and looking into Maizie's face. "The same elements would be present that led to your former depression. You'd be making yourself nothing but trouble. I wasn't sure myself till this afternoon. But now there's no question. My advice is absolutely against going back to Rudd."

Maizie looked back at him. Her face was twisted.

"I didn't realize I still love him."

"That's not love," he said. "He's got you hypnotized, the way you were during the years that built up to your illness."

"You mean I couldn't stand it," she said. "I'm not up to being in love with him. It's because I'm not strong enough. I'm sick."

"Not at all," he said briskly. "I'll tell you this. Rudd is a lot, a whole lot sicker than you're anywhere near being."

That night Maizie took her sleeping medicine and slept a fitful, restless sleep. She kept waking and hearing little sounds—a step on the porch? A door opening? But it was never anything but night sounds. In the morning when she woke she was keyed up and tense. She waited for the telephone to ring. But no one called except a neighbor, to talk, in the morning custom of Annestowners.

She wondered if Lambert had really gone, and saw him in her mind boarding a train last night, dark, furious, and alone. Once in the night she had awakened to hear the whistle of a train, and remembered that a night train stopped at Annestown bound North; lying in bed she had had the impulse to jump up, dress, go down to the station. . . . But she had not gone on with her impulse. She had to get what sleep she could. She turned on the light, then, and calculated how many hours of sleep she was getting.

During the day she was rigid with a new, strange anxiety. She told herself that Lambert must have gone. She would never see him again. He had, at last, left her life. She was free of him. He would never frighten her again, and he would never be in this house again—sitting in the living-room at night drawing, lying beside her in the darkness, going in to see Honora as the child lay asleep. Now she saw him clearly in her mind's eye, moving about in this house. He seemed more real to her than he had seemed in all the months since he had come to Annestown.

She kept wanting to cry. For the first time since her illness began she had a feeling of nostalgia for the past. Without fear, now, she kept remembering the old days, the days long ago. She had loved him so. And he had loved her, she knew he had, in his own violent furious way. She had never been strong enough for him. The fault had been in her. If she had been strong enough to endure his passion, if she had been the strong, sure, unshakable woman he wanted, they would have had together the life he wanted—large, passionate, elemental. It was her fault that they had never had it. It was the fault of her weakness, her sickness. Oh, long ago she had wanted that violent life too, she had been young and ready and eager for all he could give her. . . . It was all gone, lost in the sad weeping meshes of illness and reproach and fear and shrinking. They had never had any of it.

She went through the day following her ordinary routine, marketing, lunching, resting, playing with Honora, but all the time she was half waiting for something to happen. She knew it would not happen. He would not come back. From now on there would be nothing to disturb her calmness. She would grow strong and well rapidly, and if anything disturbed her she could go at once to Dr. Birdsong's office. Her life would be a regulated thing with nothing to frighten or tax her anywhere in it.

She had a nice life. She was in early middle age, and she was making friends in the place she wanted most to live in in the world, and she had a child, and she was loved and watched over. Her father wanted to come down and pay her a visit this winter, he had written. She was back in the world of normal, pleasant living. Later—later, when she was still stronger, she would be able to take a train and visit her family in the North, in Hampton; when the thought of travel, and of being alone, did not frighten her any more.

There was nothing to feel nostalgic about. When Lambert had been with her she had not wanted him. When she had heard about Leda her feeling had been of triumph; like a final victory over an ancient enemy. Dr. Birdsong said marriage to Lambert was out of the question for her. She could not do it. He said she was well, too; he said she had handled the situation through which she had just passed with surprising composure. But her mind, all day, was filled with an aching nostalgia like the strains of old music, sweet, tragic and lost.

She sat in the evening in the living-room before the little fire in the grate. Honora had gone to bed. LaCroix Street was quiet. All the families were living their comfortable, safe lives within their own houses up and down the street. She sat with a pile of silk stockings in her lap, and looked into the fire, wanting to cry, because everything was solved and there was no danger in life any more.

## CHAPTER LV

IN THE MIDDLE of the following winter Leda had a letter from Lambert.

She came into the house on a cold winter's afternoon, a big plaid coat wrapped around her dark blue cloth riding habit. Her dark hair was secured by a net under her bowler hat. In November she had taken up hunting for the first time in her life, and now she went out with the hounds three times a week. The Clapham hounds were not a famous pack and the country round Annestown was considered rough, not the ideal going to be found in northern Virginia; but there was generally a big field. Hunting had filled a need in Leda's life and she had thrown herself into it. The hunting people, that lived in the country houses scattered over this hilly, partly wooded land, were the people she saw, now, constantly, and it was only occasionally that she went in to Annestown or saw any of the townspeople. She knew the hunting people to be stupid, but there was still an excitement and largeness in the life which kept her mind off other things. The hunting people were unlike any sort of people she had ever known, and she occupied herself with trying to understand them; she spent all her time with one or another of them since, in these days, she was restless and dissatisfied alone.

Once in a while she went to call on Maizie as a sort of rite. Sitting for an hour in the little house with that limited, rather dull woman seemed to cancel out the uneasiness she felt sometimes.

The big house was perfectly quiet when she came in. Treat had gone away in November to spend the winter with his father. A fire was burning in the living-room, and on her way to it Leda stopped by the hall table to pick up the letters that lay on a silver tray. She walked, in her hard boots, into the living-room, shuffling through the mail.

When she came on Lambert's handwriting she stood still and turned the letter over and stared at it and turned it over again. It was postmarked Santa Fe.

She sat down before the fire and pulled the skirt of her habit above her knees and opened Lambert's letter.

"Dear Leda:

Are you still mad?

Come on out to Santa Fe. You'd like it. It ought to be good for your work.

I live in a dump with another guy. He's a lousy painter. We live on beans and coffee and take a bath when it rains, but if you came we could find somewhere to live where it would be a little more civilized.

I am trying to get at something in my work. I've been on the wrong track. This is going to hit it.

                    Love,

                                        Lambert

Don't be a sorehead. Come on out. We always got along. It gets God damned lonely out here. I wish you'd come."

It was a strange letter, and Leda felt strangely reading it.

She let her hand, holding it, drop between her knees and sat leaning forward thinking of the hours following the afternoon in Dr. Birdsong's office and how she had tried to get Lambert on the telephone at the hotel, having called all the hotels to find him, and how she had never reached him. Finally the clerk said he had checked out. She had even gone to the hotel herself, that evening, but he was not there. Afterwards, and now, it seemed to her to have been complete madness to have tried to find him.

For she had told her story, and exonerated herself, and rid herself of him and the danger and folly of her past with him. It was only that that final outburst of his in the office had excited and attracted her in an old way, a way she had not felt about him for a long time. She felt a pulse beating in her. Her reason was blacked out. She forgot the saving course of action she had planned for her own rescue. She felt she had to see him, she could not allow him that last, furious word. But she had not been able to find him after all.

She had spent the winter pushing him out of her mind, arguing against him inside herself. People seemed to be her best argument against the troubling memory of him. When she was with people she felt occupied and important; she felt attractive, and lost that fearful little nerve-throb that told her that she had been deserted, that she had lost something that meant most to her—not exactly Lambert himself, but a way of life that went with him, a sort of world to which he was the key. He had gone away and taken the key and the world with him.

In her worst moments, when she was alone, she had the odd feeling that she had sinned; that outburst of his seemed to her a denunciation of her protective worldliness. Out of fear and self-love she had cast out the free, delicate things which were the only true things for her. She had turned to the world of people to protect herself from being hurt by him. In a pinch she had clung to the orthodox ways which she had supposed herself contemptuous of.

But it was not exactly that either. It was hard to pin down the haunting feeling of guilt.

When she saw Maizie it was their way for part of the time to talk of Lambert, as though condoling with each other for the wrong he had done them. Maizie was divorcing him on grounds of desertion. They had joined hands against him. He had, no doubt about it, injured them both. Once, when Leda had called, Tom Jekyll had been at Maizie's on a visit; an old, silent man tremendously altered from the old Hampton days. Lambert was not mentioned. But in the old man's tired gentleness with his daughter, Leda could see the family attitude: Maizie was a woman who had been unutterably wronged. Leda was not Maizie's enemy now; she was her friend because she too had suffered from Lambert.

But she always had a curious twinge of hypocrisy when she left the small, tiresome house.

It was Lambert who had been in the right; both of them that had been in the wrong. He stood for something. They clung to their safety.

But now, in front of the fire this late afternoon, she felt a hot wave of justification. She held the letter up again and reread it.

She felt contemptuous and angry. He was a poor fool. He was a pitiful failure. He did not really stand for anything. What had she been thinking of? His letter was ridiculous.

She got up and went over to the desk and switched on the light and began to write a note with hard sure strokes of her pen.

"Dear Lambert,

I don't know what you can be thinking of. It seems absurd to have to tell you that I should never come to Santa Fe or any other place where you might be. I should have thought you would have had the grace not to write me such a letter.

I'm sure you can't be so very lonely. After all, you have your work. . . ."

She looked up from the page, her lips pressed together, thinking of his fumbling, over-excited painting and the way he deluded himself about its worth; her eyes fell on the clock and she saw that it was time to dress. The Ricketts, Harry Dawson, and the Palminsters were coming to dinner. She stuck her note under the blotter and went upstairs thinking of her hot bath.

Her guests stayed late drinking highballs made of rye whisky and talking of the day's run. It was a pleasant social evening. The men wore evening pink, and Harry Dawson, when he had reached a certain point, leaned, as he always did when he reached a certain point, against the mantelpiece and recited, "How We Beat the Favorite."

Leda did not think of the note to Lambert again till the next morning when she was at her desk writing up to New York about some feather-weight woollen underwear for hunting.

It was a bright, cold, sparkling morning.

She drew her half-written sheet out from under the blotter and reread it. Then she tore the page across twice and dropped it in the waste-basket.

In the spring she had another note from Santa Fe, much like the first, truculent, slapdash, and pleading. But this she never answered either.

## CHAPTER LVI

HECTOR CONNOLLY sat before a standard typewriter placed on a small table beside a window that looked out over the yard of the Connollys' house in Graniteside, and beyond it, over the ragged weather-stained picket fence to the sea. It was a late October afternoon, and the grayness and coldness of the day had only just now been broken by a round, crimson sun that lay upon the horizon beyond the land at the other side of Granite Bay.

Upon the sheet of paper in the typewriter before him one line was written: "The commercial rapacity of Horatio Starr had hitherto been underestimated."

Just so had Hector sat every afternoon of all the months since they had come to Graniteside, working or trying to work on his book on the merchant dynasty of Starr. Now that it was autumn and the old, draughty house that they heated with coal stoves was cold, he wore a pair of flannel trousers and a sweat-shirt. He would get up and dump a load of coal into the round black stove whose pipe ran into the blocked-up square of a one-time fireplace. Then he would go back to his wooden chair beside the window, light another cigarette, tip his chair back on its heels against the wall behind him, and go on looking at the line written out on the page: "The commercial rapacity of Horatio Starr had hitherto been underestimated."

All around him in piles on the floor were his notes, typed or scribbled, the accumulation of long, old months when his projected work was a madness in his brain, a torch, a triumph. In those days he had had the feeling that the book would burst out of him in a spasm of convinced writing, like an oration or a sermon.

He and Betsy had left New York and all that world in the previous January. On a tip from a man in the *Dispatch* office who had once tried to be a painter, they came to Graniteside looking for a place to live. Graniteside was all Hector had been told: a small unprosperous fishing community of a few bled-out Yankees and a larger number of poor, hardworking, silent Finnish families; there were two or three houses where outsiders lived, people like themselves who had come away from something else and sought the qualities of Graniteside for their own reasons: the Chamberlains, old Rankin who was a painter, and the Joe Crowns. But there was no one here who knew Betsy, who had ever heard of Betsy. That was what Hector was looking for, that and a place to work. They rented the weatherbeaten clapboard house from a Yankee widow, wild to get away from the loneliness and the long winters to the smelly warmth of the town seven miles away. They had rented it from her for two hundred and fifty dollars a year. There was enough of Betsy's money left to live on for that year. Nothing stood in the way of the book's writing.

It would have cost them too much to heat the whole house, once the summer had passed. The room where Hector sat was the sitting-room, which was his own for a workroom. They ate and sat in the evenings in the kitchen. So far they had done nothing to heat the bedroom where they went when they were ready to go to bed, but there was a portable kerosene stove for the bathroom. The whole house still bore, faint and ineradicable, the smell of old Yankee houses: queer, stuffy, human. This was the house that they had taken, in which their old, tormenting conflict continued to be fought out, won, resurrected, endured, suffered; and in which Hector's book must be written.

"The commercial rapacity of Horatio Starr had hitherto been under-estimated."

Hector stared at the line of words till they danced on the page and until their sound rippled like the babble of an idiot in his head. He let the chair fall back on its four legs with a clatter, and again looked out of the window. Through all the months of spring, of summer and autumn, he had sat here; looked out of this window. Outside the window was the yard. In the summer Betsy had made a vegetable garden here and he had watched her as on her knees she moved slowly along the rows of plants, weeding them. Beyond the yard was the rickety line of the unpainted fence. Beyond the fence ran the road, where in the gray increasingly cold weather little passed the house: a dog, three Finn girls, the fisherman in his old Ford truck.

On the other side of the road the shore fell sharply away in dry grass and granite boulders to the bay. Since the end of summer the noise of the sea had risen slowly, imperceptibly, from day to day, from its smooth summer singing to the loud, increasing roar that now they noticed only when they went to bed and lay in silence, and when they first awoke to hearing in the morning. The water of the bay lay gray and wrinkled like an elephant's skin; sometimes in a storm it rose to sharp points crested with bitter white.

This was all that could be seen from Hector's window.

As he looked, he heard the back door slam, out of sight around the corner, and Betsy came into the yard. She had a handkerchief tied over her head and wore Hector's old brown tweed overcoat; but even so covered her pregnancy was apparent, in the hang of the coat from her shoulders, in her slow and clumsy movements. She bent down in the brown garden and from the dry clutter of stalks and withered vines picked a pumpkin. He saw her lift it and hold it pressed to her side resting upon her hip.

She stood still looking out over the bay.

He wondered sharply what she could be thinking of. He always wondered that when he caught her thus standing, listening, watching, alone; herself without him. For he never could believe that she was not living a secret, withheld life, one that she would not share with him. In all the old, the tortured nights they had spent together she had sworn the same things: she was his, she lived for him, in him; her life away from him was lived for him. Passion, passion. They clung and clasped, they poured out the wild, the absolute words; everything, everything; everything is yours. He had shouted at her, he had struck her, he had called her the names that mounted in his head like a pile of solidified poison; all of it she endured, she stood unshaken; no, she said, it is not true, I am yours, I am all yours, I will take anything you give me, I will do anything you say. And in the end, eventually, he would take her back into his arms and believe her, recant what he had declared, hold her, hold her, and say with her, believe: we are one; we belong to each other completely. . . .

Sometimes he knew that it was a flaw in himself, that it was one of the lesions that spilled his strength, when, catching her as he caught her now, alone, unthinking, abstracted, he would feel like a wound, in a sort of collapse of everything that might have been confidence and belief: she is alone, living her secret life in which I do not exist.

Sometimes he knew it for delusion and his heart's insecurity.

But generally he believed it.

She would have her baby in late November. Her pregnancy was to have changed everything. At first it seemed to have done it. He held her in his arms, or came up behind her as she stood in the kitchen and reached around her, feeling, sometimes saying, that now she was his, a woman devoted to him in her entire being. Her body worked for him with its muscles, cooking his food, cleaning his house, attending to all matters of his living; and now it did more, it created for him, making something new in his image, that was his.

Now there was not any of her that was not possessed and employed by him. There was nothing of her he had not marked, excepting her mind and whatever was in it. She said that there was nothing in her mind but himself.

But what did she think about as she stood, unconsciously, in the dry garden looking off with her chin slightly lifted, to the sea? Who was she missing? What did she want? Was she comparing her present life of work and childbearing with her other life? What secret was she keeping?

It was like madness, to wonder what she thought; he seemed to feel a real fever mounting in his blood. His life was wrecked, his work remained undone, while this streak of poison ran through his strength like a streak in granite. A tap, and the stone falls apart. The fever mounted, and he had the terror that his life could never be collected again; she had foundered it and split it upon the fact of her past, that he had accepted, that he had taken into their mutual life in marrying her.

What had he lost? Had he given up everything that might have made him happy? He had married a woman who, his fever told him, was corrupted; was not the woman of his idealism; was not the woman his mother, his other wife, had been. What had he done? Had he sold his soul? He had accepted her life, he had married her. What might he have been if he had never met her, if this year past, this year and a half, had never been for him? Had it not set the seal on surrender from him? He had given her himself, he was her husband, and he meant much by those words: husband; wife. What would have been if he had had the strength—if he had been man enough—to put her away long ago, a year ago, in that catastrophic October, and make his own way; if he had not had to have her?

One thing he was sure of: he would have finished this book by now.

"The commercial rapacity of Horatio Starr had hitherto been under-estimated."

He ripped the sheet of paper out of his typewriter and immediately shot a fresh sheet through the roller and typed the page number, 168, neatly in the top left-hand corner. He stared at the page with his heart beating, the pulse tangible in his throat. He had to write this book. It was the book into which he had put all his resolve. He felt that his honor, his future, his chances depended on it. If he failed to write it, it would set a judgment on him, quietly, absolutely. He had to write it if it meant straining his effort through the thick mesh of tension and unhappiness.

He lifted his bent fingers and began to rap out a sentence that moved out into the fresh page, letter by letter, a growing line.

"The commercial rapacity of Horatio Starr had hitherto. . . ."

His life was stopping him.

He lit another cigarette, snatched it out of his lips, and stared out of the window again. Betsy was still there, standing in the garden with the orange pumpkin resting on her hip. Now, however, she had been joined by Claudine Crown, the French wife of Joe Crown, who lived in the stone house on the hill behind.

He stared at the two women and the little girl with them; Jeanne Crown. They stood there in the bleak weather, and now the sun had dropped behind the land and the light was hesitant and purplish gray.

They stood in the mesh of fallen stalks, in the cold twilight. Claudine as always wore clothes made by herself on peasant lines: even the coat she wore had the fitted bodice and the full gathered skirt within which she moved on little feet as nimble as a goat for all her compact solidity; above her trim body her face was calm, beautiful, and resigned. She wore nothing on her head, but stood there with Betsy looking off to sea, the wind slapping wisps of her straight black hair against her face. She wore her hair in a curiously formal style, almost a Spanish fashion, back from the face and ears and piled at the back in a high fanshape.

The child stood between the two bulks of the women, small and skinny with an ugly, angry face. In feature she looked like Joe Crown, and there was nothing French about her.

They did not seem to be talking. They only looked at the sea. The wind was rising. Hector had a queer sudden feeling that they were making it rise, the women; standing there and somehow breathing the elements, willing things, changing things. . . . That was ridiculous. But what did they think, what were they *doing*—when they stood there in the dusk, with their skirts blowing round their legs, silent, silent, powerful? Hector wondered if they really were unconquerable; women. He felt weak and tired sitting inside the house, stale and filled with absurd fancies.

He wanted to go out and join them.

He looked at the watch on his wrist. It was only half-past four. He wasn't going to stop now. He always worked till six. But it was too dark to see to write.

He tapped with his fingernails against the window-pane and both women turned and smiled in his direction. Claudine waved her hand.

He had the fancy that he was a sick child waving from its room to the strong, the well, the grown-ups. That too was ridiculous. He was a man, with a brain, writing a book; they were women who knew little. He called: "Betsy! Bring me a lamp!"

They disappeared then, and he heard the back door close. He heard them moving around in the kitchen, on the other side of the wall.

Betsy came in carrying the lighted oil lamp in her hand. He looked at her blankly as she set it on the mantelpiece where it threw light down on his typewriter. She had taken off his coat and the handkerchief. Her brown hair, braided and done up at the back of her head, was roughened. She moved slowly and it seemed to him with majesty, her figure distorted by the great child she carried before her as she walked. Even the poverty of the clothes she wore, an old skirt and a woollen jacket, seemed to him queerly grandiose; she walked in low shoes without stockings.

"Don't make such a noise out there, will you?"

"Do you want me to tell them to go?"

"No! But you don't have to make a racket."

She shook her head and went out to the kitchen again. He heard their voices speaking in low tones and he heard them hush the child. Then they were very quiet and all he could hear from them was the snapping of scissors and now and then the sound of a pot put down upon the stove. They were doing nothing to disturb him. There was nothing to disturb him. He was all alone in his workroom with a light on his work.

After a while he wrote a page more. He heard the back door slam and then Joe Crown's voice in the kitchen. He glanced at his watch and it was five minutes to six. He got up and took the lamp and went out to the kitchen.

It was a large room lighted at one end by two oil lamps, one set on the shelf above the coal stove, the other on the end of the long board table where pieces of white cloth lay cut out.

A delicious smell of onions and herbs filled the room.

Betsy's back was turned; she stood over the stove with a fork in her hand; five onions browned in the frying pan. Claudine sat on a wooden chair with her lap full of white material, sewing; Joe Crown leaned against the back of her chair with his fingers clasping her shoulders. He had on corduroys and a leather jacket; his elegant, boyish face was wind-burned.

"Bon soir, Monsieur," Claudine said. "You will have a navarin for your dinner tonight, are you smelling it?"

"Hello, Claudine . . . Joe . . . Jesus, I'm shot."

"Vous travaillez trop tard," she said composedly with her eyes on the needle she threaded.

Out of the shadows of the kitchen the child's voice spoke angrily.

"Stop talking French, Mommy."

"How does it go, old fellah?" Joe asked. He took his fingers from his wife and moved over to Hector's side of the room. At once Hector felt fortified; an alignment of himself and Joe against the women governing the room. He liked Joe very much, although he was chiefly sorry for him. Joe was a pathetic man, he thought. But he was a man, someone Hector understood.

"I have a restorative for you, my friend," Joe continued in his formal voice which carried with it the insistence that he was laughing at his own formality; a continual sarcasm. He brought out of his hip pocket a pint bottle of whisky and held it before Hector's face, lifting his eyebrows. "Shall we indulge?" he said. Hector got two glasses out of the cupboard by the door and Joe carefully poured out two neat drinks. They did not offer the women any, and the women did not look up.

Joe Crown was a drunk. Studying him, planning a book he would like to write about him, Hector had decided that he was the last flower of the 'Twenties, left unseasonably on its stem; the epitome of those days, an anachronism in these.

He had done all those things. His family had been very rich. Joe was sent to Princeton and had been one of the big boys; in those far days he had danced to the old tunes, driven a Stutz, played with the New York girls and been one of the young men Fitzgerald wrote about. He had known Fitzgerald. After college he had gone on and taken a master's degree out of some romantic vision of himself, the scholar gypsy, the scholar Don Juan. He bought a large and expensively bound library. Then he went to Paris in the great days, the dead days.

He was already a drunk, but Paris added something to his drinking. He drank at the Dome, the Rotonde, he bought champagne for the girls at Zelli's. After a few years of Francophilia he married a French girl of good bourgeois family whom he met while visiting a painter friend in the country. Her name was Claudine Labrot. Hector thought her family must have considered the match, and while seeing its weaknesses, decided that the young American with a large fortune was after all a reasonably good parti. The Crowns lived for a few years in the Rhone wine country, making frequent trips to Paris where Joe could show off his beautiful genuine French wife to the Americans in the Dome, the Rotonde, the Closerie des Lilas.

In the market crash of 1929 the Crown money had been lost. Joe had been called home but there was nothing anyone like him could do to bolster the family fortunes. He was a drunk. His wife and infant daughter came to America with him, and after some preliminary futile attempts at work Joe had fallen into a lucky berth. Friends of the Crown family, who had not lost their money, offered him the job of caretaker of their place at Graniteside, the only big estate there, set far back up a road into the moors. A salary went with the job, which meant no more than to live in the stone gate-house. He brought his library. Claudine did the work of the house.

To himself Joe was a romantic figure. He had his education, his library, his French wife, and his beautiful, vanished, golden past. His drinking was a part of that past and he was proud of it, romantic about it. When he was drinking his speech was always elaborate and formal and unblurred.

They lived in their stone gate-house on the hill. Joe made no attempt to find other work; he had enough and he was satisfied in some melancholy way with their life here. He got drunk every night and rose at noon or later except in the Fall when sometimes he did a little duck hunting. He adored his daughter and she worshipped him and saw him as he saw himself.

He never read his books and Hector realized, talking to him, that his education had been dissolved long ago in floods of alcohol; but his past did not die. After one drink he would start to talk, it might be of the New York just after the World War, or the Left Bank, or one of the heroes of that age that he had known, or the heroines . . . Hemingway, Randy Burke, Amelia Caswell, Duff Twisden. . . . Or he would sing, in his sweet, rather coaxing voice, the songs that were for him magic . . . *Lady of the Evening; A Pretty Girl Is Like a Melody.* . . .

One of the things he still had left was his wife, and he was always elaborately boastful of her beauty. He seldom called her by her name in speaking of her. He said "my wife." He was proud of her being French, of her magnificent cooking, of her Catholicism, of her un-American figure. These things belonged to him. He was the master of his house.

In this, his assumption of the male rôle of the dominator, the master, Hector felt his deepest bond with Joe. The guy might be a drunk, hopeless; he might have nothing ahead of him anywhere in life; but he was the head of his family. Things were done his way. Perhaps it was because she was French, at any rate Claudine carried out his orders and arranged for his comfort in a way that Hector approved of.

Hector liked to be with Joe, as now, having a little drink together and watching, together, the women. He did not have such odd fancies about them when Joe was there, long, sprawling, elegant in the hard kitchen chair, holding the whisky in his mouth for a moment before swallowing it and watching the women as they moved about in the acts of working for them, the men.

They had a second drink, larger than the first, and then Joe unwound his length and stood up.

"Come on, my cabbage," he drawled, "I'm ready for my own dinner. We must leave these good people to theirs. I'll leave you this, too, old fellah," he added, pushing the bottle into Hector's hand. They argued for a moment, and Joe turned away. The little girl ran and clasped him about his knees, looking up at him with her small ugly face that was made like his romantically beautiful, haggard one.

Claudine stood up. She shook the scraps of cloth in her skirt into the coal scuttle. She smoothed the cloth of her bodice down over her round firm waist and shook herself slightly so that her full skirt swirled around her knees. She was neither young nor old. She was probably about thirty-five. But she had nothing whatever of the girl about her. She was a woman. Her face, her straight fine black hair, the flesh of her neck, her arms, all were mature.

She reached for Jeanne's hand, when she had put on her own coat, holding the child's coat tucked under her arm. The little girl evaded her hand and snatched the coat from her, and squirmed into it alone.

"Button up your buttons," Claudine said.

"All *right*," screamed the child. "Leave me alone."

The Crowns went out through the kitchen door and closed it after them. Betsy had turned back to the stove and was fishing a bunch of herbs from a large earthen casserole. Claudine had given the pot to her for her to use in the French dishes she was teaching Betsy. The rising steam smelled very good. Hector sat down at the kitchen table, from which the sewing had been cleared away, and waited for his dinner.

Betsy moved about the yellow-lighted kitchen. In spite of her bulk she still, curiously, bore the look of a young girl; almost a young boy. Her face was thin, her neck long and upright. After her child was born perhaps she would come to have Claudine's look in her face. Her body was all woman. It was only the bones of her face that were a boy's. It was strange, though, how women could be changed. Hector liked the thick braided knot of hair at the back of her head. There was something about long hair for a woman. They were hardly women without long hair. Women should be women; men should, they must, be men; and they could not be men until first the women were women. Thinking about it, waiting for his dinner, he had another drink. He felt angry, for a second, because here he was, thinking about men and women when he ought to spend his thinking time on his book. There was something about the book in these days that eluded concentration. It had not been so once. It had once been engrossing. Now he found himself over and over running away from thinking of the book to think of men and women.

They ate their dinner on the kitchen table by the light of the lamps; the navarin of lamb, savory with garlic, parsley, thyme and bayleaf; with tomatoes, potatoes, and onions. Afterwards they had some cheese with the round loaf of black bread, with a hole in the middle of it, from the Finnish baker who came round three times a week. Betsy washed the dishes and pots in the soapstone sink in water from the sink pump heated on the stove, while Hector smoked. She shook down the stove, put on coal from the scuttle, tipped the lids, and went out with the scuttle. He heard the door to the bulkhead fall back, and heard Betsy walking in the cellar; the scrape of the shovel, the tumble and rattle of the coal; he heard the bulkhead close. She came in with the full scuttle and set it down by the stove; she sat down by him at the table.

She put her hand out palm up on the table and after a minute he covered it with his hand. Her hand lay flat and still, but he began to tap it with his fingers, to pat her hand nervously. After a while she took it away. There was nothing to be heard but the sea outside, swinging against the shore, doubling back upon itself, hurling again upon the rocks, swaying back and forth forever and ever. Hector reached back to the shelves for the bottle of whisky and poured himself another drink, with water. He seldom had whisky to drink in these days except when they were with the Crowns. He needed it, after the day of painful, uncertain work. Slowly his ranging anxiety shrank away and the form of his book reappeared in his mind, large and inclusive and worth any labor. When it came back to him like this the rest of his life seemed to take its place too and he could see the future, see himself, his wife and his coming child, forming some kind of order.

He began to talk.

He loved to plan. He loved to move the ingredients of life about like squares of color in a pattern, trying them this way and that. There was nothing to stay his boldness. He had only to say what he wanted, and that too became a square of color to be fitted in with the rest.

"It's the kind of book that gets taken by the book clubs, if it's properly done. You can count on a sale of—maybe two hundred thousand. . . . Of course reduced royalties. But what the hell, that's a lot of money. Enough to fix us. We could buy this house. Fix it up. I've got another book all ready to write. A novel. There's no reason why I can't make a decent living out of free-lancing without any horsing around on hack jobs. If I did a book a year, that would insure us enough to live on without selling myself down the river."

"Could you do a book a year?"

"Why the hell not?"

"I meant isn't it hard to get books published that often?"

"No . . . no. . . . Lots of writers do it."

"Then you could."

"Sure. . . ." His mind sped ahead, impatient of plans that seemed already accomplished facts. "I could be sure of enough to get this house into some kind of shape, and then, in the winters maybe, have enough left to do some travelling. There's such a hell of a lot of places I need to see. How would you like to see the world, darling? How would you like to go to Paris and have a binge? I want to go to Germany. I want to find what the hell is going on there. Bill Perkins was full of what he'd seen when he came back last year. There's something cooking. I wouldn't mind taking a job on a paper as a correspondent."

"You mean live there."

"Yeah. Oh, you mean the child. That'd be all right. It's good for a kid to get used to moving around. Our kid will have to get used to the fact his old man's a writer."

"Yes."

"I'd like to buy the piece of land behind this, running back of Joe's. I want to have a stake in a piece of property. I like it here. We'd come back to this house. It suits you, doesn't it?" he asked.

"Yes, darling. I love this country."

He glanced at her and continued, with a fresh cigarette.

"If we had that land there'd be enough wood on it to keep us supplied without buying any. I'd like to get out and chop wood."

"Man's work," she said, smiling.

It was an old joke between them. Sometimes it did not seem to be exactly a joke.

"With a little dough we'd be able to heat this house properly. Weather-strip it and put in a furnace. Then we'd be able to get some use of the other rooms, when it's cold weather. Have some room to put any kids we might have. Have someone to stay with us if we wanted to. We could do that anyway, next summer."

"Oh, darling, I'd love that! We could have a picnic, with the Crowns. And go swimming off the rocks. Could we really have people stay with us?"

"Sure. I'd like to get Hannon up some time. He'd like it here. He'd like your cooking too," he added, smiling at her. "Now that you're getting such hot stuff."

"Darling! We could have such a good summer kind of time."

"You could have your family up some time if you wanted to," he said largely. "There's really quite a lot of room."

"I could have Maizie. It gets so hot in Annestown in the summers. I could have Maizie and Lambert, now she's well. You'd like it, wouldn't you, darling? You liked him, don't you remember? And she's lovely, she's just beautiful."

"All right," he granted. "If you can keep them out of my way when I'm trying to work. What I'd like to do is this. I'd like to build a little cabin sort of job back there at the edge of the woods, to work in. Then I could be completely out of the house and have the cabin to myself."

"You could fix it up just the way you wanted it."

"I'd like to have my own can and shower so if I got started on anything I could sleep out there."

"Yes."

In her mind's eye she saw it all clearly; bright and possible. Betsy loved to think into the future too. It was her natural element. She never distrusted the hypotheses; all her life she had been able to leap from the actual into the possible without hesitation.

"And what would you be up to with me safely out of the way?" he said, but not very seriously.

"Oh, darling, don't be silly. I'd be taking the baby up to change its diapers, probably."

"Sure? You wouldn't be having the ice-man up?" He was still teasing her.

"Certainly not. The ice-man stays in the kitchen."

"Quite a lot can happen in a kitchen," he said. "Can't it, baby? Or does your memory fail you?"

She grinned and reached out for his hand again. He took hers and pulled at her, and she got up and came round and sat on his lap, and leaned her cheek on the top of his head.

"I guess I'll just have to keep you in an interesting condition," he said. "Out of harm's way. Or is it out of harm's way? Have you been true to me, baby?"

"Hector, of course! Are you crazy?"

"Okay. Skip it. I didn't mean it. I was kidding."

But he was silent. She held his shoulders to her and kissed his thick, light hair.

"Go on to bed," he said abruptly.

"Now? Do you want me to go away?"

"I've got to think about my book some."

"All right, darling." She got up and kissed his cheek. "Will you be up soon?"

"Oh, I'll be up after a while."

He sat with his face in his hands while she moved for a few minutes round the kitchen. He heard her lift the stove lids and set them back. He heard her go, and close the door, and he heard her moving over his head upstairs.

These were the bad times, and for a minute he wondered why he had told her to go away when it was always so much worse when he was alone. But he had wanted her to go away so that she could stop thinking about her. . . . In the instinctive search for a cure he made himself another drink. He sipped it slowly, waiting for the feeling of enjoyment in the taste of the whisky.

But the rhythm, or whatever it was, had begun. It wound like a relentless spiral, slowly, going a little faster as time passed. He could put aside the idea that she had been unfaithful to him because he knew, he was sure, she had not. But there were other things. . . . The evening's talk kept reappearing in snatches, now with new meanings. She wanted her family up, did she? She resented not seeing her family more, she was holding it against him. He was a mean bastard who had knocked her up and made her do the work and never helped her and didn't let her go to see her family because he needed her to look after him. Jesus God, he had his book to write, didn't he? That had to come first till it was done. He was writing it for them both, and for the child, to support them all so that they could stop living on Betsy's dough. But did she see that? Hell no. She was being close-lipped and noble about paying for everything, but he knew she held it against him. She was paying for everything. That gave her the say about how the money was spent. The hell it did. She was a woman and his wife, and if she wanted to be his wife she could damned well be his wife and take whatever he dished out.

He took another drink. The bottle was nearly empty. He sat drinking, hunched over in his chair, hearing the sound of the sea and the sound of the coals dropping secretly down through the grate of the stove. After a while his unhappiness was unbearable. What was he doing here all alone going through hell while his wife slept like a fat cow upstairs in bed?

In the cold dark room Betsy stirred when the lamp came into the room and shone in her eyes, and then Hector's voice came:

"Get out of that bed, you."

She sat up.

"What's the matter . . . ?"

Already her heart had begun to pound, knowing before her mind did what was going to happen.

"Get up and come downstairs. I want someone to talk to."

She got out of bed and put the thick cotton flannel wrapper over her clumsy flannel nightgown, and stuck her feet into the sheepskin slippers. Hector turned and went down the stairs with the lamp and she followed him. She pulled at her sleepy mind, remembering that he had been drinking, that these times had to happen, that it would be over tomorrow and he would be sorry, that he didn't mean the things he had to say.

They went back into the kitchen and sat down at the table.

"I didn't want to leave you . . ." she said.

"That's right. You're always in the right. You're pretty gracious to put up with me at all, aren't you? Pay all the bills. Do all the work. Have a baby. A God damned saint."

"I know I'm not. I know I do things wrong."

"Quit that phony humility. I know you think plenty of things you don't tell me about. It makes me shudder to think of the things you hold against me. You're tight-lipped, aren't you? You can't spill an honest gripe. Hell no, you keep it to yourself and go around being a saint, a God damned ministering angel. Do you know what I think of your meekness? It makes me want to puke, that's what I think of it. If you don't like it here, why don't you say so and get the hell out?"

"I do like it. I want to be with you. I want to be what you need."

"The hell you do. So you think I need you. You think you've made yourself indispensable, don't you? Well, you haven't beaten me down that bad yet. I can make out. I know you're dissatisfied with every damned thing about this life, and sorry for yourself, so why don't you get the hell out? You might let me have the child when you've had it, that's all I ask. After all it is my child. Or is it?"

"You know it is."

"I don't know a thing about you, except that you're a lying little hypocrite. You might have done anything. I'd believe it."

Although she knew the course such times must take, their meaning and their lack of meaning, she could not help beginning to weep. The only thing was to say as little as possible, so as not to irritate him further; but silence enraged him too. . . .

"Don't think you are getting anywhere by crying," he said, in that cold, quiet, judicial voice. It was only the words that were hot. He always sounded so reasonable, so logical, that often it was hard for Betsy to realize that what he said about her was not, after all, true. Sometimes she could not help feeling that what he said was true of her; as though he had found out some dreadful hidden thing in her whose existence she herself had not even suspected.

"I'm trying not to."

"That's very brave of you. It would be if it was true. You work every dodge of being a woman for all it's worth, don't you? Don't let me interfere. It's your privilege. If it suits you, I will simply ignore your tears. There are a few matters I'd like to clear up. What did you mean when you asked me if I could write a book a year, tonight? You don't think I can finish this book, do you? You're just sitting watching to see if I quit, aren't you?"

"Really I'm not. . . . Of course you can finish it. I only meant I didn't know whether anybody could write books that fast."

"I never heard a less convincing statement. For your information, I'll tell you something. I can not only finish this book, but it'll be a good book, and if it is, and when I finish it, it'll represent a victory against some pretty fancy odds. Did you know that?"

"I know . . ."

"What are they?"

"I don't know what you are thinking of . . ."

"Oh. You don't. Well, then, I'll just tell you, or remind you, because anybody who wasn't a cretin would have a hazy idea. Remember me? I'm the guy who was going to be a writer. I'm the poor sucker, who fell in love with the lay of New York and got taken for a ride."

She thought—now we are back to it.

From now on she knew the course the night must take. She wished that, knowing, she could stay calm and untroubled, waiting, inside. But, as ever, her eyes burned, her heart pounded; with a frantic anxiety she listened to the things he said, examining them for truth, doubting her own memory, her own judgment, feeling again the guilt that was the worst of these nights, for guilt was a panic not native to her.

The dispassionate voice went on and on, speaking the violent, the passionate words as though with an icy knife he were cutting her out of himself.

There was nothing to do but wait.

"You think you're a heroine, don't you? You think you're putting up with so much. You're having it God damned easy! You've got everything you went after. You never had to take the rap for what you did, and you had your cake and you damned well ate it too. Do you want to do one simple thing to oblige me?"

"Yes. . . ."

"Then kindly wipe that smirk of virtue off your face. You may be a heroine to yourself, but you're no heroine to me. You just don't stack up against a few women I happen to have known. For example, my mother. You don't know what work is, as she knew it. She was a good woman. She was fine and true and noble. She didn't have a drop of slut blood in her veins, and that's the only kind of blood you have, isn't it?"

"That's not true. I haven't got bad blood. I know you hate me for all I've done to you, but it's not true that I have slut blood." She was so tired that it was hard for her to make orderly sentences.

"You," he said, "shut your whining face." He leaned across the table and looked into her face. He raised his hand and struck her hard on the cheek.

She did not stir; the last stage had begun, she thought.

"Why don't you whine? Why don't you go out that door and go find somebody to crab about your husband to? Oh, go on. Get out."

"I don't want to."

"I wish you would. Don't stay on my account. You'd be doing me a favor."

She did not speak. He struck her on the other cheek, and stared at her.

"Oh, for Christ's sake," he said, and flung himself up out of his chair. Without looking towards her further, with his lips pressed together, he picked up the one lamp still lit, on the shelf, and started to the door with it.

"Are you going to bed?" she said.

"Since you ask me, yes."

She did not attempt to follow him. He closed the door and she was left sitting in the darkness, in the warm room, with only the red light of the coals showing through the tipped lids of the stove.

After a while she got up. She did not want to go to sleep in the chair. By now Hector would be asleep. She did not bother with a lamp, but felt her way to the door, closed it, and walked slowly in darkness through the house.

On the third step of the stairs she tripped on her long wrapper and fell, but not heavily, twisting herself to catch her weight on her hip, sidewise. She got back on her feet and continued, clumsily, to climb the stairs. She went into the cold bedroom and got out of her wrapper and slippers and into bed beside Hector, lying turned away from her and fast asleep.

## CHAPTER LVII

SOMETIME LATER, but while it was still the middle of the night, Betsy wakened abruptly, completely. She awoke with a full concentration, with the pains that were beginning to subside. It had begun, and a month early.

The plan had been for her to have the baby in a semi-private ward at the hospital in the town, Stone Haven, on the other side of the bay, seven miles by road. There was no provision for having a baby in this house. They hadn't made any. They were going to get a stove for the bedroom about the time she went to the hospital. Now the room was ice cold.

There was the kitchen. Women had had babies in worse places than this, a lot worse. Doctors got to them in strange, hard places.

Dr. Werner was in Stone Haven. She'd made her visits to him by bus. He could get out here in his car if she could let him know.

She could get to the hospital somehow, or she could get word to the doctor to come to her.

The Crowns didn't have a car any more than the Connollys did. The nearest means of transportation was Weino Kalinin's fish truck. The Kalinins' house was down the road.

The Crowns had a telephone. Their house was about the same distance away as the Kalinins', but uphill.

A car or a telephone. One. There was no pain nor vestige of pain now. Just this large, wide, accurate concentration.

"Hector."

She spoke out loud.

"Hector!"

He turned over heavily in the bed, throwing one arm out straight and striking her shoulder heavily.

"Hector. Wake up."

He pulled the pillow up and covered his face.

"Hector," she began again. Then she stopped.

It was simply that it all took too much time; it was too difficult, there was too much to be gone through. She could do it all quicker and more easily herself. She had no feeling of resentment. It was only that she was keyed up to a special kind of efficiency. For the time nothing at all mattered except getting everything done at once.

She reached into the dark, found the candle and matches by the bed, made a light; got up and dressed quickly. She felt less clumsy than she had for weeks. She carried the candle into the bathroom and took her toothbrush from the shelf. The neat round circle of yellow light going before her, she went down the stairs, through the rooms, into the warm kitchen where the coals still shone faintly red under the lids of the stove. She took Hector's coat from the hook by the door and got into it and put the toothbrush in the pocket. Then she unlocked the outside door and went out.

There were street-lights at long intervals down the road, but there was no other light anywhere; only a sort of luminosity hung over the great, the loud, the invisible sea. The air was strong of salt; it was damp and very cold.

The pain came and she sat down on the granite step going down to the street and waited for it to go away. It was not a bad pain, it was strong and thorough and neat. Her mind had no part in it. She sat still and her eyes grew accustomed to the night, so that everything came to have a whitish clarity. The sky was overcast and the line between the sky and the sea was distinct to her; below the heavy line the sea lay pale gray.

After a few minutes she stood up and began to walk steadily along the road. The few houses ahead stood out of the night like granite boulders. The first house was the Kalinin's, and she went up to the kitchen door at the side and pounded on it with her fist. After a minute a window upstairs was thrown open and a voice called out into the darkness in Finnish.

"It's me," she called up. "It's Mrs. Connolly. Can you come down and help me?"

The window was shut and a light went on upstairs and then disappeared, and came again on the lower floor, traveling towards the kitchen. The door opened and Betsy stepped into the kitchen. Mrs. Kalinin stood in her heavy brown man's wrapper with the lamp in her hand. The light fell on her face so that the strong spare bones stood out, the cheekbones and the sharp toothless jaw. Her hair was thin and pale brown, pulled back into a skinny pigtail. Her life of work and the bearing of her ten children had left her face stripped, drawn tight, and severely beautiful.

Betsy sat down on a kitchen chair.

"I'm having pains. The baby's started. Can Weino drive me to Stone Haven in the truck?"

Mrs. Kalinin bent her head forward to listen to the words, carefully. Like all the older generation of Finns she spoke little English. Her eyes were calm and alert and understanding.

"You sit," she said. "I get Weino."

With one hand, still holding the lamp in the other, she slammed down the tipped lids of her kitchen stove, opened the drafts, and pulled forward a large metal coffee pot.

Then she went away with the lamp and Betsy heard her going upstairs. She sat in the warm dark room and in a minute or two she began to smell the coffee in the pot. While she was alone she had another pain, but it went away just before Mrs. Kalinin came back into the kitchen. She set the lamp down on the table and walked on slow, noiseless feet to the dresser and took down three thick cups and put them on the table too.

"Weino come. He puts his pants on."

She turned and walked to Betsy and put her hand on her shoulder. With her calm, grave face she looked down into Betsy's face.

"You all right."

"I'm all right."

Mrs. Kalinin went and watched the coffee pot and the steam beginning to rise from its spout, expressionlessly, seriously. In a few minutes more she picked it up using the tail of her wrapper to hold it, and poured the coffee into two of the cups. Betsy picked hers up and sipped the strong, black coffee. It was salted, in the Finnish way; pungent and biting.

Weino came into the room putting his arms into an old torn sweater. He was a thin boy of eighteen with straight yellow hair, blue eyes as serious as his mother's, a narrow face.

"Hello, Weino. Can you drive me to the hospital in the truck?"

Another pain had begun and she felt her stomach contract to rigidity. The pain was hard and reaching and thorough. She pulled the side of Hector's coat up around to cover her.

Weino did not look at her while she had the pain. He had made a little bow from the neck with grave politeness. He filled his own cup from the pot of coffee, and sipped from it. He glanced at her, and then turned and looked at her.

"It's too bad, Mrs. Connolly," he said. "The truck broke down yesterday. I've got to get a new part for the generator in the morning. My mother didn't understand what you wanted me to do."

He spoke in quick, rattling Finn to Mrs. Kalinin for a minute, and she answered him, and they both looked seriously at Betsy.

"I can go up to Crown's and telephone Dr. Werner."

"I haven't any way of heating the bedroom in my house. There's only the kitchen. I didn't expect the baby to come for a month more."

They spoke Finnish again together.

"My mother wants to know if you want to stay here. She would be glad to help you all she can. There is a stove in my mother and father's room."

Betsy turned and smiled into Mrs. Kalinin's face. The woman, who had been watching her son speak English, looked back at Betsy and nodded several times. She held one hand out, open. On her face, as pure and simple as a skull, a faint smile began; innocent and generous.

"Tell her I thank her a million times," Betsy said. "But you're crowded even without me. I'd take up an awful lot of room. Isn't there some way I could get to Stone Haven? If there isn't, I'll stay. I wish you'd tell her how grateful I am."

The Finnish was spoken again, and, talking to her son, Mrs. Kalinin kept smiling and looking at Betsy and making small, awkward gestures with her open hand. She leaned forward and looked back and forth from one of Betsy's eyes to the other.

"You stay. I take care. Better you stay here."

"I could row you across the bay in the dory," Weino said. "It's not rough. It would be very cold, though."

"How long would it take?"

"About an hour. Is that too much?"

"I don't think so. It hasn't been long. Would you mind doing that?"

"I wouldn't mind," he said. "You want to get to the hospital."

She started to say that she was not afraid to have the baby here, that it was only she did not want to bring all the confusion and crowding into this house. But she did not say it. There was the same feeling she had had when she stopped trying to wake Hector. These people, so kind, so generous, would argue with her and deny the trouble. She had the sensation again of efficiency, of dispatch; she wanted to get things done at once, her own way. She would let them think that it was important to her to have the baby in the hospital. It didn't matter.

"We'd better go now, then," she said, standing up.

Mrs. Kalinin made little, high, inarticulate noises. She came and took Betsy's two hands and again looked searchingly into her face, from one eye to the other. Betsy pressed her hard hands and smiled and shrugged her shoulders.

"He says it only takes an hour," she said, speaking distinctly. "I've got plenty of time. I'd like to go that way."

The mother began taking down coats from the row of hooks by the kitchen door. She held open a big old dark man's coat and nodded and reached it out toward Betsy. It went on over Hector's coat. Weino took the pile of other coats over his arm. Mrs. Kalinin snatched up the coffee pot and held it toward the empty cups, nodding. Betsy shook her head and smiled.

She took Mrs. Kalinin's hand, trying to put her gratitude into her smile. But inside she was busy; composed; she wanted to get on. Weino opened the door on to the cold and they went out. Mrs. Kalinin stood in the doorway holding her wrapper around her. They went down the three granite steps and around to the back of the house. Weino stopped and picked up something under his free arm and in a minute Betsy could see the long shape of the oars.

They walked very slowly down through the small bare pasture behind the house to the rocky beach, picking their way over the small sea-rounded stones and through the harsh stubble of beach grass. The sea was deeply, softly noisy and there was that pale gray luminosity over the water. Weino found the narrow path at the back of the beach and Betsy followed him

along the smooth sea-weed-covered way to the end of the beach where the
big boulders began. He turned and held out the hand of the arm that held
the coats, to help her up on the first boulder. Then she followed him,
climbing up and down the great rocks, the huge gray shapes; the rock was
sharp and scratchy under her fingers when she had to climb on all fours.
Once she had to stop for a pain. Weino stopped and she saw him standing
just ahead of her looking out to sea, waiting for her.

"All right," she said when the contraction was released, and they climbed
on down the rocks. Now they felt damp under her hands and there were
the sharp points of the cold barnacles that grew under the line of high tide.
The dory was pulled up on the rock just above the line, farther on; Weino
threw in the coats and laid the oars across the thwarts and pushed the dory
carefully down the rocks into the water. She waited, watching him getting
into the boat, setting the oars in the locks; everything was quite plain, all in
deep varying shades of gray.

"All right," he said. He got partly out of the boat and held it against the
rocks with one foot on shore, his hand outstretched to meet hers. She
climbed on her hands and heels down the wet rocks and took his hand and
got into the boat. She walked carefully, with the boat rocking under her,
into the stern and sat down. Weino pushed the boat off with his foot and
went back and sat down facing her, handling the oars, turning the dory
around so that it faced out into the bay.

"Better put some more coats around you," he said. "It will be very cold."

Now that they were on the water a fresh sharp salty wind was blowing;
it scraped across Betsy's face. She liked the cleaning feeling, the razing feeling. In a minute more the shore was invisible and they were in the million
gray interminable waves; small, sharp-edged waves that slapped against the
side of the boat at first, and when they turned outwards into the bay, made
the dory dip first bow then stern with an enormous crisp monotony.

The pains came regularly, increasing in the range of their thoroughness,
but there was none of them that quite blacked out the sea, the great gray
heavy sky. She felt calm. The pains were a part of the feeling of complete
occupation she had and she accepted them and greeted them as more of this
going somewhere; moving towards something steadily; getting things done.
The oars creaked rhythmically in the locks, with a little jerk and squeak at
the end of each stroke, and the boat moved along, dipping, cutting steadily
through the water, crossing the invisible, breathing, unfathomable bay. Once
they passed a rocking bell-buoy.

The feeling she had between the pains was one of earned release and a
strange comfortable enjoyment. It was as though she were aware in her
whole self of the current discharge of all duty. She feared nothing. Everything had been accounted for. She trusted the soundness of the boat, the
ability of Weino to reach the other shore, the relation between man and
boat and sea to make a successful water transit for herself in her state of
full occupation. The hospital was at the other end, the doctor, the nurses,
the instruments, the bed. In this world everything was in its place. It was a
world as snug and self-contained as an orange.

In the spaces between her pains she was left free, really free with the conscienceless freedom of a child to enjoy freedom.

The trip across the cold, windy bay in the night was, in those spaces, like a pleasure-trip, a trip in a pleasure boat. It was as though there were a striped awning, music playing, blue scalloped waves with white tips, and sunshine sparkling on the smooth green scoops between the tips. The creak of the oars kept sounding to her gay, festive: She was quite cold under the coats and her cheek on the windward side ached from blown spray, but she continued to have this party feeling which spouted up in bursts from some fountain-head of satisfaction. She drew her hand out of the layers of coat and reached over the side to feel the water running past. Her hand was immediately struck numb and she snatched it back to her, rubbing it against the wools to warm it.

"Get there in a few minutes now," Weino said. "Are you all right?"

"I'm fine."

"If you'll wait on the dock I'll run up and find somebody with a car to come down and get you."

"It's too late. The hospital's only a couple of blocks. I could get there quicker walking."

"All right, if you think you can."

She considered.

"Yes, I know I can."

Now there were a few lights and the silhouetted shapes of the town on the shore, and after a while they began threading through a confusion of dark shapes of boats anchored in the cove, moored barges, motorboats; creak, creak, the oars went in unhurried rhythm, and they came up to a dock at which were drawn up a number of fishing schooners with short sawed-off masts. All was gray, all was silent and obscured. The cove water slapped against the dolphins at the corners of the dock and Weino shipped the oars and reached up one hand and caught the edge of the dock. He edged the dory along to the upright board ladder. The tide had risen and there were only two or three cross-pieces to climb.

Betsy grasped the two sides of the ladder and hoisted her weight up out of the boat. Then she thought that she would fall over backward—not fear, but an instantaneous sizing up of her inability to climb the upright ladder.

"I can't get up," she said. "You'll have to push me."

She felt his shoulder come under her and raise her steadily. She stepped up and lifted her hands higher on the side pieces. She climbed on to the wet dock on her knees and sat perfectly still where she was, with a fresh, huge, clean pain. Somebody groaned, and it was herself, but her mind took no part in the crying out.

"Are you all right?"

"I'm all right now."

When she could she got back up on her feet.

In one of the warehouses that lined the harbor street a yellow light burned, two stories up; it seemed to melt and drip like honey. No other waterfront building showed a light, but the white street-lights winked and snapped along the edge of the harbor. The hospital was up the hill, up the cold, narrow, empty street from the cove that wound up and around a curve.

They began to walk very slowly up the hill side by side. Weino kept exactly beside her, shortening his step when she shortened hers, and glancing down at her and away again.

"You left the stuff in the boat," she said.

"It will be all right for a little while."

"Somebody might take it."

"I don't think so for a little while. I will go back."

"You go home as soon as you get me there."

"I will wait and see how you are."

"I'm going to be all right."

A pain came and she stopped dead where she was, going up hill. It was enormous, expert, complete pain that ground out all around everywhere. There was a fire hydrant directly beside her and she sat down upon its short cut-off knob. Sitting down seemed to complete the efficiency of the pain. It was like something locked; fine, strong, sweet, hard, tremendous, grinding.

She had to stop once more going up the hill and around the curve. The last time was in full sight of the hospital and she watched it through her pain, ready and waiting for her: a gray concrete building, small and ugly, with a light burning inside the front door. That was where she had to get. That was where the going somewhere ended. Inside the journey would be finished and the climax reached. She would get there in time.

They rang the night bell and waited until a tall, sleepy nurse opened the door. They stepped inside. The nurse after a glance had pulled forward a wheel-chair from the side of the entrance hall, nodded to Betsy to sit down in it, gone to the telephone on the desk and was now murmuring into it in a professional, night-time voice.

"I'm all right now," Betsy said. She held up her hand to Weino. "Don't wait. Really."

"I will get the coats and the oars out of the boat and come back and sit," he said. "My mother will want to know if you are all right."

"I wish you'd go back. My husband. He was asleep, he doesn't know where I am. I wish you'd tell him where I am and that I'm fine."

It was the first time that Hector had been mentioned.

Weino's thin blond face was expressionless.

"Then I will go back and tell him. He will be able to telephone to see how you are."

"Yes."

The nurse turned from the telephone and came to them. They shook hands and Weino, in his old trousers, his mackinaw, his yellow hair wet and falling in a lock over his eyes, went to the front door and out of it. The nurse took hold of the bar of the wheel-chair and began to push it with Betsy in it toward the back of the hall, toward the swinging-doors, toward the waiting machinery of the hospital.

It seemed to her to be early dawn, because turning her face toward a window the world outside was drenched in pink light; a light exquisite, tremulous, happy beyond any light of ordinary day, quivering with delight. The buildings she saw there, the plain staff of a lamppost, were all transfigured with this light, with unbearable delicate beauty, not like any scene her eyes had ever seen. She was so happy, so much more than happy, she did not dare to move an inch for fear of breaking this iridescent bubble. She lay quite still, her body in perfect rest, her mind wiped clean of everything, her drowsily aware senses bathing in this peace, this enchantment, a new perfected world that was pink . . . luminous . . . hushed. . . .

A door opened. She had to turn her head. But the delight did not vanish, it went everywhere with her eyes.

She was in a room, in a bed, with curtains partly drawn around it. Other curtains partly hid other beds. The curtains were white . . . like fresh snow. . . . The room was full of that dawn light. She could not see the door that had opened.

But fingers curled around the edge of the white curtain . . . the curtain moved a little . . . a face looked round it at her, smiling; with dark hair and a white, white cap with wings; she had seen the face before, somewhere, in the time before the time of her long sleep. . . . The face drew back and another face came. It was Hector's. There was his big, pale face, his thick hair the color of pulled molasses candy, and his shoulders followed his face around the curtain, and he came inside it, and he was smiling too, a smile that came and went and came back again. He bent over the bed where she lay and kissed her.

"Hello," she said. She kept blinking and smiling, blinking because the light was so pink.

She saw him reach back of him and pull a chair close to the bed within the curtains. He sat down and immediately leaned forward, his eyes fixed on her face, his smile bending his face up . . . down a little . . . up. . . . He was very clean and neat, she thought; he was shaved close and his hair was cut and brushed down damp.

"You had a hair-cut," she said.

"Yes, while you were asleep. *Darling*," he whispered, reaching across the white spread and taking her hand.

"What time is it?"

"It's almost five."

"Five?"

"The sun's setting. It's been sunny all day."

"I thought it was early. . . . I thought the sun was coming up. . . ."
He laughed.

"When did I," she began. "When did it happen?"

"He was born at twelve o'clock, right on the dot."

"I had a boy."

"You had a boy, darling. I sent a telegram to your mother. Was that right?"

She nodded and went on smiling at his face.

"I saw him," he went on. "He looks just like a boy, it's the damnedest
thing. He's got the damned smallest hands. . . ."

"I saw his hands," she said. "They were waving. In a sort of crib on stilts
He had brown stuff in his eyes."

"Darling . . . we've got a baby!"

She squeezed his hand.

"Isn't it funny?"

"Isn't it funny?" he whispered. "It's terribly funny. I can't get it, yet.
You're so wonderful, darling . . . such a wonderful girl. . . ."

"When did you come?" she asked. In this dawn-colored peace, pieces of
what was past came drifting down and settled slowly in their places.

"Oh . . . Jesus. . . . I got here about seven. Got the first bus. Weino
came and told me. . . . I was asleep, you know. Listen, baby. Listen, my
sweet. Couldn't you make me wake up? What happened? He told me he
had to row you over."

"You were kind of mad at me," she murmured.

He bent his head and kissed her hand, and left his forehead lying there
against it.

Now the pink light had gone but still everything was beautiful, everything
seemed to murmur. Someone beyond other curtains switched on a light.
Betsy looked with amazement at the softness, the yellowness, of the light
trickling down the white curtains; resting in a circle on the ceiling. Quiet
. . . quiet. . . . Everything in her rested. The lights and shadows within
her vision were full of delight.

Hector lifted his head, and she turned her head slowly, comfortably, to
smile at him.

But he was not smiling.

"Why did you get that Finn boy to row you over? What were you
doing with him?"

In peace her eyes moved over his face, recognizing from far away the
signs of his anger and his suspicion. Just the same. But she was a thousand
miles, a million miles different.

His eyes were fixed on hers. She blinked her eyes slowly once or twice
and then her mouth quivered, and she began to laugh.

Her laughter came from the bottom of her, the sides of her, from deep
inside, unagitated, rolling out without any stop and without any end to its
sources.

She laughed and laughed, and someone pulled aside a curtain to look,
and laughing, Betsy caught a glimpse of a dark, fat Portuguese or Italian
face, its mouth fallen open, an absurd curly-headed woman's face. It was
so funny. She laughed and laughed.

She lay flat on her back looking up at the ceiling and laughing. Without
even trying to stop she cocked her eyes over at Hector and there he was
staring at her with his mouth working, his eyes hostile, his nose twitching.
He looked unbearably funny. She laughed and laughed.

### CHAPTER LVIII

AFTER THE HARD LONGSHORE WINTER the month of May came like a surprise.

The locust trees that had stood all winter like bare and white-bleached bones, clattering in the northeast wind, creaking, standing out pinkish-gray and luminous in the bitter silence of the great cold—now burst unbelievably into explosions of bloom. The flowering of the locusts looked like puffs of thick white smoke against the strong blue of the May sky.

The sea turned blue. Air-borne flotillas of gulls flew screeching in long scalloped lines over the blue waves and the clear clean sunlight fell on their backs, making the white gulls shine as bright as pieces of washed white linen flying in the wind. Shrieking wildly, the gulls would settle on a wave in the bay and sit there rocking on the cold blue water.

The May air had the sharpness and bouquet of a yellow ice-cold wine. All the colors of spring here were white, and yellow, and blue. The sounds of the gulls, of the sea, of hammering back in the moors behind Graniteside, carried high and exact along the air. The fish truck drove rattling along the road by the sea; the small flat waves went splash, splash, rapidly against the little round stones of the beach. Old Rankin the painter walked back into the moors every morning carrying his paint-box and a canvas, wearing a filthy old Indian topee. The old Chamberlain sisters who never went out of their smelly little fisherman's cottage all winter, emerged carrying small Persian rugs; they hung them on the line in full view of the broad blue sea and the sunny road; in their eccentric rusty hats and long, full, thick skirts, in their high button boots they crawled round and round their cottage poking with sticks at the still half-frozen earth.

After eleven, when the morning sun was warmer, Betsy would put Jerry out in the yard in his folding carriage while she did the washing in the kitchen. When she came out, with her arms full of wet white clothes, he was lying there propped on two pillows with his face as round and bright pink as a zinnia. She stopped and looked down at him. He blinked at her and blew one large, perfect bubble between his pink wet lips.

"Boo," she said to him.

The wet sheets and diapers slapped against her face as she hung them in the wind and she batted them back with her hands and fastened them on the line with the wooden pins. When they were all up she went back into the house and brought out a brown blanket and laid it down on the ground and put rocks on the corners. The round bright candid sun shone straight down and she picked the baby up out of his carriage and took off his sweaters and his diaper and his little flannel shirt. Sitting to the windward of him she put him down on his back on the blanket, naked. Lying so, flat, his cheeks fell back; his blue eyes stared at her judicially; he was a fat mass of relaxation. Betsy unbuttoned the front of her yellow peasant dress and pulled the bodice off her shoulders and down around her waist. Dressed, she had felt the sharp edge of the morning air; against her naked skin the sun was really hot. There was a buzzing, a humming, in the noonday.

Hector came in the gate around in front and Betsy heard his steps behind her approaching on the granite stepping stones. His shadow fell short and luminous over her and she reached out and squeezed one of his ankles. He squatted beside her and put down a string of silver haik where she could see it.

"Haven't you any sense of shame?"

"Nobody can see me around here."

"Hm. Hello, fat paunch," he said, poking the baby with his finger.

"You're a wonderful fisherman."

"Just a sportsman. A gentleman of leisure. Huntin', fishin'."

Hector had finished his book, *The Starrs*, in April and sold it at once to a New York publisher he had talked to about it once long ago before he had started it. The book would appear in the Fall. He had got a comfortable advance on royalties, sufficient to show the publishers expected *The Starrs* to sell.

Now all was successful, all was justified. His worst dreams had been no more than nightmares.

He was the newspaperman who succeeds in writing a book. And against odds—practically insuperable odds. Instead of being all the things he had been afraid he was, he was the author of a finished and sold book; he was a man who could make money to support his dependents. Oh, he was capable of a great deal. He was going to write a novel next. In the meantime he needed a rest from the gruelling winter. He had to have relaxation to think about his novel.

The expression of his face showed his relief at the picture he now saw when he looked at himself. A clever guy who'd done a difficult writing job successfully. He was reinstated with his kind, the clever guys, the busy, fast-talking, confident ones. Now he could look at Joe Crown without uneasiness. He could like him more; relax and view him as material for the character of the protagonist of his novel.

Now he could look at himself, living in Graniteside not because he had to and not because his wife couldn't afford any better place to keep him, not because he had been licked by other places, but because he chose to. He could say to himself that he lived here because it was a good place to write. Finishing *The Starrs* here gave him a good luck feeling about the place; it suited him as working surroundings. He could say to himself that he was here, for one thing, to study Joe Crown.

Nevertheless in the evenings he had begun to talk about taking a trip to New York. After dinner, when the hour came for the evening planmaking, he talked now about nipping down to New York for a few days; to see his publisher; to see some of the boys. He needed clothes. He had money now. More would come in. He wanted a new tweed suit and he wanted a good one. He wanted a pair of Frank shoes, he said. Sometimes for hours he would talk about clothes, a subject he knew a good deal about,

that had a curious fascination for him: the names of tailors. Wetzel,
Weatherill; other names that rolled unctuously off his tongue, Harris tweed,
Meltonian cream, Bedford cord, Tattersall checks; historical bits—the Brooks
four-button suit. In the evenings he discoursed on clothes with the same
enthusiasm and reportorial knowledge that he had evidenced in the Fall
and the Winter talking about the Starr family that then bestrode him—old
Horatio, Harrison T., the thrice-married Grace, the Senate investigation of
Harrison T. junior.

He squatted in the sunshine of the May day in a pair of blue jeans, a sweat
shirt, and dirty old white sneakers.

"Joe wants us to come to dinner," he said. "They've got a celebrity. John
Fegan, the Hollywood boy. Claudine's going to cook *moules marinière*."

"I know," Betsy said. She hugged her knees and spread her back to the
sun. "We're supposed to gather the mussels for her at four."

"You know everything," he said. "I suppose you know why Fegan is visiting them. Why he would be."

"Joe knew him when, in Paris, I think. He's going to spend the night."
He glanced at her irritably.

"He's one of the top directors! Doesn't it seem funny his having any time
to spend in Graniteside, for God's sake?"

"They used to go on wine tours with him ages ago. Claudine says he's
sort of childish."

"You women say the God damnedest things to each other. You're like an
underground railway, a grapevine, or something. You'd communicate by
drumming on the ground if you didn't see each other. You say the God
damnedest things about people. Childish! I wish I could be childish the way
Fegan is. I want to talk to him about chances on going out to the Coast—
he couldn't do anything I suppose, but it wouldn't hurt. This novel I'm
writing ought to make a picture."

"Have you begun, darling?"

"I haven't typed anything out, if that's what you mean, but I'm carrying
it around with me. I have to get things absolutely clear in my mind before
I can write anything, ever."

She said nothing. She picked the baby up and held him in her lap while
she dressed him again. When he was covered she held him to her naked
breast and he began to nurse. Hector watched them with his lips com-
pressed, his eyes abstracted.

"Are you getting after me to write my novel?" he said abruptly. "Is that
what you're after?"

"I'm not after anything, darling. I just misunderstood you."

"Because you don't know a God damned thing about how to write a
book, and I'd be obliged if you'd stop heckling me if I don't go right to
work the minute I finish the other book, as if it was a new table to build.
It's got to mill around and change and get transmuted and go through a
whole metamorphosis. If you know what a metamorphosis is."

"I want you to do it exactly your own way."

"Well, don't sound so soothing. Quit buttering me up. I know you think a lot of things you don't tell me anything about. What are you planning for this afternoon, for instance?"

"What do you mean? Going to the party?"

"Don't be innocent," he said icily. "You don't know how. I was wondering what you were planning in regard to seeing a new man. You haven't seen any man but me and Joe for quite a while, have you? I suppose you think you need a work-out."

"I don't think any such thing."

"Don't talk back, God damn it. You keep your mouth shut and try to behave like a decent woman. Do me that favor, will you? I suppose it never occurs to you what I go through in letting a man see my wife," he continued, his voice rising, expanding. "Men can tell a slut when they see one, you know. Men can tell what kind of wives other men have got. By the way, you haven't told me whether you'd ever known Fegan before. It's hard for me to keep up with your acquaintance, it's so extensive."

"No. I've never met him."

"Well, do me a favor and don't discuss your glorious past with him, will you? Don't play 'do you know,' if you don't mind."

"Of course I won't."

"Good. Good. And try to get yourself up like some kind of a decent woman. I suppose you know what you look like now," he exclaimed, getting to his feet.

"I didn't expect anyone to see me except you."

"I don't know why I let you go this afternoon, anyway," he said, snatching up the fish and walking away. The back door slammed.

He was not really angry. This was only irritability, she knew. It was familiar to her, and it would build up into passion that would appease itself. She continued peacefully to nurse her child, the high sun shining straight down on her faintly burned breasts.

In the decline of the afternoon the party of mussel gatherers clambered over the rocks carrying baskets and boxes, to pry the tight-clamped, long, dark-blue and black shell-fish out of the crevices. The day had remained clear and bright but now that the sun was setting it was colder. The two women wore sneakers on their bare feet. Both of them were dressed in cotton dresses they had made together, Claudine's pink, Betsy's red, with open sweaters.

The sea was glossy, slippery as oil; it slid back and forth against the rocks hissing and gurgling in the holes between the boulders. It was dark blue, and darker shadows spread smoothly over the water. The people laughed, and called to each other across the primeval stretch of unbroken rocks; they climbed up the dark gray rough sides, and slipped crouching down to the edges of the water where the mussels grew thick in the cracks of the rocks, their shells speckled with tiny white barnacles, clamped to the stone with meshes of seaweed. The water was icy cold.

"Wait for me, Mrs. Connolly," John Fegan called. "You keep going so fast. You don't care if I break my neck."

He was an extraordinary looking little man. Round, and compact as a drum, he had thick curly gray hair grown long and fastened down by a blue Basque beret; he wore a black woollen shirt under a tweed suit that was hyacinth blue. His nose was squashed like a pugilist's, his lips were thick, his skin fresh and pink. He looked his listeners straight in the eye and spoke in a plaintive voice.

"Listen," he said, catching up to Betsy as she stood still at the top of a boulder surveying the water line, "I want you to come and mind your baby. It misses you. I will sit next to you and tell you what ideas to put in its head. It's a wonderful baby."

Betsy had brought Jerry on the expedition, in a laundry basket which she balanced on one hip as she walked along with it. She had left it wedged securely into a crevice between two large boulders.

She gave Fegan a smile, quick and vague, and began to run down the sloping side of the rock toward the shallows that swayed and shone in the sunset.

"Sometimes I think you're evading me," he cried, and prepared to follow her down the rock on his behind, scooching along, steadying himself with his hands. "Stop being a Greek maiden for a minute, will you?"

Hector kept watching her, as all afternoon she kept a few yards ahead of John Fegan. He and Joe wore old flannel trousers and mackinaws. Joe was elated by Fegan's coming; he talked and called at the top of his voice, a flow of elaborate, formal language that ricocheted off the rocks like pebbles.

Claudine went silently about gathering mussels, her beautiful resigned face faintly smiling; she picked very nimbly and fast with strong fingers. Her body seemed too full for speed; but she ran over the rocks with tiny steps, her hips swaying.

After a while she went from basket to basket peering into them, and said that they had picked enough. They started to climb up the rocks towards the road. Betsy handed her box of mussels to Hector, looking up into his face; but he turned his eyes away from her and took the box. She picked up the basket that held the sleeping baby and hoisted it to her hip; she continued to climb the hill, through the long harsh beach-grass.

"I want to carry that baby," Fegan said behind her. "Give me that."

She laughed and shook her head and continued to climb without turning, with long, reaching steps.

But when they were walking along the road he caught up to her and walked alongside.

"I want to know about you," he said. "I want to discuss you. You are beautiful and fantastic and I don't think I ever heard of anybody anything like you. Where did you go to school?"

"Oh, I went to a whole lot of schools."

"I don't care where you went to school. Why do you look like Ceres and talk like a young boy?"

"Our Betsy will next be seen in 'Mad Passion,' a Behring Brothers production," called Joe Crown, following them along the road. "I beg of you to observe, friends, how stars are made."

"I wouldn't give you a job," Fegan said, "if the whole reeking picture business went bust tomorrow for lack of you. I think you're lovely. Why do you like it here?"

"My husband likes it here," she said. Hector was right beside Joe. "It's good for his work. And I love the way it looks and the baby likes it."

"I know. He told me. He says he's a push-over for any place you are. Why does your husband write? Is he any good?"

She turned her head, and made a slight gesture back towards Hector, but he came along without speaking. In the cold, sweet salt air, all of them: Betsy, Fegan, Hector, Joe, Claudine, and the child Jeanne, walked along the rising sea road and turned off together at the driveway that led up to the Crowns' gate-house.

"He's very good," Betsy said. "He's just sold a book. It's coming out in the Fall. It's about the Starr family."

"One of those. Like the books about the Vanderbilts, the Astors, the Rockefellers, the Goulds, the Du Ponts, everybody else. Anybody can write a book about millionaires. Phooey. Why do you like him?"

"I just do," she said, laughing.

"Connolly," he called. "Tell your wife to pay some attention to me. She flouts me. She flies past me on wingèd feet."

Hector laughed shortly.

"Oh, you bore me," Fegan said. "Look, Mrs. Connolly. I want to talk to you. Don't walk so fast, will you?"

They came to the stone house; the dry vines hanging from it were whispering in the wind of dusk. They went in and Claudine lighted the lamps. She went into the kitchen and soon the smell of garlic began to creep into the other rooms. Joe, elaborately hospitable and proprietary with his old friend, brought out a bottle of whisky in the sitting-room; Hector lit the fire. The men sat down in chairs round the blaze of driftwood, with glasses in their hands.

Betsy climbed the stairs in the dark to Claudine's room with the baby. She left Claudine standing over the stove regarding the pot before her with her deep-sunk, beautiful, dark eyes; the little girl was eating her supper at the kitchen table, hunched over, her face turned away from her mother. She left the yellow, melting lights and the men in their chairs, and the last thing she heard was John Fegan's plaintive, tough voice:

"Where is Mrs. Connolly's drink? Where is Claudine's drink? Hm?"

Betsy shut the door to Claudine's bedroom. Outside the window the vines slapped and scratched on the pane, and twilight came in and showed her the bed, the floor. She took the baby out of its basket and lay down with it on the bed. She held the warm, soft, curled body within her arm and with her other hand unbuttoned the bodice of her dress. She held the baby to her breast.

She and her child were all alone; they were together by themselves. They were in a dark, warm place in comfort, closed away. Outside and around and beneath and beyond the world continued in its driving rhythm, but here all was still, without thought, motionless, dreamless, giving and taking.

When dinner was ready they sat around the square table in the little dining-room with all the food on the table, the great casserole of mussels, the bread, the dish full of curls of butter, the bowl of salad, the bottle of red wine.

"This is like the dinners in Albec," Fegan said. "*Moules marinière*. Give me some wine, Crown, my good fellow."

"Fill your empty glass," Joe said, pouring the wine. "Empty your full glass. I cannot bear to see your glass either empty or full."

"Oh, cannot you, you old sot."

Joe laughed his melancholy laugh. His face was emaciated, bright-eyed, and beautiful. He filled his own glass.

Fegan looked down the table at Claudine, sitting behind the casserole of mussels; her face was in repose, smooth, dark-skinned, the hollows of her eyes full of shadow; her black hair made a lovely shape against the walls of the room.

He looked at Betsy, across the table from him. Her hair was braided into a crown around her head, above her large, far apart eyes. Her neck stood up from her shoulders, long and vigorous. Her body looked strong and hard, and her wrists and hands were lightly tanned as they lay upon the table-cloth; slender, muscular.

"I'll be a son of a bitch," Fegan said. "Claudine, how do I tell whether these New England mussels are poisonous or not?"

"In the cooking," Claudine said, "an onion is put among the mussels in the pot. If it turns black, there is poison. These are good."

"In this hinterland," Joe said, "the natives do not understand that mussels are put here by God for man's sustenance. They consider my good wife and me quite mad to consider eating them." He smiled at Fegan.

"How do you like living on the Coast?" Hector asked. "I hear it's a hell of a life."

"I like it," Fegan said. "And so would you, and so would you. As you well know," he added plaintively. He held out his empty plate to Claudine.

They drank three bottles of wine between them, and went back into the sitting-room. Claudine and Betsy took the dishes out into the kitchen and washed them, and the pots. When they came back into the room with the men Joe had brought out a bottle of brandy. Fegan got to his feet. He held out his glass to Claudine.

"Here's your brandy, *ma belle*," he said. He walked deliberately on his short, stocky legs to the sitting-room cupboard and took down another glass. He took the brandy bottle off the table by the lamp and poured a drink. "And yours, Mrs. Connolly," he said, handing it to Betsy. "You rococo louts," he remarked, glancing at Joe and Hector as he sat down again.

Joe laughed, but Hector's face was heavy.

"My wife doesn't drink," he said.

"Oh, well," Joe said. "This is in the nature of a celebration. We'll all partake in honor of my old friend, *mon cher collègue, ce bon monsieur Fegan. Hein?*" he queried, glancing around at them all and taking a swallow of brandy.

Betsy sat down on the small horse-hair sofa with roses carved in the curving walnut back. Holding his brimming glass carefully before him, Fegan came over and sat down beside her. He sucked off the top of his drink and regarded her with blue, bright eyes. His coarse curly hair stood straight up, a bush of gray.

"You're beautiful," he said. "Beautiful and wise beyond our generation. I'm going to tell you the story of my life."

Betsy glanced at Hector's face and smiling faintly began to slip from the sofa to the low rocking chair that stood empty beside it.

Fegan put out one pudgy, delicate-fingered hand. He did not touch her, he held his hand just above her arm.

"Don't move. I wouldn't touch you any more than I'd touch the Virgin Mary. Do you hear that, you bullying black Irish sorehead?" He turned his eyes mildly on Hector.

"Connolly," John Fegan said, leaning his elbows on his knees, "I'm going to make you a sporting proposition and we'll see how you take it. Look. I can see, I saw at a glance what kind of a guy you are. You're a fine fellow, aren't you? A prima donna, aren't you? Don't say anything," he said, raising his hand.

Hector's jaw was thrust out and his face was pale. Claudine watched as though from far away, with remote, deep, almost Spanish eyes. Joe smiled as though at a secret with himself, and poured himself another brandy. Betsy sat with her hands folded in her lap; her eyes moved from Fegan to Hector.

"You're a tough boy, aren't you, you run your women with an iron hand and all the rest of that faradiddle. You've got your wife where you want her. In the country, buried, enslaved, sure; saved up for you. What makes you so unconfident, fellow? Huh? What are you afraid of? Are you afraid you can't keep your wife? Here's my proposition. I admire your wife. I want to talk to her alone, away from you and your black looks. She wouldn't come and talk to me, no. You've got her hog-tied. You observe I'm not asking her. I'm playing your little maley-paley game. Connolly, you four-flusher, I want to take your wife into the kitchen and have a pleasant conversation with her, out of sight of you, who aren't a pleasant sight. Or are you scared, hm? How about knocking me down instead? That would make you feel fine. Go on, knock me down. Or can I have a decent, civilized conversation with your wife, whom I respect and honor?"

Hector shifted his big, muscular bulk in his chair.

"Betsy, do you want to go out with this guy?" he said after a minute.

"I knew you'd pass the buck," Fegan remarked. "Just what I thought you'd do. Then she takes the rap afterwards."

"We can talk perfectly well here," Betsy said.

"You see, Connolly? Answer my proposition. Are you enough of a guy to let me talk to your wife, or are you scared? Or are you out of your mind? Or are you going to be sick? Or are you going to knock me down? Oh, stop looking like a five-cent Firpo," he added plaintively. "I have to telescope my actions. I won't be here tomorrow."

"Betsy, go talk to Mr. Fegan," Hector said.

"We can talk here," she said.

"Go and talk to him."

"We will sit in the kitchen," Fegan said, "and if we choose we will walk in the moonlight. What are you going to make of it?"

"I said go on, didn't I?"

"Yes, dear, you did," Fegan said.

Betsy did not move.

"I don't want to go out," she said. "I'd rather stay here. I want to stay here."

Nobody said anything.

Fegan crossed his short thick thighs and drank off the whole of his glass. He held it out in his hand. Joe leaned across with the bottle and filled it. His face was filled with a melancholy delight.

"Well, I see that I am sent here by God," Fegan said, "to tell you inflated sons of bitches a few simple truths. What is this? A colony of Turks? Do you want to say anything? Because if you don't, shut up. I want to talk."

He smiled a small, secret smile; he looked down into the golden depths of his brandy.

"I know everything," he said. "It is my gift. It is my curse. I look at you all and I see everything. You disguise nothing from me. Do you know what I see? Not what you think I see, you fine, conceited Brahma bulls. You fail to impress me. Instead you turn my stomach. That is why I turn to brandy," he said, "to help me keep my sense of proportion. To help me from taking a crack at that fat Irish jaw," he glanced from under his puffy eyelids at Hector. He held his emptied glass out again and Joe, beaming, filled it.

"I see the only things of significance in this whole disgraceful picture. I see your wives. Take a look at them yourselves sometime. Take a look at your wife, you Mick four-flusher. I know better than to advise you, Joe. You haven't seen anything but yourself for years and years. I'll tell you something. You think I came down here out of enthusiasm for your fascinating personality, don't you? Your outstanding remarkableness. Look, if you died tomorrow it would fail to catch my notice. I came to see Claudine, whom I have worshipped since my eyes first fell on her. Since I worked on the Paris *Herald*. She's beautiful. She's wise, and kind, and infinitely long-suffering. I adore her.

"Virtuous wives," he said. "Loyal wives. The problem is, is it necessary to abuse them to produce them, or are some women naturally wonderful? I put my faith in the latter view.

"Connolly! Ever since I got here you've been sucking up to me. When you weren't giving your wife threatening looks when I came anywhere near her. You wife-beating Paddy. I know all about you. I know every bullying drop of blood in your body. I was raised in southern Illinois of poor and Irish parents. Farmers. My old man beat up my mother every Saturday night. He was a bastard. He was nothing. My mother was beautiful, and strong, and wise. She was a deep-browed goddess.

"Well, I wouldn't give you a job if you were the last second-rate legman who ever boasted of his newspaper experience. You're nothing. You're a nickel a dozen. It's your wife who's unique. You're jealous of her. You know she's lovely, and remarkable, and priceless, and that's why you abuse her. You hope you'll wear her out. You hope you'll take off some of the lovely bloom. You keep her all to yourself and then you abuse her. God meant her to be cherished and adored. You cheat her of everything she should have, don't you? Don't you, Connolly? Don't you cheat her?

"Mrs. Connolly. I have fallen deeply and reverently in love with you and I think your child is extraordinary. I want you both. I ask you in all earnestness to leave this preposterous colony of wife-beaters and come away with me."

Smiling, Betsy shook her head at him.

"I ask you to marry me. You are a fountain of sweetness and you were put here for men to drink from. Oh dear, why all this grimness and suffering? If you marry me I can promise you that I would never have a pang of possessiveness, or if I did I am adult enough to keep it to myself. How would you like someone to make a career of making you happy?"

"But I am happy," Betsy said gently. She wanted to laugh. The fat little man's face was glistening with sweat that ran down the sides of his broken nose. She glanced at Claudine and Joe. Claudine smiled down at her sewing, and Joe leaned forward eagerly. She looked at Hector, and his face wore his listening look; alert, concentrated, observing.

Fegan took the brandy bottle out of Joe's hand and poured his own drink. He slopped the brandy over, and ignored the wet spot on his knee.

"Yes, yes," he said. "Yes, you are. That's why I'm in love with you. That's why I am in love with Claudine. It's the sight of your heartbreaking happiness made out of nothing. Your grandeur and your calm and your immense, goddesslike beauty. I'll never get anybody like you or Claudine because I'd want to make you happy. Women like you don't want to be made happy. They grow their own happiness out of nothing—like flowers out of a sterile soil. As my mother did.

"That is my tragedy," he said. "I only love the wise, suffering women. The women in the image of my mother. It is my tragedy that none of them will ever love me. Because that's the way they are. Listen! I've got so much money I don't know what to do with it. I've got a monogamous nature, I've got everything. But you don't want that. You have to have these tough, egotistical bastards that give you a beating.

"I know everything. Everything. I know what it is. It's a religion. Connolly! You're a black Irish sorehead. Well, it hasn't anything to do with Catholicism. It's an apostate religion, it's heretic. Men and women. Male and female. The dominance of the male. The subjection of women. You make a cult out of it. I know. You have sinned, Connolly. You set yourself up as God, for your wife to worship. Well, Connolly. You're not God. You can't create. It's only women who can create. Theirs is the kingdom, and the power, and the glory. You know it, you black Irish. . . ."

John Fegan slipped down off the horsehair sofa on to the floor. His fat chin rested on his chest, and the rest of his brandy spilled over the front of his hyacinth blue coat.

"Out like a light," Joe said. He bent over Fegan with an admiring, proprietary smile. "One of the most brilliant fellahs I ever knew. He can't drink at all, though. Claudine, pick up his feet. We've got to get him to bed. He's catching a plane in the morning," he added over his shoulder as he lifted Fegan under the arms, "the intricacies of cinema politics call him back to Los Angeles at once."

Hector took Fegan's feet from Claudine and the two men carried the limp, round body upstairs. Betsy followed them, a little way behind, silently. She went into the bedroom and put the baby in its carrying basket, put on her sweater, and brought the basket downstairs on her hip.

When Hector came down again, Betsy and Claudine were facing each other, looking into each other's eyes. Claudine put out her hand and laid it on Betsy's arm for an instant.

"Ready, Betsy?" Hector said.

They went out into the pure, cold night that was splattered with stars. Great white constellations wheeled silently through the sky. They walked down the hill from the Crowns in the darkness as they had done so many times before. The red coal of Hector's cigarette came and went as he sauntered without speaking beside Betsy.

Betsy lit a lamp in the kitchen and carried it upstairs in one hand while she balanced the basket with the other. She went into the little room off hers and Hector's, and setting down the lamp, picked the baby up and laid it in its wooden crib. It slept without stirring, its pink-flushed face drowned in sleep. She changed its diapers in the crib, and once more picked it up and held it in her arm while she undid her dress. Without waking, the baby found her breast with its minute, searching lips. This was the last time she would nurse it until morning. She sat in the yellow lamplight holding the child to her. She could hear Hector come upstairs and go into the bedroom and move around.

When she went into the bedroom he was sitting on the edge of the bed, fully dressed. He had a cigarette in his fingers, hanging between his knees, and he was looking down at it. He threw it down in the bedside ashtray as Betsy brought the lamp in, and crossed the room to her in an instant. He came so swiftly she thought he was going to strike her.

But he took the lamp from her and set it down on the bureau and turned to her again and put his arms around her.

She looked at him in surprise.

He began to unfasten her dress, murmuring to her words she could not catch. He knelt down and undid her sneakers and pulled them off and held her feet between his hands. He led her to the bed and lifted her in his arms and laid her on it and squatted by the side of the bed holding her hands and kissing them, mumbling against her skin.

She felt a crazy impulse to laugh.

"I thought you'd be mad," she said.

He looked up and into her face, and put his arms up around her with an extraordinary, yearning gesture. His face in the lamplight was transformed. He looked tremulous, anxious, loverlike, sensitive, inquisitive.

Because she did not know what else to do, she leaned and kissed him. His lips were softened and loose and he lifted his face to her kiss and closed his eyes.

Hector was unpredictable. The forming of the thought in her mind settled her and stopped the desire to laugh.

From squatting on his heels he shifted on to his knees and stayed there, holding her and looking into her face.

"Darling . . . I don't know anything about you. Do you know that? You must tell me things," he said. "There's so much I want to ask you. You *know*, don't you? You must tell me the answers to things."

He never liked to have his moods questioned. It was one of the things that made him furiously angry. She thought that she had better not ask him anything about how he felt about Fegan and Fegan's talk. It would make him feel that she questioned the integrity of his emotion. The only thing to do with Hector was to take him as he came.

But she felt curiosity about what Hector felt about her own behavior.

"You aren't mad at me because of the way that man acted?"

"Oh my darling. . . . You were wonderful. He saw it. He saw that you are like a goddess, that nobody can touch, nobody can approach. He knew he couldn't get to first base. You're on a pedestal. You look so wonderful! So strong, and untouchable, and beautiful. You look like a woman who belongs to only one man. To me, darling. You look unhearing, and unseeing. Because you don't belong to anybody but me."

How strange he was, she thought.

For she had moulded herself upon the image he had held up before her, pushed before her, thrust upon her; she had done it and done it, for months and months; beginning when she first met him. She had always been good at becoming things, she thought. The kind of woman he wanted—the good woman, the faithful wife—she became. She acted upon the vision. All that time she had acted upon it.

And for all the many months that she had, propelled by desperation and fear and love, been true; been true to him and unhearing and unseeing except of him, for his sake—all that action had escaped him; he would never believe it; the tempests and the violence had come and come regardless of her actions. Was it that he never saw anything for himself, or that he did not ever believe his own eyes? For it was words that convinced him, anyone's words. Now, after months and months of hard and unavailing action, a man got drunk and talked wildly, and suddenly Hector saw and accepted and believed. Just someone's words.

Now it was no triumph to her and no ecstatic relief as once it would have been; it was only interesting and almost funny. For all the old desperation had gone.

Hector was here, and she loved him, and he was necessary to her life as she had cast its lines. But something had shifted. The old wild tension between him and her had slackened like a loose rope. It was as though, from that direct confrontation she had passed to one side; she had been shifted by events out of range; she was no longer a target; the shafts of his violence glanced just past her nowadays.

He did not fill the center of her consciousness. He had moved from it to join her in the periphery of a circle, in the center of which sat the baby.

So now he said that she was the woman he had always wanted. That was nice, she thought. He said she looked unhearing and unseeing. But it was her child and the thought of her child that rocked in her consciousness like the sound of the sea, and it was her child that she belonged to, that commanded her.

And all this now was only words. He would be angry again soon enough, she thought. He was a great one for words. They were the real things for him. Words and the past. The past had more reality for him than the present or the future. That was something she could not understand. Well. . . . It didn't matter.

Hector had his moods.

"You must tell me how you feel about things," he was whispering, urgently, eagerly. "Tell me the things you think about. Tell me when I treat you badly, will you? I want to know. I'm not like Joe. I want to understand you."

She kissed his cheek.

"I know I'm a bastard," he whispered. "I always told you I was a bastard. I've been so mixed up. But I swear to you I see it now. I know what that guy had to tell me, I know I've got a wonderful, strong, unique wife. That guy may have been drunk but he was talking the truth. You won't believe me, but I liked him!"

His face was full of an exalted light.

"Look, darling, We must talk more. You must tell me all the things you feel. I want to know every bit of you. Tell me about how it feels to be a woman. I want to understand."

He lifted himself and sat on the edge of the bed leaning down over her.

"We must talk!" he said, eagerly, coaxingly. "There's so damned much I want to understand. Tell me about you and Claudine. What are you like? What do you talk about?"

"We don't talk about anything much," she said warily.

There was nothing that made him angrier than the suspicion that wives talked together about their husbands.

In the lamplight his eyes were brilliant and intent; his face wore its expression of learning new things.

"Claudine has a hell of a time, doesn't she? With Joe. And that sulky brat. God, Joe didn't even get what that guy was talking about tonight. He didn't see the guy despised him. Smirking . . . I'm not like Joe, darling. What do you think makes Claudine put up with Joe?"

"He's her husband. She's a Catholic."

"Yes. Yes. Her religion means a lot to her, doesn't it?"

It was very late now. She had to feed the baby at six. Hector, though, looked ready for a long conversation. Oh well. . . .

"Yes, it's what gets her through everything. She gets homesick, you know, and Joe won't give her any money to go home for a visit to her family, and Jeanne screams if anyone mentions going to France. But I think she's really happy most of the time."

"Yes. . . . Her religion. Does she talk about it to you?"

"No, not much. She takes books along when we go for a walk. She's reading the letters of St. Francis de Sales."

"She is? I didn't know that. She goes to mass, doesn't she?"

"Oh, yes. She gets up early and goes to the seven o'clock mass in Stone Haven on the bus."

"I'll be damned. I never thought about it."

With his hands on her shoulders he looked off for a few moments at the lamp. Betsy yawned.

"Darling," he said, bending over her, "tell me something. Do you feel cheated? Ever? I mean, do you feel badly about my having a wife?"

"What do you mean?"

"You're my wife," he said. "You're so tremendously my wife. But you know in the eyes of the Church I'm still married to my first wife. The Church doesn't recognize remarriage. It doesn't recognize divorce, you know. But I'm not married to her. I'm married to you."

"I know you are," she said.

"I don't want you to feel cheated."

"I don't."

"You're so wonderful. I want you to have everything you should have. God damn it. . . ."

"We're married," she said. "We got married perfectly all right and we've got a child. I'm perfectly satisfied. That doesn't bother me, not any. I didn't think it did you either. You left the Church a long time ago."

"I know . . . I'm changing," he said. "Being married to you has fixed me up. Really. I feel really married to you. The whole way."

"Good."

She was very sleepy.

"Marriage isn't a civil institution," he said. "It's a sacrament. You know, if two people stood up together alone on a desert island and said 'I take you for my husband' and 'I take you for my wife' the Church would recognize that as a marriage. It's the only one of the sacraments that doesn't require a priest. Of course they would go to a priest later whenever they could get to one."

"Really?" she murmured.

"Oh, darling," he said. "I feel so strangely."

With her eyes closed she reached her arms up around his neck and he sank down with his lips pressed to her mouth. He was trembling. Dimly she realized that he was extraordinarily excited; something was going on in him; he kept murmuring words as he touched her. . . . He was such a strange man. . . . She loved him very much. . . . Somehow he could make her happy. . . .

The baby would begin to cry about six.

## CHAPTER LIX

THE FULL SUMMER CAME, and waxed, and the land and sea lay in the comfort of the heat.

The air was sweet with the smell of wild rose bushes, of bayberries, of sweet fern, growing on the sun-baked inland moors; the salt smell of the sea sharpened it from drowsiness. The sea was more green than blue; they swam every day in it; the top water was warm from the sun and underneath their legs struck the deep cold ocean water. They lay on the hot rocks and burned themselves. The baby played on the grass of the yard, in the speckled shade under the horse-chestnut tree.

In the mornings Hector used to fish off the old quarry dock, sitting in a daze in the sun watching the sea swing back and forth against the granite piles, the loud lazy gulls skim the surface of the bay. Beyond, on the rocky little beach, he could see Betsy and Claudine walking. They were always walking together; they walked along the beach in their bright cotton dresses; they climbed the hill among the hot yellow summer grasses; they clambered together over the huge gray boulders. Or, coming home, he would find them sitting on the grass in the yard with the baby naked beside them and the little girl, Jeanne, sitting scowling behind.

The summer seemed long and as quiet as the summer sea. Betsy had asked her sister Maizie to visit them in June and she had accepted, but later she had written and put the visit off till July; then again till August; then again till September. She had a summer cold; or Honora had to have her tonsils out; or her maid had left and there was nobody to leave Honora with. Bring Honora, Betsy wrote. But Maizie answered that it would be better to put off the trip up North till September. The months of the longshore summer passed like green waves rolling. Nobody came from the outside to break the long murmuring dream.

In the afternoons Hector would sleep for an hour after lunch, and wake up in the heat and lie on his back on the bed and think about his novel. He was making notes for it in the evenings. In his mind he was coming round Joe Crown from every side, closing in on him, pinning down what was there. He would lie there for a while, and then he would come up against the wall; he would jump up off the bed and button up the front of his shirt and go out into the afternoon.

Across the road, on the great shadowed rock they called Old Benjamin, Betsy and Claudine would be sitting with the children. The women wore big rough straw hats from the Stone Haven grocery store, and they sewed as they sat and talked; Jerry lay on his stomach on a blanket and played with big snails; Jeanne, with her cotton dress tucked into her drawers, went down to the pools just below the rock and waded. The green water swirled and sucked gently in circles, coming in from low tide, going out from high. The far off bell-buoy rocked and rang in the lazy afternoon.

Hector would join them in the shade, and sit staring off at the blue and green streaked stretches of the bay and the ocean beyond. After a while Betsy would pick up the baby on her hip and carry it off to the house for its feeding. All summer long Hector and Claudine talked, for hours in the soft heat, his deep tough voice and her reserved voice with the French articulation. What they said Betsy did not know; they were talking about the Church and she had a feeling of delicacy about listening; it was something deep and private, understood by them and not by her.

The books Claudine lent Hector to read now lay about the house; Betsy picked them up sometimes, when she was cleaning in the warm musty gloom of the sitting-room with the shutters closed; she glanced blankly at the names of the authors: Huysmans, Belloc, Maritain. She knew the books concerned Catholicism. It was, to her, as though they had concerned the kingdom of the moon. This thing, that Claudine and Hector could talk about together with their faces absorbed and bemused, was far, fabulous, mythical, unreal. Betsy's world was round and compact and workaday; it seemed to her that now Hector roamed in some vast ringing stratosphere. He had left her world at a tangent.

She cooked the summer meals, she bathed the baby, she swam and lay in the sun, she went to bed with Hector when it was night. His new preoccupation did not trouble her. She did not see how it affected her and her small full life. She had always gone on with the steady level of working days while he described parabolas of thought and reaction and emotion. He had gone off and up in such a curve now while she marched straight on from sunup to sundown.

In August Hector began getting up early on Sundays and going to mass in Stone Haven with Claudine. Toward the end of the month he told her that the parish priest, Father Griffin, was coming over for dinner with them. Betsy made a cassoulet for dinner, a great pot full of shell beans and lamb, chicken, pork, sausage, garlic, onions, bayleaf, all ruddy with the tomato paste that could be bought at the Italian fishermen's stores in Stone Haven.

The priest was a small, black-haired man with a sharp white face. Betsy had never met a priest before. But he was none of the things that she imagined, neither fat nor mysterious nor bell-voiced. He paid little attention to her. He and Hector talked through dinner about baseball, and sopped up the gravy on their plates with the coarse gray Finn bread. Hector had told her before the priest came that they wanted to talk alone after dinner. Betsy washed up the things in the kitchen and went out into the cool soft evening; she sat down on the grass; it was faintly damp with dew. She could hear the voices inside, through the open window, talking on and on. After a while she went upstairs and gave the baby his ten o'clock feeding. Then she went to bed.

She was awakened by Hector moving round the room in the light of a lamp. He took. his pajamas down off the closet door and took the lamp off the bureau and went toward the door.

"Where are you going?"

He turned, and came toward the bed, and stood looking down at her.

"Go to sleep," he said. "It's all right. I'm going to sleep in the north room."

But she sat up in bed.

"What's the matter? Are you mad at me?"

They never slept apart.

He set the lamp down on the bedside table and sat down on the edge of the bed.

"I was going to tell you tomorrow. I've come to a decision."

A queer explosion took place in her struggling mind. He's going to leave me, she thought. Why? He's going to leave me and the baby. Why? Without reason all at once and violently she was catapulted back into an old panic, the panic of a far away, terrible, forgotten October.

"Don't look so frightened," he said. "It's all right. You'll be glad. I'm finding myself again. I've made a decision that I want to re-enter the Church."

She thought his face had a sort of amazed light playing over it.

"Why are you leaving me?"

"I'm not leaving you. I'm coming back to you. I'm coming back to all the right things in my life. There won't be any of that fearful conflict any more. Darling, it's because I want my life in order, with you as my true wife. All that bad time I thought you were in opposition to the good things, the things I remember from my childhood. It's not true. You're good and fine. You'll be my good and beautiful and faithful wife for all our lives."

"I am your wife."

"Yes, and I want to be your husband. In the sight of the Church. Without the sense of sin. The past ten years in my life are like a nightmare. If I went on with it I'd go mad. It's all very well when you are young, but you get older. And weaker. And the sense of sin and weakness and chaos grows. I want to be able to stand up straight without a horrible weight on my back. You want me to, don't you?"

"Of course. I didn't realize we—were so awful to you."

"Don't," he whispered. "Can't you see it's partly because I honor you, darling. . . . I don't want you to be anything but my wife."

"I am your wife," she said again.

"Look. I'll try to explain it, so that you can see. I can't re-enter the Church, I can't go to confession, I can't take Communion, while we are living as we are. Because in the sight of the Church we're living in sin. The Church doesn't recognize civil divorce, you know that. I'm still married to Baby, and you're still married to Jayne."

"Can't we get some kind of Catholic divorce?"

"There isn't any divorce. Now, Father Griffin advised me to go up to Portland next week to the Diocesan Court. He'll go with me, to bring my case before it. It may be possible to get an annulment of our marriages. That is, Baby and I used to say before we were married that we didn't want to have any children and we weren't going to have any. If I can get her to state that in a letter as a fact, it would be grounds for an annulment. Because entering into a marriage on that footing makes it no marriage at all. Either you give your whole selves, or . . ."

"We gave our whole selves. I did."

"I know, darling. That's why we must be married. Now, you and Jayne didn't mean to have any children either, did you?"

"No," she said dully. "We got married in the middle of the night, you know."

"Didn't either of you say anything about whether you meant to have children or not?"

"In the middle of the night? I don't believe so. I never wanted to have any children, I know that, I was having too good a time—but I don't know whether I said so."

"Think. Think about it," he said. "See if you can't remember. You see if our marriages could be annulled, we could be married in the Church."

"And that would mean a lot to you."

"Yes," he said. "It would. It would mean everything. I could stop living in a nightmare. You don't get the Church out of your system, you know. I was raised in it. I could get along without it for a while. But I can't any longer. You wouldn't want me to, if you love me. I want to be able to confess. I want to take Communion."

"Why were you going away and leaving me?" she asked.

"I'll tell you, darling. Living together as we are now is sin in the eyes of the Church. I couldn't confess it and continue with it, and take Communion. I'd be in sin. I talked it all over with Father Griffin. The only way I can take Communion and continue to live here with you and Jerry is if we live like brother and sister. The only way I can take Communion is to be celibate—until we can be married in the Church."

She turned her face away from him on the pillow.

She had never known his voice so mild, so kind and reasonable. She had suffered from his violence but now she found herself missing it. This restraint, this gentleness came from a stranger. The man whom she had married was nowhere.

"Good night," he said, standing up beside the bed. "I love you, Betsy. I'm happier even now than I have been for a damned long time. If you love me too you'll be glad I don't have to go through any more nightmare. You'll be glad I see what to do. Darling. Be happy."

She nodded without speaking, her cheek rubbing against the pillow. She heard him leave the room, and the light went out with him.

It was after one o'clock in the morning, and this was the third night that they had sat up thus for hours in the kitchen; working; to their tired minds the scene was queerly familiar like a piece of music played again after a long time, but differently, in another key.

Hector leaned on both arms across the table with his face fixed on Betsy's; he was very pale but his eyes were intent and busy; they were full of that determination of his when he was out to get something he wanted. The dish on the table overflowed with ashes and dead cigarette butts. Betsy sat in the chair on the other side of the table. She drooped, her hands lay heavy in her lap, her neck was bent.

"Think now," he said yet again. "You must be able to remember if you go over it. Make yourself relive it."

"I'm trying," she said. "We went to Baltimore with two other people in a car. It was the Maryland Hunt Cup. We spent the afternoon out in the Greenspring Valley. Willy had some money on the favorite. We all were walking round on the grass. He had a flask and we all kept drinking out of it."

"I don't care about that. Try to remember the things you said. Did you know when you went to Maryland you were going to get married?"

"No. Back in New York . . . He used to say, let's get married, but I never really thought of doing it. It was the way people talked."

He bit his lips and lit another cigarette.

"Yes. Then you didn't decide to get married till the favorite came in first."

"Afterwards. Sometime afterwards. When we were all celebrating. Somehow we went to Elkton and got a license. These other people were all thrilled and whooping. I can't remember about how we started to go to Elkton."

"You must," he said. "You must be able to remember things if you put your mind to it. Aren't you trying? This is the most important thing in our lives, and your memory flops like an old flabby glove. How can you forget everything? Doesn't your life leave any impression on you at all?"

"Yes," she said. She began to cry. "Yes, it does now. But so much used to happen. There was so much, it all got mixed up. I don't remember conversations the way you do."

He regarded her, dragging on his cigarette, for a few moments in silence. The slow tears ran down her face.

"I'm trying to," she said. "Don't you think I'm trying? I know what will happen if I can't remember. Don't you think I'm trying?"

"All right," he said, quietly. "Let's begin at another point. I don't suppose the way you were all feeling that you would have discussed what kind of a marriage you meant to have then anyway. Now. Go back to New York. You used to sit in bars with the guy. What bars?"

"The Tony's on West Fifty-second Street. Louis and Martin's. Michel's."

"Well, now, let's go over them. Can you remember sitting at any special table in Tony's? Can you visualize yourself with him?"

"Yes. . . . We used to sit in the middle room on a sofa with a table in front. . . ."

"What were you doing? Was he holding your hand? Did he kiss you there?"

"Oh, Hector. . . ."

"Stop crying. I don't care about that, don't you see? I'm just trying to make you live over some of the times you might have talked about getting married. Did you ever talk about it when you were sitting in the middle room?"

"I don't know. . . . We might have. . . . It's all vague. . . . Oh, God, I thought I'd remembered all the past. All those nights in New York, and Reno—you don't know how hard I worked. I thought I could remember everything. . . ."

"Yes. That's all over now. Don't get it mixed up. I'm not giving you hell for anything. Keep your mind straight. But if I could make you remember things then, maybe I can now. Maybe there isn't anything to remember that will help us."

"What will you do then?"

"There's no use going into that. You can't remember anything, but you did talk with him about getting married. Try Michel's. Can you remember sitting there? Where? Can you remember talking about getting married ever when you were there?"

"Yes. . . . We were sitting in a booth in the back. We were the only people, everybody else had gone. It was late, I guess. He was sort of depressed. He wanted to get married then, go somewhere and get married. He said his life was like an old piece of Swiss cheese."

"He said that. Well, now, what did he say it would be like if you got married? Did he describe what it would be like? Did he plan anything?"

"Yes. . . . I think so. . . . He said we'd live in a cottage somewhere with flowers growing in the front yard and he wouldn't know the names of any of them. He said we could keep a large black cat to frighten us. He always talked that kind of way."

"Well, go on. Keep thinking. Did he say anything about having children?"

"I don't think so. . . . Yes. . . . He said we'd have a lady to come in to do the cooking who would be very severe with us, because we were such lousily behaved children."

"Yes. But about children of your own. Think. Did he say he didn't want to have children?"

"No. I don't remember anything like that."

He stopped again, and stared at her, and lit another cigarette. Then he leaned farther over the table.

"Now. Let's work on Louis and Martin's. Can you see yourself there with him?"

"Yes, only not any special place. We used to go there mostly in the afternoons after work. We used to stand at the bar. We used to see a lot of people we knew, and talk."

He sighed.

"How about taxis? You must have been in a lot of taxis with him. Try to remember being in a taxi and talking about getting married. Did that ever happen?"

"Yes, I guess so. I don't remember. Whenever he was depressed he wanted to get married."

"Think. Can't you hear his voice? What was his voice like?"

"Sort of funny. Cracked. He twisted his mouth around when he talked. He kept his shoulders hunched up. He always sounded as if he was putting what he said in quotation marks."

"Well, think of hearing him talk about marriage. Can you hear him saying things? Try to hear him saying something about having children."

She put her face down into her hands, and was silent.

"Don't go to sleep," he said.

"I'm not!" she said, through her hands.

Hector thrust his legs out before him under the table and sighed deeply. He passed his hand across his eyes, and shook his head sharply. Then he pulled his legs up under the chair and leaned across the table again.

"Can you hear his voice?"

She kept her hands over her face, and spoke in a low voice through them. He leaned far forward.

"He said he was a complete incompetent."

"No. About having children," he said in his hard voice.

"That's what I mean. But it wasn't to me. It was to some people standing at the bar at Louis and Martin's. He said, 'I'm a complete incompetent.' I guess he must have been talking about our getting married. Because he said, 'We're going to get married and live in a packing box on Jones Beach, like Will Cuppy. We're never going to have any children. We're going to have guppies instead.' "

"He said that?"

"Yes. I remember that."

"You're sure? You swear by everything you're not saying it because you want to stop working?"

She took her hands down from her tired, streaked, red-eyed face.

"I swear I'm not."

He smiled slowly.

"I believe you," he said. "Do you know that I utterly believe you when you tell me something is so? Betsy. God bless you. God bless you."

She only looked heavily back at him. After a minute she got up and picked the plate of ashes off the table and emptied it into the garbage can under the sink. She set it down and looked around the room.

"We can't go to bed yet," he said. He lifted his arms and flexed them and got up vigorously from the chair. "You've got to write a letter to Jayne and ask him if he remembers saying he didn't mean to have children if he married you."

He took the lamp into the sitting-room and came back with several sheets of yellow typing paper, and envelopes. He took a fountain pen off the shelf over the stove, and opened it, and shook it.

"Here. Do you know where to write to him?"

"Just the studio in Hollywood. I don't know if he's still there."

"Well. . . . Have to try it. Now. Say this: Dear Willy. Do you remember saying to— Do you remember who he said this in front of?"

"Bill Dyson. And two women. I didn't know one of them. The other one was Bill Dyson's wife."

" 'Do you remember saying to Bill Dyson and his wife that if we got married we weren't going to have any children?' " Hector hesitated. " 'That we would have guppies instead,' " he continued. "You've got to try to bring it back to his mind. Say, 'I hope you will make a real effort to remember saying this. It is more important to me than I can say. It is my hope that my marriage to you can be annulled so that I shall be able to marry my—my present husband according to the rites of the Catholic Church which do not recognize civil divorce. I assume this is all right with you. You will be doing me a real favor if you will answer as soon as you are sure you remember saying this about not having children, since this intention on both of our parts would make an annulment possible. As I remember, you said it standing at the bar in Louis and Martin's. Yours, and so on.' That's what you want to say, isn't it? Say anything you want to," he said.

She signed her name and addressed the envelope.

"There," he said briskly. "Now I'm going to write to Baby. She's bound to remember. She said more times than I can count that she never meant to have any children. Neither of us wanted to. We hardly even discussed it after we were married." He took the pen from her and began to write.

"You still think of her, don't you?" Betsy said. She stood with her back turned, at the sink, slowly scraping the dark soapstone with the wire brush.

"Who? Baby?" he said abstractedly, writing. "Not much."

"I don't feel as if I'd ever been married to anybody but you."

"Good," he murmured. She bent her head lower.

"There," he said, getting up. "I'm not sure, but I think this will all have to be done again. I think they have to sign statements in the presence of a priest. I'm not sure about any of that till I've been to Portland. But I wanted to get these off right away. The sooner the better. Start them thinking about it, anyway. I'll mail them in the morning. . . . It's such a relief to get things moving."

He stretched himself. The alarm clock on the shelf said half past three.

"Good night, dear," he said. He looked down at her, smiling, without putting out his hand. She looked up into his white, unfamiliarly determined face; her eyes searched it.

"Good night," she said.

It was the following night and the house was still; the lamps had all been turned out; Hector was asleep in the north room. Betsy got up out of bed and began to put her clothes on in the darkness. She could not lie alone in the bed any longer.

She felt her way downstairs without making a light and went out through the back door into the warm, foggy night. She had not planned this. Something was pushing her. It was only that it was impossible to stay in the house any longer.

She began to walk along the road; the street lights glowed at far intervals, patches of diffused luminosity upon the gray soft face of the fog.

Far away the foghorn half around the bay moaned. The fog was deep, solid, murmurous, impenetrable. It dripped with a faint sound from the leaves of the trees. Out on the water the muffled bell-buoy rocked and rang.

She turned off the main shore road by instinct, not seeing the hard cut granite track that led far out on to the point where years ago boats used to load from the quarries; her feet found the two hard paths of the track and she walked on, walked on, forcing her way into the fog that closed behind her. The foghorn groaned in the night, again, again. It was warm, and wet, and without thought or form; only the fog existed, blinding all, deafening all, stifling the sharp miserable world.

She did not understand her wretchedness nor try to. The fog came down and covered the points of all the knives with softness, thickness. She kept walking in the fog. She did not want to know where she was. It was a faint pleasure to feel physically lost. The fog made the world a wilderness. Wandering in it made her feel somehow tighter and contained within her mind. It stopped the sensation of being lost in a thinking world where all was bright and sharp and mysterious in purpose, and withheld.

She walked for a long time.

Suddenly out from the fog something was right there, right upon her. She opened her mouth to scream.

"Where the hell do you think you're going?" Hector's voice said loudly and suddenly. He reached out and took hold of her two shoulders and shook her. "What do you think you're doing? Coming out here in the middle of the night by yourself?"

She did scream.

"Shut your face. Are you crazy? Going off and leaving the baby. You scared me almost to death. I didn't know where in hell you'd gone. How could you go off like that?" He was very angry.

She felt better. The scream had had to come; she had had to scream. Hector turned her around, and holding her upper arm hard in his fingers began to walk her along. In a moment she found where they were; almost back on the main road.

"How did you think I could find you in the middle of a blind fog at night?" he went on. "Nobody but you would do anything so crazy. For God's sake, you've got responsibilities. To me, and to your child. You can't get up in the middle of the night and go off like this. I won't have it. Do you hear me?"

"I'm sorry," she said. Now she wanted to go home.

"You're not a child. You're not a God damned little debutante. You've got duties, and you're going to do them. What in hell made you do such a thing?"

"I couldn't sleep."

"That's no reason."

But he was silent, walking beside her in the fog.

"How did you know I wasn't there?"

"How? I had to get up, and on the way back to bed I looked in your room to see if you were all right, and I couldn't hear you breathing, and I came close to the bed and you weren't there. That was a fine thing to do. I think you've behaved outrageously. As usual," he said angrily.

The most curious flood of relief and happiness came all through her. "I'm sorry," she said again.

"That's all very well. How about Jerry, all alone in the house?"

"You were there."

"Well, I couldn't sit there and not know where in the world you'd gone to, could I? I was practically crazy. I didn't know where to go to look for you. It's only the wildest chance I found you. I suppose you think it's a fine idea, me wandering all over hell in the fog in the middle of the night."

They walked rapidly along the main road and went into their front gate and into the kitchen where a lamp burned. Hector picked it up and followed Betsy up the stairs. She went into the baby's room and he stood in the doorway holding the lamp high. The baby lay in his crib deep in sleep.

She bent over and kissed his round, warm cheek.

The lamp approached behind her. Hector stood beside her looking down at their child.

"That's a nice boy," he said. "You can't go tearing off in the middle of the night and leave a nice baby like that."

"I won't ever do it again. I don't know why I did, really. I just sort of had to. I was so—I don't know. Mixed up."

He stood with the lamp in his hand, looking at her.

His voice was still angry, but his eyes rested gently on her face.

"Don't be a fool," he said. He put his hand on her shoulder. "Everything's going to be wonderful. Don't be crazy."

She went back to bed, feeling very quiet, and fell at once to sleep. In the morning after breakfast Hector left on the bus for Stone Haven. He was going to Portland and he would not be back for two or three days, he said.

She was left alone with the baby in the house at Graniteside. During the day she followed the ordinary course, she cleaned, and played with the baby and swam and went walking in the afternoon with Claudine and the children. She wanted to talk to Claudine about Hector. But she could not begin. She did not understand, she did not know the words. Now Hector and Claudine were closer together, she thought, than she and Claudine, for all their being women; they knew something together that she was left out of. Hector had taken Claudine away from her, and Claudine, the thing Claudine was a part of, had taken Hector away from her too. Nobody needed her. They had needs beyond her comprehension.

She felt stupid and bereft.

When night came something unexpected happened.

The baby was upstairs asleep; it was late enough for bed. For the first time in years she felt afraid. She was afraid of the dark, of the night outside, the lonely coastal country, of the empty house. She went upstairs with the lamp and to bed and lay awake with her fear.

She had never thought what she would feel at being alone in a house without Hector.

She heard boards creaking downstairs. Images hurried through her mind: of tramps entering, of men looking in through the panes of the windows. The sea sounded dangerous; what sounds did its roaring hide? She thought of all the people who must have died in this house. She had never been assailed by fear like this.

She got up and lit the lamp and went in to look at the baby.

He lay on his back with his hands thrown up on either side of his head. His face was turned. His eyelids lay closed upon his flushed cheeks.

She went back to her room and went to bed. She did not feel so much like a frightened child. She was essential to the baby's safety. She reminded herself of that as she lay awake in the dark. Somehow it made her braver. She went to sleep and slept restlessly.

On the following nights she could sleep only by thinking of the baby.

On the third day Hector came home on the late afternoon bus. Betsy heard it stop and went to the gate to meet him. He came up the road carrying his bag; he looked unfamiliar in his gray suit and felt snap-brim hat. Her arms hung by her sides and she watched him come, not knowing what to say or do.

He came into the gate and set his bag down and put his arms around her and kissed her.

"Have you missed me, baby?"

But could he say baby, was it allowed? He had gone away to a world where she did not know how they behaved. Was it all right for him to kiss her? Was she allowed to kiss him back?

"Don't look so frightened," he said. He took her arm in his hand and led her back around the house to the kitchen door. He dropped the bag again with a thud inside the kitchen, and held her and kissed her again.

Some other language than any she knew was required to put the questions in her head.

Hector sat down on a kitchen chair and pulled her on to his knee.

"Don't look so like a deserted cat," he said. "Everything went fine. The annulments can get under way as soon as we hear from our respective exmates. My, those are wise old fellows, those men over there. They know so much."

She felt humble and afraid. She had no right to question anything he said any more, or to ask him things.

"It won't be long," he said. He shifted her in his lap and kissed her again. "I can get along for a while more the way I've been doing."

"What do you mean?" Her timidity made her whisper.

"I decided something. You see, I love you. You're the other half of myself. You've got to be happy or I'm not happy, did you know that? I found that out for myself. We can't live like brother and sister, because we're not. We're husband and wife. We've got to live like husband and wife."

"Is it all right to?"

"I can't take Communion till we can be married in the Church. But that's all right. I've got it ahead of me. It can wait. We're human beings. I can't have you unhappy. I'm not worried about it. It's waiting for me. Everything's going to be all right."

He held her closer and began to kiss her.

"Hector . . . I missed you so horribly. I can't get along without you. I was so scared. . . ."

"I can't get along without you," he said. "And I'm not going to. And you're not going to."

"Darling," she said.

He seemed to have come back into her world. And beyond that, she felt an overwhelming, unexpected rush of something—gratitude—love—relief. . . .

"You were thinking about me, weren't you?" she whispered.

"Of course I was."

"You were thinking about me."

In the middle of September she had an answer from Wilson Jayne in California. He said, "I certainly do remember, and I certainly never had the faintest intention of ever bringing any children into this preposterous world. I have a distorted enough life without having children, for pity's sake. I can tell you lots of other times I said so, too. But what in the name of Heaven do you think you're doing, please?"

Hector read the letter.

"That's fine," he said. "Now we're getting somewhere. Now if that little ball of fluff can pull herself together to write a letter to me. . . ."

Betsy's eyes grew very large, like a puppy's, as she looked at his face.

## CHAPTER LX

MAIZIE DID NOT COME till late in September. When she stepped off the train in the Stone Haven station she looked around at the bare, bleached, cold town and the horror she thought she had conquered, that had fingered uneasily at her in the night on the train, crept further in. This was the North. . . . A day and a night from home. . . . She had taken the step, she had left the home base of Annestown for a visit. He said she had to do it sometime. He said, "You can always just come on back home if you find your composure badly disturbed."

What a pass was this, when a short trip and a visit to her own sister meant fear and vast expenditure of courage, an ordeal? Oh, she was only half of a human being; she was smashed; she crawled about on damaged limbs; never, never, would she be like other people again. A social cure, they called it. She had heard the phrase and it echoed jeeringly in her head. A social cure meant you were not quite dead, not quite in hell. But he said, "The change may very well do you good. Going off on your own successfully ought to give you confidence."

That was why. That was the only reason. For a social cure such things as love or loyalty or free will did not exist. Neither sister nor mother nor father nor anyone except him existed, only me, me, me. Can I do it? Will it, in the end, be good for me? Take care, take care. Self came first and only, forever and ever. Take care.

I am not a human being. I am a social cure.

The two human beings approaching down the platform were not her sister and her stranger brother-in-law; they were, like all humanity, enemies.

And they were frightening; frightening, she thought as they came near her. She wanted to run away. He was a big, broad, violent-looking man. And the woman was frightening too. She looked strong and ruthless. Her hair was wound in big vigorous braids around her head and her face was not a little girl's, not Betsy's, but a big strong woman's. Oh! Will they want me to sit up late at night, will they want me to swim in deep water, will they do things that are too tiring. . . . And how can I keep them from knowing that I am afraid? How can I keep them from knowing that I am different?

"Maizie!"

The woman who was her sister threw her arms around her. Maizie smiled and hugged and laughed. That looks right. They could never tell.

"Maizie, this is your brother-in-law, this is Hector. Isn't she beautiful, Hector? Now you see what a beautiful sister you have."

The man was shaking her hand.

Oh, no. Oh, no, I cannot do this. If I do this it will begin again.

"We have to take a bus to our house, darling. Do you mind? Are you awfully tired?"

"Oh, no."

They mustn't have the faintest idea.

Hector picked up Maizie's two bags. She followed him, arm in arm with Betsy, down the platform, smiling, chattering, laughing.

This will drain me. My strength will not last. It is too much.

I must make a plan now. If it is too bad I will say I must get to Dad sooner. Betsy will understand that. She'll think that's it. When I get to Hampton I can rest; Dad won't make me do things. How much am I going to have to do? It will exhaust me. Oh, other people renew their strength when they sleep. Not I. . . .

She thought hoardingly, as she laughed and talked, of the bottle of yellow sleeping capsules in her bag; they were there; they would help her; God bless them. . . .

In Maizie's room in the house at Graniteside there was a ticking. It came and went in the middle of the night. She lay awake as tense as a violin string and listened to it. Now she heard it. Now it stopped.

But is it really there? Or is it in my head? Is it the first sign of it coming back? There isn't any clock. The ticking is right there, as if in the wall. Or is it in my head?

She went over and over the old time. There wasn't any ticking that time. There was the look of rain falling over everything. I don't see any rain now. And there was everything turning frightful outside the window. I must look out of the window in the morning when I get up and make quite sure it looks normal, outside.

But this is such a frightening place.

Why did I ever come?

He said, "I don't think there is the faintest chance of a recurrence of your sickness. That was brought on by a long period of extreme tension. There's nothing troubling you now. There's no one to put you through what Mr. Rudd put you through. There's not the slightest chance of it."

But this is tension. Suppose it's too long? Suppose it's too extreme? Suppose I break again? Oh, I couldn't endure it again, oh God, oh, the long phlegm-streaked walls, the smell of brimstone; yes, I know it was. I know the smell of hell.

Out of the chamber of her mind, beyond, Maizie heard the deep increasing roaring of the autumn sea.

It roared that way in Manchester . . . in Manchester after Honora was born. Is it a sign? Is it a portent? Will it happen again that way?

I will look out of the window in the morning, and if there is anything queer about the way it looks—*anything queer*—I will go.

But how shall I keep them from knowing? Nobody must know. Nobody must guess. He said, "You are completely normal in every aspect to the observer."

He was far away, far away in Annestown where it was warm, not chilly and queer like this. Dear Annestown that held him. A day and a night away by train. Less if you flew—but I could never fly, never, never. A few moments away on the telephone: his voice; the comfort he had to give. Don't forget. You can telephone him if it gets too bad.

But they haven't got a telephone. . . .

Perhaps I'm caught. Perhaps it will happen before I can get to help.

And in the wall the ticking began again. Tick, tick, tick—and then suddenly stop; and then begin again: tick, tick, tick.

Is it in my head? Is something ticking in my head?

I must sleep. I've got to get some sleep.

Maizie felt for the matches and lit the candle beside her bed. She opened the bottle cap and shook another capsule into her hand and swallowed it with the water she had brought in when she went to bed, laughing, calling back to them over her shoulder before she shut the door. . . .

Now go to sleep.

She put her hands under her cheek in imitation of a child. Betsy's baby sleeps like this. Oh, to sleep like a baby, really to sleep! I care nothing about that child. He is my nephew. I care nothing about him except for his sleep. I would like to drain his sleep off from him to keep for myself.

Me. I must sleep.

She crossed her arms over her chest and hugged them with her hands. Think of him. Him. I love him. Now say, he loves me. Perhaps. . . . He couldn't tell me if he did. It wouldn't be ethical. I am his patient. But say it: he loves me. I love him. Without harm, without danger; like a cloud, a dream, a feather, he loves me. I love him. Until I fall asleep, say: I love him.

In the morning Betsy brought Maizie's breakfast upstairs to her on a tray. Maizie was sitting up in bed, her cheeks very pink, her yellow hair lying in a mass against the pillow.

"Darling! I can't tell you how wonderful it is to have you here! It's like the old days to have you back."

Betsy put the tray on Maizie's knees, and climbed up on the foot of the bed and sat hugging her knees and beaming.

*She's been up for hours. She's all rested and strong as an ox. Every nerve in my body tingles with fatigue.*

"It's a heavenly day," Betsy said. "Have you looked?"

"Yes, I looked out when I got up," Maizie said, eating grapefruit. "I'd forgotten it got cold so early up here, though."

"You should have come earlier, darling. It was wonderful. We swam all summer. It's too cold now, though. I'm so sorry you had to miss it."

*So I don't have to go swimming. There's that. And it looked all right from the window—only forbidding; not queer.*

*Maybe it will be all right. Maybe I can conquer it. He said, "if you can enjoy yourself under different circumstances, it will add a great deal to your confidence."*

"Oh, I wish I could have had some swimming!" she cried.

"We're going to have a picnic tonight," Betsy went on. "For you to meet our neighbors, the Crowns. I know you'll be interested in them. She's a Frenchwoman. She's been giving me cooking lessons. We see a lot of them. They've been so anxious to meet you. They've been looking forward to it all summer."

*A picnic. How would that be? Would they stay up very late?*

"What fun," Maizie said.

"I'm afraid we're not very gay. I mean, we don't do anything much. Hector has to work on his novel, now, all day. But you and I can take a walk and you can see this heavenly country."

*A walk and a picnic both?*

"Tell me everything you hear from Ma'am," Betsy said, curling up, leaning on one elbow, on the foot of the bed.

"She's in Bar Harbor now, with Jane."

"I know. What do you think of Jane's engagement? He's one of those millionaire Rothwells, you know, in Minneapolis. Jane and Glory are so respectable and so rich! I'm the bohemian member of the family," Betsy said, laughing. "Maizie. Do you think Ma'am is going to get a divorce from Dad?"

"Do you?"

"I don't know. But she's never at home any more. She keeps going on these long visits with Jane to Dr. Cunningham's. When Jane gets married she won't have her to sort of chaperon her. Ma'am might do anything. She's got so much energy. And Dad's sort of worn out, somehow. Poor Dad, I'm glad you're going to visit him. I hate to think of him, lonely, without any of us in the house. I think Ma'am's sort of unfeeling about him, really."

"He came down to Annestown last winter, you know."

"How did you think he seemed?"

"Terribly old. And tired."

*He was just right. He was like me. Those little quiet walks we took. And going to bed early. He was so gentle; he loves me so much, he cares about what happened to me more than anybody. Not that he knows. Not that anybody can ever know—except him; him.*

"It's funny, the way we've all turned out," Betsy said. "We've split up a lot, haven't we? I never thought we would. You in Annestown and me here, and Glory's husband at the embassy in London, and now Jane'll live in Minneapolis. And Ma'am always off visiting, and so sort of part of Boston now. Dad's the only one who's stayed put."

"Dad's really changed the most, though."

*The most except me. I am a shell; not a human being. She must never know that I'm not a human being.*

"I've got to wash up the things," Betsy said, getting off the bed and taking the tray. "Then we'll go for a walk. It's so wonderful to have you here!"

In the door she turned.

"I hope the watch-beetles didn't bother you last night," she said. "This old house is full of them. When Hector was away a while ago I couldn't sleep well and they drove me crazy."

"Watch-beetles?"

"They tick like a clock in the walls."

"Oh, yes, I did hear them."

*All that strength, all that anxiety, spilled because of a beetle in the wall. I might have slept. . . .*

"See you in a few minutes, darling."

Betsy went out and shut the door, smiling around it till the moment of closing.

But she was a stranger; a big, strong, violent woman. She meant nothing any more but something to avoid; something that might tax.

*For I am alone in all the world, and I have no love to spare. Everything threatens the little safety I have hoarded. I live on shreds and snippets; on capsules. I am alone. Except for him.*

The day turned warm by afternoon.

The kitchen door stood open on the golden day, the late September, ripe, warm, glowing weather. It was half past five. The big flies buzzed in the doorway. The late sun lay in rectangles on the floor, falling through the door, the four-paned window.

The women moved about the room. There was much to be done. Claudine Crown stood over the stove, her legs planted apart, her round waist firm and full. Betsy stood by the table with the big knife poised. There was a harmony between these two; they hurried about the kitchen, they called back and forth to each other; the warm, healthy flesh of their arms touched as they leaned over a yellow bowl together.

Maizie Rudd sat in the corner of the broad sill in the east window. Her skin was pale and thin from the languid heat of a Southern town. Her yellow hair was soft and clinging and stood out from her head in moist tendrils. On each of her cheekbones she wore a spot of pink rouge. She sat quite still; her blue eyes, the pretty eyes of a middle-aged Southern girl, with fine soft wrinkles around them, watched the women at work. They were like shining round-rumped draught-horses and she a city horse, mean-boned, with peaked hips. Their flesh was full and sturdy and tanned and hers tender, withered.

Two huge lobsters, the greenish brown of the sea-bottom, lay alive on the table, on their backs, their great claws waving feebly.

"Cut off the tails," ordered Claudine in her French voice.

The knife descended upon the lobsters.

"Cut off the claws," Claudine proceeded, speaking slowly and with force, "and crush them with a hammer. Split the bodies in two lengthwise."

Maizie sat huddled in the window staring.

"What did you say it's going to be? What did you call it?"

"*Homard a l'armoricain, madame,*" Claudine said. She turned those dark, deep eyes on Maizie; they burned in her beautiful face; they were foreign eyes. "Lobster, cooked in the fashion of Brittany. We decide upon it for the picnic in honor of you."

Betsy stood, the knife raised from the dismembered lobsters, waiting.

"Remove the pocket which is found next to the head, which contains sand. Set apart the liquid of claws, and intestines. Remove the cord from the tail."

Claudine tipped the iron skillet she was holding on the stove, in which butter and olive oil sent up a fine steam.

"Give me the lobster meat," she demanded. Betsy carried the flesh of the creatures across and emptied them into the skillet. "I fry them until they are bright red, scarlet, and the flesh is hard," Claudine said. "In the mean-time prepare the casserole, with a little butter in the bottom."

In Betsy's arms appeared a monstrous earthen pot, a great golden brown thing with a cover that had a knob. She stood beside Claudine at the stove.

"Put the pieces of lobster in," Claudine said. "Add shallots, a little garlic, two small glasses of cognac previously heated—here—and on fire"—a match flared up in Betsy's fingers and then the little pan that contained brandy burst into a blue, skimming flame—"two cups of dry white wine. I left it there, upon the other shelf, Betsy. Four tablespoons of meat juice," she continued, as Betsy went with vigorous footsteps about the kitchen, "six chopped tomatoes. They are ready? Two tablespoons of chopped parsley. And a sprinkling of cayenne pepper!" she cried. She set the lid back upon the filled casserole with a thump, and lifting the great thing in her hands, leaned and set it into the oven as Betsy flung open the oven door. "For twenty minutes," she declared. Both women brushed their hands together.

"*Bien,*" said the Frenchwoman. "And for the other things. Have we put everything into the basket, Betsy?"

The basket stood over by the door into the sitting-room. It was not an ordinary, quiet basket. It was vast, irregularly shaped, woven of rough reeds that stuck out harshly. Into it they put a great round loaf of dark Finn bread; a chunk of butter wrapped in napkins wrung out in cold water; real plates, and forks, and a wooden box of Camembert cheese, and a covered bowl that held salad. The necks of two bottles of red wine stuck up from the corner.

It was not like any picnic Maizie had ever seen. It was a meal for giants. There were no little sandwiches.

"And now the sauce," cried Claudine. The two women seemed to fly about now in a kind of frenzy. The casserole was snatched from the mouth of the oven. The lobster meat was hurried from it and cast upon a platter.

"Take the meat out of the claws and body!"

The sharp knives flashed. There was the crunching, the shattering, of shells.

"Put it on the back of the stove. *Eh, bien.* Now I boil the sauce down for fifteen minutes. And you, Betsy—chop the intestines with a little butter."

The two-bladed chopper went thump, thump, thump in a wooden bowl.

"Now! Add them to my sauce. There. Now . . . in a minute . . . it must cook . . . now! Where is the *chinois?*"

A cone-shaped sieve flew through the air and hung above a yellow bowl; then the bowl's contents was again poured through the sieve back into that yawning casserole.

"Now a quarter of a pound of butter, in small pieces. . . . Now the rest of the parsley. . . . Now! put back the lobster. *Voilà!*" cried Claudine, and she popped the great cover back upon the casserole.

Maizie slipped with hesitation down from the window ledge as the others began to snatch things up in their strong arms.

"Can't I carry something?" she said.

For they were tucking blankets under their arms; hurrying things into the crammed basket; on their quick, tireless feet they darted about the kitchen. "Hector!" called Betsy. "Hector! Joe! Come now!" She glanced over her shoulder at Maizie and smiled.

"Not a thing, darling. You're the honored guest. We've got it all. Are you ready? Shall we go to the rocks?"

Maizie took her woollen coat off the back of a chair and put it on.

A procession started from the weather-beaten house by the road.

The sky was turning crimson and orange, with purple streaks above the horizon where the blood-red sun hung. Flights of sea gulls skimmed the surface of the darkened water, screaming. There was no one but themselves in sight anywhere, no boats on the broad smooth water, no one passing on the road. The sunset air was lonely; strong of salt.

They trooped across the road and down the narrow sea-weed path at the back of the beach to the rocks. First walked Claudine bearing the enormous casserole in her two hands before her. Next Betsy carried the great basket in one hand, and a mass of blankets under the other arm. Next Maizie walked, picking her way among the round, smooth stones that slid beneath her feet. Hector followed her: he wore a leather wind-jacket strained across his big, heavy shoulders; he carried a laundry basket in his hand, holding the little boy, Jerry, who sat straight up in it and picked at his father's hand. Last came Joe Crown; he was tall, slender, lighter than Hector's brutal build; his face was elegant and melancholy in the sunset; he held the hand of his little girl in his. She stumbled over the stones, gazing up steadily at her father's face.

They climbed up and over and around great boulders like prehistoric monsters, gray, rough-skinned, petrified. At the broad flat top of the hugest of the monoliths they stopped and set down the burdens they carried. Earlier in the day someone had built a fire here on the boulder-top, of dried seaweed and driftwood. Hector set a match to it and in the crimson light of late day the fire sprang up, subdued against the sweep of western sky all streaked and flaming with enormous light.

The men sat down to windward of the fire. There was a clatter of china and metal and glass as Claudine and Betsy whisked the things out of the basket and dealt them out; plates and wine-glasses were set down upon the hard, uneven rock. Maizie moved about uncertainly; she held out her hand for something to take, something to hold; but everything was being done. She sat down on a spread blanket; the wine-glass beside her tipped over and she picked it up and held it in her hand.

Claudine was passing the great vessel full of lobster, steaming now that the cover had been lifted from it. The smell of the garlic drifted past their nostrils in gusts in the faint breeze of the beginning dusk. They heaped their plates and tore hunks from the loaf of bread. Butter was cut in slabs. The dark purplish wine was poured gurgling into their glasses. In the departing light they ate, and were given more, and wiped their plates with wedges of bread, and cut off pieces of the strong, half-liquid cheese.

Maizie had three glasses of wine, astringent and faintly sour on her palate. She felt excited. The blood mounted warm and beating into her face. She had a sensation of recklessness. What was there to be afraid of? Swallow the food, drink off the wine. She thought too much, that was it.

She did not feel worried about anything. Perhaps suddenly she was cured. Perhaps everything was going to be different. Why not? She felt sturdy, rough and ready. She was conscious of the blood in her veins. She was no different from other human beings. She must exercise, get muscles, be heedless, stride about outdistancing her fears. Tonight she had got ahead of them. Hector filled her glass again in the half-darkness and she drank from it and leaned back on her elbows, laughing out loud. She turned her head and looked into the face of Joe Crown, where he lay stretched out beside her. She put something into her eyes, her smile.

*I always used to be attractive to men.*

*Why, I may be going to have a life after all.*

They were gathering together the plates and forks; everything went into the basket. The two vigorous figures of the women moved in and out of the firelight, for now the light had failed from the sky and the twilight was deep purple. They bent over and snatched up the plates, their bodies straining against the cloth of their dresses; their legs were bare, their skirts switched sharply from side to side. The dark came down, down, and the fire sent spears of orange and scarlet up into the dark. It crackled and snapped and Claudine clambered down from the rock and reappeared bearing a great load of driftwood which she hurled upon the fire. It leapt up.

"I'll bet you," Hector was saying to Joe, "I'll bet you ten bucks Italy will move in on Ethiopia before Christmas. All this about border disputes is strictly bull. Mussolini's been talking empire for years, and this is how you go about it if you're a Fascist. You pick the smallest kid in your block and then you keep pushing him until you see your way to rubbing his face in the dirt and taking his marbles."

"And why not empire?" Joe asked. His beautiful profile was clear against the fire. "Consider the excellencies of empire. An Italian empire would be an agreeable thing. Vittorio Emmanuele, Rex et Imperator. With Mussolini to manage the wires. The world needs empires. And who's to stop it? Think of processions of chained ebony Ethiopians led in triumph through the Roman arches. Decorative."

"Who's going to stop it? It's a cinch the League won't stop it. The League will sit there with its finger up its nose mumbling about sanctions till Mussolini has what he wants."

"And why shouldn't Mussolini have what he wants? You're not upholding the rights of a horde of dismal negroes as against a man of vision who has— yes, a flair. Mussolini has, I affirm, a flair. Don't you agree with me, Mrs. Rudd?"

In the darkness Maizie felt the man's hand come against her. He ran his fingers down her back.

Something cried out and choked and stammered inside her.

A man, touching her. This strange, unknown, elegant man. After a thousand years—a man touching her. Bad? Frightening? What? Her blood ran burning inside the skin of her arms. Oh . . . oh. . . .

Quick as a flash a whole future tumbled and catapulted through her mind. Maybe he has fallen in love with me and he will divorce his wife and ask me to marry him and live—here?

Would I be able to live here? Everything slowed down and queried, peered at the question, withheld itself. Live like this, do this work—live with him, go to bed, miss sleep, and. . . . How could I do without *him?*

All her false elation died down suddenly like a guttered flame and the wine ran out of her blood and the drowsy, reckless feeling out of her brain. Oh no. I couldn't do without him.

Now she was full of fears; her blood had reassumed its nature. From the confident daze of wine she came back to hearing, seeing, shrinking.

The hand on her back moved leisurely down and caressed her hip. She moved away.

*There was his wife. Did she see? Does she know he started to make love to me? Oh . . . what a great fleshy woman like a stout horse . . . perhaps he beats her. . . . Oh no . . . I am afraid of her . . . these are all giant people, terrible, great animals, oh, no, no, no.*

"Don't you think so, Mrs. Rudd?" Joe repeated.

"I'm afraid I don't know the first thing about politics," Maizie said in her Southern voice.

"Anybody would think you recommended Fascism, Joe, my boy," Hector said.

"And why not? It has a flair. I very emphatically do recommend Fascism."

"You would," Hector said. "What a fool thing to say. The oppression of the weak by the strong."

"You miss the eternal human verity underlying Fascism, old fellah," Joe said. He pulled himself up and sat crouching on his haunches. "Nations are like women. They cry out to be dominated. Especially some nations. Especially some women. A woman, a dog, and a walnut tree; the more you beat 'em, the better they be. Add nations. Give them a free rein and they wreck themselves. Masochism, my boy; consider masochism. Masochism is a characteristic of the female organism. Nations are mostly female. Dictators represent the male principle. Beat your women, your nations; kick them, work them for all they're worth; rape them, so to speak. They love it."

"That's too easy; easy thinking. You can't treat the people as though they were a bitch in heat. Because they're not. It's serious. People have a right to be free; everything moves toward that. We've spent centuries trying to fix it little by little so they can be free."

"A movement in the wrong direction. It's precisely that that has taken the *élan* out of living. What do you see, in a democracy? Dissatisfied, bored faces. I tell you, *mon vieux*, it is passion that keeps the people amused, keyed up, living. Their eyes sparkle under oppression. They feel themselves loved. Let them govern themselves and all that balderdash, and they become like a stringy, sex-starved woman with too much time on her hands. The instinct to serve is imperative. Women become impossible when they are not kept working. Nations the same. They want a master, they want to slave for him."

"You love the sound of your own voice, don't you, pal? All that would be comic if people like you didn't take it seriously. All right, suppose you abuse your nation-woman, and suppose she breaks up under the beating you give her. Because that happens. People go to pieces under abuse."

"If the people go to pieces it's as well to know it. They should be tossed aside and used as basic slaves, without privileges. The nation that comes to the top, that's the strong nation, fit for survival; it flourishes under the heavy hand. It grows stronger all the time under it, more vigorous, pregnant with it. There's a love affair between the dictator and the nation. There's a marriage."

"You're the fanciest guy I ever knew. Your images run away with you. You're as crazy as this guy Hitler. You both get reality mixed up with a whole lot of erotic images, sadism, masochism. That's not sense, boy. People are people."

"And they can't do without excitement. The trouble with your democracy is it's so dull."

"Well, I'll bet you things aren't going to be very dull around the Mediterranean soon," Hector said, beyond the firelight. "There's going to be war, boy. I don't know how much of a scrap those poor dinges can put up. But before long there's going to be guns going off and bombs falling, and I'll stake my experience on it."

The moon had risen out of the dark horizon while they were talking and now a cold and greenish light fell over the rocks; a streaked path lay on the sea, ever-broadening, a white, dancing road to the edge of the world.

"Hector," Maizie's voice spoke faintly out of the flickering light-and-dark round the fire, "Hector, do you think there's going to be a war, honest?"

"I do, Maizie. The muscle boys, the dictators, have been sickening for a scrap for a long time. If it's not Mussolini it'll be Stalin; if it's not Stalin it'll be this boy Hitler. There's going to be some kind of a show, and I don't think it will stop at Ethiopia. The last performance of this sort was supposed to be an argument over Serbia, remember? You've got to start somewhere. The muscle boys are going to be out gunning."

"But you don't think we'd ever be in another war, do you?"

"No telling. We aren't going to stand for too much pushing around."

"This is a virgin country," Joe said. "Unravished. Cold as a maiden. We resist the conqueror. But how much gayer we would be if we were put to work! We need a whipping, wisely and thoroughly administered; we need a master. Then we would not be so bored."

"Don't pay any attention to them, Maizie," Betsy called. "They get like this when they've had a couple of drinks. Hector is always talking about war. Don't pay any attention to him."

"You are a voice crying in the wilderness, old fellah," Joe said.

In the moonlight Maizie got up and went away from the group around the fire to the edge of the rock.

She felt weak as a straw; a match-stick set perilously on end in the midst of all this ominous great country in the dark: the monstrous boulders, the huge and endless sea, the flood of moonlight beating down on this giant world, cold and green and heartless.

*What if there should be a war?*

*What would happen to me if there were a war?*

*Hector said guns going off; he said bombs falling. Oh!*

She seemed to hear the explosions, the panic chaos of sound. *That I could never stand.*

*I would break again and break entirely and never be well again.*

*He could save me again. . . .*

*No, if there was a war he would have to go to it and I would be alone then. He is all I have between myself and the pit of hell, and he would go away and I would hang there on the brink and when the explosions came I would fall in again. The smell, the smell of brimstone, and the horror, the creatures crawling up the walls in the slime that drips, and no one to reach a hand down into my hell.*

*I couldn't endure a war. There must not be a war. If there should be a war, if I should read in the papers that there will be a war, then I will know that I am finished; back to hell for me, forever.*

She looked out along the white spreading pathway on the water and slowly her eyes followed it in closer, closer to the land, the pathway broadening and steadying.

In the violent black and white of the moonlight the rocks had lost contour, they were swallowed in deep shadow, and below her there appeared to be a steep abyss. From her feet at the edge of the rock down to the water was one black chasm, one sheer drop.

*It is my destiny to throw myself down this cliff.*

The command came full-formed into her mind.

*Oh, no, no, no.*

*Yes. It is my destiny.*

*Or why did I come to the edge of the chasm? Or why is the chasm here? The scene is set. The moon is up, the chasm waits, the rocks are there, the water moans very low waiting, everything is ready.*

*I have to do it because it is here to do.*

*But I never, never, wanted to be dead.*

*This is now. Why else did I come here where the scene is set?*

*I have always been afraid of death.*

*Some day I must die, I always knew that that was true. Some day I have to die and the day is tonight because here I have stepped forward and found the scene set and waiting. Here is the means, the moment, and myself. Something intends that I should kill myself. It is my destiny.*

*Go on. Go on.*

*But I never had any idea of killing myself.*

*But think what a short instant it would take. I have only that instant's movement to make; throw myself forward, lose my balance; that's all. Then I couldn't go back; then I would have to go forward; I would have to finish what I had begun. No changing my mind, just that one instant of starting the thing in motion.*

*Now. Simply to make my feet stop clinging to the rock. Simply to alter inertia into forward movement. Do it.*

*But I don't want to die.*

*I haven't any right to dispute what is ordained. Everything is all ready and waiting.*

"We're going back to the house," Betsy's voice said close to her, and Betsy's hand slipped through her arm. "All the wine is drunk up. Isn't the moon wonderful?"

The procession wound over the rocks, the beach, back to the house, all in the blank green moonlight.

Hector and Joe immediately established themselves in the kitchen with a bottle of whisky. Claudine took Jeanne home to put her to bed.

"Are you sure you aren't tired, darling?" Betsy said. "Are you sure you wouldn't like to go to bed early?"

"You know," Maizie said, "I reckon I will just go up, although I hadn't thought of it till you spoke. I'm sleepy, that is; not really tired, of course."

*That was the kind of thing people said. Human beings.*

"I'll come up with you, angel. I'll open your bed and talk to you unless you'd rather I didn't."

"No, do."

*Will I ever be able to sleep? Two capsules? Three? Three is wrong. Two, and then two later. I can say I'm sleepy.*

Betsy opened the bed while Maizie undressed, and then sat down on a chair and began to rub her ankles.

"They ache," she said. "I don't know why."

Maizie turned with her slip in her hand and stared at Betsy. Her mind seemed to begin to revolve in the opposite direction.

"Your ankles hurt?"

*She's going to break,* a clarion voice cried in her head.

*That is a sign. My ankles hurt—oh pains, up and down. I remember . . . years and years now. The ankles were the first. She's going to break. She's like me. Hector's like Lambert, he is, he is, he's violent, he's brutal. I knew it.*

*Of course she's going to break. It runs like leprosy in our veins. She is like me. Of course. It has been in my mind ever since I came.*

*Of course.*

*I ought to save her.*

"Yes, I notice it at night," Betsy said. "Maybe I'm getting old! No, I'll tell you what I think it's from. I'm pretty sure I'm starting to have another baby."

"Oh Betsy!"

"Isn't that grand?"

"But, so close together. . . . Why, you've hardly had the first. . . . You ought not to. . . ."

*This will do it. She will have this second child, and then, when she thinks she is getting over it, suddenly the world will go sour, the music will turn queer, queer. . . . Hinky dinky parlez-vous in a minor key . . . round and round. . . .*

But Betsy had stood up and, stretching herself, flung her arms out on each side, her head thrown back.

She grinned.

"I'd like to have six," she said. "Eight. I want to have all the children I can have. That's what I'm really meant for."

*But you won't. You'll break. You're like me. Next year you will be in hell. I wonder if it will be the same hell as my hell? You will be in a brick building with ivy blowing on it, blowing through all the nights and the smell of brimstone. . . .*

"Ma'am had four of us without turning a hair," Betsy continued.

*But the mould has warped. The music has gone minor. Something has changed within our blood, and these days are not like those days, these days are the bad days. Our mother was the last. We must smell brimstone, and see the legged creatures climb squirming up the walls, and sink in the horror; deep, deep.*

"I hope this next one will be a girl," Betsy said. "I'd like a girl. I think Hector would like a girl."

*How can I warn her without telling her about me? About my hell? I
can't tell anybody that. Nobody must know.*

Maizie smiled brilliantly, and let her nightgown slip over her head.

"I hope Hector treats you well," she said. "I hope he takes care of you
while you're having a baby."

"Oh . . . sure . . . I'm as strong as a horse, you know."

*I know. Those old, frantic phrases. "I can take anything, darling. I'm so
strong." And then the strength begins to curdle and turn sour, queer. . . .*

"Don't make yourself do too much," Maizie said.

*That's the most I can say.*

"Hector and I get along," Betsy said. "He suits me. He's what I want.
He's a lot cleverer than I am, you know. He needs everything I can give
him, and a lot more. He has to have something more than me in his life.

She hesitated, as though she might add something. But she didn't.

*Everything says it. Everything says the same: you will be in a brick build-
ing next year, yes, and the ivy will slap against your window pane, and
sometimes you will think it is the fingers of the damned, and sometimes you
will not dare to look.*

*But of that I must say nothing.*

"Good night, darling," Betsy said. She bent and kissed her sister's cheek
above the pillow. "Having you here is the nicest thing. I did miss you,
darling! Have a good sleep."

"Yes."

"You do feel good these days, don't you, darling? All well and strong?"

"All well and strong. . . ."

"You don't let . . . your divorce, Lambert, all that, bother you, do you?
I notice you don't speak of him."

"Oh, no. I never think of him."

*I don't. Not ever. He was only the ancient, long-ago cause. Lambert! I
hardly know his name.*

*Now can I sleep?*

As soon as the door had fully closed she reached with eager fingers for
the bottle of yellow capsules.

But in the morning Maizie awoke with a cold.

When Betsy came in with the breakfast tray she found Maizie up, bending over a suitcase.

"I made you a little omelet. . . . What are you doing, darling? You're
not packing?"

Maizie stood upright. She had her woollen coat on over her dressing
gown, and her face was flushed, her eyes uneasy and bright.

"Betsy, I'm so terribly sorry, I've got to go home. Are there any morning
trains I can catch? You see, I've got a kind of sore throat that I get, and
it always develops into a special sort of thing that I have to have treatment
for, and the only thing for me to do is to get back home quick before it
gets too bad."

"Maizie! If you're sick you mustn't leave, darling. I'll get Dr. Werner."

He's a grand doctor, he delivered my baby; he's young, and really good. I can run right up to the Crown's and call him. Angel, how horrid you're sick! Are you sure you have something bad—eat your breakfast and maybe you'll feel better."

"No, I've got to go. I know. It's something I've had before. It has to be treated. My doctor says it's not to be left without treatment for any time. I can be home by tomorrow morning."

"You're going to cut out your visit to Dad? He'll be so disappointed. Why don't you go there and get treated for your sort throat in Boston. The best doctors in the world are in Boston. You don't need to go all the way down to old slowpoke Annestown to get treatment for a sore throat."

"Yes I do!"

Would they never stop? *I must have my own way. I will have my own way if it takes hours. I must go. I am going to have a cold. How can I have a cold up here—in this place—I will get sicker, and sicker, until I die, and staying in bed it will all come back. He said, "Staying in bed probably accelerated the onset of your sickness." I must go; must; must.*

Betsy stared at her, and set the breakfast down upon the bed.

"Of course you must if you want to," she said. "I just hate to have you go right away like this. I've hardly seen you. I've hardly gotten to know you. Do eat your breakfast, though."

"Oh yes, I will. You do understand, though? It isn't that I want to go, you know that, Betsy. It makes me furious—just furious—to have to give up all the fun we were going to have. It's just that I know the nasty way these throat things act, and I've been warned by my doctor not to let it go, and I know if I don't want to have it hang on for months I must just go right on back down home and get it looked after. . . ."

Gabbling on and on. *For now she could go, she could go, she could go. But patch the picture, make it plausible. . . . Nobody must ever guess.*

"Yes, of course I understand. I'm just so sorry. I'll go down and hunt up the time-table."

Betsy went out and closed the door.

Maizie drew a long breath.

*There. Now . . . in a little while . . . tomorrow morning . . .* If she could just hang on a little longer: she would be safe. She would touch home base. She would see him. Everything would be all right. She need not die. She need not break. She need not die, not here in the evil North; not here before strangers. . . .

They saw her off on the noon train to Boston, standing on the Stone Haven platform side by side and waving to her, in the car window, until she glided slowly out of sight.

The train moved off into the sunny distance under a feather of smoke, going south, bound by connection for the Southern lands, the lusher fields, out of this pale blue atmosphere. They turned away and walked back into the town.

Maizie had gone.

They had left the baby with Claudine and now they could have a little spree by themselves. They walked along the narrow waterfront streets. The day was chilly and bright in the town and the cove water kicked up in brilliant blue points tipped with white; it was free and gay. They went into a lunchroom full of men off the fishing schooners and ordered hamburgers and beer.

Afterwards they caught the Graniteside bus at the corner by the Fishermen's Bank.

The bus was a pleasant place; they sat on the straw seat and ate Hershey bars. The bus rattled and lurched up and down the hills and the valleys, along the white road that led home. They travelled the seven-mile journey, past the calm familiar spots: Spode's Cove, the willow stretch where the trees hung over the road, the Clearwater lobster place with the bleached gray pots stacked up on the beach, tangled with nets; Merriman's Cove, and all along the quiet white way the white spare fishermen's cottages, the Finn houses, and the bleached white thorny locusts.

"She didn't like it here," Betsy said.

"Nope."

"She wanted to get back to Annestown awful bad, not even going to visit Dad."

"What's the matter with her, anyway?"

"She was sick a long time, you know."

"What do you figure was wrong with her?"

"Oh! I don't know."

"No, but how does it seem to you? Why do you think she went crazy, or whatever she was?"

"I don't understand about people, you know."

"No, but you say how it seemed to you."

"Well . . . Just it seems sort of as if she never fitted into life except just when I remember her in the old days. I can't express it. She used to be at home . . . so pretty and happy and all her beaux . . . and dressing in a flurry in her room . . . all her new clothes, new dresses and earrings and things . . . she was right in the center of something. After she got married to Lambert she never fitted into things. I mean everything was sort of lopsided. There was something the matter. She didn't seem square in the middle of her life, or something. Does that make any sense to you?"

"Some."

"Well . . ." Betsy laughed comfortably. "I never had much brains."

"I like you."

"Good."

She stuck her hand through his arm and he clipped it to his side for a moment. They looked out of the window at the stretch of open blue bay water they were passing.

"You don't seem to be having much luck with your family," he said. "I'm sorry about that."

She took her hand out of his arm and reached for another piece of chocolate.

"It's all sort of broken up now. You and Jerry are my family."

"Why not have your old man down sometime?"

"I will. He's lonely. It's all split up into pieces, our family. I suppose it always happens."

"We're not going to get split up."

"Of course we're not."

"I'm glad you feel that," he said with some hesitation. "I'm glad you know that by going back to the Church I won't be leaving you. It won't be that at all."

"I know it won't. You have to have more than just me."

"It's not that, exactly. It's hard to explain. Sometimes, in New York, when I was trying to get a piece of work straight in my head, I'd get so I couldn't think at all. I found if I went and sat in the balcony at a concert, somehow I could suddenly think very clearly and get it all straight. And listen to the music, too. It seems as if when you try to do just one thing and nothing but, you can't do it at all. You do everything better if there's more than one thing. Something like that."

"I sort of see."

"But not exactly, either. I'll tell you something. I wouldn't admit it for a long time, but I was depending on you too damned much. Nobody has a right to demand everything from anybody. Nobody can put out everything there is. I won't be leaning just on you for every single thing. We'll have a fine time."

"We do have a fine time."

Today, she thought, his disposition was like honey.

The bus racketed around the corner by their house and stopped gasping by the telephone pole that had a mailbox attached. They climbed down and the bus roared away. They stood on their street just beyond their house, and the salt strong smell of their air came to their nostrils. They began to walk back to the house.

There was something stuck in the crack of the seldom-used front door.

"Maybe it's a special delivery," Hector said as they came to the gate in their fence. "Maybe it's a letter from that God damned bat-brained little halfwit in Pittsburgh, and about time, too. I could smash her dumb face."

"No, it's not," Betsy said over her shoulder, at the door. "It's a telegram. . . ."

## CHAPTER LXI

"Goodbye, grandpa."

"Goodbye, Treat, old boy. Come and see your old grandpa."

"Goodbye, Grandma."

"Oh, goodbye, my darling child. Grandma's sweetest baby, my little grandbaby. . . ."

"I'll be back later," Leda said.

She stood leaning on a walking stick in her tweed suit, waiting, smiling and a little impatient for the embraces to be over. It wasn't as if Treat was going out of Hampton. She poked little holes with her stick in the dry October soil of the front lawn.

"Oh, and Leda, dear," Laura said. She leaned forward from the front door where she stood beside her husband, making faces at Leda, lifting her eyebrows significantly, shaking her head and glancing at the top of the little boy's head. "I wouldn't go by way of Crompton Street—you know. I'd go around by the Water Tower Road, so much prettier walk. Treat can see the cows in Mr. Upson's pasture, won't that be fun, dear?"

Since the suicide, a few days ago, of Mr. Tom Jekyll in his house on Crompton Street in particularly ghastly circumstances, crowds of people, boys, and even trippers from nearby towns, had come to stand in the street and stare at the window; the sloping tin roof outside; the gutter edging the roof; that part of the big sprawling house that now was set apart by a lurid fascination.

Leda took Treat's hand and they set off, walking down the old, carefully weeded gravel path dividing the front lawn, to the road. Beside it to the right a black and twisted pear tree grew, and out of force of an old habit Leda stepped over its shadow, right foot this side, left foot beyond. At the foot of the path they turned and waved goodbye to the two who stood still filling the front door and waving. Leda knew precisely what her mother was thinking. She was thinking that Treat's face looked heartbreakingly the same as Leda's face at that age. Leda turned forward again and looked down at her son. His dark eyes looked back at her from the clear pale oval of his face, and it was true: that was the way she had looked.

"This is the best kind of weather for walking," Leda said, and they struck out on the main road, that led down to the hill, branched off to the left into the Water Tower Road, and continued over a small bridge, across another road, along a valley, for a couple of miles until it passed the Macomb house. Treat's bags had been sent over to his father's in the morning. Dr. James March, who had married Adèle Macomb the previous June, now occupied with his wife her family's large, ugly, old-fashioned concrete house, since the old people, Mr. Macomb having retired, now divided their year between Florida and the North Shore.

The day was sharp, sunny, and blue. Leda found herself unable to think at all of the interview which lay ahead of her. Her mind had taken a fighting stance; she felt energetic and confident; resolved to have her own way as soon as she found out what it was that James wanted. James! and his new wife! She seemed to see them as tiny figures moving about down at the end of a diminishing glass.

They walked along the sun-dappled road, scuffing in the fallen leaves at the side. Treat took Leda's stick from her and thrashed at the tall grass. She took it back and spun it round and round by the crook at the end, then Treat tried to spin it too, but only dropped it again and again.

They came to the little bridge over the Water Tower brook. Leda stopped and leaned over the white fence.

"There used to be a water-rat that lived in the side, there, between the rocks," she said in an excited, hushed voice. "He had a little boat tied up to that branch. I wonder if he's still there."

"Where?" whispered Treat. He stuck his head through the bars of the fence.

"There . . . under that tree that hangs over. . . . He was an American cousin of Ratty's."

"Ratty in the book?"

"Yes, in *The Wind in the Willows*. He had a snug little parlor just inside that hole. I wonder if he's there now?"

"Does he go for picnics in his boat?"

"He used to. With lots of lunch, in a basket. I used to see him, when I was a little girl, rowing along way down the brook."

"Did you?"

Treat had changed, had loosened from the mould of his childhood; he was ready to be led. These days, when she was in the mood, when the fit of fancy was on her, Leda would tell him stories of her childhood, invent fantasies and watch his eyes grow large and dark, his face lost. He had turned from the stout sturdy little boy into this slender child, and he was no longer fat and practical. She could recognize herself in him. Lately he had become shy of people, afraid of certain things as he had never used to be. Sometimes he was one thing, sometimes the other. Sometimes he wanted most to ride on the haycart at Andorra with the little colored boys, yelling with them and getting in the farmer's way when he pitched the hay up into the loft. But sometimes he would ask not to be sent over to a neighbouring house to play with the children; she could see in his eyes that he was afraid of someone there, or something; he would sit in the shadow of the box hedge in the garden with her and she could tell him the strangest stories and he did not stir.

From staring down at the water running over the stones they stood up and began to walk along the road again.

"How long am I going to be at Daddy's?"

"Daddy has you for half the year. You'll stay with him and Adèle till next April."

"Why is there going to be Adèle?"

"Because Daddy wanted to marry her. She's your new stepmother."

Treat said,

"Don't you like her?"

Leda shrugged her shoulders. She did not intend ever to talk against anything in the other menage where Treat must spend his time.

"Yes, I like her."

"Will I like her?"

"I'm sure you will. Stepmothers aren't the same nowadays as they were in the fairy stories, you know. They can be very nice."

Treat walked along beside her in silence.

"You must write me letters, darling," Leda said. "If you ever aren't happy you know you must tell me and I'll fix it."

"Mummy."

"Yes, darling."

"Why did you and Daddy stop being married?"

"Because we found we didn't love each other any more," Leda said. "People are only married when they love each other."

Treat said nothing.

When he spoke again it was quite different.

"Mummy, will you tell Daddy so that I can have that boy come and play with me?"

"Yes, I will. You liked Tony, didn't you?"

"Yes. I want to go to his house again."

"We had fun, didn't we?"

In the morning Leda had taken Treat to see Nicola Fenton's child Tony, a year younger than Treat.

"Yes, we did. *What did we do?*" Treat whispered, coming closer to her side. And they began to play a game they knew.

"We went into the door of the little house," Leda began.

"And there I saw a boy and he had a pair of cowboy trousers on!"

"And his name was Tony."

"And he said, 'I bet you don't know what I've got in my back yard.' "

"And when you got to the back yard what did you find?"

"A delivery wagon! With rubber tires. And all the boxes of groceries."

"And then . . ."

"And then what," he said, rubbing his shoulder against Leda as they walked.

"And then," she said, "*hands* brought four beautiful Coca-Colas, and you had one, and I had one, and Tony and his mother each had one. *Hands* brought two golden chairs, and Tony's mother and I sat down on them."

It was out of the Arabian Nights.

"They weren't golden chairs," Treat said abruptly, "they were kitchen chairs and Tony's mother took them out on the back porch."

Leda shrugged her shoulders.

"Is Tony poor?" Treat asked.

"Yes, rather."

It was a strange thing, Nicola living in that horrid little cottage in the midst of a development in the Newtons; Nicola, doing her own work—and just the same, as calm and happy and assured, as if her family had not lost their money in '29 and all the things one associated with Nicola's life vanished.

"We can't afford a darned thing," Nicola had said; she gave her low, comfortable chuckle; all the old feeling of pleasure and intimacy came back; when Nicola talked it was still like a schoolgirl, polite and well-brought-up. "Cassy Low and the Debevoises asked us down on Long Island this summer, but we couldn't afford to budge out of this little horror. Our Tudor love-nest," she remarked imperturbably, gesturing at the bogus half-timbers of the house. "I did manage camp for Tony, however. He would have melted completely away here."

"Tony hasn't got an electric train," Treat said now. "His is just a mechanical one. It's no good."

"But don't you think it's nice to be poor," Leda began carefully. "It's really nicer to be poor. It's much more fun. You see, rich people are apt to be rather stupid. They don't make up any games. They just buy things. Tony has fun living in a little house—like a playhouse—with his mother, and making his own bed. You can't have half so much fun if you're rich. When I was a little girl," Leda said, "we were poor. And I used to rake the leaves in the garden, and weed the vegetables, and I had a little vegetable garden of my own and I planted radishes, and carrots, and beets . . ."

"We're rich, aren't we, Mummy?"

"Not really," Leda said shortly.

"I think it's nice to be rich. When I grow up I'm going to be rich."

"Oh, I don't think you'll want to. Not just rich, and stupid, and boring. Maybe you'll be an architect, darling. Or an artist, and paint pictures."

"I'd rather be rich."

"Nobody's going to want to be rich when you grow up. You won't want to. You'll want to be something wonderful. What do you want to be when you grow up?"

"I don't know," he said, uneasily.

They turned, from the road, into the pretentious gravel driveway that swept up to the Macomb house. Leda held Treat's hand; he came along on his thin, young legs, up toward the glass porte-cochere; following wherever he was taken.

"Treat," Leda whispered, leaning down as they walked along. "Look at that flower-bed. Isn't it funny? In the shape of a star. Those are called foliage plants. They're not very pretty, are they?" She laughed confidentially.

"Aren't they?" he whispered back. "Why aren't they?"

"Oh, you see. They're just sort of funny, that's all."

They went up the broad shallow steps and Leda pressed the bell beside the big plate-glass front door. She stood there with her child waiting admittance. She was aware that her heart was beating fast. But she had nothing to fear from this house nowadays.

James himself opened the door.

"Hello, Leda. It was awfully nice of you to come. Hello, old boy!"

"Hello, Daddy," Treat said shyly.

But turning away from Leda, James scooped him up off his feet and flung him up in the air. Treat broke into a whoop.

"Daddy!"

Leda stood and watched.

"Come along and see Adèle. Mamma's here too," James said, leading the way down the big hall to the drawing-room. His arm was round Treat's shoulders and Treat was nuzzling his head against his father's coat.

Leda followed, in her well-cut Irish tweed suit, her dark leather brogues. She wore no hat on her dark, shining hair. As they passed the doorways down the hall she suddenly wished for a hat. But it was really smarter to be hatless in tweeds . . .

The air of this house bore upon it the old, selfsame scent of faint perfume. The walls of the hall had been painted fresh white and the decoration was more modern, less ostentatious, but it was the same house: vast, commanding, imbued with its own importance, self-assured.

Did no one but herself feel this queer vibration of power? Other people could be at home here; even Treat; now that he was here he was completely at home; at ease with his father, in this house. It was not the bigness. Andorra was a bigger house than this. It was something else.

They entered the large, long drawing-room. It had been changed. It was done over in off-whites and soft blue and violet chintzes. But there was the old smell, the perfume.

A young woman in a sweater and skirt leaned against the mantel by the fire at the end of the room. She pushed herself off from it as Leda entered, and sauntered forward.

"Hello, Leda," Adèle murmured in her casual, husky voice. "How are you . . ."

The elderly lady in a chair beside the fire held out one hand.

"Good afternoon, Leda."

"How are you, Aunt Grace?"

"I hope your father and mother are well?"

"They're fine, thank you."

"Give them my love. I haven't seen either of them for some time."

Not since the divorce. . . . No more summer visits to the North Shore. . . .

There was a silence. Leda picked up a cigarette from a box on the table beside her. James came forward and lit it; he held the match questioningly toward his mother and his wife. Treat was clinging to his coat tail, hanging on him. With a veil of excitement before her eyes Leda watched Adèle return to the mantelpiece, Mrs. Treat March pick up the brown knitting on her lap. Suddenly she felt angry.

"Shall we go into the library, Leda," James said, "and get our business disposed of? Then we'll be ready for some tea. You'll excuse us, Mamma . . . Adèle . . ."

Leda followed James towards the open door at the other end of the drawing-room.

"Come here, dear," Mrs. Treat March's voice said behind her. "Come and tell your Granny what you've been doing."

James stood back to let Leda enter the library; he followed her in and shut the door.

James sat down behind the knee-hole desk, exactly, Leda thought, as if this were his professional office. She was not going to sit facing him across it like a suppliant patient. She went to the sofa at the other side of the room and disposed herself in an attitude of grace and comfort upon it and drew on her cigarette.

"I appreciate enormously your letting me have this chance to talk to you, Leda," James said. He fiddled with the leather blotter pad on the desk.

He was getting bald; the dark hair on each side of his forehead was receding.

"My lawyers advised me to hear whatever it is you've got to say that's so terribly important," she said.

It was a strange thing how after all this time his very presence at once inspired her with the old feeling of irritation and contempt.

"It was very nice of you to come," he said again.

He dropped the blotter pad abruptly and got up and came across to a leather chair beside the sofa. She had a faint sensation of victory. He put his elbows on his knees and leaned forward earnestly. Was that the same old herringbone worsted suit, or one exactly like it? Undoubtedly one exactly like it.

"The thing is, we both want this kid to grow up happy and confident and useful."

In his best, confidential doctor's manner. Appealing to the intelligence of the patient. It did not impress her.

"Of course."

"I know you want it as much as I want it for him. We both love him. He comes first. He mustn't be made to suffer for our—inability to get along, any more than can be prevented. Divorce doesn't make it easy for a kid."

"I don't believe he remembers much about our being together."

"No, I don't believe he does. It's not that. I see a lot of the effects of split environment among the children of divorced people. It's tough on them. They don't know what to make of it. They can't reconcile one set of circumstances with the other, when they divide their time between two different households. You see it more as they begin to get older, try to make sense out of what they find. I've seen some pretty mixed-up kids. I don't want our kid to waste his energy on that kind of worry, I don't him emotionally all pulled apart. I'm sure you don't either."

"Of course not."

She put out her cigarette in the brass ashtray. She leaned back into the sofa and regarded James steadily.

"I don't know whether you've noticed it, but last winter I noticed signs that the kid was confused, he doesn't know just where he belongs. He's getting that lost look, like a puppy who doesn't know where home is. There's you, and the background he finds when he's with you, and there's me, and a whole different set of circumstances that's also supposed to represent home to him. It's confusing. You can see it in different ways. He isn't the self-confident, happy little animal he used to be. He's developed a few fears that aren't at all necessary. I don't know if he told you, but he was scared to try skiis when I took him up to Windsor last winter. A few years ago he wasn't 'fraid of anything."

"He's becoming more sensitive. He isn't just an insensate little lump."

"I agree," James said carefully. "Please do understand, the last thing I want to start is an argument about Treat. I know he gets a great deal from being with you, you develop his imaginative side and of course that's a good thing. I'm not pretending that the rough-and-tumble, boy life is everything. That's not the point. The point is that we don't want him to get tied up in knots to a point where he's wasting his emotion, missing things he ought to be getting. We want him to be happy and busy. That's right, isn't it?"

"Naturally."

"It's terribly important that we shouldn't let any antagonism between us color anything that affects Treat. I'd like it to be so that we were cooperating on his welfare; you're his mother and I'm his father; the thing we both want, absolutely together, is that Treat should have a happy and successful life."

"Our ideas of happiness and of success may differ."

"They're bound to. But we agree absolutely about not wanting him to get mixed up about life, about wanting him to keep everything straight in his mind."

Leda did not speak.

"Don't we?"

"Naturally."

"I'll come to the point. Adèle's marrying me complicates the set-up Treat finds when he comes to me, of course. He's stepping into a whole organized establishment instead of a bachelor's quarters. Also, he's too old to have a nurse that might bridge the chasm between one background and the other. He has to make a big jump all by himself from one world to another. It's a bad thing for him. Now. I want you to consider what I am going to propose, very carefully, bearing in mind that it is proposed with no thought of anything but Treat's welfare—because I want to spare him as much as possible of the trauma of the split environment set-up."

James's forehead was all pushed up into ridges and he thrust his face forward toward her. His fingers tapped on the arm of the chair.

"Here's the proposition. Frankly, I'm against the six months-six months arrangement once a kid is out of babyhood. I'm against dividing a child. I propose that for the child's own welfare we make another arrangement. I suggest that in future he spend his whole time with one parent—the other to have vacations, of course, holidays and all that. What do you think of that?"

He leaned back in the leather chair and took a cigarette out of his case and lit it.

Leda held out her hand and he dropped the lighted match and snatched out his case again to offer her. Neither of them spoke as he lit her cigarette and she took a first drag. She held the cigarette tightly to keep her fingers from shaking.

"I assume," she said slowly, "that when you speak of one parent having him all the time you mean yourself."

"Not necessarily," he said hastily. "Not necessarily. If you agree to the principle of the thing we can discuss which environment would, in the long run, be more to his advantage."

"You think yours would, don't you?"

"Leda," he said. "I give you my word that the only thing that concerns me is stability for Treat. I want him to have that. I feel that he must have that. I want that for him in all events. If you decide not to allow me to be the parent to keep him I'll relinquish custody to you gladly rather than have him go on being divided. The thing is, I want you to think about it. We've got all winter to make new arrangements. Think over both sides of the possibilities. From the point of view of what's going to make Treat a happy, useful human being."

"Stop saying 'useful'," she exclaimed involuntarily.

"I'm sorry," he said. "It's only a word. You know what I mean."

"There's a great deal that would have to be considered," Leda said.

"I realize that. I do realize that. Just let me say one thing, though," he said, not looking at her, twisting around in the large chair and flicking his ashes into the brass bowl, "I hope—I'm sure—you won't let—oh, you know, old prejudices or antagonisms or—anything that belongs purely to us as grown-up involved people, affect the issue, which really boils down to where Treat will have the happiest, most normal childhood. You do want that for him, don't you?"

"Of course I want that for him!" she exclaimed.

"I don't want you to dream of coming to any conclusion now. This will take time to think out. I'd appreciate it if you'd keep it in mind this winter, though, sort of mull it over. If you feel that with you Treat would have advantages which would make for more happiness, security, than he could find here with me, why, we'll talk it over again, in the spring, and exchange views, and if after hearing mine you still think he would be best off with you, why . . ."

"But you don't want him to live with me, do you?"

"I want him to live in one place. I guess it's natural to feel that one is best equipped to give the boy a good normal childhood, I mean, as a man, and of course selfish interest . . ."

"I don't want my child to turn into a ghastly stupid *normal* little bore!"

James was silent for a moment.

"Of course there's that," he said. "I realize that I am a pretty dull workaday sort of fellow. Adèle's not especially sensitive, I suppose, she's a simple sort of person . . ."

Leda stiffened her lips to keep them from trembling.

"I don't want my child," she said carefully, "to become the kind of person who's ruthless and insensate and crashes about asserting his will and hurting people."

"I assure you, neither do I."

"I want my child to feel things, to know what beauty is, to have the life of the mind, to have a little more in his head than just the blind urge to conform."

"Yes. I want that for him too. But, do you know," he said, "I've noticed that the people who are freest to do all that, to feel beauty as you put it, and get something special out of life—are the people who are calm and integrated, who aren't afraid. I don't want Treat to crash around hurting people, but I don't want him to be the kind of person whom other people can crash around and hurt, either. I want him to be strong."

There was a pause.

"What do you feel's the matter with my life as an environment for Treat, anyway?" Leda asked. Her eyes were fixed intently, warily, on James's.

"I don't think there's anything the matter with it," James protested. "It sounds like a lovely place you've got down there, and I know the boy has a lot of fun with your farmers, all that. The only thing is—a boy, you know, really needs a man to help him grow up. Of course he needs a woman too. He needs a lot of fixed stars he can count on—home, family, all that. Ah . . . for instance, are you definitely established down there in Virginia, I mean, are you going to stay there?"

"I expect so."

"Well . . . of course I do have a feeling that it would be nice for him to grow up around Boston in his own family background—your background, too, Leda, just as much as mine. Naturally that's a minor point."

"What else is the matter with my background?"

"Nothing. Nothing at all. I wish you didn't feel I am critical. I assure you I'm not."

"I might very well come back to Boston to live," Leda said. "I don't know. Although I certainly wouldn't say that Boston is the ideal, perfect environment for a child growing up."

"Of course it's not. Boston's really an awfully stodgy, limited place, isn't it? I'm not holding any brief for Boston. Please get me straight, Leda. I just want Treat to live in one place. Maybe we'll decide that the best place is with you . . . Would you like to have him with you all the time?"

With his dark eyes he looked straight into her dark eyes.

"Of course," she said coldly.

James stood up.

"I don't want to keep you from tea any longer," he said, smiling. "There's no rush about any of this, after all. Think it over. Look at it different ways. We'll discuss it in letters, if you will, and have another talk in the spring, or sometime."

He threw open the door into the drawing-room and Leda passed before him through it. She was rigid.

A large tea-table was set before the fire, with silver polished white and immaculate in the low cultivated lights of the room; under the tall silver kettle an alcohol flame burned; there was cream in the silver pitcher and lump sugar in the silver bowl, and extra cups, thin plain white, stacked one within the other on the tray. The polished mahogany curate's assistant bore in tiers plates of bread and butter and cake, and a covered dish in the middle.

All this Leda noticed through a blur of rage, of resentment and antagonism.

Mrs. March still sat in her arm-chair by the fire with a cup of tea beside her on a table. Adèle still leaned against the mantel, with her cup in one hand and a cigarette in the other. Her saucer was on the mantelpiece.

They had not stirred except to take their tea. Nobody could know what they had been talking about.

Treat sat on the edge of a chintz sofa opposite his grandmother with a cup placed before him on a little table and a plate on which was a large slice of cake.

Leda moved forward propelled by a tingling, pulsing energy. She kept her hands pressed to her sides.

She stood over Treat.

"What are you drinking?"

"It's cambric tea, Leda," Mrs. March said. "Hot water with a little milk and sugar."

"I didn't get any taste of tea, Mummy," Treat said. He looked up at her.

"I didn't know if you let him have tea," Adèle remarked. She lounged away from the mantel and slipped into the chair behind the tea-table. She began to tip hot water into a cup.

"He can have a taste," Leda said. Her lips were stiff. She picked up his cup and went with it to the tea-table and held it out without speaking while Adèle poured into it a dash of tea that tinged the milky contents pale yellow. Leda took it back to Treat. Her fingers gripped the edge of the saucer; she glanced at the hard black marble of the fireplace as she passed.

"How you take your tea?" Adèle murmured. She glanced up at Leda standing still on the hearth-rug; an instant's blank, uninterested stare; and back at the tray where her strong hands moved about among the silver vessels.

"As it comes—nothing in it."

Leda sat down at the other end of Treat's sofa. She could not feel the cushion under her; it was as if she was suspended above it.

"Take this to Leda." Adèle held out the cup to James; he took it and picked up the curate's assistant in the other hand and came across slowly. "Cream for you, dear."

"Right," James said, handing Leda her cup. She stared at the plates of food held toward her. Her fingers reached out and took hold of a slice of bread and butter and lifted it off the top of the pile.

James carried his tea to a chair and sat down.

"This has been a shocking business, the bombing of Adowa," Mrs. March said.

She sat in her long, archaic skirts, her shirtwaist with a jabot edged with real lace, in a position of erect composure, quite simply. Her appearance had not changed in twenty years except for the increased crumpling of her pale pink face.

"It's certainly made a figure of fun out of the League," James said.

"Yep," said Adèle. Now that she had finished pouring tea she got up and went back to her place beside the mantel and lit another cigarette. Her thick legs were planted apart. She, too, had not changed, except that the bloom of her youth that had been so indescribably enchanting had slid away from her face, leaving it only what it had always been: bold, casual, boyish. She was an athletic young woman past first youth, and the committees, the horses, the women friends, the management of her life showed in her confident expression. Her eyes were still her point of beauty; they were dark, rich brown with long black lashes.

"The League is a farce," Leda said. "How could it be anything else?"

"And yet I can't believe Cabot Lodge didn't know what he was talking about," Mrs. March said. Her voice was all reason, all pleasantness. "Perhaps it really is wiser if we keep ourselves to ourselves on this side of the world. On the other hand . . ."

"On the other hand there's nothing to stop an aggressive power from stepping in and helping itself to what it likes," Leda said. It was with difficulty that she kept her voice low. "Why should we care if a whole nation of innocent people is raped?"

"We do care, of course," Mrs. March said. "There's no doubt that there should be some sort of effective world police."

"But not if we have to put ourselves to any sort of trouble."

"It's true; as a nation we shirk our responsibilities; perhaps we simply don't realize that we have become a world power."

"Most people are half-witted," Leda said, viciously.

"Most people have so much on their hands to keep their own lives straightened out that they don't realize, they can't realize, it's their duty to do even more," James said. He bit into his piece of cake.

They were calm; they were unconcerned, talking pleasantly over a cup of tea together.

"Perhaps it has something to do with the fact that it's a nation of negroes that has been violated; who bothers to care what happens to a lot of ignorant blacks?" Leda said. She forced herself to drink her tea slowly.

"Oh, but my dear Leda, thinking people care very much indeed," Mrs. March said. "Perhaps you find that racial indifference in the South?"

"They treat the darkies horribly down there, don't they?" Adèle asked; but she did not even turn her head to look at Leda.

With infinite care Leda turned to face Adèle without jerking around.

"No, they don't," she said. "People who don't know what they're talking about find it easy to criticize the South. The South has had the negro problem on its hands for two hundred years and it's evolved a system that works. The negroes look happy down there. It takes the North to make negroes really wretched—that's where the real discrimination and economic impasse comes in. In the South they have their own things—their own districts and stores and houses and doctors. When they come North they're made miserable. You only have to look at their faces. The South loves and takes care of its negroes. The North doesn't love anybody but itself."

There was a very brief pause. Then Mrs. March spoke in her soft, agreeable voice.

"You like it in Virginia, Leda? The country there is so delightful."

"Yes."

"Do any hunting around Middleburg?" Adèle asked. "They've got some good packs."

"No," Leda said. "That's not Virginia. It's all rich Northerners who've come down and bought up the country. You might just as well stay North. The so-called hunt country isn't any more Virginia than Myopia is. Just rich, arrogant, stupid, brutalized Northerners."

"*Tiens*," Adèle said.

The word snapped in Leda's mind like the tail of a whip. She caught her breath and looked around at all of them.

They were drinking their tea, smoking; invulnerable, untouched, untouchable. Armies could fling themselves against people such as these and when they fell back the people would be unscarred; unimpressed; drinking their tea.

It seemed to Leda that at a word from these people the nations of the world fell down in hopeless subjugation: the negroes, the Ethiopians, the Italians, the Southerners—what were any of these jerry-built peoples against the calm and imperturbable Bostonians? People said that Boston was a joke, an exhausted back-wash from the past; but the people of it would never be defeated because they were not paying any attention.

Suddenly she felt vastly tired. There was no point in trying to pick a fight with them. They were not paying any attention. Over Leda like a wave of tepid water crept the old defeat.

"I have a really lovely Southern house," she said slowly. "There's some magnificent box in the garden."

"How lovely," Mrs. March remarked. "That black Southern box is so handsome. I wish I could grow it. But it's impossible in this climate."

"This box is over a hundred years old," Leda said. Within her mind the picture of Andorra and its grounds began to light up. She leaned forward. "The house is older. I wish you could see the pink brick, it's the color of soft terra cotta."

"It must be enchanting."

"How do you kill time?" Adèle murmured.

"I hunt in winter. And of course I spend a good deal of time on my writing."

"Oh?" Mrs. March said.

"Still write poetry?" Adèle asked.

"Yes . . ."

"Don't see how you do it. I couldn't write a line of poetry if I sat up all night for a week! Could I, James?" Adèle laughed.

"I'm afraid you couldn't, darling."

Leda saw them as they glanced at each other, smiling.

They're married. They like being married. They suit each other. She sees something in him I never found. What did I miss? He's a man who suits Adèle Macomb. What did I overlook? He seems quite different now, now that I see him as her husband. With his mother here. He seems the way he used to seem when I was a child—mysterious, interesting.

Mrs. March set her cup back in the tea tray with a slight tinkling clatter.

"That was a dreadful thing that happened here last week," she said. "To poor Mr. Jekyll."

"Your friends," Adèle said to Leda.

"I haven't seen them for years," Leda said.

"Oh? Thought you were pals with all of them."

"That unfortunate man," Mrs. March said. "I don't think he could have been well."

"Know what would make him do a thing like that?" Adèle asked.

Nobody spoke.

"I know Mrs. Jekyll slightly," Mrs. March said. "She's on the Crippled Hospital board. She seems such a nice woman, so brisk and efficient. This must be a terrible blow for her. I understand she was away when it happened. I wish there was something I could do for her."

"I only know the one named Jane," Adèle remarked. "I like her. She did most of the work on the Vincent Show last winter."

"You knew Betsy, in school," Leda said.

"Yep. But she never liked me," Adèle said.

"Didn't Mrs. Jekyll say her oldest daughter lived in Virginia? Do you know about that, Leda?"

"Oh . . . yes . . . Maizie. Yes, I see her every now and then. She lives in a town near me."

"Thought you said . . ."

Adèle started to speak and stopped. She shrugged her shoulders.

"At any rate, it was a sad, distressing thing," Mrs. March said. "I think one always has the feeling about a suicide, that it hangs so in the balance. If something had happened, the person might never have gone through with it. The striking of a clock, perhaps, or someone coming. Almost anything."

They were all silent.

Leda got up.

"I must go . . ."

"Can't I run you home? You walked over, didn't you?" James said.

"No, I want to walk. Goodbye, Aunt Grace."

"Goodbye, Leda. Don't forget to give my love to your father and mother."

"Goodbye . . ."

"Goodbye . . ."

Leda walked out to the hall.

"Treat must be around somewhere," James said, following her. "I'll find him. Treat! Hey, Treat."

She had entirely forgotten him.

At the door the little boy joined them. Leda bent over him and kissed him.

"Goodbye, my darling child."

"Goodbye, Mummy."

The little boy and his father stood in the open doorway as Leda stepped out into the twilight and walked rapidly away down the crunching drive.

Then they shut the door and James went back to the drawing-room to his mother and his wife. Treat ran away down the other end of the hall.

"Well, dear," Mrs. March said.

"Well, Mamma."

"Let's have a drink," Adèle said. She pressed a bell by the mantelpiece.

"James, did you say anything to make Leda angry when you were talking alone to her?" Mrs. March said. She stood up and straightened her long, full, black broadcloth skirt. "She seemed to have no patience with any of us."

"I hope not, Mamma."

A maid came in in a black dress and white apron; Adèle leaned over and set her cup back on the tea tray. The afternoon was finished; the evening was beginning.

"She has grown very beautiful," Mrs. March remarked, sitting down.

"She's a very beautiful woman. A very brilliant one," James said.

"Hey," Adèle said.

She and James smiled across the hearth-rug at each other easily and comfortably.

"Don't you think so?" he asked, smiling.

"Oh, you bet. She's never liked me."

Oh God oh God, she thought, walking faster and faster through the twilight, it is a battle that can never be won. What is the use of all the years, all the tears, all the fears. Why not face it, it is a battle that I never can win, I never could. The defeat is inherent in me, I've got the defeat in the corpuscles of my blood. I can never win against those people.

I never could. Oh what a waste! For I've spent years and years on trying --unworthy, unworthy--to play that game and win at it and I never can, it wasn't born in me, I am the selfsame creature as when I was born. All the years, all the tears, all the fears. Oh, shame! I'm ashamed, ashamed.

But they can't take my child. That's where I win. It's right here in my hand. All I have to do is say no. He'd give him to me for all the time.--I wonder how much they ever heard about Lambert . . .

But I don't want Treat for all the time.

But if they think I'm going to hand him over meekly to them the conquerors for all the time. Yes you're wonderful you're the ones to have him; yes I admit I'm not a good custodian, neurotic unstable self-centered supersensitive maladjusted . . .

But it's my side. It's the sensitive, the vulnerable, the feeling, the aware against the big guns. The big guns. They were gunning for me all those years and how I worked, I certainly worked, and what do you suppose, the curtain falls to denote passage of time, put me back up against the big guns and it's all over but the music. Just the same way, just the same nerves, just the same.

Oh, God, how I hate Boston.

I love the South. I love the gentle ways the hospitality. They think I'm quite remarkable down there. I love the South, that's where I should have been born and then none of this would ever have happened. What an easy time. I love the South.

That's a lie.

It's Boston I love I fear I cannot conquer I desire.

Down South! Honeycomb accents going slop, slop, slop and no trouble, nothing to respect. When I'm down South I'm a Bostonian for all I'm worth. They don't know the difference. Doesn't it make me feel good, to notice the stains on the wallpaper and the lapses in good form; they don't do it in Boston, they do these things better in Boston. I'm an unfrocked Bostonian. I never was a Bostonian. Oh, God I'm ashamed of myself.

When I think of the things they are saying about me now in that house. I can be cheaper more vulgar more disloyal than any human being.

They are saying how very vulgar. They are saying how very disloyal. They are saying thank God you're rid of her James.

I got rid of him.

But they got rid of me.

I don't understand it, I've spent my life trying to win that battle and at the same time I threw it all away. No more visits to the North Shore in the summer. What was I doing? I don't understand. Whatever I thought I was doing, I didn't conquer. I lost. I always lost. I'm right back where I was in the beginning before all the people and the work and the planning, there wasn't any use in any of it. I might just as well have gone the other way. I might far better have gone the other way.

Then I should be whole. Integrity.

I didn't have the courage. I had to win the war first.

And the war turns to water in my hand like a bad dream and I am right back where it all began. Little Leda March with something the matter with her.

But they can't get my child.

They are saying poor little Treat, he will be ruined if that woman brings him up. He'll be just such another. Another like her.

I see now that I can make him my way. I wasn't sure. He understands, though. I can make him be just the same way. My childhood over again.

I've got a mind like a villain in a melodrama.

They are quite right, I'm not fit to bring up a child. I get everything by the wrong end. They are the people who know how to bring up children, make them their way. Strong ready easy natural pleasant in power. They know the trick.

But if they think I'm going to admit that.

Hand over the last spoils, say all right you've won the battle for keeps, I'm nothing, I'm all you think, I'm that frightful little mess I always was, I admit it, the whole thing's been an act.

If you act a thing long enough you become it. That's not true.

I can impress the life out of the Southerners but I can't impress the Bostonians worth two cents. They know. They don't care where I've been or what I've got or how I look or what I've got on or who I know. They know. I'm just Leda March.

They are saying, what a really dreadful person.

They're right. I was dreadful. I was as bad as I've ever been.

Taking the Southern point of view about the negroes—how many times have I not been contemptuous of that? The times I have picked it carefully to pieces. Democracy, I have said; down with the vicious system of paternalism. A man must stand on his own feet, a race. Taking the Southern point of view just to impress them, just to have something to fight them with, just because I hated them so. Just because it's the opposite of the Northern point of view.

I couldn't stop those words about Northerners because I hate them so. And yet that's the way I've tried to be myself. Without success.

I couldn't even be consistent. First on one side then on the other about the negroes. Disgusting, disgusting, shameful.

And coveting James because he is someone else's husband. That is Leda March all over. Oh shame! If thy right eye offend thee pluck it out. . . . And saying I write poetry *of course*. Playing every little card for what it is worth. And it isn't worth anything, not a cent. Not to the Bostonians. Even if it was true. And I know, and they don't know, and they don't care—that I haven't written poetry for a year. Oh, no. Not a line of poetry for a year. Maybe I can't any more. Perhaps the drop of the pure spirit is spilled and lost now. It doesn't make any difference to them whether I can or whether I can't. It is with me and my soul. I have sinned . . .

They don't want anything I have except my child. And there's nothing they can do about it. He's my child. He looks like me. He responds to me. I could live my childhood over again in him.

Ah, the fond mother!

I didn't even remember him enough to think of saying goodbye to him. I wonder if James knew. I got so rattled. I was so angry—and they were so . . . so . . . unconquerable . . . forever . . .

I would have walked straight out the door. But James called him just in time. I would have walked straight out the door.

But I said Goodbye my darling child. Oh God! The shameful the hypocrite and no integrity. Just exactly like my mother. She said, Goodbye my darling child. And how I writhed. I think I'm so much better. No slop. Taste. But without a moment's hesitation. Goodbye my darling child. Ah, the suffering bereft mother who didn't even remember her child was there to say goodbye to.

Who didn't even have the guts to say Yes, the Jekylls were my friends. And you lost that hand, didn't you, as usual? The Jekylls being perfectly edible after all to the conquerors, perfectly acceptable, and a whole lot more so than you are, my girl. And so without a hair turned it appears they are your friends after all, since it's all perfectly edible, it goes down. She said, *I thought you said* . . . and stopped. My ancient enemy. My enemy since my beginnings. It doesn't take you to tell her whether Jekylls are edible, whether James is a desirable husband. It takes her to tell you.

In the flash of a moment you will betray anyone, won't you? Remember your first friends. Who saved you from your loneliness and turned on the lights and made you begin to laugh. Surrounded you with their laughing selves. The Jekylls long ago, the first friends, the ones who showed you how. . . . Who started you on this way into the world, the broad way, the way of people, the happy Jekylls . . .

There's the house.

She had walked rapidly a mile or more and now stood in the deep dusk on Crompton Street opposite the great, lightless hulk of the closed house. She leaned on her stick and stared at it. No one was there any more. No people stood around gaping. It was too dark to see the house clearly.

Within that dark window I know so well he stood with the razor in his hand, all alone in the big clumsy house now abandoned of all the laughing groups, in the hall, up the stairs, the window seat in the bay window, and the giggling daughters dressing in the bedrooms. They were gone away now and he stood by the bathroom window with the razor in his hand. The open window.

And with the blood now spurting leaned against the window, rolled, gasped spurting scarlet blood, and fell.

And rolled, the man in extremest anguish, in his blood, down the short span of roof, down to the gutter of the roof.

And lay there caught fast and spurting blood until he died.

And about this shocking episode what are the appropriate emotions?

You see, she demanded of some obscure personification within herself who must be convinced, you see? I care nothing for anybody but myself. Make it myself with the shortest stab of suffering and I care; I care. But I can say, what are the appropriate emotions to have about this elderly man, who has been forced back into a position where he must kill himself? Tom Jekyll, a Southerner, a lawyer, a husband and father, by his own hand. . . . At which the mind stops short. You see? she demanded.

Why had he done it? One shrugged one's shoulders. Why do people kill themselves? Why do people do any of the things they do? Who knows?

But it must have some significance, it must mean something that applies to me, to the others sitting back there in that drawing-room; but especially to me. Does it warn me?

Or does it mean nothing at all, except as a shocking episode? Something that has made me come here to stand in the street—just as the people from the village have come—to stare at the house, the window, the roof, the gutter? Scandal! A man has cut his throat. One must stare at the window through which he fell, the roof down which he rolled, the gutter where—one sees it, titillated,—he lay caught until he bled to death.

The facts lie blank like a headline on a page.

Was I responsible for any of it?

You see? The ultimate egocentricity of guilt.

But I am guilty of so many things. Surely this empty house without lights has been touched by me, I passed through it once, I touched those people. Maizie. I am guilty of Maizie. I am guilty of Betsy. I dropped her, forgot her. Perhaps she is happy, but if she is unhappy perhaps it is on account of events which might have been different had I been loyal, had I been a friend. Perhaps not. One cannot be sure of innocence. The whole thing interlocks and twines and complicates itself and for all I know it was my hand in matters which led to the death in that lonely house.

The egocentricity of guilt.

When I and people are put together evil comes of it.

That's true.

If they are stronger than I, then I suffer for it. If I am stronger than they, they suffer for it.

But when I and people come together there is the battle; the battle that can never be won.

Lambert. That was as normal as I could ever be with anyone, as right, and still it ended in disaster. In the end, he was people; the same is true; when people and I are put together evil comes of it.

As if the direction her thoughts had taken gave her some grim relief, Leda sat back on the stone wall behind her in the deepening twilight, letting her stick hang between her knees. She felt a sort of peace as though the worst were known. She went on staring drowsily at the big vague shape of the empty house.

She imagined the house filled with lights again; she pretended she heard the sound of loud jazz music played carelessly on the old piano; figures moved dancing past the windows, and out of the house into the early evening came the sound of laughter. The Brats were climbing the stairs; Maizie, with her hair a halo of light, sparkled and chattered in the living-room to a dozen young men, and Betsy stared at them, goggle eyed and thrilled. On and on Minnie May played, racketing out the tinny tune, with smoke rising from her cigarette before her eyes.

How beautiful it was! It was as though they were all of them dead. They were embalmed in this amber forever, the lively Jekyll family from the South, who had pranced North to seek their fortunes in Boston. It had all become clear and beautiful, though tragic; though fated—it was strange that one had not always seen it—though fated from the first for tragedy.

How beautiful things are, Leda thought, when I see them, alone. When I am alone I love them, love them, for being what they are. I am full of love, when I am alone.

When I am with people—the battle. I can't see, I can't think, in the smoke of that battle.

How beautiful it all is now, now that I am alone. And, carefully, she began to turn her mind this way and that, to see if the charm held. Those others in the drawing-room—yes, they are beautiful too. They sit beside their fire like great statues, antique and bleached white, very beautiful and still.

My child—he is the most beautiful of all. I see him. The dark clear eyes, the child's hair, the upturned pointed chin, the throat, the little thin body. Yes, I love my child; I love him most of all. Yes, I really love my child. When I am alone.

But even with him, I am fighting for something. I am fighting to make him mine.

One kind of power would be mine if I kept him. Another kind of power still is there in making him in my image—and I could.

And if I made him in my image—I know the life that I would give him. Could I be evil enough to give anyone a life like mine, wrong from its beginnings in the world of people?

I could be evil enough to do anything.

I don't feel evil. Evil slides off my feathers, like water from the swan.

Power is the key. I always wanted to conquer. I always had to conquer. Is that where power lies? To keep my child? A full-time job no matter how I do it. Do I want him all the time—for the power? To make it all mine?

Mine! There isn't any such thing as mine. The world slips slithering through my fingers.

Alone it is mine. Alone I own the world. I own it with my love.

This is my way of life.

Observing all at once that it had become quite dark, Leda stood up and began to walk on. She looked back over her shoulder at the big closed house. Perhaps, she thought, people kill themselves because they absolutely cannot, are prevented from, finding their way of life.

Is that it? It feels that way. As though people are always seeking for the way of living that inside they need and must have. If I am any example. If, for once, I am any example—the way may prove to be quite different from what they plan or picture to themselves. They may refuse to recognize it, and keep on trying to find the life they've decided would suit them, trying trying trying. . . . And of course impossible. They only fit one slot. The current only goes on one way. Maybe they never know it. Perhaps the light never goes on, and in that case they wonder why, they try again and wonder why, and perhaps in the end it is bad enough in the dark so that they kill themselves. . . . Perhaps. . . .

But there is no doubt whatsoever that I was never meant to live the life of people. My spiritual home . . . my way of life is alone.

It always was.

I always knew it.

Never once did the light go on, never once, the other way. Why not at length acknowledge it? Lost in the dark smoke of battle.

Through her mind in a procession the thousand afternoons, the thousand evenings passed, of all these years; the evenings and afternoons with people; what was called a normal life. It was empty. The people in it were indistinguishable one from the other. Smiling, laughing, nodding, chattering, mouthing the words that would be acceptable, the years had passed without refreshment, slowly, slowly the invaluable gift which was all she had, being spilled away, sifted away, worn down.

It was all making and giving of what was not myself, she thought, and the time passes; it was all spending, and no gain; destruction little by little, death—yes, death, of all that's me.

Creation lives alone in a small temple. Only one may worship at a time. That was my gift at birth, that was all I ever had. I was given the private means of purification. But being mine I put it away, and preferred to try to live as the others lived because, being they, they must be right. The normal.

I've tried it long enough; for me it's cowardice, it's retreat, it's delay, it's denying not acknowledging, it's death—and all the time the other thing, the only thing, goes dripping, wasting, the only thing I ever had that made me happy. Why have I set aside the means of happiness so long, so often? I have been cheating no one but myself. All the people, all the years, and not one moment left of them that's good; all false for me; and the pure spirit goes dripping. . . .

In life and in all things, she thought, the task is to bring order out of chaos. A necessary order. Not what order one may choose, but the order which alone will hold. The order must be inherent in the chaos; one must *find* one's natural home, not try to construct it. Neither the readymade order, the order of the others—nor the sick resignation to chaos is the end. Chaos must exist, and so must order, but from this native chaos one must be strong enough, grow wise enough, to pluck this order which has no definition but to be one's own.

With a feeling of relief and delight she saw the little lights of the village sparkling below her as she climbed the hill toward home in the darkness. She had not noticed them before; but now she saw them, clearly, and they were beautiful, private and calm. The village lay twinkling below the hill; the road wound up the hill and round; street-lights showed the way at spacious intervals; and beyond, beyond the road and the invisible silent fields, against the dark gray evening sky, was the deep uneven jagged line of the woods; the woods beyond it all, lying still as they had always lain, secret and infinite.

She caught her breath with the sense of pleasure beginning.

And there is nothing to spoil the joy of loneliness but the perverse and hopeless fight to establish importance among the world of people. Surrender that . . . surrender that. . . .

Why is it, she thought quietly as she came to the bottom of the gravel path up the front lawn of home—why is it that everyone believes that people may be finally judged only by their actions? By what they do? For that is not so.

My self lies in the things that have occurred to me, the things I never did, the alternatives to the course I took; which course was always taken because it was what someone else whom I admired or feared—not I—would have done.

I have been sick with being somebody else.

She opened the front door and went in to her parents' house.

The smell of dinner cooking was faintly discernible, warm and comfortable. Laura sat beside the fire in the small living-room. She appeared to be doing nothing whatever. When Leda came in she began to stir nervously about in her chair, and smile, and stretched out her hand uncertainly.

"Well, lovie? Did you have a nice time? Was everything all right?"

Leda looked down on her, from the first step of the stairs.

"Everything was fine," she said. "I had a talk with James."

"Oh dear, I hope everything was perfectly pleasant, I hope. . . ."

"Perfectly. Why not? He wants to keep Treat with him for the whole year instead of dividing him between us. He thinks it's bad for Treat to be split up this way."

"Oh, Leda! Oh, darling, how dreadful for you! Does he have to have his own way?"

"Of course he doesn't have to. . . ."

"I know you will do all you can to stop such a thing. Your own precious baby! You want him near you, to guide him and give him all the wonderful things that only you can give him, dearest. . . . Oh, dear!"

"Don't get so upset. Of course he can't make me do anything. But I think it's very wise. I agree with James."

"I don't understand! Don't you care? You must think, Leda. You can't have thought about it, there hasn't been time. Oh, Leda, you must think about this. It's so unnatural."

"I have thought," Leda exclaimed. "There's no use discussing it. I want Treat to have a normal bringing up. They can give him a normal bringing up over there. He'll be brought up as James was."

"But, dearest, you can give him everything they can and so much more, your wonderful, sensitive mind. . . ."

"I can't give him a normal bringing-up," Leda said. "I never had a normal bringing-up myself."

She ran quickly upstairs.

She went into her old bedroom and shut the door; without turning on any lights. In the dark room she was perfectly at home, moving easily among the hidden pieces of furniture.

She went to the window and opened it, propped it open with a stick and knelt down on the floor in front of it with her arms resting upon the sill.

The sky was dark blue-gray. One by one the stars were forced out into it. She swallowed down the sharp, sweet, cold October air.

Upon the horizon lay the dark edges of the woods.

This is the only kind thing that I have ever done; the only unselfish thing.

I can't count on its always being like this, she thought. It won't always be like this.

There'll be the same old urges, the false desires. The pride, the envy, the restlessness. . . . I'll be ready to throw it all away again.

But I acknowledge it now. I say it is my way.

If it will come like this twice a year—a few times—now and then; if it is there and I can know it comes; know it; know it—that will be enough.

To be at peace; to be alone; to be myself.

To feel the splendid wave sweep silent over noise, the coming down, the overwhelming, beautiful with a thousand silent voices.

The world moving round me, round beyond me, in great beauty, wonderful, full of astonishment.

If I can remember always: it is when I am alone.

Under this cold New England sky, or under any sky, under the brooding heavy sky of Virginia; to lie alone; without desire; receiving all; breathing all; seeing it; motionless inside; listening; alone.

When I strike out it is in sin; when I rejoin the others I commit sin. All sin lies in the life of people, all virtue for me alone.

Greed, vanity, lust, self-assertion, aggression, untruth, pretence.

Simplicity, humility, understanding, truth; love.

I only love alone.

And in surrendering, conquer.

PLUME Quality Paperbacks for Your Enjoyment

☐ **LIVES OF GIRLS AND WOMEN. Alice Munro.** The intensely readable story of Del Jordan grappling with life's problems as she moves from the carelessness of childhood through uneasy adolescence in search of love and sexual experience. (259754—$7.95)

☐ **LIE DOWN IN DARKNESS. William Styron.** The eloquent story of Peyton Loftis, the beautiful desperate daughter of a wealthy Virginia family, and the tragic consequences of her intense search for love and understanding. (261287—$9.95)

☐ **PRICKSONGS & DESCANTS. Robert Coover.** Exemplifying the best in narrative art, these fictions challenge the assumptions of our age. They use the fabulous to probe beyond randomly perceived events, beyond mere history. (260310—$7.95)

Prices slightly higher in Canada.

Buy them at your local bookstore or use this convenient coupon for ordering.

**NEW AMERICAN LIBRARY**
**P.O. Box 999, Bergenfield, New Jersey 07621**

Please send me the PLUME BOOKS I have checked above. I am enclosing $_____ (please add $1.50 to this order to cover postage and handling). Send check or money order—no cash or C.O.D.'s. Prices and numbers are subject to change without notice.

Name_____

Address_____

City _____ State _____ Zip Code _____
Allow 4-6 weeks for delivery.
This offer is subject to withdrawal without notice.